The Patriot is Ray Hodgkin, alias Raimondo Occhiaccio, one of the Kings of the Honoured Society—the Mafia. His native country is Sicily, but his real affiliations lie with America—his adopted home. He has, at the age of forty-five, his own patch of Manhattan where he runs a profitable business of protection, prostitution and murder. But he also has enemies, and at the height of his illegal career finds himself convicted of tax evasion and deported to Sicily, where he has to begin all over again.

With the ruthless skill of his previous rise to power, he bribes, tortures and kills his way into the big money of a drug smuggling operation that takes him to Beirut. In achieving his eventual goal of returning to America he proves that nearly anybody can be bought, if the price is right. And the few that can't have to pay the highest price of all—in the currency of blood . . .

The Patriot

Charles Durbin

CORGI BOOKS
A DIVISION OF TRANSWORLD PUBLISHERS LTD

THE PATRIOT

A CORGI BOOK 0 552 09486 2

Originally published in Great Britain
by Michael Joseph Ltd.

PRINTING HISTORY

Michael Joseph edition published 1972
Corgi edition published 1974

This book is set in 10/10½ pt. Plantin

Corgi Books are published by Transworld Publishers, Ltd.,
Cavendish Hse., 57-59 Uxbridge Rd., Ealing, London W.5

Made and printed in Great Britain by
Richard Clay (The Chaucer Press), Ltd., Bungay, Suffolk

FOR ELLIS AMBURN

Cosmus, Duke of Florence, had a desperate saying against perfidious or neglecting friends, as if those wrongs were unpardonable. 'You shall read (saith he) that we are commanded to forgive our enemies; but you never read that we are commanded to forgive our friends.'

—FRANCIS BACON
'Of Revenge,' *Essays, Civil and Moral*

I conclude then that Fortune varying and men remaining fixed in their ways, they are successful so long as these ways conform to circumstances, but when they are opposed then they are unsuccessful. I certainly think that it is better to be impetuous than cautious, for Fortune is a woman, and it is necessary, if you wish to master Her, to conquer Her by force; and it can be seen that She lets Herself be overcome by the bold rather than by those who proceed coldly. And therefore, like a woman, She is always a friend to the young, because they are less cautious, fiercer, and master Her with greater audacity.

—NICCOLÒ MACHIAVELLI
The Prince

BOOK ONE

CHAPTER 1

A guard in the Federal House of Detention, West Street, New York City, said to Ray, 'You have a visitor.'

Ray went out to meet him.

The visitor, L. Howard Willis, senior partner of the law firm of Willis, McGowan, Courtney, & Hardin, had unofficial privileged status. That meant a private room in which to confer with his client—with a guard standing outside the door, not over the conferees and looking at the clock. The key word was 'unofficial.' There were no hard-and-fast rules about these things. Not all attorneys, simply because they were officers of the court, enjoyed such courtesies. In the final analysis, it was up to the man who administered the institution. But Willis rated whatever amenities the FHD had to offer. He carried clout, even in federal facilities.

Willis had played football for Yale in his youth. The shoulders were wide and rangy. He limited himself now to swimming and handball at the New York Athletic Club. There was no midriff fat behind the tailored suit, but his reddish sandy hair was beginning to thin. He studied his client over a pair of down-slipping bifocals and smiled encouragingly.

'Well, Ray, tomorrow is the big day.'

Ray took his time about replying. He lit a cigarette, stared at his attorney without expression, and rubbed a graying temple.

'Is that what my big legal eagle came down to tell me?'

'I came down to say good-bye.'

'Good-bye.'

Willis accepted his client's ungraciousness philosophically.

'I'm sorry we couldn't stop the deportation order, Ray.'

11

'That's understandable. I was probably your most lucrative account.'

'I wouldn't say that.'

'I would. How will you replace me as a source of revenue?'

'We'll struggle along.' Willis' smile broadened. 'Don't take it so hard, Ray. How old are you, by the way?'

'Forty-five. Why?'

'Nothing. You have the waistline of a professional tennis player. You have a good head of hair. You're a young man. You'll make a good life for yourself over there.'

Ray tilted back in his hard wooden chair. 'Are you going to bill me for this pep talk?'

Willis chuckled. 'No. It's on the house.'

'Hallelujah! This is the first free lay I've ever had from your legal cathouse. By the way, Howard, what does the L stand for?'

'Llewellyn.'

'No wonder.'

'No wonder what?'

'So you have an alibi for the initial in front of your name. You're still a stuffed shirt. As big a thief as any of your corporate clients. My kind are just peanuts compared to you legal racketeers.'

'Now, look here, Ray——'

'Did you see the editorial in today's *Daily News*?' interrupted Ray.

'I don't read the *Daily News*.'

'Pardon me, counselor, I forgot.' Ray picked up a copy of the *Daily News* from the table between them. 'I don't want to take up too much of your valuable time. I'll just read you a few lines of it.' He read:

... the United States Attorney for the Southern District of New York and the New York District Director of the Immigration and Naturalization Service are to be congratulated for having brought to a successful conclusion the deportation proceedings against the notorious mobster Raymond Hodgkin, alias Raimondo Occhiaccio. This battle was begun by Robert F. Kennedy when he was Attorney General of the United States. The conduct pattern of these organized hoodlums is monotonously unvarying. They evade their lawful taxes, putting a proportionately greater tax burden on the rest of us. They break down respect for law and order, they terrorize honest working people, and they corrupt public and law-enforcement officials. The fewer of them we have in our country, the better off we shall be. We salute the Department of Justice and urge this present team to continue the good fight.

Ray threw down the *Daily News*. 'Who thinks up that garbage?'

Willis shrugged. 'We've been through that already. They convicted you of income tax evasion.'

'My accountants deducted a political campaign contribution and I signed the return in good faith. I didn't even read it. It's being done every day. Do you call that income tax evasion? Does that rate deportation? If it was one of your own breed, all he'd get would be an audit and a penalty tax. If that.'

'I don't know about that,' said Willis. 'You could have received a five-to-ten in addition to the deportation order. We saved you from that.'

'Thanks for nothing. You didn't want my room and board coming out of your taxes for the next five years.'

'You're being very unreasonable,' said Willis patiently, with a lying afterthought. 'Understandably so.'

'They were out for my scalp—personally,' soliloquized Ray. 'Bobby-boy said as much. This new bunch is following through. The bastards.'

'That's paranoid thinking. In spite of your harsh and unkind comments, you must admit that we exerted ourselves at the trial on your behalf. I emphasized your distinguished war record, your graduation from Yale, your——'

Ray yawned. 'Harvard, MBA, 1949. When are you going to get it straight? Don't go making a Yale boy out of me. I earned my education the hard way—under the GI Bill. And I didn't wear long hair and go around bombing college labs. I worked my ass off and won a degree on my own merits.'

Willis shrugged. 'We'll continue working on the appeal.'

'Do that. But, if you fail, don't send me any bills. I won't pay them. And keep an eye on that Al Poggio. The minute I'm on the ship, he'll start stealing.'

Willis grimaced distastefully.

Ray grinned. 'Tactless of me, wasn't it? Still, representing my kind can be profitable as hell. Half the work and twice the fee.'

Willis rose from his chair and extended his hand. 'Well, I'll say good-bye now. Keep in touch and good luck.'

Ray, still grinning, shook the attorney's hand. 'And good luck to you, Lewellyn. Don't ever get careless and start defending paupers.'

L. Howard Willis left and the guard escorted Ray back to his cell.

One federal marshal drove the plain, unmarked black Chevy. The other one, a stolid, chunky ex-cop, sat in the back with the prisoner. 'Well, how are we this morning, Ray?' said the federal man.

Ray stared at him without expression. 'Fine. Couldn't be better.'

Only his friends called him by his first name. Who were these creeps to take liberties? He *could* make an issue of it. And, by the same token, they could deliver him to the ship in bracelets with a fractured jaw. The law had him by the balls. Willis was right. He was getting paranoid.

At shipside on the Brooklyn dock, the marshals turned Ray over to a pair of Immigration and Naturalization inspectors. One of them extended his hand and Ray shook is skeptically. 'I'm Wethers,' said the inspector. 'This is my partner, Inspector Kovolchik.'

'Pleased to meet you,' said Ray. He stared after the departing marshals' car and yelled in Italian: 'May all your daughters be syphilitic prostitutes! May all your grandchildren have six fingers! May your son get your wife with triplets!'

'What was that?' asked Kovolchik.

'I was saying good-bye to the boys,' said Ray. He stared up at the side of the ship. 'Is this a good boat?'

'As good as any,' said Wethers. 'You'll have nineteen other passengers for company. Let's go aboard.'

'Are you boys sailing with me?'

'As far as Ambrose Light,' said Wethers. 'We'll disembark with the pilot. We just want to see you safely on your way.'

'Very thoughtful of you,' said Ray. Once in the cabin, he rummaged through his luggage and produced a bottle of scotch. 'Make yourselves comfortable boys.' He brought three glasses from the bathroom and filled them half full of scotch. 'Cheers.' Wethers and Kovolchik acknowledged and sipped solemnly. Impersonal civil service types, Ray decided. Without the sly, malicious sadism of cop-psychos. He could smell that streak a mile away. May all your grandchildren have ten fingers—on each hand. And ten toes on each foot. May you get four flats on Canal Street, in a traffic jam, on a rainy morning, all at the same time. May you be hit by a truck. He looked out at the Statue of Liberty from the porthole and lifted his glass. 'So long, kid. I'll be seeing you sooner than you think.'

Wethers nodded. 'It's tough, Mr. Hodgkin.'

'You're my guests, gentlemen,' said Ray. 'This is my going away party.' He lifted his glass. 'I've had better company. And worse, too. Like the characters who brought me here.'

Kovolchik swallowed some scotch. 'Did they give you a hard time?'

'I just didn't like their smell. But let's change the subject. This is routine for you, I suppose.'

Wether agreed philosophically. 'We've been doing it for years.'

'You've seen them all, eh?'

'Most of them,' said Wethers. 'Kovolchik and I helped put Charley Lucky aboard the *Laura Keene* in forty-six. Remember, Iz?'

Kovolchik nodded. 'Big crowd. Reporters and photographers all over the place. All the boys came down to the pier to say good-bye to Charley. The longshoremen gave us a bad time of it.'

'It was sort of sentimental, though,' said Wethers.

'A few friends wanted to come down to see me off,' said Ray. 'I told them not to.'

15

Wethers raised his eyebrows in casual interest. A little too casually, thought Ray. Which meant that he could be more interested than he pretended. Which meant that things might not be what they appeared to be. He nursed his glass without swallowing any more scotch. 'Drink up, boys,' he said. 'I'll give you a refill. I have two more quarts in there.'

Kovolchik smacked his lips appreciatively. 'This is good stuff.'

Nicky Polo, Saldana, and Beniamino were okay, Ray was thinking. No point in their showing. They had enough headaches running the show now. The FBI would have an observer somewhere on the scene to see who, if anyone, came down. Marta Peruzzi had wanted to show. 'You're still in law school,' he told her when she visited him in West Street. 'You see me off, it will be a banana skin under your shoe when you come up for the bar exam. Stay away.' From Al Poggio he had heard nothing. It was a feeling he had about Al, just a very strong feeling. Nothing he could prove. Right at this very moment, there's nothing you can do. You're going for a boat ride to Sicilia, the home of your ancestors. So relax and enjoy it.

The freighter began to get hot flashes and undergo a change of life. Something was stirring in her bowels. Feet were clumping by in the passageway outside. Feet were scampering overhead on the boat deck. Someone was shouting orders up forward. And aft. The freighter had gas on her belly. She was coming to life, burping and grunting like a sow with a bad dream. There *was* something about a ship getting ready to haul ass and stand out to sea. Ray's last sea-change had also been from Brooklyn. On a troop transport. From Brooklyn Army Base. The sergeant at the foot of the gangway checking each man off his roster sheet. The man, duly accounted for, then went plodding up the gangplank. One duffle bag. One backpack, the rifle, and the rest of the gear. Five-tiered canvas cots stretched between iron-pipe frames. About twelve inches of space between the cots. He hadn't felt anything. He didn't remember how he felt. He hadn't felt afraid, he was sure of that. When you're young, you don't give a shit about anything. Whatever it is, bring it on.

The freighter bellowed, hoarse and mournful, like a

16

thoroughly disillusioned cow. She began to tremble and rumble more loudly.

'Here we go,' said Kovolchik.

Ray glanced out of the porthole at the widening gap of water between ship and pier.

The I and N-niks stayed put, anchored in their chairs, impersonal, stolid, incurious, uncommunicative. Ray plied them with booze and failed to loosen their tongues. They drank, grunted, and cared nothing that Ray did not drink. Or that he was surrendering the Upper East Side of Manhattan. Ray mourned sincerely for the Golden Rectangle, but kept a clamp on his own tongue and watched Wethers' eyebrows. They sent out no further signals. Paranoid, Willis had said. If that included intense suspicion, he could very well be paranoid. All capable men had a little paranoia built into their specifications, anyhow.

Off Ambrose Light, the freighter hove to, momentarily. Wethers and Kovolchik followed the pilot over the side and down the ladder into the pilot craft. Ray stood by the rail, watching them climb down. Let alone fall into the sea, the creeps didn't even stumble. Good scotch was wasted on them. Chloral hydrate was what they deserved. Or paraldehyde. Or lysergic acid. Anything to stiffen them or shake them to pieces. But giving them high-quality booze was like pouring it down the kitchen sink. Good-bye, I and N. Enjoy your pensions. Drop dead.

The Atlantic stayed calm and flat all the way across, a nothing, a blank. That was a break. Ray's fellow passengers were elderly tourist types. Who had time for freighters except retirees and deportees? There was nothing to be gained by socializing with them. He considered alternatives. If the ship docked at Naples first, he might be able to make a deal with someone to remain on the mainland. If the ship went nonstop into Palermo, that was it. In Naples and Rome he knew some of the members of the American Colony, as the Italian police called them—people who'd been sent back each year ever since the end of the war. They were big colonies, but he hadn't kept in touch too closely with anyone. No reason for it. He had been doing very well in New York City for almost twenty years, so

17

why should he? Thinking about deportees was like thinking about the dead—a morbidity. But, since he had no connections, he'd have to play things off the top of his head. Cash he had plenty of. More would be coming over by courier once he got settled. That was the word from Beniamino and Saldana. One thing was certain: As long as you could pay off, you'd find someone with whom to do business. Especially in Italy. Most especially in sunny Italia, the land of the big yoke. He had been in Sicily during the war but had skirted Palermo on his way north. He had served in a real corn pone Southern infantry outfit right through the North African campaign. Which reminded him of college. While attending Harvard, he was simultaneously running a profitable book. Nevertheless, he had earned his degree the hard way. That North African campaign had had some rough spots in it. Those Southern boys were alien yokels but good soldiers. Real fine. The skipper of his company was also a rebel with a hawg-calling dialect, a regular Army noncom by the name of Millard Patterson Colquhoun, who had himself been commissioned in the field. He had recommended Ray for a Silver Star in North Africa. That was something. You didn't make jokes about the Silver Star. They had gone into Sicily by the back door, on the south side of the island, at Licata. They had busted through, heading north behind an armored outfit, clearing the real estate of German rearguards and skirting Palermo. So he remembered nothing of the country. Whatever he did see was all smashed up. Sicily had been just a clean-up operation through a big garbage dump. Then they were shipped up the west coast of the mainland boot and Ray got a second Silver Star in the Rapido River fighting. After that intermission at Monte Cassino, he continued the march up the length of the Italian peninsula with the rest of his outfit and took part in the invasion of southern France. Some intermission! You tell today's kids about Monte Cassino, they just look at you. They don't know what you're talking about. Number one, they can't read. Number two, they don't give a shit, even if they could read. Moral: Don't talk about Monte Cassino; don't even think about it. Go dig yourself a hole, get into it, and zip it closed. Were Ray capable of it, he would have felt grief and anger for

18

all the good men who had manured the slopes of Monte Cassino. Nor was it any good hating the kids who didn't understand what you felt. You might as well hate a mindless, swarming horde of driver ants. They were twenty and you were forty-five. So you hardened your heart and just got the hell out of the way. He had returned to South Brooklyn in 1945 with a relatively whole skin, a pair of sergeant's stripes, and the two Silver Stars, which he always carried in a special little wallet like a pair of religious medals. That's what they were, in a way. So he returned and settled down in earnest to resume his interrupted career in the Business, in the real lifetime army. As a part of that resumption, he had taken the unprecedented step of enrolling at Harvard. It was inevitable that some of the boys should comment politely about the unusual. He didn't mind explaining. 'It's coming to me. While you people were making a bundle in coupons, stamps, sugar, meat, gasoline stamps, the whole bit, I was sitting on my ass in a wet dugout, when I wasn't being shot at.'

'No beef,' said the boys. 'Who's saying no? We were just asking.'

'And, in case anybody asks,' finished Ray, 'tell them that Raimondo Raffaele Occhiaccio is no ordinary button. Okay?'

It was evidently okay. Ray had also changed in that he was better armed to battle with society. His name had also been changed—by Captain Colquhoun on the occasion of his first decoration. 'Well, now, sergeant,' said Colquhoun, 'what in the hell are we going to do about that name of yours? It sounds like a couple of jay birds swearing on Sunday. Besides, my clerk can't spell it.'

'Sir,' said Ray, 'the captain has a free hand.'

Colquhoun had noted. 'That's fine, sergeant. I've been giving this a lot of thought. From now on, sergeant, your name is Ray Hodgkin. How do you like that?'

'Sir,' said Ray, 'it stinks. But it's a helluva lot handier.'

'My sentiments exactly,' said Captain Colquhoun. 'But God Almighty, sergeant, look where you're starting from! All right, I'll have the paper work thrown into the pot right away.'

So Raimondo Raffaele Occhiaccio returned to his old outfit in the real lifetime army with one more name to add to his collection—Ray Okey, Jack Oakey, Ray Malocchio, Raffles Occhi, and, now, Ray Hodgkin. Since he had developed into an individual whom it was healthier to oblige than otherwise, his friends, business associates, and enemies obliged. The real name fell into limbo. The man became Ray, that educated boy, to his friends, that mean sonofabitch to his enemies, and Mr. Raymond Hodgkin to newly introduced strangers. The pure, distilled consensus of informed opinion was—Ray is no man to fuck around with. By the time he had attained field rank in the Organization and was facing the pleasure of deportation to Sicily he had for many years been known predominantly as Ray Hodgkin.

The freighter didn't stop anywhere en route. It did Palermo the honor of heading there directly. Why would any ship want to go to Palermo? Why would any ship want to go to Sicily, a cemetery with a malicious half-life of its own? But this ship did and Ray was on it. It came gliding down the bay toward the harbor. The water was calm, with the mist coming off the surface, and it was going to get hotter at midday. A bony Minnesotan fellow passenger of Scandinavian extraction pointed toward a mountain peak off to the right. 'That's Monte Pellegrino. That's where the shrine of Santa Rosalia is at, the patron saint of Sicily.'

'Is that right?' said Ray. 'You've been reading up on this place?'

The Minnesotan tapped a book he held in his hand. 'Everything. This island's got quite a history. It was invaded over twenty times in the last two thousand years.'

'How about that!' said Ray. 'How long are you planning to stay?'

'One week,' said the Minnesotan. 'We've got a few auto tours lined up to see the whole place. Then we're going on to Rome and Florence. What about yourself?'

'Strictly pleasure,' said Ray. 'I'm going to look up some old relatives. Things like that.'

'Well,' said the Minnesotan, 'I'd better get down and start helping the wife with the bags. Then we'll have to open them up again for customs.'

20

'I don't think they'll give you any trouble,' said Ray. 'Have a good time.'

'You, too,' said the Minnesotan, and departed. Ray stared after him with a mild feeling of disgust and puzzlement. Tourists were like children—wholly incomprehensible and overwhelmingly superfluous. Why would any man in his right mind want to travel? What could the world possibly have that the midsection of Manhattan couldn't surpass?

The freighter crept in toward its assigned pier and was finally made fast to the land. Ray stared down from the main deck at the packs of ragged urchins, the shabby hotel hustlers hanging around the customs sheds, the peddlers, and the criers. At all the people gazing up at the ship from America. The same expression with which cons regarded a delivery truck from the outside. On the outskirts of the crowd a few cars and trucks waited. And, over all, the stale stink of garbage, rotting vegetables, cooking oils, and a whiff somewhere from invisible lemon groves. Over the hills to the west, that would be the heartland of the Honored Society. So this was the joint from which his father had escaped. Felice Occhiaccio hadn't found much better in an America which had killed him. For Felice, being in America had been like hiding in the mountains, cold, wet, and hungry. Still, it was better than Sicily. One was free. Ray stared down and exposed himself to the color, the noise, and smells of the shore. The strongest olfactory message which he received was that of poverty, the greatest ill, the source of all evil. Ray's past travels had taught him one truth, that the earth was small. Most of it, with people everywhere clinging to handholds, was a slum, the many squeezed by the few. Sicily, this ill-omened island, was only one among many of the planet's garbage dumps, and not the worst. Who needed the worst? Someone touched Ray's elbow. He turned to look at a man standing beside him. The man wore a rumpled cheap suit, glasses, a toothbrush mustache, and a smile.

'I am Inspector Corso of the Palermo *Questura*,' said the man. 'Are you *Signor* Occhachino?'

'Hodgkin,' said Ray. He enunciated the two syllables carefully.

'Occhachin,' said Corso gingerly, as though he were putting a foot in ice water.

'It used to be Occhiaccio,' said Ray. 'It was legally changed to Hodgkin when I served in the American Army.'

'Ah,' said Inspector Corso, 'I prefer your former name. A rather unusual one, but, at least, Italian. Well then, welcome to Sicily, *signor*. I have been detailed to escort you to your place of residence and to see that you get settled.'

Corso was bland, pleasant, and unperturbed about anything.

'You have obviously run this course many times before, Inspector,' said Ray.

Corso smiled and shrugged. 'We have quite a colony of Italo-Americans in Palermo, a large colony. You might say that we have it down to a routine.'

'I take it that I can remain in Palermo, then?' said Ray.

'I'm afraid not,' said Corso almost apologetically. 'The government has recently issued new directives. They are enforcing the rules more strictly. The *soggiorno obbligato* now has teeth in it.'

'Which means what as far as I am concerned?'

'Well, effective as of three months ago, when a deportee arrives in Sicily, or anywhere in Italy for that matter, he must go directly to the city, town, or village of his birth. He must remain within the limits of that locality. He must report to the local *carabiniere* station at least once a week. The *carabinieri* also have the option of increasing the number of obligatory visits. It's a form of regional detention.'

'I was born in Castellammare,' said Ray. 'Does that mean that I have to live there?'

Corso took a document out of his pocket. 'So it says here. Castellammare. It's not bad, really. For a fishing village. It's quite celebrated in its way.'

'Celebrated for what?'

Corso chuckled. 'It's émigrés, for one thing.'

'I like that,' smiled Ray. 'It's true, inspector, we Castellammarese have made our mark on the big city.'

'In which district of it did you reside, *signor*?'

'In Brooklyn.'

'Ah,' sighed the inspector. 'Brooklyn.'

22

'But let us not get carried away by this old home week spirit, Inspector Corso,' said Ray. He extracted a hundred-dollar bill from his wallet. 'Please accept this with my compliments and let me remain in Palermo.'

'I wish I could, *Signor* Occhiaccio.'

'The impossible has happened,' said Ray. He added four more hundred-dollar bills and pressed them toward the inspector. 'There! Three hundred thousand lire. Do you have daughters, inspector?'

'Three.'

'They will be able to marry civil servants, live in Rome, and give you many grandsons. Take the money.'

Inspector Corso shook his head. 'It's not easy, *signor*. I'm afraid I can't do anyting for you even if I wanted to. Technically, I could charge you with attempting to bribe a police officer. But I'll overlook it. You will find that things have changed a good deal in Sicily.'

'I wouldn't know,' said Ray ruefully. He put the bills back into his wallet. 'All I know is that this would never happen in New York City. All the policemen whom I knew there took.'

'I beg your pardon?'

'They accepted money for favors.'

'Ah, they must have higher living expenses than we have here.'

'Much higher than your new morals,' said Ray. 'You're absolutely right. But I'm not going to argue with you. I made up my mind on the ship that I wasn't going to fight anything. I would accept things as they came.'

'That is wise,' said Corso. 'Be a philosopher.'

A ship's steward took Ray's luggage down the gangway and put the bags into the car which Inspector Corso had waiting on the pier. As Ray and Corso got into the backseat, the uniformed policeman behind the wheel saluted informally. Ray relapsed into glum silence until they reached Castellammare.

Inspector Corso took Ray to the best hotel in town. The best room stank of mold and buzzed with bluebottles. Alberto, the proprietor, remained beside the open door armed with a defensive air. Ray noted the lumpy mattress, the soiled bedspread, and the sagging springs. 'Very well,' he said. 'The last

23

time I was in beautiful Sicily, I slept on the ground, out in the open. How much in this room by the month?'

'Two hundred and fifty thousand lire,' said Alberto.

'I don't want to buy your hotel,' said Ray. 'I just want to rent a room.'

'Two hundred thousand lire a month,' said Alberto.

'That's almost twelve dollars a day,' said Ray in a shocked tone.

Alberto looked at him sadly. Corso shrugged.

'Tell them to bring up the bags,' said Ray.

Ray dug into Castellammare and settled down to wait. He had unpacked silently. He fell into a routine of reading and walking around the principal square of the town. He sat before the café sipping vermouth. He waited. As he waited, he reviewed his birth and his family's beginnings in Castellammare. He had been baptized Raimondo Raffaele Occhiaccio. The family name meant 'a threatening glance' or 'a baleful look.' The locality was then too small to possess the dignity of an identity. One of its modest claims to distinction was in the name 'Occhiaccio.' This claim was also perceived by the thoughtful as a measure of the village's insignificance and of the monotony of the people's lives. Local gossip and rumor had it that Felice Occhiaccio, the father of the boy and of seven daughters besides, was a notable practitioner of the *mafioso* stare. This stare was the cold, unblinking, menacing, and insolent look with which men of honor pierced peaceable citizens whom they wished to intimidate. Whence arose a second rumor, to wit, that Felice was a member of the Honored Society. Yet, if Felice was a Friend—that is to say, a brother —his mode of life never demonstrated that he was enjoying any of the material benefits conferred by membership in the Honored Society. As far back as anyone could remember, he had been the impecunious proprietor of the village's solitary wineshop, a tumbledown affair with rough benches and a rude earthen floor. It served a wine which was reasonable enough in price but so rough to the palate that even Felice's inured neighbors grimaced. 'If Felice were a brother,' said some, 'surely, he would have something better to serve than this

24

wretched vinegar.'

Sarati, being the village wag, embroidered on this theme: 'The mystery of Felice Occhiaccio may be explained in this fashion: item, he is no member of the Honored Society, merely a poor soul like the rest of us. Whence it arises that his true Christian name is Infelice [the unfortunate one] rather than Felice. As for the quality of Infelice's wine, that may be ascribed to the infelicitous family name. There is nothing basically wrong with the wine until Infelice stares at it. Then it turns sour.'

'Perhaps,' suggested someone, 'the family name was at one time Malocchio [the evil eye].'

'I doubt it,' said Sarati. 'If poor Infelice has the evil eye, he certainly injures no one but himself. This black look of his is nothing but a kind of melancholy. And what is its source? That's easy. The *occhiaccio* steals into his expression when our Infelice contemplates his seven daughters. Think of it! That would give the devil himself a hangdog glare.'

There was a sublime unanswerable logic about Sarati's argument. His neighbors nodded agreement. The aforementioned *mafioso* stare was nothing but depression. Infelice was no Friend, merely another poor man like themselves whom God or fate had singled out for a particularly hard kick in the ass. Seven daughters!

Although Castellamare was so small and poverty-stricken in those days, it nevertheless possessed a church and a priest. From the ecclesiastical administrative viewpoint, the distribution of salvation to this particular locale was uneconomical. Despite some material loss to God, however, the diocesan authorities magnanimously held open the lines of communication. The bishop thought of it philosophically as a free clinic of the spirit. Charity, he concluded with a sigh, was one of those necessary evils, precisely because the beneficiaries of charity were not only ungrateful but often openly resentful. The men of Castellammare, perversely, did not often avail themselves of such spiritual solace as was offered them. In a discreet, civil, taciturn fashion, they had their reservations about God as well as about His annointed representatives upon earth—particularly the latter. Even the shabby little church in

Castellammare tended to ape the great cathedrals of the cities, to withdraw gingerly and disdainfully from a lapping tide of sweat, patches, and despair, from human poverty and misery. But such matters, like the all-pervasive presence of the Honored Society, were better left undiscussed by poor men. Being poor, they were, *ipso facto*, ignorant. And, being ignorant, they could conceivably be in error. And, being both, they could be proven wrong even if they were right. Since poverty and weakness were an irrefutable proof of innate wickedness, the villagers decided that it was better to hold one's tongue, continue the struggle for survival, and silently curse one's mother for having had the bad judgment to bring one into the world —that was to say, into Sicily—that was further to say, into the bleak, sterile environs of Castellammare.

But Infelice had been in silent, patient rebellion against fate, God, the government, the church, and the system for twenty years. By superhuman discipline, control, and effort, he had hoarded his coins and watched them grow. Perhaps he had more than people suspected. Perhaps the abject poverty of his life-style was an amplification of the Sicilian protective camouflage against the depredations of the bureaucrats, the *carabinieri*, the *mafiosi*, and of Holy Mother Church. Whatever the reason, Infelice one day gathered up his wife, his seven daughters, and his infant son. He locked the wineshop (which no one wanted anyhow, or could not buy even if they did want it), shook the dust of the place from his feet, and departed. He left the oppressed and hungry land as would any sensible Sicilian who had the means of escaping. The neighbors bade farewell to Infelice and his family, sympathetically and with goodwill, as might prisoners in a penitentiary to one who was that day being liberated. True, they were remaining behind, but it was a welcome momentary break in the stupefying routine of life to see one of their number escaping. They understood that the Occhiaccios were bound for Milan. Infelice had given it out, though only when specifically asked, that they were traveling to Milan to find work there. He was wise. Even in leaving, it was best not to impart information too freely. Why tell the wardens of the island one's destination? They might pass the word to someone malignantly inclined. It was best to simply go. Perhaps the Occhiaccios were traveling to Milan, perhaps not. If Milan, they were doubtless bound for America, which certainly made more sense. If a man was leaving this place of hopelessness and confinement, he was wiser to put as much distance as possible between it and himself. Milan would be an improvement, America an infinitely greater one. Castellammare's collective eyes observed the bare toes of the seven daughters kick up the little clouds of red dust on the village's single street. When the rains came, the dust would turn into mud. America! That was the land of dawn and hope, where children wore shoes, the land where children went to school and made something of themselves. America was, above all, the land which allowed that a man was not necessarily a broken donkey. If there was any sense at all left in Infelice, on whom fortune had frowned so long and steadily, he would continue forward and not look back until he reached America. So the people said to Infelice: 'Go with God and with Santa Rosalia.'

Replied Infelice with a wry smile: 'Better keep them both with you in Castellammare. You have greater need of them.'

Said Sarati: 'It never hurts to have them along.'

Said Infelice: 'I wonder.' Then, fixing the neighbors, whom he was seeing for the last time, with his *mafioso* stare, he added: 'I am leaving here to escape from God, from Santa Rosalia, and from Holy Mother Church. The church tells us to wash our faces and feet, to put on shoes and shirts before we come calling on her. She doesn't want our dirty feet soiling her marble pavements. She doesn't want our stink sullying her grandeur. She tolerates us uneasily. But we have no shoes or shirts, have we, brothers?'

A muttered collective sigh answered the question.

'Farewell, my friends,' said Infelice.

With these words, the Occhiaccios marched down the dusty road toward the shabby little bus for Palermo. The seven daughters walked in single file behind the mother and each bore a bundle on her head. Infelice himself carried in one arm his infant son and a bundle in the other. The people stared after the departing figures. No one commented on Infelice's final words, not even Sarati. No one had to. An invisible, bitter, choking cloud rose from the sulphur fires of their agreement. That agreement was deep—deeper than the floor of Mount Etna's crater. Then they dispersed to face the invisible bars and to go about their business.

Infelice had saved enough money to bring his brood across the sea from Palermo to South Brooklyn. The family was destitute when it came ashore. It somehow survived until Infelice found work finally as a laborer, heaving loaded cans for a private garbage disposal contractor. His health deteriorated. Within two years he developed a hard cough, a heart condition, and a hernia. Three years after his arrival in America, he died. His final words to his wife were calm: 'I cannot deny that I am not sorry to be leaving this world. I am only sorry that I must leave you with the burden. How will you manage?'

His wife replied: 'You liberated us from the prison. That is enough. You should not worry about the rest.'

The dying Infelice glanced over to the sleeping Raimondo who was bedded down on the top of an old trunk. 'The boy——' he began.

'The boy will survive,' said the mother soothingly. 'He will collect what is due to Felice Occhiaccio. Look to yourself. Do you wish for a priest?'

Infelice smiled thinly and replied: 'Put the money into your stomachs. You have greater need of it.'

His wife nodded, sober and tearless.

'Perhaps the county will bury me,' said Infelice. 'Let my employers carry me away in one of their garbage trucks. Let my body be burned and thrown into the Gowanus Canal. It is all one to me.'

His wife clasped his hand and said, 'Sleep.' Infelice closed his eyes and slept—forever. The prudent widow, however, had Infelice's body interred in consecrated ground with the rites of the church. Not because she believed in the Resurrection and in the mercy of God but as a point of practicality, to hedge Felice's challenge, that the infant, Raimondo, might enjoy a better beginning.

Young Raimondo survived to make a beginning. It was neither good nor bad. It was inevitable. He spent his childhood, adolescence, and young manhood in South Brooklyn. One by one, his sisters left the tenement flat which they and the mother had desperately held together. Four of the girls found husbands. Three of them went into orders. Having served a classical apprenticeship with some distinction, Raimondo Raffaele Occhiaccio was made as a button in the Family controlling Brooklyn. He was assigned to the crew of a *caporegime* covering the docks and the Bay Ridge area. Within a few weeks after his ordination, Ray's mother took to her bed. Once again, as many times before, she told her son the story of the past. 'You do not have to tell me what you are,' she said. 'I already know it.'

'It is not what you think,' said Ray.

'It is more than I think,' she replied. 'And I am not sorry. Now I am going to join your father. Be a strong man. Nothing else counts in the world. No tears.'

'No tears,' said Ray. 'I'll make you a fine funeral.'

'Do not trouble yourself,' she replied. 'Avenge your father.'

Nevertheless, Ray made his mother a good funeral, a better one than Infelice had been tendered. The seven sisters and the four brothers-in-law came to the funeral. So did the boys in the regime. The *caporegime* sent a handsome wreath. The boys chipped in to provide a few more floral pieces. Ray's somber, taciturn mother was accorded respect and journeyed to reunion with Infelice beneath an incongruously cheerful pall of flowers. Expressionless, without comment, Ray contemplated the blooms and saw his mother buried. He was polite to his sisters and reserved. He had never been noted for warmth, even as a child. His sisters were practically strangers to him, as he to them. 'He has that look,' said one of the sisters. 'Our father's look. Mother told us about it.'

Ray had the look but, unlike Infelice, there was more behind it than impotent resentment against fate. He left the cemetery and returned to his special world to hack his special way through the jungle. Yet, before he could roll up his sleeves to carve his initials on the great city's back, he encountered a detour and an involuntary chore to perform. Uncle Sam sent him greetings and inducted him into the Army of the United

States. Ray took leave from his crew and was sent to Alabama for infantry combat training. Then he was sent overseas to North Africa. Then he was sent to Sicily.

And now he was back in Sicily.

CHAPTER 2

After a month in Castellammare, Ray decided to visit the wineshop which Infelice had once owned. It still existed. Ray walked in and introduced himself to the current proprietor, one Pizzola. He looked around.

'My mother described the place to me,' he said. 'You've evidently made improvements since my father ran it.'

Pizzola nodded complacently. 'All new furnishings. As in Palermo. Like a real American cocktail bar.'

'What happened to that man my mother was always telling me about, the one who was always making jokes about our family name?'

'Ah,' said the proprietor, 'Sarati. A great sense of humor! It was inherited in the family.'

'And how is funnyman Sarati?'

'Many years ago he passed from this to a better world. His son now carries on the business.'

As Ray listened, he realized that he did not entirely understand the proprietor's speech. He had heard enough Sicilian in Brooklyn. This, however, was an enriched language, with an accretion of slang-coral since the American Army had passed through Sicily. New words and phrases had been coined in the past twenty years. Only a native reared on the island since the war could use them with facility. Their meaning puzzled Ray.

'What business do the Saratis conduct?' he asked the proprietor.

'They own four large vineyards and many olive groves.'

'Good for the son,' said Ray. 'All old Sarati had, from what I heard, was that sense of humor. Otherwise, like my father, not one *soldo* to rub against another.'

31

'Gold may be distilled from laughter.'

'Perhaps my father should have remained here. All he ever distilled was garbage. But, then, he never laughed much either. What did he have to laugh about?'

'I was told of your father,' said Pizzola tactfully, 'and of his countername, Infelice. It followed him around.'

'A born loser, as the Americans might say.'

'You might put it so. Infelice, the unfortunate one. But you, *signor*, seem to have broken the tradition.'

'I'll try to keep it so. As far as I'm concerned this entire country is a haunted house, a disaster. I've never seen a better island at which not to come ashore.'

Pizzola said wryly, 'This is your native land.'

'That's like saying my mother was a witch. I leave my share of it to the Saratis. They seem to have the touch. *Arrivederci*.'

'*Arrivederci*,' said Pizzola. He looked after the departing American and respected the son as he had not respected the father. And for the correct reasons.

The lesson was obvious—never go back. Ray had been pushed back by Bobby-boy, so he was not at fault. At that last dinner with the boys, while the trial was still on, he had voiced his thoughts: 'This is a personal vendetta between Bobby and myself. He's going for my jugular with a razor. He's trying to make hamburger out of me.' Nicky Polo, Tony Saldana, and Beniamino—and Al Poggio—were there listening. Ray had gotten half drunk and shouted at them, 'Are you people going to stir off your asses and help me take the stone out of my shoe?' The others had just looked at one another and shrugged. 'That Bobby-boy,' said Ray, 'someone is going to give him his buckwheats some day. If not me, then somebody else.' He shouldn't have shot off his mouth like that, not with Al Poggio around. The moral was: Don't get drunk and sound off, even among friends and business associates. Some little iron bird will swoop down and pick up your crack like a hot coal and start a forest fire with it.

That first month had been a hard one. Ray stayed on his side of the line and the Castellammarese did the same. Sicilians were the greatest for minding their own business. Ray knew the score and how their brains worked. Forearmed with the wisdom of his mother's milk, he didn't expect to be invited into anyone's home. Only close relatives and trusted friends ever got into a Sicilian's house. For the rest of the world—a high blank wall and a barred gate, even if the house was only a mud hut with a thatched roof. That was the way of it.

That first month had been the quarantine period. Incommunicado. Solitary. The Atlanta–Leavenworth–Milan–McNeil's Island routine. There was a rationale behind it. Paper work to be completed and tests to be run. The shrinks and the psychologists were sizing up the new guest. What kind of cat was he? Where should they put him? How would he shape up? Not with any personal interest, of course; they couldn't care less. In the meantime, there was the prisoner, frozen in the middle of a cake of ice, certain that nobody knew he was alive. But the prison population and the administration knew all right in a general way that the fish was alive. They were appraising him. What else was there to do? As soon as the fish was released from quarantine, they would start leaning on him a little to see what would happen. If he had faults, they would appear as faint hairline cracks. It was much the same thing here—the Castellammarese were seeking the cracks in Ray, a pinhole into which to start the point of a knife. Western Sicily was still hung up on that underground-prisoner psychology. It figured. The Sicilians had been prisoners under one warden or another for the last two thousand years. Understanding, though, didn't increase Ray's enjoyment of life. He yawned and waited doggedly.

The freeze began to thaw during the second month of Ray's sojourn in Castellammare. He had shown neither cracks nor flaws. He waited sardonically. Let the creeps come to me. That's important. Who comes to whom first. Who turns away his stare first. Dignity, respect, face. It was more important in Sicily than in Japan. I know these people. And why not?

He was sitting out on the terrace of the café one sunny midmorning sipping Cinzano and smoking an American cigarette. There was a plentiful supply of smuggled American tailormades in Castellammare. The mayor of Castellammare, accompanied by two other men, came strolling by. He stopped at Ray's table, tipped his hat, bowed slightly, and smiled.

'*Signor* Occhiaccio?'

Ray rose. 'At your service.'

'Aldo Perilli, mayor of Castellammare. My friends, Dr. Pardo, Avvocato Terzi.'

Ray shook hands all around and said: 'Will you join me in an *apéritif*?'

They accepted and seated themselves.

Perilli tasted his *Cinzano*. 'How do you find Castellammare, *Signor* Occhiaccio?'

'A heavenly, or rather an earthly paradise,' said Ray. 'I have returned home. My ancestral roots are here.'

Pardo and Terzi smiled politely.

'But, of course,' said Perilli. 'Yet, our town must be unbelievably quiet and uneventful for you, after New York City.'

'A most pleasant contrast,' said Ray. 'And I'm not lonely. As for being uneventful, true. But our town's past history makes up for its present peacefulness. I'm sure you're aware that Castellammare has stamped its imprint on New York City. The Castellammarese War of nineteen thirty to thirty-one. Little Castellammare and the megalopolis of the Western world. David and Goliath. Need I say more?'

'You need not,' smiled Perilli. 'We are not exactly strangers in New York. Each one of us has visited your great city on several occasions.'

Which put everything in a better perspective. Ray was talking not to hayseeds but to men who had been around. In Sicily you had to allow for the probability that any given man had a second face and a second role to play. Perilli had just indicated that they might be connected. Very good.

By the third round of drinks, Ray was playing the role of host.

'You are *simpatico*,' said Perilli at last. 'We are warmed by the affection in which you hold Castellammare. Roots are good. But so is travel. You no doubt plan to visit the mainland. Florence, for instance. Although it cannot compare with Castellammare, it also has something to offer.'

'The Florentines will be heartened to hear that,' said Ray.

Perilli chuckled. 'And there is Rome,' he continued. 'And Naples. And many other beautiful and interesting places.'

'There is the little matter of my *soggiorno obbligato*,' said Ray.

Perilli raised a plump, padded white hand. 'Why don't you drop into my office tomorrow? About eleven in the morning? We can enjoy a coffee together.'

'Eleven will be satisfactory,' said Ray.

Pardo and Terzi rose to their feet. After a pause, so did the mayor.

'Among men of understanding, everything can be arranged,' said His Honor.

'I hoped to hear you say as much,' said Ray. 'Gentlemen, your company has given me pleasure.'

With more expressions of mutual esteem, the three citizens went on their way. This was the southern way of doing things. Things would get done. They were in the works already, but you had to play the game by *their* book of rules.

On the following morning, while enjoying a coffee with Perilli, Ray handed him an envelope containing three thousand American dollars. 'In the name of my family,' he said, 'permit me to make an offering to the municipality of Castellammare.'

Perilli accepted the envelope, glanced into it, and put it into his breast pocket. 'In the name of Castellammare, and for the citizens of our town, I accept your gift with thanks.'

Within two weeks after his meeting with Mayor Perilli, Ray was invited by telephone to visit the Palermo law offices of *Commendator* Francisco Tamburelli. Ray checked around with Perilli. Tamburelli was a deputy with clout in Palermo and in Rome. Ray met him. Tamburelli was a tall, spare, grave-faced man with iron-gray hair and the careful manner of a monsignor playing a wealthy aged widow on a fly rod. With all of that, he was not as southern and circuitous as Perilli, who had made the connection. Tamburelli was more direct, businesslike, and American, yet light-handed. He savored his own humor. 'We are both men of the world, *Signor* Occhiaccio. We need not, therefore, waste time. Even God has domestic budgetary problems; why should not Deputy Tamburelli?'

'A good question,' said Ray. 'Why not, indeed?'

'*Signor,*' said Tamburelli, 'there is no problem so knotty that it cannot be unraveled with money.'

'That has been my experience.'

Tamburelli nodded with a hint of self-mocking ruefulness. 'In the threadbare lands of the Mediterranean littoral, and, in particular, in our Italy, officials are vastly humane and tolerant. Have you noticed how their tolerance rises in direct proportion to a man's means, until it shades off into respect and, finally, into frank admiration?'

'I have noticed.'

'Five thousand dollars,' said Tamburelli. 'It is not only for myself. Many needy members of the society will benefit from your generosity.'

'It is little enough,' said Ray. He took out the money in thousand-dollar bills and paid it over.

'Thank you,' said Tamburelli. 'Your generosity is most timely. You have no idea how much. Only this last week I have been faced with a distressing personal problem.'

'You don't have to go into details, *commendatore,*' said Ray. 'What man doesn't have constant problems and emergencies rising before him? One can always find a worthy use for money.'

'Ah,' said Tamburelli, 'true. But your generosity gives you some claim to knowledge of my personal affairs and so I do not hesitate to tell you. You are yourself a Sicilian and know how Sicilians feel about family relationships. They hold them to be sacred. One is under an obligation to assist a nephew, an uncle, even a second cousin. How much more so a dearly beloved brother!'

'How true,' said Ray.

'I'll be brief,' said Tamburelli. 'Nevertheless, I want you to fully appreciate the timeliness of your loan, for that is all I consider it.'

Ray waved his hand.

'As you know,' said Tamburelli, 'the new native revolutionary Libyan government has expelled many Italians who have long been resident in that country. As I'm sure you know, that country was once an Italian colony and many of the Italians

36

resident there were third-generation inhabitants. At any rate, my brother, Renato, went out there twenty years ago. He worked hard and established himself in a small pharmaceutical manufacturing business. After much struggle to support his wife and five children, he finally began to see the light at the end of the tunnel and to provide his family with a comfortable living. Now comes this new despotic government. It confiscates his business by decree. It arbitrarily expells all Italians from the country. My brother, Renato, and his family are told to quit the country where he worked so hard on forty-eight hours' notice. They have just arrived in Palermo, penniless. It is my obligation to support the entire family until Renato can find something—a job or, perhaps, a small business by which to support seven souls and feed seven mouths. Is this not a tragedy?'

'It certainly is,' said Ray warmly. 'Please be assured that I am happy to have been of service.'

'You Americans do not entirely appreciate the free and easy ways of your system of government,' said Tamburelli. 'Libya! Bah! Well, then, one of these days, *signor*, I should like to have you meet Renato. He will thank his benefactor in person.'

'Don't mention it,' said Ray.

Tamburelli put the money into his pocket. 'What I like about you, even above your liberal attitude, is your courtesy and quickness of understanding.'

'Thank you,' said Ray. 'After all, I have the advantage of being myself a Sicilian.'

'Quite so.'

'My *soggiorno obbligato*——' began Ray.

Tamburelli waved his hand. 'There is none, *signor*. You are a welcome visitor. If you wish to remain in Sicily, you may do so anywhere. If you wish to leave us and travel on the mainland, you may do so at your pleasure. Go with God wherever your fancy leads you.'

'That is very fair and considerate.'

'We shall do even better. We shall provide you with the necessary Italian passport and whatever documents you require, so that you may travel wherever you wish on the Continent.'

'Thank you. I shall study to repay your kindness.'

'You are remarkably *simpatico*,' said Tamburelli. 'You will do well in our country.'

Tamburelli was sincere enough. He liked Ray. Not as a person—that was irrelevant—but because there had been a meeting of minds. He approved of a man who comprehended without words his own mental drift. With a man like this Occhiaccio, wasteful preliminaries could be avoided. This American possessed that Byzantine sagacity which was the inheritance of every successful Sicilian. In a guarded, cautious fashion, the men became friends. Now that Ray was free to leave, he was no longer in such a hurry. He rented an apartment in Palermo on a short-term lease. Tamburelli introduced him to a few people. What was more, he began to give Ray the score.

'You must first of all understand that the Honored Society is going through a crisis,' said Tamburelli. 'It has less of the world's goods than you may suppose. It is steadily losing even its most prized possession, prestige, that which its members call respect. Your donation, for instance, to the Castellammare Triumvirate—that's what we call them—it was generous, more than Perilli expected. Yet it was not for themselves alone. The entire *kosca* in that area will share and benefit by it.'

'I anticipated as much,' said Ray. 'It does not go well nowadays with the men of respect, you say?'

'It goes badly. The *carabinieri* are bearing down with ever more power. As for the members, I've seen many of them sent away by the police to some obscure town in the north. There they are mocked when they walk down the street, jeered by the urchins of the town. When a *mafioso* loses prestige, what has he left? Theirs is no more a lucrative business. It operates in the poorest parts of the country.'

'But they're still operating here on the island, aren't they?'

'Certainly,' said Tamburelli. 'They're still in the building business, in smuggling, prostitution, and gambling. Some of them enjoy the pose that they are too honorable for the traffic in women. Don't believe it. As for the gambling——' Tamburelli shrugged and smiled. 'It's hardly that by your American standards, from what I hear. Nevertheless, some of them still make money. Then, there are other things. For instance, we had an earthquake here a few years ago. Millions of lire in earthquake reconstruction money were to have been siphoned off. Well, they got some of it, but the police nipped it in time. On the whole, however, most of them have become, how would you say——?'

'The literal American expression is "smalltime," ' said Ray.

'Exactly. The typical *capo* here doesn't get rich. Most of them seek respect as their reward. Our traditional southern attitude. That doesn't mean, though, that our peculiar institution has withered away. This island and Calabria are still the most backward regions of Italy. The government is using the *soggiorno obbligato* more widely now.'

'Is that what I was supposed to be under?'

'Nominally,' said Tamburelli. 'But, after all, you are an American. And I shall be frank—I have very heavy living expenses.'

Tamburelli had pocketed Ray's money with a glow of satisfaction. He would have abrogated Ray's *soggiorno obbligato* for half that amount and still had enough to pass around to others in the prefecture and the *questura*.

In his later travels about Italy, Ray met a number of these banished members of the Honored Society. The story was always the same: With the concurrence of the police, the courts, and the procurators, these brothers had been banished to small towns in distant parts of Italy and kept under careful and constant scrutiny for months or even years. Distant! thought Ray mockingly. The whole goddamned country is smaller than the state of California. A thoughtful *mafioso*, one Cortino, congratulated Ray on Felice's good sense in having emigrated to America. 'The law in America may be too easy,' said Cortino, 'but at least it is consistent. Now, in Italy the law is abominable, not because it is erratically harsh but because it is inconsistent and unpredictable. It is not for nothing that we call the law here *la sunnambula*, the sleepwalker. Italian law operates on the assumption that people are idiots and scoundrels. Very logically, the people have retaliated by despising the law. They always have; not only we who are professional denigrators of the law, but the so-called law-abiding citizens. Take this wretched little town in which we must abide. They are not happy to have us. We live like dogs in the local *osteria*. The innkeeper doesn't like us because our presence discourages what he considers to be more desirable guests. The locals here —we can hardly understand their speech or they ours. They are not about to invite us into their homes.' He sighed. 'It isn't as it used to be. The only time that the Honored Society is going to be completely eradicated from the south—I'm talking now about Sicily and Calabria, Italy's backyard——'

'Like Mississippi in the United States,' said Ray.

'Like every big industrial city in America. You Americans have nothing to be complacent about. Look at you! The American mountain labored and sent you back.'

'Only temporarily,' smiled Ray.

'Italy needs a social revolution,' continued Cortino, 'education, birth control——'

'You people, above all, aren't going to buck the church,' said Ray. 'You're hand-in-glove with it. You're talking from both sides of your mouth.'

'That's the root of the problem,' continued Cortino, as though he had not heard, 'less children, less churches, more schools for those who are born.'

'Nonsense,' said Ray. 'You're talking like the Italian Communist Party. Worse than that, like one of those liberals intoxicated with his own voice. You people are still a part of the Establishment.'

'You don't have to be a Communist to oppose the Curia nowadays,' said Cortino. 'Any intelligent man knows that the Vatican is the great fishbone in Italy's throat, the curse which keeps us poor, ignorant, and overpopulated. I, a good Catholic, believe that the Vatican must be removed from its official monopolistic position.' He stared at Ray. 'Do you believe?'

'Certainly not,' said Ray. 'Not even an emotional attachment. My father, from what my mother has related, was a priest-eater, bitterly anti-clerical. Many times he told her that the church was the source of Italy's misfortunes.'

'You have the advantage of me,' said Cortino. 'My heart still melts when I infrequently enter a church. I cannot help it. It's a childhood conditioning.'

40

Later on, when Ray talked to Crispi, another of the forlorn exiles of the Honored Society in a lonely North Italian hamlet, the man complained bitterly. 'Our people are beginning to crack, to break up. They don't stick together any more. I know for a fact that some of them go secretly to the police and tell them whatever they know, in an attempt to have their *soggiorno obbligato* eased and shortened.'

'No more *omerta*?'

Crisp snorted. '*Omerta!* Of course it is weakening. We haven't the strength to enforce silence. When the force decreases, the lack of respect rises. It is as inevitable and predictable as the law of supply and demand.'

'I'm struck by one aspect of your native Mafia,' said Ray.

'What is that?'

'I never expected to find so many knowledgeable members in its ranks. In the American connotation, a *mafioso* is a mobster—a semiliterate hoodlum—cunning, perhaps, but uneducated and parochial in his thinking.'

'Thank you,' smiled Crispi. 'What in the world did you expect—barbarians? What you call knowledgeability is our native Sicilian heritage. We are in some ways like the Jews. We have had to bow to superior strength for two thousand years, survive, and still retain our individuality. But you, *signor*, you somehow do not fit your own definition of what you call a mobster.'

'I happen to be a university graduate,' said Ray modestly, 'and a master of arts.'

'Indeed!' said Crispi admiringly. 'What a country!'

Ray reflected back on some of Tamburelli's observations. 'Sicily is no longer desirable for the Honored Society,' Tamburelli had said. 'It is being patrolled by more than four thousand *carabinieri*. And they don't accept bribes. A unique phenomenon in Italy! They are actually a military organization responsible to both the Ministry of Defense and the Ministry of the Interior. As a result of this dual command, they act with complete independence. They make their own law.'

'They really don't take?' said Ray.

'Exactly.'

41

'But you don't mind taking?'

'That's different,' said Tamburelli. 'I need the money desperately. And, besides, you're an American. What have you to do with all this?'

'Nothing,' said Ray. 'I feel alien in this country. I don't feel at home here. I'm a New Yorker.'

'Then you would feel more at home in Milan,' said Tamburelli. 'They are the New Yorkers of Italy.'

'I don't know,' said Ray. 'But here I feel as though I were in Mississippi or Alabama. No, its even worse than that. It's more like Mexico. You know, *mañana*. If you don't do it today, you can do it tomorrow.'

'Ah,' said Tamburelli, 'our *Hispanidad*. Together with the church, the greatest political problem of Italy—I should say, psychological problem—is what I would call *Hispanidad*, the southern way of doing things. It's the southerners who crowd and preempt the government offices and bureaus, you know. They operate in the traditional way—languid indifference and inefficiency. As you say, what is not done today can be done next week, next year, or not at all. When you get on a government payroll, you have a secure job. It's almost impossible to discharge one of those paper shufflers and it takes ten people to do the work of one. It's the southern style. Everything is accomplished after a fashion by time-wasting ceremonious personal contact. We call it *personalismo*.'

'We call it fuckupismo,' said Ray.

'I beg your pardon?'

'Let it pass. It's untranslatable.'

Tamburelli cocked an eyebrow in Ray's direction. 'You joke, *signor*, but I am serious. Ours is a heritage from the times that Spain controlled Sicily and southern Italy. If you want a new public urinal built in a Calabrian crossroads village, you have to go through channels and interviews. You'd think an international treaty was being thrashed out. Then these little clerks think they are doing you a favor when they finally stamp the last document. What Italy needs is American methods.'

'We aren't doing so well, either,' said Ray. 'Back in Washington, D.C., even the Republicans are full of that *Hispani-*

dad.'

'It could never be that bad. *Hispanidad* involves paying off, going through extralegal channels, making contact with someone influential to get something done—the smallest thing, getting a permit to fix your toilet. The government clerks look at the citizen on the other side of the window as if he were a criminal. If you want a permit to build a doghouse, they won't look at you till you produce your birth certificate. Without the necessary papers, you can't travel, choose a trade, take a job, or even die.'

'Sleep with a girl?' said Ray.

Tamburelli chuckled. 'Italians would take to the barricades and go Communist if that happened. In the meantime, the citizen doesn't officially exist. He stands all day in line in the corridor of some government office on some stupid errand. Some of the clerks won't even talk to the citizen on even dates. They are only open for business on odd dates. I'm not joking. I saw a seventy-five-year-old man the other day who wanted to renew his driver's license. They said he would have to produce his grammar school certificate.'

Ray began to laugh.

'I'm serious,' said Tamburelli. 'If your house is robbed and you complain, they won't listen to you unless you can produce the five hundred lire for the government stamps which have to go on the duplicate copies of the official complaint. If you're an Italian, you have two choices—you can either hang yourself or go insane. That's why Italians always laugh. If they didn't, they'd be running berserk and killing the civil service clerks. What a country! That's why Italians have gotten into the habit, as some politicians point out, of setting fire to a forest in order to boil an egg—so long as the forest is public property.'

'That's why so many Italians went to America,' said Ray.

'Ah, America,' sighed Tamburelli. 'You have capitalism, a capitalism that works. Long live *laissez-faire*! Poor Italy! Never was such an amiable country so badly misgoverned by pigs and idiots.'

'But you're part of it,' said Ray. 'Deputy Tamburelli is only another pinch of emery dust in the gears of government.'

'What choice do I have?' said Tamburelli. 'If I don't play the game, a hundred others would be glad to step in and replace me. I conform to the system, but I despise it.'

Descending from Tamburelli's lofty theoretical heights, Ray fully agreed that, based on his own experience, things just didn't function in Italy. The people worked hard. If one had a little patience, they accomplished the job in a sort of half-baked way. It took longer because one had to show them how. More of them could paint pot-boiler landscapes than fix toilets. If you flushed the john in a good place back in the U.S.A., it worked. You took that for granted. If it didn't, you called maintenance. Somebody came up with a bag of tools and made it work. If you were living in an apartment in New York City, a window, a faucet, anything, you called the super, he sent up a handyman, and the thing was done. If you weren't handy yourself, you called a plumber, or an electrician, or a roofer, or whatever you needed, and the job got done.

Here? All thumbs, everything uphill, ass-backward, *Hispanidad*. Pure fuckupismo. The Romans, really the transplanted southern bureaucracy which controlled the heart pump of Italy's capital, had a style all their own. Ray discovered that the best way of expediting his business, whatever it was, and getting quick results was to pay off—baksheesh, graft, bribes. He thanked his stars that he had the wherewithal, the ice, to spread around. The government clerks were secure, but their salaries were incredibly small. They moved and bestirred themselves for the American deportee because he paid a generous fifty percent in advance and the balance promptly upon completion of the favor. Money, money, money—that was what made this fucking Western civilization go round. It was probably the same way in the Communist countries. Those con artists in the Communist Bloc were no different. Human nature was the same all over the world. And when a government ran everything from one main central spot, even the placing of a village privy, everything was bound to get all screwed up. Free enterprise. It wasn't the best, but it worked better than anything he'd seen. *Laissez-faire*, and the more *laissez*, the better. When he got home, he promised himself, he would join the Republican Party, the most conservative wing of it.

But all of this was mere icing on the cake. Ray finally struck pay dirt with Tamburelli when he casually observed: 'You might be interested to learn that my *cumpare* back in America, my beloved mentor, once told me that there is, in fact, no so-called American Organization. All we have, according to him, is a loose industrial association of people in the same business. It is not really a monolithic organization but rather a great public market where the vendors all carry on their enterprises by a license or a franchise.'

'Whatever it is,' said Tamburelli, 'it certainly has no connection with this inglorious, bedraggled ghost of a Sicilian Mafia. There is only one tenuous link left, the narcotics traffic. In this area, we——' he caught himself, '—they are still able to cooperate with American businessmen to move the drugs from the Middle East to the refining laboratories in Milan and Marseilles. And from there to America. But that, too, is shrinking. I understand that the Mexican growers of inferior opium are cutting more and more into the traffic.'

Ray had not been particularly enjoying this idle chatter with Tamburelli and was becoming restive. Still, his patience as a good listener had paid off. Tamburelli's slip of the tongue offered a small opening. He decided to take the bear by the snout.

'*Signor* Tamburelli, let us be frank with one another and more specific. If I may change the subject, I am very much interested in entering the pharmaceuticals business in Italy. I have capital to invest and some small experience in that business.'

Only by a small flicker of his eyelid did Tamburelli indicate that he understood. 'Indeed? How can I be of assistance? I know nothing of that business.'

Ray took another stab in the dark. 'Perhaps not. But you may be able to give me entrée, introduce me to some people or person with whom I can come to terms.'

Tamburelli made a show of being deep in thought.

'If I establish myself and begin operating,' said Ray, 'you will not lose by it. In fact, you will profit handsomely. I will set aside a specific percentage of the profits for you.'

That was what Tamburelli had been waiting for. He nodded

slowly.

'Someone does come to mind,' he said at last. '*Signor* Roberto Greco, my colleague in the Chamber. He may be interested in your proposals.'

'I'm listening.'

'Greco makes his home in Rome. He's quite a man, of many diverse interests.'

'Now that I'm a free man, I've decided to make my permanent residence in Rome also.'

'You could do worse,' said Tamburelli. 'When are you leaving?'

'In a week. There is nothing further to keep me here.'

'I will write you a letter of introduction to Greco.'

'Perhaps you should just telephone him.'

'I'll do both,' said Tamburelli. 'But the letter of introduction remains the cornerstone of our southern system. And Greco is one of our own. Which reminds me—I think my brother, Renato, will soon be entering the employ of Greco.'

'I'm glad to hear that,' said Ray. 'He'll feel good to be paying his own way again. Nothing is more bitter than to accept help from others, even if it is a close relative.'

'How true,' said Tamburelli. 'Dante said that once. And Renato is a proud man who has always worked for himself.'

'What kind of position will he be taking?' asked Ray.

'Greco has many interests, aside from politics. He is also in the pharmaceuticals manufacturing business, the same industry in which Renato has experience.'

Ray did not press further questions. He was not really interested.

'Very well, then,' he said. 'I have a feeling that your introduction may prove profitable for all of us. I will keep in touch with you.'

Tamburelli rose and so did Ray.

'It has been a pleasure to know you, *Signor* Tamburelli,' said Ray. 'Despite my deportee status, I must concede that travel is broadening.'

'The pleasure is mine,' said Tamburelli. 'For an American, you are a most civilized man.'

Standing at the stern rail of the steamer, Ray waved his hand at the receding mountains of Sicily.

'A lovely sight, isn't it?' said a Palermitano beside him.

'The loveliest,' said Ray. 'No spectacle more beautiful than Sicily sinking into the sea.'

CHAPTER 3

The true Italian vice was talk. They adored conversation, even when the world was crumbling under their feet. Every step toward disaster must be accompanied by ten thousand words. Ray talked, perforce, and finally settled down in a Roman luxury apartment like a tired chicken hawk. Tamburelli had also tipped him off to another deal. A financially distressed princeling, was trying to sell his villa on the coast near Anzio at an exceptionally low price. 'I give you this information because we are friends,' said Tamburelli. 'It is an incredible bargain.'

'I won't be staying in Italy that long,' said Ray. 'At least, I hope not.'

'It doesn't matter. At the offering price, you will always be able to resell it at a profit. Have no doubts. That blue-blooded idiot has squandered his entire fortune. He is a compulsive gambler and a drug addict and so are his wife and mistress. And the price of heroin keeps rising.'

'Man!' said Ray. 'Does he have hemorrhoids?'

'No,' said Tamburelli, 'but his children are homosexual, I hear.'

'I'd say he has problems.'

Tamburelli varied his usual urbanity by spitting. 'These titled degenerates are one of Italy's problems.'

'Fine,' said Ray, 'I'll go down there and look over this big sleeper.'

For the asking price, it *was* a sleeper. Ray purchased it and engaged a contractor to commence renovations. These people were real screw-ups, but, at such prices, the property was worth it. It had originally been a farmhouse, actually a manor.

Fortresslike, old, with massive stone walls. Ray laid out money to soften and disguise the hostile architecture with sinuous, slender pillars that supported the roof of the loggia. Over the great fireplace in what was now a kind of living room-cum-library with a lofty vaulted ceiling had been carved a coat of armorial bearings, the colors faded and flaking off. Ray despised these heraldic reminders of impotence in this haunted house of an ancient sunny land. They were a reproach, paper dragons. He also had the contractor improve the dour medievalism of the entrance hall. The floor had been of roughly cut stone slabs. Ray had the area repaved with white and black marble squares like a chessboard. He also had the contractor face the harsh stone walls with a soft warm marble with many rounded niches. In those niches he had placed busts on pedestals. When the job was done, the house began to assume an air. But such trouble! Italians, his own people, were the greatest stonemasons, artisans, and artists in the world. Yet the brain work, the planning, was always uphill, the hard way. One step forward and two steps back. Never had a people as talented as the Italians been saddled with such a lousy system. No wonder the Italians had emigrated to the Americas, anywhere, all over the world, to get away from that system. The upstairs rooms had been left unimproved and sparsely furnished with a few dark, heavy pieces of furniture. Masochistically, Ray had left those rooms undisturbed to remind himself that he was in Italy, not Florida. His place on Key Biscayne had been all glass and stone, but softer, with a broad green lawn all around and a big kidney-shaped swimming pool, with the bay waters seen through the palms. Those who could bought the right screening to shut out the real Florida, a sleazy flat swamp, the palmetto state, scrambling for a living. The only part of Florida that mattered was the southeastern coastal strip where the boys had entrenched themselves and where they had good working relationships with the local politicians. Miami Beach was now a forest of twenty- and thirty-story high-rises, a monument to the boys. Florida was okay as long as you had it. There he had had it. Here in Italy he still had it. But it was different; the atmosphere was oppressive. Not like New York City, where he had ridden high for twenty years before being deported. Ray had landed in Italy feeling unfriendly. Italy reciprocated his feelings.

Having started the villa on the road to rehabilitation, Ray returned to Rome. For his money, the capital of Italy was an overrated cliché. It's charm was lost on him. It should never have been. While waiting for his introduction to Greco to jell into something tangible, Ray began to examine Rome more closely. Grateful to have escaped from Sicily, he made a dogged attempt to enjoy life. His three *caporegimes* Nicky Polo, Tony Saldana, and Beniamino, were remitting faithfully by courier. From Al Poggio, his subboss, he heard nothing. That was bad. Knots never unraveled themselves. Problems never solved themselves. You had to do it—in person. You. Nobody else. Nevertheless, he was here in Rome, Poggio was in New York, and frustrated rage and anxiety were a waste of energy. Whatever the three honest *capos* were remitting wasn't enough to finance an escape from Italy. More important, it wasn't enough to engineer a comeback in New York via a legal acquittal. Anyone could slink back to the United States. The idea was to return openly and to make it stick. No question, Al Poggio was working behind his back with that thief Don Leonardo Codi and stealing him blind. And figuring ways to muscle out the boss altogether. Ray had no doubt that he would eventually be able to take care of Poggio. In the meantime, he would have to play along. His only regret was that Al Poggio had only one life to lose. But, first things first. A few good narcotics deals were the logical answer. He had to organize these now, while he still had plenty of funds. He had to be looking ahead a year, maybe two years, from now. While waiting for Greco to act—these Italians moved like frozen molasses—he began visiting Monte Carlo as a means of distracting his mind from his unease and inner worries. The documents provided by Tamburelli shielded him from interference from Italian, French, and Monegasque authorities. Why should anyone object? Ray was quiet, of good appearance, well mannered, well dressed, and spent his money freely as well as judiciously. In certain official minds the thought occurred that it would be pleasant if more legitimate tourists conducted themselves as decorously as this man, for he was obviously not one of their tribe.

Sitting at a baccarat table in Monte Carlo, Ray studied his surroundings. It shouldn't be hard to heist this place if it was set up right. But doing so meant having the right people. Where would you get the right people? Anyhow, heisting was a losing proposition. He needed far more money than that and with less risk. Not that Monte Carlo couldn't be knocked over. It wasn't what he'd seen in Vegas. That town had a tough security system set up by men who'd been in illegal gambling all their lives before settling in the legal paradise of Nevada. Wherever there was gambling and money, there were hustlers, kooks, psychos, angle artists, and mechanics. Money always brought the maggots swarming out. All you had to do was read the *Wall Street Journal* and note that the SEC never had enough budget and people to police the legit crooks on the Street. Right to the very top of the government, there were never enough watchers to watch the watchers who were watching the watchers. Larceny in the human heart was a vulture which flew in ever-narrowing circles till it arrowed up its own rectum and robbed itself by devouring its own entrails. Perhaps the security people in Monte Carlo knew their characters and who to watch. The weak spot, however, was that there was no way to close off this place as Vegas could be snapped shut. But, then, Vegas had more to lose. Compared to this operation the Vegas take was so big it was no contest. American knowhow had put gambling on a mass-consumer basis. The casinos flew the little people to Vegas for twenty-five bucks round trip, with the trimmings included. Just bring money. Per John, the casinos figured they made back their twenty-five bucks three times over, and that included the pink champagne in paper cups. There *had* been a few attempts in recent years to heist Vegas. The police there and the sheriff's deputies could get the town sealed off in eight to ten minutes. By that time everything had been covered—the highways, bus stations, rail tracks, and airport. Within a half an hour, a mouse could not have sneaked out of town without hitting a police roadblock. After the town had been clicked shut, the cops tapped an internal intelligence network—bartenders, waitresses, bellmen, shills, pit bosses, stickmen, porters, and everything in between, a lot of eyes that could notice anything worth noticing—to nail down the heisters, on the assumption that they were still inside.

Ray tried to focus his atention on the game before him and grunted with the effort. His mind kept skidding into the past. There had been one particularly profitable crap game he had run that kept moving along from one big hotel to another or from an apartment house along the Upper West Side and as far down as 57th Street. The Upper West Side was at its sleaziest in those days, which was okay with him and other crap game entrepreneurs. The Puerto Ricans and the blacks had been moving south steadily until they were at 96th Street, then at 72d Street, and, finally, at Columbus Circle and there was no place farther to go because that was where Auto Row started—at least it did in those days. The games were often held in the big old apartment houses on Riverside Drive somewhere between 72d and 116th streets. Some of those apartments were big ten- and twelve-room layouts, monster-sized rooms from the old days when the well-heeled German Jews had lived there on the Drive and West End Avenue. New York Jews and New York Italians, New Yorkers with middle-class money and middle-class tastes. His own tastes. He talked their language. He was a part of that world, understood it, knew his way around, and felt secure there. You just didn't change your life-style no matter how much money you stepped into. This European scene, Ray admitted, made him nervous; he didn't understand it. Where were the powerhouses in this Europe? What and who called the turns? He groped, tried to understand, and disliked what he saw. The titled beggars and the aristocratic hangers-on of the Roman and Monegasque jet-sets made no sense to him. Why titles? What were titles, especially Italian titles? He had already met a few Sicilian *baroni* and *conti*. They had been on the bum so long, they had become a special type. The Mafia *gabellotti* had taken over their worthless eroded acres so long ago, it was forgotten ancient history. Where did they get the price of admission into this joint, or a presentable dinner jacket, or a clean shirt, or chips with which to play? Maybe they had their wives and daughters out hustling on the street. There was more sense of honor in a Sicilian peasant than in a Roman aristocrat. What the peasant resisted with all his might, the aristocrat conceded. Something about having a title, perhaps, made a pimp not a pimp. No doubt there were some among the blue-bloods who were honest as well as broke. So what did they do? Maybe they had emigrated up to Turin, working as auto mechanics and making Monte Carlo once a month. Who knew how they existed? No question, New York middle-class Borax was best. Play it cool. Keep down the overhead, give yourself a wide money margin. If you can afford a Rolls, drive a Chevy. Don't draw gunfire by waving a red flag with a dollar sign on it sticking out of your tail. So why was he driving a Ferrari? He made a mental note to dump the Ferrari as soon as he returned to Rome and to get a Fiat. But he recognized this line of association for what it was—an underlying unease scratching at the fabric of his rationalizations. He must start throwing a few parties as soon as he returned, broaden his local contacts, and get going on a junk deal. The sooner, the better. The money stream from New York was slowing to a trickle. The crap game cut had stopped altogether. His most lucrative game had been in a big auto assembly plant over in Jersey. Then, there were three more on the Upper West Side that Poggio was running for him. He had even tried phoning Poggio. The man was never in, never returned his calls, never wrote, never sent messages. He was being clipped, all right. That was the greatest sin of all. Poggio was going to wish that his mother had never borne him.

There had been that no-limit crap game he used to run in a fifteen-story dump around Needle Park—what was the name of it?—the Nebraska. Some name for a flea bag in Needle Park! A roach-ridden ruin rising above that loser's paradise. With the junkie kids, their bones sticking out of their backs, lying around the benches on the nod. During the day you could see them down there on the benches. At night, who knew what holes they crawled into? Or what they ate, or how they slept? Or where they got the money to buy the adulterated horse which the pushers peddled? A junkie could die in a dozen different ways—from an overdose of horse, an air bubble, an infected needle, a jolt of rat poison, or just plain collapse of the entire power plant. Perhaps they crawled down a manhole and pulled the cover over themselves. Or jumped into the Hudson River holding a NO PARKING stanchion in their arms. Was his a callous contempt for the junkie's predicament? Of course it was. Drugs were one business where your customer needed you desperately and hated you just as desperately. It was also the riskiest business of all. Most of the boys avoided it, some because the *infamita* of it bothered their consciences, most because of the ferocity of the 1956 law. He examined his own conscience. It still twitched in a kind of deadened fashion. What fascinated him about junkies was the insane ease with which they condemned themselves to a slow and painful form of suicide. After he returned to the U.S.A. he would never again get mixed up with the junk business. He promised himself that. He would stick to relatively moral enterprises—books, numbers, and gambling. His crap game customers had been Broadway people mainly. There were enough of them around in those days, still making it big in the legit theater and spending it just as fast. Or some visiting show business people from the West Coast who were making it even bigger and who were just as anxious to get rid of it, as if it were dirt in their pockets. It was hard to have any respect for the show business crowd. They received an invitation to a game and couldn't wait to get in with a wad of green stuff clenched in their hands. The cab drivers picked up the customers at their hotels and drove them to the corner where the watchers waited at the drop. The watchers paid the cab driver his cut and called the room to get the okay. Then the customer was given the room number or was taken up. It was usually in a three- or four-room suite with two bathrooms and a man behind the buffet feeding the players free drinks and sandwiches. The doorman frisked the customers as a matter of course. It wasn't the Broadway or Hollywood kiddies he was concerned about. As a matter of fact, showbizniks rather liked the idea of being frisked for a gun. It was flattering. There was a danger—from real crap game heisters, guys stupid enough to try and take a protected game. Heisters, being outlaws, were a running expense. If they got too stupid, the word went out to take them —any way. They were taken, but there were always new punks

54

coming up and willing to try. There was one gutsy rock head who heisted ten protected games before they nailed him. It was decided to make an example of him. They drove him to a meat-packing house in the lower East Bronx, rammed a barbed pig hook up his rectum, hoisted him to the rafters, and let him hang there screaming for two hours. When they let him down and pulled the hook, his intestines came out with it. Did that stop the heists? Only for two weeks. Outlaws were thick, of course. More to the point, they were ignorant. Protected games couldn't be knocked over without a reaction. You just didn't do those things. Ray had kept his games simple, straight craps, no layout, come bets, no side bets. The house took the shooter's money on all come-outs with double aces, not the cover money. The least a customer shot was one hundred dollars. If, by chance, he got too hot, there was always a house mechanic on standby to cool him down. Right. That game at the Nebraska had been a money-maker, even after expenses for the fix and the payoff to the main office for the franchise.

Ray's mind returned to the present. He looked up at the massive chandeliers over the baccarat table, the formally garbed croupiers, the women in their evening gowns, each one with her *cavaliere* beside or behind her. He took in the scene and laughed. The croupier-dealer looked at him in a puzzled way. Ray smiled and made a new bet. This was fun, like Alka-Seltzer for an ulcer. Like a diet of Drambuie when all one wanted was a glass of water. Gambling was a business for Ray and he took a jaundiced view of the player's risks. Money was ammunition and the act of committing it to chance was irrational. Money was something you had to make seriously, no excuses accepted. Gamblers were trying to prove something by losing it. Gambling was a crippling vice, like drugs or lushing. But—one accepted the fact of other people's hang-ups without trying to understand. One tried to profit by the kinks and go one's way. So what else was new? Food, with the right vintage wines. He was in the right diggings for it. This area had some of the world's finest chefs at one's service. It was all a cult, with excess calories he was trying to avoid. He needed the sauces and the sommeliers like a hole in the head. Food was something one ingested to keep one's power plant going, so one could avoid doctors and stay on target. Then there was the mystique of travel which he somehow viewed through the wrong end of the telescope. How did those travel agents stay in business? But they did. Look at all those hordes of tourists overruning Italy! What were they gaping at through their cameras? What were they seeing that escaped him? There was that German who had stumbled on the Spanish steps the other day. The man's spectacles and light meters went flying one way, at least six assorted cameras the other way. Photography was evidently a thing. Ray tried to be tolerant.

As a kid, any kind of car had been beyond his dreams. Now he had a twenty-grand Ferrari and someone else drove it for him. It was just as well. The Romans drove without hands and turned corners on one wheel. They moved in all directions without signaling, squeezing between obstacles, making jack-rabbit starts and stops. Never trust their hand signals; they're discussing politics or women. Rome's auto traffic had increased a thousand percent in the postwar years, while the narrow streets remained the same. Rome had piled up the world's highest accident rate, fifteen times that of New York City. So what was fun? Getting back into the action, back to the U.S.A. Getting squared away with Poggio, Codi, *et al.*, and stopping the leak in the money-dike with their heads. That was fun.

On one of his visits to Monte Carlo, Ray met Anthony Ponchielli, also known as the Punch. The Punch was a tall, jolly character with white hair and a rubicund complexion, a man who obviously enjoyed the pleasures which Ray sourly questioned. The federal government had deported the Punch twelve years before Ray's arrival in Italy. He had made the big adjustment, had gone native, as Ray defined it, and was reasonably happy. From his style of life, the Punch evidently enjoyed a substantial income. He had a sense of humor and a keen intelligence. He and Ray hit it off from the beginning.

A few months after their first meeting, the Punch observed: 'I notice when you're alone, you get lost in thought and your mouth turns down. You're not happy?'

'Who's happy?' said Ray.

'You've got it made. Lots of money. In good health.' The Punch patted his well-stored pot affectionately. 'You've got the waistline of a man of thirty.'

'I work at it.'

'It's indecent to poop everything the way you do. You should take a cue from the Italians, the saddest people in the world. With that goddamned system they've got around their necks, they have a right to be. But they laugh it off. Aren't you ashamed of yourself? I'll tell you what—open up a Boys Town, maybe. Like that priest in Nebraska. Italy is full of kids, all running loose like homeless cats.'

'You're not serious,' said Ray.

'Why not? It would be good therapy for your type.'

'Kids,' said Ray, 'are the source of every trouble. I'd sooner start a Snake Town. I think there should be a moratorium on reproduction over all the world for the next twenty years.'

'You feel that way about children? No kidding?'

'No kidding. I'll tell you the truth, Tony. I have a feeling the human race won't be around much longer. Also, that it wouldn't be such a bad thing.'

'You sure you're Italian? Maybe you need a good shrinker.'

'I know what I need—to get back to the States.'

'You'd be crazy to try it,' said the Punch. But he asked for no details and Ray did not volunteer them.

For two such apparently dissimilar men, they got along. Ray accepted the Punch's outward presence for what it appeared to be. There was obviously more to the man but Ray forbore to inquire further. For his part, the Punch was aware that Ray sensed the reserve behind his extroverted volubility. The reality was a guarded caution in their conversations. Each man respected the other's intelligence and did not ask the wrong questions.

The Punch made his permanent home in Rome, proclaimed a private love–hate relationship with the city, and lavished a sardonic eloquence on it. 'You know the standard crack about this burg? It's the town of the six P's—*papa, preti, principi, puttane, pulci, e poveri* [pope, priests, princes, prostitutes, fleas, and the poor]. Also fags, fucked-up traffic, fake art, a climate like Washington, D.C., too many churches, too many cops, and a government that doesn't know its ass from its elbow.'

'You're wrong about the government,' said Ray. 'The Sicilians have the political racket sewed up tight. They know what they're doing.'

'Yeah,' said the Punch. 'But then, again, where else can you find such polish, such genius, amid the majestic memories of the past?'

'Okay, Tony. Where?'

'Nowhere,' said the Punch emphatically.

'If you say so.'

'Don't you agree?'

'I'll even take Cleveland first. Even Philadelphia.'

'Man! You have it bad. This is the city of the Americans. You should feel at home here. The beautiful, crazy Americans with so much money and so much imagination. Where else can you find such a concentration of film, stage, and TV talent?'

'Where else?' echoed Ray.

'You're kidding me.'

'And you're conning me. I'm one of the boys, remember? I've been all through it with these showbiz fags, butches, junkies, lushes, kooks, and exhibitionists. I'm seeing the film the second time around. You don't have to knock yourself out with me.'

'You're sore because they deported you.'

Ray shrugged. 'You haven't bought the carny-pitch of this old whore town either. You're too smart. What's Italy? It's not even a has-been. It doesn't exist.'

'Man, you're a real hater.'

'A respecter.'

'What do you respect?'

'Muscle.'

'America?'

'I want my piece of it back,' said Ray.

'You're doing your time hard. It's like an acid. You're liable to eat out your guts.'

'This part of it I believe.'

'Okay, so you're going back. In the meantime, what?'

'Two or three good deals. Even one. That's all.'

'What kind of deals?' asked the Punch.

'Junk.'

'Are you ready to buy weight?'

'Only from someone I know. From someone who checks out all the way.'

'Maybe I can put you onto something,' said the Punch.

'You talk a lot, Tony. What's your angle? Do you have credentials?'

'The best,' said the Punch.

'Good. Maybe we'll do something.'

But, privately, Ray decided to have the Punch checked out. Junk was a no-joke business. Par excellence, a game where you had to know for sure whom you were talking to.

In Rome Ray experimented with young virgins, Italian, Swedish, Greek, Arabs from Tunis, and on two occasions a pair of matched nubile Negresses from the sub-Sahara, who were brought to the villa by Petri, the Neapolitan woman-trafficker. When Petri delivered the third matched pair, Ray telephoned him. 'Look, enough is enough. What do you think I'm doing here, collecting bookends? Get down here and take one of these broads back. I don't care if I am breaking up the set.' And he hung up.

The best piece of merchandise supplied by Petri was a young Japanese girl whose name was Truthful Fern.

'You should be aware, *Signor* Occhiaccio,' said Petri, 'that she has had three years of experience. I'm aware of your preference for the intact hymen. Truthful Fern, however, is unique.'

'How so?' said Ray.

'Her Japanese training. The Japanese are sexually superior in an absolute sense. Think of her as a Mercedes-Benz. A used Mercedes is preferred by connoisseurs to a new car of any other manufacture. So it is with Japanese women. You will never believe she is anything but a virgin. Like rock gardens and bonsai trees, the Japanese do that sort of thing well. For a man of your disposition, I would recommend her. She's like a Japanese dinner—bland, light, innocuous, and not much of that either.'

'As a matter of fact, that's what I prefer at the moment— low-calorie sex. How old is she?'

'Seventeen,' said Petri.

'Very well. Deliver your little fern tomorrow night. After dinner.'

'As you say, signor.'

The fact that Truthful Fern was far from extraordinary in bed recommended her to Ray. She spoke a wildly improbable French, some insane Italian, and had a fair store of Tokyo cocktail bar English. 'Supposing I call you TF,' said Ray. 'How many verbs do we need to make love?'

'Oh, not much,' she giggled.

'I'll tell you how it is with me,' said Ray. 'I'm not looking to climb any walls or blow any gaskets when I'm making it with a girl. I have heavy matters on my mind, you *capisce*?'

'Oh, yes,' giggled Truthful Fern, 'you are a tired business-man.'

'Right,' said Ray. 'I like a quiet life. Let's keep it peaceful and relaxed. Do you have any problems?'

Truthful Fern repressed a muted giggle. 'Oh, no. No problems. I am very happy.'

'Great,' said Ray. 'I like people with no problems. You know, Italian people laugh a lot also. That's because their hearts are breaking. You're sure your heart isn't breaking about something or other?'

'Oh, no,' smiled Truthful Fern. 'My heart is fine.'

Ray nodded approval. 'You had a good coach, kid. Very sensible people, the Japanese.' He stared down at the girl lost in the monstrously wide bed. 'What's the matter? You act like there were horseshoes under the sheet.'

'No, no,' said Truthful Fern. 'Too soft. I am used to a quilt on a tatami floor. It is much better for to make love.'

'No problem, kid,' said Ray. 'Let's get on that tiger skin rug.'

He slapped his hard belly muscles and slid off the bed. He dragged the sheet from the bed and spread it on the tiger skin. Truthful Fern rolled off the bed and walked quickly to the sheeted tiger skin. It was a sinuous, flexible, flowing movement, mincing, yet fast. It was all over before it started, like a crooked blackjack dealer with a deck of cards. She lay down on her back and parted her thighs. 'Much better,' she smiled.

'There is support for the back.' She glanced at Ray's erect organ approvingly. 'You are very large.'

Ray regarded his success complacently. 'Not bad for a man of forty-five.'

Truthful Fern caressed his body and punched his abdominal muscles gently. 'You are more like a man of twenty-five.'

'That's my girl,' said Ray. 'I can see you were raised right.' He positioned himself and entered her gently. He placed his hands under her firm little melon buttocks and pressed forward. She put her arms around his neck and gripped his hips with her crossed legs. 'Is it not so?' she said.

'It is so,' said Ray, 'except that I'm too tall for you.' Still in Truthful Fern, he rolled over on his back and reversed the position. She remained in the saddle and giggled softly.

'You ride me,' he said. 'Like a horse.'

She leaned forward, put her hands against his shoulders, raised herself a little and plunged down on his erect organ with a twisting motion. 'This is very good,' she said. 'Japanese men do not make love in this way. At least, I was not so trained.'

'You're a real kamikaze, babe,' said Ray. 'I can see you've done it this way before. You like?'

'I like,' said Truthful Fern and plunged harder. Ray played with her peachlike little breasts, pinched the nipples softly between his fingers, and nibbled at them with his tongue. She breathed heavily and rode him hard, intent on her orgasm. He concentrated on his end of the seesaw and gripped her waist hard, his big open hands almost enclosing it. A small rivulet of sweat trickled down between her breasts.

'We're going to make it together,' said Ray. 'Right?'

'*Hai*,' she said and nodded. Then she sighed, shuddered, and a small moan burst from her as her own orgasm let go. She fell forward and lay with her left cheek against his left shoulder. Her black hair was in his face and he inhaled the faint flowery perfume. He put his arms round her and they lay quietly for a few minutes.

'You're all right,' said Ray. 'Made in Japan.'

'Made in Japan is good,' she giggled. Then she stirred and Ray released her. The sexual connection was broken. She rolled off the rug, kneeled, and bowed to him in one move-

61

ment.

'Please. Excuse me.' She ran out of the bedroom.

Ray stretched, yawned, wrapped a big towel around his waist and sat up cross-legged on the tiger skin. The girl re-entered the room wearing a kimono and still combing her hair. She pattered toward him on small bare feet and bowed again.

'What did you say your name was?' said Ray.

'Truthful Fern,' she said.

'Helluva name,' he said automatically. 'You like it here?'

'If I please you.'

'You please me plenty. Would you like to stay here?'

'If it is all right with Petri-san. He owns me.'

'You don't believe that. He just owns your contract. Right?'
She nodded.

'I'll talk to him,' said Ray.

He did on the following day. 'That Japanese chick you sent me——' he began.

'You like her, *signor*?' asked Petri, alert.

'She's all right. I want to make a deal.'

'For how long?'

'A month. Maybe longer. Depends on how I feel. How much?'

'Four hundred thousand lire a month, *signor*.'

'You're kidding,' said Ray. 'I just want to rent her. Even first-class hotels give you a little break on a monthly rate.'

'Three hundred and seventy-five thousand lire.'

'Three hundred thousand lire,' said Ray.

'Three hundred and fifty thousand lire,' said Petri.

'Three hundred and twenty-five thousand lire,' said Ray.

'Make it three hundred and forty, *signor*,' said Petri.

'Done,' said Ray.

The next morning, breakfasting at the pool with Ray, the girl wore Japanese costume. They ate in silence. She picked delicately at her food and waited for him to speak.

'You're sure you're going to like it here?' he finally said.

She made a little bow. 'Very much.'

'I like you,' he said magnanimously. 'I will treat you well. One thing—no European clothes in this house. You kids don't have the figure for it. Japanese costumes only.'

She giggled. 'You like Japanese clothes?'

'On you, very much. The only thing.'

She bowed. 'I am here to please you.'

'Good show,' said Ray. 'We'll get along fine.'

And they did.

Of all the females, Ray reflected, Japanese were the best. They knew their place and were easy on your nerves, a silent massage between the shoulder blades.

'I will leave you now,' Truthful Fern was saying. She rose from her chair, bowed, and backed away from the table.

'Take care,' said Ray benevolently and watched as she disappeared into the apartment. Nice kid. Properly bred. Petri was right about that Mercedes-Benz quality. No question about it. He felt something toward Truthful Fern as close as he had ever come to tenderness. In a mildly euphoric mood, he lit an after-breakfast cigarette.

He repeatedly renewed his lease on Truthful Fern month after month and until he left Rome altogether, at which point, her face smiling impassively, she went back to Petri.

A nice broad, a really nice little broad.

CHAPTER 4

When the Chamber of Deputies reconvened, *Commendatore* Francisco Tamburelli came up to Rome to perform his duties as a servant of his constituents. Since his legislative duties did not preempt his entire time, he enjoyed ample leisure. He devoted much of it to the theater and the opera and, particularly, to a young actress whom he maintained in Rome. Being a gregarious man despite his grave outward appearance, he also delighted in the company and conversation of friends. He had many of them in Rome. Raimondo Occhiaccio, the obliging and generous exile with the barbariously unpronounceable American name, became one of Tamburelli's favorites. They had already attained a first-name basis. Precisely because Ray impressed Tamburelli as a man with a disinterested and unsusceptible heart, a man uninclined to petty intrigue, and the Sicilian legislator imparted the details of his arrangements with the actress.

'Don Francisco,' said Ray one day, 'since you have done me the honor of trusting me, I'll speak the truth about this business.'

'Please do, Raimondo,' said Tamburelli.

'I don't like it,' said Ray. 'A professional woman, a *puttana*, in whom one does not confide is one thing. Such are the females which I use and I am, on all points, far less vulnerable than you are, I have less to lose.'

'Oh, you're much too careful,' smiled Tamburelli. 'You see snakes beneath every bush. What are you suggesting?'

'That you break off with this actress of yours. Discharge her. Pay her off. Get rid of her. Softly, gently, and amiably. Without rancor. Disengage yourself cautiously, as you would from a bear.'

'For heaven's sake! Why? In any case, I don't have the character to do so. I frankly admit it. She is half my age, a lovely young woman of twenty-five. Her voice is a viola even when she is indulging in idle gossip. Which she does, often, I admit. But she has breasts like two ripe melons. She has the most delightful nipples in the world and buttocks of polished ivory. She makes love like a little leopard. She would arouse lust in a dessicated saint. And I, Francisco Tamburelli, have her. And I need her desperately.'

'As an antidote to your wife and five children in Palermo, I suppose.'

'What have you against her? You haven't even seen her.'

'You're a fool, Francisco. I don't have to. I already know her.'

'Then describe her,' challenged Tamburelli.

'She is young, she is voluptuous, and she is in show business.' Ray spat deliberately. 'That is enough. She is treacherous, greedy, mercenary, calculating, and unfaithful. She will do more than waste your money, my friend. She will break your political neck and tumble your bones and career into a spiked grave. Better men than you have fallen into that hole.'

'What a harsh, vindictive judgment on no evidence ! ! !'

'Believe me, Don Francisco, these remales are poison. Many an otherwise astute man has been ruined by them. Break off with her, in friendship only. Stick hereafter with the *puttane*, as I do.'

Tamburelli shook his head. 'You're much too suspicious.'

'Adequately so. That is why I have survived. Sleep with them to your heart's content. But never confide in them. The breasts, the hips, the secret place between the thighs, it does something to a man's judgment. You begin to feel kindly and eventually you succumb to the poison of tenderness. When you love a woman, sooner or later your tongue will slip. When it does, she will cut off your hair. That is a woman's secret and greatest pleasure.'

'You are very sure of yourself,' said Tamburelli mockingly.

'It is a religious principle with me,' said Ray. 'That is why I never married.'

'Surely, there is some woman in your life whom you love or have loved.'

'There is a woman in America who loves me. Thus far, I have risen above it and evaded the trap. Love is an enervating web, a bog. It saps a man's judgment. And in our business it is fatal.'

Tamburelli shook his head. 'There are good and honest women.'

'The honest ones bear other penalties.'

'You are a most unnatural Sicilian.'

'An exceptionally superior one. And I say it soberly. Women—yes. Make mine whores, prostitutes, courtesans—in a word, *puttane*. Treat them considerately as chattels and servants. They will serve you better and more safely than those who worm their way into your heart.'

'What a bleak picture you paint! No wife? No children?'

'Neither,' smiled Ray. 'And it is no bad life. As for children, I tell you seriously, Don Francisco, that the greatest injury a man can do himself is to father children. Wives are a necessary evil for most men, I'll concede that much. Mistresses are a risk. But children are a thousand times more dangerous than both.'

Tamburelli laughed. 'This is revolution and heresy. Even Heinrich Himmler had a wife. And so did Iago. Even the devil himself must have a favorite female tucked away somewhere, with whom he relaxes after a hard day of tormenting sinners.'

Ray chuckled. 'I like that. But listen to me. When I see a plump infant suckling his mother's nipple, chuckling, kicking his rosy little feet, opening his tiny hands and gripping your finger in his little fists, do you know what I see?'

'What?'

'An infant cobra. Newly emerged from the egg, but with its venom sacs already charged and fully as lethal as those of the adult.'

'Very pretty,' said Tamburelli dryly. 'Are you serious?'

'Quite. The infants have only one virtue in my eyes. They are easier to destroy.'

'I can't talk with you. You are simply too fantastically unbalanced on this subject.'

'So I've been told. No matter. I've warned you.'

'So you have. There is a streak of gruesome inhumanity in you that I never noticed before. I should say, an a-humanity, a kind of alienation which I find incomprehensible. Particularly in an Italian, the most humanized family group in the race of man.'

Ray gestured. 'I've been through all of this before. I want to discuss something of more pertinence, something more basic.'

'What, in God's name, could be more basic than these questions?'

'Stop being an Italian for a second,' said Ray. 'Do you know a man by the name of Anthony Ponchielli? Presumably an Italo-American deportee? Have you heard of him? Do you know him?'

'Nothing. What about him?'

'I was just asking. Very well. A second matter. I need two good men. You are my friend. If you can find me two such, I will make their fortune. And your own also, Don Francisco.'

'What kind of men?' said Tamburelli.

'Strong, faithful men, servants to whom I could trust my life, if necessary.'

'Ah,' said Tamburelli, studying Ray. 'If I know you, I have an idea of the kind of men you seek. *Sicarii*, life-takers.'

'Strong and skillful life-takers,' agreed Ray. 'But it's also important that they should have minds, that they should be men of judgment. I want them primarily to dig intelligence for me and to guard me. Their talents for destruction are important but almost secondary.'

'I do know of two such men,' said Tamburelli. 'Our Palermo Friends used them on a few delicate missions and they acquitted themselves with distinction. Yet they are not brothers.'

'Why not?'

'Because they are not Sicilians.'

'Tell me about them.'

'One of them is a Corsican,' said Tamburelli, 'a former *caid*, banished from Marseilles on pain of death. Some complicated internal affair concerning which I did not get the full details. These Corsicans seem to have a little Vatican of their own in

Marseilles which regulates the business affairs of their groups. I gather that he was convicted and expelled by his brothers. In that respect they differ from the Friends. A parallel might be Portuguese bullfighting as against Spanish bullfighting. At any rate he is now a masterless free-lance, existing on odd commissions and, no doubt, eating out his heart. Really, an outlaw.'

'What is his name.'

'Dominique Maestracci.'

'Such a man may interest me. Where is he now?'

'In Palermo, I believe.'

'Can you pass the word down to have him sent to me in Rome?'

'I think our Friends down there will be glad to see the last of him,' said Tamburelli wryly. 'He is like a reproachful ghost, a not entirely trustworthy skull, an alien *memento mori*. Remember, he's not a Sicilian.'

'I'm not parochial in my thinking. The Corsicans breed some good men. I'll give this stray Corsican cat a saucer of milk and make him mine. What about the other?'

'Even stranger. A wandering exotic bird who fits no cage. A Spaniard, a veteran of the Foreign Legion. An old soldier without indoctrination.'

'But a man seeking to make a living.'

'That, indubitably.'

'What is his name?'

'Juan Torres, I believe.'

'What a memory you have for names! No wonder that you are so successful in politics. I am interested in both, but I want Torres even more than Maestracci.'

'What is there about Torres that takes your fancy, Raimondo?'

'He was a soldier. I know soldiers. I understand them as some men understand horses, some tigers, some snakes. I can make even an unfaithful soldier faithful. I can make a cowardly soldier brave.'

'Now that you say it, yes, it is true. You should have been a soldier.'

'I was a good one,' said Ray. 'I took to the soldier's life like a seal to water.'

'I can believe that.'

'I will handle this team well. As my friend, have them sent up to me. You will do me, and yourself, a service.'

'It is done,' said Tamburelli.

'Now, the last thing.'

'God! What a man! What is it now!'

'The most sensitive and critical matter of all,' said Ray. 'Your colleague. Roberto Greco. Is he a trustworthy man? Can I do business with him?'

Tamburelli smiled ironically. 'Greco is a power. You can do business with him. You will have to, because you have no choice.'

'A big man, eh?'

'A powerful man. An intelligent man. Never underestimate him. A Sicilian. Like yourself, an exceptional Sicilian.'

'Tell me something about him.'

Tamburelli smiled. 'Ah, Greco! His biography will be written some day. I know the family. He was born the son of a Palmeritan cobbler. His parents and relatives helped him scrounge his way through the university till he became a country lawyer. He originally entered politics through the Catholic Party in Sicily. Under the Fascisti he remained unscathed. Under the Nazis, he remained on excellent terms with them. He, his friends, his mistresses, and his family never missed a meal. I'll concede he saved many people from being executed by the Germans, but his own pocket was always his first concern. In the postwar years he became an active mover in the Democratic Christian Party. Our own Sicilian Talleyrand. When Greco finally dies and goes to heaven, I have no doubt that he will persuade God Himself to vote for Greco.'

Ray nodded. 'I know such men. I have done business with them in America.'

'Never take Greco for granted. If you do, he will take your arm off.'

'My business has always been a risky one,' said Ray. 'I am eternally grateful to you, Francisco. I shall not disgrace you. I think I shall be able to dance with your friend Greco.'

Tamburelli nodded. 'Very probably. You even have something which Greco lacks, a typically American *brutalita*.'

'A good point. That is where many people underestimate the Americans. They are the real Romans of the twentieth century. Their mistakes and excesses are great, but their strength is even greater. Yes, Francisco, I am a willing American because they will hold the winning cards for many, many years to come. They can and will smash anything which opposes them. This I respect. I won two Silver Stars from them. Because of those stars, I respect myself also. I will deal with your Greco.'

'Raimondo,' said Tamburelli, 'you are a mysterious, many-layered onion.'

'As long as I don't make you weep. By the way, did your brother Renato start work for Greco?'

'He's doing very well there. His salary is liberal, although there is some risk attached to the work he does—if you know what I mean.'

'What kind of risks, physical or legal?'

Tamburelli looked mysterious. 'Perhaps you will find out for yourself when you meet Greco. You know, if one wishes to make a lot of money, one must be willing to take some risks. Is it not so?'

'That has been my experience,' said Ray.

And so they parted.

Ray thought about Tamburelli's cryptic remarks concerning brother Renato. It all added up rather vaguely. Renata was very probably in junk. Something to do with junk. Therefore, Greco was also in junk. Not a very brilliant deduction. A rather simple one, in fact.

Roberto Greco was a tall, broad-shouldered, and slim-waisted man with large, soft southern eyes and a masterful nose. An immensely prepossessing man, Ray decided. A man to make the women wet their pants before he takes them. Ray and Greco had finally met. The politician moved slowly, *piano, piano*. He was sizing up Ray for something. Okay. Ray relaxed and waited for the southern *modus operandi* to run its course. When Greco was ready he would bring matters to a head. Of the fact that there were matters, Ray had no doubt. Of Greco's sloth in this instance, Ray approved. Junk, the heart of the

70

matter, was murder and dynamite. Know with whom you are dealing. That held for Greco as well as for Ray. In the meantime, there were the little and enjoyable *antipastos* through which to wade. Through Greco, Ray began to meet some holders of Italian titles, the red, the black, and a sandwiched subspecies. With his mane of beautiful white hair and his noble Roman head, Greco cut a good figure. He wore a fashionable tan, tailored British suits, and, for an Italian, a minimum of jewelry. The little he did wear was good—a very thin Patek Phillipe wristwatch, plain platinum cuff-links, and no rings. Greco's voice was suave. A sexy sonofabitch. He spoke English with an Oxford accent, which against his mother tongue was pleasant, which gave the *contesse* pseudo-orgasms, even the white-haired ones. Greco was a voluble conversationalist. It was impossible to know what he was thinking, when he was lying, when he was not. Ray played it safe and believed nothing. While awaiting developments, he listened patiently as the politician attacked his favorite target, the Italian nobility. That means, Ray concluded, this character would himself like to be sporting a title. But it was against the law to assume one, wasn't it? And, anyhow, Greco wasn't the kind of a cat that would be satisfied just kidding himself.

'Our aristocracy,' Greco declared, 'is a special breed, the most unexclusive in the world, the easiest to meet, the poorest. At the moment, it is chic and in to include Italo-Americans within their circles. You are not a deportee, Occhiaccio, my friend, you are, if you please, an exile. How many illustrious Italians have been exiles at some period of their lives! It is a mark of distinction. Hence, your friendly welcome at the affairs where I have introduced you. Next week or next month, things may change. At the moment, the blue-bloods fancy Americans. The people dislike the blue-bloods; hence, they dislike Americans. You, Occhiaccio, is your American name ready Hodgkin? Permit me to advise you as a disinterested friend. Take that name out on a dark moonless night, bury it quietly in an unmarked grave, and drive a stake through its heart. You, I say, are somewhere in neutral territory. You are of Italian ancestry, of our people, A Sicilian like myself. You dress and speak well. You have means. For the moment that is

71

sufficient for these frauds of the *Almanach de Gotha*. As you know, according to Article 14 of the Italian Constitution, titles have no validity here. And, when the empty title is compounded by a real poverty, the pretensions of those red, black, and blue-blooded mongrels with their armorial bearings is doubly absurd.'

Ray listened and observed. Tamburelli had been as good as his word. He had sent up the two strays cats, Torres and Maestracci, from Palermo. Ray took them into his house and into his service with a strong and generous hand. They did homage willingly, and Torres even gladly. There were some farmers who could extract edible grain from a stony desert. Ray was such a farmer. He extracted respect from the stony desert of Torres' heart. The first task to which Ray set his new vassals was a more detailed report on Roberto Greco. They did their work well and Torres was the spokesman. '*Padrone*,' he said to Ray, 'this man, Greco, speaks from strength. He owns a six-thousand-hectare citrus plantation in Sicily. It is managed for him by *gabellotti* of the Mafia. They are glad to deal honestly nowadays. They send him his fair share. The pickings are no longer as good as they used to be. You have no doubt heard of the severe new government policy anent the Honored Society. The *soggiorno obbligato* is being rigorously enforced.'

'I have heard,' said Ray. 'For an outsider, Torres, you seem to be well informed on the activities of the Honored Society. It is—how would you say?—irregular.'

'It is a measure of their present weakness, *padrone*,' said Torres.

'That is also true,' said Ray. 'What else?'

'South of Milan,' said Torres, '*Signor* Greco owns another two-thousand-hectare estate where he raises pedigreed cattle.'

'A duke without the title,' said Ray. 'What else?'

'Let Dominique continue,' said Torres.

'*Padrone*,' said Maestracci, 'I took Rome and the north because I know it better. Your friend maintains a luxurious seventy-five-foot twin diesel yacht. It moves from one fashionable watering place on the Italian and French Rivieras to another, as *Signor* Greco's fancy dictates. He also owns a villa

72

at Portofino and a luxury cooperative apartment in Rome.'

'Good,' said Ray. 'There are other things, but I already know them.' His estimate of Greco rose. That sort of thing took important money, the kind which Greco could never have managed on his political perquisites. For a man who had risen from humble beginnings, this Sicilian, Greco, had done well. When Ray received confirmation from Torres that Greco had, indeed, been born the son of a cobbler, he almost admired this politician who obviously trusted no one, cheated most people, and was interested in cheating everyone. He laughs, he smiles, thought Ray, he puts his arm around your shoulder, he tells jokes to make other men laugh, and his own eyes never laugh. A good man to do business with. To have risen as high as he has in this sinkhole of a country takes a Sicilian brain. It is harder here, infinitely harder, than in America. Ray was making progress with the politician. Greco was implying without words that his association with Ray could be profitable for both of them. As Greco discoursed on aristocrats, Ray listened and thought, he must seriously hate them, since they are apparently his favorite subject.

'As in your America,' said Greco, 'their children go to certain schools, the right schools, the Sacred Heart, or the San Gabriele. They belong to the right clubs, the hunting club, the chess club, where no one, of course, plays chess, the golf club, where a few of them play it badly. Golf, being American, is in high favor among them. They even patronize American-type hamburger places.'

'Real swingers,' said Ray. 'Are they alive or just forty years behind the times?'

'Four centuries behind the times,' said Greco. 'Take the black nobility, for instance, the pope's lapdogs. They are so exclusive, even the spiders in their huge Roman palaces will not receive spiders from other palaces without a proper introduction. They keep large staffs of liveried servants. God only knows how they maintain themselves! Their children are openly homosexual and addicted to narcotics.'

With an effort, Ray had been maintaining a show of polite interest. Had someone wasted his time in this fashion back in New York, he would have had the bastard's head slapped off.

'How,' he said, 'do they pay for such an expensive habit?'

'Ah,' said Greco, 'they make themselves useful. Perhaps the elders owe their children more than they know.'

'Only one thing about these people interests me. Can they be useful to me?'

'You move like a true American,' smiled Greco. 'Very directly. The answer is—they can. But, first, let me tell you about our red nobility.'

'Here we go again. What are you on now, the Italian Communist Party?'

'But, no,' laughed Greco. 'The red nobility covers everyone whom the Holy Father has not preempted. The black crowd is especially devoted to the Pope. The red crowd would be like the old French nobility of the sword. You've heard of them, I'm sure?'

'Not a word, my field was accounting and business administration.'

'Well, then, like your American Four Hundred.'

'Oh, that! I've got news for you. There is no Four Hundred in America. Only about sixty family groups with the real muscle, and several thousand people connected with the tangle. It's a different ball game today.'

'A naked oligarchy,' nodded Greco approvingly. 'You Americans are much more realistic and honest about these things than we Italians.'

'In a way. The U.S.A. has money, the best toilets and ice-boxes in the world. That's how we disguise the stink and we're going to be able to do it for a long, long time yet. Italy is what we would call in American piss-poor—bad iceboxes, bad toilets, so you can't ignore the stink. We even have a Mafia in America. It's listed daily on the stock market page. It's the guts of America's Honored Society.'

'And you, my friend?'

Ray shrugged. 'I'm only a small businessman, deported for having run afoul of the American Mafia.'

'Exactly. And how do your affairs go?'

'They could go better. I was interested in what you said about those playboy types, the jet-setters. We've got something like that in the U.S.A., money without the titles.' Ray hunted for the right question. 'You say you've got some kind of working arrangement with these characters?'

'I find a use in my affairs for the gilded youth. These Bubis, Nikkis, Pepitos, Rudis, Tittos, Foffos, and the rest of it, with their American hippie-isms. The young ones, they dress like scarecrows, they never bathe, and consequently they stink. But they still race custom-built cars and they never dip a finger in cold water. They play and they spend.'

'What do they spend?'

'Money. As long as it's easily come by, without work. Take myself.' Greco tapped himself in the chest and a cold Sicilian hatred glazed his eyes. 'I had to work hard, at least, in the beginning. And I still work and pay taxes to my government. Whatever I have to.'

'God help your government, then, *commendatore*,' grinned Ray. 'I hope you never meet up with the American IRS. Those abortions have absolutely no sense of humor about taxes. Well, then, what is your real game?'

'In good time. I'm still on the gilded Bubis. They play at gambling and drugs and show business, as Marie Antoinette used to play at being a shepherdess.'

'Fine. So you have a big hatred and you're nursing it along. Now what keeps up your balloon?'

'Dreams,' said Greco. 'The drug business.'

'Is that what you've been telling me in ten thousand words?'

Greco laughed. 'A bad Italian habit. There's really no point in being so mysterious about it. Drugs are sold openly in Rome. The penalties are relatively light.'

'Then the prices must also be light.'

'I don't do business in Italy. The distribution and retailing in the large cities of Italy is all right for Greeks and Tunisians, not for me. It's the export end, the American market, I'm interested in.'

'Let's get down to cases.'

'We will,' said Greco. 'You're in the right country to do business with America. Italy is the world's largest supplier of heroin. True, the best refining laboratories are in southern France. But the impetus of the traffic arises here. The stocks of heroin in Italy are conservatively estimated to be about ten times the officially admitted quantity. Italy is a drug aircraft carrier. The mid-carrier between the Near East–Marseilles complex and New York. I tell you this so that you may drop your habitual American caution reflex. Here, things are—how would you say?—relatively wide open.'

'How does the heroin come here?'

'A considerable quantity is refined in Rome, Milan, Turin, and other large cities up north. Wherever there are considerable pharmaceutical manufacturers. I happen to be in that business also.'

'That interests me greatly,' said Ray.

'A great deal of it enters the country in the anchor lockers of ships, the nuts and bolts of aircraft, in fuel tanks, barrels of animal fat, cans of fish, any sort of tinned goods, tennis balls, chocolates, tourist suitcases, false auto compartments—in any way.'

'In the bras and panties of airline stewardesses?'

'But of course,' said Greco.

'It should be profiitable.'

'It's worth the risk. Let's put it that way. Right now, I have an interesting negotiation pending in Beirut. A large purchase can be made there. Would you be interested?'

'Definitely,' said Ray.

He did not like mysteries. Now that he had Greco in focus, he felt easier. The politician was obviously the chief of a drug-exporting outfit. Probably in the flesh business as well, on the financing end of it. Undoubtedly, in a number of smaller rackets. Everybody was in something over here that could make a fast buck—smuggling gold, cigarettes, women, munitions, stolen jewelry, or just peddling their bodies as did the young Italian cocksmen to elderly well-heeled American females, American fags, anybody. Why stop with Americans? Greco had still another good racket, Ray had learned from Tamburelli, one that went with his position. It was even better, possibly, than drugs. He speculated in land and concentrated on the construction of luxury apartments. The gimmick was that Greco was favored with government help, getting a thirty percent government subsidy before he even started the excavation. Once he had the buildings up, the violations of building regulations

76

were overlooked by government officials, who looked the other way as they held out their hands. Greco made it simple for himself most of the time. He bought the land just before the announcement of public improvements or land on which construction had hitherto been forbidden. After getting his construction permits, he resold the land for thirty times the price he had paid. Great, just great.

During subsequent meetings, Ray and Greco explored the proposed joint venture.

'I also do business with Esposito,' said Greco, 'the biggest opium grower in Mexico.'

'I'm not interested in Mexican opium,' said Ray. 'I plan to limit my deals to the Middle East.'

'There, too. We have contacts with laboratories, not only in Marseilles but also in Athens. If you want to get into the softer trade, we have a wholesale drug jobber in New Jersey who handles two tons of benzedrine each month and at least two tons of yellow jackets. On the really light merchandise, we have in Tijuana a warehouse where the marijuana is stored like baled hay.'

'I'm sold,' said Ray. 'We'll do business. There's one more matter I want to check out. Do you know a man named Anthony Ponchielli?'

'What about him?' said Greco casually.

'I met him a few times in Monte Carlo and here in Rome. We became friendly. I hinted at what I was interested in. He said he might be able to arrange something. Do you know him? Is he in this business?'

'What did you say to him?'

'I said I was interested in buying weight.'

'Were those the words you used?'

'Yes.'

'And what did he say?'

'Only that he might be able to arrange it.'

'Did you mention any names to him?' said Greco.

'None.'

'You did unwisely to say as much to him as you did. You have alerted him. For all you know, you may already be under surveillance. What you tell me now changes the situation.'

'It may abort our venture?'

'Precisely.'

'Go ahead.'

'A part of what Ponchielli told you was true,' said Greco. 'He was deported about twelve years ago. He now makes his living, the principal part of it, as a paid informer for the American Treasury, the Federal Bureau of Narcotics. As you know, they have a resident office right here in Rome.'

'Oh, my prophetic heart,' said Ray softly.

'You were saying——?'

'I had a vague feeling about Ponchielli. Repeat it carefully, *Signor* Greco. Is that man an informer?'

'Yes.'

Ray nodded somberly. 'Don't be concerned. Despite Ponchielli, our venture will go through.'

'What will you do?' smiled Greco.

'What would *you* do?'

'I would wipe him off the face of the earth. I would kill him.'

'As long as you said it first, *Signor* Greco. Very well, then.'

'When?'

'As soon as possible. Immediately.'

'I like your American dispatch,' said Greco. 'To seal my good faith, I make myself your willing accomplice.' He opened a drawer and passed a stack of bank notes across the desk. 'Here is my contribution to a praiseworty endeavour, the equivalent in Swiss francs of seventy-five hundred American dollars. Enough to destroy three Ponchiellis.'

'He has upset your operations, I take it?'

'Grievously, on two different occasions. I haven't been in a position to retaliate. If you can exterminate him, you'll make me very happy.'

'My pleasure,' said Ray, 'for myself as well as for you.'

'If I may make a constructive suggestion. Don't let Ponchielli die too speedily. Question him at length on his connections, his principals, and his *modus operandi*. Milk his brain before you disconnect it. It may be of invaluable assistance to both of us. Don't you agree?'

'Any reasonably intelligent man would agree,' said Ray.

'Let's leave things in abeyance for the moment. When I contact you again, you'll be satisfied that our security is intact.'

'You speak with confidence,' said Greco skeptically. 'How will you make certain?'

'Ponchielli will tell me how much he knows or doesn't know,' said Ray. 'He'll tell me whether or not he has passed pertinent intelligence to others.'

'How will you know he's speaking the truth?' persisted Greco.

'I suppose that's a matter of technique, isn't it? I'm not without resources. I think I can elicit the pure, unblemished truth from Ponchielli's lips. *Arrivederci, Signor* Greco.'

'*Arrivederci,*' said Greco.

Heroin had been around ever since Ray could remember. It rad always been a relatively small market and a modest business even well into the fifties. Somewhere around the middle sixties it began breaking loose and expanding fast. Not only H, but all kinds of softer mind-benders, the depressants, stimulants, hallucinogens, and marijuana. Even that venerable old hustler, cocaine, had made a comeback. It was in the act again and coining money, like a has-been Hollywood star with a contract, after twenty years of rotting idleness. How could intelligent people, apparently in their right minds—college students, for instance—let themselves get hooked? The phenomenon surprised Ray without eliciting his sympathy. His sole editorial position was one of sardonic neutrality and he could only conclude that they didn't know what they were getting into. This new, bright, turned-on generation was, in terms of its drug kick, the stupid generation. Ray was some twenty-five years older than his new crop of drug devotees, but, in terms of conditioning, the chasm was unbridgeable. Supposing I had children, he thought, and they became hooked, what would I do? I'd throw them out like garbage, for good and forever. And, if their mother objected, I'd throw her out also. The next man couldn't do it, but I could and I would. By Ray's standards and experience, these people were made of straw, concerned with matters which were irrelevant and unimportant. Of what significance could it be that the human race should survive? What if it *did* go down the drain? Better that it *should* go down the drain. Perhaps these people, their being bugged by such heavyweight bubbles, had driven them to the drug route. That was giving them the benefit of the doubt. More benefit than they deserved. Things had bugged Ray and his generation also. Remembering, he felt his old body scars. They were real, not just soul scars, whatever that was. His generation, too, had felt bored, frustrated, hostile, and impotent. But they hadn't broken down and dropped out into pills, acid, and mainlining. They had taken their lumps, picked themselves up off the canvas, and come up for the next round. For a lot of them, the next round had been the gas chamber, the electric chair, a cement kimono on a river bottom, or a stretch in the joint. That was a risk of the business. Meanwhile, the world about him was changing with bewildering speed. There were more drug users around than he had realized, and more new kinds of drugs. There were just more people around. Where were they all coming from? This thing with drugs wasn't being controlled; it was growing. Every high school kid who lit a reefer was a prospect for the harder stuff. If the college campuses all over the U.S.A., if the military bases all over the world, were demanding and buying the stuff, the junk game would climb to a permanently higher plateau. If he didn't get into the action and supply some of the demand, someone else would. Ray didn't need that chestnut to rationalize anything to himself. The first step was to get in there and start buying for resale.

Ray's previous experience in junk had been marginal and vestigial. As a kid, he had worked briefly for a pusher making deliveries around the midtown West Side. His instructions were—get the money before you hand over the envelope. 'No credit. A lot of the customers are hustlers who'll try to pay you in trade.' All users were actually or potentially dishonest by the very fact that they were users.

Ray had also seen the other side of the coin. It was during a night when they were holding him in a precinct house. That was the time they had picked him up with policy slips. During the evening they had pushed a youth into Ray's cell. The boy came from a well-heeled family. He told Ray his father was a bank vice-president. He had an expensive habit that his pocket money couldn't support. So this young junkie had tried to pull a heist. The cops had nailed him the first time out and had shoved him into a cell to wait for the morning magistrate's court. Ray had listened unsympathetically to the independent amateur's tale of woe. The junkie hadn't had a shot for several hours before going on the stickup. Poor judgment already. By the time the cops had put him into Ray's cell, the junkie was really trying to climb the walls. He kept screaming, moaning, gurgling, and waking up everybody along the corridor. The overnight guests began cursing: 'For Christ's sake, give him a shot of something and shut him up, so we can all get some sleep!' The cops couldn't care less. In the meantime, when the junkie wasn't trying to climb up the wall, he was crawling around the floor on his hands and knees, with the vomit running down his chin and chest. When he wasn't doing that, he was shaking. Yes, he was certainly shaking. His legs were going one way, his arms another, his head a third way, as if they had no connection with the rest of his body. And his teeth were rattling like loaded dice. Then he grabbed his stomach with both hands and began to scream that his stomach pains were killing him. Then he vomited some more, except that he had nothing else to give out. That was bad, heaving up on an empty stomach. Ray had sat on the top bunk with his feet out of the way, looking, listening, and cursing the cops for having put the junkie into his cell. What could he have done for the poor bastard? Nothing. No question, they had done it on purpose. Cops and screws were like that—sadistic in a sly way. Cops and screws weren't made sadistic by the job; they took the job in the first place because they liked to push people around and because they got a kick out of inflicting pain. Like New York cabbies—a guy had to have a screw loose in the first place to become a hack driver. That wasn't all. The mucus was running from the junkie's nose and he was perspiring. Not like a pig. Ray, at that age, was already of the firm opinion that pigs were more civilized and well behaved than most human beings he had met, even though he hadn't met too many pigs. The junkie would scream and try to reach his back muscles. He was going it cold-turkey all right. That meant he was getting cramps and muscle spasms, like a charleyhorse all over—in the belly, the back, legs, any muscles.

Ray watched and remembered.

That was H, the big fish hook, and Ray prepared coldly to go into the traffic. The reports from New York City were growing more and more ominous of late. Something was going sour at home. He was getting the big squeeze play. Since he was, for all purposes, dead here in Italy, somebody was going to take over, and what could he do about it? For openers, he would do something about it—make a stake in junk and then head back home to straighten things out. The memory of that junkie in the cell hadn't shocked him. The contemplation of possible treachery on someone's part did shock him. His reaction was to counter-attack.

CHAPTER 5

Ray had warily forborn to question Torres at length regarding his past. The little which the Spaniard had volunteered was sufficient. In Ray's previous experience, engaging personnel had been relatively simple. Every man who had eventually entered the Family back in New York had been a twig of the same historical–ethnic–cultural shrub. Ray was familiar with the botany of it; he himself had bloomed from the same species. Nature herself had provided the security clearances. Even the Jesuit order did not boast a tighter checkrein over its soldiers. Certainly Ray had made mistakes, as in the cases of Al Poggio and Len Codi. He would rectify those mistakes as soon as he was able to escape from Italy. Torres, now, was another matter, something unique beyond the perimeter of Ray's experience. On intuitive first impressions, he had accepted the Spaniard without hesitation. After two decades in the Business, he had sufficient confidence in his own judgment to conclude that he would not regret Torres. The Spaniard was a tall, leathery-skinned man in his mid-forties or early fifties, with close-cut black hair, a hawk nose, and stony eyes forever squinting against the Saharan sun. The brand of the Legion had been sledge-hammered into his face, the battered thoughtfulness of the Resting Boxer. He was entirely typical of those noncoms who were the heart and entrails of that military brotherhood. It had been said that when the devil was inducted into military service, a sergeant of the Foreign Legion was assigned as his drill instructor. Such a one had been the Army captain under whom Ray had served in World War II— Millard Patterson Colquhoun, a regular noncom, commissioned himself in the field. These pros were a breed, perhaps fashioned in a woman's womb but more probably compounded of inorganic materials, ground to powder, and baked into hard-tack with the fat rendered out. Torres would probably be harder on a prisoner or any enemy than Colquhoun, and, at the same time, quieter about it. The American had had the Geneva Convention and the United States of America, as well as the American Army and his regiment. The Spaniard had had only *La Légion*. A fine piece of cutlery was Torres. What a pity that the times were out of joint and the Torreses must rust! It was too late to reinvade and reconquer Mexico and Peru. Sicily wasn't worth bothering with and neither was New York City. Since the world's loot had all been apportioned, what was one to do with a sharp knife like Torres? If the United States Marine Corps had any judgment, it would send its recruiting sergeants to Spain. Ray mentally drafted a letter to the Commandant, United States Marine Corps. Dear General: I hear that you people are having draft troubles, what with everybody putting their own good housekeeping seal of approval on their own wars and wanting to do their own thing. I know you Marines have always depended on volunteers but now there's talk of an all-volunteer armed force. If you Marines want to steal a march on the Army and Navy, take a look at Spain. It's full of unemployed Torreses, prime leatherneck material. They'll go for your deal. You just give them a home and they'll take the whole world apart for you—that is, if you want it taken apart. Respectfully, Ray Hodgkin.

Ray had succinctly outlined the problem of the informer Ponchielli to Dominique Maestracci and Juan Torres. 'This joint venture with Greco means much to all of us,' he concluded. 'Nothing must be permitted to go sour, particularly since it can be avoided by careful planning.'

'As I see it,' said Torres, 'it's a simple enough problem. The first step is to take Ponchielli. The second to persuade him to talk. The third, to kill him quietly and let him disappear. By your own account, you didn't give Ponchielli enough information to place us under police surveillance. I'd take a chance on that. Ponchielli's tongue should certainly be loosened—but against Greco. *Signor* Greco is potentially more dangerous to us than the police.'

'You make a nice point,' said Ray. 'The more we know about Greco, the better. In particular, how honestly does he deal?'

'Then Ponchielli must be interrogated,' said Torres. 'Even discounting the troublesome loquacity of a subject under torture, Ponchielli may reveal something useful to protect us from Greco, not from the police.'

'Agreed,' said Ray. 'What methods of persuasion would you suggest?'

Dominique Maestracci stirred and spoke for the first time. 'There are ten thousand. One man persuading another to speak is the history of the human race.'

'We need only one,' said Ray.

'Since we have the generous *Signor* Greco's funds,' said Torres, 'sufficient time, and a free hand, I'd suggest persuasion by fellation, the torment of the oral caress.'

'You mean a blow job?' said Ray.

'Is that what you Americans call it?'

'The common people do.'

'Are there such in golden America?'

'Oh, yes,' said Ray.

'And what do the cultured classes call it?'

'A blow job. But, seriously, Juan, are you trying to tell me that a blow job is torture?'

'I wouldn't know, but an eight-hour fellation with resultant hemorrhage can be disagreeable.'

Ray gestured impatiently. 'Why do we have to waste so much time and trouble on a mere ratfink? What's the matter with an honest gasoline blowtorch?'

'Nothing, I suppose,' said Torres with a shrug. 'But you're on vacation now in wicked, lubricious old Roma. When in Rome, give rein to your imagination.'

'I suppose,' said Ray. 'Still, eight hours does seem a drag.'

'We can expedite the process by having the fellatrice bite *Signor* Ponchielli's organ or incise it with a knife to expedite hemorrhage.'

Dominique began to laugh.

'Santa Maria!' said Ray. 'Is this your *own* idea, Juan?'

'Oh, no, *padrone*, it's a Chinese refinement.'

'Why not a fellator? Or a vacuum milking machine?'

'There you go, being technical, American, and innovative,' said Torres reproachfully. 'It must be a fellatrice. The Chinese are supremely conservative purists. The ritual must not be varied.'

'Very impractical and cumbersome,' said Ray. 'Overelaborate.'

'Admittedly so,' said Torres. 'This torture was a set piece for connoisseurs and inflicted, though very rarely, in imperial China on nobly-born matricides.'

'Is that so?' said Ray. 'Well, Mr. Ponchielli is no nobly-born Chinese matricide. He's just a common, ordinary, garden variety slob of a Calabrian stool pigeon from Brooklyn, U.S.A. He won't appreciate such exotic treatment.'

'Not exotic at all,' said Torres. 'The Chinese have always been an elderly people on short rations and one cannot help admiring their ingenious simplicity. They were always forced to stretch their budgets and imaginations to make ends meet. Much like the French people, or, for that matter, like we Spaniards. There was never enough money or frills to waste on malefactors; hence the guillotine, the garrote, our Spanish contribution, and the kang board. Have you ever seen a kang board in use, *padrone*?'

'No.'

'I have, in Indochina when I was there with the Legion. Before Dienbienphu. A cultural export from China, you might call it. There's nothing more drastic than the kang's cumulative effects.'

'Very well,' said Ray. 'I'll go along. Let it not be said that I am a parochial American. What's the next step?'

'Procure a qualified fellatrice to be turned loose on Ponchielli,' said Torres.

'Petri would be the man for that,' said Ray. 'I'll go to see him.'

Petri, the trafficker in flesh, confirmed the dictum that in time all men come to resemble their callings. Petri's striped, pinch-waisted suits, his wildly-flowered, large-knotted necktie, and thin-soled pointed shoes trumpeted 'pimp.' He wore his modishly long coiffure, his exaggerated sideburns, and his drooping guardsman's mustache with an air. His heavy five o'clock shadow had been powdered to subdue it. A cloudlet of French cologne followed him. In an Edwardian fashion, *Signor* Petri was definitely chic.

Ray had reluctantly purchased Anitra during their initial meeting.

'Petri,' he told the merchant, 'can you rent me an expendable female, preferably an alien with a record, who will be reluctant to go to the police? I have a rather monotonous task for her to perform.'

Petri commanded one of the most extensive and varied inventories in Rome. He could supply females in age range from nine to seventy, with milk teeth or with no teeth at all, jet black, yellow, nut-brown or albino-white, sane or insane, nuns, debutantes of the *jeunesse dorée*, moonlighting housewives or battered gladiators from the North African arena, hermaphrodites, monsters of ugliness, and even fetuses. He could, of course, also supply males in the same rich variety. Petri also possessed the proud distinction of having provided a heroic Roman *contessa* with a carefully trained young giraffe. The giraffe had a pair of testicles like velvet-covered bowling balls and a sexual organ like a baseball bat. The *contessa* grunted and survived, her avidly watching friends applauded enthusiastically, and Petri gained much valuable publicity. In this affair, he had quite out-performed the ass of Apuleius. He had been instrumental in breaking a record unchallenged since antiquity.

Over and above the armpit, the breast cleft, the navel, the hand, and the ear, females had three utilizable sexual orifices. A noble client had once asked Petri for a female with a fourth sexual orifice. He reflected for some time and finally suggested that the client have his purchase surgically customized to his own specifications. The client followed Petri's advice, with indifferent results. When he complained, Petri shrugged. 'Your Excellency is being unreasonable,' he said. 'Am I God to work miracles? Go and have yourself a plastic doll fabricated. Then you will be able to furnish her with holes to your heart's content. But, if your Excellency will take my advice, you can save yourself money.'

'What is that?' said the connoisseur of exacting tastes.

'Buy yourself a Swiss cheese,' said Petri. 'It should serve your purpose admirably.'

The client, hampered by an aristocratic lack of humor, indignantly rejected Petri's well-meant suggestion.

'Have you ever tried a Persian melon?' said Petri blandly.

'A Persian melon?'

'It is exquisite,' said Petri, 'the supreme sensation, the delicate end product of an incredibly refined civilization. In this regard, there is a celebrated Persian proverb. Since you look so scholarly and cultured, you are not doubt familiar with it.'

'What is it?' said the client suspiciously.

'A woman for duty,' quoted Petri, 'a boy for delight, and a melon for sheer ecstasy.'

'Have *you* ever tried it?' said the client.

'I! Good Heavens, no!' said Petri. 'I have a wife with whom I'm perfectly content. And three children. But for you, Excellency, a Persian melon, definitely. Or even a fat-tailed Circassian sheep. Neither will ever nag or bore you. Or cuckold you, or become pregnant. Or inflict ghastly relatives on you. And you will enjoy an added advantage. After you have satisfied your noble libido, you will be able to devour your love object and obtain wholesome nourishment. Sliced melon and broiled lamb without the heartburn of human love. A dish for Omar Khayyám! No wonder he wrote such exquisite quatrains.'

The client departed, baffled but intrigued.

Such was Petri.

Ray commenced negotiations with Petri through appropriate small talk.

'How is Truthful Fern, *Signor* Occhiaccio?' said Petri. 'Does she still please you?'

'Ah, my little Japanese kitten!' exclaimed Ray. 'Splendidly! I will purchase her also and give you a generous price.'

Petri shook his head regretfully. 'Alas, *signor*. Truthful Fern is not for sale. She is rentable only, to my prime clients. And, then, only on short-term leases.'

'Her Italian is abominable,' said Ray. 'She massacres the double L.'

Petri shrugged. 'She has other virtues, *signor*.'

'That she has,' admitted Ray. 'When I finally return her to your collection, she will be doubly valuable, a real money-maker. I've taught her some new erotic techniques.'

'Indeed?' said Petri.

'The triple-spin,' said Ray. 'An interesting sexual exercise. The male partner, of course, must provide a strong and reliable phallic vertical axis.'

Petri sighed. 'Interesting. However, my prime-rated patrons are not always so fortunately equipped as you are.'

'Wasn't it always so?' said Ray.

'If I may inquire, *signor*,' said Petri, 'this—er—expendable female which you require, to what purpose do you propose to put her?'

'I need a sturdy and durable fellatrice,' said Ray. 'One sufficiently disciplined to remain at her workbench for long hours, without murmuring.'

The qualifications which Ray laid down rang a warning bell in Petri's sensitive ear. To give himself time to reflect, he stroked his mustache. If Don Raimondo Raffaele Occhiaccio, alias Mr. Raymond Hodgkin, late of New York City (Mother of God! What a pair of names!), specified so precisely, he had something ominous in mind. Petri swifted reviewed his current stable. Don Raimondo, Petri suspected, would return the merchandise in a battered condition. No! In such case, renting would be unwise; like leasing a shiny new Lancia to be driven over the mountains of Sardinia.

'I have just the thing for you,' said Petri. 'A reliable North African girl. I'm told she once fellated an entire company of Zouaves in Algiers during an uninterrupted twenty-four-hour session.'

'Impossible!' snapped Ray. 'You lie like a politician.'

Petri shrugged. 'It was told to me,' he admitted. 'But she is tough. And she had been through the mill of love.'

'I don't want any wornout bags. How old is this one?'

'Considering her experience, remarkably young. No more than twenty-five.'

Ray elevated his eyebrows. 'So young? And so steeped in depravity?'

Petri held his open upturned palms close to his chest. He thrust his palms forward from his chest in sharp short stabbing movements. 'She was raised in an older culture where such talents are highly prized. As an oral manipulator, she is an artist. She's even attractive, the child of a French father and a Kabyle mother. But you'll have to purchase her outright.'

'How much?'

'Five thousand American dollars.'

'Is she sound?'

'I can't lie, *signor*. She's being presently treated for a gonorrheal indisposition. Those North African military brothels are hard on girls.'

'Two thousand dollars,' said Ray.

'*Signor*,' said Petri in a shocked tone, 'considering the purpose you have in mind, her temporary malady is irrelevant.'

Ray snapped his fingers disdainfully. 'You offer me a diseased, battered prostitute and have the impudence to ask me five thousand dollars! If it were not for an extraordinary circumstance, I wouldn't have such refuse under the same roof with Truthful Fern.'

'Four thousand dollars,' said Petri.

'Twenty-five hundred dollars,' said Ray. 'Take it or leave it.'

Petri took it and duly delivered to Ray's apartment one poor, humble North African prostitute. She had been born in the image of her Maker and her name was Anitra Houssayne. Ray had her installed in the vacant maid's bedroom, there to await her call to duty.

It had been bright and sunny on the morning after Anitra's arrival. At 11 A.M. Ray, Anitra, Torres, and Dominique breakfasted together on the terrace overlooking the swimming pool. Ray, at forty-five, was a man of medium height, broad-shouldered, flat-stomached, and slim-hipped, with closely-cut glossy black hair, thin-lipped, long-nosed, with a cleft in his chin. His eyes were black-brown, a cold opaque. An infrequent smile cracked the muscle of his left cheek, which had been severed by an old knife slash. He usually wore dark, conservatively cut lightweight suits. His button-down stone-gray shirts and narrow, dark neckties were old-fashioned against the new flamboyant modes. Today, as a concession to the relaxed morning, he, like Dominique Maestracci, was garbed in casual slacks, sandals, and a jersey. Only Torres, in a dark-gray suit and a thin black knitted necktie, despite the rapidly warming sun and the easy atmosphere, seemed immersed in a private, formal Spanish shell. Torres looked what he was, a soldier in civilian clothing. He had glanced once at Anitra and frowned. She was well tanned and had seated herself, wholly at ease in bikini and halter. Ray divined the Spaniard's thoughts—the impudence of this naked little slut! Sitting down so boldly among three men. For Torres, all of female Gaul was divided into three parts: the native animals, the prostitutes in the military brothels, and the officers' wives. Bayonet-edged distinctions.

Most negligently, Ray had neglected to mention Anitra's veneral malady to Dominique and Juan Torres. The latter, having established himself as senior to Maestracci by the strength of his personality and by the loftiness of his outlook, was conceded the right and courtesy of the first night. He tasted in all innocence and was stricken with an attack of gonorrhea. Maestracci, having been spared a like fate, was thankful for himself and solicitous for his colleague. Ray was conscience-stricken for his faithful Torres and furious with Petri, whom he summoned instantly.

'But, *signor*,' protested Petri, 'I apprised you of the condition of the girl. How am I at fault?'

'You shouldn't have sold her to me,' said Ray sternly.

'But, *signor*, pharmacists sell poisons every day. Are they then to blame if the purchaser drinks a plainly labeled preparation?'

'It's indecent,' shouted Ray. 'You've brought down my best man.'

'I, *signor*?' Petri curled the fingertips of both his hands against his chest. 'I don't even know the man.'

'You will, you Neapolitan pimp! Wait until I tell him. He'll make a cold pizza out of you.'

'*Santa Mamma!*' said Petri weakly.

'And, furthermore, I'm not going to pay you.'

'But that is grossly unfair!'

'What an ignominy!' fumed Ray.

It was obvious to Petri that *Signor* Occhiaccio was genuinely disturbed. Since the *signor* was such a prized customer, Petri decided to be liberal. '*Signor* Occhiaccio,' he said, 'I own myself at fault here and will deduct five hundred dollars from the price of the girl for this mishap to your servant.'

'Well,' said Ray, mollified as much by Petri's humble tone as by the credit deduction, 'that is something. Now, clear out!'

Petri bowed himself out.

When the physician had confirmed the Spaniard's gonorrheal infection, he was angry, though, fortunately, not at the *padrone*. Torres was a sensitive, unpredictable package. Although he dissembled philosophically, he was irked. Ray sympathized. Torres was a man whose personality extorted respect. There was no way of knowing how casually, or uncasually, he had accepted the mishap. Ray preferred a conservative conclusion; that Torres, a peculiarly fastidious man in his own fashion, regarded the venereal infection as an affront to his Spanish dignity, a dignity which was exceeded only by his contempt for human life. As for his attitude toward women, Torres might as well have been a mountain Berber.

'Consider, *padrone*,' said Torres to Ray, 'in all these years of military service I never contracted a venereal disease. It may be difficult to believe, but it is so. I respect my body. I have preferred to deny myself rather than dip into sewers. Finally, I fall victim to the perils of the civilian jungle, in the holy and accursed city of Rome, no less.' His eyes looked inward and he smiled reminiscently. 'My ancestors sacked this florid, flabby city of Rome some four hundred and forty years ago. I should like to have been there. I should certainly have been there. Now, this! Bah!' Torres spat.

'I should have warned you,' said Ray almost apologetically.

Torres dismissed the implied apology with a wave of his hand. 'I took the risks of a taster.'

Ray finally invited Anthony 'the Punch' Ponchielli to dinner at the apartment. The guests included Anitra Houssayne, the innocent North African grenade. It also included Dominique Maestracci and Juan Torres, the afflicted one.

Ponchielli presented himself at Ray's apartment, his usual jolly, ebullient self. He reminded Ray of the Western Airlines parrot.

During a momentary break before the five sat down to dinner, Ray took Dominique and Torres into his study for a final preattack briefing. 'What do you think of Ponchielli?' he said.

'A bag of wind,' said Torres. 'Give him a half hour to digest his dinner. It will be his last. Then we'll take him into the small bedroom and tell the girl what to do.'

'She may be difficult,' said Ray. 'Prostitutes are sometimes temperamental.'

'She may be,' said Torres.

'How long were you in the French Foreign Legion?'

'Some twenty-five years.'

'Is it true that you supervised a penal battalion at Fort Laperrine?'

'There, and even farther south,' said Torres. 'An inhospitable, an inhuman country.'

'I only wish I had had you in New York City,' said Ray. 'Bah! One overblown informer and one Nordaf prostitute. For you, sergeant major, it will be child's play. And, for all your trouble, take the pair. Kill the man and sell the woman.'

While Ponchielli was sipping a brandy after dinner and conversing with Dominique and Torres, Ray gave him the bad news.

'What's this I hear about you, Tony?'

'What do you hear?' said Ponchielli.

'That you work for the Federal Bureau of Narcotics.'

'Where did you hear that?' said Ponchielli calmly.

'From the usual unimpeachable sources.'

Ponchielli stared at Ray impassively. 'What's on your mind?'

'You said you might be able to put me next to something.'

'Did I say that?'

'Your very words. You also said you had the best credentials. Whom do you work for, Tony?'

Ponchielli did not reply.

'Think up a good one fast,' said Ray. 'You haven't got much time. Maybe I'll put *you* next to something.'

'What do you mean by that?'

'Next to hell,' said Ray. 'Do your bosses know where you are tonight?'

'You're in a risky business,' said Ponchielli. 'You won't get away with a thing.'

'You won't be around to see whether I do or not,' said Ray. 'Do you know Roberto Greco? Ever do business with him?'

'I don't know what you're talking about.'

'Of course you do,' said Ray. 'There's nothing wrong with your memory that a little deep scaling won't correct. Start spilling while you can still do so painlessly.'

Ponchielli finished his brandy, lit a cigarette, and stared at Ray without expression. 'You're trying to scare me. I don't bluff that easily.'

'Gutsy bastard,' said Ray. 'Your last chance. Start talking and I'll give you a break—two slugs in the back of the head.'

Ponchielli shrugged and rose from his chair. Ray nodded and walked out of the room.

While Torres leveled a gun at Ponchielli's heart, Dominique slugged the informer and handcuffed him.

Anitra was brought into the sacrificial chamber but perversely refused to turn to. When Dominique ripped Anitra's dress from her back, she resisted, though without screaming. Dominique casually backhanded her across the face and knocked her to the floor. She lay still, breathing heavily and quivering.

Torres touched her with the toe of his shoe and said in a flat voice, 'Go to work, girl.'

Anitra did not respond.

'Isn't this your job?' said Torres. 'Move, then! Start swallowing the tiger.'

Dominique bent down to seize her by the hair, but Torres restrained him. 'No need. She has already been broken to obedience.'

Anitra finally capitulated. She struggled to her feet, went over to the couch, positioned herself over Ponchielli, and began fellating him, her head bobbing up and down with a slow,

94

regular movement.

Ray returned to the room and watched Anitra at work. 'No trouble?'

'As you see,' said Torres.

Ray nodded. Anitra Houssayne had obviously worked the North African circuit. She had just as obviously met the Torres breed in her travels and feared them like the devil on a stormy night. She had not cried out. She had turned to like a mutinous galley slave, but she had turned to.

The three men watched silently for fifteen minutes. Ponchielli's organ was not responding to Anitra's oral ministrations.

'He is afraid, and confused,' said Torres, 'and even embarrassed and disorientated. Later on he will have an erection. Not from sexual excitement, but from sheer physical irritation.' He gestured toward Anitra. 'That creature has a hard night's work ahead of her. Before it is over, *Signor* Ponchielli will ache and she will be very tired.'

Ponchielli was now breathing stertorously and his eyes were closed. Dominique had bound his arms and ankles firmly with cord. The prostitute, Anitra, had been fellating him under duress for a full hour. At the end of the hour, Torres curtly told her to take a five-minute rest period.

'She'll be at for several tedious hours yet, *padrone*. Dominique and I will keep her at work.'

'I'm not waiting around till he talks,' said Ray. 'This is not only disgusting, it's tedious. Get the tape recorder out and start questioning him. Dig into his connection with the FBN. Also what he knows about Greco's reputation in the drug business. And if you're smart, you'll dump this fancy routine and use a blow torch.'

'He'll talk,' Torres assured Ray, 'and we'll get it down on tape. When will you return?'

'In about six hours. I think I'll go out to dinner and then to the theater.'

'Enjoy yourself, *padrone*. When you return, Ponchielli will have talked freely. No one can withstand the blandishments of Oriental love.'

Ray actually returned eight hours later. Anitra, now haggard and twitching in every muscle, was still at her drudgery.

Ponchielli, the paschal lamb, still breathed. Ray's return had been felicitously timed. Ten minutes after his arrival, Ponchielli hemorrhaged, Anitra Houssayne rolled aside, gagging and spitting out the informer's blood.

Dominique rose from his chair, clutched her by the hair and dragged her away from the trussed victim. She sank to the floor and began vomiting.

Dominique was dark-skinned and heavy-bearded. He shaved twice a day and used much talcum powder which helped but little. His mental processes were adequate for standard procedures. This, however, was an unnecessarily complex and elaborate operation. He rubbed his chin thoughtfully, uncertain as to the next step.

'Now the man will begin to suffer in earnest,' said Torres.

'Did you get the information out of him?' said Ray.

'Enough,' said Torres. 'It's safely down on tape. You can play it back.'

'He is, in fact, an informer?'

'Greco was telling the truth. Ponchielli is an informer and Greco is a thief who cheats those with whom he deals.'

'Just as you had suspected,' said Ray.

'Just as I suspected.'

Ray gestured toward Ponchielli. 'Get him out of here. Take him at least twenty miles offshore. Weight him well before you drop him off. We don't want him returning like a tactless piece of driftwood.'

Dominique nodded, produced a short lead-cored rubber truncheon from his pocket, and walked up behind Ponchielli. He raised the informer's head by the hair and laid a sharp blow across the nerve complex at the base of the skull. Then he lowered Ponchielli's head to the couch. 'Tonight, *padrone*.'

Anitra was lying on the floor, moaning softly. Her eyes were closed. Torres stared impassively at her smooth, dark haunches. 'She's not hurt, just tired and afraid. What do you want done with her, *padrone*?'

'As I mentioned, I give her to you. She must have *some* value. There's value in scrap metal. There should be some in her.'

Torres appraised the girl with a horse dealer's eye. 'If she stung me, I suppose it was my own fault. One must be fair about these things. She's a graduate of the house of Siddi-bel-Abbes, if I'm not mistaken. Unusually durable. I could sell her to Makarios and split the proceeds with Dominique.'

Dominique shook his head. 'No, no, Juan. For the inconvenience she caused you, she's rightfully your little piece of tripe.'

'I'll share with you,' said Torres.

'Very generous of you, sergeant major,' said Dominique.

'It's nothing,' said Torres. 'She's healthy yet, and young. If Makarios retails her in Meknes, say, the people down there could squeeze at least three more year's work out of her. Trust the Arabs for that. They know how. I'll ask Makarios two thousand American dollars and he'll probably beat me down to one. I'm a baby in the hands of that wily Greek.'

'How much is that in lire?' asked Dominique.

'A Corsican should certainly be able to calculate that,' said Ray. He turned to Torres. 'As good a plan as any. The sooner you get started, the better.'

Dominique drove Ray's Ferrari down the *autostrada* leading south from Rome. He swung off at the desired exit ramp, rolled down, and saw the rutted crossroad too late. He tramped on the brake pedal and the Ferrari bounced.

'Softly,' said Torres, 'you'll awaken *Signor* Ponchielli.'

'This is the first time I've ever seen something like that,' said Dominique.

'I've seen it carried to a conclusion both in China and in Indochina,' said Torres.

Dominique shuddered and spat out of the open car window. 'Ugh! Why should we not simply have shot him through the head, like a man?'

'That would be too good for an informer,' said Torres. 'He wished to injure the *padrone* who plucked us both from the misery of the Capo District and who treats us with respect. Is it not true?'

'It is true.'

'For such a *padrone*, one stretches one's imagination,' said Torres. 'He makes me feel again like a noncommissioned

97

officer.'

'He has a way about him,' admitted Dominique.

'Watch the road,' said Torres.

Dominique grunted and proceeded more carefully. The road headed up a hill flanked by two groves of gnarled olive trees.

'Since I have been here before,' said Torres, 'I'll give you directions. After we get over the hills, you'll see an old stone barn. The road splits. Bear off to the right. That will take us straight down to the *padrone*'s villa.'

'This was all one estate?'

'It used to be, I understand. He told me that he bought the entire place from a nobleman. It starts at the top of the hill. The olive groves are the markers. *Signor* Occhiaccio must have spent a fortune remodeling the old farmhouse. That is where they have the parties.'

'What sort of a boat does he have?' asked Dominique.

'A good one. A little slow, but big and seaworthy. A forty-eight-footer. Let's go directly to the boat. We don't have to bother the caretaker.'

Dominique swung the Ferrari down the curves toward the sea.

Torres opened his window and snuffed the air. 'It's good to be buried at sea. It's what I would wish for myself.'

'What difference does it make?'

'It's a distinctive fragrance, like a family kitchen. It awakens in me nostalgic memories. I'm from Cádiz. My people were always fishermen or sailors.'

'You were a soldier,' said Dominique, as though uttering a profound truth.

'True,' said Torres patiently. 'I broke the family pattern. Did I do well?' He shrugged. 'But I was satisfied with my life as a soldier.'

'Do you find this much different?'

'Not really. This is also a form of soldiering. What is important to a professional like myself is a superior officer who trusts one to do one's job properly. This the *padrone* does, and it is the most durable expression of respect.'

Torres throttled down the boat's diesels to idle and the hull rolled in the swell. The western coastline of Italy had long ago sunk over the horizon and the sky was starless.

'Strip off his suit,' said Torres. 'We can sink his clothing in the grotto or burn it ashore. Let him leave the world as he entered it—naked.'

Dominique undressed the limp body methodically. 'It's hard to tell if he's still breathing. He busied himself roping the spare anchor to Ponchielli's body.

'It will be easier in a moment. Hold his feet.'

While Dominique did so, Torres positioned Ponchielli's head over the side, opened fire with a submachine gun, and shot off Ponchielli face. 'In case he should come ashore.'

'They go by fingerprints.'

'True. But a face is a face. Why leave them one when you don't have to?'

Dominique laughed. 'Ah, La Légion, La Légion!'

'A university,' said Torres, sliding the naked, faceless corpse over the side. 'But one I was not sorry to leave. Toward the end, even before Dienbienphu, she was a shell. We no longer believed, no longer revered even the little she had to offer us. Like the fall of an oak tree. Like seeing one's mother becoming a prostitute.' Torres shook his head and his eyes filled with tears. 'What a pity! How sad! She was the only real mother and sweetheart I ever knew.'

Dominique nodded with respectful sympathy.

'The truth is that I am lonely,' said Torres. 'I could return to Spain and live there. But I have grown away. What is Spain to me now? Nothing. Little better than this tired whore of an Italy. My motherland was the Legion and now she is gone.' He opened the throttles and swung the craft shoreward in a wide arc.

Ponchielli disposed of, Ray's two men at arms returned to Rome and Anitra. The thought that she might try to escape had occurred to Dominique. It was true—cows sometimes wandered away from the pasture. One either found them, or one did not. Where would this one go? To the police? With her dossier and her alien status? It was unlikely. The *sbirri* had no interest in righting the alleged wrongs of a transitory soiled pigeon with a broken wing. The *sbirri* were a big piece of the system, with a basic callousness, compounded of indolence, indifference, corruptibility, and two profound articles of faith; a conviction that the weak are iniquitous and a conviction that all human nature is inherently incorrigible. Dominique, the Corsican, did not know these things with his brain. He felt them as a cat feels a steady wind ruffling its fur.

Anitra had not wandered away. She slept on the same couch which had supported the late informer. Torres went over and seized her by the hair. In one sweep he lifted her to her feet.

'Tired?' he said in a neutral voice.

Anitra's eyes opened and narrowed again to hate-filled slits. She swung her small palm and slapped it hard again Torres' left cheek. The white mark on the dark leathery skin began to fade immediately. Torres' expression remained grave and he did not react.

'Bitch,' said Dominique, coming over.

'Let her be,' said Torres. 'She has some work to do cleaning up the room.'

'She struck you.'

'No matter.' Torres addressed Anitra. 'You! Girl! Where did you work on the other side? Tunis? Algiers?'

Anitra replied by lunging for Torres' eyes.

Dominique swung an easy edge-chop across her forehead and sent her reeling away.

'How far down did you get, girl?' said Torres. 'Fez? Meknes?'

Anitra stared sullenly at the two men and did not reply.

'An experienced one,' said Torres. 'The troopers made them work hard. Take her into the kitchen, Dominique. Get her a bucket of hot water, a scrubbing brush, some cloths, whatever she'll need. We have to get this room polished up.'

Dominique's eyes swept the room's disorder and he grimaced. 'Then you can play with her a little,' Torres concluded.

Anitra scrubbed with detergents, mopped, and wiped for a full hour before Torres was satisfied. All of the equipment was returned to the kitchen and put away, clean and dry. Dominique, the cleaning foreman, finally returned to the bedroom with Anitra in tow.

'No trouble?' said Torres.

'She seems calmer now,' said Dominique.

'Fatigue. And the pacifying influence of wholesome work. Prostitutes don't exercise all of their muscles. Not the honest muscles, at least.'

'You're a particular man.'

'My training,' said Torres. 'Now she's all yours. Go to it.'

Dominique slapped Anitra's buttocks lightly. 'What about you? And don't you want to sell her?'

The Spaniard rubbed his left cheek thoughtfully. 'No. Sergeant Torres already has his little souvenir and has changed his mind. He bequeaths his share to you. Have a good time. And don't catch anything.'

Torres left the room.

Dominique thrust a finger under Anitra's chin and lifted her face to his. 'Little animal, you did unwisely to strike that man. As you did unwisely to give him the clap.'

Anitra pushed his hand away and made a dash for the window. Dominique got to her before she reached it. He slammed his hand over her mouth before she had a chance to bite. He threw her down on the rug.

'Now we will play. *Au naturel*, eh?'

Anitra looked up at him. 'You're going to rape me?'

Dominique laughed. 'How can a whore be raped?'

'And what if I don't want to?'

'Then want to. Isn't it your profession?' Dominique took a bundle of lire notes from his pocket and threw it down beside her. 'There! As you see, I'm not being ungenerous. And you're a very lucky girl, my dirty little sparrow.'

Anitra sneered, yet her body seemed to relax.

'That's better,' said Dominique, lowering himself beside her. 'Now you're sensible. You'll be able to leave here tonight with your head on your shoulders and a bit for a marriage portion.' Dominique grinned. 'It's true. Your life has no more meaning than a sparrow's in winter. Another would have had you——' He made a chopping motion with his hand. 'But I am not a hard man.' He touched her cheek. 'Now that that fat informer's blood is off your face, you're almost pretty. Come!

I'll treat you well. Perhaps I won't even sell you. Though I will if you don't behave yourself.'

Ray breakfasted on the terrace with his two men at arms after Anitra's departure.

'Did you make tricks with the girl?' he asked casually.

'Protected tricks, *padrone*,' said Dominique. 'She gave herself willingly.'

'You alone?'

'Only I.' Slyly: 'Torres was not in the mood for swimming in a polluted river.'

'That is true,' said Torres.

'I did not abuse her,' added Dominique. 'I gave her money and she left here contented.'

'You should have sold her,' said Ray, 'and split the proceeds with Torres.'

Torres shrugged. 'It is no matter. I do not like to sell women. It is unsoldierly.'

'Very well,' said Ray. 'If you are both satisfied, then I am also. Even a prostitute is a human being. And I must say that both of you have displayed a certain magnanimity and liberality which pleases me. Neither of you are petty and I commend that.' Ray turned to his coffee with a sense of righteous benevolence.

CHAPTER 6

On June 5, 1968, Robert Francis Kennedy, Senator from the State of New York and candidate for the Presidency of the United States, was assassinated at the Hotel Ambassador in Los Angeles by Sirhan Bishara Sirhan. On that same day, Ray Hodgkin and Roberto Greco were getting down to hard figures.

'What do you think of the news from America?' said Greco.

'He was an abrasive man,' said Ray. 'He had many enemies.'

'Do you think this Sirhan was in it alone?'

Ray opened his hands, stared at Greco, and did not reply.

'My own answer,' said Greco. 'In this matter, at least. There are two kinds of Sicilians—those like myself, who love life, talk, and laughter, and the other kind, the joyless ones, the silent monomaniacs.'

'I am still alive,' said Ray. 'I follow my own track. To work, Don Roberto.'

'To work, then,' agreed Greco. 'Have you heard of Tufarelli Pharmaceuticals, A.G., of Milan?'

'Who has not?'

'I hold the controlling stockholder interest. As I mentioned before, Italian law as it concerns narcotics is relatively lax. A certain amount of heroin is legitimately used in this country. Many physicians claim to find some medicinal value in the drug. The fact is that all the pharmaceutical firms in Italy produce far more heroin than the small legitimate market calls for. Tufarelli is among the front-runners. We are now beginning to produce a better end product than the clandestine laboratories of southern France. To review: much of the crude morphine base enters Italy directly from Yugoslavia and Beirut. Concerning the production figures on heroin, the books are manipulated. Every pharmaceutical house does so. All those who count, including the control authorities, are aware of it. The situation is shrugged at. That, in sum, is the picture.'

'I would say it is much like the production of alcohol in the United States during the Prohibition period,' said Ray.

But Greco did not seem to be listening. His mind had wandered away. He came to and smiled. 'I'm sorry if I seemed rude. A totally irrelevant thought just struck me. *Signor* Ponchielli seems to have disappeared from his usual places of resort. None of his friends, apparently, have seen anything of him lately or heard from him. Have you seen him lately?'

'Now that you mention it,' said Ray, 'no I have not. He is probably off on a holiday somewhere. A convivial man who loves baccarat. Perhaps he is up in Monte Carlo.'

'Probably,' agreed Greco. 'Please forgive me, you were saying——'

'I was likening the Italian narcotics situation with our Prohibition period.'

'Oh, it is much more open than that. Now!—if you want pure heroin, we can supply you right here in Rome or Milan. Ninety percent pure and as good as anything from Marseilles.'

'How much will you charge me?' said Ray.

'Fifteen thousand dollars per kilo. We want only American money or Swiss francs.'

'That is high. Why are you asking so much?'

'As you know, there is a confused political situation in the Middle East. The pipelines from Beirut are blocked and the supply of morphine base is shrinking.'

'No doubt,' said Ray. 'But a wholesaler in New York, a one-kilo buyer, pays no more than twenty thousand. If I have to pay you fifteen thousand at this end as an exporter, there will be very little profit for me, too little to make it attractive.'

'I agree with you. But you will find the situation no different anywhere else in Italy. The market is very tight at present. Moreover, I need not emphasize to you the importance of knowing with whom you are dealing. Tufarelli is reliable and honest in what is an exceedingly risky and unreliable commerce.'

'I'll grant you that,' said Ray. 'Nevertheless, if I buy at fifteen, I will not be able to realize a justifiable profit.'

Greco nodded. 'Very well, then. We will just have to wait. We cannot fight the market. We must bow to it.'

And there the matter rested until July.

A little more than four weeks later, Greco sent a message to Ray: 'I hope you can join me for luncheon in my office on Thursday of this week. I promise you delicious food.'

The food *was* delicious. Greco had had it sent in from Guardelli's. Both men ate silently, each preoccupied with his own thoughts.

When the waiter came in and cleared away the dishes, Greco rose, locked the door, went back behind his desk, and settled himself comfortably.

'Have you ever had this office thoroughly checked for electronic listening devices?' said Ray.

'Several times,' said Greco. 'But that is only because I believe in extraordinary precautions. This room is thoroughly soundproofed.'

'Have you had it checked out by an electronics technician who knows what to look for?' repeated Ray.

'Considering the conversations we have had in here already,' smiled Greco, 'isn't it rather late to be raising this point? But, rest assured, Don Raimondo, this room is free of electronic surveillance. Italy is not as electronically sophisticated as the United States. In that area, we are still in *circa* 1940.'

'I'm glad to hear that. In my country, it is an ever-present consideration. So, then!'

'I think I have a situation which will interest you and which may benefit both of us,' said Greco.

'Ah?'

'This is an extraordinary circumstance. First of all, are you familiar with the latest—I emphasize, the latest—New York Market in heroin?'

'Truthfully, no. I'll take your word for the figures.'

'You can double-check me later. At the present time the importers in New York are paying between sixteen and eighteen thousand per kilo, ninety percent pure, delivered. It's closer to eighteen thousand. The importers sell to the whole-salers for twenty. The wholesalers used to be able to buy at between eighteen and twenty. Now they have to ask about twenty-two and a half to turn a profit. The retailers, of course, have raised their prices proportionately.'

'What has all this to do with our end of the business?'

'I impart this to give you the outer guidelines,' said Greco. 'Then you can calculate back. The art of merchandising is to be able to lay your hands on a consignment of merchandise which, for whatever reason, is unusually cheap at the source, and sell it in an area where, for a number of reasons, the supply is scarce and the price unusually firm. That describes the situation in New York. Now, I have received confidential word that the leaders of an Arab guerrilla organization in Bei-rut are offering an extraordinarily large quantity of morphine base for sale at a truly spectacular price. They have in their hands two thousand kilos of morphine base.'

'What are they asking?'

'Five hundred American dollars per kilo, or the equivalent in Swiss francs.'

Ray did some mental calculations. 'Why don't they follow the usual channels? With such a low price, the simplest route would be the best. Why don't they sell it to the Corsicans in Marseilles?'

'A good question, with a number of answers. The most im-portant one is that, providentially and fortunately for us, the Marseilles importers and refiners are temporarily disorgan-ized. Three months ago the American Treasury Department worked out a new agreement with the Narcotics Bureau of the Marseilles Sûreté, one with teeth in it. In essence, the Mar-seilles Sûreté has been drastically expanded. With American funds, naturally. One can hardly imagine the French spending their own money on this sort of thing. So what do we have? A renewed vigorous drive is being mounted against the drug traffic in and out of the port of Marseilles. The net result is that the Corsicans have closed up shop and are temporarily out of the market. This situation won't last, of course. Under nor-mal circumstances, the Corsicans would jump at the oppor-tunity.'

'The heat is on in Marseilles?'

'Exactly,' said Greco. 'Another thing, since this cache is very large, these Arab revolutionaries wish to dispose of it immediately, in one lot. Several Lebanese politicians are undoubtedly involved, politicians with pro-guerrilla sympathies. Officially, the Lebanese government is trying to steer a neutral course between these groups and Israel. It frowns on these guerrillas who are using Beirut for a headquarters in which to replenish their war chest. The situation is fluid. The Lebanese government could act at any time. In the meantime, the revolutionaries—I suppose you can call them that also—want to get rid of their cache of morphine base and turn it into money. If boils down to morphine base for bullets. This is the picture —the seller is anxious and jittery. He is seeking a buyer who can take the entire shipment off his hands. To such a buyer he will offer a wonderful price, as I said before—five hundred dollars per kilo of morphine base.'

'A million dollars?'

'Cash on the line,' said Greco. 'That is only the beginning, of course. Getting two thousand kilos of morphine base out of Beirut will be a truly challenging task. You will need Tufarelli's facilities and resources in order to be able to bring off such a coup.'

'That's what I'm waiting to hear.'

Greco picked up a sheet of paper. 'I have already made some tentative plans. It will take at least two months, I am calculating conservatively, to get the entire shipment out of Beirut. If less, I shall be happy. Let us break it down into four five-hundred-kilo lots. One lot could be shipped from Beirut to Hamburg by ship with a consignment of general merchandise. It would then be transshipped from Hamburg by rail across Europe as electrical equipment to Milan. The other three lots, I tentatively propose, would be shipped to Genoa, Naples, and Trieste. From there they will all be carried to Milan. As you see, it will be quite a logistics problem.'

Ray was mentally reducing two thousand kilos of morphine base to two hundred kilos of heroin. 'That is only the beginning, I suppose.'

Greco nodded. 'Tufarelli will convert the morphine base at

107

a price of one hundred dollars per kilo. That is another two-hundred-thousand-dollar expense item for you. You can assume that shipping costs and extraordinary expenses for safeguarding the merchandise will be charged to you. That will probably be another two or three hundred thousand dollars. Say a million and a half dollars, all told. Even if your organization receives fifteen per kilo in New York, you will realize a profit of one and a half million.'

'A net profit?' said Ray skeptically.

'I didn't say that. After all, Tufarelli is entitled to a broker's commission for its services—what you might call a finder's fee.'

'How much?'

Greco gestured negligently, as though he were speaking of an insignificant sum. 'Twenty five hundred dollars per kilo of heroin. A total expense to you of two millions. A net profit to you of one million. But that is based on a price to the wholesaler in New York of fifteen. Let us say your people receive eighteen per kilo. That would mean an additional profit to you of six hundred thousand. Not bad.' He looked at Ray. 'Are you prepared to commit yourself to a transaction of this magnitude? Do you have such funds available?'

'I am,' said Ray. 'I have. I'll take it.'

'I knew you would. There is one more thing. You'll have to go to Beirut in person to conclude the deal.'

Ray looked sharply at Greco. 'Why? Don't you have people in Beirut who can handle it? I'm willing to back the financial end of the transaction. I don't, however, like to get that close to the merchandise. In fact, I don't even want to see it.'

'Of course. But this is an unorthodox situation. These revolutionaries are inexperienced in this business and extremely suspicious. All they want to do is to sell it, get their money, and clear out of the picture. They want nothing to do with the shipping details. Naturally, they know nothing about that end of the operation.'

'All right,' said Ray. 'Let's sum it up. You suggest that I go to Beirut and close the transaction with certain people?'

'Just one man. Their spokesman. I will arrange the meeting for you with this man. You will meet him in Beirut, pay him, and take title.'

'Just like that? It would be easy for them to take my money and simply cut my throat.'

'This man will deal honestly with you. You will see the merchandise first. You will test it and have it weighed. Only when you are satisfied concerning the weight and content will you pay over the money.'

'One little deported American lamb surrounded by a circle of Arab brigands on their own terrain. You paint an overly simple picture.'

'I will provide you with bodyguards if you wish.'

'I have my own,' said Ray. 'Men whom I trust.'

'That is good. In addition. Tufarelli has two honest agents working in Beirut. You will not be groping in the darkness all alone. You will then have four good people working with you.'

Ray thought it over. 'Done.'

'Bravo,' said Greco. 'I think this transaction will turn out profitable for all of us.'

'It sounds all right,' said Ray. 'By the way, isn't Francisco Tamburelli's brother working for you?'

'How do you know about that?'

'Why shouldn't I know? Francisco himself told me. Renato Tamburelli. Isn't that the man? I should know about him. It was my assistance to Francisco which helped get Renato started after he was kicked out of Libya. And Francisco was instrumental in getting us together. Isn't that how things work out? One good turn deserves and leads to another.'

'I meant nothing by it,' said Greco. 'I just don't like the details of my business spread around carelessly.'

Ray shrugged. 'That would hardly apply to me at this point. What does Renato do for you? Is he a heroin chemist?'

'Not quite,' said Greco, thinking that the American was much too inquisitive. 'Just a laboratory assistant. Some men just don't have the knack of it. But I'd say that Renato is quite adequate as an assistant.'

'I'd like to see your laboratory someday,' said Ray.

'We'll discuss that some other time,' said Greco. 'After all, despite Italy's lax laws, heroin-making is still a highly confidential and guarded operation.'

109

Ray rose to his feet. 'All right. We have a deal. I'll be in touch with you.'

'*Arrivederci*,' said Greco.

Two weeks after that conversation, Ray flew from Rome to Beirut to meet Hassan Mahmoudi. A redoubtable man from what Greco had told him. It encouraged Ray that Juan Torres knew Hassan Mahmoudi intimately. Maestracci and Torres flew to Beirut separately. A rendezvous had been arranged in Beirut where the three men would meet for the negotiations with Mahmoudi.

Juan Torres and Dominique Maestracci were already installed at the Royale when Ray arrived in Beirut. They had engaged a five-room suit with two bathrooms on the sixteenth floor of the hotel and settled down to wait.

'When did you get here?' said Ray.

'We arrived three days ago, *padrone*,' said Torres. 'We have been enjoying the sights and sounds of the city while waiting for you.'

'You've been here before?'

'A few times. It is a good city. A man can be hurt here, of course, not because it isn't a civilized place, but because it is politically unstable.'

'Political violence puzzles me,' said Ray. 'Business disputes? That is rational and understandable. But politics!' He shrugged. '*Dei gusti non si discute*. All I seek from life is to be allowed to manage my affairs without interference.' Which summed up the ghost of Robert F. Kennedy in Ray's mind. If Kennedy had only minded his own business and let Ray mind his. But Kennedy's had been a fatal restlessness. His luck had finally run out and he had walked into a gun held by a punk.

Ray had come into the room carrying a small suitcase, which he deposited carefully on a couch. His luggage was brought up within a few minutes after his entry.

'Dominique,' he said, 'telephone Room Service for menus and waiters. Give me something to drink if you have it here.'

Torres produced a bottle. 'I have some good cognac here with me, *padrone*.'

110

'Perfect,' said Ray. 'Pour for all of us, Juan. And pull up your chairs, both of you. Before the waiters arrive, I wish to speak.' He looked at his two men at arms. 'You have both been with me, how long?'

'Six months, *padrone*,' said Torres for both of them.

'Are you satisfied with my service?'

'I am satisfied,' said Dominique.

'For myself,' said Torres, 'since I am no longer in *La Légion*, I would not wish to be anywhere but here.'

'I never make compliments, *padrone*.'

'If there is anything you want,' said Ray, 'if there is anything I have failed to do, speak. Ask it now.'

Dominique remained silent and Torres shook his head.

'Very well, then,' said Ray. 'From this moment forward, you are no longer my servants. Perhaps I should not use the word "servants." It has an unfavorable connotation in America.'

'I see none,' said Torres. 'In its true sense, the word has an honorable meaning. I am content to be your servant.'

'It is well,' said Ray. 'But, from this night on, you are both my partners and associates as if you were true-born Sicilians and my sworn brothers.' He paused. 'I put my trust in you and shall have no secrets from you.'

'I shall not betray your trust,' said Dominique.

Torres rose to his feet, went over, and extended his hand. When Ray clasped his hand, Torres bent over and kissed Ray's hand. 'Don Raimondo,' he said gravely, 'I give you my allegiance and my faith.'

Ray smiled to mask his emotion and a fierce exultation in the pleasure of the new bond. 'Thank you, Juan,' he said. 'This I have heard of but have never seen. You are a man from another age. I felt it in my bones when I first met you.'

'This may be,' said Torres.

Ray raised his glass. 'To our new relationship and to our success.'

The glasses clinked and they drank solemnly.

'Juan,' said Ray, 'and you, Dominique—I hold you both the equal of twenty ordinary men. I tell you this, we shall carry through our business here successfully and we shall return to Italy. We shall all play our parts properly and we shall emerge wealthy and powerful men. You will both return with me to America and I have greater plans for us there.' He clenched his fist and his face hardened. 'I was taught to love my friends and to hate my enemies, and so I shall.' Then he relaxed. 'You know why we are here. I have already given you the outlines of our mission.' He pointed to the suitcase. 'This piece of luggage contains one million American dollars. Dominique, it will be your duty to guard it constantly. You will remain here in the hotel with the money. Juan and I will go to meet Mahoumoudi. Is that understood?'

Dominique nodded.

'You know the city well, Juan?' said Ray.

'Well enough, Don Raimondo. I shall be your guide.'

'Good.'

There was a knock on the door. Dominique went to open it and two waiters came in with a large table. Two other waiters carried in a serving table bearing heavy, silver, covered casseroles. The waiters began setting the table and opening bottles of wine. Ray rubbed his hands, poured himself a little burgundy, rolled it over his tongue, and smacked his lips. 'To the table,' he said. 'No more business. Now we shall eat and enjoy ourselves.'

The waiters filled the three glasses and began serving.

At Ray's request, Juan Torres gave him a thorough dry run tour of the entire city of Beirut. 'As with all cities,' said Torres, 'there is a dark side to this one.' He drove the car into the Nahr District, which ran along the Nahr River on the northern boundary of the city. 'This is the Casbah of Beirut,' said Torres. 'Here live the poor and the lawless ones. Here life is cheap.' He piloted the car carefully through narrow, crooked, cobbled streets and alleys where high stone walls, ominously blank and topped with jagged glass, hid the houses behind them. These houses were interspersed with crumbling makeshift huts constructed of mud, wattles, and flattened oil drums. 'Here the police do not enter except in four-man

112

squads,' said Torres. 'This is like the Capo District of Palermo.'

'Or Harlem, or the South Side of Chicago,' said Ray.

'You have such districts in rich America?' asked Torres.

'In America, we do everything bigger and better. The inner cores of all our large industrial cities are gradually turning into Casbahs. In time, each decayed core will be abandoned, left to its own devices, and ringed by invisible gun muzzles on the suburban perimeter.'

'Why should this be in America?'

'You will see for yourself when you go there. The Nahr District doesn't worry me. We can take care of ourselves. Let's now return to the smiling side of Beirut.'

They returned to the newer, sunlit districts and Ray absorbed what he saw with a clinical concentration. There was a hint of Vegas in Beirut's anything-goes atmosphere. The promise of it in Vegas was questionable; in Beirut, real. It was the porno-scene difference between Copenhagen and Los Angeles.

'What do you think, Don Raimondo?'

'An interesting place. It reminds me somewhat of our Las Vegas. You have heard of it?'

Torres nodded.

'I smell a license here,' said Ray. 'Vegas has a pseudo-license. Here, I suspect, it is real.'

Torres smiled. 'What is license? Go into the southern Sahara for a year. When you return you will see that all cities are fat and soft and that your license is childish. I have seen men staked out naked on the sand and smeared with honey. That is license. But, this *is* a city, half a million townsmen, a history, a distinctive atmosphere. It is as unique in its way as Paris or Rome.'

'You speak well, Juan. How is that?'

'Ah,' said Torres, 'when I was not performing my duties as a soldier, I read instead of drinking and consorting with prostitutes.'

'So I suspected. As to Beirut, we had such a city in America called San Francisco.'

'What happened to it?'

113

'It was overrun by hippies.'

'What are hippies, Don Raimondo?'

'You will meet them when you go to America. They are the American counterpart of the long-haired scum of Rome and Naples.'

'Ah,' said Torres.

After a three-day wait, word arrived by messenger from Hassan Mahmoudi. He would meet the buyers at a half hour after midnight in the gardens of the Grande Casino, on the marble terrace above the casino.

'I am familiar with it, Don Raimondo,' said Torres. 'It is a safe, anonymous meeting place.'

On the evening of the rendezvous, Ray and Juan Torres sat at a table in the subterranean nightclub of the Grande Casino. They sipped a light wine and watched the belly dancers perform.

'They are good,' said Ray, looking across the huge dim area of the nightclub. 'These producers have nothing to be ashamed of. Their technical skills are on a par with Las Vegas and New York.'

'Dominique would have liked to see this,' said Torres. 'Those bellies have a lascivious life of their own.'

'I will buy you a pair of them. Pick two that please you.'

Torres smiled and looked at his watch. 'I think it is time for us to leave, Don Raimondo.'

Ray left money on the table and the two men strolled through the carpeted elegance of the nightclub toward the exit and the upper terrace. When they reached the agreed-upon place, the seller still had not arrived. 'We still have ten minutes,' said Ray, glancing at his watch. They looked down from the balustrade to the Grande Casino high upon a cliff. The lights glittered along the long coastline and the illumination of the city spread out beneath them. A metropolitan center and a garden spot, thought Ray. This is how Miami Beach would like to look. The fact that Beirut was a nervous time bomb as well somehow enhanced its attractiveness.

'Do you know the Beirutis, Juan?' he asked.

'A little, Don Raimondo. A formidable people in their chosen skills. As a simple soldier I would never try to compete

114

with them in trade.'

'How so?'

'A Beiruti will rise at three in the morning to sell you a dozen rusty nails, or an obsolete battleship, or a vial of the true pre-Creation darkness. If you wish to hold your own, you would do well to rise an hour earlier and to guard your teeth. If you do not, you may well find yourself without your purchases, as well as toothless, as well as eyeless. The Beirutis are legendary traders and this is by way of a compliment to them.'

'We're fortunate in one thing, Juan. The men with whom we shall deal are not traders but soldiers and politicals. They will be easier to handle.'

'Hassan Mahmoudi will give you no difficulty, Don Raimondo. He served in the Legion with me and was a senior noncommissioned officer. He is a native Algerian and he served in other units of the French Army also. When the Algerian War of Independence began against France, Hassan deserted and went over to the Algerian Nationalists.'

'How long was he in the Legion with you?'

'Five years. After that affair in Indochina began, he transferred to a crack paratroop regiment. He made sergeant major there, I understand. Had he been a Frenchman instead of a native Algerian, I do not doubt that he would have been at least a captain. I met him again in Indochina. He watched the Viet Minh work and learned how to set up intelligence networks and a good politico–military organization. When he deserted the French, he used everything he had learned about guerrilla warfare against the French. When the French lost Mahmoudi, they lost a good soldier and made a bitter, implacable enemy.'

'He won plenty of medals from the French, did he?'

'A chest full of them. And his hatred was so great that he turned all his military experience against the French. A handful of men like Hassan Mahmoudi turned the tide and helped the Algerians win independence.'

'And now he wants to do the same thing here in the Middle East.'

'He's evidently training the Palestinian guerrillas in the latest methods of revolutionary warfare. That takes money.

Mahmoudi needs money.'

'We'll know more about it soon,' said Ray as he studied the area. The terrace was a perfect meeting place. It was deserted. Standing in the darkness, the two men were indistinct from the brightly lit entrance of the casino. At the parapet they had privacy and could stand hidden and unrecognized.

A figure materialized on the terrace as though from nowhere and walked silently toward them. He might have been standing behind one of the pillars. Torres touched Ray's arm. The man came closer, recognized Juan Torres, and smiled.

'Ah, my good friend, Juan Torres,' he said extending his hand. 'How good to see you again. And how strange to see you in civilian clothing.'

'I might say the same thing, Hassan Mahmoudi,' said Torres. 'I wish to present my friend, *Signor* Pietro Cornaro.'

Mahmoudi shook hands with Ray. 'A pleasure, *Signor* Cornaro,' he said in Italian. 'Has my good friend Torres been showing you around Beirut?'

'Very competently, *Sidi* Mahmoudi,' said Ray. 'Your Italian is very good. Better than my own.'

'I'm sure you've detected the Tunisian taint in my Italian,' said Mahmoudi. 'That's where I learned it. My mother language is French.' He grinned sardonically. 'And, of course, I speak Arabic and a few of the local dialects. I used to practice them on Juan.' He looked at Torres. 'Do you still remember any of the lesser ones, Juan?'

'A little,' said Torres.

'Juan is quite a good Arabist. Did you know that, *Signor* Cornaro?'

'No,' said Ray, 'but I wouldn't be surprised.'

He was appraising Hassan Mahmoudi. The man had confidence and an air of command. He was about six feet tall, lean, and athletic-looking. He wore a tailored suit, from the cut of it, and a conservative necktie. His face was lean, hard-muscled, very dark and scarred.

'*Signor* Cornaro,' said Mahmoudi, 'do not think me rude if we get down to business immediately. The less time we spend up here, the better.'

'Proceed,' said Ray.

'Greco has already been in touch with me,' said Mahmoudi. 'I understand you have all the basic figures. Are you prepared to act immediately?'

'There will be no bargaining?'

'None whatsoever. The price is firm.'

'This will be the first time then that a transaction was completed in Beirut without the pleasure of haggling.'

Mahmoudi smiled. 'It *is* a drastic innovation, isn't it?'

'When can I inspect the merchandise?'

'As soon as it reaches Beirut.'

'Where is it now?'

'Somewhere in Syria,' smiled Mahmoudi. 'A large country relative to Lebanon.'

'How do you intend to get so large a shipment across the border?'

'In an Army truck. With the cooperation of the Lebanese Army. Certain military elements here sympathize with us. The official administration does not. We cannot waste time. The truck will cross the border between now and dawn. It will be preceded by an Algerian Legation automobile carrying a Lebanese Army colonel and myself. We enjoy a further safety factor. I have diplomatic status in Lebanon.'

'Where is the truck now?' said Ray.

'In Syria. Naturally, we enjoy even greater sympathy there than here in Lebanon. The Syrians do not have the sensitive commercial interests of our Lebanese friends. If you're satisfied after examining the merchandise in Beirut, you can pay me. I assure you that everything is as I say. Trafficking in drugs is not my business.' He made that statement disdainfully.

'I prefer to examine the merchandise in Syria,' said Ray. 'If I'm not satisfied, it will save you a trip. Torres and I will go with you. I may not have another opportunity to drive the historical road to Damascus.'

'Why Damascus?' said Mahmoudi sharply.

'How many good paved roads do you have on this border?' said Ray.

Mahmoudi smiled. 'It was a stab in the dark, wasn't it? Very well, then. Please follow me.'

117

Mahmoudi led Ray and Torres to a 300 SEL Mercedes-Benz flying the Algerian flag. He got in behind the wheel and introduced a man who was sitting in the right front seat.

'Colonel Abdul Malik,' said Hassan Mahmoudi.

Ray, sitting in the rear left-hand seat, studied Malik. An Army man evidently. Lean, well set up, with a small, dark mustache.

Mahmoudi drove well and fast. He knew the city. He made his way down a very narrow curving road from the Grande Casino at the top of the cliff, spiraling down and handling the wheel with fast, sure control until the road reached sea level. Ray looked back through the window and could see the lights of the Grande Casino far above sparkling in the black velvety night. He tried to keep his sense of direction; everything was good to know. Now Mahmoudi swung the Mercedes in a complete U-turn toward the heart of the city. He drove through an empty wide boulevard. In a few moments they were out of the city and heading at high speed on a flat straightaway.

'*Sidi* Mahmoudi,' said Ray, 'if I am not being too curious, how did you manage to get twenty thousand kilos of opium across the Turkish–Syrian border?'

Mahmoudi drove fast, looking straight ahead. 'If I may say so without offending you, *Signor* Cornaro, you *are* being too curious.'

'Then do not tell me,' said Ray.

Mahmoudi suddenly laughed. 'But I will tell my friend Juanito. What difference does it make now? We had teams of the best border-runners on both sides working in relays for weeks. Ten men were killed in the land mine belt. Another four were shot down by the Turkish gendarmery. A small price.' He peered ahead intently and added, 'You are now on the famous road to Damascus.'

Ray had been studying maps of the roads between Beirut and Damascus. Damascus was the logical way station on the route between the opium country of Afyon province and the port of Beirut. He did not know what the driving conditions would be, but he calculated that they would arrive in perhaps two hours, a distance of approximately seventy miles, in the meantime he decided it would be a good idea to go to work on

118

Malik. It might be useful to find out what kind of cat this Lebanese soldier was. 'Colonel,' he said, 'your country in its attitudes and outlook reminds me of my own native land, Sicily. Lebanon, however, is a much more sophisticated country than Sicily. And more fortunate in a material sense.'

The colonel was friendly and replied in a very fair Italian. 'Thank you, *signor*. We like to think of ourselves as the Switzerland of the Middle East, at least, insofar as Beirut is concerned. We believe we can hold our own even with the Swiss when it comes to banking and international commerce.'

'It's interesting that an Army man should have such a high opinion of merchants,' said Ray.

'Every Lebanese is a merchant,' said Malik, 'even those of us who are in the Army. Commerce is the breath of life to our people. The Phoenicians, the traders of antiquity, were our ancestors. Like Switzerland, we are a small country without industry or natural resources. We trade and bank in order to live. We are the financial bridge between the East and the West. Beirut is a free port. We offer every service that the Swiss do, and with less trouble to the client. Our living comes from trading commissions. Narcotics?' The colonel shrugged. 'From our viewpoint, it is only another commodity. People want narcotics. We merely expedite the flow from the point of origin to the ultimate market.'

'Your government doesn't see it so simply,' said Ray.

Malik laughed. 'Our Lebanese politicians are like politicians everywhere else in the world—scoundrels and hypocrites. They pay lip service to American opinion in order to retain power.'

Mahmoudi was now speeding along a narrow two-lane highway which at times widened into three lanes. He flicked on his high-beam headlights. Hills followed long sinuous downgrades which, in turn, were followed by hairpin curves. Mahmoudi did not slacken speed.

'*Signor* Cornaro,' he said, 'my driving does not make you nervous?'

'Every man's fate is written on his forehead,' said Ray. 'We are all in the hands of God and of *Sidi* Mahmoudi.'

Mahmoudi chuckled. 'Well answered, *signor*.'

119

'You are an excellent driver,' said Ray. 'I think you would enjoy driving in the mountains of Mexico, as I did not. There are roads in Durango and Chihuahua which can turn a man's hair white.'

'Actually, I never trust this road,' said Mahmoudi. 'It can happen suddenly around a down curve, a slow-moving oil truck, another car crossing the center line, or a flock of sheep.'

The Mercedes wound steadily up into the mountains. 'We are at the six-thousand-foot level,' said Mahmoudi. He straightened out on the summit and slowed to a crawl through clouds and fog. They began to descend. Mahmoudi shifted into a lower gear and gave the road his full attention as he negotiated the curves with the right side of the Mercedes on the outside open rim of the cliff. 'We are coming down into the Bekaa Valley,' said Mahmoudi. 'A beautiful fertile place. It is worth seeing by day.'

They finally reached the floor of the valley on the straightaway. Mahmoudi depressed the accelerator and the car flashed away. 'For that road at night,' he said, 'give me a Mercedes. It has rack-and-pinion steering, the most accurate, sensitive steering, and the best disc brakes of any car in the world.'

They sped across the valley in forty minutes and pulled up at the Lebanese border post. The guards peered in, stepped back, saluted, and the Mercedes went through.

'Thank you, colonel,' said Hassan Mahmoudi.

'I'll share honors with your legation flag,' said Malik. 'And with your impressive automobile. It is the choice of oil sheiks and pashas.'

'Not Cadillacs?' said Ray.

'They are simply not in the same class, *signor*,' said Malik. The Mercedes sped on through the empty border country and reached the Syrian border guard post. The Syrian guards came over and colonel Abdul Malik spoke with them in Arabic. The guards stepped back and saluted. The Mercedes sped east on its way.

'I asked them if they wished us to show passports,' said Malik. 'They said it was not necessary. They were pleased to extend diplomatic courtesies and welcomed us to the Syrian Arab Republic. I informed them that we were were going into

Damascus to escort back a Lebanese Army vehicle with important secret electronic equipment, a truck which had been lent to the Syrian Army. We were planning to return the same night. They were impressed.'

'Who would not be?' said Ray.

'Consider,' said Colonel Malik, 'the people on this border work long hours for small pay. This road is the most heavily traveled one between Beirut and Damascus. It carries several hundred vehicles a day, mostly trucks. They couldn't possibly check all the vehicles that go back and forth, certainly not thoroughly. Occasionally they will spot-check one, but they are aware that a great deal of contraband goes through. It is not so, Hassan?'

'We have the odds in our favor,' said Mahmoudi. 'Professionals are seldom caught at borders with gold, diamonds, or drugs. Only when informers give the border advance warning. Amateurs of petty contraband are invariably caught. The seller of the contraband often informs the border for a reward or to curry favor against the time when he himself may be stopped. Our credentials, however, are tight. We are beyond reproach with both border controls.'

The Mercedes picked up speed and began to rise into the Anti-Lebanon mountain range heading for Damascus.

'*Sidi* Mahmoudi,' said Ray, 'I'll concede that the security and credentials with which you are providing us command a definite market value.'

'That is a fair statement,' said Mahmoudi. 'I need not point out that neither Colonel Malik nor myself have anything personal to gain from this transaction.'

'I'm aware of that,' said Ray.

They entered the New City area of Damascus. The Mercedes drove down an enormous eight-lane modern boulevard gleaming coldly under the tall, modernistic, fluorescent mercury streetlamps. The glass expanse of modern office buildings on either side of the boulevard reflected the intense illumination of the lamps. Within a few minutes Mahmoudi had piloted the Mercedes out of the New City and up into the Old City in the hills. He slowed down and they began to bump over narrow cobbled streets, twisting and turning in the darkness. Then he entered streets which were so narrow that the Mercedes slowed to a five-mile-per-hour crawl to negotiate and squeeze its way between the flanking structures. Old Damascus had never been built for a wide-hipped Mercedes. Mahmoudi finally pulled into a driveway and they faced a high sheet metal gate of a brick warehouse structure. The colonel left the car and walked swiftly toward a narrow door beside the gateway. He rang a bell and waited. The door opened and he entered the building. The sheet metal gateway began to rise like a portcullis. A flashlight beam flicked on and off. Mahmoudi put the Mercedes in gear and rolled forward in the black cavernous maw of the warehouse. 'Remain in the car for a moment,' he said. He got out from behind the wheel and disappeared into the darkness.

'What do you think?' said Ray to Torres.

'It will go well,' said Torres. 'He was always a good organizer.'

Hassan Mahmoudi returned to the car. 'Everything is ready. Please follow me.'

Ray and Torres followed Mahmoudi's flashlight into the echoing blackness of the warehouse. The Algerian opened a side door and they followed him into a room also in darkness. When they had entered, Mahmoudi slid a bolt and switched on a light. They were in a large, windowless, inner room. Before them, stacked in fours, were ten columns of metal boxes which resembled ammunition cases. They bore Arabic script and the insignia of the Lebanese Army.

'You have forty cases here in all,' said Mahmoudi. 'Each one contains fifty kilos of morphine base in triple bags of five kilos each—that is, ten bags in each case. You are free to spot-check any case you wish.' He smiled. 'I suppose, as a careful and prudent buyer, you should open and examine each of the bags. I assure you that it will take all night and would be impractical. This is a moment for trusting one another, although I admit that this is a strange place and an unusual situation for the mention of the word "trust." '

'You make a good point, *Sidi* Mahmoudi,' said Ray. 'This is a problem for a wise man. Give me a few moments apart with Juan Torres.'

He and Torres went aside, out of earshot.

'He is right,' said Ray. 'Spot-checking one or two bags would be useless. We would make fools of ourselves. Tearing open the entire lot is, as he pointed out, impractical for either of our sides.'

'Don Raimondo,' said Torres, 'we must go by the man in this situation rather than by the merchandise that he is selling us. What do you think of him?'

'He is not a drug smuggler, or a smuggler of any kind. He is not a criminal or a liar. He is probably a madman in his own specialized way, a fanatic, but he is also a soldier.'

'You say well. I will take a moment to briefly tell you a story about him. When Mahmoudi was with me in the Legion, we also had an Algerian lieutenant in temporary command of our company when our Captain was away on furlough in France. This Algerian, he may have been a Kabyle, I recall his name was Mouhadienne, was a compulsive gambler. Without going into detail, this Mouhadienne embezzled and gambled away the company funds while on leave in Algiers. Mahmoudi was a sergeant at that time. A fellow Muslim in the company, Mouhadienne's orderly, secretly told Mahmoudi what had happened. Mahmoudi bided his time, ambushed the lieutenant one night, and stabbed him to death. He made it appear as though the lieutenant had been the victim of a robbery. Then, through the orderly, Mahmoudi replaced the embezzled company funds with his life savings from Army service. For he was a frugal man and a devout Muslim who denied himself every pleasure and relief from the harshness of duty. Be that as it may, the replacement represented Mahmoudi's life savings. A week later, our captain returned from leave to find that his lieutenant had been murdered by thieves. But, of course, the company funds which had been entrusted to Mouhadienne were all quite in order. Mahmoudi told me about it later. "Mouhadienne was a traitor to Islam," he said. "He brought shame upon all of us. Never shall these Christian dogs be given the opportunity to point the finger at us and call us thieves." He said smiling, "I except you, Juanito, despite that you are a Spaniard. I know you are a heathen and not a Christian. I wish you well, Juanito. Accept Islam and I will call you 'brother.' " ' Torres paused. 'I did not, of course, accept Islam, but I tell you this to point a self-evident moral.'

'Are you satisfied?' said Ray.

'On my head,' said Torres. 'I will lay it on the block of that man's word.'

'Then I am also satisfied.' They returned to the two waiting Muslims.

'*Sidi* Mahmoudi,' said Ray, 'it is not in my mind to offend you by questioning your word. I will examine nothing.'

Mahmoudi smiled. 'I am a stranger to you in an illicit transaction. Why do you trust me?'

'I know something of men and the world. I am, in a small way, a psychologist.'

'You are gambling with a million dollars. And you will never see me again.'

'If I never do,' said Ray, 'I wish you well.'

Mahmoudi looked slyly at Torres. 'I see a fine Spanish hand in this matter.'

'It may be,' said Torres.

Mahmoudi turned serious again. 'It is well that you trust me. As you see, each case is sealed with an official seal. Had you insisted, we would have had to break open each case and reseal them.'

Ray checked his watch. 'We should be thinking of returning. Whatever arrangements you have made to transport this merchandise, perhaps it is best that you activate them immediately.'

Colonel Malik rose and signaled with his flashlight.

Four men in Syrian Army uniform materialized in the darkness and began taking the cases out of the inner room. A truck motor began rumbling. They saw the big Army truck with tarpaulin covers being moved backwards. The soldiers had the cases loaded into the truck in a half hour and the covers were firmly secured. Two of the soldiers jumped into the truck bed with the merchandise and two of them got into the cab of the truck.

'We are ready for the return trip,' said Mahmoudi. 'Get in, gentlemen.'

The four men reentered the Mercedes. Mahmoudi backed

out and began the slow, rocking return to the New City of Damascus. Looking back, Ray could see the bulk of the Army truck behind them. It was following the rear lights of the Mercedes.

Driving back towards Beirut, Ray felt more optimistic that he had made a good deal. The powerful engine of the 300 SEL purred softly as the road slipped away beneath the tires. There would be no problems in reentering Lebanon. The tricky part of the journey was now behind them. Still, there remained a number of tasks to be accomplished before he and Torres parted company with Mahmoudi and Colonel Malik.

CHAPTER 7

The Mercedes-Benz was sedately opulent and innocent of any contraband. The Algerian Legation flag whipped about bravely in the breeze on the other side of the radio aerial. The four passengers within could have been going to or coming from a festive affair. As the automobile sped along, the grimly functional Army truck lumbered along doggedly, trying to keep up. Torres and Ray were in evening clothes, Mahmoudi wore a tailored suit, and Colonel Malik was trim in a summer uniform. The purchase money was in a suite at the Royale Hotel and Maestracci sat over it with a gun in his lap and dexedrine in his stomach. The operation was solid thus far. Take Greyhound and leave the driving to us. But there was the second act, getting the junk out of Lebanon, a problem planted with land mines every step of the way. Greco's men—his two resident agents, as he called them—were supposed to take care of that angle. It would be the most logical thing in the world for them to take care of other angles as well—to kill the buyers, for instance, after the buyers had paid off Mahmoudi. The agents and the principal had everything to gain by killing and would be fools not to try it. Put that aside for the moment, reflected Ray. Even if Greco attempts no double-cross, which will amaze me, the junk is bound for four different ports—Genoa, Naples, Trieste, and Hamburg—there to await transshipment to Milan. Ports are always swarming with thieves. The grayish-brown gold of morphine base is not as precious as the pure white gold of refined heroin, but it is precious enough. Anybody at any one of those ports could steal or hijack a quarter of the shipment, five hundred kilos of base. The people in this traffic would cheerfully murder you for a quarter of a kilo. For five hundred they would unhesitatingly bring down the whole world. Compared to narcotics, cut diamonds were mere glass. Supposing, then, that this happened, what recourse to Greco? In the unlikely event that he played honestly, he, Greco, would be in the clear. If he arranged a hijack somewhere along any of the four routes, how could it be proven? And what steps should be taken if it was proven? Ray glanced out of the window at the road. Land mines everywhere, and sharpened stakes smeared with putrid dung and serpent venom.

'Drug smuggling techniques have become increasingly sophisticated over the years,' Colonel Malik was saying. 'I worked for a few years with Customs Intelligence and I've come across most of them. A long time ago, in the old, simple days, contraband used to cross the border in caravans.' He laughed. 'Imagine a column of plodding camels entering modern Beirut! It would cause the same sensation as a caravan train entering London or Paris. They even smuggled the drugs in double rubber bags in the stomachs of the camels. Quaint and obsolete. X-ray photographs took care of that. Then there were the stomachs of infants in arms.'

'The infants were killed at the end of the trail, of course,' said Ray.

'Of course,' said Colonel Malik. 'But the small amounts which could be successfully slipped in in this manner were uneconomical. Today, car and truck caches have been refined down to the point of no return.'

'Do you have a heavy truck traffic on this road?' said Ray.

'An enormous one. Mainly oil and produce trucks. The Border Service now has instruments sensitive enough to detect drugs buried beneath a load of stinking uncured hides or sunk in oilproof canisters at the bottom of a petroleum tanker truck. But they still rely principally on informers.'

'And on the jealous or angry wives, mistresses, and sweethearts of the smugglers,' added Mahmoudi.

Could Mahmoudi and/or Malik have alerted Lebanese customs? Why? How could it possibly serve their interest in this particular situation? Ray crossed it off his list. They could attempt to kill Torres and me after we pay them and attempt

127

to resell the merchandise to a new buyer. That was a possibility. What would be their *modus operandi* in that case? Unknown for the moment, but it was a possibility. To an idealist, all things were permissible, even praiseworthy, for the cause. Mahmoudi's fanatical honesty and hatred of infidels and Westerners, as relayed by Torres, strengthened that hypothesis. This was a stiff poker game. At least no women, the most unpredictable quantity of all, were involved in the transaction.

The halt at the Syrian border took a moment. The guards saluted Colonel Malik and waved both vehicles through. The personnel at the Lebanese border saluted twice, stiffened to attention, and presented arms. No question, no question at all. Mahmoudi's big fix was worth the stomachs of forty thousand camels. It was like strolling into Fort Knox as the Secretary of the Treasury's personal guest. How would matters work out if the boys could get their feet firmly planted in a country like Lebanon? It wouldn't be a country anymore. It would be an operational base. What a base! They could set up their own government, they could license banks, collect taxes, send out ambassadors, and put the button men in uniform. They could appoint judges, prosecutors, and district police chiefs. Santa Mamma! They could print currency and stamps. And issue bonds. And borrow money from the United States. And join the United Nations. National sovereignty. Ray sighed. What a racket! The best in the world. There would be problems also. The boys would have to learn not to steal from themselves because they would be the people in charge and it would really be Cosa Nostra. The problem was the prisoner psychology. Or, still better, the tenant psychology. That was the Organization hang-up and they were still crippled by it. If they owned the setup outright and in fact, the rules would force them into a radical and unaccustomed honesty. It would be just like table stakes in poker. The dynamite of high stakes would force you to play correctly in spite of yourself. When the landlord owns the pad, you piss on the rug. When you own it, you don't. It was as simple as that. Right.

The Mercedes-Benz came down from the mountains, crossed the Nahr River, drove through downtown Beirut, and entered the Nahr District. The Mercedes and the following truck now bumped and jolted through narrow crooked streets as tight as anything in Old Damascus.

'This is a dangerous district,' said Colonel Malik. 'The Beirut police, if they do come in here, go heavily armed.'

Ray patted the .38 in his shoulder holster. He assumed without knowing that the two Muslims in the front seat were armed.

The Mercedes finally halted before a verminous-looking two-story warehouse building. This would be the stash where Greco's boys, Polizzi and Cadri, would be waiting. The building had one thing in its favor, an eight-foot wall all around the front, with shards of broken glass embedded in concrete on top of the wall, as well as three lines of barbed wire running along the top on embedded iron posts. Two of the Syrians jumped out of the truck carrying short fat burp guns. A man came out of the warehouse and peered through the bars of the double gate. He unlocked and swung the gates inward and Mahmoudi drove into the courtyard. The driver of the truck backed it in skillfully. Even with both gates swung back, the opening was so narrow that the truck barely scraped through. Then the man who had come out of the building closed and padlocked the gates. He came over to the Mercedes. He was a powerfully built bruiser. 'Is *Signor* Cornaro here?' he asked.

'I'm Cornaro,' said Ray.

'I'm Polizzi. Cadri is waiting for you inside.'

The Syrians and Polizzi began carrying the cases into the warehouse. Ray touched Torres' sleeve and led him over to the courtyard wall. 'I don't like those burp guns at all,' he said. 'You can assume you are facing eight potential enemies. If this were a trap—I'm not saying it is—but if it were, we couldn't do a thing about it.'

Torres patted the bulge under his left breast pocket. 'I agree that it's militarily untenable. We are in a faulty position.'

'At least keep well in the background near the wall and don't let anyone circle behind you,' said Ray. 'Give me plenty of cover.'

Torres nodded. They spread out, waited in the shadows, and watched the unloading. Mahmoudi and Malik went into the warehouse office. Polizzi came out and saw Ray and Torres by the wall.

'They are waiting for you in the office, *Signor* Cornaro,' he said.

'We'll be right in,' said Ray. The truck had been completely unloaded and the Syrians with their burp guns climbed back in. The truck rolled out into the street and Polizzi locked the gates behind it.

'I'm glad to see those burp guns leave,' murmured Torres to Ray. 'That leaves only four people to watch. The slugs from those weapons can mangle a body.'

'Let's go in and meet Cadri,' said Ray. He had been briefed by Greco on this man. Cadri was somewhere in his sixties, hence not too dangerous. He had lived in Beirut for many years. His mother was a Lebanese Copt. He was supposed to be the office man, the brains of this pair. Ray and Torres walked into the warehouse office. Considering the scabrous exterior of the warehouse and the stark, grim slum in which it stood, the warehouse office was surprisingly large and luxurious. There were good Turkish rugs on the polished hardwood floor, lamps, prints, and paintings on the wall. Mahmoudi and Malik were relaxing in leather chairs and smoking cigarettes. Cadri rose from behind a big walnut desk covered with a glass top. He was dark-skinned. Italian father or no, he could very well have been a Levantine of some kind. He had a big shock of white hair and the long sinewy hands of a professional pianist or guitarist. He was cadaverous, lean, and wiry. He extended an arm to Ray across the desk and said with a big toothy smile: 'Welcome back from Syria, *Signor* Cornaro. *Sidi* Mahmoudi tells me that everything went well.'

Cadri's Italian was flavored with the faint musk and cloves of an undefinable Arabic accent.

Ray extended his hand, clasped Cadri's, and hoped that Torres had plenty of clear shooting room. A man in the act of shaking hands was in a vulnerable situation. But the instant passed and Cadri and Ray completed their handshake.

Polizzi brought in a silver tray with a bottle on it.

'Old French cognac,' said Cadri, 'at least a hundred years old. I know that *Sidi* Mahmoudi does not take alcohol. But

130

perhaps the colonel will.'

'Thank you,' said Colonel Malik. 'I am not as strict an observer as Hassan. Pour me a drink.'

Cadri poured drinks for Ray and Torres as well as for Polizzi and himself. Ray put his glass to his lips but did not drink until the others had done so. Then he sipped cautiously and played with his drink. The fact that all the others appeared to be at ease and behaving normally reassured Ray somewhat, but he remained on guard. Mahmoudi, the strict Muslim (his piety evidently did not inhibit him from the pleasures of tobacco— he was therefore not as puritanical as a back-country Wahabi) lay back in his chair with his eyes closed, relaxing from the tension of the round trip. Like a good soldier, the man knew how to ease his muscles into passivity when it was safe to do so. Ray had once been able to do that, to drop down for a ten-minute rest break during a night-long route march and fall asleep immediately like a cat.

Mahmoudi finally opened his eyes. 'I will repeat my offer, *Signor* Cornaro. If you wish to check the merchandise, there are four of you here. Now is a good time for it. The colonel and I don't mind waiting. In view of the sum involved, I would even urge it in order that you may completely satisfy yourself.'

Ray thought of Torres' story. He weighed that against a surprise attack while they were busy checking the merchandise. He came to a quick decision. 'My mind has not been changed, *Sidi* Mahmoudi, by a distance of seventy miles. Your word is good enough.'

Mahmoudi smiled and nodded, unimpressed. This Italian, he thought, is trying to feint me off guard with compliments. 'In that case,' he said aloud, 'we should complete our transaction.'

'I do not have the money with me,' said Ray. 'I would hardly be carrying such a sum on my person.'

'Naturally,' said Mahmoudi calmly. 'What arrangements do you suggest?'

'The best plan would be for you, and the colonel also, if he wishes, to come to my hotel tomorrow evening. Be my guests for dinner. Then we can go up to my suite and I will pay you

131

what I owe. Is that satisfactory?'

'It suits me,' said Mahmoudi. He looked at his confrere. 'Can you make it, Colonel?'

'I shall be there,' said Malik.

Some sellers might have objected to such a payment proposal. There was no trust in the junk business. Mahmoudi's reaction was reassuring. Ray tried once again to thaw the Algerian.

'I am pleased by your trust, *Sidi* Mahmoudi.'

'I am not concerned,' said Mahmoudi. 'I am probably as good a judge of human character as yourself.' He looked at Torres. 'My insurance is Juanito. He and I served together. Even if some man were tempted, Juanito would keep him honest, even if he had to kill him. It is not so, sergeant major?'

Torres smiled wryly. 'Almost so, Hassan.'

'By God!' said Ray, 'I have brought a good man from Italy.'

'Better than you know,' said Mahmoudi. He rose and so did the colonel. 'Well, gentlemen, we shall see you tomorrow night.'

'I am at the Royale,' said Ray. 'Eight in the evening?'

'That will be satisfactory,' said Mahmoudi. 'Good night.'

He and the colonel walked out with Polizzi. A few seconds later the Mercedes purred into life. It rolled out and the gates clanged shut. Polizzi reentered the office. There was a long silence.

'Well, *Signor* Cornaro,' said Cadri, 'what do you think of Hassan Mahmoudi?'

Ray stared at Cadri without replying. One did not have to wast urbanities on this pair.

'You were not wrong in your estimate of him,' continued Cadri.

Ray rose from his chair and took off his jacket. So did Torres. Cadri looked at the revolvers in the shoulder holsters.

'It was not necessary to go armed,' he said.

'I wish to see the merchandise,' said Ray. 'You and your man, start opening the cases and the bags.'

'Of course,' said Cadri. 'We will help you.'

'You will not help me,' said Ray. 'You will do it. The morphine base has a long road to travel before it reaches Milan. Let us, therefore, make a good beginning. To both of you I say, if any of the merchandise is missing when it arrives, if it does not arrive, if any small part of it is adultered, if there is any short weight, I will chop off the hands and feet of your wives and children. I will have their eyes torn out and let you watch. That will be only the beginning.'

Polizzi turned pale with anger.

'That was not necessary,' said Cadri uneasily. 'We have been Tufarelli's trusted employees for the past twenty years.'

'I commend your honesty,' said Ray. 'In the meantime I will kill anyone who deals treacherously with me, including your employer, *Signor* Roberto Greco. Is that clear?'

Cadri shrugged. 'You will have no cause to complain about Polizzi and myself. We are at your service.'

'Good,' said Ray. 'Now produce an accurate scale and let's get to work. I intend to record the weight of every bag out there.'

Cadri rose from behind his desk. 'Follow me, please.'

Cadri and Polizzi got to work. They opened the cases and broke the seals of the bags. Each outer bag was of double linen. The inner bags were of nylon firmly tied with thin nylon cord. As Cadri passed each opened nylon bag to Ray, he examined the grayish-brown powder within and spot-checked at least five bags by taste. Then he called out the weights to Torres, who marked the figure down on a sheet of paper. By the time they were done, the dawn had long broken and the sun was rising. Torres added up his column of figures for all the bags. 'Don Raimondo,' he said, 'we have by actual weight, considering that many of the bags have a fraction over five kilos, a grand total of two thousand and five and a half kilos.'

'Do you vouch for the accuracy of that scale, Cadri?' said Ray.

'It is accurate enough,' muttered Cadri. His face was darkly under control.

'Good,' said Ray. 'Your personal happiness was also being weighed on that scale.' He sat down on a case and lit a cigarette. 'Leave the cases open. You and your man remain here with the merchandise until tomorrow morning. I will be back

133

at that time to check them once again and to review with you arrangements for shipment.' He stared at Polizzi. 'Is something bothering you, my friend? You look as though you wish to say a word.'

'Nothing, *Signor* Cornaro,' said Polizzi tightly.

'Good,' said Ray. 'Remember, you are earning here more in two days' work than you could in ten lifetimes in Calabria. You *are* from Calabria, are you not?'

'I am a Calabrian,' said Polizzi.

'That's what I thought. Then be content. You are a fortunate man. Now drive *Signor* Torres and myself to my hotel.'

Both the radio and the television set were blaring at full blast when Ray and Torres entered the suite in the Royale Hotel. Dominique Maestracci, in shirt sleeves, was sitting on a couch with the lights still on. The suitcase was secured to his left wrist by a length of nylon cord. He had a revolver stuck in his waistband. He looked up, his face pale and haggard, his eyes bulging out.

Ray looked at him keenly. 'Too much dexedrine, Dominique.'

Dominique's jaw muscles knotted spasmodically. 'A little too much,' he said tightly.

'No phone calls? No visitors? No thieves?'

'Nothing, Don Raimondo. A quiet night. Did all go well with you?'

'Smoothly,' said Ray. 'You are relieved from sentry duty. Juan will now take charge of the money until the Muslims arrive this evening.'

He threw his coat on the floor and flung himself down in an armchair.

Juan Torres lowered himself into a chair slowly and carefully. The only outward sign of his weariness was the deepened lines on his brown, carved face.

'Don Raimondo,' he said, 'you did well to take a firm tone with that one. His type is honest enough after a fashion, as long as they have to be. But the pure cold terror of God must always hang over them, the terror of instant destruction.'

'Did you think I was making idle threats?' said Ray.

'Since you committed yourself by voicing your thoughts, no.'

'That is correct, Juan.'

'Don't doubt for a moment that your statement concerning Greco will get back to him.'

'I so intended,' said Ray. 'There is no choice. If he plays games, he must die, even if I am also killed.'

'Assassination at the cost of suicide?' said Torres judiciously. 'Yes, that is practically impossible to prevent.'

'He has a son,' said Dominique, 'a son whom he loves dearly.'

'Still better,' said Ray. 'We will consider this son, if necessary.'

Torres nodded. 'The attack in overwhelming force is a sound tactic. It is the safest. The attack while the enemy is still attuned to talking.'

Ray's sustained murderous mood began to pass. As his adrenaline fell, he began to feel a weariness. He tossed down a double jigger of scotch and slumped lower into the couch.

'When this business is done,' he said, 'we will go to America. I will make you rich men, rich beyond your dreams.'

'I'm not sure I'd like to leave Marseilles forever,' said Dominique, with a suggestion of a croak in his voice. 'Only in Marseilles am I not an exile.'

'I am not that interested in wealth, Don Raimondo,' said Torres.

'I will make you rich anyhow,' said Ray. 'Yet my problems will not be over when I return. They will only begin.'

Torres grinned like a saturnine idol. 'But Francisco Pizarro faced greater odds, didn't he?'

'Ah,' said Ray, 'but he had an infinitely greater love of gold than you do. The suitcase is in your keeping, Juan. Guard it. I am off to bed.'

'Good night, Don Raimondo.'

Ray staggered into his bedroom, took a hot shower, two sleeping pills, and fell into bed, all his muscles aching.

CHAPTER 8

At four in the afternoon, Ray, Dominique Maestracci, and Juan Torres sat about a table in the living room of the suite and conferred. The waiter had already cleared away the break-fast-*cum*-luncheon dishes. He had left them two big electric percolators filled with hot coffee and departed. Dominique bolted the door after him.

Ray lit a cigarette. 'I don't like the picture. There are too many loopholes. If any one of them is neglected, there will be failure.' He stared at the other two. 'Give me your ideas.'

Dominique did not reply.

'I am waiting to hear your views first,' said Torres.

'Theft or adulteration can be accomplished at any stage en route,' said Ray. 'Four ports are involved, a danger and a weakness of itself. Once the merchandise is aboard ship, we're at the mercy of unknown seamen-couriers who will stow the merchandise and remove it from the shipyard or dock area at the arrival port. Whether these couriers are in Greco's employ or not is irrelevant. Whether Greco, Cadri, and Polizzi are honest is also irrelevant. The chain is too long. There are too many links in it. It's a statistical probability that one of the links will prove faulty. I am seeking total safety and security. What we need is a blanket insurance policy to cover us for any contingency. We cannot afford to depend on blind circum-stance and hope. We can't scurry after a hundred rats to keep them honest.' He leaned forward. 'We must place Greco in a position where he will have more to lose than we, where he will be more anxious than we to deal honestly.' He turned to Torres. 'What did you want to say?'

'I move we eliminate the Hamburg consignment entirely,'

said Torres. 'Ship seven hundred kilos to Genoa, seven hundred to Naples, and six hundred to Trieste. We can supervise delivery of the merchandise here in Beirut to the three selected vessels. Cadri is making those arrangements with the couriers who are part of the ship's crew. Finally, each one of us can take passage on the vessel with our portion of the merchandise.'

Ray nodded. 'That's a simplification; hence an improvement. Good enough. But it doesn't solve the basic problem. People in this business aren't frightened easily, especially if they're resolved on dishonesty. Your suggestion is good, but not good enough. By accepting responsibility for security of the three shipments, by trying to maintain too close a personal supervision over the goods in transit, we advertise our vulnerability and insecurity. The key phrase here is "responsibility for the security of the shipments."' He slammed his fist on the table. 'We must shift that responsibility to someone else's shoulders. We must insure that, no matter what happens en route, we shall not lose. Think it over for a moment, both of you.'

Ray sipped his coffee and looked out of the windows at the sunny Mediterranean far below them. The sailing yachts off the beach appeared as toys. Yes, Beirut did look like Miami Beach, only far more elegant and beautiful.

'Mahmoudi and Malik will be here at eight,' said Dominique. 'Juan, Mahmoudi is your friend. Perhaps you can enlist his manpower to aid us here.'

Torres shook his head. 'No, on two counts. It's neither his métier nor in his interest. He has neither the skills nor the motive to assist us. To him, this transaction was merely a means of laying his hands on funds for arms. Hassan Mahmoudi is a political animal. Cross him off your list.'

'Juan,' said Ray, 'when we returned, you mentioned the overwhelming attack. That was your phrase. You were on the right track there. Think about it.' He turned to Dominique. 'You spoke of Greco's son. Think about that son for a moment. We must have a blanket insurance policy which will secure us, no matter what happens.'

'Overkill,' said Torres at last, 'a policy of deliberate *terror-*

ismo.'

'You're getting warm,' said Ray. 'Who is the key man here, the crucial figure, the heart of the problem?'

'Greco, obviously,' said Dominique.

'Correct,' said Ray. 'He is the cornerstone on which the structure of this transaction rests. He controls the situation. If he remains honest and deals fairly, all the other minor gears will mesh and function.'

'Greco is our insurance policy,' said Torres.

'Our insurance company, rather,' said Ray. 'He must be put in a position to reimburse us in full for any loss. Our self-interest must be transferred to his shoulders. He must be saddled with the insurer's role so that our well-being becomes his. Greco maintains a large inventory of heroin in Milan and Rome. If our merchandise is pilfered through whatever circumstance, he must be forced to replace it. The question is—how?'

'The son,' said Dominique. 'Luigi Antonio Greco.'

'Yes,' said Ray. 'He is one lever to compel Greco's honesty. Juan's *terrorismo* is the other. We must force Greco's complete and wholehearted cooperation through two of the strongest human emotions—love and fear. Does that make sense to you?'

'The general proposition is sound,' said Juan Torres. 'I'm trying to translate it into specific tactical terms.'

'We shall do precisely that,' said Ray. 'We shall now implement your theory of overkill. Listen closely, both of you. This is what you will do.'

For the next fifteen minutes Ray outlined his plan. Dominique Maestracci and Juan Torres gave him their concentrated, silent attention. There were no interruptions.

'What do you think?' said Ray at last.

'Drastic,' said Torres. 'A powerful vermifuge.'

'Right,' said Ray. 'It should expel many worms, the living as well as the dead ones. What is your opinion, Dominique?'

'Beautiful,' said Dominique.

'Improvise and accomplish it in your own way, as circumstances dictate,' said Ray. 'I will sail with the Genoa consignment. Go into action before or after my departure, at your convenience. It does not matter. When your task is completed, separate. Juan will accompany the Trieste shipment. You, Dominique, will go with the Naples lot. Is everything understood?'

'Perfectly,' said Dominique. 'Cadri, of course, is making arrangements for four five-hundred-kilo shipments on four different vessels.'

'I'll amend his instructions,' said Ray. 'No problem there. A courier prepared to smuggle five hundred kilos aboard a ship will also be able to handle seven hundred.' He paused. 'Now we will examine what Dominique suggested, the lever of love. Dominique, you have investigated Greco's personal life to come extent. Does he have any other weaknesses? A secret wife somewhere whom he loves dearly?'

'None that I could run down,' said Dominique.

'An old mother perhaps? A dearly loved relative?'

'Nothing.'

'A mistress to whom he has opened his secret heart?'

'Nothing. He has many women, but his heart is never involved.'

'The son, then,' said Ray. 'This Luigi Antonio Greco.'

'The son,' nodded Dominique. 'I went into that well. *Signor* Roberto Greco truly loves that young man.'

Ray nodded with satisfaction. 'We must be grateful for that much. Even a Roberto Greco must have something to love. Perhaps as an antidote to his own wickedness. If a man like Greco did not love something, he could very well sting himself to death and die by his own poison. Dominique, give us the details on Luigi Antonio.'

'He is twenty-three, a law student at the University of Rome. He is Greco's crown prince, a bright and handsome young man. I would assume that *Signor* Greco hopes to pass his interests on to his son.'

'A reasonable assumption,' said Ray. 'Roberto Greco spent thirty years amassing his little empire with much effort and some danger. Where is young Greco now?'

'Where should he be?' said Dominique. 'In his law classes.'

'A typical enough picture,' said Ray. 'Roberto doubtless envisions a brilliant career in politics for his son. Since the father is a Sicilian, he is, by definition, a dynast and a nepotist to his fingertips.'

'The son's heart is the father's heart,' said Dominique. 'The young man sleeps with many women. There are always women in his bed, never less than two at a time. He plays, no doubt, more than he studies. This displeases the father. Luigi Antonio is handsome, athletic, with the virility of a young bull. The women adore not only his overhanging inheritance but his balls. He is distinguished for the largest and strongest cock in the School of Law.'

Ray sighed. 'Oh, Christ! To be twenty-three again and have a few women in your bed all at the same time! Doesn't that fire your blood, Juan?'

'No,' said Juan Torres.

'I don't believe you,' said Ray. 'Every man in his forties envies the virility, the attractiveness, and the opportunities of youth. The only phlegmatic, blind, unconscious and discontented pig in the entire picture is youth itself. I envy Luigi, yet my envy hasn't turned into hatred because his cock is bigger than mine, which it undoubtedly is, and because he can probably achieve six orgasms in a single night, which I cannot. Age has a way of dulling our desires as it gradually steals away our powers. It's a form of merciful anesthesia. No, I don't hate Luigi, I merely envy him, but with goodwill. I am interested in him only because his father loves him.' He turned away to Juan Torres. 'Juan, we must find you a woman. We must awaken your heart so that it will beat again and help you discover the pleasure of loving and the pain if your love is not requited.'

'Why are you so concerned with my heart, Don Raimondo?' said Torres.

'I, myself, am dying for love,' said Ray. 'My heart is withered and stale. It's full of nothing but pain.' He rose from the table and began to walk about the room in his excitement and agitation. 'By the blood of Jesus Christ, when this business is finished I'll make a celebration which will leave those Roman abortions, those misbegotten sonsofbitches, gabbling for weeks to come. We'll wade knee-deep in naked girls. Then we'll go home.'

140

Juan Torres smiled and shook his head. 'One girl will suffice me. A man's lusts are insatiable, but the muscles of the penis and the blood supply from the brain never measure up to his expectations. And what if you had a cock as large as a strong man's right arm, large enough to kill a woman? And what if you could flood her with twenty orgasms? Would that cure your fever? Never. Show me a man who kills too easily and I'll show you a man who is sexually frustrated to the point of madness.'

'Dominique,' said Ray, 'are you one of those?'

Dominique shook his head. 'No. I think I am like Juan. I kill only in the course of business. I would prefer not to kill, because it can lead to complications. Are you like that, Don Raimondo?'

'I could be,' said Ray, 'if I did not control myself. When I return to New York City, I intend to fall in love with a woman who already loves me. Then my heart will stop hurting and one woman will give me everything which I need.'

'I truly hope so, Don Raimondo,' said Torres.

'The ridiculous, the ignominious aspect of a man is that he needs to love and to be loved by a woman. I need to love, therefore I am shit.'

Dominique looked at Ray, glanced at Juan Torres, shrugged, and maintained silence.

'I don't follow your logic, Don Raimondo,' said Torres. 'You say there is a woman who loves you. I congratulate you. You are a fortunate man. It's more than I have. What about you, Dominique?'

'I have a wife,' said Dominique shortly. 'She is my heart and all I need.'

'You see, Don Raimondo?' said Torres. 'What are you tilting at?'

'The heart is a weakness,' said Ray. 'I have a need to tear it out.'

'Who are you to say that? You are only a man of flesh and blood like the rest of us. This woman, if you return and she still wants you, you may count yourself fortunate. It's no weakness, nothing of which to be ashamed. If I found a woman to truly love, what a happiness! I would kiss her hands. I would even begin believing in a God and start going to church.'

'You, Juan?' said Ray with surprise in his voice. 'You the Berber?'

'Yes, I. What am I? You know what I am and what I have done. What have I ever known in my life? Barracks and whorehouses and fighting.'

'By God! You hold yourself too cheaply.'

'No, I don't. It's you who hold yourself too dearly. All this thrashing about to achieve a kind of idiot autonomy isn't strength, it's a real inner weakness.'

'The devil drives me and makes this existence too painful,' said Ray. 'I feel sometimes as though my skull were going to burst with fury and frustration. My eyeballs swell, my heart pounds, my hands tremble, and the whole world becomes a blurred curtain of red, as though the blood were seeping out of my eyeballs.'

Juan Torres stared at Ray calmly. 'All I see is that you are in many ways still a boy, a boy of forty-five. You are still growing up.'

Ray flushed, turned pale, and stared fixedly at Torres. He controlled himself with an intense physical effort and finally laughed. 'From you, Juan, I'll take it. It's the measure of my friendship.'

'Friends were made to speak the truth.'

Ray nodded. 'Good enough. But we've strayed far from the main thread.' In a calmer voice: 'Dominique, have you taken Luigi Antonio Greco hostage?'

'In my mind,' said Dominique. 'With the help of Juan.'

'Do it as soon as you reach Rome. As soon as your business here is finished. And do this part of it well, in every detail, as I instructed you.'

Dominique nodded.

'Where will you hold young Greco?' asked Ray.

'In your villa on the coast. It is the most natural place in the world.'

'And what if something goes wrong? What if the heat rises?'

'We will transfer him to Marseilles. We'll drug him first.'

142

'But you're a condemned man there.'

'I won't go into the city,' said Dominique. 'We can hold him elsewhere. I have cousins in Gardanne, in Toulin, and in Hyères. If it's necessary to kill Luigi, it's the easiest thing in the world to drop him into the sea. As we did with Ponchielli.'

'Give me your plan.'

Dominique shrugged. 'I have made none. It will be no problem to pick up Luigi. I will work out the details after we reach Rome. As a matter of fact, I have several friends who are connected with the university. Two of them are building custodians. They can be a useful connection. But I think we will take Luigi in his apartment. He rents one near the School of Law.' Dominique grinned. 'I suspect we'll have to pluck Luigi from the arms of a beautiful, naked young woman.' He paused. 'Don Raimondo, are you sure that Roberto Greco will not misinterpret—that is, underestimate—the kidnapping of his son and'—here he gestured toward Juan Torres—'this other business on which you have briefed us?'

'Roberto Greco is a Sicilian,' said Ray. 'He will read the message like the Lord's Prayer, like the *Fioretti of Saint Francis*. At this very moment, he is following our conference in his mind, step by step, as though on a duplicate chessboard.'

'If that is so,' said Torres, 'if he has not already done so, why doesn't he take safety precautions for his son?'

'It is possible he may have done so already,' said Ray. 'In playing this game of Sicilian chess, it is the speed of the attack which is all-important. True, Greco may be anticipating such a move on my part. But he may not be anticipating it so quickly. He may not be giving us credit for sufficient initiative. I am certain that he will be entirely unprepared for the shock value of the Beirut prong of our attack. I read Roberto's mind—a Spaniard, a Corsican, and an American. *Bene!* They will try to kidnap my son. But only after I have cheated them. And I will have taken my safety measures by that time.' Ray paused. 'Don't kill young Greco unless you absolutely have to. He is a refundable insurance premium, nothing more.' He turned to Torres. 'Well, Juan?'

'Don Raimondo, it is a good plan. It is tactically sound.'

'I believe so,' said Ray. 'One final thing. Do you anticipate any difficulties when the two true believers come tonight for their money?'

'None whatsoever,' said Torres. 'In any case, there will be three of us here. Armed.'

'I think we should kill them,' said Ray. 'It would be the easiest thing in the world to do so. It would be, as we say in America, a natural. We would save a million dollars. What do you think?'

Torres reflected for a long time. 'You would be introducing new, unknown factors,' he finally said. 'Mahmoudi is no man to walk into a trap. If you killed him, you might very well not get out of Beirut alive. You would be overreaching.' He paused. 'Besides, there is my personal friendship with Mahmoudi. He trusts me.'

'That is an important factor with you?' said Ray.

'Yes,' said Torres. 'Cheat Greco if you wish. Do not pay him if you can engineer it. Kill Greco and his son together, if necessary. But pay Mahmoudi and let him go. That is my advice.'

Ray sighed. 'I suppose you are right.' He struck the table. 'Then we can dismiss Mahmoudi and Malik. They have been paid. They are already off the board, ancient history.' He rose from the table. 'I am going to take a siesta until it is time to dine.'

Dominique Maestracci and Juan Torres left the room.

The dinner with the two Muslims went well. Five men sat about the dinner table for two hours as the elaborate courses were served. Finally Ray said, '*Sidi* Mahmoudi, Torres and I will leave now. Dominique Maestracci will bring you and Colonel Malik up thirty minutes after we leave.'

When Mahmoudi and Colonel Malik entered the suite preceded by Dominique, Torres was relaxing in an armchair smoking a thin black cigar. Ray was pacing the length of the long living room.

'Don Raimondo,' Torres had said just before the Muslims entered, 'you are too agitated about something. If it's about Mahmoudi, be at ease. It will go well.'

144

'He is my last and smallest concern,' Ray replied. 'I'm thinking about young Greco and his women.'

'Then have a woman, or three women sent up here after Mahmoudi leaves. It will calm you.'

'It's not that,' snarled Ray. 'I want young Greco's youth and the youth of ten more like him. God Almighty! Why are the young so unhappy, the undeserving bastards?'

'Ah,' said Torres, 'that! Now you are being an unreasonable man.'

'My unreasonableness will destroy me some day,' said Ray. 'It has a name.'

'What do you name it?'

'Hodgkin's disease. It is my own private malady.'

'There is such a disease,' said Torres, 'named after a British physician, I believe.'

'Mine belongs only to Ray Hodgkin.'

Torres grinned. 'The name itself is a disease. Why don't you quietly dispose of it?'

Ray laughed in spite of himself. 'I have already been advised to do so.'

'But seriously,' said Torres, 'there are other men like yourself.'

'Impossible,' said Ray. 'I am unique.'

'The Buddhists would say that you are in hell for sins committed in some former life,' said Torres. 'But no man is wholly unique. There are even other Torreses walking this world.'

'Impossible, by God!' shouted Ray. 'There is only one Torres.'

Their conversation had been interrupted by the arrival of the sellers.

'Ah,' said Mahmoudi, strolling through the room toward the window and looking out. 'What a magnificent view! What a coastline! What beauty!'

'I shall be sorry to leave this wonderful city, *Sidi* Mahmoudi,' said Ray. 'I shall return again, I hope, on a more relaxed occasion.'

Dominique and Malik seated themselves in armchairs.

Ray went into another room and returned with the suitcase.

'Here is the money, *Sidi* Mahmoudi,' said Ray.

145

Mahmoudi took the suitcase and smiled. 'Shall I take your word as you took mine, *Signor* Cornaro?'

'I insist that you open the case and count the money. The physical and temporal obstacles which made inspection of the merchandise inadvisable do not apply here.'

'Very well,' said Mahmoudi.

He opened the suitcase. Twice he and Colonel Malik counted over the stacks of thousand-dollar American bills.

'The full sum is here,' said Mahmoudi. He repacked the stack of bills, snapped shut and locked the suitcase. 'It has been a pleasure to do business with you, *Signor* Cornaro.'

'The pleasure is all mine,' said Ray. 'I am curious about one thing. Perhaps a naïve question. In my country it is sometimes a problem handling a large number of thousand-dollar bills and getting them into safekeeping. Institutions make a record of such denominations and report them to our Internal Revenue Service.'

'We have no such problems here,' said Mahmoudi easily. 'In that regard we are more progressive than the great United States of America. Beirut has more banks than Zurich. We, or rather, the Lebanese, rival, and, indeed surpass the Swiss in handling secret and coded numbered bank accounts. Lebanese banks are stringently protected by law and no questions are asked.'

'Lebanese banks even pay interest on checking accounts,' put in Colonel Malik.

'I congratulate you,' said Ray. 'You have here a sensible country.'

'We must operate in this way,' said Colonel Malik. 'Consider! The funds pour into the country, particularly from the oil-rich lands and sheikhdoms of Saudi Arabia, Kuwait, and Trucial Oman. Many of the rulers of those countries never feel safe, and quite rightly so. Switzerland is far away, but Beirut's banks are near. These rulers use Beirut to provide themselves with insurance against revolt in their own countries. The banks trade with the money or invest it and then reconvert it into more money. We Lebanese, as I said before, are traders and commission men. That is how we live.'

'Wonderful,' said Ray. As a pad, as a fortress, as a base of operations, Lebanon fascinated him. What could not the Organization do if it ever got a real foothold in this country! When he got back to the United States and reorganized himself, he would bring up the matter before the national commission. There was nothing visionary about the concept. If the planning was sound, the mission could be accomplished. Crusaders had been able to do it once, why not the boys? Who in hell were the Crusaders? A rabble of hillbilly yokels from the dung heaps of northern Europe, egged on by priests. Strongholds had been taken and held through the ages. With organization, it could be done again. This Lebanon was a small country, just right. It could be taken.

'*Signor* Cornaro,' Mahmoudi was saying, 'I wish you all success. Juanito, may Allah have you in his keeping.'

Torres grinned. 'Take care of yourself Hassan. You travel a hard road.'

The polite leave-taking continued between the sellers and the buyers. When Hassan Mahmoudi and Colonel Malik finally walked out of the suite with the suitcase, Dominique bolted the door behind them.

Ray sat down and moodily lit a cigarette. 'Now we are poorer by a million dollars. Perhaps we should have killed them after all.'

'I think it would have worked out badly, Don Raimondo,' said Torres.

'Perhaps you are right,' said Ray. 'Well, then, it's done. It's finished.'

'You gave yourself away in that last exchange with Mahmoudi,' said Torres. 'When you referred to your tax collection service. He thought that you were an Italian national.'

'I realized it as I spoke the words. But it doesn't matter now. I've changed my plans. I won't sail to Genoa in that freighter. Considering our altered plans, it doesn't matter whether I am here to see the loading or not. Juan, you and Dominique can work with Cadri and Polizzi on the entire transfer. When the merchandise is loaded, go into action.'

'What are your intentions?' said Torres.

'I'm flying to Rome in the morning. I will go to the apartment first, then to the villa. Meet me there.'

147

CHAPTER 9

The Italian merchantman *Doge Loredano* rode at anchor in the bay one mile from the Beirut waterfront. Standing on the pierhead, Juan Torres and Dominique Maestracci examined it carefully with high-power binoculars. In the bright moonlight which bathed the ship and the calm waters of the bay, the profile and details of the big freighter were clearly visible.

Polizzi sat at the wheel of the Lancia and waited. Cadri raised his own binoculars and studied the ship intently. The *Loredano* showed two masthead lights and an anchor light. Otherwise it was dark except for three circles of light in three widely separated portholes.

'A few of them are aboard,' said Torres. 'The harbor watch, I suppose.'

'Yes,' agreed Cadri. 'You may be sure that at least three-quarters of the crew are ashore sampling the fleshpots of Beirut.'

'It's on in the morning,' said Dominique to Cadri. 'When will the ship heave anchor and move in to load the cargo?'

'According to my information,' said Cadri, 'at six in the morning. There are no special watches, lookouts, or guards out there. No need for it on an empty freighter in peacetime. Now is the ideal time to put our goods aboard. The courier is waiting.'

'We're eliminating the Hamburg consignment,' said Torres. 'The *Loredano* will have to take seven hundred kilos instead of the original five hundred.'

Cadri shrugged and looked surprised. 'If you wish,' he said dubiously.

'What difference should it make?' said Torres, with a touch

of irritability.

'None, I suppose,' said Cadri carefully. 'It can be accomplished.' He did not like this Spaniard, nor his saturnine Corsican companion. He disliked them almost as much as the Sicilian who had already departed, the one who called himself Cornaro. There was a damp and moldy smell about this trio, the smell of an open grave. Cadri felt the chill of it through his meager flesh and into his sun-dried bones. They were unlike the peaceably inclined smugglers and *contrabbandieri* with whom he customarily dealt. There was something about these men which made him feel uneasy. For all his fine ways with Mahmoudi, that Cornaro was the most savage brute of all. Cadri envied Rossano Polizzi his thick, unimaginative phlegm. The brunt of this business was being laid on his tired frame. He wished he were at home with his wife and daughters instead of out here on the exposed waterfront.

'The *Loredano*,' said Torres, 'is this the ship which is bound for Genoa?'

Cadri nodded.

'Would it be possible to put the entire lot, two thousand kilos, aboard the *Loredano*?'

Cadri shook his head emphatically. 'Never! For a hundred different reasons. The time element alone is prohibitive. The danger is too great. No! We must never put our eggs in one basket.'

'I was just asking,' said Torres.

'Do you expect any real difficulties?' said Dominique.

'Not with our equipment,' said Cadri. 'You will see my boat. I have one of the finest sport-fishing craft in the Beirut Yacht Club.'

'Let's go then,' said Torres.

The three men got into the Lancia and Polizzi drove them to the yacht club. Cadri's craft, the *Swallow*, lay secured fore and aft at her moorings in a bath of antifouling solution contained in heavy plastic sheeting.

'She has twin diesels and can make twenty-five knots,' said Cadri. 'Polizzi keeps her in top condition.'

For such a big man, Polizzi was moving around *Swallow* with ease. Plainly, he knew his way about a boat. He started the port engine into life. Then the starboard engine. While the engines warmed up, Polizzi moved with the leisurely caution of a sailor to clear away and stow the canvas coverings. The morphine base lay in the wheelhouse on the main deck under the upper open flying bridge. There were fourteen packages in all, each one containing fifty kilos wrapped in heavy waterproof plastic and securely tied with thick nylon fishing line. Two fishing chairs had been bolted to the deck of the cockpit immediately forward of the transom. Two heavy fishing rods with the reels already secured rested in the chair sockets and overhung the transom.

'It's unlikely that we'll be stopped and questioned at this hour by the harbor patrol,' said Cadri. 'But if we are, we're getting an early start because we have a two-hour run to the fishing bank.'

Polizzi cast off the fore and aft mooring lines. *Swallow* moved out slowly, the diesels barely rumbling and gently snorting out water from the exhausts. The run was a short one. As they approached the *Loredano*. Polizzi cut the engines and drifted down toward the side of the freighter. Cadri began putting out fenders on the starboard side of the *Swallow*.

'It must be his boat,' said Dominique to Torres. 'Look how gently he treats it.'

Cadri pointed up toward an open freight hatch in the sheer side of the freighter, fifteen feet above them. 'Watch the porthole just to the left of the hatch.' A second later, the four waiting men saw a series of three flashes from the porthole. Cadri acknowledged, his own flashlight blinking on and off three times. Then they bumped gently alongside under the open hatch. A man stood dimly outlined in the open hatchway above them. Polizzi and Dominique each took a boathook and held the *Swallow* to the side of the *Loredano* by hooking the boathooks into two open portholes. Despite the fact that the sea was calm and there were no swells or waves, it was clumsy and difficult. 'It's better this way,' said Cadri in a low voice. 'If there were a swell running, we'd have to hold her against the side of the ship with the engines.'

The man silhouetted in the freight hatch overhead sent a heaving line snaking down into the cockpit of the *Swallow*.

Cadri secured a single fifty-kilo package to the line, gave it a tug, and the man hauled it up. The operation was repeated fourteen times. Then the freight hatch in the side of the *Loredano* closed silently. Polizzi started the engines. The *Swallow* fell away from the side of the freighter and headed slowly back toward the Beirut shoreline.

Torres and Dominique seated themselves on the naugahyde-covered settees which ran along the wheelhouse bulkheads.

'Well, that's finished,' said Torres to Cadri. 'What's the next step?'

'The *Albertine Peyreau* will be arriving the day after tomorrow,' said Cadri. 'She's out of Le Havre and will call at Trieste and Naples on her way home. She also will anchor on her arrival night. Then she will come alongside the pier in the morning to take on her cargo. It's a routine procedure.'

'Then I'd like to put the balance aboard her,' said Torres. 'Thirteen hundred kilos.'

'Impossible,' said Cadri. 'The stowage of it would take too long. There's only one seaman-courier aboard the *Peyreau*. He's not equipped to handle such a load single-handed.'

Torres grunted noncommittally.

Dominique, observing Cadri carefully, thought to himself, The man seems cowed enough. Don Raimondo may have crashed into him too hard. A little friendliness is in order here to ease the man's mind and soften him. There's safety in honey as well as in knives and bullets. 'Signor Cadri,' he said, 'I've been watching and admiring your own and Polizzi's handling of the *Swallow*. It's a beautiful craft.'

'Yes,' said Cadri, with some surprise in his voice. 'I love her.'

'You were evidently a professional sailor at one time.'

'For many years I used to sail in freighters out of Genoa,' said Cadri. 'I had a second officer's license.'

'I thought so. And Polizzi also. He is also a sailor.'

'I hold a boatswain's rating,' said Polizzi briefly and without turning his head. He did not like these two men. The departed Sicilian's words still rankled in his heart.

'Let's be friends,' said Dominique. 'Since we still have two more missions to accomplish together, let us work in harmony.

151

There will be still a third vessel after the *Peyreau*, no?'

'The *Giorgio Alberoni*,' said Cadri. 'From here, she is bound directly for Naples.'

'When do you expect the *Alberoni*?'

'In a week.'

'How long will she remain in Beirut?'

'Three days.'

'Then our work will be done.'

'If all goes well.'

'It will go best, then, if we work together amicably,' said Dominique. 'I apologize to you and Polizzi for *Signor* Cornaro's harsh language. He is our employer. We could not say anything in his presence. He is an unpredictable man with a heavy tongue. Don't take his words to heart.'

Juan Torres caught the drift. 'My friend Dominique speaks the truth, *Signor* Cadri. Our boss did not speak for us, only for himself. I am willing to learn from you. Dominique here has had deep-water experience and speaks your language. We are staying at the Royale. Polizzi, you, also. You and Cadri come to the hotel tomorrow night. Be our guests for dinner. There, and at the Grande Casino nightclub. They put on a good show there. Beautiful girls. The best belly dancers in the Middle East, and French artistes.'

'I wouldn't know,' said Polizzi, still suspicious. 'On my wages, I cannot afford to visit the Grande Casino and still support a wife and four children.'

'It will cost you nothing,' said Torres. 'Come as our guests. That is the least we can offer for your hard work and conscientious service.'

Cadri seemed somewhat mollified. 'If you wish,' he finally said. Perhaps, he thought, my imagination has been working overtime.

When they finally parted company with the two agents of Tufarelli, Torres said, 'You did well, Dominique.'

'I hope so,' replied Dominique.

On the following night Torres and Dominique put themselves out to regale their guests. Cadri was impressed by the luxury and elegance of the Grand Casino nightclub and enjoyed it. Polizzi was impressed and rendered uneasy. Torres beckoned to the waiter and ordered Five Star Hennessy brandy to follow the rich and heavy food which they had consumed.

As Cadri sipped and began to relax, he felt more at ease.

'I envy you men with experience on the sea,' said Torres. 'My people were all sailors and fishermen from Cadiz. I was the only one who became a soldier. Ships are a mystery to me. How do you manage to successfully conceal this merchandise aboard a ship so that it will not be found?'

Cadri puffed forth a cloud of fragrant smoke from a Corona Corona which Dominique had offered him.

'Ah,' he replied, 'it has been claimed by experts that there are between twenty and thirty thousand hiding places on a vessel for anyone minded to do some smuggling. The experts with whom we match wits know most of the hiding places, but they never know all of them. For large quantities of merchandise such as we are handling in this operation ships are always the best, better than aircraft. After all, there are so many more ships plying the trade routes than aircraft, and they are far more difficult to search than planes. Genoa and Naples, for instance, have so much shipping going in and out of port that it is impossible for customs men to search each entering vessel thoroughly. Again, unless the customs men are tipped off ahead of time, the odds are very good that they will never find the contraband. Polizzi and I both know most of the places because we have both worked on ships. There are places below the decks, behind a bulkhead or an overhead, or in the piping and behind the wiring where a mechanically minded man, moderately skilled with screwdrivers, pliers, and wrenches can hide a surprisingly large amount of contraband. The most original place of which I heard was an old-fashioned coal burner of a ship. A fireman was used as the courier. He hid the contraband behind the firebrick wall of a boiler when it was cold. Only the most ambitious customs agent would wait about for a dirty, sooty boiler to become cool enough so that he could get in there with overalls on and start tearing down the firebrick in the dim recesses of the boiler. It is one of the dirtiest jobs in the fireroom.'

'This man who took in our shipment on the *Loredano*,' said

Torres, 'is he trustworthy?'

'He's one of our regular couriers,' said Cadri. 'An oiler. He works in the engine room. He and the second assistant engineer work for us steadily. They have been with us for the last five years and have never slipped up yet. Their bonuses for cooperating with us earn them more in one trip than three months' wages. The second assistant, for instance, happens to be a specialist on pumps and piping. He can and has custom-designed pumps to perform a highly specific task, equipment that is not usually in the engine room when the yard delivers a ship to the shipping line. This man has installed three so-called sump pumps beneath the engine-room floor plates on the *Loredano*. They look very impressive but they are actually dummies which have no functional value. The interior of those pumps provide us with some very valuable space for carrying contraband.'

'That's the ship that's going to Genoa, isn't it?' said Dominique.

Cadri nodded. 'Consider the size of the port of Genoa. Our shipment, seven hundred kilos of morphine base, a little over fourteen hundred pounds, is an insignificant item. Genoa is one of the busiest ports in the whole of Europe. It stretches for miles along the waterfront.'

'I've been there,' said Dominique patriotically. 'I think that Marseilles is larger and busier.'

'Genoa handles perhaps fifty million tons of cargo annually,' said Cadri, beginning to enjoy himself. In such shop talk he was most comfortably on his own home ground. 'There is a movement in and out of the port of some twenty-seven thousand ships a year.'

'Ah,' said Dominique, impressed. 'You may well have the advantage of us, *Signor* Cadri.'

Even Polizzi, the surly one, was beginning to relax. Perhaps these were not such bad fellows, after all. They were certainly sports. The rich food sat comfortably in his belly. This evening's entertainment had surely cost Torres and Maestracci the equivalent of a month of Polizzi's wages. And the brandy which they urged on him was superb. Never had he tasted such liquor in his life. Polizzi, too, began to hold forth on the arcane skills of smuggling. 'The stowage of merchandise on a departing ship is delicate work,' he said importantly to Dominique and Torres, 'but the removal of it at the port of destination is even more sensitive.'

'How do you mean that, *Signor* Polizzi?' said Dominique, giving the Calabrian close attention. Even Juan Torres removed the cigar from between his lips to listen more attentively to the ripe wisdom of an expert.

'Well,' said Polizzi, 'when a ship arrives in port, let us say, as when the *Loredano* arrives in Genoa, do you think that the merchandise will go ashore immediately?'

'What else?' said Torres. 'Well, doesn't it?'

Polizzi smiled. 'Oh, no. It is not disturbed in its place of concealment for the first three or four days at least. Remember this—contraband does not move from man to man. It moves from place to place. There is a difference. This merchandise we're talking about is moved only after the first flurry of activitity and confusion is over, after the stevedores have unloaded the ship and the crew has gone ashore.'

'Ah,' said Torres.

Dominique looked at Polizzi admiringly.

Cadri leaned forward confidentially across the table with his cigar between his teeth. 'Let me tell this part of it, Rossano,' he said to Polizzi. 'I think I am more familiar with it.'

Polizzi finished the balance of his brandy and waved his hand in generous permission to his colleague. Dominique refilled Polizzi's glass. Rossano Polizzi could not remember when he had last seen a waiter ordered to leave an entire bottle of Five Star Hennessy brandy on the customer's table.

'The thing is this,' said Cadri. 'The crew member who receives the merchandise on the departing ship is not the same man who takes it ashore. There a different man is employed. The man who receives it aboard knows only who handed it to him. The man who takes it ashore at the other end does not know the consignor. He does not know the consignee either, for that matter. All he knows is that he must deliver it to someone else in the shipyard or just outside the yard area. This buffer chain is a safety measure. Each man in the chain knows only his immediate link. This is a security step, in case

155

he should be arrested and questioned. He will honestly be unable to give the authorities a clear and complete picture.'

Torres smiled wryly. 'There is always the *cassetta*.'

Cadri shrugged and turned his palms outward. 'The *cassetta* will hurt but will not help. The principle is that each man involved in the operation knows only his own part of the job. Only the ultimate consignee knows all the steps involved.'

With tipsy solemnity, Dominique patted Cadri lightly on the shoulder. 'You speak the truth, my friend. Do you know how I know it?'

It reassured Cadri that the Corsican was more awash than himself, and hence, more vulnerable and the lesser man. He therefore humored the man from Marseilles. 'How do you know it, *Signor* Maestracci?'

'Call me Dominique,' said the Corsican ponderously and enunciating his words slowly. 'Let there be no formality among friends. I will tell you how I know. I served in the French Resistance during the war and we employed the very same security measures. That is how I know.' Dominique looked around triumphantly and winked at Cadri.

'Dominique,' said Juan Torres paternally, 'perhaps you have had a little too much.'

But Dominique did not reply. His chin rested on his chest and he snored very gently and softly.

Torres looked at Polizzi and Cadri apologetically. 'You must excuse my friend, *signori*. He really has no head for liquor, certainly not for brandy of this quality. These Corsicans! Their mothers nurse them at the breast on pastis, on anisette and similar garbage.'

Cadri laughed and waved his hand charitably. Even Polizzi was somewhat amused at this Corsican whose mouth was perhaps larger than his capacity for drink.

'I think we should call it a night,' said Torres. 'Will you help me with my friend, *signori*? We will take a taxicab at the stand in front of the club. I will take you both to your homes and then I will get my friend to bed.'

'It is considerate of you,' said Cadri, 'but it is not necessary. Polizzi and I can find our own way home. We do not live so far from here.'

'I insist on it,' said Torres. 'It is the duty of a host to ease every step of the way for his guests.'

The four men left the club, Dominique assisted by Torres and Cadri. Torres said to Cadri, 'Give the driver directions to your house and to Polizzi's. Then we will continue back to our hotel.'

Cadri was the first man to be dropped. He shook hands cordially with Torres. 'Thank you for a most pleasant evening, *Signor* Torres. And thank Dominique for me when he wakes up in the morning. He is really a jolly fellow and a good companion.'

'A little simple, with a weak head for brandy,' agreed Torres, 'but his heart is in the right place. You will get word to us when the *Albertine Peyreau* arrives?'

'Immediately,' said Cadri. 'Good night and sleep well.'

The cab drove away. Cadri, at peace with the world, walked into the lobby of his apartment house. Cornaro was one thing, but he had misjudged these two fellows. They seemed decent types, like the normal, respectable smugglers with whom he had worked so successfully for so many years as Tufarelli's Beirut agent.

At the warehouse office the next morning, Cadri said to Polizzi, 'Well, Rossano, did you sleep well?'

'Like a log,' said Polizzi. 'It was a good evening, Enrico.'

'What do you think of them?'

'I may have been wrong. They are our kind.'

'That's what I think,' said Cadri.

CHAPTER 10

Alda Quirini was a major and solid glory of the Italian film industry. She would have been of any other country's because of what she was, a driving fanatic reaching for *virtú* in her profession. She could have chosen other mediums, but it was impossible to think of her as other than actress. Sheer vital energy aside, she possessed cruel intelligence. The climb up the mountainside had burned some humanity out of her. She had lost patience, a tolerance with and sympathy for those whom she had outdistanced. There were those about the world who earned more money. *Bene!* Alda had long ago ceased to trouble about money. Her mission was to continue perfecting herself until death. Alda never permitted her identity to become entangled with the illusions of the role. She maintained control with a strong hand and a clear head, smashed the role into something malleable, and reshaped it to her own interpretation. Her ability to remain her own role was a formalin which preserved her from corruption. Given this context, she had resigned emotional fulfillment and happiness with open eyes. *Aut Caesar, aut nihil.* Alda had made her choice and paid the price. The price had incinerated her soul and refined her face. For Alda, with everything else, had beauty. Her body was one thing, a long book. Beyond that, it was her face which made perceptive artists thoughtful. Alda's delicately boned cranial and facial structure, as coldly symmetrical as that of a Grecian statue, was framed in flowing masses of golden hair. The nose of a duchess with an undoubtedly clear title. The mouth straight, the lips thin, sinuous, and arrogant. From such lips had raucous squawks or dead silence issued, it would have been enough. But Alda had a low, resonant voice, a cello to utter an implacable 'No.' Time and her own will had tautened the facial muscles and accentuated the hollows of her cheek-bones. Time had creased two horizontal hairline wrinkles across the pure forehead. Time had painted a faint darkness under the cold clear eyes. This sign that Alda was only perishable tissue made the hearts of discerning men melt all the more. 'How could any woman have such a beautiful face?' said one artist. 'She is a somber Medusa,' said another. 'You are wrong,' said the wisest-eyed among them. 'Do you see those little wrinkles? They make her more human and approachable. They make her even more beautiful. When she grows older and more wrinkled, I'll allow myself to fall in love with her.' It was, of course, ridiculous for grown men, competent in their own art, to talk so about a mere female. And, yet, they were not ashamed to do so. Because of what they saw and were, beauty stirred them in a thousand ways. It was more than a desire to climb into bed with Alda. Far beyond that, they wanted to mother and father her, to protect her, to drown her in tenderness, to wallow in loving her. But they also had their own egos and identities to consider. To love an unresponding statue was corrosive and self-destructive. So the artists appreciated from a distance. 'She could conceivably love a man,' was the general consensus, 'but not one of us.' The quality of that hypothetical man posed a knotty problem. 'He would have to be a hero,' said someone, 'a man who would overshadow and overpower her. By a hero, I mean a fanatic even more remorselessly dedicated to greater goals than her own, a man who would not notice her. To such a man Alda might surrender what is left of her heart. And, by falling in love, she would destroy herself. Personally, I prefer her alive, as she is, so that I can look at her.'

Alda had often listened to these discussions of which she was the center. She listened with a stony lack of expression, because painters and sculptors were extravagant idiots, worse than women, who loved to talk instead of work. At this particular moment she was turning on her right flank and regarding Roberto Greco thoughtfully. He lay on his back beside her in the oversized ornate bed. His hands rested clasped on the graying hair of his abdomen. His legs were stretched out and close together. His noble head rested on two pillows. His eyes were closed and his sharp profile was outlined against the lighted reading lamp on the marble night table beside him. In addition to the lamp the table bore a polished human skull set in an alabaster base.

Alda stretched out her left hand, seized a handful of gray hair matting Greco's chest, and pulled it sharply.

Greco opened his eyes and stared at her coldly. 'Why did you do that?'

'You so resembled a corpse,' said Alda. 'I wanted to make certain you were still alive.'

'I assure you that I'm very much alive.'

'Why do you keep that skull beside your bed?'

'To remind myself of my beginnings.'

'You've wilfully turned it around,' said Alda. 'The skull should be to remind you of your mortality and your end. As usual, you're thinking crookedly.'

She reached down and gripped the shaft of Greco's penis in her left hand. She squeezed it hard and tugged it upward twice.

Greco winced.

Alda smiled, opened her hand, and the flaccid penis fell back.

'*You* may be alive,' she said, 'but *that* is very much not alive. Perhaps you should call in a priest to give it extreme unction.'

Greco stared down without expression at his limp organ. 'Bitch,' he said tonelessly.

Alda laughed. 'Why blame me?' She raised and tautened her magnificent left breast. The rosy nipple stood out from the surrounding aureola. 'Ten thousand young men here in Rome would be giving ten years of their lives to be lying in bed with me at this moment, to be sucking my nipples and nibbling at my clitoris. Ten thousand young men with furiously upstanding cocks, small, large, thin, thick, black, white, straight, crooked, but all reared upward respectfully, praying to God, ready to do battle with Alda Quirini. Even Saint Simeon Stylites would come sliding down from his pillar like a brave fireman with his stinking rags all tucked up, ready to fuck me. And I would let him do so, body odor and all.'

'Shut up,' said Greco, with a murderous calm in his voice.

'I was fucked by a young painter the other night,' said Alda. 'He could not have been more than twenty-five or twenty-six. Nor was his body so impressive either. In fact, it was even plump and flabby. No muscles, no golden coat of tan. No gladiatorial manliness. His cock, in repose, was about as impressive as a lukewarm cocktail sausage with an inferiority complex.'

'Don't use that word,' said Greco sharply.

'What word?'

Greco scowled at her.

'Cock?' said Alda. 'Why not? Men with cocks like to hear my sensuous yet virginal lips form that word. It excites them.' She flicked her fingers teasingly and stingingly at the head of Greco's mutinous penis. 'As it does not excite this one. But I was telling you of my painter.'

'I don't want to hear about him,' snapped Greco.

'Since you can't fuck,' said Alda coolly, 'at least, listen. Perhaps you will learn something, my tired statesman. This little painter is certainly the most wretched, the most untalented artist in the world. I believe my spaniel could do better with a brush tied to its tail. No, my painter can't paint. But he can certainly fuck. How is this possible? He is no athlete.' Alda laughed. 'Good heavens, no! But the blood and fire are somewhere in his poor brain. He has an imagination and it is evidently good for something. The fiery heroic visions in his fevered mind which he cannot transfer to a blank canvas he is able to transfer to his prick. Do you like this synonym better?' Alda shook her head with admiration. 'It is not a big prick, dear Roberto, but it is a tireless, dutiful, obedient, and indefatigable prick. What a prick!'

'Silence!' shouted Greco, shifting his position uneasily.

'I won't be silent!' screamed Alda. Then she laughed again. 'My little painter plunged into me and kept pumping away until I had three orgasms. Then he flooded me with his own burst like the fountains of Versailles.' Alda smiled in tender remembrance. 'That's where his talent lies, in his balls and his prostate gland.'

'Why,' grated Greco, 'must you be so deliberately vulgar?'

' "Vulgar" means "common," dear Roberto. I am never vulgar. *You* are infinitely vulgar.' Alda smiled again. 'My little Michelangelo! My Raphael! Having flooded me so generously, do you think he withdrew a limp little penis for the American pause which refreshes?' Alda laughed, a laugh of pure, silvery glee. The critics adored her voice and her bell-like enunciation. She poked a playful left forefinger into Greco's navel. 'No, Roberto. Without withdrawing, this hero of mine, this warrior, hardened immediately and drove forward into me as though he intended to split Alda Quirini's skull. And he repeated the performance a third time without withdrawing.' Alda's glorious luminous eyes widened in wonderment. 'How could that shriveled little orphan of a cocktail sausage have expanded into such hard, magnificent wrath, into such implacable inflexiblity? How? He is not extraordinarily big, Roberto. But he is hard as the Arch of Titus. Harder than your heart, Roberto. He has an angle of erection like a ninety-millimeter cannon throwing shells at a distant city. That's what a woman needs. How is this, my dear? You are a big brain. Tell me.'

Greco shrugged, controlled himself, and did not reply. The bitch was playing her customary sadistic games with him.

'Then I will tell *you*,' said Alda. 'I know it's painful and humiliating for you to analyze this distressing phenomenon, so I will do so. My painter is a no-talent. He has neither brains, nor vision, nor the technical competence to execute visions. Therefore, merciful nature has compensated by endowing him with the ability to fuck. Where else should his blood flow but into his cock? What else does he have to think about?'

'He is half my age,' said Greco grimly.

'You deceive yourself, dear Roberto,' said Alda. 'It's not a matter of years. My most mediocre lovers have been men of intellect and talent. Their libido flows into their work. They sacrifice their cocks to art, to literature, music, philosophy. Very well! I still respect them as human beings and love them, even though I derive no personal physical pleasure from them. They have surrendered their potency on a worthy altar just as an honest priest vows chastity for the love of God.'

'Listening to you is an education in itself,' growled Greco.

'You will do well to believe that seriously, my friend,' said Alda coolly. 'My worst lovers, the most atrocious, the most pitiable, the weakest, have been men like yourself, men of business, politicians—that is to say, thieves, hypocrites, intriguers, and money-grubbers. You pay off generously with money what your heart and sexual organ cannot deliver. I take because I love beautiful things. But it is impossible to respect your breed, Roberto, as one respects an honest artist or a man of intellect who uses his mind with integrity. Your prick is engrossed and monopolized by the love of gold. How much more money and power do you need in order to compensate for your failure as a lover and for your self-hatred? The worms won't be impressed by an additional million or two or three.' Alda paused and stared at Greco's defeated penis disdainfully. 'That thing I can see, and it speaks silently for itself. Your heart I can only deduce. It is probably a decayed blackened morsel of pork. Why don't you have your doctor give you an intravenous infusion of molten gold?'

Greco shook himself deliberately like a sodden dog emerging from a river. He sat up slowly and punched up the two pillows behind him. He leaned back against the pillows and blew out his breath.

'Are you done, Alda?' he said in a flat, empty voice.

Alda Quirini also sat up and looked at him.

'I am done.'

'Luigi Antonio has been missing for five days,' said Greco. 'Saracino has been in daily touch with me.'

'The *Questore*?'

Greco nodded. 'He has not been seen at the university. He has not been home at his apartment.'

'How terrible,' said Alda, trying to infuse some sympathy into her voice. 'He is probably away on a trip. Why have we seen nothing about it in the papers?'

'I asked Saracino to keep it quiet for the time being. Saracino is certain he has been kidnapped.'

'What a pity!' cried Alda. 'I hear your son has a beautiful cock.'

Greco looked at her with tired disgust. 'Is that all you think about?'

163

'When I'm not seriously engaged with my own art—yes.'

'I'm worried.'

'Naturally. It's reported that you sincerely love your son. A miracle, if it's true.'

'I love my son,' said Greco heavily.

'You love the extension of your own monstrously swollen ego, the extension to which you will pass your loot and your name. Cheer up, Roberto. Luigi will turn up.'

'He has been abducted,' said Greco tightly. 'I know the signs. I received his severed forefinger in the mail yesterday, with a signet ring on it which I gave him on his last birthday.'

Alda practiced a convincing shudder, one which her director might be satisfied with. 'How gruesome! It sounds like some of your playful business associates.'

'I know the signs,' repeated Greco.

'A visitation from God undoubtedly,' said Alda, 'because you have been such a sinful, wicked man.'

Greco smiled crookedly. 'Pious comments from a whore.'

'You know better than that,' said Alda. 'With my golden hair, my high, pure forehead, my white skin, and my luminous delicate face, I make the perfect nun. The directors always seek me for such a role. Did you know they are planning to cast me as Saint Theresa of Avila?'

Greco laughed hollowly in spite of himself.

'I'm glad that I can cheer you up,' said Alda. 'Let me cheer you a little more while you're awaiting news from Saracino. Did you see today's *Messaggero*? A little item there tickled me. Where is the paper?'

Greco reached down to the floor on his side of the bed and handed her the paper. She folded it back to an inner sheet. 'Listen to this, Roberto:

The cardinal-vicar for Rome has complained that only about a third of the city's three million residents attend Sunday mass. And many who live in this Eternal City do not believe in heaven, hell, or any afterlife, he says. The vicar described this as incredible in a city of five hundred churches, the world center of Roman Catholicism. The cardinal's complaint confirmed the opinion held by many

Romans that the city is short on the practice of formal religion. So evident is the lack of belief in afterlife, said the cardinal, that parish priests are reporting an increase in those who die without receiving sacraments. The prelate said that the average Sunday mass attendance was thirty-five percent of the population. He pointed out that many of Rome's faithful pray to obtain temporal favors. However, to pray as worship and an action of thanks is less practiced. The prelate said that the remedy is a change in the mentality of priests, a new attitude emphasizing missionary action.'

Alda flung the newspaper to the floor. 'What do you think, Roberto?'

Greco shrugged and did not reply.

Alda slid out of the bed and stretched her arms high above her perfectly proportioned body. She swayed her hips and regarded her breasts, her flat stomach, and her long legs complacently. 'It is true,' she said. 'I am a beautiful woman, taut, fit, and healthy. And what is most important, an able artist in my profession. All the critics say so and I say so, too. I need to depend on no man. I am superior to most of them. Yes, I am a success, which is more than I can say for you.'

'Where are you going?' asked Greco.

'Home. Where else?'

'Why?'

'You're a bore. You're dull. That is even worse than being impotent.'

Alda dressed carefully, made up her face, and drew on her gloves. 'On my way home,' she said, 'I'll stop at one of the good cardinal's five hundred churches and say a short prayer for the safe return of Luigi Antonio. *Arrivederci*, dear Roberto.'

The door closed behind her.

Greco fell back on the bed, writhing with self-hatred, self-disgust, self-pity, and fear—fear, a cold, clutching fear in his bowels and his heart. Whoever had Luigi had sent no ransom note. They were demanding nothing—yet. They were waiting. They had nine more fingers to go. He stared at his limp penis and spat at it. He felt like slashing it off with a knife. He could not perform because of his sick fear for Luigi's safety. And his fear of the enemy against which he could not strike back. The Honored Society? Perhaps. But, in Greco's experience, the Friends were more urbane in their approach. There was something too brutally direct and savage about this salutation to the father of the abducted young man, something barbarian. Something American. He turned away from that line of reasoning. He could not perform because of Luigi. But that was also a lie. Even if Luigi were safely in his own apartment peacefully fucking the female of the moment, he, Roberto Greco, would have been unable to obtain an erection. He floundered and squirmed in the poisonous quicksands of his reflections. He tried to thrust the hatred away from himself and push it onto the world all about him. Ah! The women of Rome, the tourists, the Germans, the Spaniards, the English, French, Americans, the young and old, the beautiful and the ugly ones, the poor and the rich, the cunning ones on some business mission, the prostitutes, full- and part-time, amateur, professional—all were or had become Romans, whores and harpies. The women of Rome were Rome. Into the fire with all of them, together with the men and the city, the new apartment houses, the ancient yellow walls, the five hundred churches, the obscene accretions of two thousand yars of misguided piety, the oily, sluggish river which had seen too much, Saint Peter's and the Vatican, the palaces, the hills and the fountains, the shops, the nightclubs, and the restaurants—into the fire with everything. *Roma!* No worse than any of the other great cities of the world or the smaller urban outposts on the rimland of the planetary garbage dump. No worse, no different. But because I, Roberto Greco, am here, into the fire with you, ancient *Roma*. What you need is fire without end. Fire to burn away the uncombustible rubbish, to melt the stones, fuse the iron, turn bones into clean, drifting ash, polluted water into steam, floating carcasses into cinders, noise into silence, evil into good. Fire was the medicine to reduce not only Rome but all of earth into a small, tumbling, black ball. Rome is my prison cell. The people of Rome are dolls living under glass. Dolls who scratch out a bare living, who write and act and posture in television and the films, wet-mouthed, empty-skulled dolls who dream up advertising copy, who shuffle paper in endless government offices. Dolls in a world of fantasy who don't even know they are dolls. The beginning of wisdom was to be able to touch a tree and to say, 'This is a tree.' Of this feat, the dolls were incapable. From this tree emerged the relatively accurate appraisal of power balances, of relationships and estimates of probability. The struggle to recognize reality was like the struggle in the Sicilian game of *zicchinetta*. Wishful thinking could not enter into it. The cards had no memory, no predisposition to repeat patterns, to do one thing before another. There were only the percentages. Since you could not see into the future, you had to guide yourself by the percentages. The stronger you were (and it was a feat in itself to recognize just how strong, in fact, you were) the less need you had to oppose the percentages and to take chances. Because, what was the game all about? To win. That was all that mattered. Roberto, you are sweating out the poison of an undirected inner rage. And fear. Like an impotent child, you are throwing mud at a world which presents no fixed target. You have escaped into some primitive, magical outer orbit. Drag yourself back. There are no miraculous formulae. You are wasting precious energy. With a feeling of sick exhaustion, Roberto Greco finally halted the runaway horses of his corrosive negativity. He finally brought the team to a halt and reshuffled his thoughts like cards in a game of solitaire in which he was trying not to cheat. You have an addiction, Roberto, as vicious and compelling as any narcotic addict's, an addiction for money and power. And, as Alda had pointed out, the worms would not be impressed. But the conviction of truth was deep in his bones. You *had* to have money. There was no way around it. It was as stupid as that and it was the only truth. That was the only secret. Suddenly, the overwhelming blatancy of the secret, its crass transparency infuriated and irritated him anew. Money was the sanctum sanctorum of the Western world, the most impersonal of gods. Which came first, the chicken or the egg? The answer was money, the heart and primal thought, even of those who did not understand. If you were mad and had no money, you were a clown.

167

If you were mad and had money, you were not mad. The secret was to be mad in the beginning, to gamble, so as not to have to gamble later. If you accumulated the original capital and survived, you invested and held out physical coercion as a reserve force. After all, other men were also trying to gamble and survive. The higher you climbed, the less risks you had to take. You passed the money about like oil on a stormy sea and the storm abated. You passed money about and people did what you asked them to do. People were honest, they obeyed because they were terrified, or confused, or blind to the reality of the tree. Roberto Greco never ceased to marvel at the vast excess of honest over dishonest ones. And you always kept a skull by your bed to remember the beginnings, in spite of what that bitch had said. He reached out his hand and stroked the polished skull. Money and power were one and the same thing, like energy, a duality which could never be destroyed. The snakes, including the kidnapping of Luigi, would untangle themselves. They always had. If he lost control and patience now, he would only end by knotting the snakes more hopelessly. Rage and hatred would not help him to solve the puzzle. Could it be the Honored Society which was behind this business? He, Roberto Greco, had his ties with the Society, as did many of the Sicilian landowners and aristocrats who lived in Rome in a blind, stupid ostentation. A part of his own money came from Mafia *gabellotti* who sweated peasant rents out of his estate. The *gabellotti* used the law to keep the peasants in line and the peasants had, until now, gone along with the system, keeping their mouths shut on the theory that testimony was all right as long as it hurt no one. It *could* be the Society which was behind this affair. Its heart was still beating in spite of what many people said. It kept no books and no lists of members. It made no mistakes and had rules, none of them written. Everyone knew who belonged and who did not. In what way had he displeased the Society, if he had? Who were his enemies? Groaning, Roberto Greco rolled off the bed and staggered into the bathroom and vomited into the toilet bowl. A bitter after-bile welled up into his throat and he spat it out. He looked at himself in the mirror and saw a pale, haggard face with deep dark pouches under the eyes. He fingered them.

168

The pouches of fear. 'You have enemies, Roberto,' he murmured to himself. He opened a vial, threw three sleeping pills down his throat, and followed the pills with a full glass of water. He felt his way back to the bed and flung himself on it full length. As he was desperately thinking 'sleep, sleep,' sleep overtook him.

CHAPTER 11

Pierre Levaque was a tall, slender man with a blond mandarin mustache, thick glasses, and a preoccupied absentminded manner. He was not a chemist by profession. He had actually been trained as a doctor of medicine and he had practiced obstetrics and gynecology in Grenoble for a decade. It had been unfortunate when the patient on whom he had consented to perform a therapeutic abortion had eventually died. The subsequent investigation disclosed that death had, in fact, ensued through causes which were not a direct result of the procedure undertaken by Doctor of Medicine Levaque. But he was forced to drag through the formality of a trial and retain an able lawyer to defend him before the justice of France. The expenses of his defense consumed all of his savings. Moreover, while the trial was in progress he had been forbidden to practice his profession. He was also suspended from the post at the hospital in Grenoble with which he was affiliated. Dr. Levaque was eventually and reluctantly acquitted by the court. There is a vindictive and vengeful quality about French justice, Dr. Levaque thought, as he sat, day after day, in the courtroom and followed the proceedings. My compatriots, expressing themselves through the majestically leisurely processes of the Napoleonic Code, simply do not like to acquit defendants. They do not relish it any more than they relish paying their taxes or obeying their government of the moment. The only reason they have acquitted me is that they dislike maintaining me in prison. There is a sly, hardhearted malice about my countrymen, the malice of miserly old age. There is also the harsh cruelty of the French penal code, a reflection of parsimonious, niggardly old age, a reflection of France.

170

Whether or not Dr. Pierre Levaque was justified in his generalized condemnation was irrelevant. He had become an impoverished and an embittered man. Following his acquittal by the court, the private and professional ordeal before a board of his medical peers in Grenoble did not soften his conclusions. In fact, their verdict alienated him still further. Levaque's colleagues decided that, despite the acquittal, his usefulness as a practitioner of medicine in Grenoble, and elsewhere in France, was ended. Dr. Levaque's license to practice was permanently revoked. Levaque thought, The smug, comfortable bourgeois swine delight in sitting in judgment on me. They are throwing me out in order to better divide my practice. A mean and petty motivation, but a very French one. Aloud, he said to them, 'Let him among you who is without fault cast the first stone at me.' But he had said it too late. Nor would it have mattered if he had said it earlier. His fate had already been decided. His erstwhile brothers in the practice of medicine smiled at him coolly and said, in effect, 'Go your way in peace.'

'You are taking the bread out of my mouth,' said Dr. Levaque. 'How will I make my living?'

His colleagues stared at him, this time without a smile, and repeated: 'Go.'

So Dr. Pierre Levaque went home with a stone in his chest and black bile in his throat. There he found a note on the kitchen table indited by his wife to her careful, schoolgirlish scrawl. The note informed the fallen physician that Mme. Cécile Levaque had left him forever. She had a lover with whom she intended to live, in sin or otherwise. Also, it would be vain and foolish for him to attempt to seek her out. 'Pierre,' the note ended, 'even if this wretched business of yours had not arisen, I would eventually have left you. You have never satisfied me sexually. You are undersexed and not the partner for me. During the past few years, my life with you has become intolerable. I have finally met a man who has opened new vistas of ecstasy to me, happiness of which I never dreamed or imagined during my twelve years of marriage with you. There is no ill-will on my side. I hope there will be understanding on your side. Cécile.'

Dr. Levaque remained in Grenoble long enough to get rid of

his house. In the opinion of some, he sold it overcheaply. The real estate agent, however, did not complain. He was highly pleased with an overanxious seller. The house disposed of, and the furniture also, Dr. Levaque packed his personal belongings into his old Citroën and drove toward Italy. Before crossing the border, he halted his car, stepped out, spat on the soil of France, and said, 'May France became a blackened radioactive crater.' Then he continued his journey southward to the land of sunshine, carefree joys, and oranges. He eventually reached the great city of Milan, where he found neither sunshine, carefree joy, nor oranges, but some reasonable opportunities for employment. He could have found a new niche in the medical profession. Perhaps because of his new frame of mind he might not have been as good a physician as he had been before. At any rate, he entered the service of Tufarelli Pharmaceuticals, A.G. When the chairman of Tufarelli's board, *Commendatore* Roberto Greco, offered to train Levaque in the techniques of converting morphine base into heroin, the Frenchman accepted the offer without hesitation. Indeed, the prospect of again practicing medicine had become abhorrent to him. The prospect of manufacturing heroin for ultimate consignment into the veins of thousands of faceless and unknown addicts had become postitively congenial to him.

The general informed consensus of opinion in narcotics circles was that it was easier to train a professional criminal in the techniques of making heroin than it was to turn a genuine chemist in a lawbreaker. Pierre Levaque, however, proved a felicitous exception to all the rules. He was positively motivated and quickly mastered the relatively simple techniques of heroin-making. Each kilo of ninety percent pure heroin which he produced in Tufarelli's large and superbly equipped laboratories left him with a feeling of satisfaction, a sense of personal gratification. His secret dream was to find some way of flooding all of France with heroin, of turning the French people into a nation of addicts. It remained a dream, of course, but each kilo of snowy-white heroin was a symbolic swordstroke. He worked hard at the tedious, unpleasant, and sometimes dangerous task of converting morphine base into heroin. Although he observed all the safeguards, he nevertheless ran the

172

risks of becoming himself involuntarily addicted, considering the large quantities of base which he handled in each operation. Greco watched Levaque work and concluded himself well satisfied with his chemist. Greco was familiar with Levaque's background. He understood the Frenchman's motivation. Let me have men about me that are lean and bitter, thought Greco. They will turn out the best quality of merchandise.

Levaque, in his turn, trained three others to assist him. One was Alois Manoury, an ex-pharmacist, a French *pied-noir* from Algiers who had lost his family and his business during the Algerian War of Independence. The second was Paul Kurzlicht, a German. Kurzlicht was a stolid, bald-headed man in his sixties who had been a hospital orderly in the German Army of the late Third Reich. Due to some postwar unpleasantness (questions had arisen as to whether or not ex-Medical Corpsman Kurzlicht had actually injected carbolic acid into the hearts of Jews, gypsies, Russians, Poles, and other human garbage) Kurzlicht left for Italy. Like many, many other Germans before him, Kurzlicht had an affection for Italy. He found there a *Gemütlichkeit* which he missed in his native land. Despite Milan's miserable climate and hectic pace, he settled there—because the job was there. He also entered the employ of Tufarelli and came under the tutelage of Pierre Levaque. Kurzlicht did his work methodically and carefully. He became a reliable heroin chemist. The fact that he was not driven by the emotional motivation of Levaque did not detract from Kurzlicht's stolidly consistent performance.

The fourth man was Renato Tamburelli, the brother of *Commendatore* Francisco Tamburelli and the beneficiary of Ray's generosity. As Roberto Greco had indirectly indicated to Ray, Renato lacked both the intellectual capacities and the manual dexterity to become a really dependable maker of heroin. He had been a businessman and a trader all his life, not a technician. Despite the fact that he found the work boring, Renato was a hard, obedient worker. After training, he proved to be a dependable laboratory assistant, but no more than that. He maintained the big laboratory and the expensive equipment in an immaculate condition. Renato had other virtues. He was of Sicilian ancestry and he had kinsmen in Palermo who were

173

members of the Honored Society. He was himself imbued with the honorable traditions of *omerta*, although he was not himself an active member. Like his brother, Francisco, he thought of himself as an inactive associate. For obscure reasons of delicacy, perhaps, Francisco Tamburelli had forborne to mention to Ray the extensive and seasoned connections of the Tamburelli family with the Palermo *cosca* of the Honored Society. Renato was a few years older than his brother, the *commendatore*, and much resembled Francisco. In addition, Renato had no qualms of conscience about being involved in the manufacture of heroin. Indeed, in his own pharmaceuticals business in Tripoli he had carried on a sideline business of narcotics and cigarette smuggling in a small way. Nevertheless, he was secretly discontented with his position with Tufarelli Pharmaceuticals, A.G., no matter how well the position paid. He had always been his own master, an entrepreneur of modest dimensions. He thought of himself as a proud man and it irked him now to be employed in what he considered to be a menial position and beneath his dignity. His employer, Roberto Greco, irritated him continually with a manner of brusque arrogance. Whether Greco was aware or not, he had a decidedly abrasive effect on Renato Tamburelli. He orders me around like a servant or a schoolboy, thought Renato. Nevertheless, he schooled and disciplined himself into an impassive obedience as he went about his work. He was even honest enough to admit to himself that there was a factor of jealousy and envy involved. Renato, the businessman failure. Roberto Greco, the businessman success, the sophisticated political success. Many men hated Greco for much less.

As for Roberto Greco, he was unconcerned and wholly unaware of his negative effect on Renato Tamburelli. In fact, Greco was quite pleased with the team in his heroin laboratory. A good team, he thought. A fine team to undertake the challenging assignment of converting two thousand kilos of morphine base into heroin.

These, then, were the Four Horsemen who undertook to start the witches' brew from Beirut on its way to the golden marketplace of New York City.

When Levaque entered the laboratory on the morning of the

174

big job, he looked around him with satisfaction. He had fallen into the habit of regarding that laboratory as his personal domain. How much more satisfying to make heroin than to deliver babies! Definitely, smiled Levaque to himself, I am no longer psychologically attuned to the practice of obstetrics and gynecology. The laboratory was fifty feet long, set with gleaming white tile from floor to the midpoint of the wall, enameled brightly from the midpoint to the ceiling, which was brilliantly illuminated with the finest of fluorescent equipment. The laboratory contained four forty-foot counters equipped with stainless steel sinks, Bunsen gas burners, multiple electric heating plates for the critical brewing processes, running water, balloon flasks, serpentine glass tubing, suction pumps, and low-heat and high-heat electric dryers.

As Levaque was fond of pointing out to his colleagues: 'Our little kitchen here is undoubtedly superior to the best of the clandestine laboratories in southern France. The difference is that we are a legitimate firm in the business of manufacturing pharmaceuticals. We do not have to conceal our conversion activities, at least, not entirely.'

And, as Roberto Greco deigned to point out to Levaque: 'The authorities here know that we refine heroin from morphine base. The only difference is that there is an alteration of records as to the amount we put out on the legitimate market. Everyone knows that there is a legitimate market here in Italy for heroin, although, admittedly, a relatively small one. The Italian police and the government claim to follow a strict and severe policy anent the manufacture of heroin. That is, of course, propaganda, a sop for world opinion. Do your work well and carefully, be loyal to Tufarelli, and you will prosper.'

The Four Horsemen did not have to be reminded of that. They were all prospering. Levaque, in particular, as well as engorging his hunger for revenge was on his way to becoming a wealthy man.

When the two thousand kilos of bagged morphine base had been brought up by elevator into the laboratory, Levaque, Kurzlicht, Manoury, and Tamburelli took charge. Their first task was to weigh and record the weights of the merchandise on their very accurate laboratory scales. Together with the

175

morphine base, a rectangular wooden case was also brought up. It was three feet long by eighteen inches high and the lid was nailed on. A label on the case was addressed to SIGNOR ROBERTO GRECO, TUFARELLI PHARMACEUTICALS, A.G., MILAN, ITALY. FOR THE PERSONAL AND PRIVATE ATTENTION OF SIGNOR GRECO.

Levaque came into the laboratory at that moment to see how the weighing was proceeding.

'There's something else here,' said Alois Manoury, 'an extra package of something for *Signor* Greco. It doesn't look like base.'

'I'll go and tell him about it,' said Levaque. He went out and returned with Roberto Greco, who stared down at the box suspiciously. 'Who brought it?' he asked.

Manoury examined the label. 'It came by rail freight. I don't think it's part of this consignment.'

'Renato,' said Greco, 'take the box into my office, take the nails out of the lid, and leave it on my desk. Can you handle it alone?'

'*Si, signor,*' said Renato, 'it isn't heavy.'

'Just pull out the nails,' said Greco. 'I'll examine it later. Then get back here. We have a lot of work to do.'

'*Si, signor,*' said Renato. He took a nail puller, quickly drew out the nails, carried the box in the office, and placed it on Greco's big, ornate desk. Then he returned to help with the weighing.

Greco lingered out in the laboratory with the three chemists.

'We have obtained a final count here of exactly two thousand and six kilos of morphine base, *Signor* Greco,' said Levaque.

'What do you think of the quality?' said Greco.

'I must admit,' said Levaque, 'they did a good job of reducing the original Turkish opium to morphine base. It's much cleaner than the usual stuff we get from Beirut. Nevertheless, to be on the safe side, we shall start to repurify it before beginning the actual conversion process.'

'Good,' said Greco. 'The sooner we get started, the better. This is the biggest consignment that we've ever handled.'

He thought of the box which Renato had opened and went

back into his office.

Roberto Greco removed the covering boards from the top of the box and placed them carefully on the floor. Within the wooden box was a smaller container manufactured out of plywood. Tissue paper and straw packing had been wadded firmly all around the plywood box to hold it firmly in place. Greco removed the stuffing, lifted out the plywood box, and placed it on the desk. He cleaned up the stuffing, threw it all back into the outer wooden box, and put it on the floor. He examined the plywood container before him. It was secured with a single hasp through which a piece of piano wire had been twisted to hold it in place. A bomb? He listened intently. There was no ticking sound. Perhaps he ought to have someone else open it elsewhere. A bomb? Ridiculous! He was still smarting from the verbal lashing which Alda Quirini had given him yesterday. Moreover, his curiosity had by now also been aroused. A bomb? *Bene!* Let it be a bomb to kill or maim me. To such a state has Luigi's disappearance and that whore's forked tongue reduced me. He untwisted the piece of wire and raised the lid. A pungent stench arose from the contents. A stench from what resembled two soccer balls wrapped in bandages. Greco recognized the heavy reek as that of formalin. The soccer balls were half-buried in coarse rock salt. Greco touched one of the soccer balls and ran his fingers over the topography of a human face. He nodded grimly to himself. So that was it! With a feeling akin to relief, he carefully unwrapped the ball which he had fingered and finally held in his hands the preserved and embalmed head of Rossano Polizzi. The sliced-off edge of Polizzi's neck was wrapped in blood-caked bandages, now dried to a heavy crust. Very considerate of these people! Greco grasped the head by the matted black hair and lifted it. Polizzi's eyes, open wide but clouded and glazed, stared back at him reproachfully. A thin rivulet of blood had dried while issuing from Polizzi's nose. At the corners of the mouth, also, streaks of dark dried blood. 'Did they think that I would faint to meet you in this condition?' said Greco to the head. 'This is how I faint.' He spat in Polizzi's blind, dead face and dropped the head back into the tangle of wrappings. Then he noticed a folded sheet of paper lying on the rock salt. He picked it up and opened it. There was writing on the paper. It had evidently been written with a heavy-nibbed pen. The script was ornate, almost Spenserian, to match the ornate floridity of the style. Said the note:

Respected and Distinguished *Signor*—Be pleased to receive the heads of your servants, Rossano Polizzi and Enrico Cadri. They did their work well and served you faithfully. By way of admiring their loyalty, we herewith send you their mortal remains. It is our earnest hope that you will take an example from them, that you will continue to deal honestly with others, even as you have done hitherto. With assurance of our highest esteem, we remain, and shall always remain.

And the note ended with a big ink splotch, as though the writer had stabbed through the paper in an access of approval for his powers of composition.

Roberto Greco smiled. Very pretty, *signori*. After we have come to terms—and we shall—I may even ask you to practice your art on the lovely head of Alda Quirini.

He picked up the second wrapped soccer ball and hefted it. 'And this, I suppose, is Enrico Cadri,' he said aloud. 'Do you hear me, you stupid son of a prostitute?' He tore off the wrappings and lifted Cadri's dark-visaged head by the big shock of blood-smeared white hair. 'Enrico,' said Greco, staring at the head, 'if you're missing a body, you deserved nothing better.' He spat into Cadri's unprotesting face, threw the head back into the rock salt, and tossed the wrappings in over it. He slammed down the lid of the plywood box, went into his private bathroom, and began scrubbing his hands carefully with antiseptic soap and a nail brush. He deliberately dried his hands and returned to his desk. He pressed the intercom button and said to his secretary in the outer office, 'Have them page Renato Tamburelli in the Laboratory and send him in to me.'

Five minutes later Renato entered Greco's office. '*Si signor.*'

'Put this plywood container back into the wooden box,' said Greco. 'Renail the lid.'

'*Si, signor*.' Renato left and reappeared a few minutes later with hammer and nails. He nailed down the boards.

'Pick up the box and lead me to the incinerator,' said Greco.

When they reached the incinerator chute, Greco said, 'Will the box fit?'

Renato jammed the box into the chute. 'I think it will just make it, *signor*.'

'Into the fire with it,' said Greco. 'Push it through.'

Renato kicked the box hard a couple of times with the full sole of his shoe. The box finally cleared and went tumbling down into the furnace.

'Thank you, Renato,' said Greco. 'Now get back to your job.'

'*Si, signor*,' said Renato.

Roberto Greco returned to his office in a thoughtful, even a cheerful, frame of mind. At least the mystery of Luigi's disappearance had been solved. At least Luigi would live. His respect for the American, Don Raimondo Occhiaccio, rose somewhat. In the game of *zicchenetta* if one was convinced that one held the weaker hand, it was no disgrace to throw in one's cards. Any man who added more money to an initially dubious wager to determine if his opponent was lying, to prove it for the satisfaction of his pride, was a great fool. Such a man would not recognize the tree when he touched it, not even when he split open his head against it. Cadri and Polizzi? That was just a love token, so to speak, a gentle admonition, not to play games, any games except *zicchenetta*. *Bene!* The abduction of Luigi, that was more serious. The maiming of Luigi, the theft of the young man's finger, yes, that had also been necessary. While Roberto Greco's paternal heart churned with fury and humiliation for the mutilation of his own flesh and blood, another Roberto Greco within and behind the real one conceded that Don Raimondo Occhiaccio had handled the affair well, had carried it through correctly, with balls, with big Sicilian balls, just as he, Roberto Greco, would have done it, had he been in Raimondo Occhiaccio's place. That did not, by any means, mean that he, Roberto Greco, was throwing in his hand. It remained to be determined what Raimondo Occhiaccio wanted—or rather, how much he wanted. The first priority was to get Luigi back alive. The second priority was to pay no ransom for Luigi's restoration to the bosom of his father. If that were possible. Who could tell at this point? The third priority was to kill Raimondo Occhiaccio and his two *sicarii*. If that were possible. But killing the American would be such a wanton waste of opportunity. How much more sensible to saddle him with a heavy heroin habit and to keep him alive in some secluded, secure place! He caught himself firmly and grimly. This was not a time for dreaming.

He would soon be hearing from Occhiaccio and everything would fall into place.

The four witches had gone into a huddle and the brewing of the dream was about to commence.

'Renato,' said Levaque, 'are the sinks ready? Can you vouch for their absolute cleanliness?'

'Every single one of them, *Signor* Levaque,' said Renato. 'I scrubbed them with detergents and disinfectants. Then I sterilized them three times with boiling water. They are surgically clean.'

'Are the stoppers in good order?'

'I installed new ones in all the sinks, to make certain.'

'*Bien*,' said Levaque. 'Kuzlicht, Manoury, this is going to be a long and tedious operation. There is no point in moving carelessly. We have ten sinks. Place ten kilos of morphine base in each one and fill each sink to the top with acetone.' He looked at his wristwatch. 'It is now about ten minutes after seven. The base will have to be thoroughly mixed with the acetone. Then the mixture should stand until at least three in the afternoon.'

'Why so long?' asked Manoury.

'I'm being particular,' said Levaque. 'This merchandise looks good. Still, I want to make certain that we separate out all the other opium alkaloids.'

'A hundred kilos a day,' said Kurzlicht. 'That means we have at least twenty days work ahead of us.'

'It will be closer to a month,' said Levaque. 'Since it's such a large amount, I emphasize again, don't get careless. I want no accidents. We'll all pitch in and get the first batch soaking in acetone.'

The morphine base was put into the sinks and well mixed up with acetone. 'Since we don't have the facilities,' said Levaque, 'there's really nothing more to do at this point. Get the mixtures well stirred up and call it a day. After we've gotten the first batch under way, it will go faster. We'll really get started at seven sharp in the morning. In the meantime, keep your stomachs full of food and get plenty of rest. I don't want any involuntary addiction.'

On the following morning, the first hundred-kilo morphine base-acetone batch was rapidly filtered by the use of high-speed suction pumps. Then it was placed in low-heat drying ovens for the removal of remaining impurities and secondary alkaloids.

While the three chemists were engaged in this operation, Renato Tamburelli was scrubbing and preparing the sinks for the reception of the second hundred-kilo batch of base.

When the first batch had been thoroughly dried and all the moisture was evaporated out, it was no longer morphine base. It was pure morphine. Levaque was now ready to convert it into crude heroin. He telephoned Greco. 'We will need more glassware from the storeroom and at least three more men to help Renato. He cannot handle all the details by himself. The extra men can keep the new batches stirred in the sinks and clean the sinks after. We're going to need Renato to help us.'

'I'll have the men sent over,' said Greco. 'What else?'

'We're going to need twenty of the largest balloon flasks we have in stock,' said Levaque. 'I suggest that the men start bringing them in from the storeroom into the laboratory so that we can get them set up.'

'What size?' said Greco.

'Eight-kilo capacity,' said Levaque.

'Why twenty?'

'We have ten burner plates,' said Levaque. 'We will cook ten flasks at a time. And that is about as much as we can supervise safely. While that is being done, one of us can be filtering and purifying the previously cooled batch.'

When the balloon flasks were brought in, the chemists began filling each one with four kilos of morphine and eight kilos of acetic anhydride. The flasks were equipped with fixed internal thermometers and topped with coiled glass tubing to procure condensation of the vapors. Then the flasks were set in double boilers and the critical brewing process began. Levaque also began his customery safety lecture to Manoury, Kurzlicht, and Tamburelli. 'We've been through this before,' he said, 'but we can't repeat it too often. Making good heroin is much like cooking good food, distilling good liquor, or, a homely example, brewing good beer or fermenting good wine. A careful man is a lover of his work, or is it the other way around? But you know what I mean. The by-product of love is greater accuracy in every phase of the operation. Love implies accuracy, attention, and care. A careless cook turns out mediocre food. A careless, inaccurate chemist turns out low-purity heroin. This I will not tolerate. Be most vigilant and careful that you use the right amount of reagents. Watch your temperatures carefully. You have only a margin of five degrees on either side of the critical temperature point. At eighty degrees you will not procure acetylation. At ninety-one degrees you will destroy the morphine. At one hundred degrees you will cause an explosion and blow all of us into hell. Do I make myself understood?'

The others nodded. They had listened to the lecture many times before and looked bored.

'Renato,' said Levaque, 'I tell you this particularly. Watch those thermometers in the balloon flasks constantly. The temperature must be kept as close to eighty-five degrees Centigrade as possible, and constantly. Wear your masks at all times when the brewing process commences. Start the ventilation fans and let's get started.'

The balloon flasks were set in double boilers on the electric burners and the cooking process began. All ten burners had been pressed into service. Since they were cooking ten flasks, each one containing four kilos of morphine, at the termination of the six-hour cooking operation the chemists would obtain forty kilos of impure heroin. The critical factor was the cooking temperature. At Levaque had stressed, the acetic anhydride-morphine mixture had to be kept at a constant eighty-five degrees Centigrade. The ventilator fans hummed and the masked chemists went about their work with careful concentration. The reagent which they were using was miserable stuff to work with because of stench. They wore gloves constantly. Not only was this acid dangerously corrosive, it had an acrid, pungent, overpowering reek. After a time, one became accustomed to the stink of the acid, just as one became inured to the odors of a slaughterhouse, an embalming room, or a tannery. All smoking in the laboratory was strictly forbidden. Not only were the fumes of the mixtures cooking on the ten burners noxious, they were highly inflammable. Therefore the amateur chemists—for that was what they were—worked as carefully as they could. They were quite aware of the dangers of toxification, acid burns, addiction, and explosion.

The brew was finished after six hours. The excess acid had been distilled off. Levaque, Kurzlicht, and Manoury removed the balloon flasks from the burners to allow them to cool. They now had forty kilos of diacetyl morphine acetate, or impure heroin, in solution.

In the meantime, the three helpers, under the direction of Renato Tamburelli, were preparing the sinks and mixing up a new batch of morphine base with acetone for the first stage of impurity removal.

At this point, Levaque called a halt. This six-hour period had been one of strict and concentrated attention. The temperatures of the flasks in the double boilers had to be kept under constant scrutiny. Everyone was fatigued.

'Renato,' said Levaque, 'have your helpers put everything in order and lock the laboratory. We will continue tomorrow.'

On the following day Levaque and Manoury prepared a new batch of morphine and reagent for ten fresh flasks. In the meantime, Kuzlicht began the operation of purifying the diacetyl morphine acetate which had been obtained in the previous day's operation. The desideratum was to remove the acetate. He did so by washing his impure heroin in distilled water and bone black for whitening. After he had filtered out the mixture with suction pumps, he placed it in low-heat driers. He repeated the washing-filtering-precipitation-drying-sifting process three times. It was monotonous, tedious work, yet each step had to be performed with the utmost care. As

183

Levaque had said, this was the secret of good cooking. Yes, thought Kurzlicht, we are chefs. When he had completed his work, Levaque came over to test the net result for purity. 'Eighty-seven percent,' he finally said. 'Only fair. Run it through again, Kurzlicht, we are chefs.' When he had completed his work Kurzlicht began the final hydrochloration procedure. He poured his batch of heroin, kilo by kilo, into boiling acetone and added exactly predetermined amounts of hydrochloric acid and ninety-degree alcohol. This procedure rendered the heroin soluble so that the addict could dissolve it in water and inject into his bloodstream and attain happiness. When the interaction of the acid and the alcohol had been completed, the heroin was deemed to be completely soluble. After it had cooled overnight, Kurzlicht would put the heroin crystals once again into the low-heat ovens and start the pulverizing and sifting process.

'That is also important,' Levaque had often said. 'I want the final product to look as white, soft, and fluffy as dusting powder for a baby's ass. Now that I think of it, it wouldn't be a bad idea to dust a newborn baby with pure heroin.'

Such was the routine of the three witches and their familiar, Renato Tamburelli, and the master of the coven, Roberto Greco. Like any other form of necromancy, the casting of spells, the drawing of pentacles, and the summoning up of potent spirits from the netherworld, it was a procedure involving hard work and attended by personal danger.

Even with the extensive facilities and excellent equipment provided by Tufarelli, the process of heroin-making was necessarily a slow one. The men could not work in the laboratory more than five or six hours a day, nor more than three or four days a week. In this regard they were like deep-sea divers who had to make time to depressurize themselves so that they would not be seized with the bends. The heroin chemists, despite their dust masks, rubber gloves, and full stomachs, had to make time to detoxicate themselves. No matter how much care they exercised, they could not escape breathing in some acid fumes and heroin powder in the air. Above all, they must avoid the danger of having their body chemistry altered by heroin addiction. Tufarelli paid them liberally for their work.

But they knew that once they became addicted their usefulness to their employer would be ended. They would not only be considered unreliable for the performance of their exacting work, but they would be an actual security risk. And if they became security risks, there was only one conclusion which the employer could reach. There was too much at stake, and any one man's life was nothing in the balance.

CHAPTER 12

Dominique Maestracci got in touch with Petri, the flesh peddler. He made an appointment to meet him in a small out-of-the-way *birreria* in a workingman's neighborhood across the Tiber. When Petri sat down, Dominique wasted no time.

'Do you remember Anitra Houssayne?'

'The fellatrice?'

'The cocksucker,' said Dominique. 'Where is she now?'

'In Regina Coeli, I believe.'

'You believe! Don't you know!'

'I don't run her any more. She's on her own now. Besides, she has become syphilitic. Altogether too ripe for my clientele.'

'Why was she picked up?'

'Heroin peddling. In a very small way. It would be logical, since her ass can't be selling very well.'

'What do they usually give those girls?'

'Oh,' said Petri, 'a fine and anything from three to six months. Anitra's better off in Regina Coeli. At least they're treating her syphilis there.'

'I suppose. My boss paid you twenty-five hundred dollars outright for that unhygienic piece of garbage. Do you remember?'

'True,' said Petri. 'He was generous.'

'She gave my colleague the clap and I fucked her only once. Then we sent her packing.'

Petri grinned. 'You were a brave man.'

'That I was. I used three rubbers. I suppose I should have worn gloves and a mask as well. And kept my prick in my pants. Anyhow, I didn't catch anything.'

186

'Your boss didn't buy Anitra for fucking,' Petri pointed out. 'He was very specific about it.'

'Yes, yes,' said Dominique impatiently. 'I know all about it. The point is, we want her again.'

'I told you, she's in jail.'

Dominique threw a thousand dollars in American money across the table at Petri. 'Get her out then. Hire a lawyer. Pay her fine. Bribe someone. Do whatever you have to do. But get out out and deliver her to my boss's villa. You know the place. When you do, I'll give you another thousand for yourself.'

'I don't know——' began Petri, as he counted the bills.

'Look, pimp,' said Dominique. 'You're not talking to my *padrone*. You're talking to Dominique Maestracci. My boss is a very easygoing gentleman, but I'd just as soon hammer a cucumber up your ass as look at you.'

Petri put the bills in his pocket and grinned placatingly. 'Another big blow job?'

Dominique stared at him witheringly. 'Get her over to me. And don't take more than four days. I'm in a hurry. Tell me, is Anitra an addict?'

'Of course.'

'Tell her this. It won't be a hard job. No marathon cock-sucking. We'll treat her well and pay her a thousand. Dollars, not lire. We'll also give her a thousand dollars' worth of heroin for her own use. We won't need her for more than a week. We'll even call in a doctor to give her her penicillin while she's with us. What do they give the girls now, anyhow? Then she can return to Regina Coeli or wherever she wants to go. It's a fair proposal. She'll jump at it.'

'What is she supposed to do?' said Petri.

'If it's any of your business, a very short blow job. The easiest and the best-paid work she's ever had in her life.'

Due to the excessively starchy diet in Regina Coeli, Anitra Houssayne had put on some weight. Otherwise, she seemed to be in better physical condition than when Dominique had first met her.

'Ay, my little white lamb,' said Dominique. 'What's this I hear about your having bad blood?'

'I'm sick,' said Anitra shortly.

Petri had gotten her liberated without too much difficulty. The female wing of Regina Coeli was overcrowded with diseased prostitutes.

'Petri said you'd give me a thousand dollars,' continued Anitra. 'Is that true?'

Dominique took the money out of his pocket and handed it to her. 'Count it.'

Anitra counted the money and put it in her purse.

Dominique opened a drawer. He produced a syringe, a piece of rubber tubing, a glassine envelope of white powder, and a tiny vial of colorless liquid.

'Here,' he said, 'have a jolt of good heroin on the house.'

Anitra looked at it suspiciously. 'What strength is this?'

'It's been cut enough,' Dominique assured her. 'It's safe. If someone wanted to kill you, they wouldn't be going to all this trouble, would they now?'

'I suppose not,' said Anitra. 'Petri said you would give me an extra supply for myself.'

'Right,' said Dominique. 'Correct. A thousand dollars' worth. All for yourself. Go ahead, give yourself an injection; you'll feel better. There is exactly one-tenth of a gram in that envelope. It has been cut down to safety. I doubt if you've ever had service like this before. Do you want me to inject it for you?'

'Yes, please,' said Anitra.

Dominique tied the rubber tube above her left elbow. 'Open and close your hand. Make a fist.'

Anitra did so and the vein stood out.

Carefully, Dominique poured the white powder into the vial of distilled water. It dissolved instantly. He inserted the needle of the hypo syringe into the vial and sucked up the solution into the syringe. Deftly, he pierced Anitra's skin and slid the needle into her vein. She winced briefly. He pressed down the plunger and the solution disappeared into her arm. He withdrew the needle and pressed a bit of gauze padding down on the needle prick. 'There! That didn't hurt.'

Anitra leaned back and smiled coolly at him.

'Well,' he said, 'what do you feel?'

'Nothing yet. Absolutely nothing.'

'You will.' He offered her a cigarette and lit it for her.

'How did they treat you in jail?'

'The food stank,' she said. 'All pasta.'

'Looks that way. I think you're getting a little belly.'

Anitra smiled at him sweetly. 'What is it you want me to do this time?'

'Suck off a special customer. A nice handsome young man with a big cock. Just once. No hard work. Not like the last time.'

Anitra giggled. 'You bastards really made me sweat.'

'This will be different,' Dominique assured her. 'A breeze. Here! Let me look at you.' He took her face between his hands and studied her eyes. Anitra's pupils had become tiny. They were pinpoints which had practically disappeared and the whites of her eyes were abnormally huge.

As Dominique looked at the prostitute, a faint memory tugged at his heart. It was so faint that he did not recognize it for what it was—sympathy. Then it returned to him. When he was a boy of ten walking the streets of Bastia, a small and hungry black mongrel began to follow him about hopefully. Wherever Dominique stopped the mongrel sat down patiently and waited. Dominique had gone into his aunt's house and she had given him a delicious meat pie or pasty which she had baked that morning. He was supposed to take the pasty home and share it with a brother and a sister. His aunt had scoldingly emphasized that the pasty was for all three of them. Young Dominique had sat down on the doorstep of his aunt's little house and began pulling pieces out of the deliciously hot pasty and eating it. The little black mongrel was irresistibly drawn closer by the heavenly odor. It crept to Dominique's feet. He broke off a morsel and threw it to the dog. Not believing its good fortune, the dog bolted it down and stood waiting for more, although its eyes plainly revealed that such an incredible windfall could not repeat itself. Dominique gave the mongrel still another piece of pasty, which it swallowed down without chewing. Dominique had laughed at the animal's ravenous, wolfish, frantic appetite. He got up and set out for home. But he had now made a lifetime conquest. The little dog was now his, heart and soul. It trotted at Dominique's heels, emotionally secure in the new alliance with the boy. Suddenly Dominique became irritated by the fact that the dog was crowding his heels so closely, as though afraid that it would lose him. The irritation turned into perverse anger, which itself masked the thrilling plan which was already forming in his mind. He stopped and shouted at the dog: 'Go! Go home!' The dog looked at him and its eyes said, Where shall I go? Dominique threw a stick at it and struck it. The dog ran off a few feet, stopped, and returned again, almost crawling on its belly. Then Dominique's sly plan bloomed out from the petals of his anger which had had its source in his original irritation. He broke off another little piece of the meat pasty and threw it to the dog. In humble thankfulness the dog seized and bolted it down. In the meantime, Dominique had picked up a jagged, sharp piece of granite block from the unpaved road. He hefted it and studied the dog calculatingly. The dog returned his stare trustingly. Dominique hurled the rock and sent it crashing down on the mongrel's bony muzzle. It screamed, a shrill scream of pain. Not a yelp, a real scream. Then it ran, the blood dripping from the wound down both sides of its muzzle. Even after the dog had disappeared around the corner, Dominique could still hear it screaming. His heart had gone cold with puzzlement for an instant concerning the mystery of his act. Why had he done it? That miserable animal's pain reechoed in Dominique's ears for many years after. Was he sorry or not? He did not know. There was one very brief period when he shuddered with a kind of self-hatred for what he had done to the dog. Then he forgot about it for many years. Sometimes he remembered it for a few fleeting moments. Then the memory would drop out again into a black ocean of unconsciousness. Now Anitra Houssayne was reminding him all over again of the little black mongrel and he shuddered with a kind of pain of the memory. Yes, she was that wretched little mongrel. He groped trying to summon up a kind of sympathy for her to atone for that villainy of his childhood. And, while he was groping, the moment passed. The little dog faded into an invisible ghost and Anitra was again only Anitra. She was grinning at him and he noticed the heavy tartar deposit on her teeth. She had square, well-shaped teeth, but they were neglected and yellowed. Too many cigarettes and not enough brushing. 'Go look at yourself in the mirror,' he said.

'I don't have to,' she giggled. 'I'm flying. Where's this good-looking boy of yours? I'll suck him off for you right now.'

'Don't do it for me,' said Dominique. 'Time enough. In the meantime, I've got a nice room for you here. You'll get your penicillin and heroin shots regularly and a balanced diet. You can sit on your ass and take it easy. Fair enough?'

'No rough stuff?'

'None,' Dominique promised. 'After a week you can go wherever you wish.'

Anitra giggled again. 'You're not such a bad one. Maybe I'll want to stay.'

'That's understandable. Now get to your room and get yourself settled down. I'll see you later.'

Dominique went out of the villa and down to the boat dock. Juan Torres was in the wheelhouse of the boat. He had two Rollex cameras beside him and several rolls of film.

'You won't need that much film,' said Dominique.

Torres loaded a spool of film into the camera he was holding and looked up.

'Is the girl ready?'

'As ready as she'll ever be.'

'Does she know what she has to do? Is she in a cooperative mood?'

'As cooperative as a good jolt of heroin can make her.'

Torres rose. 'Then let's get started.'

'Perhaps we should wait until tonight.'

'We can finish it tonight,' said Torres, 'but we may as well clear the first stage of the operation now. Get the girl and meet me down in the cellar.'

Dominique went back into the villa and up to Anitra's room. She was lying on her bed, reading a magazine, or, rather, looking at the pictures, leafing idly through the pages and dipping into a box of chocolates which Dominique had left her.

'How is everything, Anitra?' said Dominique. 'Do you feel

like another shot?'

Still under the soothing influence of the first injection, Anitra smiled and nodded. 'I could use one.'

'You have an expensive habit,' said Dominique dryly. 'I rather anticipated you'd be wanting a lift so I brought everything along.' He took the syringe out of his pocket, together with a vial of distilled water and a glassine envelope of heroin. He produced a tiny plastic vial from his handkerchief pocket. 'Here's a new sterile needle for the syringe. An extra one. Do you know how to change it?'

But Anitra had changed her mind. With the providence of an addict who has known former lean days she said, 'I really don't need it yet. I'll save it till after dinner.'

'Smart girl,' said Dominique sarcastically.

'When do we eat?'

'*You* will eat at six. Right here in this room. You can have anything you want. I'll bring it up. In the meantime, let's go. Your lover is ready and eagerly awaiting you.'

The cellar room in which Luigi Antonio Greco was being held was windowless and had a heavy iron door. It was ventilated by a grate in the ceiling and brightly lighted by three fluorescent fixtures. It was sparsely furnished with a bed, a table, two chairs, and two floor lamps. The walls were painted a gleaming white. A spotlight had been mounted over the door and was focused directly on the bed. Luigi, his hand bandaged, sat sullenly on the bed, his head downcast to avoid the strong glare of the spotlight.

Dominique brought Anitra into the room and locked the door behind him. Torres was seated on one of the chairs, holding a camera.

'There's your lover,' said Dominique. 'How do you like him?'

Anitra appraised Luigi Antonio Greco objectively. 'He doesn't look very pleased.'

'That's because he still doesn't know how talented you are. He doesn't realize how happy you're going to make him.'

Torres placed his camera carefully on the chair, went up to Luigi and stood over him. 'All right. Luigi. Get your clothes off. Strip.'

Luigi stared up with dark hatred and menace on his sensual, handsome face. 'You won't escape. My father will have your balls for this outrage.'

Torres smashed Luigi across the face with the back of his hand. 'Be content we didn't send your father *your* balls instead of your forefinger. Now get undressed. The sooner we get this chore finished, the sooner you'll go free.'

'Anitra,' said Dominique, 'take off all your clothes. Strip naked.'

Anitra obeyed.

'What are you going to do?' said Luigi.

'Take a few photographs,' said Torres. 'While you're being sucked off by this beautiful young girl.'

Luigi scowled up at the Spaniard. 'Blackmail! Nothing can make me——'

Torres seized Luigi by the hair and jerked him to his feet. 'On your feet, scum.' He flicked out a switchblade knife and pressed the point of it against Luigi's cheek. 'Have you ever had your facial nerve pierced? You'll never forget it if you do. Now take off your clothes or I'll slash them off.'

In cowed, silent fury, Luigi stripped naked. Torres seized his wrists and cuffed them in front. 'Now stand here, just where you are.' He turned to Anitra. She was still euphoric and waited, docile and naked. 'You, girl, get down on your knees in front of him and go to work.'

Anitra obeyed. She took Luigi's limp penis into her mouth and began sucking.

'What's the matter, handsome?' said Dominique. 'Don't you enjoy her? You're supposed to be the best cocksman in Rome.'

Torres went back to the chair, picked up the camera, focused it, and began clicking off pictures of the fellation from several different angles. He handed the knife to Dominique. 'All right, put it into the idiot's hands. And watch yourself.'

Dominique came up behind Luigi and thrust the hilt of the knife between Luigi's cuffed hands. 'Here, grip it, stupid.' He took care to remain behind Luigi at all times. His palm slammed into the back of Luigi's head. 'Bend over, my boy. Bend over, just as if you were going to stab her in the throat with the knife.'

Torres loaded another roll into the camera and snapped several more shots.

'This is the stalest trick in the world,' said Luigi thickly, as he recovered his balance. 'It's been done a thousand times before.'

'That only proves how reliable it is,' said Dominique. He suddenly clamped a strong wrist on Luigi's bandaged left hand and squeezed hard. Luigi screamed with pain and dropped the knife. 'The stump still hurts, eh?' said Dominique.

Torres had finally put the camera into his pocket and had moved up behind Anitra. She turned her head and looked up. As she did so, Torres smashed down a lead-cored sap on the top of her head. It was a crushing blow. She crumpled to the floor.

'Luigi,' said Dominique, 'as a lover, you're very disappointing.' He seized the manacled young man around the neck, heaved him over his back with a judo grip, and sent Luigi crashing into the wall. 'Patience, my friend. You'll soon be back in the bosom of your family.'

He picked up the unconscious Anitra and slung her over one shoulder and walked out. Torres followed Dominique out, slammed and locked the door.

'This one,' said Torres, staring at the limp, unconscious burden on Dominique's shoulder, 'she's likely to pollute the waters and poison the fish.' He shook his head gravely. 'A poor *disgraziata* if ever I met one. A true friendless one. Born to suffer and die young.'

'Even in her profession, she did not distinguish herself,' said Dominique.

'That is their hallmark,' said Torres, 'an overwhelming mediocrity.'

Ray studied the glossy prints which Torres had handed him.

'Crude,' he said, 'and obvious. A good defense lawyer in an American courtroom could tear the whole thing to pieces. He could demonstrate in twenty ways that it was a frame.'

'This is Italy,' said Torres.

'Fortunately for us,' said Ray, 'Roberto Greco would never let it get that far. Too many people hate him already. The scummy scandal sheets of Rome would have a real *festa* with this trash.'

'We should save an extra set for *L'Osservatore Romano*,' said Dominique.

Ray smiled. 'This old whore town has seen much worse. But these photos certainly have the ingredients of a good sermon, don't they?'

'As long as they'll hold up,' said Torres.

'They will,' said Ray. 'Tamburelli—remember him? He has consented to act as our middleman and to conduct the negotiations with Roberto Greco. He wanted a five percent commission, but I cut him down to three percent. For sixty thousand dollars American that man would sell his wife. If he's successful, it will be the easiest sixty thousand he's ever made.'

'He speaks Greco's language,' said Dominique.

'That's why I thought of him,' said Ray. 'His greed aside, he's a good politician, just as Greco himself is an intelligent man. That's what makes a politician—greed, a certain amount of low intelligence, and the morals of a skunk. I have Don Roberto in a box and I think he knows it already.'

'Have you been in touch with Greco at all?' said Torres.

'Tamburelli has, twice,' said Ray. 'They have a meeting arranged for next week.'

Francisco Tamburelli had been delighted to negotiate an agreement with Roberto Greco on Ray's behalf. Aside from the fact that he would gain sixty thousand dollars, the complex convoluted, tortured quality of Greco's dilemma struck him as droll and, therefore, interesting. Of course, Greco might at the last moment find a way to counter the threatening mate which no one else had perceived. In that case, Greco would counterattack with lethal effect and that would be the last of this bold and interesting American, Raimondo Occhiaccio. It would be too bad. In any case, he, Francisco Tamburelli, was acting in a strictly neutral capacity to untangle a distressing Gordian knot.

When Tamburelli sat down with Greco, the latter was certainly not disposed to reveal how much he knew or did not know. He waited to hear the worst. If he absolutely had to bow to the worst, he would at least be able to do so without loss of face. He would, in effect, be throwing a hopelessly outclassed hand into the discards, with no witnesses to his defeat.

After the amiable and ceremonious preliminaries had worked themselves into a cul-de-sac, Tamburelli went into his performance. '*Signor* Greco,' he said, 'I have been asked by certain persons to approach you in this unfortunate affair touching your son.'

Greco stared at Tamburelli steadily. 'I am delighted that it was you who were chosen. I could not think of a more able—ah—negotiator.'

'Thank you,' said Tamburelli. 'The nub of the matter is this. I have been informed, through third parties, of course, that young Luigi Antonio is safe and unharmed——'

'Except for the loss of a forefinger,' said Greco sharply.

Tamburelli sighed. 'A distressing circumstance.'

'Isn't it?' said Greco. 'Well, how much do they demand?'

'They demand nothing. They ask for two million dollars. Or the equivalent in Swiss francs or English pounds.'

'Is that all?' said Greco. He carefully controlled his face in order not to wince. 'The English will be flattered to learn that the pound sterling has been readmitted among the world's sound currencies.'

Tamburelli smiled his appreciation of Greco's wit and sportsmanship. He opened his hands sympathetically.

'And what is your commission?'

Tamburelli closed his fingers and touched his chest delicately with his fingertips. 'I, dear friend? Not a lire. I come to you in a totally disinterested capacity.'

'I can see that. Very clearly. Is the amount negotiable?'

Tamburelli sighed again. 'I have no instructions to that effect. It would appear that they are very firm.'

'A most un-Italian aproach,' said Greco pointedly. 'A rather barbarous, American approach. What do they actually say?'

'Upon delivery of the monies, your son will be released to you immediately, and alive.'

'What if I refuse and ask Saracino to redouble his efforts?'

Tamburelli rolled his eyes upward. 'You will place your beloved son in mortal danger.'

'I shall retaliate,' said Greco, watching Tamburelli covertly.

'It will not help that promising and brilliant young man. If the authorities are brought into this affair more deeply than they are already involved, Luigi Antonio will surely be murdered.'

'So I am dealing with assassins?'

'Let us say, with a very determined group of people,' said Tamburelli, 'who also have an interest in photography.'

'How do you mean that?'

Tamburelli bent over and extracted a brown manila envelope from his briefcase on the floor. He handed the envelope to Greco.

Greco opened the envelope and examined the ten photographs. His face remained expressionless. 'Obviously a piece of crude and disgusting blackmail.'

'Of course,' said Tamburelli, 'but the scandal rags are not interested in good photographic art.'

'My son would be acquitted in court,' said Greco. 'From the manner in which he is holding that knife, it is plain that it was thrust into his hands. Don't forget, I, too, am a lawyer. His entire posture is artificial, strained, and unconvincing. They were, of course, photographing him allegedly stabbing this female while she was fellating him.'

'Of course,' agreed Tamburelli, 'these are precisely the facts which would be brought out in open court. Luigi Antonio would indeed be acquitted.'

Greco tossed the photographs across the desk at Tamburelli. 'Swine,' he said to himself between his teeth. 'Francisco, how do they propose that this money transfer be effected?'

'Of course, they insist on an immediate response from you. If you are agreeable, you are to hand me the funds. I, in turn, will place it in the hands of their emissaries. When the money is in their hands, Luigi Antonio will be driven into Rome and released.'

'They do not say where or when?'

'Of course not,' said Tamburelli, 'but they do stress that if there is any attempt at police surveillance, Luigi Antonio will be delivered very dead upon arrival. Despite payment of the money.'

'Of the ransom.'

'They do not think of it in those terms.'

Greco was too much of a realist to waste time expressing indignation or surprise. The tree, the tree, the blessed tree, was the central shade point of his personal theology.

'So!' he said. 'And what guarantees do I have?'

Tamburelli permitted himself to look surprised. 'None, of course. As in all such cases, they hold the winning cards.'

'Tell me, Francisco,' said Greco, 'is the Society involved in this business?'

Tamburelli nodded cautiously. 'It would appear so.'

'I am not so much concerned about putting the money into your hands. After all, we have been colleagues for twenty years in the service of our constituents.'

'Exactly,' said Tamburelli. 'That is why I undertook this sad mission. I could not go astray even if I wished to. My ties with the Society do not go deeply, I admit, but they have always remained pure, honorable, and unblemished. No man shall be able to say of me that I did not behave with the highest integrity. I am acting here in a totally disinterested capacity.'

'I understand. Well, then, after I have handed you the money, how long will it be before I see Luigi Antonio again?'

Tamburelli reflected deeply. 'I would suggest that you give them thirty-six hours at least. That is, after the delivery has been made.'

Greco was a man of decision. He shrugged philosophically. 'Francisco,' he said formally, 'tell these industrious and imaginative people that I accept their proposal.'

'I am overjoyed,' said Tamburelli. 'May I say that you are taking this in a most statesmanlike fashion?'

'You may.' Greco smiled. 'There are times when the cards perversely go against one.'

'That has been every man's experience,' said Tamburelli.

CHAPTER 13

While Francisco Tamburelli waited, Ray completed the count of the money. Tamburelli's chauffeur had carried it into the villa in two suitcases. What Roberto Greco had described as the ransom had been paid over in francs, lire, pounds sterling, and American dollars. 'One million, nine hundred and forty thousand dollars,' said Ray at last, 'or its equivalent. Francisco, I see you've already deducted your commission.'

'Of course,' said Tamburelli.

'In what currency?'

'Dollars,' said Tamburelli reluctantly.

'Where do you keep this income which you don't find it necessary to declare to the Italian government?'

'In Lugano,' said Tamburelli, 'right across the border.'

Ray sighed and looked at the tall stack of lire notes on the desk before him. He counted off thirty-six million lire in one hundred-thousand-lire notes and snapped a rubber band around the stack. 'Then you really don't need dollars. Give them back to me. Here's the equivalent in lire.'

Tamburelli looked at Ray and shrugged. Still reluctantly, he took the American currency from his briefcase, handed it to Ray, and looked dubiously at the lire which he had accepted in exchange.

'What's the difference?' said Ray. 'Once it crosses the border, you turn it into Swiss francs, don't you?'

'Immediately.'

'And the bank invests it for you, right?'

'In American securities only.'

'Very prudent,' said Ray. 'People all over the world shoot off their mouths about how the U.S.A. is being flushed down

199

the toilet, how it's being split apart. The shitheads have a fancy new expression now. They say the U.S.A. is being polarized. Don't believe it, Francisco. All the money you can drag together, stolen or otherwise, have your Swiss gnomes put into American blue chip commons and American triple-A corporates. The U.S.A. will outlast all the horses' asses with the pointed heads who've been predicting its imminent doom for the last thirty years.'

'What are these horses' asses? I don't believe I'm familiar with the term.'

'It's an American expression,' said Ray. 'It means academicians, prophets, forecasters, economic analysts, social theorists, fast-buck polltakers, that sort of thing. They usually belong to the political party which is out of power.'

'Ah!' said Tamburelli. 'In Italy, we usually invite them into a coalition cabinet.'

'That figures. That's why you have such a fouled-up country here.'

Tamburelli opened his hands. 'Italy is a democracy. What else should we do with them?'

'Did you ever consider making chemists out of them?'

'Why chemists?'

'From what I've observed,' said Ray, 'your local horses' asses have a genius for transmuting hard money into soft shit. That connotes a chemical talent of some kind. Six hundred of your lire equal one American buck. There's something obscene about a ratio like that. Anyhow, I'm going to need all the American paper to pay Greco for my buy. I have to make it look convincing.'

'I admire you,' said Tamburelli. 'A certain severe integrity is required to hand a man a million dollars, even if it is actually his own money.'

Ray seemed lost in thought. 'If I may change the subject, how is your brother Renato doing at Tufarelli's?'

'Financially, quite well,' said Tamburelli. 'But it's interesting that you should ask me that. It's a coincidence, but I've heard from my sister-in-law, his wife. Since he's not really happy there, she wants him to leave, resign his job. She tells me that he now has accumulated enough capital to get started again in his own business. You know, once in business for yourself, always in business for yourself.'

'What does he have in mind?'

'He has an opportunity to go into business in Tunis. Besides, he dislikes Greco. He considers him too exacting and tyrannical an employer.'

Ray reflected a long time. 'I'm delighted to hear this, Francisco. Since I was instrumental in helping bring your brother back, he owes me a favor, doesn't he?'

'At any time.'

'I have a plan whereby both you and Renato can profit substantially. Listen to what I have in mind.'

When Ray was done, Francisco Tamburelli said, 'Well, there doesn't seem to be too much risk in it for Renato.'

'None that I can see. If it goes through successfully, there will be fifty thousand dollars in it for you and one hundred thousand dollars for Renato. With capital like that, Renato should be able to establish himself very well in Tunis.'

'For a figure like that, I accept for him.'

'Good,' said Ray. 'Then do this. Telephone Renato in Milan. Tell him to ask for a week's leave to visit some of your relatives in Palermo. A sick aunt or uncle should do it. Have him come directly here to the villa and stay with me. I'll give him the details and work it out with him.'

Francisco Tamburelli was already counting the fifty thousand dollars which he would receive from Ray in extra commission. 'You can count on it, Don Raimondo. I'll get in touch with Renato immediately. I must admit it's a very generous offer on your part.'

'I'll keep my word. A deal is a deal. That's how we Americans do business. Now, getting back to Greco, how did he react?'

'Very sensibly, I must admit. He analyzed the position, recognized the pending mate, and resigned.'

'What did you tell him?'

'That those holding Luigi Antonio would release him as soon as the money was paid over.'

'Then I shouldn't upset Greco's analysis by unexpectedly strengthening his position. I'll conclude my deal with Greco first. I'll pay him and take delivery of the merchandise. Then I'll release Luigi Antonio. The fond father has waited this long, he'll wait a little longer.'

'It would reflect on *me*,' said Tamburelli protestingly. 'Since I presented a different proposal to Greco, he might misunderstand.'

'You may be underestimating him. He's a Sicilian, like you and I. You may be certain that he's still studying the board. If I overlook some shift or variation, he'll surely take advantage of it, and very properly so. Do you recall what Machiavelli said about brains?'

'He said many things.'

'And this among the others: There are three different kinds of brains—the one understands things unassisted, the other understands things when shown by others, the third understands neither alone nor with the explanation of others. The first kind is most excellent, the second is also excellent, but the third is useless. Roberto Greco belongs to the first group. You know, Francisco, I have a personal theory that Niccolò Machiavelli was a Sicilian.'

Tamburelli smiled. 'Tell that to the Florentines.'

'I haven't the heart. Those Florentines have been on relief for the last three hundred years. What do they do up there, anyhow?'

'Keep the flame of culture burning,' said Tamburelli dryly.

'Culture and a few hundred lire will get you a plate of ravioli and a half bottle of red vinegar. Which reminds me, how are you managing with that little show girl of yours?'

'So far, so good,' said Tamburelli.

'I detect a note of insecurity. It's a constant concern, isn't it? Do you remember what I told you? That's what happens when a man takes up with a female half his age, especially one in the theatrical profession. They'll deceive you with the first virile cock to come their way. They'll deceive you just to keep in practice.'

'I already know your thinking.'

'Take my advice, Francisco, invest your money prudently and patronize whores. I'd like to meet your piece of tail though. As soon as my merchandise is safely cached and Luigi

Antonio is out of here, I plan to relax and have a little fun. It's time I began to enjoy life.' Ray looked about the large living room in which he sat with Tamburelli. 'This villa should lend itself admirably to my purpose.'

'What do you have in mind?'

'A good old-fashioned orgy. With semen and vomit all over the rugs. I suppose that's inescapable. Rome seems to have everything else, political corruption, nepotism, straight and gay sex, gambling, bribery, and so on. Would it have something like a competent orgy-arranger?'

'That depends on how much you want to spend.'

'I intent to be very liberal.'

'Then I can recommend a most unique individual.'

'What's his name?'

'Quinto Babbi.'

'Tell me something about him.'

'Well,' said Tamburelli slowly, 'I'd describe him as a major-domo and master of revels. He has a truly creative imagination. I've attended some of his productions. Without my wife, of course. He's a plump, smooth-faced man of middle height, as innocent in his effect on those about him as a tapestry, a portrait, or a piece of furniture. He's the essence of self-effacing anonymity, the faceless, inoffensive, and, hence soothing archtypal servitor, the distillation of a hundred generations of specialists whose only interest in life is the pleasure of those whom he serves. A truly professional. Quinto can program your orgy well enough. It's all a question of how much budget you wish to allocate.'

'A good man, eh? What's his experience?'

'It parallels the history of Rome,' said Tamburelli. 'He insists he's a direct descendant of Quintus Maximus Baber, who performed a like function for the retired Emperor Tiberius at the imperial Capri villa. As is well known, Tiberius regaled his guests with the group sexual performance of his troupes of Greek dancers and acrobats, the *spintriae*. These Greeks were double-jointed artistes, capable of copulating in foursomes while hanging from a swinging chandelier.'

Ray laughed. 'Fucking in fours on a chandelier! What an act for Las Vegas! It would even stop the crap-shooters. Still, isn't it a little——'

'Pointless? Yes, I suppose by modern standards it would be. Like playing a Paganini violin concerto while standing on one's head. But it was the robust taste of the times. The Emperor Tiberius commanded and Quinto's ancestor executed.'

'Okay. But you're going back a long way. What have the Babbis been doing lately?'

'You must remember that everything in Rome happened only yesterday,' said Tamburelli. 'The Babbis are history, the private history of potentates. Another of his forebears, for instance, was Pope Alexander VI's master of ceremonies. For the intimate parties, of course, not for the public ecclesiastical functions.'

Ray shook his head and grinned. 'I just can't get with the sense of time of you Italians. You make a century sound like a week.'

'Well, I'll bring you up to modern times, the mid-eighteenth century. At that time, another Babbi operated the most exclusive brothel in Venice. It was far superior to and more elegant than Madame Jourdain's in Paris. It offered anything from virgin boys for aging pederasts and virgin girls for aging lesbians to slightly rotten corpses for necrophiliacs. This is Quinto's art. You might call him an impresario. He has good working relationships with the most exclusive flesh dealers in Rome.'

'Does he know Petri?' said Ray.

'Petri? The Neapolitan pimp? Petri simply isn't in the same world with Quinto. *This* man is an artist.'

'He sounds good,' admitted Ray. 'If he delivered for a pope, he should be able to do a job for the son of a Sicilian wineshop keeper.'

'Ah, you're entirely too modest.'

'Why don't you ask this Babbi to come around and see me?'

'I can do that.'

'You're invited, of course,' said Ray. 'Bring your little theatrical jewel with you. Don't worry, I won't try to steal her. Can you get me an introduction to the *questore* Saracino? I'd like to invite him, too. Greco will also come.'

'Greco! After all this? How can you be so sure?'

'My dear Francisco, when a Sicilian is unable to avenge his wrongs and has no other choice, he continues to be the most amiable fellow in the world. *You* should know that.'

'What audacity! Well, as long as you can carry it off.'

'I try. I try. If I didn't, my heart would break with home-sickness. Now, my friend, I must get ready for the big confrontation with *Signor* Roberto Greco.'

Tamburelli rose to his feet. 'Good luck, Don Raimondo. And watch yourself. Greco may be your performing bear for the moment, but bears are the most unpredictable creatures in the world.'

'Very true. *Arrivederci*, Don Francisco. Don't forget to send Renato down to see me.'

'I have already done it. *Arrivederci*. Go with God.'

A week later Ray called in Dominique Maestracci and Juan Torres. As they seated themselves, Ray began pacing around the room.

'We have problems,' he said. 'Everything appears to be going well, and yet it is not going well. Let's take it from the beginning. We made a deal with Greco. We went to Beirut and, at considerable trouble, purchased merchandise from Mahmoudi for which we paid him one million dollars of our own money. I assume that the merchandise reached Greco in good order and has been converted. This merchandise, two hundred kilos of heroin, if we can successfully export it to America and sell it to the wholesalers at fifteen thousand dollars per kilo will gain us the sum of three million dollars. But I'm getting ahead of myself. In the meantime, we returned to Italy and abducted Greco's son. We have obtained a ransom of two millions and still hold Luigi Antonio. We have recouped our original outlay and gained an additional million dollars, less the commission to Tamburelli. Greco still holds the heroin. That's the situation as of this moment. Let's assess it.'

'All Greco has laid out is the cost of conversion,' said Torres. 'Even if he exports it at between five and ten thousand per kilo, he can still make a profit. Why should he sell it to you?'

'Our agreement was that he would charge me one million for conversion, shipping costs, and finder's fee,' said Ray. 'Exactly five thousand per kilo of heroin. But, now, what motive would he have for adhering to his original agreement with me?'

'The risks of undertaking the export operation himself, perhaps,' said Dominique. 'After all, he's a legitimate businessman and a political figure of some importance.'

'True,' said Ray. 'But that's really a feeble argument. Does it convince you?'

'No,' said Dominique. 'But, perhaps, he'll keep his word and deliver because he wants Luigi Antonio back. The fact that the people for whom Francisco Tamburelli was allegedly acting have not kept faith would not surprise a man like Greco. Therefore, being certain of the identity of the abductors, he will deliver on the original terms in the hopes of retrieving his son alive.'

'That argument is a little stronger,' admitted Ray, 'but still uncertain. Let's follow out the line. I meet Greco. We both maintain the fiction that I know nothing of his son's abduction. I pay him and take delivery. Immediately thereafter a very much alive Luigi Antonio is united with his family. How would we stand then?'

'We would have the ransom money, one million dollars,' said Torres. 'We would also have two hundred kilos of heroin for which we paid nothing and which is worth three millions on the export market. We would also have two extremely dangerous and able enemies united in their efforts to destroy us.'

'Exactly,' said Ray. 'Just what course they would take, I have no idea at the moment. But I would never underestimate Roberto Greco's ability. How did we get into this situation? First, we, or rather I, threatened Greco through his agents. Second, we killed Polizzi and Cadri to warn and intimidate him. These steps had the effect of throwing him off balance. Third, we kidnapped his son. Greco is still off balance. Why did we do so? Necessary or not, it was a form of preventive warfare to discourage his possible dishonesty. Whether it was the wisest course is now irrelevant. That is what happened.

Greco is now an actual enemy and we are running out of clamps, with which to keep his jaws closed. We still have the initiative. However, if we don't produce a fourth step, we'll surrender that initiative and he'll then go over to the offensive. What can he do? I don't know. He is a powerful man, well connected, and on his home ground. And the moment we release Luigi Antonio and take possession of the heroin, we assume a passive role and become vulnerable. Do you really think that Roberto and that very able, intelligent young man will allow us to enjoy the fruits of our labor in peace? Remember what Machiavelli said: When you harm a man, you must either reconcile him entirely or destroy him. Has Greco been harmed? Definitely. Can Greco be entirely reconciled so that he will be as harmless to us as our dead mothers?' Ray laughed. 'Would *you* relax your grip on Greco's jaws and turn your back on him?'

'Supposing,' said Torres, 'after the heroin is in our possession, we kill Luigi Antonio—what then?'

'If we do that,' said Ray, 'we maim the bear in one paw only and enrage him all the more. Trying to break off the engagement in this way won't work. I certainly want the heroin and will make every effort to get it. But, whether we get it or not, our only safety lies in the death of these two men. Here is the conclusion I've reached. They must be destroyed if we are to survive.'

'Preventive warfare can lead to unexpected complications,' observed Torres.

'How do we know it would have gone better had we dealt honestly?' said Ray.

'Men conclude deals honestly every day and it goes smoothly,' said Torres. 'Look how it went with Hassan Mahmoudi.'

'Mahmoudi was one of those exceptions which prove the rule,' said Ray. 'And so, for that matter, is Greco. And so is the entire narcotics traffic. You can't judge this particular transaction or the drug business by normal standards. *You* know that, Juan.'

'I think Don Raimondo is correct,' said Dominique. 'Why should Greco adhere to his original agreement and sell us the

207

heroin?'

'Why, indeed!' said Ray. 'He would be insane to do so. And Greco isn't insane. Given the circumstances and his grievances. I can come to only one conclusion: Greco and son must die. We already hold Luigi Antonio. But how do we get at Roberto? At this point, considering the trap we're in, getting the heroin would be merely frosting on the cake. But, very definitely, father and son must be killed. There's also a time problem. If I wait too long before moving, I only give Greco additional time to reinforce his position. We must strike immediately. But how?' Ray looked from Dominique Maestracci to Juan Torres. 'No suggestions from either of you? Very well. Then I have a modest proposal to make. Excuse me for a moment.' Ray left the living room and returned, followed by Renato Tamburelli. He waved Renato into a chair and took one himself. 'Juan, Dominique, this is Renato Tamburelli. He is Francisco Tamburelli's brother and he works for Greco. He is an assistant in Tufarelli's heroin conversion laboratory. In fact, he helped to convert our entire consignment. I might add that he has personal reasons for not loving *Signor* Greco. Do you wish to ask him some questions?'

Juan Torres studied Renato with interest. 'Where,' he asked, 'is our heroin now?'

'In Milan,' said Renato. 'Specifically, locked in the strong room off the laboratory.'

'Can it be gotten at?' said Torres.

'*Signor* Greco has one key. Pierre Levaque, our chief chemist, carries the other one. I can tell you this much. I saw your goods packed up into four big fiberboard suitcases and put in.'

'So you have no access to the strong room?'

'None. But I do have a key which permits me to enter the laboratory. Levaque carelessly let me have his for a short while. I secretly had a duplicate made before I returned the original to Levaque.'

'What are you doing here away from your job?' asked Torres.

'Renato got a week's leave, ostensibly to visit some relatives,' Ray explained. 'At this moment, he's supposed to be in

208

Palmero.' He turned to Renato. 'What's going on in the laboratory now? Do you have any ideas?'

'I know this,' said Renato. 'They've just gotten a new lot of morphine base which has to be converted fast. Levaque dropped some words to the effect that it was a rush order. Since my absence leaves them shorthanded, the three of them—Levaque, Manoury, and Kurzlicht—are working late every night.'

'Tell us about the layout up there,' said Ray.

'About Greco's office, you mean?'

'Yes.'

Renato replied: '*Signor* Greco has two offices. One, his big official one, so-called, is in the pharmaceuticals division of the plant. Then he has a small office which is right off the heroin laboratory. It's a very private place.'

'Would you, by chance, have a key to it?' said Dominique.

Renato shook his head. '*Signor* Greco trusts no one in that office when he's not there. He has the only key.'

'It doesn't matter,' said Dominique. 'I have a set of picks. If necessary, we can always shoot off the lock.'

Ray studied the three men. 'I smell a certain infernal creativity being generated here. I smell brimstone. Renato, how large is that laboratory in area?'

'About fifty feet long by about thirty feet wide. Quite a big place.'

'And Greco's private office?'

'About twelve by eighteen, I should say.'

'Juan,' said Ray, 'you've had experience with explosives and incendiaries, haven't you?'

'With military devices, yes,' said Torres.

'We wish to destroy Greco and we wish to obtain the heroin,' said Ray. 'An unavoidable necessity is that we will also have to destroy the three chemists who will be on the premises. Hence, our problem is a three-pronged one.'

'Well, as for Greco,' said Dominique, 'I can install a bomb in his automobile, under the hood or under the driver's seat.'

Ray shook his head. 'Too uncertain.'

'My installations are quite reliable,' said Dominique with some pride. 'I usually attach the dynamite sticks to the fire wall on the driver's side of the car. The auto battery provides the current. I attach one alligator clip to the input side of the coil and connect the other to a common ground. The ignition key naturally acts as the trigger. To make certain, I can install a second pressure trigger assembly under the driver's seat.'

'Such hookups are reliable enough,' conceded Ray, 'but only where the target suspects nothing. Greco, however, has already been forewarned. He will certainly not be using any of his own cars. If he does, he will have them thoroughly checked. The automotive approach is out.'

'Keep it simple,' said Torres. 'After removing our merchandise and destroying the chemists, all we need is two or three bombs, one for Greco's office and, say two for the laboratory. Six dry cell batteries, three cheap alarm clocks, and sixty sticks of dynamite.'

'Sixty!' said Ray in mildly shocked tones. 'Are you trying to start a war? Six sticks would be more than enough.'

'I'm merely stressing thoroughness,' said Torres.

Ray shook his head. 'Six or sixty, I don't like overkill. I don't want any civilian noncombatants affected by this operation. Tufarelli has a great many employees.'

Dominique looked surprised. 'Is that important, Don Raimondo?'

'You're not using your head, Dominique,' snapped Ray. 'This isn't a matter of humanitarianism. Wanton, irrelevant killing of the uninvolved is synonymous with clumsiness and usually boomerangs in a very unpleasant way. A soldier's job is to destroy his opposite number as expeditiously as possible, not to push unarmed civilians around.'

'Atrocities sometimes do occur in military operations,' said Torres.

'Sad but true,' agreed Ray, 'but it's avoidable in this case. Why irritate the authorities more than is necessary? All we want is our merchandise and Greco. The three chemists are unimportant. The authorities will not pursue that aspect of the case too seriously.' He turned to Renato. 'You say the chemists are working there every night?'

'Yes. In fact, they have rooms in the plant. They are sleeping over and eating there because of this rush job.'

'And you can get Torres and Dominique into the laboratory?'

Renato nodded.

'Very well,' said Ray. 'We have to get the merchandise out of the strong room. We have to get Roberto Greco out of this world. But with the minimum necessary amount of force. I don't want a city block destroyed and innocent people killed simply to suppress one scoundrel. The public reaction would be appalling. Don't mistake my meaning. No one is really innocent. I mean those who are uninvolved.'

'If you'll be a little more specific, Don Raimondo,' said Torres.

'As you've gathered,' said Ray, 'I don't like the indiscriminate use of explosive devices. There are always policemen about who enjoy patiently reassembling detonated fragments and studying them, just as others enjoy solving jigsaw puzzles.'

'Specifically,' said Torres.

'Specifically,' said Ray, 'I suggest four small booby traps. One is an ordinary telephone handset such as I have here on my desk. Pick up a set anywhere and substitute it for the one presently on Greco's desk. When booby-trapped, the charge is in the base, a few ounces of TNT and a simple percussion cap. When the receiver is lifted, a small tension spring is released. A striker pin swings over and strikes the percussion cap. Greco's face will be sheared off but no one else will be affected. This is the sort of thing I favor.'

'Beautiful,' said Dominique. 'It sounds German.'

'It is,' said Ray. 'It was.'

'Very good,' said Dominique, 'but supposing Greco doesn't happen to lift the receiver?'

'Booby trap number two,' said Ray. 'Juan, are you familiar with miniature antipersonnel land mines? Or you, Dominique? Perhaps you ran across them in the Underground days. The Germans used to leave behind beautiful little specimens for us. They resemble a small discus. A pressure of twenty pounds on the pressure plate initiates the striker unit. Just one ounce of TNT and it used to shear away an infantry soldier's foot. Do you know those?'

Torres nodded. 'I've had experience with them in Algeria and Indochina.'

'And I, in La Belle France,' said Dominique.

'Good,' said Ray. 'Pick up one from the arms dealers here. There's always a surplus of that sort of devilry around. Slip it under the cushion of Greco's office chair, or in the seat of the chair.'

'One ounce of high explosive,' said Torres thoughtfully. 'It wouldn't necessarily kill Greco immediately. He might live long enough to answer a few questions.'

'That toy would sympathetically detonate the telephone handset,' said Ray. 'But, for insurance, here are two more backstops. Place one of your quaint alarm clock devices in the lower drawer of his desk and set it. Three sticks of dynamite should be adequate. If the mine doesn't detonate it sympathetically, it will trigger itself at the proper time when the alarm goes off. Also a smaller timed device to be placed in something on top of his desk. A standard three by five index file box should serve quite well. I've seen them made up with small, cheap timing units which release a spring-loaded electric switch. They hold a half stick of dynamite, or even a quarter stick, or a few ounces of TNT and a tiny electric fuse cap. That should take care of Greco with a minimum of debris.'

'What about the main laboratory?' said Torres.

'Ah,' said Ray, 'there, you can improvise to your heart's content. Except for one thing—I want incendiaries, not explosives. You will need dynamite, of course, but only to ensure the successful launching of your incendiary chemicals. Use magnesium and powdered aluminium mixed with iron oxide. A thermite mixture will set off the magnesium. And you can use an ordinary dynamite device to set off the thermite. Do you follow me? There's nothing quite like magnesium. It's hot. It's the piranha of metals. It melts everything in its path and it's hard to extinguish. It will be far more difficult for the authorities to reconstruct the events after a carefully prepared magnesium conflagration than after an ordinary explosion. That's the broad outline. Take it from there.'

'I think I have the solution,' said Dominique.

'I think we all have,' said Ray. 'Don't you, Juan?'

Juan Torres nodded. 'Yes. It should go off fairly simply.'

'Can you get them in, Renato?' repeated Ray.

'Without question,' said Renato. 'I was thinking of something along these lines—pushing the temperature of the burners, pushing it up high during acetylation. That's the process of converting pure morphine into crude heroin. Above one hundred degrees Centigrade the cooking mixture would explode and wreck the entire plant.'

Ray shook his head. 'Too much random uncertainty in that approach. Too much inaccuracy. You don't hack down a whole tree for kindling. Just get Dominique and Torres into the laboratory, Renato. They'll handle that end of it.'

'As you wish,' said Renato. 'About the money you promised me——'

'I said one hundred thousand dollars,' said Ray. 'You'll return to Milan with Juan and Dominique. As soon as the job is done, Juan will pay you the money. Have you planned your destination?'

'Tunis,' said Renato. 'My family is already there waiting for me. I'm already packed.'

'Excellent,' said Ray. 'You can take a plane directly from Milan airport.' He turned to the other two. 'Anything else on your minds?'

'I think we've covered it,' said Torres.

'That's it, then,' said Ray.

Renato Tamburelli rose and extended his hand. 'I'm satisfied. Thank you, *Signor* Occhiaccio.'

Tufarelli Pharmaceuticals, A.G., in Milan was a four-story dark-red building, one block in length. Behind it sprawled an extensive railroad marshaling yard area. Renato Tamburelli sat at the wheel of the Lancia across the street from the plant. Dominique Maestracci and Juan Torres were sitting in the backseat. Renato scanned the cobbled street which had no sidewalks in both directions. It was deserted. 'As you can see,' he said, 'this is an industrial area. No one comes down here at night and very few police patrols.'

Dominique checked his wristwatch. 'It's almost twenty

minutes after midnight. Can you see the laboratory windows from here? Where do they work?'

'They're up on the fourth floor,' said Renato. 'You can't see anything. The windows are shuttered.' He pointed across the street. 'Do you see that small metal side door? That's where we go in. That's the door for which I have the key.'

'Any night watchmen around?' said Torres.

'Not at this end of the plant. *Signor* Greco doesn't want them snooping around here. They make their rounds in the so-called legitimate areas which cover about three-quarters of the entire plant. It's a huge place, a one-block frontage.'

'Well,' said Torres, 'we're about as ready as we'll ever be. Say the word, Renato.'

'Let me swing the car around first,' said Renato.

'Hold it,' said Dominique. 'Are you going to park across the street in front of the door?'

'Yes. That's what I had in mind.'

'And what if a patrol comes along?'

'They never do in this area.'

'That's why one may come along on this night,' said Dominique. 'We'd look good coming down and finding no car or a few *sbirri* waiting for us. Drive down the block. We want a better hiding place than the open street. That's elementary.'

'It will be a long walk,' said Renato. He started the car and drove toward the railroad yard. Between the rear wall of the Tufarelli plant and the wire-link fence of the boundary of the yard was a small cobbled alley.

'Turn in here,' said Dominique. 'It looks nice and deserted. Turn on your high beam.'

The Lancia crawled along for another hundred feet. 'Keep going,' said Dominique. 'Up there. What's that?' He pointed to what looked like a ten-foot stack of lumber. The car pulled up alongside.

'Cargo pallets,' said Renato. 'Probably damaged and about to be broken up for scrap wood.'

'That should do it,' said Dominique. 'Pull up ahead a little and then back in right against the stack. That way they can't see you from the street. What's up at the other end of this alley?'

'I'm pretty certain that the fence of the rail yard makes a right angle there and continues along.'

'A dead end?' said Dominique. 'Well, this is still better than leaving the car sitting out in the open street like a squatting duck.'

Renato backed the Lancia in carefully until the rear bumper gently touched the stack of cargo pallets. He switched off the headlights. The darkness in the alley behind the building was absolute. 'Leave all the doors unlocked and the trunk unlatched,' said Dominique. 'Lead the way, Renato.'

Juan and Dominique, each man carrying a suitcase, followed Renato back to the street. They turned right. Renato had the door key in his hand. He opened the door and waved the others in. When they brought the suitcases in, he relocked the door.

The areaway in which they stood was very small and dimly lit by one small bulb. Renato pressed the freight elevator button on the wall. 'This is where the merchandise comes up. It leads directly to the laboratory on the fourth floor.'

'What's on the second and third floors?' said Dominique.

'Just empty warehousing space. When we get up there, we step into a small hallway. There is one small door. That leads directly into the laboratory. I have the key for that door.' Renato seemed nervous. 'You'll have to work fast.'

'Why?' said Torres. 'What's the hurry? Do you expect to be interrupted?'

'I don't know. I hope it goes well.'

'Don't worry. We'll handle it all right.'

'Now,' said Renato. They got out on the landing with their suitcases and waited while Renato unlocked the door. They followed him into the laboratory and placed the suitcases on the floor. Torres blinked in the brilliant lighting of the big room. He drew a .38 from his holster and fitted a silencer tube over it. Dominique followed suit. Renato was down at the other end of the room talking to three men in white coats. Torres and Dominique walked toward them rapidly. The descriptions tallied. Manoury was the slight, dark one. Levaque, the tall, slender, blond man with the drooping blond mustache. Kurzlicht, the tall, burly, bald-headed German.

Renato moved away on the other side of the counter.

Torres pointed his gun muzzle at Levaque's heart. Dominique covered Manoury and Kurzlicht.

'I want you to unlock the strong room,' said Torres.

'I don't have the key,' said Levaque calmly.

Dominique took careful aim and shot Kurzlicht between the eyes. The German crashed to the floor. Dominique fired into his head twice more.

'We are serious,' said Torres. 'The key. Unlock the place.'

Levaque shrugged and made no move.

Dominique spun the slight Manoury around and fired a bullet into the base of his neck. The Algerian crumpled to the floor.

'As you see,' said Torres.

Levaque was no faithful steward defending his master's premises. This laboratory was his private little kingdom. He resisted fear and gave ground doggedly. Seeking to gain time, he spoke to Torres in Spanish. 'You're a Spaniard, *señor*?'

'Yes, but it won't help you,' said Torres in the same tongue. 'You know the saying—*mi venga la muerte de Spagna* [let my death come from Spain]; for, then, it will be sure to be long in coming. But not in this case, *Señor* Levaque. Your death will come with a most un-Spanish dispatch if you disobey.'

Clinging to hope, Levaque finally complied, though still reluctantly. He turned around and began walking slowly toward the strong room. He unlocked it and swung the door open. Torres pushed Levaque into the room and shot him in the back of the head. Levaque fell to the floor. Torres holstered his gun, took off his coat, and hung it on a hook. 'Dominique,' he called, 'bring the other two in here also. Now we can work at ease.'

Dominique and Renato dragged the bodies of the other two chemists into the strong room. Torres examined the space in which they stood. It was a small area, about six by eight feet—actually a steel box embedded in the brick-and-concrete of the wall and fitted with metal shelves. Renato pointed out the fiberboard suitcases on one of the shelves. 'There it is.'

'What are you waiting for, then?' said Torres. 'Drag them down and get them over to the elevator landing.' He reconsidered. 'Hold it. Open one of the suitcases, so we'll know that we're getting the right thing.'

Renato pulled down one of the suitcases, undid the webbing straps, and lifted off the lid. 'I packaged it myself. There are fifty one-kilo bags of ninety percent pure heroin in here. I put them up in double-waxed paper bags.'

'Open one of them,' said Torres.

Renato slit the scotch tape sealing the top of one of the bags. Torres lifted out the bag, moistened his finger, and took a pinch of the white powder on his finger and tasted it.

'So this is the stuff.'

'It's good heroin,' said Renato. 'I watched them make it. They did a careful job. Just tasting it won't tell you much. There are better tests than that.'

'Never mind,' said Torres. 'Seal up the bag. Get all the suitcases down and set them by the elevator.' He stared once more at the bodies of the three dead heroin chemists sprawled on the floor of the strong room. 'Come on, Dominique. We have two more little jobs to complete.'

They came out of the strong room and Torres left the door unlocked. 'Renato,' he said, 'when you come back, bring our bags back with you. They're standing by the elevator.' To Dominique he said, 'I think we'll rig one incendiary right here in the strong room to cremate these people thoroughly. And another one out in the main laboratory to demolish it completely. The second one should be larger and in a well-concealed place, where it won't be easily located. But, first, let's prepare Greco's office.'

They waited till Renato returned, carrying the two suitcases with the explosives.

'I want an obscure place to plant the bomb out here,' said Torres.

'Here,' said Renato. He led the other two over to a deep metal cabinet six feet in height. He unlocked it. 'We keep carboys of acetic anhydride in here.'

'This will be fine,' said Torres. He opened one of the suitcases, taped up two bundles of ten sticks of dynamite each, and placed them in a corner of the cabinet between two carboys of the acid. He carefully bored a hole in the middle of a stick of dynamite, inserted an electric blasting cap into the stick, and secured the connection with friction tape. One of the electric blasting cap wires connected with two dry cell batteries in tandem. Torres connected a second wire from the blasting cap to the alarm lever of a small clock. A third wire connected the clock to the dry cells. When that was done, he wedged a ten-pound container of the magnesium-powdered aluminium-iron oxide mixture between the two bundles of dynamite sticks. Then he placed a five-pound can of thermite on top of the magnesium.

'After we've prepared Greco's office,' he said to Dominique, 'we'll set this clock. You know these silly civilian devices better than I do. How does it look?'

Dominique examined the hookup judiciously. 'Looks all right. The alarm goes off, the metal surfaces come into contact, the electric circuit is completed. *Bon!* The current will flow from the dry cells into the blasting cap. That will set off the dynamite, the thermite, and the magnesium successively. Very pretty.'

'Thank you,' smiled Torres. 'Go, thou, and do likewise, Dominique. Take the suitcase and rig up a similar device in the strong room. I'll just relax and smoke a cigarette till you're done.'

Fifteen minutes later Dominique returned from the strong room.

'All set?' said Torres.

Dominique nodded. 'We've done our duty for the dead.'

'Fine,' said Torres. 'Now lead us to Greco's office, Renato.'

Renato led the way to the other end of the laboratory and the passageway leading off to Greco's office. Dominique tried the door handle. 'Locked, of course.' He knelt down and took out a plastic case of lock picks from the suitcase that he had carried along with him. Kneeling in front of the door lock, he probed delicately with one pick after another. 'The tumblers are giving a little, but only a very little.' He slid an eight-inch piece of celluloid into the edge of the door. 'Too flexible,' he grunted. He left the celluloid sticking in the door and selected a piece of flexible steel that resembled a nail file from the case. He greased it and forced it in alongside the celluloid.

'Be careful not to leave any marks,' said Torres.

'I'd like to shoot that damned lock off,' grumbled Dominique.

'Try the picks again,' said Torres, 'We depending on you. They never taught us these arts in *La Légion*.'

Dominique began probing with the picks again, trying one after another patiently. 'No good,' he finally said. 'I can't seem to swing the tumblers all the way over.' He suddenly struck his forehead with his doubled fist. 'Idiot! I have a set of master keys in the suitcase. You get so damned hypnotized trying to do it the hard way, you forget about the obvious way. This looks like an ordinary American Yale lock. I probably have something for it.'

He extracted a ring containing twenty different keys and began fitting them into the lock methodically, one after the other. 'Even if I get one to turn the lock a quarter of the way, I think I can do the rest with the celluloid.'

By the eleventh key Dominique said: 'I think we've got it. It fits. It's turning. Halfway at least. Juan, I've got the key turned as far as it will go. Push that piece of steel in harder.'

'I've got it in another half inch, at least,' said Juan.

'There's another expander in the kit,' said Dominique. 'Force it in alongside. If it can widen the gap even an eighth of an inch, it will help.'

Renato handed Torres the third steel expander and he began sliding it in slowly, without forcing it. 'Don't bend too hard,' said Dominique. 'They're flexible. Just press it forward gently. I think we'll get it this time.' He removed the key from the door and studied it. 'I think I have another blank that's closer.' He selected a new key blank and tried the lock again. 'Juan, force all three pieces in as far as you can, the celluloid and the two expanders, while I turn the key. Now...' He turned the key.

'It's sliding in more easily,' said Torres.

'Now it's coming,' said Dominique. 'Put some pressure on.' He turned the key slowly and strongly. The lock sprang open.

Roberto Greco's office was furnished sumptuously. The walls were paneled in walnut and the floor covered with a Kirman rug. Dominique went directly to the big polished walnut desk and pushed the leather swivel chair back from the desk. The desk was a six-drawer model, three on each side. Dominique tried both top drawers. They were locked. 'I know this type. You unlock the top drawer and the other two on the same side are also released. These locks are more ornamental than anything else.' He inserted a long master key blank delicately into the keyhole and released the spring catch of the top drawer. 'The bottom drawer is always the big one. That's where we can leave our little present.' He lifted a small attaché case carefully from the suitcase. 'This one is a pretty job. Only the timer has to be set. Renato, what time does the boss usually come into the office?'

'He's usually here by ten in the morning.'

'*Bon!* We'll set it, say, for eleven A.M., one hour after his arrival.' Dominique opened the attaché case. 'This one utilizes C-3 plastic. It's a favorite with our Algerians. A very lively, vivacious high explosive. None of your cheap alarm clocks here. This one has a military-type demolition timer. It utilizes a spring-loaded firing pin and timing disc internally. This knurled knob sets the time on the gauge face.' He turned the knob on the side of the timer and the clocklike hands crept around until the long hand stood at twelve and the short hand at eleven. 'It's like setting an electric kitchen oven in which your wife is roasting a chicken.' He closed the attaché case gently and placed it softly in the bottom of the big drawer. The papers which he had removed from the drawer he now replaced in the same order and pushed the drawer closed.

Dominique took a small carton from the suitcase and opened it carefully. He removed a small, shiny gray metal discus. 'This is a Krügeller antipersonnel land mine. One of the smallest ever manufactured. I know these toys as well as you, Juan. We used them against the Boche in the Underground. This one is old but very much alive and it can bite.' He raised the rubber seat cushion, placed the mine carefully on the seat of the chair, and very delicately placed the cushion on top of the mine. '*Le* hot seat. What else, Juanito?'

'The telephone set,' said Torres. 'I've already disconnected the genuine one. Here, let me have your new one.'

Dominique carefully handed over the pressure-triggered

telephone handset. Torres set it down where the original one had stood and dropped the cord over the edge of the desk. 'He won't notice anything dangling. Now the wooden file box.'

'I didn't make one up,' said Dominique apologetically. 'I didn't have time.'

'It doesn't matter,' said Torres. 'These three gifts from the wise man of the west should be adequate.' Carefully, he pushed the swivel chair toward the desk. 'Renato, wipe up the desk a little and make everything look neat and undisturbed. Check it all over but don't touch the telephone set. There's nothing like a nice clean job. That's a self-locking Yale on the door. Set the lock and wipe down both sides of the door around the lock. Then close the door.'

As the three men walked down the aisle in the laboratory toward the acid storage cabinet, Renato said, 'Perhaps we should have worn gloves.'

'Not necessary,' said Dominique. 'There won't be enough of this part of the building left to find any fingerprints.'

'Dominique,' said Torres, 'go and activate the hook up in the strong room. We'll synchronize everything for eleven A.M. I'll take care of this one.'

Dominique went off in the direction of the strong room.

Kneeling in front of the open cabinet, Torres delicately completed the task of setting the alarm for eleven A.M. He finally rose from his knees. Renato locked the cabinet and wiped down the door.

Torres took a long manila envelope from his pocket and handed it to Renato. Renato opened the envelope and counted the money quickly. 'I've never seen this much at one time. Many thanks. And thank *Signor* Occhiaccio for me again.'

'Don't mention it,' said Torres.

Dominique returned from the strong room. 'I locked the room also.'

While Renato put the elevator on HOLD, Torres and Dominique stacked the four bulky suitcases containing the heroin and the two empty suitcases in the elevator. In the areaway Torres said, 'We'll have to make two trips.'

Renato slowly backed out the Lancia along the narrow alley into the street and swung it around. He drove himself to the airport and got out from behind the wheel in the parking field. Dominique slid in behind the wheel and Torres got into the right-hand front seat. 'Have a good trip, Renato,' said Torres. 'You'll read about it in the papers. *Adios*.'

Ray finished his third cup of coffee in the villa and tossed *Il Messaggero* across the table to Torres. Torres picked it up and reread the headlines and the lead article:

MAJOR EXPLOSION AND FIRE IN MILAN—TUFARELLI
CHEMICAL PLANT ALMOST ENTIRELY DESTROYED

... the police investigation is hampered by the fact that firemen are still searching in the ruins for bodies. It is still unknown how many persons were killed when the plant exploded yesterday morning. It has been tentatively ascertained that *Commendatore* Roberto Greco, an executive of this large and well-known pharmaceuticals manufacturer, one of Italy's largest, was in his office in the plant when the explosion occurred. Police are working on the theory that illicit heroin manufacturing operations were being carried on in one of Tufarelli's laboratories. They theorize that the destruction and the ensuing conflagration was set off by an accidental explosion in a clandestine heroin laboratory somewhere in the building. The investigation is continuing.

Together with the Death of *Signor* Greco, police are also investigating the mysterious disappearance of his son, *Signor* Luigi Antonio Greco. The younger Greco has been a student in the School of Law of the University of Rome. Whether or not young Greco, if found, may be able to cast some light on the death of his father. . . .

'Don't believe that newspaper article, Don Raimondo,' said Torres. 'No one was killed there except those who were supposed to have been killed. There were no accidents.'

'I hope so,' said Ray. 'I hate accidents. Did you take care of Luigi Antonio all right?'

Torres put down his cup of coffee. 'We dropped him, I would say, almost over Ponchielli's body.'

'Then I'd say we're safe on first,' said Ray.

'What does that mean?'

'It's an American game called baseball. It means we still have three spans to leap, three more bridges to cross before we are home safe. Still, having reached first calls for a celebration.'

'For my part,' said Torres, 'I'm glad this step is over.'

'No more than I am,' said Ray. 'This is my first and last venture into the narcotics business. It's like the real estate business—nothing but worries. I have no temperament for it. I worry too much. It's like having to go to tenants every month and collect rent from them. And then some tenant loses his job and can't pay his rent and you have to hire a lawyer to get him evicted. I remember once owning an old tenement apartment house in Brooklyn. The place practically gave me gray hair. I got it on a foreclosure. I would have been smart to have walked away from it and let it fall into the bank's lap. Then the plumbing would go out or the wiring or the roof had to be fixed. Always some damn thing. It used to annoy the hell out of me. You either love the real estate business or you don't.'

Torres and Dominique both began to laugh.

'I'm serious,' said Ray. 'That's the way the junk business is.'

'Will you attend the funeral, Don Raimondo?' asked Torres.

'Oh, yes. Out of respect for the man's memory. Since there's no corpse, it's not a funeral in the real sense. But I understand that there will be a memorial high mass in Rome. I hear that all of his colleagues will be there. After all, he was an important figure—a leader and a statesman.'

'I will say this,' said Torres. 'He was a most able man from your descriptions. I hope we never become entangled with another.'

'Amen,' said Dominique.

'Amen,' echoed Ray gravely. 'Let him rest in peace.'

CHAPTER 14

Quinto Babbi took Ray, step by step, through the preparations which he had made. 'I was going to set the buffets and bars out in the patio around the pool,' he said, 'with the garden for a background. It would have been most attractive. However, the evenings are becoming cool and clammy. The weather isn't too promising, so we'll remain indoors.'

The big central hall or living room of the villa had a broad balcony running in a U shape on three sides. Staircases on either side of the room led up to the balcony, which gave access to the bedrooms. A long, crescent-shaped buffet table flanked by two bars had been set up at one end of the sixty-foot-long hall. The bartenders and the food servers were also entertainers of Quinto's selection. The open expanse of the central gathering area was spotted with couches and armchairs. Tiger skins and polar bear furs were spread at irregular intervals over the rugs.

'This stuff is out now,' said Ray, pointing at the skins.

'So I hear,' said Quinto. 'However, these animals were shot by the prince before ecology became fashionable.'

'That man shoot?' said Ray. 'The way he impressed me, the only thing he could shoot was a load of horse into his vein. But, you know, I never noticed the quality of this stuff before. He certainly didn't spare the expense.'

'He had good taste,' said Quinto. 'This room is magnificently dimensioned. The secret of beauty in interior decorating is dimension—generous size and lofty ceilings. When you have that, everything falls into place naturally. You achieve a majestically underfurnished effect. The most carefully designed thirty-foot room can never equal the dignity of one twice the size.'

'Forget it, Quinto,' said Ray. 'You're talking about a pre-income tax world when the big spenders could really spend it all. In Manhattan we just don't have the space for this sort of thing. Compared to this setup, the biggest Park Avenue apartment looks like a group of packing cases.' He looked around. 'The American robber barons of the Gay Nineties would have dug this. When they sat down to lunch in their Newport cottages, they had fifty flunkeys handing the soup around. You can't do that nowadays; it's a different kind of world.'

Quinto smiled. 'When Louis the Fourteenth sat down to lunch the first course alone consisted of thirty different kinds of soup. When the cardinal Alessandro Farnese partook of a light luncheon alone, three hundred footmen in the livery of the Casa Farnese attended him. His entrance was announced by trumpeters and a full orchestra, his own private one, played while he ate.'

'How about that! What was *his* racket?'

'If I take your meaning, his lovely younger sister was Pope Alexander the Sixth's mistress. They called him the Petticoat Cardinal. That was his first step on the ladder to sanctity. We Babbis supervised Il Farnese's domiciliary arrangements also.'

'It does make the Du Ponts and the Vanderbilts look like country cousins,' admitted Ray. 'What did he have for lunch, whole roast boars stuffed with gilded swans?'

'Oh, no. Il Farnese was an ascetic eater. He usually contented himself with a chicken wing and a glass of white wine. Sometimes a peppered hard-boiled egg and a plum tart.'

'Three hundred flunkeys, eh? And a lot of people blowing on bugles when you walk into the room. You know, Quinto, I like that. It has class.'

'Il Farnese fed, clothed, and maintained these people,' Quinto pointed out. 'Of course, he had twenty times as much space in his palace. He supported between eight hundred and nine hundred souls in his household. Would *you* be able to do that?'

'And pay in social security benefits on all of them? Not on today's dollar. With a layout like that, I wouldn't be able to get my own work done.'

225

'It was a way of life. It also had its disadvantages. One was, in a sense, the prisoner of protocol, etiquette, and one's dependents. Come, *Signor* Occhiaccio, let me show you some of the bedrooms upstairs.'

They entered a room upholstered in dark-green silk. The floor was covered with wine-colored deep pile carpeting. Quinto pointed out the mirrored ceiling.

'I see,' said Ray. 'You're spending my money like it was going out of style. Look at that bed. It looks like it could hold three couples, with room to spare for the in-laws.'

'It was so designed.' Quinto raised the bedspread and indicated the shimmering black sheets. 'Pure satin.'

'It's because they're black, not because they're satin.'

'It heightens the effect and pleases the eye of discerning persons.'

'A girl's white butt on black sheets,' said Ray thoughtfully. 'Very effective. It should make for good photography.'

'I have three excellent photographers standing by. They are specialists for this type of work and their lighting is already installed. It can be switched on immediately for a long sequence.'

'I want some studies of Donato Saracino in action. Keep your boys on close tap. I'll give you the word.'

'The *questore*? Isn't that risky?'

'In my business, you have to think big, Quinto. Like that Al Farnese of yours. I'm not playing for buttons either.'

Again, Ray took in the entire room. 'Yech! It's like a cordial that's too heavy and too sweet. Real whorehouse modern.'

'No, no. Not modern at all. This was inspired by François Premiere, the greatest libertine of the sixteenth century. The mirrors and the black sheets were of his design. The background heightened his enjoyment.'

'He's the one that caught the Big Joe, wasn't he?'

'I beg your pardon?'

'Syphilis.'

'Oh, that! They all had it. I suppose better personal hygiene might have prevented it. But they didn't think along those lines. Huge, drafty bedrooms, gold-and-ivory chamber

226

pots, and never enough bathrooms. The odors were never entirely masked by perfume and lofty ceilings.'

'They still aren't,' said Ray. 'Give me a nice snug Holiday Inn Motel suite any day.'

Quinto smiled. 'You remain incorrigibly American, *signor*.'

'I'm glad to hear that. I'll tell you something, Quinto. You Europeans don't know how to live.'

The late Roberto Greco had been a personal friend of *Questore* Saracino's. The cop's bloodhounds were beginning to nose and sniff too closely. It was rumored, though unproven, that the *questore* had attained his high post in part through Greco's influence. I'll lay odds, thought Ray, that Saracino was on Greco's private payroll for a piece of the action. It would have been Greco's style to have given Saracino some key details of his dealings with me, just in case anything went wrong. So the name of the game is to try to discourage the cops. Let the bloodhounds go loping around for clues in the Greco case all they wish. Let them come up with some plausible theories and make it look good for the press. Just keep it away from Mrs. Occhiaccio's boy.

No question, Saracino was a swinger. He took and he played. After Ray had compiled a little file on the *questore*'s personal sexual preferences, he put his plan into effect. He had tossed a few preliminary warm-up bashes at his apartment, just to get the feel of the thing. It was at one of these that he had lighted on an American actress named Leona Downing. Leona was a tall, voluptuous, leggy redhead. She was also broke and impressed Ray as a likely mullet with which to hook Saracino. The particular party during which he had spotted Leona had been something of a washout. Ray had been inviting the Bubbis and the Nikkis. He wanted to look them over as possible courier material for the junk which was packed and ready to go, if, as, and when. 'Some of them make useful couriers,' Greco had said. 'Those who themselves have expensive habits to support take their pay in drugs.'

'Can you trust them with a valuable shipment?' Ray had asked.

'Up to a point, yes,' said Greco. 'They don't have the enterprise or the capital to become entrepreneurs. The central concern of their lives is to maintain a sure personal source of supply. In that context, you can trust them.'

'Have you had any double crosses?' said Ray.

'Relatively few,' Greco replied. 'Though addicts, they're intelligent enough to realize that they are vulnerable. After all, they inject chemicals into their bloodstream on faith. They are, thus, the easiest targets in the world. Perforce, they must be honest.'

'It adds up,' said Ray.

His party invitations were enthusiastically accepted. It was still chic among the blue-blood and the Italian rich kids to be not only American and Bohemian but hippie. The American showbiz freeloader contingent also showed up regularly. And this interesting Mr. Ray Hodgkin seemed to understand what amused the kids. The sprigs with the old titles and the long names turned up at Ray's bashes readily enough, fashionable in an amorphous shabbiness and exuding a vague unisexuality. One had to feel them in the crotch if one was interested in identifying them. Ray made his way through the crowd studying them as he went. The vacant and vapid expressions of the females—that was the in-pose of the moment. Perhaps pot or the stronger depressants. A freakish, unprepossessing lot. His apartment was now often filled with bearded, unwashed young men. The longer their ancestry the ranker their odor. Following one party, Ray and Quinto Babbi surveyed the mess and the wreckage after the last guest had departed. This was, indeed the body odor generation.

'Quinto,' said Ray, 'when I was a boy, it was a difficult matter to take a bath. Most of the time I went to the public bathhouse and paid a quarter. It was less trouble than at home. What about you?'

'Fortunately, *signor*, we Babbis were always in comfortable circumstances. I never had difficulty in maintaining high standards of personal cleanliness and hygiene.'

Ray gestured after the departed guests. 'These people aren't exactly poor, if that's what you mean. They have bathrooms in their homes, even if this *is* Italy. They know what soap is.'

'Indeed, *signor*, these young people come from aristocratic and affluent homes. They certainly know what soap and bathrooms are.'

'So what do you make of it?'

'It's the new religion, *signor*. The expression is, I believe, the in-thing. My private theory is that what you describe as the body odor generation has regressed to a form of primitive Christianity, to the Dark Ages, to the self-mortifying hermits who equated dirt with godliness—that sort of thing.'

'Look at what they did to my Persian rug. They defecated on it. Deliberately. Look at those drapes. They burned cigarette holes in them.'

'Think of it as their form of mysticism,' said Quinto serenely. 'They are retreating from the world in their efforts to achieve a closer communion with the Universal Spirit.'

'Fine,' said Ray, 'but do they have to leave a trail of excrement behind?'

'From their viewpoint,' said Quinto, 'your concern with mundane objects is excessive, unworthy, and irrelevant.'

'That rug cost me five thousand dollars,' said Ray. 'Since when was five grand irrelevant?' His eyes turned dreamy. 'I have a final solution for these types. I'd turn them all over to Torres. I'd let him take them down into the Tuareg country.'

'To do what, *signor*?'

'Shovel sand, stark naked. Drag it from one place to another. And Torres standing over them with a whip and a gun. And the sun beating in their skulls till they go up in smoke.'

Quinto nodded. 'It may come to that.'

When Ray approached Leona with his proposition, he expected from her neither anger nor sharp rejection. He knew her financial straits. The sum of money he offered would be enough to give her pause.

Leona listened calmly. 'I've never worked stags before,' she said.

'Good enough,' said Ray. 'I just thought I'd ask.'

Leona sighed. 'I'd certainly like to go home. I'm tired of this imitation New York. I have a passport. I'm an American. All I need is return flight money.'

'You're one up on me,' said Ray. 'I don't have the passport. The money? Well, if you want to get back badly enough——'

'What do you want me to do?'

'A blue spot,' said Ray testing the water. 'With that stud we had here last week, Giovannino. He's American—well, half American.'

Leona grimaced. 'I've never done anything like that.' She stared at Ray. 'Before cameras?'

'Of course, before cameras. But they'll be concealed.'

'And the photographs?'

'They'll go into the wholesale market.'

'Man!' said Leona. 'Are you in a dirty business!'

'No business that shows such a high percentage of profit is dirty.'

'The photos will start circulating and they'll get back to the States,' said Leona. 'Somebody will get their hands on them, trace me, and have me over a barrel for blackmail.'

'That's the chance you have to take.'

Leona shook her head. 'Uh, uh. Too dangerous.'

'Very well. I have another proposition for you. After all, I'm not twisting your arm.'

Leona shook her head decisively. 'I don't even want to hear it. That blue stuff is out.'

'You're being unrealistic. No job. No money. Where do you go from here? Call girl?'

'Why not? It's private and it certainly should pay better.'

'To get into the call girl business here you need connections and protection. This isn't America. You get on your uppers here, I mean, really against the wall, and you're liable to wind up in Tangier with nothing to say about your hours and working conditions. And Tangier is only the launching pad. From there, it's all south and all downhill.'

Leona tried to conceal her uneasiness.

'I have a friend here,' said Ray. 'He served in North Africa for twenty-five years. In the Foreign Legion. He can tell you how it is when you gradually start getting down farther and farther south. It's hard on a girl, worse than the old wild West. It's wild all right, Arab wild. To them, a female is a few cuts under a riding horse. You won't last long.'

Leona was contemptuous. 'What are you trying to do, frighten me?'

'Just giving you the lowdown.'

'I'll go to the American consul.'

'That might have worked in the old days. Not any more. He's got more goddamned hippies, freakouts, and bums on the loose now than he knows what to do with. He's not equipped for the kind of cultural fallout he's getting today. All American citizens and he hates their guts. I know—I've talked with him. Now, this new deal I have for you——'

'Leona gave him a flat stare. 'All right,' she said wearily, 'let's hear it.'

'I'm hosting a party next week,' said Ray. 'I have a certain high Italian official coming to the party. No names. Incognito. He likes American girls like you. Tall ones. Redheads. He'll dig you. All I want is for you to be nice to him for one night. Then I pay you off the same night and you can blow.'

'How much?'

'Five thousand American dollars. And I'll throw in one first-class seat on Pan Am.'

'What do I have to do?'

'Are you kidding? Are you trying to play games with me? Get smart, Leona. You're meat, just live meat. You're less than nothing. You're a female, an alien, and broke. You're dirt.'

'I just asked what I have to do.'

'What in the hell do you think you have to do? Just lie back and open your legs. What else have you got to offer—talent?'

Leona bit her lip and gripped her frustrated anger. 'Is this politician a sadist of some kind? Does he like to hit girls with leather belts, burn them with cigarette butts?'

'You're goddamned lucky you're not getting that kind of a deal,' said Ray. 'It so happens this man's civilized. All he's crazy about is to go down on an American broad. That's how he gets his jollies.'

'That's all?' said Leona skeptically. 'He eats, that's all?'

'That's all. Maybe he might want to ball you straight once. Or twice, if he's got delusions of grandeur. After all, this guy's no stud, no chicken. He's just a nice family man in his early sixties with a wife and children, and maybe grandchildren. Hell, this man's just hunting for a little American glamor.

Everybody gets a different screw loose, especially when they get older. His wife is a very pious, strict woman.' Ray grinned. 'He has no joy of her. Basically, this guy's an eater. Very innocent.'

'And, of course, you're going to take photos?'

'You'd better believe it, kid. That's the point of the game. But not of you. Only of the John. He may be a big wheel in Italy, but he's only a john to me. It's his face I want, clear and recognizable, eating you.'

'And me?'

'Stop worrying,' said Ray. 'Your head will be positioned on the pillow so your face won't be identifiable.'

'I wouldn't trust you or your photographer.'

'Good-bye. Good luck.'

'Can I put a scarf or something over my face?' said Leona.

'You can put a potato sack over your face, for all I care. You're not reading your hand right, kid. You've got a busted straight and I'm calling.'

Leona finally shrugged. 'It's a deal.'

'The easiest five grand you ever made. You've done it for free with men, with women, dozens of times——'

'Never,' said Leona.

'Tell that to the seals in Central Park,' said Ray. 'You play this new hand right, you'll soon be seeing them. Get smart! Give this poor family slob a little fun and get paid for it. You'll be a real boy scout.'

'Go to hell,' smiled Leona with hatred in her eyes. 'Maybe I'll have a chance to pay you back.'

'You're like all American broads,' said Ray, 'a stupid, snotty castrater. You overestimate your own value. You'll never pay me back anything.'

'Only the man's face?' said Leona. 'You're in a big dice game, Mr. Hodgkin.'

'You just worry about your end of the picture. Okay?'

'Okay,' said Leona.

While the American expatriate freeloader bums and the blue-blooded wop bums were swinging at Ray's expense, while Quinto Babbi was lining up his big bash, Ray was busy

232

with New York. He passed the word by courier to Nicky Polo and Tony Saldana: What's the current market on ninety percent pure? The word came back: The importers were offering seventeen and a half per key. Which meant a profit of three and a half millions. The buy money to Mahmoudi had been canceled out by the snatch money for the late Luigi Antonio. Three and a half millions. That would buy a lot of good legal talent when he surrendered in the U.S.A. on an unlawful re-entry charge. The talent alone, no matter how capable and willing, might not be able to swing an acquittal by itself. But there would still be plenty left to buy a few more trump cards, even after he had paid off Juan Torres and Dominique Maestracci.

Saldana, Polo, and Beniamino didn't handle junk. They had never wanted to. In any case, they didn't know the business. The only one in the Family who had been active in this traffic on his own had been Al Poggio, the subboss. Poggio used to go in on deals with Len Codi, who was one of the biggest importers in New York. Ray's negative attitude toward Al Poggio was based in part on the fact of Poggio's constant dealings with Don Leonardo Codi, one of the slipperiest, trickiest bastards outside of a cemetery, where he properly belonged. Codi was a short man, not more than five foot five. He wore highly polished elevator shoes. A long time ago, Ray had come to the conclusion: Beware of small men. He made no generalization of it. It was simply the resultant of his own experience. Small men were touchy, peppery bantam cocks. The paranoia was built into their lack of height. Codi was going on sixty-five and physically defenseless on a personal basis, which was an academic point. Personal strength was as irrelevant in a boss as in a modern general or a federal judge. The executive had available plenty of muscle to do his bidding. The strength was in Codi's eyes—the strength and the singleness of purpose which had raised him from slumhood infancy to wealth, the ownership of pieces in fifty different corporations. And there was one more point against Codi. He was as ruthless about taking a man's last dime as his last million. Success had not inculcated into Codi that primitive magnanimity which restrained people from stealing a beggar's pencils and tin cup.

233

Codi, on the heights, had only recently become the subject of a joke going the rounds with those in the know—he had become involved in an argument with a blind news vendor whom he had tried to shortchange. Those who knew Codi were neither shocked nor surprised. Mean, cheap bastard was the general verdict. He's always been that way. He's still got the first two bits he ever rolled from a drunk.

Codi was and had always been hungry. This, despite the fact that he owned a two-hundred-acre landscaped estate in Connecticut, another waterfront estate in Fort Lauderdale, and a seventeen-hundred-acre ranch in Arizona which specialized in the breeding of Santa Gertrudis cattle and in harvesting substantial tax offsets. Codi also had oil wells in Texas, high-rises in Miami Beach, tract developments in San Diego (completed and sold before high interest rates had hit the construction loan money market), and lucrative rapid transit franchises. Codi had all of these things, but he was the kind of man who wanted to be able to sit on six toilet seats simultaneously. '*Ma*,' said those who knew him best, 'it's a tapeworm in his belly, a fever that will not abate.'

Ray had heard these stories about Codi from Don Oliverotto, the elder statesman, godfather, patron, and all-powerful protector of Ray's Brooklyn beginnings. Don Amerigo LoCroce, a boss emeritus now retired in Princeton, New Jersey, who knew Codi best, had once told Oliveretto, 'It won't surprise you to learn that Codi is having two custom-designed burial caskets constructed for himself secretly. He does everything secretly. I understand that the caskets will be vacuum-sealed. The engineering firm is equipping them with all the amenities of a Gay Nineties private railroad car.'

'You're not serious,' said Oliverotto.

'Indeed I am,' said Amerigo. 'Codi intends to make the big jump like a pharaoh—always secretly, but in style.'

'One of the caskets is for his wife,' said Oliverotto.

'Never,' said Amerigo. 'Codi is too mean for that.'

'Then, why two?'

'That is style,' said Amerigo. 'One of the beginnings of wisdom is to accept the fact that many men are selectively mad. Such a one is our brother, Don Leonardo Codi.'

So on this junk exporting deal, the way it broke down, Ray was stuck with Poggio, the man he trusted least, and with Codi.

The merchandise had gradually begun to move. The first fifty kilos of it went over cached in the specially built compartment of a 280 SL Mercedes-Benz sedan. Dominique flew up to Stuttgart to pick up the car. He drove it down to Naples. There he had a mechanic who specialized in customized body alterations go to work on it. The mechanic removed the fuel tank and installed a new one almost twice as large, yet unobtrusively so. The new tank had been internally fitted with two liquid-tight compartments, each one holding twenty-five kilos of heroin. When the new fuel tank had been installed, Dominique had handed the transaction to a customs broker who had been approved by Francisco Tamburelli. Dominique paid the freight charges and prepaid the import duties on a used car. By courier, Ray had notified Tony Saldana, who reluctantly accepted delivery of the Mercedes in New York. Tony had reported back later that it had all gone well enough. The customs people in New York had checked the car over a bit and put their release stamp on the windshield and one of Tony's boys had driven it off the pier and up the West Side Highway. Sure, it took nerve, at least twenty years in a federal pen worth of nerve. But Tony had handled that step of the route for old time's sake. Tony had turned the Mercedes over to Poggio, who had disposed of the shipment to an importer at the agreed price of seventeen and a half. On this fifty-kilo shipment. Poggio took off a small acceptable commission for services and forwarded the net sales proceeds to Rome by courier. Ray received the money with a feeling of relief and surprise.

Since the pattern had worked well, Ray decided to repeat it. He got in touch with Francisco Tamburelli on this occasion.

They met and had a leisurely lunch together. After the lunch, Ray asked: 'What do you hear from Renato?'

'He seems to be doing well,' said Tamburelli. 'He has received a good offer to purchase a fine retail pharmacy and he is presently negotiating it. At any rate, he and his family appear to be happier in Tunis. With his present nest egg he feels more secure. And I feel easier about his future. Thanks to you.'

'Glad to hear that,' said Ray. 'I had in mind the possibility that you might be able to do me a small favor.'

'If I can.'

'I understand you have some connections with the student exchange program between Italian and American universities.'

'True,' said Tamburelli. 'As a matter of fact, I helped set up the exchange program between the University of Rome and the University of Chicago.'

'Then you know or have means of finding out certain Italian students who may be going over to the U.S.A. on the exchange program, and when.'

'I can find it out.'

'Please do, indirectly and discreetly.'

'What do you have in mind?'

'A friend in New York wishes to buy my Ferrari. It's now two years old and he'll give me an excellent price for it, practically as much as I paid for it. Of course, I must deliver it for him in New York City. Find me a clean-cut exchange student to take the Ferrari over on the ship as his own car. He'll get two hundred and fifty dollars before he leaves. When the ship docks, he'll be met at the pier by this friend of mine who will give him another two hundred and fifty. These young people get little enough in the way of scholarships. I'm sure they can use the money.'

While Ray awaited word from Tamburelli, Dominique drove the Ferrari down to Naples, where the same mechanic modified the Ferrari's gas tank for the reception of fifty kilos of heroin, as he had the Mercedes. Tamburelli notified Ray that he had located a suitable candidate, one Carlo Riccioni, who was traveling to the United States and who would be entering the Graduate School of the University of Chicago in economics. This young man would be glad of the opportunity to declare the automobile as his own and to earn a five-hundred-dollar commission. Ray did not meet Riccioni. He turned the prepared Ferrari over to Tamburelli who, in turn, had it delivered to Riccioni.

Ray passed the details as well as how to identify Riccioni to Nicky Polo in New York. Like Beniamino, Nicky Polo was reluctant. Nevertheless, he picked up the Ferrari when it arrived, paid off Riccioni, and delivered the merchandise to Poggio. Nicky Polo sold the car in New York and sent the money back to Ray. This was something which Poggio would not have done. Meanwhile, Poggio disposed of the second shipment of the heroin and sent back the proceeds, less his usual commission.

For the time being, Ray decided not to press his luck too far. It was time to vary the routine. Half the consignment had been shipped across and disposed of successfully. A new method was in order.

The new method materialized in the person of Lieutenant Desmond O'Brien, U.S.A.F., who had attended a couple of Ray's parties with Leona Downing. The Air Force man, Ray found out, had a job ferrying planes back and forth between Italy and the United States. An angle player. A guy who had ways of cutting himself in on anything that wasn't nailed down, including extra furloughs that he didn't rate. O'Brien was a liberator of things, for O'Brien. At the moment he was on furlough, living high off the hog and having a ball in Rome. Ray recognized the type. He had met enough of them in the Army. They were the guys who always organized the crap and poker games and took their cut off the top. They always had watches and booze to sell. They performed wonders for themselves whenever they got their hooks into an officers' or enlisted men's service club. They always had cozy connections on the local black market when one was in existence. They were the merchants of the Army and the Air Force. From the few things O'Brien had said when he was a little drunk, and from Ray's own experience in sizing up people, O'Brien was a man with whom one could do business. He phoned the lieutenant at his hotel and made an appointment to meet him in the bar. The hotel was plush—too expensive for a lieutenant's pay. From Ray's viewpoint, that was promising. This fly-boy had big tastes and liked to play around. He had a wife and two kids back in the States. From Ray's viewpoint, O'Brien's cheating on his wife was also good. It nailed down the picture tighter. This guy would handle. Right.

O'Brien was pleased. He knew the score as to Ray's status. Not only didn't he care, he was definitely interested. Wherever hoods came down to rest, could a little easy money be far behind? The two went together. O'Brien was money-smart, too—smarter than an O'Brien should be. But why should one say that? thought Ray. The acquisitive drive in one form or another wasn't the exclusive property of any particular ethnic group. The Irish had done very well for themselves in the big cities of America, if not in actual cash, then in political clout, which was even better. The Irish had carved themselves a solid niche in America.

'Glad to see you, Hodgkin,' said O'Brien. 'What's on your mind? Throwing another party?'

'Pretty soon,' said Ray. 'A real big bash this time. Will you still be in Rome next week? It'll be at my villa down on the coast, not in the apartment.'

O'Brien nodded. 'I have ten days leave left. Count me in. You got a country house also? You must be loaded.'

'You get nothing on the cuff,' said Ray. 'I have to hustle to support my layout. It takes plenty of loot.'

O'Brien narrowed his eyes and continued to grin. 'I'll bet it does.'

Ray's gesture took in the elegant, luxurious barroom and the quiet, skillful waiters. 'It's none of my business, but isn't this place a little steep for a looie's pay?'

'I manage,' said O'Brien. 'A fellow tries to develop a little income on the side. With a wife and two kids you have to. You know, a little here, a little there.'

'Well, now that there's no real black market operating in this country, it must be a little tough to make money. I mean, some real money.'

O'Brien shrugged. 'I do all right.'

'You ferry planes back and forth. Right?'

O'Brien nodded.

The fly-boys were a natural, thought Ray. Better than ships, which went through customs, much better than civilian aircraft. The fly-boys went straight from one military airfield to another. Eventually someone got careless and the pilot who took a chance would get nailed. But the odds were good that a man like O'Brien would get through at least once. Maybe more than once; but Ray would be satisfied if the pilot got

238

twenty-five keys across for him.

'I know something about your side operation, lieutenant,' said Ray. 'Swiss watches, perfume, a little gold, crap like that. Right?'

O'Brien was noncommittal. 'It's a few hundred bucks a month on the side.'

'Chicken feed,' said Ray. 'I can offer you a better deal.'

'Go ahead.'

'When you get back to your base, where will you be flying to in the States?'

'Westover.'

'That's the one up in Massachusetts?'

'Right.'

'How would you like to take a package over for me?'

'What kind of package?'

'Just a package. Somebody will meet you in the nearest town and take it off your hands.'

'How big and heavy? You know, they watch weight on a plane.'

'Say, as heavy as your loaded Val-A-Pak. You'll still be able to put some of your personal gear into it, not too much. But it'll be worth it to you.'

'How heavy?' asked O'Brien.

'A little over fifty pounds. Fifty-five pounds to be exact.'

'I won't be able to take any of my own personal gear.'

'For the money you'll be earning, you'll be able to do some tall shopping.'

'Sounds very valuable, that package,' said O'Brien casually.

'Not to you, sonny. It wouldn't be worth a lead slug to you.'

'But I might get Leavenworth if I'm picked up with it. Right?'

Ray raised his eyebrows. 'The higher the return, the higher the risk. Let me give you a friendly piece of advice about this package. Don't get any ideas about it. You think about it as anything but sand, you're a dead pigeon.'

'How much?'

'I'll have the package delivered to your hotel here with twelve hundred and fifty bucks. The man who picks it up at the other end will give you another twelve hundred and fifty in

239

an envelope.'

O'Brien nodded and at the same time felt annoyed with himself. If he had shown more initiative and asked for five thousand, they might have settled for thirty-five hundred. But it was too late now. 'Okay,' he said. 'Done.'

'Good show,' said Ray. 'I'll have the package dropped off here the night before you check out to return to base.'

They shook hands and Ray got up to leave. 'I want you to come to my party, O'Brien. Next week. You'll have a real workout.'

'How do I get there?'

'Don't worry about that,' said Ray. 'One of my friends will pick you up at your hotel and drive you there and take you back. Deluxe service.'

Ray departed well satisfied. Twenty-five keys was about the maximum that the pilot would be able to handle in one flight. If there were only more people around with larceny in their hearts and the guts to implement their larceny, life could be a lot simpler for him. In the meantime he was moving steadily closer to the promised land. It was easy enough to get yourself thrown down the cliff. It was hard as hell to climb back up. But he would do it.

CHAPTER 15

The muted, cunning lighting arrangements in the big hall camouflaged and blotted out the tired lines in human faces. The vulnerable faces, throats, and hands of women were softened and smoothed by the skill of Quinto Babbi's lighting men. Some hundred people milled about in the hall, on the staircases, and on the U-shaped balcony, chattering, exchanging greetings, looking for some person in particular, or cruising for anything which looked promising. Both bars were busy serving and the guests were loosening themselves up with a slow but steady intake of alcohol.

Ray, in a dinner jacket, stood on the balcony and examined the crowd beneath. O'Brien, in civilian clothing, stood beside him.

'That's a pretty well-dressed crowd,' said Ray, 'not like the young creeps who've been breaking up my place in Rome.'

'Quite a few young ones here tonight,' said O'Brien. 'Very attractive looking kids. They look like they scrubbed their necks and ears well and took haircuts.'

'Those are the people from Quinto's agency,' said Ray. 'They're here to make sure that the guests have a good time. No man is going to be brushed off because he's bald and pot-bellied—that is, if he's in the mood for a little fun. It works the same way for the woman. Just because a chick is sixty years old and doesn't have competitive equipment doesn't mean she doesn't want to get laid. If she does, there's going to be some polite, capable young man around to lay her any way she wants. To me, that makes sense.'

'What are you personally getting out of this?' said O'Brien.

'I sometimes wonder,' said Ray. 'I enjoy seeing people

241

swinging and balling it. It seems to relax me a little. Also, this is going to be a sort of going-away party.'

'Going away—where?'

'Back to the U.S.A.,' said Ray. 'Just thinking about it makes me feel friendly toward the human race, and that's something. The last time I was in Italy, that was during the big war, I felt the same way. I just wanted to get home. But I didn't for a long time. I had to slog through North Africa, Sicily, Italy, and southern France.'

'That so? What branch of the service were you in?'

'The real Army, the infantry.' Ray touched O'Brien's arm. 'See that tall, leggy blonde, the one in the pale-green evening gown? She's holding onto that tall man with the iron-gray hair.'

O'Brien looked. 'The one with that padded, pointed uplift bra?'

'That's no padding, son. Those two things are real.'

O'Brien emitted a low growl-grunt-wolf-whistle. 'Yum, yum.'

'That's Alda Quirini,' said Ray, 'the gal thousands of men keep thinking about when they're screwing their wives.'

'Mighty fine,' said O'Brien. 'She looks good in skin, even better than on screen. Who's the lucky character she's with?'

'Nobody. Just the man she came in with. As far as males are concerned, Alda makes her own schedule. What makes her even more attractive to a lot of people is the fact that she's loaded. Alda is not only a good actress, she's a damn good investor. Believe me, that enhances her sexuality. So Alda can take her pick, and she does. Very active hormones that girl has.'

'She's a charger, eh?'

'If you mean by that she likes to fuck, you're right.'

'Mmmmmmmmmmmmmm! How do you get on the waiting list?'

'Do you want an introduction?'

'You know her?'

'Well enough. She was a close friend of a close friend of mine.'

'Was?'

242

'Poor guy passed away. Maybe he died in Alda's arms.'

'I'd love to die like that,' said O'Brien with feeling. 'Please do introduce me. The Air Force will take over from there.'

Ray looked O'Brien over. 'You look pretty sharp in tailored clothes. You're about twenty years younger than I am. Handsome guy, good physique. What sport did you go in for at the academy?'

'Boxing mostly.'

'Good thing they didn't flatten your nose. On the other hand, with certain females, scars and busted bridges sometimes make a man sexier. Alda might just go for a blue-eyed black Irishman like yourself. With a man-eater like Alda you have to deliver, though.'

'Deliver what?'

Ray slapped his stiffened right forearm with his left hand. 'The goods. Looks alone cut no mustard. She wants action, not talk. You notice the ratio down there? About one and a half females per male. And a lot of the males here are gay, or too old, or out of condition for a number of reasons. Not too many boys around here who can handle that mare. So maybe you'll get yourself a ride. It'll be something to keep you company on you're homebound flight.'

O'Brien stared after Alda's slim, gracefully undulating hips and nodded. 'Yessir. That could keep me warm all the way back to Westover. If I'm not being too personal, have you ever made a play for her?'

'No,' said Ray. 'I'm not in Alda's division sexually. After I've blown my load two times, three tops, I'm ready to sit back and talk philosophy. A gal like Alda's just getting started. She expects a fucking machine. Also, she's a little too aggressive for me, too American. I like my broads small, peaceful, and easygoing. A gal like Alda can chew up a man and spit him out. I prefer the Japanese school, Thais, Hindus, Chinese. They have a different slant about men. Even when you can't get it up with them, they still make you feel like you are really the emperor of Siam. If you feel like fucking, they'll fuck. If you don't feel like it, or can't, they'll listen to you like you were Christ Almighty delivering the Gettysburg Address, you know what I mean?'

'Well, I'm willing to square off with that broad, if I can. She can chew me up all she wants.'

'Fine,' said Ray with a show of interest. 'I'll see what I can do.' He was studying Donato Saracino, the big cop. The man was tall and rangy with a hollow-cheeked face, deep-set, restless eyes and a wide, sensual mouth set in a fixed smile. A good manhunter. That was his rep. Maybe. That was what had gotten him to the top of the heap. That, and a talent for politics. Ray was willing to bet that it was the ambitious wheeling and dealing more than the merit which had boosted Saracino to top dog. He was running the investigation on the Greco case, not because he gave a damn about his late buddy-buddy (the Saracinos of the world kept their eyes on one target only) but to boost his own political stock. So this obviously political cop had brains. Brains he had plenty of. Would he fall for the stale trick which Ray had set up with that American broad? He really didn't have to fall for anything. Leona Downing was good eating stuff on any menu for those who dug that kind of apple pie. And plenty of people did. And nothing wrong with it, either: low in calories, low in heartburn, high in protein. Although he himself was not of the partakers, he took a tolerant, even a benevolent, view of cunnilinctors. That part of it was okay. What Saracino wouldn't hold still for was the blackmail threat posed by photographs. So why was he going to all the trouble if Saracino would just laugh and spit at the art work? A good question. The man wouldn't be intimidated exactly: Saracino didn't look like the kind of guy that scared easily. But, because he was politically ambitious, he wouldn't want any scandals either, or publicity from the news rags, which he hated. Besides, it wasn't really blackmail. Ray wasn't trying to squeeze money out of the big cop. On the contrary, all he wanted to do was to give the cop money to lay off. All Ray wanted was: Bury the Greco thing, file it, period. Saracino was a reasonable, intelligent guy. Ray felt confident that, on this two-pronged basis, he would be able to deal with the cop. So much of Ray's activity was excessively preventive in nature. Maybe he was wrong in being so careful, in anticipating so much ahead of time. Maybe, but it had paid off up until now. The Greco business had worked out well because he had chopped off every threat in sight and come out ahead. As long as it worked, he would continue to follow that policy.

'Come on, O'Brien,' he said. 'Let's go down and join the crowd. Since we're now business buddies, I'll see if I can't get you next to that Roman bomb. If you can get into her, it'll be a free bonus, like, on the house.'

'Lead on, Macduff,' said O'Brien.

They moved slowly down the staircase through the crowd and threaded their way through the groups on the main floor. Most of the faces were unfamiliar to Ray. Marvelous how people turned up from nowhere, from the woodwork, for a party. You didn't have to know people. Just provide the place, the food, and the liquor, and the friends of the friends you're not sure you ever met will be sure to bring *their* friends. Be popular. Be a host. Yeah, right. This mob was already three-quarters loaded and getting noisy. A rock band had started to smash up the decibel count like a squad of marine jets screaming down into your middle ear. You couldn't hear yourself think. That, on top of the weird flashing, shifting lights which made people look like vampires with facial neuralgia. The pulsing, whirling multicolored lights and the massive sound assault from the fiendish rock musicians were providing an effective blanket of privacy. Better than total darkness, it somehow gave people the illusion of being completely alone. It coaxed them to put their alcohol-tenderized fantasies into action. There was a guy who had his hand up under a broad's dress and right into her crotch and she was loving it. Two. Three. Two broads feeling up each other. Two boys clinched in a passionate kiss. And nobody was looking. Everybody was doing is own thing. Great. Great. With O'Brien in tow, Ray caught up with Quinto Babbi in the crowd and yelled in his ear: 'That goddamned rock band, was it your idea?'

'One must keep up with the times,' Quinto yelled back.

'Al Farnese would never have stood still for this,' shouted Ray.

Quinto shrugged his shoulders and opened his hands. 'One must keep an open mind,' he shouted. He beckoned Ray and O'Brien to follow him into a small side room off the left-hand bar. They went in and Quinto closed the heavy fumed-oak door. The murderous cacophony of the rock musicians muffled down to a dull, thumping roar, like distant artillery. 'I just wanted to say,' said Quinto, 'that I've made a little study of the combined effects of these noise-and-light patterns. The lighting is hypnotic—that's a fact. The noise can injure your eardrums—that's incontestable. But it does have a sexually stimulating effect on people en masse. The audio-visual assault actually hammers their inhibitions out of them. After a while, each individual feels himself to be alone and free to do whatever he wishes. Add a pinch of drugs and a lot of them out there are flapping their wings. Among a smaller group of intellectually minded persons who know one another, say, a multisexual *festa* can be launched into motion as coldly and deliberately as a minuet. But with a large, amorphous mass such as this, they have to be stampeded over the cliff like the Gadarene swine.'

'Why do you have to try so hard?' said Ray. 'What's the matter with playing charades?'

'Why?' said Quinto. 'That's my function. Isn't that what you wanted?'

'True,' said Ray. 'I bought it, so I may as well enjoy it. Come on, O'Brien, no use being party-poopers. Let's get into the spirit of it. Quinto, see that the bartenders and the waiters don't steal too much. If there are any disturbances among the guests, report to Torres and Maestracci. They'll take care of anything that gets out of control.'

'I expect no violence from this crowd,' said Quinto. 'They'll find an abundance of other outlets for their energy. Noise and orgasms should keep them relatively peaceful.'

Ray and O'Brien pushed through the crowd and finally found Alda Quirini in the center of an admiring coterie of well-groomed limp-wristed young males. She turned to the newcomers with a pleased expression. 'Ah, a man! Two men!'

'Hello, Alda,' said Ray. 'May I present my friend, Lieutenant Desmond O'Brien?'

With an appraising smile, Alda offered the pilot her hand. 'What happened to Saracino?' asked Ray.

'He's probably off hunting something young and fresh,' said Alda. 'You know his tastes. Besides, he knows that I'm not interested in him.' She pressed against Ray and gripped his forearm between her long, sinuous fingers. 'But I'd like to become better acquainted with you.'

'You'd be wiser to make your selection from Quinto's stable of studs,' said Ray. 'They're all here tonight and most of them are already in the nude. Besides, I'm not that interested in sex.'

'Perhaps that's why I'm interested in you,' said Alda. 'You're an average in external appearance, but I'm rather attracted to preoccupied, ambitious men. They're a challenge, I suppose.'

'A thankless one, Alda,' said Ray. 'Besides, I'm on duty.'

Alda examined Ray with a smile which was sultry, skeptical, and, at the same time, indifferent. 'Why should you be off limits? You're at least a well-built man.'

'Don't pine,' said Ray. 'I'll give you a rain check. In the meantime, deign to consider my friend the lieutenant. He's dying to become better acquainted with you. He's twenty years younger than I, strong as a bull, and in complete agreement with your philosophy.'

Alda turned to the pilot. 'You come well recommended.'

'Thanks,' said O'Brien to Ray. 'That's quite an introduction.'

'Give it the old college try,' said Ray. 'See you later.'

'Raimondo,' said Alda, 'when you locate Saracino, make certain he enjoys himself. He wields considerable influence and has something to say about how successful and pleasant your life in Rome will be.'

'True,' said Ray. 'Take good care of our guest.'

Alda smiled up at O'Brien like a maternal and undernourished spider. 'He's in good hands.' She drew O'Brien after her and they vanished into the press of the crowd.

Quinto Babbi had silenced the rock-and-roll assassins by raising his hand. The breaking waves of shifting multicolored lights ceased from troubling and dimmed down to an eerie glow. With relief, the various groups halted their laborious conversational exchanges.

'Those who wish to disrobe are free to do so,' said Quinto. 'As you see, the professional among us have already done so.'

There was scattered applause.

'Our motto is tolerance, which is the mother of love,' continued Quinto. 'To disrobe is a psychologically constructive step because it's easier not to do so. As you shed the clothing which conceals your physical deficiencies, you also shed your irrational prejudices, inhibitions, and guilt feelings. The truth of the matter is that people are more acceptable in our eyes clothed than naked. Of course, if all the men were bronzed, muscular Adonises and all the women lithe, symmetrical nymphs, it would be a different matter. We all begin life as beautiful babies. See what happens as we run the gauntlet of time. If you think you can discern a partner's beautiful spirit through the imperfect flesh, by all means don't hesitate. The greater your reluctance, the greater your credit if you try. Obviously, many of you are not Venuses or Apollos. All humanity is flawed, so I say have no fear. We'll love you just as much.'

The guests cheered.

'Just be certain to safeguard your wardrobes,' concluded Quinto. 'Cupidity is easier to arouse than erotic desire.'

An hour later Ray spotted Alda Quirini and Desmond O'Brien coming down the staircase to the main hall. Alda, who was leading the airman possessively by the hand, was the most spectacular woman in the crowd. Ray went forward to join them, thinking, If only everyone else had a body like Alda's.

She returned his greeting with a radiant smile. 'Ah, Raimondo, still the self-abnegating host, I see.'

'Still,' he replied. 'And how are you two managing?'

'Famously,' said Alda. 'Desmond and I find that we have many interests in common.'

'We certainly do,' echoed the airman.

'It all sounds very domestic,' said Ray. 'As long as you two are making it on a first-name basis.'

Alda squeezed the pilot's hand. 'We're making it, as you Americans would say, aren't we, Desmond?'

'Great,' said Desmond heartily. 'Great.'

A nude Francisco Tamburelli came up to join them. He was accompanied by a small, shapely brunette with pert, upturned breasts. Tamburelli looked as uncomfortable as his female companion did not.

248

'Ah, Don Raimondo,' said Tamburelli with forced casualness, 'meet Liliana.'

Ray smiled and completed the introductions. 'Don Francisco,' he said judiciously, 'you look as insecure as a defrocked monsignor in a whorehouse. Does something here displease you?'

'Only that you have an unfair advantage of us,' said Tamburelli.

'Duty,' said Ray. 'Stern duty. The host is obliged to retain his trousers and see that everyone else is happy and at ease. Look around you. Only a relatively few of our guests now seem to be self-conscious. The initial trauma is disappearing. I agree, men are somewhat at a disadvantage in the nude, compared with women. Women, being less intelligent than men, are probably more accepting of themselves. That's my theory. You can also comfort yourself with this thought, Don Francisco. It's because men are innately more moral.'

'Innately more silly,' said Liliana, 'with all that awkward dangling equipment.'

'*Ma!*' said Ray opening his hands and shrugging good-naturedly. 'Look at all those handsome young men strutting around out there. They don't seem impeded by their genitalia. In fact, they're pirouetting about like peacocks.'

'Oh, they're not really guests,' said Liliana, 'they're *effeminatos*, swishy professionals who come here to entertain us. But, of course, they are more attractive physically.'

As they displayed themselves, Quinto Babbi's male agency referrals did seem to be quite at ease in the nude. Their female counterparts exuded a similar air of freedom and unconstraint. Obviously, their greater physical attractiveness had imbued them with confidence and a pleasant feeling of superiority over the opulent yet often more decrepit patrons whom they were there to service.

'It's difficult to distinguish here between the aristocrats and the prostitutes,' said Tamburelli. 'One can understand how the Communist Party feels about these people.'

'Charity,' said Ray. 'You'd be the first to go to the wall.'

'It won't happen in my lifetime.'

'Don't be so sure.'

'Don't smack your lips,' said Tamburelli peevishly. 'They'll get you, too, Don Raimondo.'

'I'll be home free by that time, in the good old U.S.A.'

'They'll find you there, also.'

'In this ragged little boot of an Italy, perhaps,' said Ray. 'In America, never. I know my country.'

Quinto Babbi dominated the festivities. He was that immemorial prototype who managed such festivities without taking part. That was plain from his bland, relaxed, and pleasant demeanor. He was the devil who did not partake, the madam who did not copulate, the procurer who did not sample his wares, the gambler who did not gamble, the classical course of all license who was not himself a sinner.

'I admire that man,' said Tamburelli. 'He is professionalism personified.'

Ray beckoned and Quinto came over, immaculate in full evening dress. 'And how does the affair suit you thus far, *Signor* Occhiaccio?' he said.

'Do you know what you remind me of?' said Ray.

'I have no idea,' said Quinto.

'An eminent proctologist peering up an emperor's rectum for suspicious tumors.'

'In my position it's necessary to be neutral and detached,' said Quinto.

'Exactly.'

'What I admire about you, Quinto,' said Tamburelli, 'is your ability to remind everyone, queens, saints, and geniuses included, that they all have anuses.'

'And he never sits in judgment,' put in Alda Quirini.

Ray raised his glass. 'To your good health, Quinto. You're holding up a mirror here to a most convincing collection of asses.'

Quinto raised a deprecating hand. 'I don't even see nudity.'

'That's what I mean.'

'You've referred quite a few homosexual men here, Quinto,' said Alda.

'Does it meet with you disapproval?' said Quinto.

'I suppose not,' she replied. 'Aside from my personal needs, I actually prefer them as people. I find gay men somewhat

250

more civilized.'

'Gay people, male and female, are fine in my book,' said Ray. 'They tend to underreproduce, which is the best recommendation.'

Alda cast an appreciative glance at the oversized phallus of a passing stud. 'Goodness, Quinto,' she said, 'it that creature from your stable?'

'That's Peppino Ingrao, one of my prize young bulls,' said Quinto. 'He is much in demand. His is a veritable flagstaff, a symbol of the majesty of the people, a weapon of offense with which that lad could drive all the titled parasites of Italy into the sea.'

Liliana pointed to the pseudo-engorgement of Francisco Tamburelli's organ. 'Francisco, why does yours look so dejected and indecisive?'

Tamburelli glanced down hopefully. 'Because it's an intellectual. I call it Hamlet. Don't discourage it any more than you need. It needs all the morale it can get.'

'It's almost a mathematical precept,' said Alda. 'A man's pride in his erections rises in inverse proportion to his ability to achieve them. Francisco, your feeble turgidity reminds me of the bowel movements of that nun who was recently beatified. I can't remember her name. So many perfectly impossible people are being beatified these days, one can't possibly keep track of all of them.'

Tamburelli detested intellectual conversation at such critical moments.

'What about her bowel movements?' he said grudgingly, and ruefully also as he watched his hitherto promising erection inexorably droop.

'I understand,' said Alda, 'that she achieved peristalsis and a resultant bowel movement once every six months. For which reason she enjoyed a considerable reputation in the provinces for sanctity.'

'Very orthodox and proper,' nodded Quinto. 'Constipation has always been equated with piety. The ideal, of course, are the angels who lack anuses altogether.'

'They do?' said Tamburelli mournfully and absently. The aborted erection was now a ghostly shrunken memory. Liliana

251

smiled maliciously.

'Courage, *Signor* Tamburelli,' said Quinto. 'No man's gonads are proof against the malice of women. Even when they're squirming and yowling in the height of heat, they never lose the vindictive desire to castrate a man. I would say, in fact, that they take more satisfaction from emasculating a male partner than from achieving orgasm with him.'

'That's not true, Quinto,' said Alda. 'You're just being disagreeable.' She appraised the lieutenant's semiturgid phallus dubiously. 'Desmond, you're not very impressive either, except by comparison with poor Francisco here.' She turned to Liliana. 'I'd say your friend appears hopeless.'

'I wouldn't put it with such finality,' said Liliana, patting Tamburelli's cheek tolerantly. 'Francisco is mediocre, but not entirely hopeless. His mind, his work, his wife and five children, and, of course, his age, are always getting in the way.' She sighed. 'That's the world. What we women need, Alda, are reliable, uncomplicated young male morons. It reduces itself to a matter of a good blood supply, healthy muscle tissue, and motivation. And the less intellect, the better.'

'I have the interest,' admitted Tamburelli. 'But, true, all the factors you mentioned get in the way. Including my Sicilian sense of propriety. It's ridiculous, after all, for a man of my years and station in life to divest himself of his clothing which conceals his deficiencies.'

Alda turned to O'Brien. 'Well, lieutenant,' she said impatiently, 'do you think *you're* ready?'

'Let's sit this one out,' said O'Brien resignedly. 'My blood supply has been monopolized trying to keep up with this brilliant chatter.'

'That's an admission of defeat,' said Alda briskly. 'What about you, Raimondo? Being fully clothed should give your ego some advantage over the rest. Don't you want to come to bed with me?'

'I'm the host,' said Ray loftily. 'My first duty is to see that all my guests are happy.'

'I don't believe that,' said Alda. 'You're just putting the best face on your lack of confidence.'

'Why don't we just talk and work this out intellectually?'

252

said Tamburelli.

'No,' said Alda stubbornly. 'I feel the need for privacy and an adequate functioning male.'

Everyone turned to the handsome Air Force lieutenant. 'Looks like it's up to you, O'Brien,' said Ray. 'It's your turn at bat.'

O'Brien regarded his now wholly limp organ dolefully. 'I'm afraid the Air Force has struck out. I like sex as well as the next man. It must be this overexposure to women with brains.'

'And your American conscience, probably,' said Alda.

O'Brien shrugged apologetically.

'Never let it be said that a Babbi left a lady frustrated,' said Quinto. 'Let's see what we can do. Ah, here is someone for Alda.' Quinto motioned over a young athlete, the one who had passed by a short time before. He was of middle height, with black curly hair on his chest and muscular arms and calves. He wore a high pompadour of slicked back black hair and a thin mustache. His phallus at rest, gave the impression of being a leashed tiger awaiting only some encouragement to spring from its cave.

'Alda,' said Quinto, 'this is Peppino Ingrao, heterosexual, obedient, in good health, and not too bright.' He turned to the young man. 'Peppino, this is *Signorina* Alda Quirini, one of the cornerstones of the Italian film industry. She has heard of your ability as a seven-orgasm man and is interested in making a personal test of it.'

Peppino bent over Alda's hand and kissed it. 'At your service, *signorina*. May I say that I have seen all your films five times.'

'How delightful!' cried Alda. 'No intellectual could possibly sit through that rubbish five times. I don't know which I like better, your manners, your physique, or your low intelligence. A woman shouldn't have to throw herself at men. And with such unrewarding results.' She glanced at Ray. 'Our host insists that he has duty on his mind.' And at O'Brien. 'And the American Air Force has turned out to be a paper dragon. A lady might as well go to sea in a leaking boat.' She put her arm through Peppino's and pinched his bulging bicep. 'Come, young man, I feel like fighting. And the rest of you are welcome to come and watch two virtuosi. Especially you, Francisco. Perhaps it will stimulate you.'

'Ah, for my lost youth,' sighed Tamburelli.

'You, too, Raimondo,' said Alda.

'I prefer to sit down somewhere, take off my shoes, and smoke a cigar,' said Ray.

'And you also, Quinto,' said Alda.

'Go with God,' said Quinto. 'I have to take care of my guests.'

'Ah, *signor*,' sighed Quinto, 'sex play is not really for amateurs, no more than is skiing or ballet dancing. Certainly not for disgracefully unfit amateurs like some of our guests here, with their pot bellies, leaking ventricles, stiffened muscles, prostatectomies, hysterectomies, slipped discs, bad breaths, and psychic inhibitions. Making love properly is a form of calisthenics. One must be in form. One does one's best, but some of these people! Their hearts and heads are stuffed with dirty lire instead of love. There is more pure eroticism in the coupling of two bluebottle flies on the lid of a garbage can.'

Ray clapped Quinto Babbi on the back. 'You're a poet, my friend. Come on, let's leave these pigs to their struggles and have a nightcap together.'

They went off together to the bar.

'Give me a little tonic water please,' said Quinto to the bartender.

'The same for me,' said Ray. 'I'm wrapping it up for this evening.'

'I think you missed the spirit of the evening,' said Quinto.

'The spirit of it, for me, was to keep my pants on and my eyes open. A man is a man, not a purple-assed baboon. To hell with nudity. Give me a good tailor anytime.'

'The human body is beautiful.'

'As far as I'm concerned, man is the ugliest ape of all, as well as the most disagreeable. I didn't see you take off your pants.'

'But I'm a Babbi.'

'And I'm an Occhiaccio. Which reminds me——' Ray lowered his voice. 'Has your photographer been keeping Saracino and that American girl under surveillance?'

254

'All evening,' Quinto assured him.

'The photographer knows exactly what to do?'

'I gave him explicit instructions.'

'I want a set of clear photographs. Another thing, did he get some good shots of the American pilot and Quirini?'

'As you ordered. But, in this matter, frankly, I'm surprised.'

'Surprised? Why?'

'Alda Quirini,' said Quinto. 'A fine person. A classic. The salt of the earth. Why should you move against her?'

'Hell!' said Ray. 'I have nothing against her. I like Alda. She's the only one around here with balls. It's the American I want a half nelson on. Just in case. Do you understand?'

'No.'

'It doesn't matter. As long as you obtained the photographs. If that young man plays games with me, I'll bury him ten ways to Christmas.'

Ray finished his tonic water and set his glass down on the bar. 'Quinto, you've been the hero of the night. Keep my honored guests amused and get me those photographs.' He yawned. 'I'm going to bed.'

'Good night, *signor*' said Quinto.

'Good night, Quinto. Keep the swine off balance and count the silver after they leave.'

CHAPTER 16

Poggio had received the twenty-five kilos flown in by O'Brien and had remitted.

Seventy-five kilos to go. Worth one and one third millions on the export market.

One morning at the villa, Ray said to Torres, 'I'm going to shoot the works.'

'How?'

'I'm going to send over the balance in one lot. I want to clean out this stash. It's making me superstitious.'

'Since you distrust the man, is it wise to commit your reserves?'

'I suppose, deep down, I want a showdown with Al Poggio,' said Ray.

'You're hoping he cheats you?'

'In a way. Then I can collect from him on location. In a way, I'm playing games with myself.'

'Sometimes you're too cautious,' said Torres. 'Now I think you're being too rash. This Poggio has salt in his brains.'

'I have more,' said Ray. 'If he steals, I'll collect anyhow.'

Tony Saldana had three foreign car agencies out on the Island, the main one in Mineola. Ray had made arrangements to have five Fiats driven down from Rome to Dominique's mechanic in Naples. The seventy-five keys were split five ways and stashed by Dominique in the five modified fuel tanks. Then the Fiats were delivered to the broker for shipment in three different lots—two, two, and one—on three different vessels.

While the Fiats were being primed, Ray passed the word to

Tony Saldana. The consignment would come dribbling into his Long Island City storage warehouse and parts department.

Tony Saldana was unhappy. Accepting the first lot in that Mercedes had been an accommodation. He had sweated coldly as long as the H had been on his hands and on his premises. Now this. Tony S. was the son of a New England boss. He had been sent to the Occhiaccio Family of Brooklyn to start at the bottom and work up. Old Saldana hadn't believed in nepotism. Since Tony S. had such good antecedents, and native ability, too, Ray had pushed him along fast. Too fast, some people thought. Ray had long-range plans: Tony S., young *capo*, up to subboss. Al Poggio subboss and fink, down to the bottom of Long Island Sound. Tony Saldana, thirty-one, below average height, stocky, a cheerful crewcut extrovert, had been okay from the start. He had pitched in his share of heavy work and had executed his assignments efficiently, without beefing or cracking. He didn't like it, but he had delivered. Who did like it? Only psychos, which made them unreliable and not good to have around. Hitting people was nothing to enjoy. If you did, you were marked lousy. Anyhow, Tony had worked out fine. Too many sons or relatives of bosses took the attitude that they should skip the heavy stuff and start on an executive-trainee level. Tony had taken his chances right along and was okay in Ray's book. But this second call to hazardous duty, accepting and delivering seventy-five keys of junk was not okay in *Tony's* book. With three auto agencies, a healthy loan business, an auto-scrapping yard, and a small regime of his own, Tony was doing fine. He needed junk like he needed lung cancer. His father up in New England had never handled it, and neither had he. Tony was sensibly afraid of junk. The 1956 law carried a mandatory twenty-year sentence for the first offense, without probation or parole, for conspiracy to import heroin into the United States. By this time, the five Fiats were already under way. Tony S. awaited their arrival and slept badly. When they were finally delivered into his Long Island City warehouse, he slept worse and debated whether he should himself unload the cars or deliver them straight to Poggio. On that same night, while Tony slept on it, the five Fiats were stolen out of the warehouse. It had been a silent, peaceful hijack. Some very fine pros had gotten into the warehouse, wire-jumped the engines into life, drove the cars away, and that was all there was to it. Tony didn't report the loss to his insurance carrier. Naturally. He made up no fake bills of sale which could start a train of new complications and the Department of Motor Vehicles snooping around. He passed the word to Ray and continued to carry the five vanished automobiles on his books as inventory. Al Poggio was contacted from both ends of the line and answered: 'I know nothing. I'm still waiting for Tony to deliver.'

Go prove otherwise, thought Ray. The hand has finally come out of the wall and written: *Mene*, someone has boosted the Fiats and stolen your junk. *Tekel*, you have been screwed, Ray Hodgkin, but good. *Peres*, you are up the creek without a paddle, one and a third million dollars' worth. Isn't that what you were sort of expecting, even hoping for? Okay, it's time to pack it in.

He called a little breakfast meeting and said, 'This is the hand of Poggio.'

'We've been hearing of his hand for a long time,' said Torres.

'It's a serious loss,' said Ray. 'If I don't move now, while I still have ammunition, I wither on the vine, I rot in the foxhole.'

'Another drug purchase in Beirut?' suggested Dominique.

'Never,' said Ray. 'I'll never repeat that.'

'Your mind is really pointed toward New York,' said Torres.

Ray nodded. 'I finally hear the bell. Will you go with me?'

'I'll go,' said Torres.

'Dominique?'

'To speak the truth——' began Dominique.

'You must,' said Ray. 'Now is the time.'

'For me,' said Dominique, 'America is another Tibet, the end of the world. If it wasn't for that mess I got into, I'd be in Marseilles, where my heart is. Failing that, Switzerland, a peaceful, civilized country.'

'Not Italy?' grinned Ray.

'Italy is a sauce. You can't make a meal of it.'

'How will we go, Don Raimondo?' said Torres.

'As crew members with seaman's papers to Montreal. There we buy American citizenship credentials and cross the border by car to New York. That's the simplest way. Dominique, do you want to come to Montreal?'

Dominique grimaced and shook his head. 'Eskimo country.'

'You'll be able to speak French there.'

'Still, no,' said Dominique.

'Very well,' said Ray. 'This is what you'll do. Tomorrow, I'll turn over to you titles to the villa and the apartment.' He took an envelope out of the desk. 'Here's twenty-five thousand to keep you going till you wind up everything. Will that be enough?'

'Plenty,' said Dominique.

'Good. Then you can convert the real estate, the furnishings, everything into cash at your leisure and get the best price.'

'You're giving all this to me? It's too much.'

'That's your share since you're remaining behind. Are you satisfied?'

'More than satisfied.'

'Very good. This arrangement will speed things. I'm returning with a minimum of baggage and a maximum of cash. After you've cashed in everything, you should be able to buy a pardon from your pope up there in Marseilles.'

'No question,' said Dominique.

'That's what I thought. You Corsicans can't be that much different than Sicilians.'

'No problem,' said Dominique. 'I'll be set up for life.'

'You've earned it,' said Ray. 'One more thing.' He took a manila envelope out of the desk drawer, opened it, and took out some photographs. 'These are pictures of people making love, after a fashion. Quirini and that pilot. Since he delivered, we don't need them anymore.' He studied the photographs and sighed. 'That Alda—when I look at her lovely face, it makes my heart ache. It makes me want to cry.' He selected a half dozen glossy prints, tore them across, put them in a large ceramic ashtray, and lit a match under them. 'Now for the rest. They show Saracino and the American girl in action.' He tossed them across the desk at Dominique. 'Since I'm leaving,

259

I don't care what Saracino does or doesn't do. It's now academic. But he may come bothering you. If he does, hold these in your sleeve as a reserve card. They'll work, believe me.'

Dominique studied the photographs without expression. He put them into the envelope and slid it into his breast pocket.

Ray turned to Juan Torres. 'Do you know where you're going, my friend?'

'With you.'

'Correct. To the war. Right up to the front line.'

Torres opened his palms upward and chuckled mirthlessly. 'I will see America.'

Ray sighed. 'Ah, America! Now that I've been away three years, either I'm getting double vision or I'm seeing another picture.' He took a flat wallet from his breast pocket, unfolded a piece of silk, and carefully laid the two Silver Stars on the desk. 'America gave me these when I was young and brave. Though not very law-abiding even then.'

Torres picked up and examined the stars and the vertically striped red-white-and-blue ribbons to which they were attached.

'These are what sort of decorations?'

'The third highest,' said Ray. 'It is not awarded lightly.'

Carefully, Torres put down the stars. 'Then, perhaps, she will forgive you.'

'Never.'

'What do you plan for yourself, then?'

'After settling accounts with Poggio, I'll surrender to the Immigration and Naturalization district director in New York.'

Torres raised his eyebrows. 'Isn't that a drastic step?'

Ray smiled. 'That's because you don't understand how the American system works. I'll give you your first lesson in a citizenship which is beyond your wildest dreams. I go to I and N with my attorney. I am arrested and released, after giving bond. A United States Attorney takes it from there, from the I and N. He goes to a federal grand jury.'

'What is a grand jury?'

'Patience. He says to them: Indict Raimondo Occhiaccio for violation of Section 1326 of the United States Code—reentry of a deported alien, two years in prison and/or one thousand dollars fine. The grand jury listens and says, *Bene*. It returns a true bill. That means that I must appear before a judge and be tried on the charge. Then I give them some more bail money.'

'And all of this time you are free to come and go?' said Torres.

'As long as the court is satisfied that I will appear for trial.'

'And you will appear?'

'Yes. Otherwise, I may as well remain here. I shall be convicted, acquitted, or the government's case will be set aside. Whatever happens, the I and N recommences new deportation proceedings against me.'

'Cannot the court order you reexpelled? You are guilty on the face of it.'

'Not in America,' said Ray. 'Deportation is a civil procedure. I have many remedies at my disposal. I can drag it out for a few years.'

'You have great confidence in the American system,' said Torres wonderingly.

'You do not even begin to comprehend it. The burden of proof is always on the government. Unrestrained, it could crush me like a crippled fly.'

Torres frowned. 'Don Raimondo, if America is so permissive, benevolent, and patient, then why do you laugh at her?'

'I don't laugh at her,' said Ray grimly. 'On the contrary.'

'Ah.'

'Yes. I respect her. That means nothing. When I'm back on American soil, she will never cease from her efforts to reexpell me. Ultimately, she may succeed.'

'Then why are you returning at all?'

'A good question, to which I have no answer. To protect my interests. To retain what is mine. That's a good rationalization. Poggio and Codi, a strong combination. They'll naturally do their best to kill me. Their thinking is: The government kicked you out. Stay in Italy and rot. *We* now have the chair.'

'But you disagree with them.'

'I shall kill Poggio,' said Ray. 'That's a foregone conclusion.

261

Even if he's innocent, which he isn't, I'd kill him anyhow because he irritates me. The point is, I can. The other one, Codi, I'll draw his teeth for good. But you asked why I was returning.'

'You have a woman there,' said Torres. 'You spoke of her when we were in Beirut.'

'It goes beyond the woman, as it goes beyond money,' said Ray. 'It's something between that country and myself.'

'You said that you have a good chance of remaining there because of the foolish laws, that it may take them years to uproot you again. Then what difference does it make?'

'The difference between a cockroach in the house and an owner of the house.'

Torres rubbed his chin. 'You said in Beirut, I recall, that you wanted back your youth. Is this the same thing?'

'Yes,' said Ray reluctantly.

'And I said that you were an unreasonable man.'

'I remember.'

'So you will slink about like a beggar at the gate——'

'In the house,' interrupted Ray.

Torres shrugged. '—in the house, hoping against hope. For what? This is like a woman who has cut you out of her heart. How can you reawaken her love and forgiveness?'

'How?' echoed Ray.

'It's impossible,' said Torres.

'I'm going back anyhow. Maybe she'll kill me.'

BOOK TWO

CHAPTER 17

Palermo's noise, when deportee Ray Hodgkin finally stepped ashore, had hit him like a falling brick wall. That and the tangle of smells. After he had left Castellammare and settled down temporarily in Palermo, he began to note a parallel to his own early life. As in South Brooklyn, the raucous rhythm of the Palermitan streets died down on occasion. The decibel count fell to nothing. Sudden silence was the same alarm bell which meant trouble, that someone was being hit or worked over in the streets. The cops came swarming in. What a change then! No more noise. No more people. So had it been in the South Brooklyn of his childhood, the same pattern of dispersal. No witnesses when the police began asking questions. People in Ray's childhood neighbourhood had had the worst eyesight in the world and a passion for minding their own business. Here, in Palermo, they were selectively blind. They wouldn't see you dead if you lay in the middle of the Via Roma in a big silver coffin.

Ray as a kid had been no different. He had instinctively followed the same cultural pattern. When he saw his first street hit early one evening, he was up the stoop and into the flat while the gun reports were still echoing. His sisters, Rosalie, Joanna, and Maria, were sitting in the kitchen eating, as usual. The black button eyes in their pudding faces shifted as Ray tumbled into the kitchen and slammed the bolt.

'That sounded like a gun,' said Maria.

'That was a car backfiring,' said Ray.

'You saw something out there,' said Maria.

'Mind your own business,' said Ray dispassionately, 'or I'll bust you one.'

'Don't be chicken,' said Maria. 'We won't tell mamma.'

Ray punched her in the nose skillfully, just hard enough to start the blood flowing. 'You keep forgetting what the old lady is always telling us—don't see nothing you ain't supposed to see.'

Maria began to cry. The other two joined her in sympathy. 'You two shut up,' said Ray calmly, 'or I'll really give you something to cry about.'

Rosalie and Joanna sensibly turned off their tear ducts. After a while, Maria brought her nose under control. The sisters resumed their three-way argument while Ray sat silent. The afternoon dragged on like a mired fly. Dusk fell. Ray turned on the kitchen light. Mrs. Occhiacio finally came home from work. She had already heard of the killing on the block and she questioned Ray obliquely after the dinner dishes had been washed.

The sisters kept interrupting. 'It's hot in here,' Maria whined. 'Can't we go out and sit on the stoop?'

'In hell it's hotter,' said Mrs. Occhiaccio. 'Tonight you girls will remain indoors. You will not go out.'

Maria's whine rose to a slightly higher pitch and Mrs. Occhiaccio banged her across the ear. 'I am the mother and the father,' said Mrs Occhiaccio calmly. 'Obey. You three girls go into the bedroom.'

When the girls had left the kitchen, she said to Ray, 'This thing I heard about that was supposed to have happened in the street—you saw nothing?'

'Nothing,' said Ray, remembering quite clearly what the killer looked like.

Mrs. Occhiaccio nodded approvingly. 'May my friends never lack for food and see only angels,' she said in the mother tongue. 'May my enemies always be hungry and see blood wherever they look.'

'I saw nothing,' repeated Ray.

'Good,' said his mother, 'then you won't be hungry.' And she told him a little more of the past. 'You left Sicily as a baby. It's a small, poor island. It was invaded a hundred times since time began. We worked like donkeys or we starved. Most of the time we starved. The women drudged forever. No matter how hard the wind blew, they bore the children and held the family together. And all was determined by the strength of the man.'

'The old man was always sick,' said Ray. 'It sounds like you held things together.'

'Your father wasn't strong in his body but stout in his heart. He was a good man who did his best for his family. His heart was courageous and he brought us all away from Sicily.'

'You make it sound like a jail,' said Ray.

Unsmiling, Mrs. Occhiaccio raised her chin and eyebrows and closed her eyes. The gesture implied, You don't know the half of it.

'Yeah,' said Ray, watching her.

'However hard this may be,' said his mother, 'it's better here, a thousand times better. You can build yourself a shield against the world. In the old country, never. Your father did well for all of us.'

By the time he was fifteen, Ray and his lieutenant, Fat Beniamino, were leading a mob against Louis Nitti and his Night Owls and usually getting the worst of it because the Night Owls were older and heavier. The weapons were bicycle chains, straight razors, jack handles, and baseball bats. It was bad. 'I don't want no heroes in this crowd,' said Ray to the boys. 'Any guy goes off half-cocked trying to take on more than one is going to be on his own. Grandstanding is for bums.'

Another lieutenant, Nicky Polo, asked, 'So what are we supposed to do if we meet them?'

'If there's more of them than of you, turn around and run like hell,' said Ray. 'If there's more of you than of them, kill them. Never give nobody a break.'

'Sometimes they just want to talk,' said Nicky Polo.

'When you're weaker, you talk,' said Ray. 'When you got no out and think it will help. When you're stronger, don't talk, just hit. But don't rumble if you can get out of it. We're trying to make a living, not get our heads broken. Any bum can do that.'

About this time serious love descended on Ray and his associates. The gang bangs began.

One day Ray saved Marta Peruzzi, a neighbor's daughter, from being banged by Louie Nitti's Night Owls. After that she tended to carry a torch for Ray Occhiaccio. Her appreciation was understandable. Had she been raped by ten or twelve husky teen-agers, she might have been turned into a hustler.

The week after Ray had played Saint George for Marta, he was ambushed and beaten up by Louis Nitti and the Night Owls. Louie Nitti, seventeen and twenty pounds heavier than Ray, had made special plans for Marta Peruzzi. He had been particularly irritated by the fact that Ray had run interference.

While his skull healed, Ray avoided the Night Owls. He would have, anyhow, as a matter of common prudence. The week before the Night Owls had nailed Ray, they had gouged out a fifteen-year-old kid's eyes with a broken Pepsi-Cola bottle. Ray had a tender regard for his eyes. You got two handed out to you, two eyes, two arms, two balls, and one head, no more. The plan formed in his mind. So that he, Ray Occhiaccio, could stop worrying about his eyes, Louis Nitti would have to go. Marta Peruzzi's cherry, if she lost it, she could live without. But your eyes gashed out by a dirty broken pop bottle, screw that! 'That's what I've been trying to tell you,' said Ray at a war council. 'You can't do business with those guys. You have to catch one of them alone and jump him. You can't buy no peace. You got to make it expensive for them, then they'll let you alone.'

But Ray could barely explain to himself why he had defended Marta against the Night Owls. It wasn't right, he felt, to bang a girl of one's own people. Maybe it was because he had the liability of his own sisters. He recalled his mother's account of the episode in the old country, when Sarati, the village wise-ass, had sympathized with Infelice for the misfortune of having fathered seven daughters. Girls were a responsibility. They required strong fathers and brothers to guard the honor which the mother had impressed on them. There was no halfway stuff in the old country code. A girl was either good or bad. If she'd lost her cherry, she didn't get a husband. And if she didn't get a husband, what was she? What would become of her? Who would protect her? Certainly a girl needed watchdogs around her with big sharp teeth to protect her virtue. Lacking those, she could wind up in the wrong guy's bed without a marriage contract in her hand. Girls, after all, weren't supposed to have brains; that's what fathers and brothers were for. That was the uncomplicated old country code. And the people were as merciless as their code. They sneered at families insufficiently clever and vigilant to protect the virginity of their daughters and sisters. They respected families which took good care to forestall such disasters. If a girl lost her virginity unlawfully, her menfolk did something about it. They had better, or life wouldn't be worth living. No leper so odious, so worthless, as the father or brother who couldn't or wouldn't exact retribution. Who did Marta have to protect her? No father. The old man was dead. Ray had undertaken an obligation of honor to protect the neighbor's daughter and had done so. Not that he had thought at that time of Marta for himself. It was an instinctive act on young Ray's part. He had violated his own rule about noninvolvement and had gotten his head broken for it. Now he had a personal reason for getting even with Louie Nitti.

The fact that Louie Nitti was bigger, heavier, and bossed the Night Owls didn't make him smarter. He really wasn't, but he had a grapevine on the neighborhood cops, the ones you could deal with, the ones you had to run from. As a kid, Ray had grown up relatively neutral about cops. Even at that age, without sympathizing, he could see that cops themselves had a tough time. He wasn't excusing their petty shakedowns. Maybe it was a good thing that they did take. As Uncle Oliverotto, who later appointed himself Ray's godfather, observed: 'Like I told you so many times, it's not because our people are so smart or something special that we stay in business. The pay-off to the cops is a legit expense. Without the fix, even in the smallest thing you are out. They won't let you operate. It goes all the way to the top from the cop on the corner to the big politicians in Washington.'

By the time Ray was sixteen, he had added a new wrinkle to his modest extortion operations among the neighborhood storekeepers. He set himself up as a commission man between a fence and the twelve-year-olds who specialized in swiping small packages off the trucks. This middleman line added modestly to Ray's income. Every buck counted.

After his skull had knitted from the shellacking administered by Louie Nitti and his Night Owls, Ray apparently accepted Louie's suzerainty and paid in a weekly tribute from his own take. He came around and was even tolerated as a player at a Night Owl-run crap game. Ray knew why he was being tolerated. He had flashed a hundred dollars in bills. The Night Owls didn't know where he had gotten it, and they didn't care. They wanted it and figured this Occhiaccio punk for a pushover. All the Night Owls were there, five visiting Aces from East Harlem and a few unconnected kids who were the marks that everybody, Ray included, were aiming for. Ray got hot that night and kept making his point. By midnight, he had busted the five Aces. They departed for East Harlem, accepting their losses, so it seemed. They had an understanding with Louie Nitti—when the Night Owls slugged and rolled Ray Occhiacco at the night's end, they would get back a piece of their stake. Louie had agreed to this arrangement as a reciprocal courtesy to the visiting uptowners. It was an angle he had learned from big brother Castaldo. Not that the Aces trusted Louie Nitti to keep his word. In fact, they went on the assumption that he would try to double-cross them. If and when he did, they would eventually catch up with him and reimburse themselves as fully as possible. Promises, contracts, and obligations were good only insofar as they could be enforced.

The crap game heated up. Ray had a grand of winnings in his pocket. It was more money than he had ever held at one time in his life, all in sweaty, dirty fives, tens and twenties. He had been too engrossed in the game to note the departure of the Aces. Then he suddenly realized that he was there all alone with the Night Owls. The other independent kids, the busted marks, had also left. The hot streak was over. One way or another, Ray sensed, the Night Owls would see to that. Paco, the tall, thin kid with the long hands, a skilled bust-out guy for the Night Owls, had the dice. That should have been the tip-off. It was. They were going to take him down.

'Shooting a hundred,' said Paco.

Louie Nitti grinned at Ray. 'Go ahead, rich boy. Cover.'

Ray covered.

Paco made his point. Then again. And again. That lanky sonofabitch with his own special dice. Why not? He, Ray, would never get the chance to examine them.

Between them, Paco and Louie worked Ray down steadily to his last fifty. That figured.

Then Louis handed the dice over to a third guy and began leaning on Ray and giving him the needle. That also figured.

'Friggin' hero, ain't you?' said Louie. 'What is that Marta Peruzzi, your special lay?'

'It's a cinch, she ain't yours,' said Ray.

'I don't think you could lay an oilcloth,' said Paco. 'You look like fruit to me.'

'Your sister asked me,' said Ray. 'I told her I don't touch whores.'

'You talk very strong for a motherfucker,' said Paco.

Ray smiled, grabbed up the queer dice from the table, and threw them hard in Paco's face. 'Kind of heavy, ain't they? But on the wrong side.'

As Paco retrieved the dice, Louie put his arm around Ray's shoulder. 'Hey, fruit, I kind of like that sister of yours, the sixth or the seventh one, I'm not sure which. How about fixing me up? You know which one?'

Night Owl Joe Grandi put in his comment. 'With pleasure. Just give him the four bits in advance.'

'With pleasure,' repeated Ray. He smashed down his iron-shod boot heel on Louie's instep and sidestepped.

'Hey, kid,' laughed Joe Grandi, 'we're just riding you a little. Get off his ass, Paco. He's no fruit. Hey, Louie——'

But Louie Nitti was still hopping around on one foot trying to ease the pain.

Joe Grandi moved in warily.

'From one fruit to another,' said Ray. He drove his rigid fingers into Joe's eyes. Joe recoiled. Ray kicked him in the groin. Joe doubled up. Ray drop-kicked a steel-shod toe into Joe's face. 'Here's a cherry—for free.'

Louie Nitti bore in, limp and all. The other Night Owls followed in a crescent. Paco had an open switchblade in his hand, low, blade up, with his thumb along the edge. That was when Ray drew out a stolen .38 Colt.

'It's old,' he said, 'but the slugs are fat. They'll take a piece out of your backbone.'

That gave the Night Owl crescent pause. 'Okay, kid,' said Louie Nitti at last, 'we believe you.'

'The spic don't,' said Ray. He fired deliberately at the switchbade. Paco, his hand suddenly covered with blood, dropped the knife.

'Ain't that a shame,' said Ray. 'There goes the best mechanic in the business. You better start looking for a new one, Louie.'

Louie stepped forward reluctantly. Ray put a second bullet between the Night Owl boss's thighs. 'Next time, I'll take your balls off. I been practicing with this thing.'

Louie stopped and the Night Owls looked at him. 'Okay,' he said, 'you made your point.'

'Thanks,' said Ray. 'Just between us, Nitti, you fuck with me, I'll kill you.' He kept backing up till he reached the door. 'Hey, Paco!' he shouted, 'start practicing with your left hand.' He hit the door hard with his shoulder, went down the stoop, three steps at a time, and began running.

The word got around. That was the end of tribute to the Night Owls, and a beginning. That was how respect was accrued. It was harder in the beginning. You had to be ready to tap at any moment, to go the whole distance if necessary. The only way to keep the cats away was with fire. You had to be ready to use the fire, not your mouth. In other words, you had to be a little crazy or have bigger balls. Ray's balls were just a little bit bigger than the next punk's.

That crap game stopped the weekly payoff to Louie. It had been on the strength of Big Man Castaldo that Louie had been muscling a weekly cut out of the weaker and younger gangs. Ray was the first to break loose. The lesson was not lost. Other people were always trying to cut themselves in and feed off you. If you didn't learn to defend yourself, you'd get nibbled to death. Ray was satisfied for the time being. He reflected on the problem and kept out of Nitti's way.

It must have been Louie Nitti, Ray reasoned, who tipped

off the cops about him. A month after the crap game, Ray was arrested with a pocketful of policy slips. Who knew how the cops knew? The stools were also being developed young. This stool smelled like Nitti, who was angry about Marta and the lost tribute. Louie was the kind of character that wanted a cut of everything, even if it was only a dime, He wanted everything in sight. He wanted.

At the precinct house the cops worked Ray over hard. Ray told them nothing. Uncle Oliverotto himself went down to the precinct house with a lawyer and someone from the local political club. Whatever they did, they got Ray sprung and Uncle Oliverotto assumed the role of Ray's protector. Only later did Ray discover how potent Uncle Oliverotto's connections were in the precinct houses, in the courts, and in the clubhouses. By that time, as an adult, he was able to fill in the big picture to his own satisfaction. The world was composed of mobs, all in the business of taking. Small fry like the Nittis and himself. People like Uncle Oliverotto. The cops. The independents or unorganized outlaws, who were fair game for everybody. The politicians who, like the cops, took their cut from those who took the risks. Then there were the legit businessmen, so-called, who worked in a never-ending series of shifting alliances, deals, and understandings with cops, politicians, and mobsters. There were square Johns also. There had to be. They picked up the tab for everybody, because there were more square Johns to go around. Everything rested on them. The entire interlocking structure was supported by people who paid their taxes and ran every morning to catch the subway to work.

It took Ray all of six months to square accounts with Louie Nitti. He finally caught up and shot Louie from ambush one night with the old .38 that had remained stashed away. One bullet, and it took a piece of Louie's head away. Ray put the gun back into his pocket, even though he knew that he should get rid of it immediately. Then he knelt over Louie's body, zipped down the Night Owl's pants, and used a knife in the traditional way. Louis had not been a rapist exactly, only an unsuccessful rapist. It would make no difference now. The

273

cops could draw their own conclusions. Since their case loads were excessive, they sensibly drew none, except that they had one punk less to worry about. The people who knew about such things reasoned, Louie Nitti is dead with his bird in his mouth. Therefore, he must have misbehaved himself. They promptly dismissed Louie from their minds. It was lucky for Marta, Ray reflected, that Louie had not gotten into her. That would have put her out of the running, maybe with him, maybe with some other right guy. The fact that it wouldn't have been her fault was irrelevant. Blame or no blame, the merchandise would have been secondhand, not marrying stuff.

When Louie's mutilated body was found the Nittis raised undirected hell in the neighborhood. They went to Uncle Oliverotto, who showed them the door with small ceremony.

'What are you coming to us for?' he said. 'Since when are your young bums our responsibility? What are we, some kind of social agency?'

From Uncle Oliverotto's viewpoint, the killing of Louie Nitti was really unofficial kid stuff, a neighborhood rumble. Still, the Occhiaccio boy had handled it with a kind of aplomb which awakened nostalgic memories of his own youth in Uncle Oliverotto. He summoned Tony, his personal aide.

'I want you to keep an eye on that young Occhiaccio,' said Oliverotto. 'He seems like a nice boy. I think he was raised right. He has character.'

CHAPTER 18

Two months after Louie Nitti's passing, Ray was invited as a guest to celebrate Uncle Oliverotto's birthday. No one knew the old man's age and Ray didn't ask. He came and respectfully presented gifts—a big box of Oliverotto's favorite cigars and a bottle of potent Misilmeri.

The slender, white-haired man accepted the gifts gravely and said, 'Thank you, my boy.'

After the heavy meal, he took Ray into his private little study, poured him a glass of the Misilmeri and handed him one of the black cheroots. Ray looked at it dubiously and said, 'This thing's liable to floor me.'

'Nothing will floor you,' said Oliverotto. He puffed forth a cloud of smoke and continued: 'How did you know the right thing to do, seeing that I had not taught it to you? Felice, may his soul rest in peace, died when you were a baby.'

Ray worked on the cheroot. 'What didn't I know?'

'What you accomplished so well.'

'It seemed the natural thing to do.'

Oliverotto smiled dryly. 'It is as I always tell Tony, who grunts like a pig in reply, so one is never sure if he is agreeing or disagreeing. You were born to it. There are thing you do not have to be told. You do them naturally. That is the important thing.'

Ray did not reply.

'Now I will tell you what I want you to do,' said Uncle Oliverotto. 'You will go back and finish high school so that you can graduate.'

'The hell with that,' said Ray. 'Who needs it? I'm doing okay right now. The second thing is I got to help out my old

275

lady with money.'

Uncle Oliverotto raised his hand. 'The first thing you will learn is not to speak to me like that. But that you will learn. The second thing is that you need the high school because I say you do.'

Ray wanted to ask who had given the old man the right but decided not to.

Oliverotto smiled. 'Your mother gave me the right. She asked me to take over. So, already, I know what is in your head before you speak the words. The third thing is that she is your mother, not your old lady. The fourth thing is you will learn to talk not like a bum. The fifth thing is that we will take care of your mother's living while you go to the school so that she doesn't have to work any more. She has done enough.'

'My mother don't take from nobody,' said Ray. 'So far she hasn't.'

'From her son's *cumpare* and from her own people she will take,' said Oliverotto, 'because she has already come to me about it.'

Ray's mind refused to orient itself to what the old man was talking about. 'A lot of going to school I'll get done with the Nittis looking to break my head.'

'The Nittis aren't going to do anything,' said Oliverotto, 'nor is anybody else. The Nittis have already been told that everything is finished and to forget it. They have forgotten it. Believe what I say. Besides, you will go to a private high school. It is uptown. It makes people ready to go to a college.'

'What?' said Ray.

'College. We are going to need people who understand about business, accounting, taxes, and law. That is going to be more important than the big balls, which you have already.'

Ray wasn't sure what the old man was talking about but he knew enough not to talk back either. 'You mean the old lady— I mean, my mother—says it's okay for me to live away from here in another town——'

'It's all the same place,' said Oliverotto. 'New York City.'

'Okay, but about Benny, Nicky, Collucci, the Bug, all those guys. They're my friends, they depend on me.'

'They are one thing. You are another. Beniamino and young

276

Polo will get along fine without your leadership. I have other plans for them. Every boy has his own level. Collucci also. And this Bug. I don't know the boy, but, if he's your friend, I'll have Tony talk with him also. And another thing, don't give or take nicknames. That's for bums. You will go and finish high school in a place where they don't know about those kind of nicknames. And you will study and that is all you will do is study. If I hear about your getting into trouble on the side, I will not like it very much and you will hear from your mother and from me also.'

'Yeah, sure,' said Ray. 'But I got this reform school rap already. That ain't going to help me.'

'That is already taken care of. Nobody cares nothing that you were in reform school nine months. From now, it is important that you should keep your nose clean. That is how I want it, because, when you finish high school, I want you to go to the college at Fordham.'

'What's that?' said Ray.

'It's a college. That's where you will study the things which I said.'

'Jesus Christ!' said Ray.

'That's another thing. No more swearing. You will learn to talk right if you're going to be a businessman and talk to people in politics, with lawyers, with high-class people. In college you don't talk like a hoodlum.'

'Me, a college boy?' Ray was going to say something but caught himself. 'What's the matter with the way I talk now?'

'It don't sound right in my ear,' said Oliverotto calmly. 'It sounds to me that you talk like a bum. That I don't want.' He leaned over and tapped Ray on the chest. 'You listen to me good now, with both ears. If you got ears in your hands and feet, throw that in also. Also your belly and your whole head. You will go to a high school where there are people who don't know about the things that you know. You keep your mouth shut and watch and listen. And learn. That's what I want you to do. And don't get into no trouble there with the boys and the teachers, with nobody, even if you are right. If I hear of anything, there will be big trouble for your mother, for me, and especially, for you. Do you understand what I say?'

'Yeah,' said Ray.

'Yes. That is the first lesson. You will learn to talk like a boy from a good family, because that is what you are, not like a bum. Now go back and talk about these things with your mother. And come back. I want to talk to you some more tomorrow.'

When Ray returned on the following day, Uncle Oliverotto said, 'Did you talk to your mother?'

'Yeah. Yes.'

'Was it like I said?'

'Yes.'

'You will go and live in the house of my nephew Gaetano in the Bronx. Your room is ready there. Also, your clothes, which will be different. You will not need the big buckle to cut somebody's face with. Or the steel in your boots to kick somebody in the balls. These things are not done. You will not get mixed up with anybody in the Bronx, because they know about you already so nobody is going to bother you. You will not come back here.'

'What do you mean, not come back here? I want to see my friends.'

'On big holidays you will come back and see your family,' said Oliverotto. 'Your friends will get along fine without you. I will take care of that. Now you will give me your hand and swear that you will obey me in these things which are good for you.' He put out his hand and Ray took it and waited.

Uncle Oliverotto stared at Ray and said, 'Look into my eyes.'

Ray stared at Uncle Oliverotto's opaque, hard black eyes.

'There are no words to be spoken out loud,' said the old man. 'Do you know what I want?'

'Yes.'

'You will obey?'

'Yes.'

'If you do not, it will go badly for your family and for yourself. But I do not say this to make you afraid. The thing is, you will obey willingly because it is for your good. Do you understand this?'

'Yes,' said Ray.

278

'If you fail,' said Oliverotto, 'it will be because you didn't want to, not because you couldn't. That will be disobedience. You have given me an oath. Now go. And I don't want to hear from you, although I want to speak with you whenever you come home because the school is closed. You will report to me. Do you understand?'

'Yes,' said Ray.

'Then go,' said Uncle Oliverotto.

And Ray went.

When Ray graduated from high school, Uncle Oliverotto gave him a massive and expensive wristwatch for a graduation present. Ray buckled the broad, heavy leather strap on his left wrist and looked at it. 'If you cracked someone across the bridge of the nose with this,' he said, 'you could flatten the guy's nose.'

'This is for telling the time,' said Oliverotto, 'not for breaking people's noses.' He took in Ray's neat dark suit, gray shirt, conservative necktie, and cordovan loafers. 'I see you do not wear the boots any more with the steel toes. You found you did not need them?'

'No,' Ray admitted.

'As you did not need the knife and the brass knuckles,' said Oliverotto. 'These things must be in your brains, not in your hands.'

'Okay. I finished high school as you wanted.'

'As you wanted. Don't put it on me. Now you will go back and study some more.'

'I'm finished.'

'You're starting,' said Oliverotto. 'Now you will go to the college. The brains were there all the time, like I said. Go.'

And, again, Ray went.

At the end of Ray's first year at Fordham, Oliverotto said: 'Now I will speak with you as man to man. When you are finished you will come back to join your own people. When you do, move slow and careful. Feel your way. Listen. Don't talk. When you start getting around on a job in other cities, they will want to know who you are, how much money you have, who you know, how strong you are connected. That is

279

the heart of it—how strong you are connected.'

'How strong will I be connected?'

'Very strong. Even so, they will push a little to see what you do. If you don't push back, they will push harder.'

'So?'

'So the first time around, push back so hard, there will be no second time. With these people words are smoke. They don't hear good. Do you know what I mean? Never give up the initiative. That is the word I want. You remember that, eh?'

'I'll remember.'

Oliverotto relit his cheroot. 'You know, boy, it's a hustling world. All kinds of wheels inside of wheels. You'll hear all kinds of loose talk when you start getting around. Words about Outfit, Organization, Combination—words like that. All kinds of people claiming this or that. Don't believe what you hear. There's no Organization, just all kinds of tough hustlers making believe that there is, thousands of people in all kinds of businesses, crap shooters, pit bosses, bartenders, bookies, people who think they know and are sharp. They don't know nothing. They don't belong to nothing.'

'You're saying——'

'Not much. Only this: You either belong or you don't. You see me here in my small office which costs me a hundred and fifty a month? You see my shoes which I have had resoled? I belong. I don't have to prove nothing.'

'So?'

'You belong. You don't have to keep hitting on your chest to prove something.'

Ray grinned. 'You mean I can't even wear a tailored suit? I have to resole my shoes?'

Oliverotto chuckled. 'You can wear tailored suits. You will. It's all a part of having been born into it. You're a brother or you're not. You get it now?'

'No.'

'You will.'

'I've been around to see Benny and Nicky,' said Ray. 'How're they doing?'

'Good boys,' said Oliverotto. 'Occhiaccios they are not, but they got their own kind of brains.'

'What kind of work are they doing for you now?'

'What you don't have to know, you don't have to know. How is the school, the business administration?'

'Fine,' said Ray.

Uncle Oliverotto nodded. That checked with the reports he was getting directly from his connections at Fordham.

'So continue. I have nothing more to say to you now.'

While Ray was away at school, Uncle Oliverotto kept his eye on Beniamino and Nicky Polo. They were developing along a predictable curve. 'How are they on heavy work?' he asked Tony.

'Very good,' said Tony, 'especially Benny.'

'That's good. From now on, for a while anyhow, keep them on enforcement. Also let Beniamino help keep the dock people in line for Brigiddo. How's he doing on collecting?'

'He brings in the money,' said Tony. 'He can't count too good, but he's never short. I got no trouble.'

'The count is always right?'

Tony grunted.

'I have a new young man coming down from Boston,' said Uncle Oliverotto. 'Tony Saldana.'

'The old man's boy?' said Tony, raising his eyebrows.

'The same,' said Oliverotto. 'You will put him to work at the bottom. Old Saldana doesn't want his son spoiled, it should be too easy for him.'

'Old Saldana is smarter than you are being about young Occhiaccio,' said Tony.

'Don't worry about that,' said Oliverotto. 'Raimondo has character. He will be all right.'

'One of these days he has to make his bones,' said Tony.

'When he does, it will be a good one. What I tell you now, put it away in your head.'

'Like you say,' replied Tony.

The next time Ray came visiting he showed Uncle Oliverotto his draft card and his notice from the draft board.

'Forget it,' said Oliverotto. 'I got other plans for you. I'm not making an educated boy out of you to waste you in some-

281

body else's business.'

'Why? I think I ought to pitch in against that sonofabitch Hitler.'

'You're not finished with school yet.'

'I'll finish when I come back. I owe it to Uncle Sam.'

Oliverotto slammed his palm down on the desk. 'You owe Don Oliverotto,' he shouted. 'Not Uncle Sam. You are my man, not his.'

Ray smiled. 'With all due respect, Don Oliverotto. This is not what they have been teaching me in the school. They tell me it is a citizen's duty to defend his country.'

'Then they have been teaching you the wrong things,' snapped Oliverotto. 'This is not what I wanted. I need you for my business, not Uncle Sam's.'

'*Cumpare*,' said Ray, 'when I return from the war, I will obey you in all things.'

But Oliverotto remained unmollified. 'Uncle Sam has a wider choice than I have. Let him take care of his business in his own way. You belong to us.'

'But the draft board says I have to go.'

Oliverotto waved his hand. 'This is childishness. I can arrange it with the draft board so that you will have a heart with rheumatism in it. Or six children, or that you have been dead for twenty years. Now, with a war going, we are going to be very busy. We will need you with your new brains.'

'That's dishonest,' said Ray.

Oliverotto swore a ferocious Sicilian oath. Then he closed his eyes and slapped his forehead with his fingers, his mouth set in long-suffering lines. He finally opened his eyes and stared at Ray. 'I have spent my money to fatten a mule. Stay at least until you graduate, Raimondo. I will fix the delays with the draft board. Then you can go as an officer, at least.'

'That's no guarantee I won't get killed,' said Ray.

Oliverotto looked at Ray and shook his head in silent exasperation. 'All my good work is undone. That accursed school has corrupted you. Nevertheless, your blood belongs to me, not to Uncle Sam.' He shrugged resignedly. 'You are still going with Marta Peruzzi?'

'We see each other pretty regularly,' said Ray. 'I take her

out on dates.'

'I'm going to send her to law school to become a lawyer,' said Oliverotto.

'Is that so!' exclaimed Ray. 'She didn't say anything to me about it. You! I thought you didn't believe in that sort of thing.'

'I don't. But she is the only one in that family with the brains. She's going to college at night on her own wages.'

'I know that,' said Ray. 'She's one smart secretary.'

'That's not enough. One must keep up with the times and have an open mind. Another woman, let her stay in the house and cook for a husband. But I want Marta for you. Is it not better to be in bed with Marta than in a war? I can fix that, too.' He looked at Ray. 'You like the girl?'

'Fine. But right now I don't want her getting too close. Not with this war on. As it is, I'm getting too used to her. Where does it end up?'

'In bed, fool, with Marta as your wife. Where else? In marriage. What's wrong with that? She's a fine girl. I will make her an educated girl for you. She loves you and that is good enough.'

'I don't know,' said Ray. 'Not with this war. Maybe I don't get home from overseas. Then, if I do and go into your business—— You don't have to tell me any more. A wife and your business don't mix.'

'Ah,' said Oliverotto, 'you make too much of it. Look at me. I was married to my wife thirty-eight years before she died. Look at Tony. He's got two grand-kids. Sure, there is angles against it. But you have to be married, Raimondo. What other way is there to live?'

Ray shook his head. 'I don't know. I've heard from some married men when they go to jail they do their time twice as hard just thinking about their families. That's no good. I notice some of them try to play it conservatively, too close to the chest. That's the surest way to lose. There's no way to play it safe in your business. It's like playing scared poker, the worst kind of poker.'

'What is all this talk about jail?' said Oliverotto. 'Listen, boy, you're telling me things I've been through forty years ago.

Sure, what you say about marriage slowing a man up in the business is right. But you're making too much of it. You can't insure yourself on all sides. You live single, like a dog, you'll still make mistakes. And if you have to do a stretch, it'll be no easier for you. It'll be harder. You'll be a dog, all alone. Marriage is bad'—Oliverotto shrugged—'but being single is worse. In any business. You might as well say being alive is bad. Just being in the world, you're taking a chance. What you are really trying to do is play it safer even than a married man. No, I don't agree with you.'

'Well, it's all academic,' said Ray. 'I don't have to make up my mind about marriage just yet.'

Oliverotto stared at him. 'You have made up your mind about this?'

'I am going to the war,' said Ray and held out his hand.

When Oliverotto clasped it, Ray bent over and kissed his hand. Then he walked out in silence.

The following Sunday, for the first time in twenty years, Oliverotto went to mass.

CHAPTER 19

When Ray returned from the wars three and a half years later, still in uniform, he went around to see everybody in the old neighborhood.

When everything had quieted down and they got to the nut of things, Beniamino said, 'So how was it? You never wrote much.'

'Sometimes good, sometimes bad,' said Ray. 'I was never much for writing.'

'That's a lot of fruit salad you got there,' said Frankie Rondelli.

'You stay alive long enough,' said Ray, 'they pin stuff on you. You got nothing to say about it. How's it been with you, Benny?'

'I been in a war, too,' said Beniamino, 'only I didn't get medals, only plenty of headaches.'

'How's the old man?'

'You ain't seen him yet?' said Nicky Polo.

'I'm going up there tomorrow for dinner.'

'The old man don't change,' said Beniamino. 'These skinny guys they just get skinnier and better tanned, like an old piece of leather.'

'Me and Anita was out in California last year,' said Frankie Rondelli. 'We stopped a few days in Albuquerque. I got an uncle living out there. What for, I don't know. Personally, I'd go crazy there. Well, you see these old Indians around the Santa Fe railroad station. They look maybe about a hundred and ten years old and they ain't got no pot on them. My uncle says they could outwalk you and me. Well, what I started to say, that's how the old man is, like those Indians.'

'So why don't you just say it?' said Nicky Polo.

'What I mean is,' finished Frankie, 'they don't change. They just get preserved.'

'I wouldn't like to have you making speeches at my funeral,' said Nicky Polo. 'They'd never get the grave filled up.'

'Which reminds me,' said Ray. 'I have to go out to the cemetery where my father and mother are buried. I wrote them last year from Europe and sent them money for perpetual care. I come over there yesterday and you know what it is? All hay all over the plots and everywhere around also. And the graves sunken in. I told them, raise up the graves, clean it up and green it up and keep it green. That's what I'm going to see now—if they did it.'

'Those damn cemeteries,' said Beniamino, 'bunch of robbers if you don't keep on their tail.'

'If the hay is still there,' said Ray, 'they're going to eat it. If the ground isn't filled up, they're going to fill it with their heads. I'll see you boys around after I've talked with the old man.'

After Ray left, Pecci said: 'I asked him before about all that stuff on his chest but he ain't talking.'

'I heard about one of them medals from another guy that was in his outfit,' said Beniamino. 'This guy that told me ain't got no feet. They get frozen off or something after you stand in water long enough. Anyhow, it's a Silver Star. They give you that when you hit a lot of guys who by rights were supposed to hit you.'

'So what did he do?' said Pecci.

'This medal I'm talking about,' said Beniamino, 'Ray was supposed to have got that for strangling twelve Germans with a wire. That was around Anzio–Nettuno. Then he blew up their gun and the whole goddamned house it was in and everything. Then he went back.'

'I thought it was a knife,' said Nicky Polo.

'It was a wire,' said Beniamino, 'a short piece of thick piano wire with hand grips at each end. They teach you how to use it.'

'How do you know?' said Frankie Rondelli.

'This other guy without the feet told me,' said Beniamino.

'Twelve guys!' said Rondelli. 'They must of been sleeping.'

'Sleeping is also good,' said Beniamino. 'You want they should of been awake?'

'For that they give you a Silver Star?' said Rondelli.

'That's all,' said Beniamino. 'Nothing to it.'

When Ray finally met Uncle Oliverotto again, he recalled Frankie Rondelli's description. The old man must have been taller before the war. Now he seemed to have shrunk into himself and become thinner. Right. Like one of those ageless Indians. He tried to remember what he knew about Uncle Oliverotto. Nothing really. The old man had always been there like a monument. And without a record of any kind that anyone knew of.

The table was spread for a feast and Oliverotto's few relatives were there. Also Ray's sisters and their husbands. Also Marta Peruzzi and her mother.

Uncle Oliverotto embraced Ray and kissed him on both cheeks. 'You are the guest of honor,' he said. 'Tonight we drink to you and no business.'

After that first *festa* and the round of visits, Ray put the uniform and the fruit salad away for good.

'Now,' said Oliverotto in a subsequent meeting, 'you got a lot of catching up to do. I have a lot of work for you to take care of, like a cow that's got to be milked. If you don't milk it, the cow gets sick—you know what I mean?'

'The cow will have to wait a little longer,' said Ray. 'I'm going to get some more schooling under the GI Bill.'

'Didn't I give you enough?' said Oliverotto.

'You gave me the appetite. Now I'm going to go to Harvard and get me an MBA.'

'Is that good?'

'Very good for your business. Keep things running. I'll be back before you know it.'

'How long?' said Oliverotto. Now, Ray noticed, the old man was asking, not telling.

'Two, three years,' said Ray. 'How's Tony?'

'Dead. Peaceful in his bed. Like a good Christian. You're supposed to take his place. Well, if I got to hold things down till you get back, I've got to. I need a strong young right arm. That's what I was trying to tell you when you were a stupid kid, when you didn't want to go to high school.' Oliverotto looked at his gnarled old arm. 'It's not so strong as it used to be. After all, I'm getting along. You make that MBA quick because you may have to take over my place quicker than you think. Everybody goes.'

'You're good for another thirty years yet,' said Ray.

Uncle Oliverotto closed his eyes and raised his eyebrows and chin in mocking irony. 'You just be ready to step into my shoes when you get the word. You say you need some more college, okay, but God ain't interested in no college timetables. The Family has agreed and I have cleared it with the commission. When I go, you step in. That is the clear agreement and understanding.'

'The other people understand it that way? I don't want any trouble.'

'Beniamino and Polo are your *capos* and your old friends,' said Oliverotto. 'They will keep the others in line. Also, there is a third *capo*, a very good man you will meet, Tony Saldana. But they are *capos*. You, I trained to be a boss to take my place.'

'Otherwise things are going okay?'

'Very okay. The war you were fighting made us some more. Before the war we were doing all right, but small compared to what it is now. Now we are legit and it is complicated so maybe a little more schooling won't hurt. And now, because I am training you to put on my hat, I will tell you the greatest secret of all.'

'What's that?' said Ray.

'That there is no secret. That's all.'

'What are you getting at?'

'What I'm telling you. There is no secret. There really is no big center table of big brains floating around and saying to everybody: Do this, do that. There is no court saying: This is the law; obey, or else.'

'No Organization?'

Oliverotto gestured impatiently. 'What is this Organization everybody that doesn't know talks about? Is it something you can see like the Washington Monument, the Empire State Building? There is no such thing.'

'So what is there?'

'Businessmen,' said Oliverotto. 'In the same business, the franchising business, one man here, another man there, all over the country, all in the same business. They have conventions, they talk about prices and fair practices and government regulations, like another business. What is good for one man is good for another. You think they're something special, extra smart in some way? No, Raimondo, very ordinary people. Only this—they hustle, they work hard, and they think in the same language from the old country, without words.'

'I don't believe it.'

Oliverotto smiled. 'You have been seeing too many pictures, Raimondo. What do you think, we Sicilian people are some kind of magicians? Even if you work hard, it guarantees nothing. The people, the customers, want what we got, that's what makes us so smart. We just happen to be in a good franchising business.'

'The government doesn't like the way you run it.'

'Sure they don't. The muscle gives us a little edge. They don't like *that*. Other things. The taxes,' Oliverotto shrugged, rolled his eyes, and sighed. 'America! Such a wonderful, beautiful country. So many good people.' He opened his eyes wide and stared hard at Ray. 'And so may thieves, also. From the top to the bottom. We're a very small business, Raimondo, when you think of how big America is.' He sighed again. 'I will never understand it. But we will not be a thorn in Uncle Angelo's ass much longer.'

'You mean the Organization's going to fold?'

'I didn't say that,' said Oliverotto cautiously. 'I only think that our people will slip away, *piano, piano*, out if this business. We will disappear and become Americans.'

'Just like that, and leave a hole?'

'No hole, Raimondo. Plenty of new people will come in, Puerto Ricans, black people, Polacks, Jews, Germans, the polenta eaters from the north of Italy——' Oliverotto paused and spat. Then he chuckled. 'Even the Protestant Yankees who were the first robbers in this country. When you see the pictures of the wild Western *banditi,* what are you looking at, eh? Protestant heretics, all good Americans.' Oliverotto paused to take breath. 'As long as there is an America, the way she is now, there will be this business and the people in it.'

'That reminds me,' said Ray. 'I always wanted to ask you. What is this Mafia the papers and the government people keep talking about?'

Oliverotto laughed. 'Ah, La Mafia! Sure, Raimondo, there used to be a Mafia in the old country. In the west—Partinico, Monreale, Correale, Palermo, Trapani—only in the west. It was the rackets dressed up fancy. It was a part of the life.'

'It isn't there any more?'

Oliverotto shrugged. 'How would I know what goes on in the old country? I am an American.'

'So that is the secret?'

'That is the secret. That there is none.' He paused. 'Now I wish to speak of something which concerns you. I have raised this before.'

'I listen,' said Ray.

'I have seen you grow up into a young man of respect and good habits. I have not seen you in much time but I judge that you will do your work well and live quietly. I do not think that you are a drinker, a gambler, or a chaser of women. You speak low and show respect. That is all to the good. Now that you have returned alive from the war, there is only one thing.'

'What's that?'

'You need a wife. It's time you were settling down.'

'I'm not ready yet. I have a lot of things on my mind outside of women. I'm not sure of anyone yet.'

'She is sure,' said Oliverotto. 'She is waiting for you to go to her and ask her.'

'Who?'

'Do you speak with a stranger? I don't have to tell you who. She is your right eye. She will be better than your right arm. Every man needs one, even you.'

'Marta Peruzzi?'

'You knew it all along as well as I. I warn you to marry her. If you don't, your good fortune will run out and you'll meet death himself on the staircase.'

'How can you be so sure?'

'How? Because I am old and have had a lot of experience. With her beside you, you will be fortunate. Without her, who knows?'

'You have a point,' admitted Ray. 'But I have this priority. When I come back, I'll think about it.'

'You do that, busy man,' said Oliverotto. 'Come back fast. I do not think I have that much time.'

CHAPTER 20

In the years which immediately preceded his deportation, Ray attained the zenith of his career. When Uncle Oliverotto died, a major emotional link was severed for him. When Oliverotto's soul parted from his body, Ray pressed more fat from his own heart, that soft, self-deluding quality which he had hitherto unconsciously thought of as humanity. He hardened his heart with satisfaction and said to himself, Now I finally see clearly. Only later did he come to realize that, like the infinity of calculus, full clarity was a theoretical ideal and a constantly receding unattainable. At the commencement of each year he had been saying to himself, Now I see clearly. Now I am down to bedrock. But, at the year's end, he always found that he had perversely reserved to himself some ragged tag-end of self-deception and illusion. He finally realized that only the dead were perfectly wise and skeptical, because their hearts were perfectly hardened. As long as a man breathed, he would harbor somewhere in his being the virus of folly and a tendency to error. Only the dead, indeed, were wholly autonomous, and, hence, wholly immune to error. So, at the end of each year, Ray was forced to say to himself: If hate is a sickness which distorts reality, love is an even worse sickness. All feeling weakens and impedes. But feeling is an inescapable component of life. One is compelled to feel as one is compelled to breathe, urinate, and defecate. Even Joseph Fouché, a better man than myself, was compelled to obey the Law of Feeling. Just as birth is the prime misfortune, so is feeling an organic disadvantage of being alive. Moreover, in a world of flawed and feeling men, the perfection of unfeeling is a disadvantage. It's like playing sound logical poker with beginners.

They'll steal your drawers, precisely because they don't know what the hell they're doing. So I'm still a fool, but at least I'll keep punching.

Ray's office had been in downtown Manhattan for the past several years. Now he moved his place of residence from Brooklyn and cut the cord. He agreed with the opinion that Brooklyn was a monstrosity. It was a hideous borough (whatever that was) which would never succeed in becoming a city. Brooklyn was an elderly drooling idiot with hardened egg stain on its bib and a propensity for spasmodic viciousness. Brooklyn was a drab, stale, stinking bedroom, the ultimate in unrelieved sprawling ugliness and dreariness. It was a prime and worthy candidate for instant atomic obliteration and the world would be relieved by the passing of Brooklyn, as by the lancing of a ripe boil. And yet he had lived in that goddamned place how many years? He had even experienced some happy days there. Uncle Oliverotto lay buried there. His mother and father slept there. The old woman, Marta's mother, still lived there. Nicky and Beniamino still worked there. Brooklyn had claims on Ray, but he tore them up coldly and turned his back without regret. At the same time, he sensed that his new strong hatred for the place was irrational and, therefore, suspect. It was safest to feel nothing.

After returning from Harvard, Ray had leased an apartment in Brooklyn Heights and had commuted to the office in the Wall Street area just across the river. With the opening of the decade of the sixties, he moved up to Beekman Place. I like this, he thought, looking at Beekman Place. It's good for me. Through merger with another group, his interests were now citywide. As a result of that merger, Ray's financial strength had increased. A negative result, however, was that he had been forced to accept Al Poggio, the representative of the new group, as subboss of the Occhiaccio Family. Poggio was one of the conditions on which the consummation of the merger rested and Ray had reluctantly acceded. Indeed, Ray's original prejudice against Poggio had been born on the day that he was forced to accept a stranger over his three trusted *caporegimes*. Even if Al Poggio had been the soul of rectitude, Ray would have hated and resented him because the man had been imposed. And Ray had always been a man slow to love and quick to hate.

Beniamino and Nicky Polo were left behind to hold down the Occhiaccio satrapies in Brooklyn. By this time, Tony Saldana had entrenched himself predominantly in Queens and nearby urban Long Island.

At the time that Ray made his push across the river, Beniamino was courting Janie Califano in an elephantine fashion. Beniamino did so not because he had original inclinations in that direction but because the late Oliverotto had commanded him to do so. 'Look at it this way,' Beniamino had explained to his associates. 'You gotta get married some day, right? You're gonna get hooked sooner or later, right? I admit I don't know shit from shinola when it comes to picking a wife. If I went shopping on my own, I'd more'n likely wind up with some lousy bimbo. The old man had more brains in his left tit than I got in my whole body. So the old man says to me: "Benny, you marry Janie Califano. She'll be okay for you. She won't give you no trouble." So I figure this way, that I got like an expert shopper picking over the broads for me. What am I gonna do, spit in the man's hand? The man sees something I don't see, so I figure I'll play along and take advantage. That way I'm being smarter than a lotta guys that always try to pick their own stocks. I got experts doing it for me.'

The crack about stocks was meant for Nicky Polo, who prided himself on being an astute trader in securities. 'Benny,' said Nicky disdainfully, 'you sound like one of those chicken-shits who buy mutual funds.'

'Fuckin' right I do,' said Benny blandly, 'and I'm doin' a helluva lot better than you are. I got expert professional management.'

'Shit,' said Nicky contemptuously. 'Any time you want to match performance results, let me know.'

'You'll be sorry, wise-ass,' said Beniamino cheerfully. 'But I'm talkin' now about Janie. I got expert advice and I'm takin' it.'

Beniamino and Janie threw a party for Ray which included the other two *capos* and their wives.

'Well,' said Beniamino to Ray, 'now that you're a big executive, you gonna have to turn in your Buick and get yourself one of them new Eldorados.'

'So happens I have an order in for a new car,' said Ray.

'Yeah?' said Beniamino. 'A big Caddy?'

'Caddys are old hat,' said Ray.

'Not in my book,' said Beniamino. 'You seen the new sixty's? Man, they got real class! I love them sharp tail fins. That's it; you can't go further than that. That's the livin' end.'

'Nothing's the living end,' said Ray. 'Besides, there's no production control on those bathtubs.'

'Yeah?' said Beniamino. 'So why do people buy them?'

'Lots of people don't know any better. Lots of people still on the make.'

'All right, so what're you gettin'?'

'A little quiet Mercedes-Benz.'

'You must be nuts, Ray,' said Nicky Polo. 'You pay in tariff duties almost as much for one of those jobs as you would for a Caddy.'

'They're worth it,' said Ray. 'They're engineered right. They have quality, not a big mouth.'

'Danny Danielli won't look right driving you around in one of those,' said Nicky. 'It's too small.'

'Let that be my biggest problem,' said Ray.

'What color you gettin'?' said Beniamino.

'Charcoal gray.'

Beniamino looked disgusted.

Ray poked his finger into Beniamino's belly. 'A Mercedes is quiet. It doesn't flash. You don't remember it. Never forget what the old man always used to say—don't splash in the tub. The IRS is always watching. Keep it low key, pay by cash, and remember the net worth yardstick. Aside from the book-keeping, you boys always remember one thing: Don't live in a style that won't square with the figures you hand the IRS. Especially you, Nick, because you always keep a boat. If you're going to run a forty-footer on top of everything else, you can't go reporting a twelve-, fifteen-grand annual income.'

'So, if you can't spend it,' said Beniamina, 'what's the use of piling it up?'

'It's a fact of life you have to live with,' said Ray. 'Like dying. There's no escaping the IRS. The tax boys are your first wives. Every step you take, keep them in mind. The only out is to legitimize your income. That's what we're going to start doing now. When you hit the big time, you develop a philosophy about money or break your neck. Money isn't for buying beans, it's for reinvesting. We're at the point now where we don't need income except for emergencies and that kind of cash can stay stashed outside the U.S.A.'

'I don't know what the hell you're talkin' about,' said Beniamino.

'So listen,' said Ray. 'You can only eat three meals a day. You can only wear one suit at a time. A man making fifty grand a year is as well off as a man making five hundred grand or five million. When people get greedy and start splashing, that's when the IRS kicks them in the balls. I'm talking to you, Benny. Keep it down, keep it low, don't splash.'

Ray now had a busy job shaking down his new Manhattan organization. In the morning, Danny Danielli, neat in a black suit and black tie, behind the wheel of the Mercedes, drove him downtown from Beekman Place. He spent his time reviewing figures sent in the day before, daily reports from the books and the numbers bankers, weekly reports from the slot operators and the juke combines, monthly reports from the breweries and the whiskey distributors, everything which the reorganized outfit owned and controlled, legit and illegit. The other outfit had lost its identity and the new merger was known as the Occhiaccio Family. We have enough to go public, thought Ray, over-the-counter, or on the American. The first balance sheet showed such a robust ratio of assets to liabilities that the Occhiaccio conglomerate could probably get a direct listing on the New York Stock Exchange. Be interesting if we could, thought Ray sardonically. Imagine selling the public shares in the rackets! What we really ought to do is set up as a closed-end investment company. It may come to that some day. By that time, we'll be strictly and entirely legit. In the meantime, it was pleasant to look at all the clean pages of neatly typed figures and to check off one thing against another. He had come a long way from that first insurance company which he and Benny had operated in Brooklyn as kids.

At noon, Ray would ride uptown to Jerry's barbershop for a shave and a massage. Jerry's was a second office where he met those who had business to discuss—more cash for the retail shylocks, an argument over juke territories, a beef among the books and controllers, and sometimes the humble, homely items which recalled Brooklyn: this one, after a touch, that one, after a job, somebody else, a fix to be put in with the law. Each day they waited for him to show. Even on Sundays, Jerry kept open to take care of Ray and his petitioners.

Ray lunched at Pucci's in the East Fifties, where there was no menu for those on the preferred list and the captains knew whose patronage to discourage. Whether or not he showed, Ray had the same corner table continuously reserved. He did not have to ask twice for anything and appreciated Pucci's service and attention. But, after all, it was his money which had helped open Pucci's in the first place.

Pucci's, Ray cautiously conceded, was fun. The bar prices were two hundred percent higher than they would have been in a just very good place where the same quality drinks were served. The dining room was just as right, in the same price range, and for the same reasons. In every big city in every country, there were the places where you paid a premium not for the food, booze, and service but to keep out the crowd, which was strictly cholera. What with the world becoming daily tighter, Ray accepted the premium for a place in which to relax, kick off his spiritual shoes, and catch his breath. Although Pucci's existed for the insiders, room remaining, a stranger who had the what-with was allowed in grudgingly. It was Ray who finally called over Massimiliano, the proprietor of Pucci's, and made the Edict of Toleration official. 'You know, Massimo,' he said, 'there's no point in keeping the place as just a hangout for the boys. They're liable to become inbred and develop too restricted and parochial a viewpoint.'

'Whatever you wish, Mr. Hodgkin,' said Massimo.

In the same tone in which God had once proclaimed, 'Let there be light,' Ray replied, 'Let the world in. But only if you have extra room.'

'Of course,' said Massimo.

297

'After all,' said Ray, 'the world is interesting. We can learn something from it, especially from the legit. Besides, I, personally, enjoy observing people from other milieus.'

'You've got something there, Mr. Hodgkin,' said Massimo and cautiously eased Pucci's standards of admission.

So Pucci's became a focal point of infection for several random groups which had in common gall, nerve, and a big hunger for the world, as they understood it. All were ambitiously on the prowl for something, young would-be tigers with empty bellies and ceaselessly switching tails. The girl swiveled around the man she had in tow, constantly appraising him through the small talk. The girls hunted hard. It took a lot of scratch to keep a girl in the right dresses through a New York summer, in an apartment at a sound address, in Bermuda, Southampton, and Pucci's. It took money to live in New York City, to believe in the ads, and, simultaneously, to think beautiful. Many were called and few were chosen. That was why the girls at Pucci's studied their Johns so intensively. That was why the feminine archers aimed higher than the target so that their arrows might hit the bull's eye on the down-leg. One had to check out ever so many hopeful young males to locate the right one. And then one was never sure. The proof was on the young man to deliver, and who knew how long he'd be able to maintain the pace before cracking? Because, in addition to all else, the girl expected him to get it up in bed. That often became a problem. After a day of batting out his brains to keep this piece of fluff in the style to which she wished to become accustomed, the young man's weariness braked his potency. And the girl would finally ask, 'You never used to be so cold. Don't you love me any more?'

Not all of the girls made it. Most of them missed not only the bull's eye but the entire target and ended up settling for less and less. Women were fortunate, reflected Ray. Like cats, they adjusted and accommodated themselves. They tried for the best seat in the house and the two-hundred-buck dresses. If they didn't make it, they aimed for the hundred-buck or the fifty-buck dresses, and, even if they had to settle for a ten-ninety-five number on special sale and eighty-nine-cent hamburger, half of it fat, in a suburban supermarket, they still didn't crack. Their bones bent like a cat's. They rolled with the punches and said what the hell. That was the strength of women. By that time the young men with whom they had paired when skin and jawline were still tight were dead. Or, if they still survived despite worry, fear, anger, and disappointment, they owned ulcers and coronaries. In this regard, Manhattan was an undesirable town. One had to make it, no excuses accepted. The majority didn't. Who knew the percentages? The minority who did had nothing to worry about except their medical and hospital bills. New York City was a worm which ate up a man's eyes, hair, heart, guts, and balls as termites devoured a house, leaving only the coat of outer paint. But the boys and girls on the make kept coming and trying, and loving Pucci's in the process. The girls were along for the ride, like pilot fish hooked up under the shark's jaw, hoping they'd connected with the right shark. If their shark sickened or was ripped to pieces, they dropped off and sought another. That was *their* problem, and it was quite a problem. Ray sympathized.

You had to have *some* money to withstand the Puccian tariff two, three, or four times a week. But not big money, which didn't come there anyhow. The very rich interested Ray as they had interested F. Scott Fitzgerald. But Ray was unimpressed, because he had the lever of muscle to offset the deadweight of legit superwealth. That made all the difference. Still, he was interested in the specialized, narrowly unique intelligence of the very well heeled. They weren't all-around intelligent or street-smart, as he himself was, but they understood what money was, what it would do, and, most important, what it couldn't do. Since big money didn't satisfy and couldn't really protect, the very well heeled were constantly running scared and haunted and big money became mere compensatory damages for lives otherwise wretched. Which reminded Ray of gloomy septuagenarian Paul Getty being interviewed before his English mansion. 'Well, Mr. Getty,' said the brisk BBC man, 'now that you look back on it, how would you sum it up?' Paul Getty had cleared his throat glumly and replied: 'I've increased the net worth of this trust and am leaving it in better condition than I found it. Mine has been a satisfactory stewardship.' Well, what else could the poor guy say, seeing that he knew in his heart he'd been screwed? What he really meant was: 'I'm glad I've had a job all my life and a reason for being.' Ray Hodgkin sympathized and congratulated himself on being in that lower echelon which could enjoy the passing parade and the human comedy at Pucci's. People from the name publishing houses dug the joint; their lives seemed to revolve around lunch. The snakes and the weasels from the big ad shops on Madison Avenue were there. The tiger cubs with delusions of grandeur from the big TV networks. The fiery young bulls from the performance funds which turned over their portfolios quarterly, trying to steal a march on the bulls with whom they were lunching. Show biz types paying to be seen. They, too, had problems. All the arthritic aches of wealth without the wealth. Models who were making it. Expensive call girls glowing like athhletic drum majorettes. Shrewd, waspish, business-oriented faggots in interior decorating or garment designing who could swish daily to the bank. Occasional young inherited money just taking in the scene for kicks. Some talent. Some brains. And, finally, the majority with plenty of nothing and enough gall to fill a three-mile freight train. That was Pucci's and its duplicates in midtown East Manhattan. One really didn't have to step out of the joint. Pucci's could play you the entire tape and you'd get only a repeat, neither better nor worse, at the next place. In sum and total, no big money, only on-the-make money which could be shoved off its foundations because the mortar was still wet. So what did it all boil down to? Only this: An intelligent man should keep a skull by his bed and read his will weekly to remind himself of the folly of piling up excess. The heart of Pucci's, the Organization bosses, knowing this truth, accepted good fortune stolidly. They had inherited nothing and had started from the gutter. They knew that they were lucky to be alive. They weren't worrying about the problems of setting up foundations for useless great-grandchildren. There were emeriti there who had made their original nut in bootleg, lived through the gang wars, and teamed up with the Jews to push out the Irish and make peace. Sympathize with Organization bosses, Paul Getty, thought Ray, as I sympathize with you.

We, too, have our problems, even if we survive to retire without a bullet in the head or a stretch in a federal can. Were Organization bosses happy? Who was happy? An Organization boss, being mortal, died like anyone else. He was laid out in a ten-grand bronze casket in a three-hundred-dollar suit. His hat was placed on his chest, a rosary was shoved into his hands, willy-nilly, he was stuck into the ground, and the state, the lawyers, and the *caporegimes* wrangled over what was left.

Late in the afternoon, Ray had another regular spot. It was the cocktail lounge in a little family hotel off Park Avenue, the Burford, which no one but elderly people frequented, people in a bracket so high they could not afford to show off. It was here that Ray kept his appointments with the judges and politicians who did not care to be seen going in and out of his downtown office. It was here that Ray made the important pay-offs for fixes and connections. It was in this phase of his life that Ray recalled Colquhoun for bestowing upon him that harsh, ugly, and supremely unmelodious English name, Hodgkin. Because of its intrinsic defects, 'Hodgkin' blended with his present milieu. He had no need to hastily Anglicize an Italian name, as had so many of his confreres upon attaining a plateau of significant respectability. Not that Ray accepted without resentment the world's casually neutral approval of 'Hodgkin.' He had looked up the name's antecedents. There were several in the telephone book, all apparently obscure, unknown, average people. It was an overwhelmingly mundane and plebeian handle, like Smith, Jones, Taylor, or Carpenter. The only bearer of note he could discover was an English physician who some hundred years before had discovered a rare and apparently fatal disease. This disease had been named in the Englishman's honor, to wit, Hodgkin's Disease. He had mentioned it once to old Doc Freyer in Brooklyn, who had snorted and laughed. 'Hodgkin's Disease! Right. The cause is unknown and the outcome fatal. Don't contract it, Ray, you hear me?'

It was irksome as well as interesting that Anglo names should enjoy such universal acceptance—perhaps because of their frequency, which provided a bland protective anonymity and coloration. Who were the English that their names should retain the prestige of Swiss Francs and gold bullion while Italian names did not? Perhaps because the U.S.A.'s roots were Anglo. No chauvinist in this matter, Ray appreciated the blank, bony stare of Hodgkin. Yet, privately, he enjoyed the palatable clatter of Occhiaccio, the Baleful Stare. There was a sound with guts to it! What was he, then? Sicilian? Italian? American? English? None of these. Simply Ray Hodgkin or Occhiaccio, and he had made his mark. Let others have the publicity. All that interested him was the substance, protection against a hostile world. He was of the species of M. Joseph Fouché, that agile genius who had survived five regimes and died a multimillionaire. He, too, was one of the joyless ones who saw too clearly. It wasn't the money that counted, it was the satisfaction of having beat the game, as Fouché had done. Whatever the manager of the Burford thought about it did not matter. The manager was a well-paid employee who watched his tail and properly performed his duties. Mr. Raymond Hodgkin held the first and only mortgage on the Burford.

At any time between 7 and 8 P.M. Danny Danielli called with the Mercedes and drove the boss home to the Beekman Place apartment. Ray had vetoed too predictable a pattern of movement and had two unobtrusive buttons in the background from the moment he left his apartment in the morning until he returned to it in the evening. The buttons occupied a table at Pucci's or lounged at the bar. They held down a rear table at the Burford during Ray's visits there. When he left with Danny, they trailed the Mercedes in a Chevy driven by a third button.

While Ray hadn't achieved domesticity in Beekman Place, it wasn't the stern, stark bachelorhood of Brooklyn Heights either. Marta Peruzzi was there on occasion, waiting to have dinner with him. Not bed, just dinner. Ray had never quite noticed how she managed it, but she had done so. He explained it to himself as an apathy following the daily competitive grind, so he gave tacit acquiescence. He had been able to regulate many things, but not Marta Peruzzi. By omitting to voice a specific negative vote, he had consented to this female's positive drive toward himself. Talking to her had been useless. No matter what he said, Marta had an answer. In any case, he always had broads available for sex on a strictly commercial basis. That was safest: Pay them off and show them out.

And so had the routine gone until Robert Francis Kennedy lowered the boom on him.

Oliverotto had often said to Ray: 'Let's not kid ourselves, Raimondo. We are in the rackets. The people who protect our rackets to fatten their own wallets are the politicians and their enforcement arm, the police. When things are going smoothly, the cost of the fix keeps going up. When the voters every once in a while demand reform and investigation, the politicians drop everything and run. They bow to the voters, not because they want clean government, but to protect their own interests. They start a crime investigation and throw enough racket people to the voters to turn away heat from themselves. As long as you are in the rackets, Raimondo, you'll have to pay off. But never trust them. Politicians are interested in only one thing, keeping their jobs and the graft that goes with it.'

When it came Oliverotto's time to die, he did so as inscrutably as he had lived, disdaining to show anything, even relief. The physician had telephoned Ray up in Beekman Place and said, 'The old man wants to see you immediately.'

'How is he?' said Ray.

'Sinking,' said the physician. 'That's why he wants to see you.'

Ray drove down to Oliverotto's. No one was in the house except the physician and Perciata, the house button who attended to the old man's wants. Oliverotto seemed small in his big black four-poster. His white hair was neatly combed, his face was pale, and the sheet and coverlet were drawn up to his chin. His voice was low but quite clear.

When he saw Ray, he gestured without expression and motioned the visitor to be seated. 'I have sent for you because I am leaving,' he said.

'Do you want a priest?' said Ray.

Oliverotto smiled. 'Raimondo, my boy, your mother once asked your father that question. I give you in substance the answer he gave her. No, I don't want a priest. What would I

303

do with one? I have never believed at any time.'

'Do you wish me to call your sisters from Jersey?' said Ray.

Oliverotto shook his head. 'When a man is dying, it's foolish to have old women about. They cry and become noisy. Their tears are as meaningless as a puppy pissing on the carpet.'

Ray went aside with the physician and asked the question with his eyes and chin.

The man of medicine shrugged. 'His heart and kidneys are failing. He's dying because the power plant switches are being shut down; literally, of old age. Someday we may be able to keep a man such as Oliverotto alive to the age of one hundred and thirty. But, today, he's slipping away.'

'You could keep him going, though, couldn't you?' said Ray.

'Of course,' said the physician, 'for three months, six months, perhaps even a year or two. But he won't permit it. He absolutely refuses.'

'I agree with him,' said Ray.

'So do I, in a way,' said the physician. 'With an ordinary man, it would be a different matter, but not with Oliverotto.'

He and Ray once more approached the bedside.

'Don Oliverotto,' said the physician, 'in the presence of your godson as witness, it's my duty to remind you that, in conformance with my Hippocratic Oath, I must attempt to prolong your life.'

'For how long?' asked Oliverotto sardonically.

The physician shrugged.

'To hell with your Hippocratic Oath,' said Oliverotto. 'I make my own schedules. Save your pills and fluids for someone who seeks them. I have business to discuss with my godson. Go and wait in the other room until he leaves.'

When the physician walked out, Oliverotto said, 'Well, Raimondo, my boy, I'm one of the very fortunate ones. How many men are privileged to leave so easily?'

'May my own end be as good,' said Ray in Sicilian.

Oliverotto nodded. 'You say well. My affairs are all in order. Ricci has the will and you will go over it with him. You are the executor of my estate as well as the principal beneficiary. I've set up income trusts for my sisters. You know how women are. No brains. Ricci will go over it with you. That's all I can think of. Good-bye and go.'

Ray knew what the answer would be, but he asked the question nevertheless: 'Do you want me to remain with you until the end?'

Oliverotto grimaced. 'What end? Who knows when it will come? No, don't wait. If you do so against my wishes, you will behave as a woman and it will displease me. A man with balls should always meet death alone. That's how I want it. Do you see, Raimondo, how I'm leaving by my own will and at a time of my own choosing?'

'I see,' said Ray.

'Then remember my example when your own time comes. This is a good end, not that of the priests. Now go.'

'You're sure?' said Ray.

'I'm sure and it's important,' said Oliverotto. He lifted his hand from the coverlet. Ray raised Oliverotto's hand and kissed it. Then he went.

Ray recalled that final meeting many times in the years which followed. He always returned to the original conclusion. There had been no fat in Don Oliverotto's heart. He had reasoned well, chosen well, and died well. The worms would break their teeth on Oliverotto. He would rust in the ground, but very, very slowly. Truly, a good example.

BOOK THREE

CHAPTER 21

Ray dialed Tony Saldana's house in Mineola. When Tony answered, he said, 'That you, Tony? No names. Do you know who this is?'

Tony hesitated for a second and replied, 'Yeah. When'd you get in?'

'Last night,' said Ray. 'We drove all night.'

'We?'

'I have a man with me.'

'Where you calling from?'

'Midtown.'

'Give me the address. I'll send a car out to pick you up.'

'Your phone okay?' said Ray.

'As okay as it can be,' said Tony. 'I check them all out twice a week.'

'Still, there's no use in your taking any chances of a tail. We'll take a cab out to your place, not where you're talking from, the one in Long Island City.'

'I'll start right out,' said Tony Saldana.

'What day is this?' asked Ray. 'I've lost track.'

'Saturday afternoon.'

'Still better,' said Ray. 'It will be quiet out there.'

'I'll meet you there in an hour,' said Tony Saldana.

Ray emerged from the booth on the lower level of Grand Central Station. He and Torres walked up the stairs and emerged on the Vanderbilt Avenue side between Forty-second and Forty-third streets. A cab was just discharging a passenger. They got into it. Ray gave the driver the address in Long Island City.

'It don't pay me to drive you out there, pal,' said the driver.

'It's dead out there Saturday afternoon, I come back empty, I'm losing money.'

'Now I know I'm home,' said Ray. He handed the driver a five-dollar bill. 'This is for you, outside of what we put on the meter. Go across on the Queensboro Bridge. I want to take a look at it again.'

'You been away, mister?' said the cab driver in a friendlier tone.

'I've been living in Wichita,' said Ray.

'Wichita? What's that?'

'A disease,' said Ray and laughed. 'Where I'm going in Long Island City is only about a half hour from here. You trying to crap an old New Yorker?'

'It's a tough hustle,' said the driver. 'On a Saturday, only around here in Midtown can you make a buck.'

Ray sank back into his seat with a sigh of pleasure.

'What did the driver tell you, Don Raimondo?' said Torres.

Ray grinned. 'He was scolding me.'

'Why?'

'It's a mental disease peculiar to the cab drivers of this city. They're compulsive talkers, grumblers, gossips, and scolds.'

'Well, if you ain't been here for several years, like you sound,' said the cab driver, 'there's a lot of new places they been building——'

'Shut up,' said Ray. 'I'll do my own looking.'

The cab sped out on the bridge gratings heading across the river to Long Island City. Ray said to Torres, 'Look out on the right. That street is simply called Fifty-eighth Street, East Fifty-eighth Street, to be exact. Do you see the little house at the end of the block? The one overlooking the river?'

'I see it,' said Torres.

'That little house has always symbolized this island of Manhattan for me. I have always had my eye on it. I was afraid it might be gone when I returned. But it's still here. Pretty. Like a little doll house.'

'What about it?' said Torres raising his eyebrows.

'If all goes well, I shall buy that house and live in it,' said Ray.

'How do you know the owner will sell?'

310

'When I am ready to buy, they will sell,' said Ray.

'What is so unusual about this house?' said Torres. 'A little nondescript house, dwarfed, overwhelmed by big buildings, in a windy, gloomy city, overlooking a dirty industrial river.'

'To understand the desirability and peculiar appeal of that house,' said Ray, 'you have to have New York City in your bones. Not all of New York City, just this little enclave. There is a charged, throbbing excitement humming through every street here.'

'I feel nothing,' said Torres.

'How could you?' said Ray. 'I feel what a Parisian feels when he returns after twenty years in Brazzaville, or a Londoner after twenty years anywhere. This city is my native place and I know all its nuances. For me, this neighborhood, this district, is charged with sexual excitement, a huge erection and an orgasm that never stops pulsing.'

Torres listened politely and Ray laughed. 'Tell me Juan, have you ever felt a particular affection for some city and for some particular area in that city, a place where you would like to spend the balance of your life?'

Torres smiled and shook his head. 'There's none in my memory. The great sands of the southern Sahara, the mountains of the Atlas and the towns of the North African coast are all too violently removed from this. Barracks, troop ships, and the stark, alien Maghreb. Nothing of that has stayed with me.'

'Alien? Even after two and a half decades?'

'After a century it would still be alien,' said Torres. 'The Africa I have known was a moonscape, a hostile land, no doubt because we made it so. It was a no-man's land to hurry through.'

The cab sped down Queens Boulevard going east.

'Look at those dirty, old, tired, flat-assed little buildings,' said Ray. 'They call them taxpayers. Brown, dull, dirty red brick. Yessir, we're in crumbly old Long Island City all right and even *it* looks good.' He pointed to the elevated tracks to their left. 'That's the IRT, Juan, part of the dirtiest, most fucked-up subway system in the world. Look, the damn thing it still running, just as if I was never away.'

'Your friend Saldana is waiting for us at the warehouse?'

asked Torres.

'That's what he said,' replied Ray.

'We could be walking into a fusillade,' said Torres.

'It would be a beautiful opportunity, wouldn't it?' said Ray. 'I've always played it strictly fair with Saldana. He has always been aces with me.'

'But men do change,' said Torres. 'Conceivably, he, and the others also, could be better off with you buried in Italy. Even if they think well of you, nevertheless your return upsets a pattern of living which has begun to harden. That is always vexatious. It can be irritating and men can be like a horned viper in the sand. Something irks it and it lashes out.'

Ray nodded. 'I could reason: If I can't trust Tony Saldana, who *can* I trust? And it would be quite irrelevant.' He tapped the driver on the shoulder and said, 'That number I gave you, drop us three blocks before you get to it.'

When the driver finally pulled up at a deserted curb beside a silent factory building Ray paid him with another five-dollar bill and got out after Torres. 'Let's kind of stroll up to the place—and keep your gun handy, Juan.'

The warehouse fronted Queens Boulevard. One block from their destination, Ray turned down a side street going east. They kept walking until they came to a sleepy little luncheonette which was open. 'That's something,' said Ray. 'These places by rights should close up on a Saturday afternoon. It's dead around here as Kelsey's nuts. Let's go in.' There was an open pay phone in the luncheonette. Ray dialed the warehouse and Tony got on.

'Look, Tony,' said Ray, 'I'm here in this little greasy spoon about two or three blocks from your place. Write the address down. You get in your car alone and drive over here and pick us up. We'll wait for you till you get here.'

Tony's voice was unsurprised. 'Sure, Ray. You just stay put. I'll come right over.'

Ray hung up the receiver. 'Smart boy. He understood all right.'

Five minutes later Tony pulled up in front of the luncheonette in a dark chestnut brown Cadillac with a padded top. Ray was sitting at a table with his back to the wall sipping a cup of coffee. Torres was sitting at another table in the corner where he was not visible from the doorway. Tony walked in and Ray beckoned him over.

Tony sat down and said, expressionless, 'Hi, boss.'

'You all alone, Tony?' said Ray. 'Everything okay?'

'There's nobody in the place. I came alone.'

'Fine,' said Ray. 'We'll go back with you.'

'We?'

'That's what I said on the phone. I have this man with me.' He pointed to Torres, who was sitting at the corner table behind Tony. He beckoned the Spaniard over. 'Tony, this is Juan Torres. He knows a lot of languages and speaks Italian better than both of us, but not English. So speak in Italian.'

Tony Saldana and Juan Torres shook hands.

'Being kind of careful, aren't you, Ray?' said Tony.

'Don't read anything into it. Let's go.'

Ray and Torres followed Tony out and got into the backseat. Tony swung around and headed back to the warehouse.

'You got the drop on me,' said Tony calmly.

'I'm peaceably inclined, as usual,' said Ray. 'Just careful.'

'So am I, Ray. Everything I'm doing is on the level.'

'Don't worry about anything, Tony.'

Tony got out of the Cadillac, unlocked the gate controls, and pressed a button. The gate began to rise. Tony got back into the Cadillac and drove it in. The three men got out of the car. Tony pressed the close button and the gate came down. 'Now we're private,' said Tony. He led the other two through the warehouse area toward a small glassed-in office in the back. He took a bottle of Teacher's scotch and three shot jiggers from a wall cabinet and filled them. He lifted his. 'Welcome home,' he said. 'Glad to see you again.'

'Tony,' said Ray, 'as I said before, talk in Italian. I want Juan to know the score on what we're talking about.'

Tony nodded.

'We came in across the border from Montreal yesterday,' said Ray. 'We've been doing a lot of driving. We have a lot of things to do. In a few days I'm going to phone Willis Howard and turn myself in to the feds. But, first, there are a few things we have to do.'

313

'They'll throw you in the can,' said Tony.

'Not quite,' said Ray. 'We'll post an appearance bond immediately with the I and N people. After all, I'm coming in voluntarily. Then there will be some more time before the U.S. Attorney makes his presentment to the grand jury.'

'Yeah, well—I guess you know what you're doing.'

'That part of it I've got zeroed in. Now about Poggio, what is the score on him? Did you find out anything else?'

'It was Poggio all right,' said Tony. 'It couldn't have been anyone else. About those Fiats—we've never been able to prove anything. But you have to go by the way he's acting.'

'How's he acting?' said Ray.

'Strong. Right out in the open. He's gone over and joined Len Codi, with his whole crew. He took all his buttons with him.'

'Did he have to twist their arm to go along with him, or did they just go?' said Ray.

'Some went, no questions asked, like they were going to a picnic.'

'Do you know which people they were?'

'I know some of them,' said Tony. 'Those I missed maybe Nick and Benito know.'

'Good. So get a list of their names,' said Ray. 'That's the last thing we'll take care of. Now this wholesale walkout, did the commission okay it? How about Amerigo LoCroce? He's in with the commission. Did he just lay down and say okay to Codi and Poggio?'

'From what I heard he voted against it,' said Tony, 'he and a couple of other guys. But the majority went along. Why not? Look at it this way: Remember when you were shipped over, Poggio was subboss and acting boss of the family? So he wasn't out of line. Also Codi himself sits on the commission. There's four or five other guys that don't want to rock the boat. So, seeing that you are out of the country, they think what the hell and just go along. You know, all these guys want is not to disturb their own setups. What they are saying is this is a private matter inside the Occhiaccio Family and no outsider should get into the act.'

'A very convenient ruling,' said Ray. 'Those guys change

the law and make new rulings every day to suit themselves, it seems like. So, maybe, *I* might make some rulings to suit myself. Now, about you, where do you and Nicky and Benito now stand about this thing?'

'We don't,' said Tony Saldana. 'We are *capos* in the Occhiaccio Family. But, according to Poggio, there is no more Occhiaccio Family and Poggio says we have to go along with him and join up with him and Codi. Okay, the three of us—Benito, Nicky and me—got together and talked it over. We said to Poggio we want to think about it before we move.'

'What did Poggio say?' asked Ray.

' "Sure," he said. "Think if over till the first of the month." ' Tony touched the desk calendar. 'That's two weeks from now.'

'So what happens by the first?' said Ray.

Tony shrugged. 'You read what he's saying: If we don't come over with our regimes and get squared up in the new arrangement before the commission, we are not friendly, we are on our own.'

'What does that mean?'

'You go figure it out. It could mean anything from he will forget all about it and let us go our own way and set up our own outfit to he will pull out as many of our buttons as he can and then he can knock us off like clay pigeons. The fact is, we don't have the muscle to take on a Poggio–Codi combination.'

'How do you feel about it?' said Ray.

'How do I feel? That Poggio is trouble for all of us. He has to go.'

'How about Nick and Benito?'

'Well, you know how it is with Benny. He's your boy. He'll put his head on the block for you. Nick is the same way. They're solid.'

Ray turned to Torres. 'Juanito, you're following all this?'

Torres nodded. 'Quite clearly.'

'Nick and Benny,' said Ray, 'have they got a good hold on their outfits? There's not going to be any of that cop-out stuff like with those people Poggio pulled along with him?'

'If I'm going to be sure,' said Tony Saldana. 'I can't speak for Nick and Benny. That's their business. When you see

315

them, you talk with them about it. Like my saying their people are okay doesn't mean anything, you know what I mean? *I* think they're all right, but you ask *them* to make sure. For my own buttons I can talk. *Them*, I know.'

'Before we move I'll check it out with them,' said Ray. 'You have in your crew—how many people?'

'Twenty-two,' said Tony. 'I can vouch for all of them. There's not a bad apple in the bunch.'

'So, figuring that Nick and Benny have at least as many in their own crews——'

'More,' said Tony.

'Okay. At least sixty men. And Juan Torres here is an assault team all by himself. I want you to stash him out of sight till we're ready to move.'

'What do you have in mind?'

'From what I hear,' said Ray, 'we have to go after Poggio immediately, now, without delay, before I surrender to the feds. I want to move fast on him, before I am spotted and the word gets around.'

'Move how?' said Tony. 'You want to hit him? What good is that? Does that get your money back?'

'I'm going to snatch him. After he pays up, he gets buried.'

'If you do it that way,' said Tony, 'you just alert Codi. He'll louse you up good in some way. That's one man, don't underestimate him. He and Poggio, they have one head.'

Ray thought a long while. 'You know something, Tony? You're right. You're absolutely right. The play is to take both of them. What we don't get out of one, we get out of the other. If you want the arithmetic, I don't have to tell you there is cash one and one-third million dollars involved. That's aside from all the other lumps those two gentlemen have coming.'

'There's one more little item,' said Tony. 'The commission says you can't snatch a member for ransom. Also that you can't snatch and/or hit a boss without you first clear it with them and get their okay. And Codi is a boss.'

'My heart bleeds for them,' said Ray. 'We'll just have to make an exception this time, maybe two or three exceptions, because this is such an exceptional case. As you say, those fat cats don't want to rock the boat. The only thing they respect is the accomplished fact. Well, they are going to get a few—right in the puss. You know what they accept? The thing that has been done. If you can do a thing and make it stick, that's all that counts.' Ray toyed with his empty shot jigger. 'Right, between those two cookies, we should be able to squeeze the money owing out of them.'

'Then what?'

'Then we hit them both.'

'Kill Codi? Without an okay?'

'I'll take it to the commission and lay it on the table,' said Ray. 'Those two *gonifs* tried to give me the shaft. I gave it to them first. They'll square it somehow. Besides, Amerigo LoCroce is a friend of mine. I'll get *his* vote.'

'Man, you're playing wild,' said Tony.

'Man, I'm just scooping up grounders,' said Ray. 'This is a real fast game. This is how we have to do it. Then we have some working space to wheel and deal. We have money and muscle. We have breathing space and bargaining power. Right. This has to be settled first. Then I will worry about the feds.'

'Okay,' said Tony. 'Let me get on the phone with one of those guys. I'll call Benny. He'll bring Nick out.'

He dialed the number and waited. 'That you?' he finally said into the receiver. 'How you been? Yeah. I got company here. An old friend of ours. Who do I mean? Yeah. Well, I'll put him on.'

He handed the receiver to Ray. 'It's me, all right,' said Ray. 'Yeah, I haven't heard your voice in a long time either. You get over here. Pick up our other friend on the way. One hour. Okay. See you soon.' Ray hung up. To Tony he said, 'He knew my voice right away. They're both coming over.'

The three men sat and waited until they heard the outside bell ring. 'That's them,' said Tony S. 'Wait here.' He went out alone into the warehouse. Ray and Torres sat silently and heard the overhead door slowly rising. Tony finally came back into the office with Beniamino following and Nicky Polo last.

When Beniamino saw Ray, he began to cry. He threw his arms around Ray and kissed him on both cheeks.

'For Christ's sake,' said Ray, 'you're acting like you were

317

my mother.'

'Yeah,' said Beniamino. 'Jesus, Ray, I can't help it. When I am moved, I start bawling.'

'There's a lot of you to move, kid,' said Ray. 'You look like you put on forty, fifty pounds since the last time I saw you.'

Beniamino sighed. 'Blame my wife.'

Nicky Polo came over. He and Ray embraced. 'Skip the kissing, for Christ's sake,' said Ray. 'That Benny is like an old country wop. How've you been, Nick?'

'Okay,' said Nick, nodding his grizzled head. 'Just seeing you again, I feel twenty years younger.'

'We're talking in Italian here, not English,' said Ray, 'on account of my brother. I want you two guys to meet Juan Torres. As I told Tony, he talks a better Italian than you guys. I don't care what you call him. Giovanni or Juan, he's my brother and I officially declare him a Sicilian going back a thousand years.'

Beniamino and Nicky shook hands with Torres. 'If Don Raimondo says that you are his brother,' said Beniamino to Torres in Sicilian, 'then you are his brother and our friend. Welcome, Giovanni.'

Ray was moved to be viewing Beniamino again. This was the childhood friend with whom he had worked his kid rackets. They had screwed the broads in grade school together and fought side by side against the Nittis until Oliverotto had split them up. Beniamino had been faithful. 'Okay,' he finally said, 'Roll up the red carpet and put it away. We have to talk. You still in the old neighborhood, Benny?'

'I never left it,' said Beniamino. 'Nicky and me have been working together all these years. We work everything partners—the books, numbers, the loan money, crap games, everything.'

'You said you were married?'

'Yeah, I'm an old married man now. I married Janie Califano. You remember her? She was in grade school with us.'

'You got kids?'

'Three,' said Beniamino. 'And I think Janie has got a new loaf in her oven.'

'You old fat bastard,' said Ray. 'With all that beef you're

318

carrying around on you now, it's a wonder you can get it up to knock out four kids.'

Beniamino threw his arms once again around Ray.

'For Christ's sake,' said Ray, 'stop acting like a Saint Bernard dog. I know you're glad to see me. I'm glad to see you too. Tell me, how's Marta Peruzzi?'

'She's doing great. She's a lawyer now. A good one, I hear.'

'So she made it,' said Ray.

'Yeah,' said Beniamino, 'the old man, may he rest in peace, he bankrolled her all the way through, like he said he would. She's now a junior partner in your law firm. The one that handled your business, you know——'

'How about that!' said Ray. 'She's now a part of those WASP bastards?'

'Yeah,' said Beniamino, 'it's now Willis, McGowan, Courtney, Hardin & Peruzzi.'

'Isn't that something!' said Ray. 'All they need now is a Shapiro and they'll be a real wake-up-and-live New York law firm.'

'She asks about you,' said Beniamino. 'Every once in a while, she gives me a call at home. She doesn't give her name and it's the only unbugged unlisted number I got left. She says, "How's Ray doing? You hear from him?"'

Ray sighed. 'We're wasting a lot of time, Benny. We have work to do. All right, so what do you say?'

'I don't tell her nothing,' said Beniamino. 'Naturally. I say, "Yeah, Ray is a great guy, but I don't hear from him." Once I met her at Frankie Rondelli's funeral. You remember him? He got a heart condition working too hard or something. Marta came up to me and said, "You really don't hear anything from Ray?" I said, "Honest to God," and she said, "If you're ever in touch with him, say hello to him from me special."'

'Little Marta,' said Ray. 'So she's an attorney now. How does she look? Did she get married?' Ray looked at Tony and Torres apologetically.

'Don Raimondo,' said Torres, 'this is more important than all the business in the world. Even if the world is falling apart, these things must be said first.'

'You're goddamned right, Giovannino,' said Beniamino.

'That's the way I feel.' To Ray he said, 'She's single, eating her goddamned heart out. What're you going to do? Hey, Nick, come on over and join the human race. I'm getting dry in the throat.'

Nicky Polo had been sitting alone on a couch just looking and listening.

'You still in the junkyard business, Nick?' said Ray.

'Tony and I are still running the old scrapyard in Greenpoint,' said Nick. 'We just bought another one out in Jersey. We also just bought a garbage collection business here on the Island.'

'Look at your hair,' said Ray. 'It's all gray.'

'What the hell, Ray! I still got more hair left than you have.'

'I'm doing okay. No bald spots yet. You haven't had the worries I've had. So now *you* tell me something about Marta.'

'So she's going to be an old maid,' said Nicky. 'She looks good. You know, a figure like a young girl yet. No fat on her. She don't eat pasta like my wife and Janie. She's getting a little gray in her hair, just around the edges like. So she's a lawyer. So she's still sleeping alone.'

'What makes you so sure?' said Ray.

'When a broad's sleeping alone, you can see it in her face,' said Nick. 'Whyn't you give her a break and call her up?'

'I'll be talking to her,' said Ray. She and her forty thieves will have to take care of my unlawful reentry charge.' Ray paused. 'Tony, give them the scoop on what we've been discussing. We can't waste any more time.'

When Tony Saldana was done, Ray said, 'We lay plans right now to take Al Poggio. Start planning.'

'It's like this,' said Beniamino. 'Poggio's gone high class. He's got himself a big place out in Sands Point with an English tailor and a butler and he takes lessons from a special teacher on how to talk right in public and stuff like that. I remember him when he was running a book and a few whores and peddling junk. There's been a lot of changes.'

'How do we get at him?' said Ray.

'Not through the front door,' said Tony Saldana. 'You'll see the security I got out in my place in Mineola when you come

320

out there. Poggio's got twice as much. And where he's at in Sands Point, there's only one two-lane dirt-and-gravel road leading away from the place. One call from his house and the cops can block it off. He's supporting them out there. The best way is land on the water side, by boat. Poggio's got a pier for his boat and everything. I got a guy in there. You remember Al Franzelli? Well, Al went with Poggio. Now he's sorry because—I'll tell you about Poggio, he's greedy. I won't go into details.'

'Don't,' said Ray. 'Let's get going.'

'Well, anyhow,' continued Tony Saldana, 'Poggio promised Al a crap game that they took away from some other guy. The name's not important. Instead, Poggio gave it to a nephew of his that just graduated college. Poggio made him also. Some snot-nosed punk, that's all he's been doing is going to college, for Christ's sake.'

'Skip the details,' said Ray. 'Get to the point.'

'Al Franzelli is sore,' said Tony Saldana. 'That's the point. So we made a deal. He gives us the word when Poggio comes out to the Point for a weekend. We go out there by boat and take Poggio.'

'Who's he got out there?'

'Nobody. Just Al Franzelli and a houseman and a gardener and his family. He don't do no business out there.'

'His family, eh! I ought to chop off their hands and feet for openers.'

'That might spoil things,' said Nicky Polo uneasily. '*That* the commission might really make a stink about.'

'But I won't,' said Ray. 'Just Poggio. Also, we have to take Codi the same or the next day.'

'*There* you got a break,' said Tony Saldana. 'Him and Poggio are neighbors out there. Country gentlemen. Golf players.'

'Get the word out to Franzelli,' said Ray. 'Let's get going. This weekend. Now. Tonight. Tomorrow. It's a weekend, isn't it?'

'So fast?' said Tony Saldana. 'We got to plan a little.'

'Nothing to plan,' said Ray. 'Let's move on the sonofabitch. I remember in the war we had a general who was always way up ahead of us and we were chasing him and the *Red Ball*

Express was chasing us trying to keep us in boots, bullets, and rations. He went through those goddamned Germans like epsom salts through an eel. His name was Patton, you remember him?'

'Yeah,' said Beniamino, 'he was the guy with the pearl-handled guns that slapped that wounded kid in a hospital.'

'He should have kicked the punk's ass through his shoulder blades,' said Ray. 'That's what I would have done. The point is, we attack. Juanito, am I right?'

'Totally right, Don Raimondo,' said Torres.

'Call Franzelli right now at Poggio's house,' said Ray.

'Ray, it's risky,' said Tony.

'Screw the risk. Call him.'

When Tony Saldana put down the phone, he said, 'I took a helluva a chance. Al Franzelli is in Poggio's house alone at the moment. He says Don Leonardo is staying at Poggio's this weekend. It's a big party for the two families. One of Codi's daughters is getting graduated from college or engaged or something. Franzelli took one helluva chance talking.'

'We move now, Franzelli will be in the clear in forty-eight hours,' said Ray. 'Okay, the boat. Nicky, you still got yours? I always remember you kept one even when you couldn't afford it.'

Nicky Polo grinned. 'What I got now, it'll knock your eye out. With two big Chrysler engines. It drinks gas like a wino drinking rotgut, but it goes—boom!'

'Where's the boat?'

'City Island,' said Nicky.

'Let's go then.'

'You don't have to go personally,' said Tony Saldana. 'Why take a chance?'

'This I wouldn't miss for anything,' said Ray.

'I got a man in Mineola, Fats Mazzi,' said Tony. 'In case we got some locks to open, he's a genius.'

'Tell him to go right out to City Island direct and meet us at Nicky's boat,' said Ray. 'Have you got any guns at your house?'

'I shouldn't but I do,' said Saldana.

'Tell Fats to take all his tools and six pieces with him. Tell him to check and load the pieces carefully. Do you have any dynamite at your place?'

'Yes,' said Tony reluctantly.

'You're a helluva citizen,' said Ray sardonically. 'Tell Fats to take along a whole case of it, priming caps, cord, the works.'

'What do you want to do, blow up Sands Point?' said Tony.

'The way I feel now, yes.'

'Let's eat first,' said Beniamino. 'I can't work on an empty stomach, especially I'm doing button's work, which I'm not used to any more.'

'You'll eat Poggio after we get finished with him,' said Ray. 'I'm not waiting for you to eat. We got two cars here. Let's go.'

Ray and Torres got into Nicky Polo's car and Tony drove off with Beniamino.

'I'll head right up for the Whitestone Bridge,' said Nicky. 'As good a way as any.' He took off but kept within the speed limit. 'We got to wait for Fats and get the boat ready. Then we have to wait till after dark before we shove off.'

'Do you keep any guns on the boat?' asked Ray.

'God, no!' said Nicky. 'You can't keep anything of value on a boat. The kids come around the boatyards and break into the gear lockers and steal stuff out. It's so bad you can't trust nobody no more. No, I have nothing like that aboard. I've got some canned goods and coffee and wine in the locker. Benny can cook us something before he dies of hunger. That man's got no sense of humor when it comes to eating.'

'When do you figure on starting out?' said Ray.

'We should shove off from City Island about ten thirty,' said Nicky.

'You know your way on the water—the lights, the buoys, all that stuff?'

'I've made the run several times,' said Nicky. 'I got all the charts. Not that I'll need them.'

'How long do you figure on taking to get there?'

'Going very easy, about three hours. Say we get there about one in the morning. That's a good time.'

Nicky tooled the car over the Whitestone Bridge and up the Hutchinson River Parkway and turned off at the City Island ramp. They drove into the boatyard. Saldana and Beniamino were already there.

'Come on,' said Nicky and led the way to his slip.

Ray surveyed the cruiser in its gleaming white paint and polished brass. 'This is some big hunk of wood, Nick.'

'Not so big,' said Nick modestly. 'Only forty feet. I want speed mainly. It's a Matthews. Very conservative. Like a Buick in cars. But fast. It's a good thing I'm making a living to support this thing.'

Fats Mazzi drove into the yard and began bringing two suitcases aboard.

'You got everything, Fats?' said Tony Saldana.

'Like you said,' replied Mazzi.

'We can't leave till after dark anyhow,' said Nicky. 'Benny, there's a lot of groceries in the locker. Start cooking something. It'll keep your mind off your belly.'

Beniamino tore all the canned goods out of the locker and said, 'You guys better go into the wheelhouse. Like this place is very confined and I am very big. I'll call you when it's ready.'

'Make enough for Fats also,' said Tony Saldana. 'Open up everything you got.' He turned to Fats. 'Open up one of those suitcases. Let's look at the pieces.'

Fats Mazzi, a five-by-fiver, grunted and complied. 'There's six thirty-eights here,' he said, 'and six boxes of slugs. I just grabbed it all up and threw it in the case. The guns are empty. You can load and check them yourselves.'

Torres examined one of the revolvers. 'They look brand-new.'

'They were taken off a West Side pier only a couple of weeks ago,' said Saldana. 'Brand-new merchandise. If one gets used, which I hope it ain't necessary, it should get dumped immediately.'

Each man loaded his gun and put it in his belt.

'Let Beniamino check and load his own when he gets finished cooking,' said Ray. 'That way, he'll be sure.'

Beniamino brought down a couple of pots of strong black coffee. 'This'll take the edge off. The food will be ready soon.'

While they were sipping coffee they waited patiently. Beniamino finally called them. 'Soup's on. There ain't enough room for everybody. Three of you guys stay where you are. I'll bring the stuff over to you.'

They began to eat. 'You're a lousy cook, Benny,' said Tony.

Beniamino shrugged. 'Canned goods on a two-burner hot plate. What do you want, miracles? How can spaghetti and meatballs from a can be good?'

'There's a couple of apple pies in the fridge,' said Nicky. 'Warm them up and cut them up. It'll take the taste away from this crap.'

Ray finished his cup of coffee, lit a cigarette, and sat silently. He finally stretched himself out on a bunk. 'I'm going to take a nap. Call me when you're ready to shove off.' He promptly fell asleep.

Nicky came down into the wheelhouse. 'Another couple hours yet,' he said. He pointed to Ray. 'Let him sleep. Don't wake him up. It's a long pull.' He said to Torres, 'you, too, Giovannino, stretch out.'

'Thank you,' said Torres. 'We were driving hard.'

'So sleep,' said Nicky. 'We'll wake you in plenty of time.'

Torres stretched out on another bunk and promptly fell asleep.

'Do we take those two finks,' said Saldana, 'where do we hold them? Where's the best place?'

'The best place I got is that railroad flat in Greenpoint,' said Beniamino. 'I was using it for a numbers bank up to two weeks ago. Then we moved it. It's a natural. It's got four bedrooms and goes through from front to the back of the building.'

'You can tell Ray when he wakes up,' said Saldana.

'If Greenpoint was crumby then, he ought to see it now,' said Beniamino. 'This place has got a lot of privacy. I fixed up one room in the back without windows. I had the window taken out and bricked up. It don't matter anyhow because this rat trap backs up on a railroad siding, a kind of spur track with the ass end of a factory on the other side of the track. We can put them both in that room.'

'Show it to Ray,' said Saldana.

'Even the door,' continued Beniamino. 'I got that fixed up

like a fake bookcase, wallpaper behind so you don't even know there's a room there.'

'Tell it to Ray when he wakes up,' said Tony.

'It's got its own can and enough ventilation to keep them alive,' said Beniamino.

'All right, already,' shouted Saldana. 'I don't care if it don't keep them alive.'

'Keep your voice down,' said Beniamino. 'Let him sleep. Listen to him snore, for Christ's sake. Like Enrico Caruso belting out *Rigoletto*. The other guy too. Beautiful.'

Nicky Polo came into the wheelhouse and started first the port engine and then the starboard engine. 'I'm going to let them warm up ten, fifteen minutes,' he said. 'Benny, you keep your fat ass inside. You're too big to move around out there in the dark. I'll use the flying bridge controls. Tony, when I give you the word, just cast off the fore and aft lines and I'll back out of the slip.'

Ray woke up and sat up on the bunk.

'Who asked you to wake up?' said Nicky Polo. 'You can knock in at least two, three, more hours sack time.'

Ray stood up and yawned. 'I want to see this. I don't want to miss anything.'

'How you feel, Ray?' said Beniamino.

'Great. I was dreaming how you and I were beating the crap out of Louie Nitti. Look at Juanito. Sleeping like a dead man.'

'He sleeps good,' admitted Beniamino almost enviously.

'This man could sleep on razor blades, end up,' said Ray. 'He has done things that would put dry ice in your balls.'

'If you say so,' said Beniamino.

'You know me,' said Ray. 'I don't talk loosely.'

Nicky Polo pushed the throttles out farther and the cruiser hull began to vibrate a little. 'Okay, Saldana,' he said, 'get out there up forward and cast off one line. I'm going topside.'

'I think I'll join you,' said Ray. 'I want to get a lung full of this nice stinking City Island air.' He climbed up the ladder and sat down next to Nicky.

'Okay, Tony,' Nicky shouted, 'Cast off the stern line.'

He reversed both engines gently and drifted backward clear of the slip. Still holding the port engine in reverse, he pushed

326

the starboard engine throttle over gently. The cruiser swung slowly on its keel until it was pointing out into the blackness with its transom toward the end of the slip. Nicky put both engines on SLOW AHEAD and moved into the darkness.

Ray watched the shore lights falling away and said, 'These range lights and buoys got me all confused. I've lost my sense of direction out here.'

'It's like a parkway,' said Nicky. 'All you have to know is what you're doing. We're going to head across to the north shore of Long Island. The channel is marked out clear. Then we just stay on course heading east along the north shore till we make the Sands Point buoy. Then we start heading in.'

'I hope you know where you're going,' said Ray. 'Don't wind up in Port Jefferson or something like that.'

'Don't worry,' said Nicky. 'You want to be smart, go below, relax, make some coffee, get some more sleep. We got a long ride ahead because I'm going to make it at half speed. I don't want to get there too early.'

'Okay, skipper,' said Ray. He climbed down the ladder and reentered the wheelhouse on the main deck. 'It's black as a whale's gut out there,' he said.

'Nick knows where we are,' said Beniamino.

Ray stretched out and began to doze off and finally fell asleep again, lulled by the gentle roll of the hull and the throb of the engines.

He finally awakened because Saldana was shaking him. 'Okay, Ray, we're going to go in. We just passed the marker buoy.'

Ray sat up. 'How long was I asleep?'

'More than two hours,' said Saldana.

Nicky had come down into the main wheelhouse. He had throttled the engines down and the cruiser was barely crawling. 'I can con her in from here just as well. Turn off all your inside lights. I'll just keep the riding lights on. We'll just drift down nice and easy with as little noise as possible.'

'How do you know where you're going?' said Ray.

'There's a channel marked out with poles, each one with a number on it,' said Nicky. 'Fats Mazzi is out there on deck watching for me. If you ever get a boat, remember, it's red

327

right returning. It's like signal lights on a main drag. We ought to be there in another ten minutes.'

Ray kept peering into the darkness.

Finally Nicky said, 'You see ahead of you a few lights there? That's Poggio's place. It's got a long bulkheaded waterfront and a little pier sticking out from it where he keeps his boat. You see that place sticking out there in the dark? That's a mast he has at the end of the pier with three red lights one over the other.'

The cruiser drifted down on the lights and the outlines of Poggio's own boat were now visible.

'The boat over there belongs to me,' said Ray. 'Everything here does.'

'Yeah,' said Nick, 'old Al Poggio has developed a lot of class. His daughters go to a private school out here on the Island, you know, one of those places that puts a simonize job on dumb broads to help them find a husband. It's great how easy you get used to good things. That bum took to it like he always had it.'

'We'll see if it works that way in the opposite direction,' said Ray.

Some fifty feet away from the pier, Nicky pulled the engine throttles back to neutral. When the bow of the cruiser gently bumped the pier, he reversed the starboard engine and swung the port quarter of the cruiser toward the pier. Fats Mazzi scrambled out and made the stern line fast. Tony Saldana was up forward. When he had secured the bow line. Nicky killed the engines. 'Hah!' said Nicky. 'Any Sicilian of fisherman stock, you give him a boat, he'll piss rings around some of these Sunday yachtsmen. Even Fats. You see how he moved?'

'Fats,' said Tony Saldana, 'take your tool kit and come along. There may be a gate between the pier and the grounds.'

There was one padlocked gate, but Fats Mazzi opened it in a few minutes with the first pick. The house was entirely dark except for a large room in the rear. 'That's the kitchen,' whispered Saldana.

'Nicky,' said Ray, 'you and Juanito stay right here near the gate. If they're in the kitchen they might try to get out by the back. Tony, Benny, and I will go by the front door. That's a long pull from the kitchen if someone's in there. Fats, come along with those picks.'

The four men went around to the front door. Saldana held the flash while Fats examined the lock. 'He could have an alarm system hooked to this door.'

'That's the chance we have to take,' said Ray. 'If they go dashing out the back, they'll get knocked over anyhow. Go ahead.'

'I can open it,' said Fats. 'It would take about fifteen minutes. This is one of those double-tumbler locks. Then, he could have a couple of bolts inside above the locks.'

Saldana played the flash over the door. It was a genuine or a replica of a Sloopy Seventies front door with colored glass around the sides and stained glass side panels. 'This is the kind of crap the decorators are using now,' said Tony Saldana. 'It's coming back in style. The hell with the lock, Fats. Cut out a whole pane down at the bottom.'

Fats Mazzi extracted a glass cutter from his bag and grooved out a rectangular panel of glass with precise incisive pressure. He tapped it out, donned a glove, and inserted his forefinger. Holding the cut glass between forefinger and thumb, he began to cut the entire pane of glass nearest the lock. He went down all around twice to make sure he had a clean cut. There were no wasted motions in his work. Still holding the pane between thumb and forefinger, he tapped the entire section of glass softly. It went back clean. Still holding on, he tilted it to an angle, slipped the pane out, and laid it on the welcome mat at their feet. Then he inserted his entire hand and flipped back the lock and tumblers and a bolt. 'See,' he said, 'there *was* a bolt, a big one.'

'Fats,' said Ray in a whisper, 'you can reopen my grave any time you want.'

Fats grunted and opened the door, while Saldana played the flash down the big hall which led to the kitchen. 'The bum should have had a big dog of some kind sleeping out here in the hall,' whispered Saldana. 'He ain't expecting no surprises.'

'That's what Patton used to say about the Germans,' whispered Ray.

They walked down the hall over soft, deep rugs.

'No creaking,' whispered Saldana. 'That's a break.' He pointed to a curving staircase. 'If there's others up there, they must be asleep by now. Maybe he does have a dog of some kind around here. Maybe Franzelli fixed that up. I'll ask him about it.' He turned the knob of the closed door noiselessly and slowly opened it. The light was shining from under a closed door at the end of a service hall. 'That's the kitchen,' whispered Saldana. 'Somebody's sitting in there.'

He led the way with his gun out and the others followed. Without hesitation, Saldana opened the kitchen door softly, but fast. Ray, Beniamino, and Fats Mazzi walked in swiftly with guns pointed.

Al Poggio and Leonardo Codi were sitting at the kitchen table facing one another. Poggio looked up first because he was facing the door. He stared wordlessly at the four guns pointed in his direction and at the back of Codi's head. Codi, feeling something and noticing Poggio's face, turned around quickly.

Saldana put his finger to his lips.

'What are you boys playing?' said Ray.

Poggio stared at Ray wordlessly.

'What the matter, Al?' said Ray. 'You look like you're seeing your dead grandfather. I asked you a question.'

Poggio did not respond. Ray walked over and banged his gun butt across the bridge of Poggio's nose. 'I asked you a question, creep.'

'Gin,' mumbled Poggio.

'Okay, Fats,' said Ray, 'tape and cuff them.'

The five-by-fiver moved quickly, like a dancer with small feet. He already had two rolls of two-inch friction tape in his hands and began strapping it over the mouths of the two prisoners. Poggio jerked his head once and Mazzi cracked him across the ear with his gun butt. Then he cuffed the wrists of the two men behind their backs.

'Let's go,' said Ray. Fats Mazzi opened the kitchen door and shoved the prisoners out ahead of him. Walking down the dark path toward the open gate and the pier, Codi tripped and fell. Silently, Fats kicked Codi in the side, seized him by the hair, and lifted him to his feet. Alongside Nicky's cruiser, Saldana and Nicky were about to throw the prisoners over the rail onto the deck.

'Take it easy,' said Ray. 'You might kill them. They don't rate any breaks.'

Codi and Poggio stumbled aboard and were thrust into the cabin.

'Fats,' said Ray, 'tape up their eyes. If you have any left, slap some more over their mouths.'

Nicky started the engines into life. Tony Saldana and Ray cast off the lines. The cruiser fell back until it was clear of the pier. Slowly it swung around and headed out into the sound until it came up with the Sands Point marker buoy. Once seaward of the buoy, Nicky shoved the throttles all the way forward and roared back toward City Island with his engines wide open.

In the cabin the five men looked at their two prisoners sitting on the deck, shackled, gagged, and blindfolded.

'Well,' said Saldana, 'it looks like we got our Cornish hens, like we touched first base.'

Ray thoughtfully tapped Al Poggio's back with the toe of his shoe. 'That's what I said in Rome,' he said tonelessly. 'But I'm beginning to think there's more than three bases in this ball game, maybe five or six, maybe more.'

CHAPTER 22

As dawn was breaking, Nicky Polo's cruiser was tied up and made fast at its City Island slip.

'Nick,' said Ray, 'keep our boys stashed on the boat. I don't want them transferred in daylight. You and Benny move them after midnight. Fats, you hang around till seven or eight o'clock and keep an eye on them. Don't untape or uncuff them.'

'That's like twenty hours,' said Fats.

'They'll live through it,' said Ray. 'Tony, let's shove off for your house now. Juanito, you too I think we all need a bath and some clean clothes and some sleep.'

The three men stopped at a diner for breakfast during the return trip. 'Ray,' said Tony Saldana, 'you going to get in touch with Marta now and tell her you're here?'

'Time enough,' said Ray, 'first I have to get the money out of those two babies.'

'This additional day on the boat in their present condition,' said Torres, 'it will make them reasonable.'

'That's the general idea, Juanito,' said Ray.

Saldana halted the Cadillac before the gates of his house in Mineola. The gates swung inward. 'I got an electric eye hookup,' he said. He pulled the car into a three-stall separate garage and said, 'Before we turn in, let me give you the quick twenty-five cent tour.' He led the other two through the grounds. 'I got three acres here of wet grass. Always in the morning it's wet. Plenty of shrubbery around it. Very private.' He indicated a ten-foot wire cyclone fence with four strands of barbed wire jutting outward from the top of the fence. In many places, the shrubbery had grown and curled over the

332

barbed wire. 'I've got an alarm system hooked up with the fence and the gate. That's what Al Poggio should have had.'

'He didn't figure on a boat snatch,' said Ray.

'He didn't want to on account he likes the idea of having waterfront. Class was always a big thing with Al.'

'Your layout is secure enough,' said Ray, looking around. 'Alarm systems can always be cracked, of course.'

'I figured on that also,' said Saldana. 'I have five Doberman pinschers on the place. They're trained to take off a man's hand if they don't know him and they don't know too many people. Also, there's always a couple of buttons on the place. Fats is one of them. The other man is Jack Dumdum. Their front is they're gardeners. Jack is an old pineapple man, one of the best in the business. He makes up all his own parts. He can wire up any kind of job.'

'They don't make those old artists any more,' agreed Ray.

'They're good when you need them,' said Saldana.

'Good deal,' said Ray. 'How do you like it, Juanito?'

Torres nodded approval. 'Very tight and orderly.'

'I'm for a bath and some sleep,' said Ray.

'Follow me, gents,' said Saldana.

The three men entered the house.

Fats Mazzi checked in at nine in the evening.

'How's it going over there?' said Saldana. 'Do they have things under control?'

'They're going to move the two guys to Greenpoint right after midnight,' said Fats. 'They'll pick up the phone and buzz you eleven sharp. You want me for anything else?'

'Nothing. We'll go over there. You stay here with Dumdum. Turn the dogs loose and don't go to sleep. I don't want no surprises. The word is out already. One more day, there'll be buttons all over the place and they'll know where to look. They can put two and two together just like we can. Okay, Fats, take off.'

Fats Mazzi left.

'Ray,' said Saldana, 'you're sure no one knows you're back?'

'By now, I think they all know I'm back. I haven't seen your

333

wife and kids around. Where do you keep them?'

'In the other end of the house where they belong,' said Saldana. 'This is the business end. You want a little more Galliano?'

Ray and Torres nodded and offered their glasses. Saldana refilled the three glasses and slouched lower in a big leather chair. 'So goddamned comfortable in here, I hate to stir out again.'

'As that cab driver observed,' said Ray, 'it's a tough hustle.'

At eleven sharp, the telephone rang. Saldana picked up the receiver. 'Yeah? Okay.'

He hung up. 'They're starting out. We better get moving. We'll meet them there.'

Torres sat in the right front seat of the Cadillac beside Saldana, and Ray lolled in the back as they sped down the parkway.

'There's a good chance,' he said, 'you're going to have a tail on you.'

'You'd better believe it,' said Saldana. 'Once we get into Queens, I'm going to start doubling back and forth. I know the streets around there as good as anyone.'

The doubling, twisting, and turning added a full hour to the trip.

'When I feel I have a tail,' said Saldana. 'I got a trick. I suddenly hit a one-way street and go up the wrong way. That is, if there's no cops around. It seems to work. Something about a one-way sign always makes the tail hesitate for a few seconds.'

'Do you have a BAR in this car by any chance?' said Ray.

Saldana shook his head.

'I know a good way to shake a tail,' said Ray. 'Let him get up close to you and let him have a burst right through the windshield. That usually cools their curiosity.'

'Very old-fashioned,' said Saldana, 'and it's a tough rap in New York now. It don't pay. Anyhow, if we had a tail, I think he's shook already.'

They rolled slowly through the dark streets of Greenpoint.

'Nice place to lose your wallet,' said Ray.

'Ain't it,' said Saldana. 'It really looks worse than it is. I'm going to pull into a garage a half block from the flat. It's part of the drop. The guy keeps it open all night for me.'

'Juanito,' said Ray, 'do you remember the Nahr District in Beirut?'

'Very well,' said Torres.

'This is one of our little Nahrs,' said Ray. 'We have several in New York, including an all-black one.'

'What is this Nahr?' asked Saldana.

'A tough neighborhood in Beirut where Juanito and I went,' said Ray. 'Helluva place. A real swinging town. You ever go into Harlem, Tony?'

'Harlem? God, no! A law-abiding citizen ain't safe there. Too much crime and violence and stuff.'

'I used to read about the situation in New York when I was in Rome,' said Ray. 'It wasn't exaggerated?'

'It's even worse than the papers say,' said Saldana. 'What do you think I moved my family out to Mineola for? The whole thing is out of control. Terrible! You know, that Lindsay, he's a nice guy and all that, and he tries, but what can one man do? I ask you, Ray, what can one man all by himself do?'

'Nothing,' said Ray.

'Right,' said Saldana. He drove the Cadillac into the garage and gave the keys to the all-night attendant. 'Wash her down, Joe. I'll be back in a few hours.'

'Okay, Mr. Saldana,' said Joe.

Beniamino and Nick were already at the apartment.

As the three newcomers entered, Ray raised his eyebrows inquiringly at Beniamino.

'We got them bedded down nice,' said Beniamino. 'I'll show you.' He led them through the long, empty flat, swung back the empty bookcase, and opened a heavy wooden door behind it. The five men walked into a room which had no windows in it, only a grating in the wall, high up near the ceiling. The room was illuminated by a small lighting fixture flush with the ceiling.

'The switch is on the outside,' said Beniamino.

There was an alcove off the side of the room with no door. It contained a toilet and a washbowl and that was all. There

335

was no furniture in the room, just an old green linoleum.

'Do you have any other tenants in this building, Benny?' said Ray.

'Yeah,' said Beniamino. 'You notice the candy store on the corner of this dump? Well, that candy store used to be a numbers drop. Then we turned the whole building into a bank. Then we moved the bank. But the guy that ran the drop still lives here, rent free, to kind of take care of the place. He lives downstairs in the back right under this flat. And the guy that runs the garage where Tony put the car, he has the front flat downstairs, also free. This flat up here takes up the whole floor. I had the wall between busted through. It used to be two flats up here. It's tight up here. Solid.'

'How about the cops in this area?'

'We got the whole precinct house on the pad here. Their bagman comes around every Friday. It's a very quiet neighborhood as far as we're concerned. It looks a lot worse than it really is—you know what I mean? The cops don't give us no trouble and we don't give them none.'

Ray finally studied Poggio and Codi, who were sitting on the floor still cuffed and taped as they had been on the boat the night before.

'They look like they need a pressing and cleaning,' said Saldana.

'Go ahead, Benny,' said Ray. 'Unseal them. Leave the cuffs on.'

Benny began peeling the tape off. Although some skin and hair came away with the tape, neither of the prisoners complained.

'Don Leonardo,' said Beniamino finally, 'welcome to your new home.'

'Codi,' said Ray, 'can you hear me?'

'I hear you,' mumbled Codi through cracked, torn lips.

'Then I'll make it quick. You and your buddy here screwed me on that shipment. You know it. I know it.'

'It could have been settled with talk,' mumbled Codi. He winced as he spoke.

'Len,' said Ray, 'if you want to live long enough to enjoy that customized burial casket of yours—both of them, in fact

—listen carefully. I'm going to talk slowly. We don't have much time. You know what you owe me, you and your friend here. For the extra trouble you've given me, it's going to be a little more. In round figures, two million clams. Now. Right away.'

Poggio interrupted in a mumbling monotone. 'Where am I going to get that much money?'

Nicky Polo aimed and kicked Poggio in the face. 'Nobody was talking to you, fink.'

Poggio began to bleed from the mouth. 'For God's sake,' he groaned, 'give me a drink. I haven't eaten in two days.'

'As usual, you're lying,' said Ray. 'Benny, go make some coffee. Give them a slug of something before they die on us. Codi here looks like he's just about to go under.'

'It's a good thing I brought some stuff along,' said Beniamino. 'I *figured* they might want to eat something.' He went out into the bare kitchen and began bustling around.

Saldana began to laugh. 'You know something? You two guys are lucky you got Benny to look after you. Always something to eat, that's all Benny thinks about.'

'What makes you think you can get away with this, Ray?' said Codi.

'I'll give you credit for more guts than this other bastard here,' said Ray. 'You're *still* wasting time. You've sold the seventy-five keys by now. You've got the money stashed away. Get it up.'

'It hasn't been sold yet,' said Codi.

'So sell it. From what I hear, the market is even stronger now. I want seventeen and a half each. The rest is collection expense. Between you and Al, you have it. Two big bosses. Two millions in cash is nothing for you.'

Codi shrugged. 'You'll let us go?'

'I'll let *you* go. Al is my personal pot roast. *You* know that.'

'I had nothing to do with that part of it,' said Codi. 'What was between you and Al, I didn't know anything about. He came to me with the merchandise and said he had paid you off for it and he made a deal with me to sell it.'

Good spot to drive a wedge between two thieves, thought

Ray. 'I have nothing against you, Don Leonardo,' he said in a friendlier voice. 'All I want is the money. Then you can go home. You have the merchandise, you can sell and retrieve.' He studied Codi's face as he spoke. Money meant nothing to the older man where his own life was at stake. He didn't care two cents about Al Poggio. He would sell Poggio down the river as well as anyone else.

'What about me?' said Poggio through swollen lips.

'Well, what *about* you, Al?' said Ray.

Codi ignored Poggio. He had already written him off. He was thinking ahead to save his own life. Finally he said, 'It's a deal, Ray. You'll let me go home?'

'Safe and sound.'

'I believe you.'

'Thanks,' said Ray.

'You have a good credit reputation,' said Codi grudgingly.

'A better one than yours. So give.'

'Call Sal LoRicco and give him the word,' said Codi. 'Set it up with him. He'll have the money delivered.'

'Your own *consigliere*? He won't believe.'

'I'll talk to him on the phone,' said Codi.

'Benny,' said Ray, 'do you have a phone around here?'

'The drop man has one in his apartment,' said Beniamino. 'We'll go down there.'

'Give us LoRicco's number, Len,' said Ray.

Saldana wrote the number down.

'Okay, let's go downstairs,' said Ray. He and Saldana lifted Codi to his feet and walked him out of the flat and down the stairs. Beniamino followed. 'I better come along so you don't scare the guy.' He pushed ahead and opened the door of the flat with his own key. The drop man came running out, wearing a bathrobe and frightened expression on his face.

'Go back to sleep, Sam,' said Beniamino. 'I just want to use your phone a minute. Blow.'

Sam disappeared.

'Tony,' said Ray. 'You talk to LoRicco.'

Saldana dialed the number and waited. 'Sal?' he finally said. 'Hold on, your boss wants to talk with you.'

Codi put his lips to the mouthpiece and Saldana held the

338

other end of it to Codi's ear.

'Listen, Sal,' said Codi calmly. 'I'm being held. Right. Snatched. Two million dollars. That's what I said. The quicker you get it over to them, the quicker they'll let me go. Right. That's what they promised. Deliver it wherever they say. Okay? Now I'll put someone on. They'll give you the rest of it.'

Saldana took the receiver. 'Sal? Okay, this is how you do it. You got a couple of buttons with brains? Okay. Put the money in a couple of suitcases. In large bills. The less bulk the better. Twenty-four hours from now they are to drive to Long Island City.' Saldana spelled out the address carefully. 'They drive into a parking lot there and wait. We'll be waiting for your boys. If the count is right, they can take off. Yeah, we'll have Len with us. They can drive him home. They'll be in an Olds station wagon. Okay.'

Ray tapped Saldana on the shoulder and waved his hand violently.

'Hold it a second, Sal,' said Saldana. 'Somebody's trying to tell me something.' He put his hand over the mouthpiece of the receiver.

'No good,' said Ray. 'You'll be setting yourself up and walking into something. Tell LoRicco one button to drive the car and he comes himself with the money.'

Saldana uncovered the mouthpiece. 'It's a new deal, Sal. You come yourself with the money. One man to drive. Yeah, tomorrow. Right.' He looked at Ray and nodded.

'That's better,' said Ray. 'Hang up.'

Saldana cut the connection.

'When LoRicco shows,' said Ray, 'we take and hold him.'

'He thinks he's going back with his boss.'

'We can't help what he thinks,' said Ray. 'If it works out, I'll make it an even exchange.' To Codi he said, 'You behave yourself and shape up when you get home, I'll send Sal back alive. It won't look good if the word gets around that you let your own *consigliere* get hit in the head, so try to behave honestly for once.'

They dragged Codi upstairs again and uncuffed him. Beniamino brought in coffee, sandwiches, and a bottle of rye. He uncuffed Poggio and forced a jigger of rye down his throat. Poggio gagged and began to vomit. 'No brains,' said Beni-amino disgustedly. Codi accepted a cup of coffee. He sat on the floor with his back against the wall and began to sip. He was calm and cool. 'Where are we going to sleep?'

'Right in here,' said Saldana.

'On the bare floor?'

'Benny,' said Ray, 'bring in one mattress.'

'What about me?' said Poggio.

'You're not a paying customer.'

Benny dragged in a rust-stained cot-mattress and dropped it at Codi's feet.

The food and hot coffee were gradually reviving the two prisoners.

Torres, who had been observing silently, said, 'So this is the man who stole from you, Don Raimondo?'

'This is the man,' said Ray, pointing at Poggio. 'The old one steals from the entire world. He is a great thief. Poggio is a little thief who stole from me.'

'He was with you a long time?'

'Long enough to know better. He was a *capo* for many years. Then, when I was deported, he became subboss of our *borgata*. I don't recall how it was.' Ray prodded Poggio with his toe. 'Did I make you subboss, creep?'

Poggio maintained a sullen silence.

'And what will you do with him now?' said Torres.

'He will die, of course,' said Ray.

If Poggio felt fear, he did not show it. 'Who is this guy, Ray?' he said.

'Only my friends call me by my first name,' said Ray.

'The money is going to be paid,' said Poggio.

'By your business partner,' said Ray. 'For himself. You don't get off the hook.'

'Give me a cigarette somebody,' snarled Poggio.

Beniamino threw a pack of Marlboros and a book of matches at him.

'He doesn't seem afraid,' said Torres.

'He probably isn't,' said Ray.

'Why are you letting the old one go?' said Torres. 'Isn't it better that he too should die?'

'It would, indeed, be better,' said Ray. 'But it will also make much trouble with the commission. And I need their co-operation. To release him alive is the lesser of two evils. The old one is a boss. The men who sit at the table are also bosses. They don't like to see one of their number killed. It decreases respect and sets a bad example for the rank and file.'

'Yes, of course,' said Torres. 'Like the execution of a general.'

'Very apt.'

'Still, it seems to me that the old one is equally guilty,' said Torres. 'Doesn't your law apply equally to all members?'

'It would be nice if everything were black and white,' said Ray. 'When you come right down to it, the law in the Organization is only what the bosses say it is. The only thing they watch on the commission is not to stretch the law too far out of shape. The idea is to get the people to accept a ruling without too much gagging. If it's not too much out of line, they'll swallow a decision. Poggio they'll swallow. After all, he always belonged to me. Codi I'm not so sure.'

'Dominique and his people do it a little better in Marseilles,' said Torres.

'I'll have to see that before I believe it,' said Ray. 'How many people were killed before those Corsicans settled the Combinati affair several years ago? Thirty-five or forty, I heard, from what Dominique told me. I'll tell you one thing— over here, we operate on a bigger scale. We don't go around hitting people for a few carloads of smuggled cigarettes. Just watch and listen.' He turned to Beniamino. 'Benny, you and Nicky make the meet with LoRicco. When they pull into the lot, one of you come up behind. The other guy covers. Bring the money and LoRicco to Saldana's house. We'll be there waiting. Bring their button along also.'

'LoRicco is going to be one surprised man when his boss ain't there,' said Nicky.

'Maybe, maybe not,' said Ray. 'A good *consigliere* isn't supposed to surprise too easily. He may have made allowance for that angle already. Anyhow, you bring him with the money out to Mineola. If the count is right, you two can go back and take

Codi home. Watch your ass that LoRicco doesn't try to pull any fast ones.'

'Nothing's going to happen,' said Nicky.

'Juanito,' said Ray, 'you'll have to stay with Poggio. Cuff him up again and keep an eye on him. I don't want the bum trying to kill himself.'

Nicky Polo and Beniamino turned up with LoRicco at four in the morning. Dumdum and Fats Mazzi took Codi's button in charge and told him to wait. Saldana and Ray shook hands with LoRicco in friendly fashion. The *consigliere* was a plump, white-haired man with spectacles, who looked like a high school teacher within five years of retirement. Or, perhaps, the boss of a small town barbershop. He was a peaceful-looking office-type man. 'Ah, Don Raimondo,' he said, 'in spite of these irregular circumstances, I can truthfully say that I am happy to see you again. After all, I'm a neutral man just doing my duty.'

'Exactly,' said Ray. 'Believe me, I wish it could have been handled differently.'

LoRicco shrugged with a carefully bland expression on his face. 'You know my position. It's a difficult one.'

'The money,' said Ray.

At that moment Fats Mazzi and LoRicco's driver brought a suitcase into the room and laid it on the table.

'It's in thousand-dollar bills,' said LoRicco. 'By all means, count it.'

Saldana and Ray made a careful count. Ray examined a few under a strong light. 'You're sure you don't print this stuff in your basement, Sal? Some of them are very new.'

LoRicco smiled. 'They're genuine enough, Don Raimondo.'

'We'll let the Swiss be the judges of that,' said Ray. 'They're pretty good at judging American bank notes. In the meantime, you'll be our guest for a while.'

'That was not my understanding,' said LoRicco calmly. 'If the count is right, why should I be held?'

'Merely a precautionary measure,' said Ray. 'Our people will now return with your man to pick up Don Leonardo and take him home.'

'He hasn't been injured?'

'Just normal wear and tear,' said Ray. 'He's being released unharmed.

LoRicco decided to make the best of it. 'You were always a man of your word, Don Raimondo.'

'I still am,' said Ray.

'How long will I remain here?'

'A week at the outside. You've got nothing to worry about. Don Leonardo will get back home. As long as he doesn't go making noise and steam about this thing, we'll take you home in a week. If you trained Don Leonardo to behave himself like a gentleman, nothing drastic is going to happen. After all, Sal, it's said that a boss is the handiwork of his *consigliere*'s guidance and advice. Frankly, I don't envy you your close associations with that man. Outside of that, don't try to get away on your own.'

'Me?' LoRicco finally chuckled. 'No, I wouldn't do that. I'm not a man of violence. When I'm released, I'll go. If and when I must die, I'll die.'

'You've got it taped right, LoRicco,' said Saldana. 'Come on, I'll show you your room. I might even have some shirts your size.'

'Can I call my wife?' said LoRicco. 'She'll be worried.'

'Wait till the middle of the day,' said Saldana. 'This would be a helluva time. Get some sleep first. After you eat, you'll feel better. Call her then.'

'Thank you. That's a good idea.'

'What the hell, Sal,' said Saldana, finally turning a little mellow. 'You and I always got along good. So did Don Raimondo. Did we ever do you harm? Did we ever deal dishonestly with you?'

'On my mother's head, never,' said LoRicco. 'Believe me, I'm very unhappy about this situation. I counseled Don Leonardo against taking the course which he took.'

'You we believe, Sal,' said Ray, also relaxing. 'We have nothing against you. Your boss will be returned home unharmed.'

'Thank you,' said LoRicco. 'Now I would like to get some sleep. I'm very tired.'

'Go ahead. Fats,' said Saldana, 'you show him the room.'

343

After Fats Mazzi and LoRicco left, Ray said to Saldana, 'Your wife's in the house.'

'So she's in the house,' said Saldana. 'So Sal LoRicco is visiting us for a week. It's no skin off her nose.'

'Right. You've got her trained right, Tony.'

'I'd be in a helluva spot if I hadn't.' Saldana leaned back in his armchair and let out a deep breath. 'Well, boss, we're in business again.'

Ray counted off twenty of the thousand-dollar bills and handed them to Saldana. 'This is for you personally, Tony. You did an okay job. As of right now, you're the subboss of the Occhiaccio *borgata*.'

'Thanks,' said Saldana. 'I'm a little surprised, though. I thought Benny was your best friend.'

'He's more than my best friend. He's my brother and I love him like a brother. But you know, and I know—and he knows —that he's no boss type. He doesn't have the head for it. He would be the first to admit it. If he was put in the job he'd only be miserable. You know that, Tony.'

'Like you say. What do you want done with the rest of the money?'

'Put it into a safe deposit box and give me the keys. Make up a name for me. Put it right here in Mineola. This money isn't going to Switzerland. We're going to spend it right here before we're finished. The lawyers will have to get a big piece of it. Also, I owe Juanito a lot of money which he is going to get right now so he'll know he's being treated right.' Ray paused. 'And Al Poggio is going to be paid off. You know something, Tony? There's only one man here who's being screwed all around.'

'Yeah? Who's that?'

'A man back in Italy, name of Roberto Greco.'

'You didn't tell me about him.'

'I will when we get a breather. Sometimes I think the only people that work harder than we do are writers and ballet dancers.'

'And auto body men,' said Tony, 'and IRT track walkers.'

'It's a tough hustle,' said Ray thoughtfully. 'I'm going to bed. Good night, Tony.'

CHAPTER 23

The morning dawned bright and sunny. Ray had had a good night's sleep, yet he had awakened in a glum mood. It was the impending unavoidable confrontation with the Immigration and Naturalization Service and the laborious uncoiling outcome of that confrontation. The reward of honesty was a blissful unfamiliarity with the ponderous impersonal machinery of the United States government. He dressed carefully in his conservative, old-fashioned way. As he knotted his necktie he thought, It's a long time since I woke up with a big hard-on making a tent in the blanket. And, if I did have one, who would I ram it into? Alda Quirini? Marta Peruzzi? The Jap doll, Truthful Fern? Or poor Anitra Houssayne who had given Juanito the clap? Anitra was now drifting on the floor of the Tyrrhenian with the sardines slipping through her empty eye sockets. Juanito had evinced a kind of acute unflinching compassion for Anitra. But, then, Juanito was a more compassionate man than himself—or, at least, a more understanding one. He was not as anesthetized and exacerbated by frustration as Ray was. No time for broads and screwing. And, what was worse, no desire for it. Not in midcourse. Several rounds yet to go and only a minute's rest between rounds. Ray sighed, put on his jacket, and went down to Saldana's study. Study! What the hell did Tony study here? He watched the fights and the ball games on TV here, he played a little poker with the boys here, and he counted money here, where he wouldn't be interrupted by his ever-loving.

Fats Mazzi was setting up a table and arranging place settings for three. He had a fifteen-cup electric percolator plugged in.

345

'Good morning, Don Raimondo,' said Fats.

'Good morning, Fats,' said Ray. 'Where's the boss?'

'He'll be right in. What will you have for breakfaast, Don Raimondo?'

'Let's see. Bring me a tall glass of fresh-squeezed orange juice, two pieces of raisin toast, dry. A cup of coffee now, strong, hot, and black.'

'That's all?' said Fats disapprovingly.

'My usual, Fats,' said Ray, patting his midsection. 'I have to keep this down.'

'That wouldn't hardly keep a bird going all day. You sure?'

'Okay. Then bring me a bowl of grape nuts. But with nonfat milk.'

Fats grimaced. 'Grape nuts? What the hell's that?'

'That's the crap the boss's kids eat. Ask the cook. She probably has some in the cupboard. Hey, Fats, I'll bet I know what you had for breakfast.'

Fats Mazzi's vast, neckless face collapsed into a big grin. His eyes disappeared completely behind rolls of blubber.

'You think so, Don Raimondo? So what did I have?'

'A big hunk of peppered Genoese salami,' said Ray. 'The embalmed kind.'

'Sicilian salami,' said Fats gleefully. 'It's much hotter.'

'You'll die young and painfully,' said Ray. 'Half a loaf of sourdough bread, hot from the oven, dripping with melted butter.'

'Jesus, Don Raimondo,' said Fats, 'you're making me hungry all over again.'

'A pint of lousy coffee, half hot milk and half grappa.'

Fats slapped his belly. 'Very close, Don Raimondo, very close.'

'I know all about wop breakfasts,' said Ray. 'It's almost as bad as the stuff the Jews eat. The only food that's worse is Mexican. Take my advice, Fats, and start hitting the toast and grape nuts. You're getting too much cholesterol.'

Fats slapped his belly and roared with laughter. 'Cholesterol! Grape nuts! Oh, my god!'

'A doctor would charge you for this advice,' said Ray severely. 'And stop smoking those black, dried, horseshit cigars.

They're bad for your lungs and digestion.'

Fats Mazzi collapsed into a chair, his belly shaking with laughter. Tony Saldana walked into the study.

'What the hell's going on here?' he said, looking around. 'What's he doing to you, Fats?'

'He wants me to eat grape nuts, Don Antonio,' said Fats. 'He wants me to quit Nobilis.'

Tony grinned. 'That'll be the day. The Nobilis ain't a bad idea. All the time you're here the place smells like a stable. Fats, take Mr. LoRicco's breakfast up to his room. He ain't coming down.'

Fats replied, 'Sure, Don Antonio,' and walked out of the room.

'Where's your family, Tony?' said Ray.

'Like I told you. At the other end of the house. This place is a two-wing job. One for the wife and kids. One for business. They stay the hell out of this end.'

Fats returned with Ray's orange juice and grape nuts, which he set down gingerly. Then he brought over a plate containing the toast, as ordered, and a cup of coffee.

'Fats,' said Tony, 'tell the cook to make me some ham and eggs. Scramble the eggs soft. Give me some coffee now.'

'Yes, Don Antonio,' said Fats.

'Too much animal fat, Tony,' said Ray.

'What the hell,' said Saldana. 'You got to have *some* fun.'

When Fats left to fill his boss's order, Ray said, 'After breakfast, send Fats out to Greenpoint with the word. It's okay for Nick and Benny to take Codi home.'

'You don't want to wait till tonight?'

'What for? We have LoRicco and the money. We're performing a benevolent act. Let the sun shine as hard as it wants.'

'And Poggio?'

'Tonight.'

'Who do you want to show?'

'You and me, to read him off. Benny and Nick need a rest. They've done plenty. About that auto-scrapping yard you have in Greenpoint——'

'Like Nicky mentioned, we have another one in Jersey, in case you're interested.'

'This one will be good enough. You have a hydraulic press there for baling cars?'

'Yeah, we use it right along.'

'Then we're set.'

'That's how he's going?'

'You got a better way?'

'There's a million ways,' said Saldana.

'I wish everything else was that simple. We could sink him in the sound from Nick's boat, but I don't want to bother Nicky any more right now. He's been busy enough. This thing is going to be private. Poggio just disappears and send your flowers to the Cat Protection Society. If we take him out to Jersey it means driving, and the less riding I do right now, the better. Something might go wrong and we are spotted. This yard out here isn't more than fifteen or twenty minutes from where Al is right now, right?'

'Right.'

'So we cut down exposure.'

'You have a point there.'

Jack Dumdum was dispatched to the yard at nine in the evening to make the preliminary preparations. Saldana and Ray left for Greenpoint at ten. When they entered the flat they found Fats Mazzi there conversing with Torres. He rose to his feet when the two bosses entered.

'So?' said Tony Saldana.

'All quiet,' said Fats. 'This man's teaching me a lot of Italian I'd forgotten.'

'That you never knew,' said Ray. 'I know the kind of Italian you talk.'

'What do you expect?' said Fats. 'I'm an American. I was born in Brooklyn.'

'How's our boy doing?' said Tony Saldana.

'He ain't making no noise,' said Fats. 'Maybe he's sleeping. I fed him a couple hours ago and took off his cuffs.'

'He's not scared about anything?'

'Not that I can tell. He knows the score all right but I don't think he'll make trouble.'

'Codi got home all right?'

348

'Yeah. From what I hear, it went without a hitch.'

Ray interrupted. 'Okay. Let's get going.'

Fats pushed back the bookshelf and the four men entered the prison room. Poggio was sleeping on Codi's vacated mattress. He was haggard, dirty, and had a heavy growth of beard on his face.

Fats bent ponderously over Poggio and shook him. 'Wake up, Mr. Poggio. You got company.'

Poggio opened his eyes blearily and yawned.

'It's time to leave, Al,' said Ray.

'How about a bath and a shave?' said Poggio. 'I'd like to leave clean.'

'No time,' said Ray. 'Cuff him and tape his mouth, Fats.'

'I won't say anything,' said Poggio.

'You might change your mind,' said Ray.

Poggio submitted without resistance.

'You want his eyes taped, Don Raimondo?' said Fats.

'No, let him look,' said Ray. 'You and Juanito take him along to the yard. We'll be down there in a little while.'

Fats and Torres heaved Poggio to his feet and led him out. The downstairs door closed.

'Well, they're on their way,' said Tony Saldana.

'I think you have something on your mind,' said Ray.

'Yeah,' said Saldana. 'You think you did right letting Codi go?'

'Yes,' said Ray. 'There are two sets of reasons for it. The first set I already explained to Torres and you heard it. The second set is that Codi alive is more unhappy than Codi dead. I only wish there was some way to keep Poggio alive. Since a man only has one miserable life to lose, always remember that when you kill a man you're liberating him from prison. That's what I'm doing for Poggio right now. What a pity!'

'Yeah,' said Saldana. 'But about Codi. He won't try to come back at us?'

'Why should he?' said Ray. 'He came away cheaply. Over and above what he paid us, he'll even make a profit when he sells the merchandise. He came out of this smelling like a rose. No, I'm not worried about Codi. What I'm thinking about is the fact that I have to turn myself in.'

'Yeah. You can't go on this way.'

'Not if I want to operate, I can't.' Ray sighed. 'Well, let's go and get it over with.'

At night, the scrapyard seemed more huge than in daylight, with ghostly hills of gutted auto bodies and mounds of scrapped parts. Saldana led the way through stacks of axles, wheels, and old engines to a wooden office shack. Fats Mazzi, Jack Dumdum, and Torres were keeping Poggio company in the shack.

'Take the tape off his mouth,' said Ray.

When Fats had done so, Ray said, 'Last words, Al.'

Poggio shrugged. 'Do my wife and kids get my money that I earned before this happened?'

'Why should they? It's all forfeit to the Family.'

'Why take it out on them?'

'What do you want us to do, reward the family of a fink? For a stand-up guy, yes. But, why for you? You brought it on them. They get nothing.'

'Ah, the hell with you,' said Poggio tonelessly.

'You got it all set, Fats?' said Tony Saldana.

'Yeah,' said Fats. 'We got an Edsel positioned in the press pit.'

'Sounds like the right make for Al,' said Ray. 'Take him out.'

Fats and Jack Dumdum raised Poggio to his feet and led the procession down to the press pit. Jack opened the right front door of the beaten-up Edsel and pushed Poggio into it. Poggio slumped forward in the seat and his head touched the dashboard.

'Shove him off, Jack,' said Ray reluctantly. 'He's had enough.'

'Right,' said Jack. He unholstered a revolver, thrust it in through the windowless Edsel, and fired two bullets into Poggio's head. There was no steering wheel in the Edsel and Poggio rolled off the seat.

Fats Mazzi had started the press. It came down crunching the condemned Edsel into a small bale of pressed scrap steel.

Ray spat, shook his head, and said, 'Not good.'

'What's not good, Don Raimondo?' said Torres.

'Revenge and justice. It's like stale bread. Everything is stale bread.'

'Not everything,' said Torres.

The office of the district director of the Immigration and Naturalization Service in New York City was standard mid-echelon bureaucrat. No criticism, thought Ray, looking around. It was a large one, with dark-green nylon carpeting. The district director sat in a high-backed leather swivel chair behind a wide mahogany desk. In a tray in the outer right-hand corner of the desk lay a stack of folders. The Ray Hodgkin folder lay open before the district director. Two big windows in one of the walls looked out over lower New York Bay. Ray admired the prospectus of Governor's Island. The other two walls were fitted with mahogany bookshelves. These shelves contained rows upon rows of forbidding law books, The United States Code, bound volumes containing reports and proceedings of the service, miscellaneous state and federal codes. The law was a monster which crushed you to death under a mountain of calf-bound words. Ray felt a tickling in his nose and wanted to sneeze. It was the deadly arid dustiness of the law, the slow, grinding, patient malice of the law, from which only lawyers, presumably, were immune, because only they knew their way through the mined jungle.

The man behind the desk was lanky and firm-jawed with thinning dark hair, darker than the sandy locks of L. Howard Willis. He, too, wore half-spectacles, just the lower bifocals portion, and they kept slipping down his nose. He wore the standard uniform—dark-gray suit, dark-blue-black-red striped necktie, and a white button-down shirt. Just like L. Howard Willis, except that the Willis shirts and suits were tailored.

The district director puffed thoughtfully on a long straight briar and toyed with the tobacco humidor to the right of the Hodgkin folder. He seemed loath to speak but finally did so.

'Well, Mr. Willis, it's all pretty cut and dried, isn't it?'

'It would seem so,' agreed Willis.

'Since Mr. Hodgkin came in voluntarily,' said the district director, 'I shall set the appearance bond at seventy-five hundred dollars.'

Willis nodded without speaking.

They all knew that the amount of the appearance bond was an academic point. It would, however, be in bad taste and undesirable to emphasize the obvious to a relatively underpaid civil servant. The play was to defer to the civil servant's legal leverage.

'With your approval, Mr. Lathrop,' said Willis gravely, 'I can post bond now for Mr. Hodgkin. Our firm's check is acceptable, I presume?'

'*Your* firm's check is, Mr. Willis,' said the district director. 'I have *some* leeway about those things.'

'Thank you,' said Willis.

While he was writing out the check, a gaunt, dusty woman in her vague fifties entered the office. The district director handed her the various forms that Ray had already signed. The woman was also wearing half-spectacles, except that hers had heavy gold rims. She also wore a determined smile engraved there by years of communing with a hypnotic routine. That hard-earned pension was finally beginning to rise on the horizon.

'You should receive your copies in about a week or so, Mr. Willis,' said the district director. He studied Ray with a dry, quizzical smile.

'Well, Mr. Hodgkin, how does it feel to be back?'

'Well, despite the circumstances, sir,' said Ray, 'I find it exciting. I think you have the finest view of New York Harbor.'

The district director stared out of the window skeptically. 'I suppose I take it for granted.'

'I don't,' said Ray. 'Sometimes I think that's why I came in. So I could sit in your office and admire the view of the ships in the bay.'

There was a weary humor in the district director's eyes. 'As long as you understand very clearly. Whatever the outcome in court, this service will commence proceedings to redeport you. In fact, such proceedings have, in a manner of speaking, already begun. And I rather think that we'll succeed handily.'

'I understand,' said Ray.

Willis handed over the check and the district director clipped it carefully to the documents in the folder. 'Let me also add this, in all fairness. I shall do my utmost to see that the Department of Justice makes the strongest possible representations to the Italian Ministry of the Interior that you be incarcerated. You may find that Poggio Reale and/or the Ucciardone lack the amenities of our federal institutions.'

Willis raised his hand in mild protest. 'Surely, Mr. Lathrop, the Italian government doesn't usually take such drastic measures. I mean, it isn't the customary pattern.'

'They may do so in this instance,' said the district director smilingly. 'After all, Mr. Hodgkin has occasioned them embarrassment and considerable additional work. The least we'll recommend is that he be restricted to regional detention within the confines of Castellammare and that he be required to report daily to the police. I suspect he won't find that amusing.'

'The Italian government is master in its own house,' said Willis diplomatically.

'True,' said the district director. 'But we have ways of making our attitude clear—that is, when we are really and personally interested in a case. I must admit that I am very much interested in that of Mr. Hodgkin.'

'For an impersonal administrator,' said Ray politely, 'aren't you being—well—somewhat zealous?'

The district director chuckled. 'You wanted to say "vindictive," didn't you? You bet I am, Mr. Hodgkin. It's a bit late now, but let me give you a tip. The surest way to make a bureaucrat like myself vindictive is to upset the even tenor of his ways with an unexpected flood of paper work. That's what you have done.'

'I'm terribly sorry, Mr. Lathrop,' said Ray.

'So am I,' said the district director. 'Believe me.' He rose from his chair. Willis, taking the cue, got up and ceremoniously shook hands.

Ray extended his hand. 'Will you at least shake hands with me, Mr. Lathrop? It's by way of welcoming me back to the United States.'

The district director smiled ironically and accepted Ray's hand. 'There's nothing in the regulations which says that I can't. I can hardly say to you, though, "Welcome home," can

I? We all know that I shall do my utmost to throw you out of this country as speedily as possible. And if we can persuade the court to impose the maximum fine and prison term prior to deportation, I'll be ever so pleased. There's no point in being insincere is there?'

'Absolutely not, Mr. Lathrop,' said Ray. 'The Congress enacts the laws and your duty is to keep the wheels turning. I don't take it personally.'

'Thank you, Mr. Lathrop,' said Willis.

The district director nodded. 'Good day, Mr. Willis.'

Back in the office of L. Howard Willis, Ray sank back luxuriously into a deep leather armchair opposite his attorney's desk.

'As Lathrop pointed out,' said Willis, 'it's all rather routine. The charge is Unlawful Reentry of a Deported Alien, Title 8, Section 1326, of the United States Code. Upon conviction, you are liable to two years in a federal penitentiary and one thousand dollars' fine within the discretion of the court. As he also mentioned, the machinery for a new deportation order is also in motion.'

'I know all that already,' said Ray. 'How will it move from this point on?'

'You're as well up on this sort of thing as I am, Ray. Lathrop will hand his material to the United States Attorney, who will make his presentment to a federal grand jury. You can safely assume that you'll be routinely indicted.'

'How much bail?' said Ray.

'Since you surrendered voluntarily, I'd judge between ten and fifteen thousand. The district director may hold onto your appearance bond separately. Or he may return it after you make bail before a U.S. commissioner. But the bookkeeping of it isn't very important, is it?'

'So I go on trial.'

'You go on trial. Before a federal district judge.'

'And, in the last analysis, it's up to the judge.'

'Let's project the best possible outcome,' said Willis. 'The judge dismisses the U.S. Attorney's case against you on grounds of insufficient evidence——'

'I don't see how he can,' interrupted Ray.

'At the moment, neither do I,' agreed Willis. 'But this is what I was getting at. The trial, however it goes, will have nothing to do with Lathrop's actions. As you know, deportation is a civil procedure.'

'I know it very well.'

'We can delay it, of course,' said Willis. 'If I and N's decision against you is ultimately adverse, and I'm pretty sure it will be, we can appeal to their board of appeals in Washington. And from there, all the way up to the Attorney General. To be realistic, Ray, while it will gain you more time, perhaps as much as three years, I don't think there's much doubt about the final decision. Whether six months, or a year, or three years from now, you'll have to return to Italy, even assuming that you escape the prison term.'

Ray replied from left field. 'You know, Howard, this is a great country, a really great country.'

'*I* think so,' said Willis.

'What the hell! You *should* think so. What has this country done for you that wasn't always absolutely first-class deluxe?'

'Oh, come on, Ray,' said Willis with an edge in his voice, 'I'm growing tired of your constant bitching.'

'Constant? You haven't seen me in three years.'

'I haven't forgotten our last conversation in the Federal House of Detention.'

'Got under your skin, didn't it?'

'It certainly did,' said Willis. 'And let me stress the obvious. I can no more help having been born a Connecticut Yankee than you can help having been born a Sicilian. I can no more help being a Presbyterian than you can help being a Roman Catholic. I can't help it if my great-grandfather made a lot of money and I went to Yale.'

'Willis, baby,' said Ray, 'I forgive you everything except Yale. You become almost human when you're browned-off.'

Willis smiled. 'All the Willises went to Yale.'

'All the Occhiaccios went to jail,' said Ray.

'Very funny,' said Willis. 'But this is no laughing matter. And don't underestimate Lathrop. Mild, dry exterior and all, he's stainless steel inside and he carries a lot of unofficial clout with the Attorney General. He's the kind of man who'd move against his own brother, even if that brother had won two Congressional Medals of Honor.'

'What brought that up?' said Ray.

'Your war record. Don't count on it. If Lathrop ever does redeport you, you can believe what he says. You'll spend the rest of your life in Castellammare and you'll report every day for the rest of your life to the local police. The good old days seem to have ended. Justice and Treasury are now working very closely with the Italian government and the Italians are listening.'

Ray leaned across the desk. 'Oh, I'm serious enough. Irwin Karpstein's up from Washington and I've talked with him. I've done him enough favors. I financed his last campaign.'

'Irwin can only do so much,' said Willis.

'I asked Irwin to introduce a private bill on my behalf directing the Attorney General to cancel deportation proceedings against me,' said Ray. 'He promised he would.'

'Don't bank too much on Irwin,' said Willis. 'Certainly, we'll try for postponement till the end of the Congressional session so that he can slip in the bill. He'll do it, but these riders that they tack on for the relief of some private citizen lack the old magic nowadays. It's a new and stuffier climate. It all began with Kefauver. Then Robert Kennedy lifted public awareness to a permanently higher plateau.'

'Don't remind me,' said Ray. 'The next item of business is that I've been in touch with Senator Thurmond Magruder, the indirect cause of my deportation. That contribution I made was to back his campaign. You remember him, don't you?'

'Quite clearly,' said Willis. 'Can he do anything?'

'Perhaps. Here's the word from Magruder. Get my case postponed for another four months. By that time, according to the federal judiciary schedule, Judge Breckenridge will be up here from Charleston. If we get Breck, we'll be all right. Know him?'

Willis smiled wryly. 'The Honorable Warner Hanley Breckenridge. I know of him. Real three-hundred-proof bourbon. Before he became a federal judge, when he was still a Congressman, they used to call him the Demosthenes of the

South. Picturesque old coot. They don't make them like that any more. When he dies, there won't be any more of them left.'

'I'm flying down to see Magruder and Governor Truscott,' said Ray. 'They want some facts to pass on to Breckenridge. Since he'll be hearing the case, it would be indiscreet for me to meet him directly.'

'To say the least,' agreed Willis dryly. 'How well do you know Magruder?'

'Only to say hello to,' said Ray. 'My real contact, the only one I really know, is Governor Truscott. You might call him the bag man for that gang of swamp bandits.'

'Well, if you have clout with that Confederate Mafia,' said Willis, 'don't be squeamish about using it. Anything you can do to prepare the way and soften the ground will certainly assist us when we come into court. As it stands now, the government has a prima-facie case against you. I'm pretty well restricted in what I can do and can't do for you.'

'Don't worry,' said Ray. 'You and Yale will emerge from this squeaky clean, no matter how it goes. I hope to settle the cloak-and-dagger preliminaries on this forthcoming trip to Dixie. When you finally enter that courtroom, hopefully, the opposition will be in a state of shock.'

'Don't tell me about it, Ray. Whatever you can do, do it. If I get the ball, I'll carry it as hard and as far as I can.'

'Fair enough. To change the subject, I understand you have an old friend mine as a partner in your firm now.'

'Oh?'

'Marta Peruzzi.'

'Indeed! Would you like to speak with her?'

'It would be nice to say hello,' replied Ray.

Willis pressed a button under his desk. The voice of his secretary came through metallically. 'Yes, Mr. Willis?'

'Will you please ask Miss Peruzzi to come into my office?'

When Marta entered, Ray rose from his chair and completed his survey in the half second before words were spoken. Marta's heavy crown of black hair did have that suggestion of graying around the edges which Nicky had mentioned. Maybe canities ran in the Peruzzi family. Nothing wrong with gray hair as long as one had plenty of it, as did Marta. She was wearing a black sheath dress with a single strand of pearls and had a cashmere sweater thrown over her shoulders and fastened with the top button. She had a pencil stuck in her hair and was wearing an austere pair of horn-rimmed spectacles. An Alda Quirini she wasn't, but quite a dame for all that. His own speed, really. And she came well recommended, not only by Uncle Oliverotto, but by her own feelings about him. A dame who liked you was a dame you could trust, most of the time, anyhow. Nothing so recommended a female as her good judgment in liking you.

Marta held out her hand and smiled. 'Mr. Hodgkin, I believe.'

Ray took her hand. 'Hello, Marta. Very good to see you, very good after all this time. I didn't expect you'd be so tall.'

'I've probably lost some weight wrestling with the law.'

'As good a theory as any,' said Ray. 'Your name looks very fine out there on the front door.'

'Thank you. Welcome back to the United States.'

'Thank *you*,' said Ray dryly. 'I suppose you've been studying my case.'

'Quite thoroughly.'

'Well, what do you think of my chances, counselor?'

An unobtrusive mask slipped over Marta's face. 'You're in very competent hands here,' she said with a faint smile. 'You'll have to excuse me now. I'm expecting a telephone call.' She turned around and walked out.

Ray shrugged and reseated himself. 'These are hardly the most auspicious circumstances under which to be meeting.'

'A bit of an understatement,' said Willis impassively. 'All right, Ray, I'll keep you posted as things unfold.'

CHAPTER 24

Governor Henry Allison Truscott was a fine figure of a man. Erect behind his massive desk in the executive mansion, flanked by the Stars-and-Stripes and the Confederate Stars-and-Bars, he looked properly noble. Truscott was as happily cast in his gubernatorial role as Warren Gamaliel Harding had been in his Presidential role. Actually, thought Ray, appraising Truscott across the desk, these Ku Kluxers were no less tough than the WASPs in the big Northeastern cities. Southern shrewdness was camouflaged by a homespun congeniality and a deceptive courtesy which gave off no warmth. But these KKKers were preferable to their Northern counterparts; they were, at least, less hypocritical. One might say that they were to America what Sicilians were to Italy. Parallels were deceptive, but they exhibited the same *simpatia*, which, however superficial, at least eased the friction of living. There was the same clinging to punctilio, ceremonial, and *personalismo*. The same resentment of a rural society left at the starting gate by a bustling, hustling, money-grubbing North. Truscott was a Dixiecrat *capo mafioso* complete with magnolia blossoms and institutionalized bigotries all done up in the ribbons of that drawl. These Southern boys had that Sicilian trick that the bleak, prim-lipped *Herrenvolk* of the North lacked: charm. My house is your house, and the rest of that corn. But you weren't supposed to take them literally because they were poor, just as Sicilians were poor. And just as proud. What other armor could a culture of poverty have? It must be the Sicilian in me, thought Ray. I like these rebs because they're the underdog as well as poor. I'm identifying with them. On the other hand, why should native, white five hundred percent

American Protestants be poor to begin with? How could a native American possibly suffer handicaps unless he naturally had rocks in his head? It was like being able to go to college full-time all day with your tuition paid for you. Any kid who couldn't get himself not a BA but an MA in four years in that kind of setup, and a straight A average, wasn't worth bothering with. But there it was. Which demonstrated that, in addition to Holy Mother Church, there were other causal historical villains around. The American Southerners hadn't been atrophied at birth by an excessive concentration on faith. That alibi was valid enough for the blighted cultures of the Hispanic Catholic belt, but it couldn't be applied to Dixie. No, it wasn't that. These rebels weren't stupid or intellectually malnourished, but they *were* fixated—well, enough of them were, with their eyes staring nostalgically into a simpler past. Only now were they beginning to tear away their eyes from their long, hopeless love affair with what was dead and buried. Only now were they becoming reluctantly aware of how much ground they would have to cover if they were ever going to catch up with those go-go Yankee bastards. Being high school freshmen at the age of twenty-five was enough to make anybody sore. Ray smiled inwardly and sympathized with the conflicting turbulence in the Southern soul—bitter resentment against the raw deal of the past, shame for present inadequacies and lack of qualification, pride in the heritage of fighting honor. And, finally, anger at Northern inability to understand the South's peculiar problem. It was easy enough for mush-mouthed Northern liberals to sound off about Southern racial bigotry. The South wasn't anti-black men. On the contrary. It had had the black man in its house, at its table, in its bed and bones for three hundred years and it was trying to cope. Could the Yankees have done better? Were they doing better now—now that they were getting a taste of things? Like hell they were! Yeah, right; these rebels were America's own Sicilians. Anything they could tear out of the Yankee's hide, by fair means or foul, was laudable. Ray's hopes rose. Here in the land of magnolia blossoms, of melancholy memories, of the highest VD and homicide rates, of the lowest per capita income rates, here in ass-dragging, soul-weary Dixie, sentimental Ray Hodgkin would fix himself a deal on foundations that would never be tolerated in the fat-cat North. To screw the Yankee is a pious and blessed work. Amen, brother. Governor Henry Allison Truscott echoed that sentiment, and so did Senator Thurmond Magruder, and so did Ray Hodgkin.

Ray had boarded the morning plane in New York City and had landed in Atlanta three hours later. Then another hour on a twin prop local trunk flight and the governor's limousine was waiting for him at the airport. Irwin Karpstein had duly and dutifully introduced his private bill for the relief of Ray Hodgkin:

A BILL
For the relief of Ray Hodgkin

Be it enacted by the Senator and House of Representatives of the United States of America in Congress assembled, That the Attorney General is authorized and directed to cancel the deportation proceedings presently pending against Ray Hodgkin, and that the facts upon which such proceedings are based shall not hereafter be made the basis for deportation proceedings.

The bill had been voted down and had come a cropper just as he and Willis had anticipated it would. In fact, the bill had attracted considerable and unfavorable attention. When Willis had relayed the news by telephone, Ray had observed sardonically, 'I didn't know that I was such a celebrity.'

Willis had replied cryptically, 'Oh, people are aware of you, Ray.'

Well, now, between these two sterling *sicilianos*, Governor Truscott and Senator Magruder, God Almighty, he should be able to wangle something! Magruder, representing a tired, bare-assed, soil-exhausted Confederate state, had as much clout in the world's most exclusive and powerful club as a Senator from Michigan, Ohio, New York, and Illinois. More. Seniority was what paid off and these Claghorns had dug in their claws where it counted. There was a lot which their redneck, wool-hat constituents didn't understand, but they sure as hell understood seniority. The South may have lost the Civil

361

War, but it was doing fine.

When Senator Magruder was ushered in by the governor's secretary, Ray and Truscott both rose to their feet. Magruder was a tall, slender man with crew-cut white hair, gold-rimmed spectacles, and a pleasant smile. People looked at Magruder and were soothed by the Magruder suggestion of Kiwanian, Sunday school superintendent, small-town editor, homespun friend of mankind. Magruder had a political bedside manner more valuable than platinum. He exuded, when on stage, a wholesome, uncomplicated amiability which, as intended, threw all but the most alert off guard.

The handshakes completed, Truscott waved his guests into armchairs. 'Let's make ourselves comfortable, gentlemen. Care for anything now, Thurmond?'

'Thank you, no,' said the Senator. 'Much too early.'

Ray relaxed. It wasn't hard to guess who called the tune down in this stronghold. Thurmond Magruder. Smart, and sharp, and hard. And, since he wasn't on display winning votes, chilly, like a wind blowing off an iceberg. He knew all about the deportation and had evinced no surprise. A good brain he had and better than average sources of information, which was also good; they could avoid waste motion and superfluous explanations. Ray hadn't really met Magruder before. Governor Truscott had always been the bag man. Ray had bankrolled Truscott's three consecutive gubernatorial terms. In return, Truscott had blessed Ray's endeavors and had permitted Ray to operate slots, books, gambling casinos, and nightclubs across the river just beyond the limits of the big city. In addition to campaign financing, Truscott had always received a generous piece of the action. Whenever a question arose, Ray gave his accountants standing instructions to decide the question in the governor's favor, the Senator's favor, the police commissioner's favor, the favor of any other politician who might be involved. It made no sense to be petty about these points. There was plenty to go around and to keep everyone happy. So it had remained a mutually profitable arrangement. This state was and had always been one of Ray's major bailwicks, better even than the New York complex, where he had five other hustling Families with which to contend.

Magruder appraised Ray coolly. 'I'm not surprised to see you down here,' he said. 'That's because I just don't surprise easily. However, I'm sincerely glad to meet and talk with you.'

'I didn't think you'd be surprised,' said Ray. 'You have a pretty good intelligence system.'

'Well, the governor has filled me in on your problem.'

'Did he tell you that back in sixty-three I contributed fifty thousand to your campaign kitty?'

'He certainly did,' said Magruder. 'I'm delighted with this opportunity to thank you in person.'

'Not at all,' said Ray. 'At any rate, in preparing my income tax return for fiscal sixty-three, my accountants deducted that contribution.'

'And you, of course, signed the return without checking,' said Magruder.

Ray nodded. 'And Mr. Robert Kennedy, who was then Attorney General, jumped in and made a big federal case out of it.'

'It was an honest mistake, Thurmond,' put in the governor. 'Ray had no intention of defrauding the government.'

'That's where you're wrong,' said Ray to Truscott. 'It wasn't an honest mistake at all. I just couldn't see paying taxes on money I'd kicked in to someone's political campaign.'

Magruder chuckled and nodded approvingly. He turned to the governor and said softly, 'Henry, you don't have to convince me about anything. Why don't you take a cue from Ray? We're not on exhibition for the voters here. All I want are facts. If I'm going to suggest to Judge Breckenridge the correct handling of this matter, I should have the basic details, shouldn't I?'

'Of course,' said Truscott.

'Fortunately,' continued the Senator, 'Breck feels quite as I do about the late Mr. Robert Kennedy.'

'All I was trying to point out,' said Truscott, 'is that if it were anyone else the government, at worst, would have called in the man, disallowed the deduction, and slapped a fine and penalty interest on him. In Ray's case, Kennedy intervened, overrode the objections of his subordinates, and personally inaugurated deportation proceedings against Ray. He did so even before there had been a judicial decision. He was an extremely vindictive man. I can't prove it, but there's a sound reason for believing that Kennedy applied some of his well-known pressure tactics against the judge who was hearing that particular case. It was a form of political vengeance. Over and above all else, Kennedy hated Ray for his unstinting support of the South.'

'I'm also the proud possessor of two previous felony convictions,' said Ray. 'Otherwise the government could not have made deportation stick.'

'I couldn't care less,' said Magruder. 'Henry is up on a stump, you're denigrating yourself unnecessarily, and I don't give a damn one way or the other. I want a good story to pass on to Breckenridge. He's the man who has to be sold.'

'I thought you were top dog,' said Ray bluntly.

'It's not that simple,' said Magruder. 'A judge should be guided by his personal and uninfluenced convictions, not by the arbitrary wishes of others. Even in a matter as relatively simple as this. Illegal reentry of a deported alien. That's hardly murder or treason or piracy or rape, is it? Still, I like Breck. The decision to acquit or to set the government's case aside for lack of evidence must come from Breck himself. And it must be palatable and convincing, so that he'll be able to rationalize it and live with himself. Do you follow me, Henry?'

'Of course,' said Truscott.

'We have adequate negative motivation for Breck,' said the Senator encouragingly. 'The Kennedy angle will fire up his hostility and certainly incline him in Ray's favor. What I want now is something positive about Ray, something favorable and praiseworthy.'

'That's easy,' said Truscott. 'Tell Breck that our friend is a real Southern boy.'

'Come on, Henry,' said the Senator. 'Ray is a New Yorker.'

'I'm talking about his war record. In World War Two, he comported himself in a way that any Southern man would be proud of.'

'Well, Breck is an all-out military buff,' said Magruder. 'Are you one of those war heroes, Ray?'

'Hardly that,' said Ray. 'All the governor means is that I fought through the war in Southern outfits.'

'Oh, hell,' said the governor, 'he's being much too modest. Ray didn't sit out the war in some safe office. He was a combat infantryman all the way through three and a half years of some of the hardest fighting in the ETO—in Southern combat outfits, with our Southern boys who fought and died there.'

'Well, that's more like it,' said Senator Magruder.

'Oh, it was a sort of an accident,' said Ray. 'I was down in Camp Polk in Louisiana training in the Third Army under Kreuger and Hodges. Then we were activated under General Patton and I went overseas and through the North African and Sicilian campaigns. Then someone screwed up some paper work and the next thing I knew my outfit had been shifted over without a break under General Mark Clark and I was at the Anzio landing and the Rapido River fighting. And at Monte Cassino. Believe me, it wasn't my idea.'

'Monte Cassino, eh?' said Magruder. 'I'll *bet* it wasn't your idea. I was there.'

'Did you have to be?'

'Not really.'

'I would think you'd have been too—well——'

'Too old, eh?' Magruder chuckled. 'As a matter of fact, I *was* too old. I had to pull wires to get myself into it. Of course, I didn't wallow around in the mud and snow in the hills, as you fellows did. I was snug in a command post. Still, I was there. All joking aside, Ray, no Southern man is too old to fight for his country.'

'I wish I'd known that in 1940,' said Ray. 'I'd have given Dixie a wide berth.'

'It's a tradition in these parts,' said Magruder blandly. 'We Southerners tend to follow the sound of the guns and to gravitate into harm's way.'

Ray grunted. 'A bit rock-headed, I'd say. You can get killed doing that.'

'Can't you, though,' drawled Magruder.

'What Ray hasn't mentioned,' put in Governor Truscott, 'is

that he won two Silver Stars for gallantry in combat.'

'Is that so?' said Magruder in a genuinely amiable tone of voice.

'Ray served under Milly Colquhoun,' said the governor. 'Milly told me personally that Ray should really have received the Distinguished Service Cross for one of those actions.'

'The hell you say! Millie is a neighbor of mine, and of Judge Breckenridge, down in Tarleton. Does he know you, Ray.'

'Pretty well,' said Ray. 'I served under him all the way through.'

'Henry,' said Magruder, 'would you kindly ask your secretary to give the colonel a ring. I'd just like to say hello to him. What about you, Ray?'

'Pleasure,' said Ray. 'Did you say "colonel"?'

'Colonel Millard Patterson Colquhoun, United States Army, Retired, a fine Southern gentleman and my neighbor. And Judge Breckenridge's particular crony.'

'If I may use that expression, Senator, he was a helluva skipper.'

'You certainly may, and I'd be inclined to agree with that judgment.'

'Still and all,' said Ray, 'he was a noncom when the war began. He was commissioned in the field. I know of chicken colonels who were put back to lieutenant after the war. I'd say my old boss did all right for himself if he retired with the permanent rank of colonel.'

Magruder grinned and winked. 'Well, we're poor in worldly goods, mister, but we're not without influence in the halls of government. We believe in taking care of one another. Not that Milly doesn't fully deserve his permanent retired rank. That man, sir, is the salt of the earth, the South at its very best.'

For the first time, Ray sensed that a cold, invisible plastic sheathing around Magruder had dissolved, that the politician was taking a personal interest in this affair, that Magruder's feelings were involved. It was now perhaps beyond cold repayment of a five-year-old campaign contribution.

Magruder took the receiver from Governor Truscott's hand.

'Hello, Milly? This is Thurmond. How have you been? Yes, I'm up here visiting with Henry Truscott and a friend of his, someone you know. Ray Hodgkin. The same. I'll put him on in a little while. Can you tell me something about Ray? Yes, a matter of business, you might say. Yes, I want it directly from his old boss. All the time in the world, Milly. Right.' Magruder listened for several minutes and chuckled occasionally. He began to smile in a broad and mellow fashion and, finally, to beam. 'I'll do that Milly. Just hold on now.' He handed the receiver to Ray. 'Wants to talk with you.'

Ray spoke into the mouthpiece. 'Colonel? This *is* Ray. I didn't know till the Senator told me. I'm down here visiting Governor Truscott. Yes, we're friends. We have been for quite some time. Yes, I'd like to come down, but I was planning to return to New York tomorrow.' He listened and finally said, 'Well, if that's an order, I have no choice, have I? I'll come down as soon as I leave here. Good talking with you, colonel. Right. I'll put the Senator back on.'

Senator Magruder took over and drawled back and forth with Colquhoun. He finally hung up and stared at Ray. 'Well, Milly sure enough recommended you for those two decorations. I'm inclined to agree that one of them should have been a DSC. We set some store by those things in the South. Milly says he baptized you himself, gave you your name, made a Southern boy out of you, so to speak. Well, he feels responsible for you, in a way.'

'That's right,' said Ray. 'The colonel picked my name for me.'

'Good one, too. Whenever Milly did something he did it thoroughly. Well, at this point, it's becoming something more than the repayment of a business debt. This rather puts you in the family, not only with me, but with Judge Breckenridge also.'

'I'll match Ray's war record against that of Robert Kennedy any day,' said the governor. 'That's the entire case, open and shut. Ray fought and bled for this country. He wants to remain here and those Yankees want to turn him out of it. That's the size of it. Whatever Ray may have done in the past as a hotheaded, misguided young fellow, he has made it up to this country with interest. I say that he is a good American who has more right to live and to work in this country than many people I could think of.'

Magruder applauded sardonically. 'Very moving, Henry. And totally superfluous. I was sold on Ray from the beginning. It will now be my pleasure to present Breck with a convincing case.'

'No problem?' said Ray.

'None,' said Magruder, 'even without Colonel Colquhoun's concurrence. With it, well—I just wouldn't worry about it any more. We Southerners feel strongly about personal relationships, about certain qualities of heart and character. We tend to elevate them above the cold letter of the law. Unlike the Yankees, we are people of the heart. We feel. Not a good thing, but we do.'

'I know,' said Ray. 'I speak that language myself.'

'Not a good thing,' repeated Magruder mechanically, as his mind concentrated on the problem. There would be no difficulties with that old fire-eater, Breckenridge, who was furiously subjective even when he was fast asleep. Deep within themselves, many men had passionate bitter hatreds bottled up. Warner Hanley Breckenridge, like Magruder himself, was such a man, a hater, an iron hater with a long memory and his own arrogant definition of Americanism. As for Senator Magruder, he had no more illusions about himself than about this New Yorker. He knew a good man when he met one and Ray Hodgkin, Milly Colquhoun's boy, was good, which in Magruder's book meant hard, tough, capable. Ray's courteous deference had pulled no wool over the Senator's eyes. He had no need to indulge in the vain rationalizations of his friend Henry Allison Truscott. That he, personally, as well as Breckenridge and Truscott, would profit financially by protecting Ray was a foregone conclusion. Every federal judgeship in this state was a political party selection, a Magruder selection, and there was nothing of superficial cynicism in Magruder's cold recognition of that fact. The concept that federal justice was impartial was nothing more than a popular myth, pap for the common man. A federal judge in Georgia was a Georgian first. A federal judge in Louisiana was a Louisianan first. In practice, the sovereignty of the state was equal to the sovereignty of the political machine in power, which meant the Magruder–Truscott machine. And a damned good thing, too, reflected Magruder grimly behind the bland smile. Loyalty to his political machine, to his party, and to his own kind, took precedence with Magruder, first, last, and always. In theory, federal judges were nominated by the President with the advice and consent of the Senate. But almost without exception the appointment was based on the personal wishes of the Senator from the state involved. In this case, the Senator was Thurmond Magruder, whom Judge Breckenridge would oblige voluntarily, because they were basically in accord. What was political corruption? Only the description applied by a political enemy to the circumstances of his own discomfiture. And political enemies should be cut down without quarter. In the case of the United States versus Raymond Hodgkin old Breck could be depended upon. Magruder had already appraised Ray and weighed him against the James boys and the Younger boys. The Americans had produced some pretty fair scalawags through the years and they hadn't always been road agents. A lot of them had been bankers, Senators, and railroad builders. Ray Hodgkin came under the heading 'our own kind' and so rated loyalty. He had been recommended by Millard Patterson Colquhoun and persecuted by Robert Kennedy. Magruder was one of those who loved his friends and hated his enemies. Milly could do no wrong. Robert Kennedy, dead or alive, could do no right, the quibblings and the pettifogging hairsplittings of the law notwithstanding. There were worse men by Magruder's scale, hypocrites who were getting away with far more. Hodgkin had at least been a good soldier. Milly, whose credit rating was at least as good as God's, had said so. If there was any mysticism in Magruder's temperament, it inhered in his approach to the profession of arms. The military was to his mind the noblest of all professions. He had wanted himself to be a soldier and would have become one if he had been able to pass the West Point or the VMI physical. Magruder knew in his bones that he would have made a competent general. Those bones despised the fussy niceties of the law, just as they despised the corrupt Yankee commercialism of the big Northern cities. Magruder, like Breckenridge, had his own code of honor and justice, a Southern rather than a Yankee code. It would undoubtedly shock simple people to realize that judges had emotions and unabashed bigotries. Old Breck had his, and no nonsense about emotional conflicts and split loyalties. The shifting parts coalesced with the hard, permanent whole of Magruder's rigid prejudices. The question as to whether Hodgkin was guilty or innocent within the framework of the case that would be presented by the United States Attorney weighed as nothing in the balance. Old Breck would free this defendant and hurl him into the prosecution's face as a boulder from a ballista. There was the practical problem, of course, that of acquitting Hodgkin on grounds that could not be reversed upon appeal, or of reasonably dismissing the government's case on the ground of insufficient evidence. Breck would work that out.

Truscott's voice broke in on his thoughts. 'Perhaps we should take a break at this point,' the governor was saying, 'and enjoy some refreshments.'

'An excellent idea,' said Magruder.

The governor spoke into the intercom on his desk. Several moments later an elderly Negro servitor in a white coat entered the office. He carried a large silver tray laden with an ice bucket, glasses, bottles of liquor, and mixes.

'I have some unusually good cognac here, Thurmond,' said the governor.

'Thank you, Henry,' said Magruder. 'I'll have the usual, if you please. Three fingers of Wild Turkey, neat. What about you, Ray?'

'I'll have the same,' said Ray.

'A classical tipple,' said Magruder. 'Remain faithful to Wild Turkey and you'll never become sick.'

When his drink had been served, Magruder raised his glass. 'Gentlemen, I propose a toast: Health to our friends and confusion to our enemies.'

'Cheers,' said Ray and drank solemnly. 'The extent to which we agree, Senator, is nothing short of remarkable.'

'That toast isn't original with me,' said Magruder. 'It has always been a favorite sentiment of Milly Colquhoun's.' He gestured with his glass. 'You go down to see him before you leave, Ray. He's a lonely man now that his wife has passed on. He wants to talk with you.' Magruder took another swallow and chuckled. 'And I have some idea of what he'll talk about— war and fighting. Get set to do a lot of listening.'

'I'll do that, Senator,' said Ray.

And the serious drinking began.

CHAPTER 25

L. Howard Willis listened intently, without interruption, until Ray had ended his report.

'No question,' he finally said. 'Your trip achieved some positive results. This jurist of yours is certainly a colorful man. His usefulness, however, is limited, no matter how benevolent his intentions. Remember, he lacks arbitrary freedom and is restrained by clearly defined boundary markers. If he violates those markers too obviously, he's subject to reversal. You did a constructive job, but it's only half a job.'

Half ironically, half seriously, Ray said, 'American law is a wonderful structure, isn't it?'

'It is,' said Willis, 'even when it's working against you.'

'All right, let's be more specific.'

'Very well,' said Willis. 'As I see it, Breckenridge's usefulness is limited. Let's consider the alternatives. The jury could either find you guilty, or the court could dismiss the charge against you on grounds of insufficient evidence. If the former, Breckenridge might be compelled to impose the prison term. Suspending sentence would be too raw and obvious in such a case. In such case, I predict that the U.S. Attorney would appeal and probably win a reversal and, indirectly, blemish the good judge's record.'

'You say nothing about an acquittal.'

'Not a chance,' said Willis. 'When the U.S. Attorney brings into court Lathrop's little file folder on Ray Hodgkin, the jurors are going to find against you. Assuming sentence is not suspended, it will be relatively light, a mere bagatelle.'

'Two years' worth of bagatelle.'

'I wasn't really minimizing it,' said Willis. 'Two years is

two years. What I'm getting at is this, you really have to aim for a dismissal of the charge.'

'I see.'

Willis nodded. 'If you've analyzed the picture correctly, just as Breckenridge is only half the solution in the pending trial, so is a dismissal of the charge only half the solution of the major problem. After all, you *do* want to remain in this country without further harassment, don't you?'

'I certainly do.'

'And, as Lathrop pointed out, no matter what the outcome in court, the Immigration and Naturalization Service will renew its efforts to deport you. At this moment, I see no way of blocking them.'

'Neither do I.'

'There's only one bright spot in this matter of deportation proceedings,' said Willis. 'It's a cumbersome, ponderous affair.' He glanced at Ray with sly irony. 'Under the American legal system which you admire so greatly, it, this process, can be delayed interminably and the big picture may change. I'd advise this: Let's stick to short-range tactics and get this pending charge off your back. Once that's disposed of successfully, if it is, we have gained a tangible benefit—time. Time is an element, an entity with very definite value.'

'It seems to me that I've heard that before from someone.'

'Whoever it was,' said Willis, 'he made a sound diagnosis.'

Ray sighed. 'Well, back to the lathe.'

The lathe before which Ray finally paused was a man and his name was Amerigo LoCroce. He could not be described as a boss in the active, functioning sense of the term. He had been active at one time with a small *borgata* in the South Jersey–Philadelphia area. Now, in retirement, with the benevolent acquiescence and consent of the powerful Families to the north and south of him, he puttered disinterestedly in Organizational affairs and supported a nucleus of faithful retainers, no more than thirty people. It was actually more a matter of maintaining a certain state and dignity in retirement than anything else. The practice was that retirees of established rank carried their closest retainers into pasture, always, of course, with the retainer's free consent. Those who elected to remain active could transfer to other Families which were willing to accept them. The strong Family which operated in Philadelphia to the south of Amerigo LoCroce and the dynamic confederation in the industrialized urbanized areas of New Jersey just across the river from New York and Brooklyn liked and trusted him.

Amerigo, in retirement, enjoyed considerable clout with the national commission because he was a very wealthy man and, more important, because he was a neutral man. Since he no longer had personal axes to grind, and since his retainers were no longer out hustling, he was unofficially invested with the toga of elder statesman. His views were listened to by actively functioning executives. Those views were not always necessarily accepted and implemented, but he was listened to. Don Amerigo was what Uncle Oliverotto might have become had he survived, an Organizational repository of history and precedent, a tribal bard, a *consigliere* to the whole rather than to one particular family. 'In the simplest terms,' said Don Amerigo, 'you might think of me as a staff adviser to the commission. My only effectiveness lies in the fact that I have withdrawn from the world of interest, which, of course, means the world, since the terms are synonymous. In this element alone lie my powers of moral suasion with the commission.'

Amerigo LoCroce was one of those men who reveled in anonymity and obscurity. Even by his retainers, very little was known about his personal life which was, in fact, impeccable. He conducted no social activities and seldom, if ever, invited anyone into his home. What further recommended Don Amerigo to the territorial executives who surrounded him was his total lack of what was vulgarly known as a rap sheet. The Census Bureau of the United States had Don Amerigo somewhere in its files. So did the Internal Revenue Service, to whom he remitted promptly, correctly, and quarterly, invariably shortchanging himself by a trifling amount. So did some department of Motor Vehicles, because Amerigo possessed an automobile and a driver's license. So did a Registrar of Voters, because Amerigo, like a good citizen, voted in all elections which pertained to his area of residence. And, finally, so did the Social Security Administration, because Don Amerigo had been assigned a Social Security number. Although he was eligible therefor, Amerigo made no claim for Social Security benefits and Medicare. 'Let less fortunate citizens than myself,' said Amerigo modestly, 'enjoy my portion of those benefits conferred by the generosity of our nation.' What was Amerigo LoCroce, then? As he himself said, merely a member of the great silent majority.

Don Amerigo was fond of discoursing on the virtues and benefits of obscurity. 'This principle,' he was wont to say on occasion, 'is one of the philosophical foundations of our Organization. Just as obedience, humility, poverty, and chastity are cornerstones of Holy Mother Church, so is obscurity one of our cornerstones. As in the ecclesiastical realm, this virtue of ours is often more honored in the breach than in the observance. It nevertheless remains a basic tenet of our effectiveness.' To listening executives, he often said, 'When you weigh men for promotion, avoid the brilliant individualists. Consider seriously those of the second echelon, those who are loyal, obedient, unimaginative, and dully conventional. The first group may bring off more spectacular coups. To counter that, they also harbor within themselves built-in disabilities. Always bear in mind that, like churches and armies, we adhere to the hierarchical principle. An unimaginative man who accepts ideology unquestioningly and who works well with a team will ultimately perform better than the unorthodox individualist. My conservatism, admittedly, has its drawbacks. The sort of men I recommend and favor tend to become hidebound by tradition. And yet, weighing everything together, I must conclude that they are the lesser of two evils. Like the church, we must always strive for cohesion, unity, and continuity.'

Yet the problem which principally preoccupied Don Amerigo in a brave new world was that of flexibility and modernization. 'Consider and observe the church's problems of recruitment,' he said. 'To what extent should it resist the pressures for liberalization? It's an important question. We here in the Organization are not immune to it. We also are faced with the problem of attracting promising young men to an Organizational career. We must always be on the outlook for bright young men who demonstrate a genuine vocational call to join us. I would recommend for your consideration two general propositions. First, a relaxation of the ethnic requirement. By insisting on that qualification, we run the risk of becoming too rigid and too inbred. Sagicity, after all, is not the monopoly of our people. There are surely men of talent and character in other ethnic groups and we should welcome them. Secondly, I recommend an increasing stress on legitimacy in our business enterprises. That trend is already well underway. I welcome it and say it should be encouraged even more strongly. Now, these two propositions may seem to run counter to my proclaimed attitude of conservatism. The fact is that an intelligent conservative must force himself toward a flexible approach if he is to survive at all as a conservative.'

Some executives demurred. 'Don Amerigo,' they pointed out, 'if your general tendencies are followed, they will result in dilution, assimilation, and ultimate disappearance of our Organization in its peculiarly distinctive form.'

'Quite so,' said Don Amerigo to these objectors. 'It may very well come to pass and there's no avoiding it. If you examine our Organization from a broad historical-sociological viewpoint, you will perceive that it is no more than a chip of wood borne up by a powerful current. There is certainly a possibility, even a probability, that we may disappear entirely in our present form. But is that such a significant eventuality? Even today, at this moment, while we sit and speak together, the Organization is already an anachronism. Everything passes away—monarchies, empires, religions, ecclesiastical hierarchies, even geological stratifications. Why not our little Organization?'

'Very impressive,' said some of his listeners with ironic overtones in their voices. 'You can afford the luxury of the long viewpoint because you are retired. We, however, are immersed in the headaches of the immediate moment. You are like an astronomer, Don Amerigo, interesting to listen to, but only for a short time.'

'Thank you, gentlemen,' said Don Amerigo, smiling. 'I understand and appreciate your preoccupation with the here and now. Thank you for listening to me as long as you have.'

Yet Amerigo LoCroce did not exist entirely on a lofty,

fleshless plane of theory. He maintained contact with homely reality by operating three factories in the vicinity of Easton, Pennsylvania, which manufactured women's garments. Since certain of his trusted retainers were the active managers of these enterprises and since his daily attendance was not required, Don Amerigo made his home in Princeton, New Jersey. To an executive who had once come to ask his advice on some problem, he had observed, 'Living in the shadow of a university is like living in the shadow of a great cathedral. The shade cast by such noble institutions upon a given individual is soothing and beneficent.' When the executive, an irreverent man with a sense of humor, replied, 'I'd say it's more like sitting next to a lucky poker player,' Don Amerigo looked at his visitor reproachfully. But, all in all, Don Amerigo was a prized and invaluable man. In addition to his ripe wisdom, he was an adept in the techniques of what was known as baksheesh, khabar, shtup, shmear, and the thousand and one delicate ways of distributing *La Mordida*, the Bite, so as to keep everyone happy. Don Amerigo had his quiet channels of communication in the byways of New Jersey and Pennsylvania politics. He also had a happy talent for bringing minor local politicians into a reasonable frame of mind. Don Amerigo unquestionably possessed the faculty of rationalizing the fears, doubts, and prejudices of politicians for the benefit of the Organization. While some overscrupulous critics might have tended to think of Don Amerigo as a corrupter, he preferred to think of himself as a dispenser.

Uncle Oliverotto had been one of Don Amerigo's close friends and had mentioned him to Ray on a few occasions. 'If you should ever need sound counsel when I'm not around,' Oliverotto once told Ray, 'try to obtain an audience with Don Amerigo.'

'You mean "interview," ' said Ray.

'I mean "audience," ' said Uncle Oliverotto. 'In other words, don't go to him lightly.'

' "Audience" has comical overtones,' said Ray.

'So it has,' agreed Uncle Oliverotto. 'The entire world has comical overtones. I still say, don't waste Don Amerigo's time with trivia. He's like a fire alarm. Smash the glass only when

377

there's an emergency.'

So Ray, in casting about for a lathe on which to complete the turning of his key, reminded himself of Amerigo LoCroce. In a cryptic, indirect fashion, two competent men had already warned Ray that the fashioning of the key was only half completed. Another factor which inclined Ray to take counsel with Don Amerigo was the elder statesman's known aversion to Don Leonardo Codi. Ray was aware, as were many other bosses, that Don Amerigo had on several occasions spoken out against Don Leonardo before the commission as a disinterested friend of the court. Even though the commission had never kicked out Len Codi, they had always listened carefully and respectfully to Don Amerigo's scornful criticism of Codi's shoddy business practices. 'Don Leonardo,' Amerigo had warned, 'is a classical example of everything which a boss should not be. He is a nepotist, a thief, niggardly and illiberal with his *capos* and soldiers. He is a man who will end by getting himself kidnapped or killed. More seriously, the anti-social behavior of Don Leonardo will discourage the recruitment of the sort of new blood which our Organization is seeking. His conduct will bring us into general disrepute.'

What particularly warmed Ray's heart toward Don Amerigo was the latter's criticism before the commission of the Poggio–Codi alliance while the implementation of Ray's deportation was still warm. 'This entente is immoral and dishonorable,' said Don Amerigo, 'hence undesirable. It reminds me of nothing less than the marriage of Hamlet's mother with his uncle. Since Al Poggio has posted with such unseemly haste to incestuous sheets, this matter will become a *casus belli* in the future.'

And so, indeed, had it come to pass. The deported boss Don Raimondo had returned to Italy. Al Poggio had been duly executed, and the relationship which existed between Ray and Codi was now a frigid and precarious one.

'This is exactly what Don Amerigo had predicted,' observed an admiring executive at a minor meeting. 'He is certainly a sage man.'

'And a cultured man,' agreed another. 'What was that business about the sheets?'

'Hamlet,' explained the first complacently. 'God damn! I've been to a lot of meetings, but I've never heard anyone belt out a little Shakespeare the way Don Amerigo can. Do you know what that man has? Class. That's the only word for it.'

Ray examined all of these thoughts with the deliberation of a haruspex examining the entrails of a fowl. For what he had in mind, decidedly, Don Amerigo LoCroce was the man with whom he must take counsel.

CHAPTER 26

As part of his overall strategy, Ray had visited Cartier's and blown in two grand on a wristwatch for Marta. He had had it sent to her downtown office with a carefully worded note:

MY DEAR MARTA:

After such a long absence from home, it was wonderful to see you again. It brought up memories.

Although I didn't write from Italy, you were very often in my thoughts. If the old man were alive now, how happy he would have been, and how proud of you!

I hope you'll approve of my little gift by accepting it. It tries to express a feeling of friendship, respect, and admiration.

Sincerely,
RAY

The gift had worked, as gifts were supposed to work on women—like Drano. Marta telephoned Ray and he came in from Mineola to see her. He was ushered into Marta's office. When the secretary had closed the door, Marta came around from behind her desk, went up to Ray, hugged him, and kissed him on the left cheek.

'What's that for?' said Ray.

Marta extended her left arm. 'The watch.'

'You like?'

'It's lovely. But your note! It was as cautious and hedged as a legal brief.'

'I'm not much of a hand at letter writing.'

Marta smiled. 'That's an understatement, isn't it?' She

seated herself behind the desk. Ray slid into an armchair before the desk and stared at the stack of blue-jacketed briefs and documents before her.

'What's all this?' he said.

Marta placed a pair of half-spectacles on the documents, leaned back, and closed her eyes. 'The Occhiaccio pyramid, Ray.'

He studied Marta casually. She wore a tailored tweed suit over a black cashmere sweater, a double string of pearls, and an antique Maltese cross brooch on the lapel of the suit. Her shining black hair fell to her shoulders.

'The whole pyramid?' he finally said.

'All of it.'

'My biography is in that portfolio.'

'It's in pretty good shape,' said Marta, 'although you're somewhat overdiversified.'

Ray nodded. His portfolio was indeed diversified. Big pieces of big mortgages on big office and apartment buildings. Geographically diversified also, not concentrated in Manhattan, which was a bad basket for all of one's eggs, because it was out of control and going to hell anyway, gods or no gods. Pieces of contracts of big TV stars. Pieces of hotels and restaurants. Always pieces, never the whole thing. Pieces of distilleries and breweries, heirlooms from the dear dead past. Pieces of insurance agencies which wrote the policies for big labor unions. Always pieces, so that if someone double-crossed or something went honestly sour, the odds would hold up. A little piece of Vegas broken up over four casinos, all strung together in a maze of holding companies like a tangle of snakes. To hold on, you needed good accountants and lawyers. Above all, human nature being what it was, good muscle. Muscle could accomplish in thirty minutes what the law in its majesty couldn't accomplish in thirty months. Just as gambling houses operated for the benefit of their proprietors, just as brokerage firms for the benefit of the general partners, so the law operated for the benefit of lawyers. Litigation as a poisonous swamp and muscle an efficient pirogue in which to navigate the surface of that swamp. Muscle was basic to the rest. To get the good accountants and lawyers, you had to have something to bring them so they could earn their fees protecting your property. It was the original crazy muscle which had built the nut. No miracles or magic formulae. Ray had built it up slowly, the hard way. He gestured at the documents before Marta.

'How does all this bear on the present charge?'

'It does indirectly,' said Marta. 'We want to make sure that the United States Attorney doesn't drag in some nasty surprises. Like new evidence of income tax evasion. As it stands, time *has* put a plausible varnish on your affairs. It would take a conscientious team to sand things down to the bare wood.'

'Who, for instance?'

'The Special Investigating Unit of the Internal Revenue Service, for instance.'

'They'd strain their eyes for nothing,' said Ray. 'I'm cleaner than a Swiss bank.'

'You'd probably be better off if you were as inaccessible to the SIU as a Swiss bank.'

'What's the matter, have you found a hole somewhere?'

'Not yet,' said Marta. 'I'm just checking to make sure the SIU can't sneak up on you somewhere. Later in the week I'm going to double-check all of this with your accountants.'

'I thought Willis was taking care of me.'

'He is. What's the matter, Ray? Embarrassed with a lady doctor?'

'Yes,' said Ray with a suggestion of surprise. 'Sort of. I guess it's the Italian in me. Marta, what was on your mind, something special?'

Marta looked at him gravely. 'Very special. You.'

Ray returned her searching stare. 'You're on my mind also. It's not a good situation, is it?'

'Supposing you got clear,' said Marta. 'I mean, really clear.'

'So I could remain here without being bugged all the time?'

Marta nodded.

'I'd do what Uncle Oliverotto was after me for years to do. I'd propose to you.'

'Thanks,' said Marta. 'You know, Ray, were I so inclined, I would have been married by now. I've had offers from some eminently qualified citizens, legitimate ones, I might add. Of

382

course, they all lacked the fatal Occhiaccio charm. I suspect that neither of us will ever marry and it's not important. Marriage in its present form has become passé. Are you interested in fathering children, Ray?'

'I consider it immoral to reproduce,' said Ray.

'Very un-Italian,' smiled Marta. 'I've met some good men who wanted me to settle down and bear their unlawful children.'

'You make me jealous.'

'Don't be. Occhiaccio still leads the pack. I don't know why, but he does.' There was a note of appeal in Marta's voice. 'We're not getting any younger, Ray. We're not kids any more. Marta is ready to move in on you, without benefit of clergy.'

'With Uncle Sam in bed between us?' said Ray. 'Uh uh.'

'But if you *were* in the clear.'

Ray sighed. 'I'd like that. I'd get a job and join the PTA and the local garden club. I'd be so goddamned square, I'd have eight sides.'

'Be serious.'

'About you, I am. And about staying in the U.S.A. Marta— I'm sick and tired of traveling.'

'There's one more little thing,' said Marta. 'Your *amici* and your *fratelli*. There'd be problems, wouldn't there, if you announced your retirement?'

Ray grinned mirthlessly. 'You'd better believe it, my friend. People do retire of course, when they're judged by their peers to have served their time, and with the consent of the whole. In my case, now, I'd get a big fat No. Hell, Marta, you know the score.'

'I wish I didn't,' she replied somberly.

'Baby——' began Ray.

'Call me "baby,"' said Marta with a smile. 'It makes me feel good. I haven't heard that in such a long time.'

'Baby.'

'Do you love me, Ray?'

'That's an unfair question. I'll have to consult with my lawyer before I answer it. No one knows what that word means. Let's say, I dig you. You fit me like someone I'd been married to for thirty years.'

'You don't know me at all, Ray. Not after all these years.'

'Let's find out, baby. Supposing I were tossed out of the U.S.A. and had to return to Italy permanently. Would you give up your friends, New York City, your profession, everything you have here, and return with me?'

'I'll level with you,' said Marta slowly. 'No.'

'A good, honest answer. And the right one. You come through loud and clear for me. You always have.'

Marta toyed with her spectacles. 'What's the use of kidding myself? Perhaps I don't love you as much as I'd like to think I do.'

'You're great,' said Ray. 'Most people jerk their motives around to put themselves in the best possible light. Anyhow, I'd never ask you to do it.'

'Raimondo! How noble can you get?'

'Way out noble, when I work at it. Look, can you play hookey from the office this afternoon? If we have to be sad, at least let's eat. May I take you out to lunch, counselor?'

'I was hoping you'd ask,' said Marta. 'A terrible thought just occurred to me, Ray. Do you realize that you and I have never been in bed together?'

'Yeah,' said Ray slowly, 'it's true, isn't it?'

'You've made it with many other women, haven't you?'

'With certain kinds,' said Ray. 'Women who don't try to drill too deeply into me.'

'I won't,' said Marta. 'I promise.

'Put it on ice, Marta. Between you and me it's serious. At heart, I'm just an old-fashioned wop, so behave yourself with me. Right now, I want to make you another little proposition. If you'll arrange to take the rest of the day off and help me with an important shopping mission, I'll take you to dinner at Pucci's and then to the theater, if you wish.'

'Raimondo,' said Marta. 'I'm not generally curious. I just happen to be about anything which concerns you.'

Ray rose to his feet. 'Plenty of time. I'll give you the full scoop. You'll enjoy it.'

Marta went into the adjoining office and returned with a tailored coat over her arm. 'Ray, I'm not properly dressed for the evening bit.'

Ray helped her into the coat. 'You I'd take to Pucci's and anywhere else even in patched jeans. You have the waistline of a high school kid, Marta. How do you do it?'

'Worrying about you,' said Marta shortly.

He held open the door and followed Marta out of the office.

'This little shopping thing,' said Ray over the luncheon table, 'it's a straight-line project. It concerns my case so it should interest you professionally. What it boils down to is this. I have to talk with a man who can deflect the heat. You don't simply contact this man, request an appointment, and tell him you have a problem. You give him the word through an indirect move. He gets the message. If he wants to listen, he lets you know.'

'Still, if you're acquainted with the man,' said Marta, 'why can't you simply telephone him?'

'In the first place, I don't know him that well, though he knows of me. He was a friend of Uncle Oliverotto's, not of mine. I know him officially, let's say, not personally.'

'Ah, Byzantine protocol.'

'Sicilian protocol,' said Ray. 'It's important to these people. The steps must be taken in order. You don't contact him; he contacts you. A little of that divinity that hedges in a king hedges in a top don.'

'Oh, come on, Ray.'

'I kid you not. They take themselves seriously.'

'I never realized how—well—medieval you were. Or Oriental, or something.'

'Not I. They.'

'Oh, very well. What sort of an indirect move?'

'You're sharp,' said Ray approvingly. 'Well, a favorite ploy is a gift. It must be a strong gift to jog the man's eye and memory. I use the word "strong" in its Sicilian sense. It must make an impression. Am I sending it because I seek a favor? Nothing of the kind. I, the godson of Don Oliverotto, have just come back from Italy. I offer him a gift on my return to the United States to demonstrate respect for the highly placed friend of my beloved godfather. Beyond an expression of respect, the gift implies a request for his protection and assist-

385

ance.'

'Unnecessarily cumbersome and elaborate.'

'That's how these things are done,' said Ray.

'So you want me to assist you in selecting a gift for this person?'

'You could be very helpful. The gift, as I said, must be strong. I know you have considerable appreciation and knowledge of art. Painting. I have none.'

'I have a little.'

'More than I,' said Ray.

'So you're going to lay a painting at this VIP's feet, is that it?'

'This afternoon. And you will be gracious enough to select it.'

'And then you're going to sit back and wait for the desired chemical effect?'

'Exactly.'

'What delicacy!' said Marta. 'What subtlety! How fascinating!'

'That's how these things are done. Don't laugh, baby.'

'I'll try not to. What does this important gumbah of yours fancy, oversized baroque pot-boilers in expensive gilt frames?'

'On the contrary,' said Ray. 'I understand he's a sophisticate, a man of exacting tastes in art. He's a collector. You'd better take him seriously, Marta.'

'That's different, isn't it? What does he like? Some people are interested in the top-dollar favorites; others pride themselves on their ability to pick up unknowns whose work will appreciate astronomically.'

'Art isn't my bag, so I'll try to steer a middle course. This man is predisposed to Italian painters. Moderns, okay too, but Italian. He's proud of Italian cultural achievements. And, of course, he's crazy about the old Renaissance stuff. That doesn't mean I'm going to blow him to a Titian or a Tintoretto, which I couldn't do anyhow. What I had in mind was a good, solid Italian modern, a man whose work is well known on both sides of the water. But if I overspend, this man is going to think I'm a damn fool and lose respect for me. Sicilians are quick to catch a false note.'

Marta sipped her coffee and lit a cigarette. 'Well, Raimondo, I'm becoming interested.'

'Would you care for a liqueur?'

'Can't afford it. Would your benefactor-to-be go for a Giglio?'

'Never heard of him,' said Ray.

'Fifty-seventh Street has for quite a while now. He's a solid young blue chip. Not an Eastman Kodak or a Sears, Roebuck, but he'll get there. If your friend's a connoisseur, he'll know Giglio's work, all right.'

'All I know is price,' said Ray.

'That's not enough. The galleries show artists at a higher figure than Giglio who aren't as good. In my opinion, at least. Precisely for the price buyers.'

'So how do you pick them?'

'How does one pick horses?' said Marta. 'Or stocks? Or husbands? Or dresses? One's own taste, an awareness of what the critics, the public, and the galleries are favoring—that is, if one is seeking appreciation of the original cost value.'

'Well, how does this Giglio stack up?'

'Quite respectably,' said Marta. 'The critics favor him rather consistently. A Giglio would probably be a reasonably safe investment.'

'Do *you* like his work?'

'I, personally? Yes. He's a fine draftsman and a sound technician. I like his ideas and his manner of expressing them. Oh, Ray, you know the experts can drown you with their convoluted phraseology. They do a lot of Delphic hedging and double-talking like financial analysts. You really have to have an instinct about these things as well as some sound knowledge of your own. But, after everything has been said, I'd like to have a Giglio hanging in my own apartment. Is that good enough?'

'Good enough for me,' said Ray admiringly. 'What a cultivated, knowledgeable girl you are! How did I do without you all these years?'

'That's what I've been wondering, Raimondo,' said Marta ironically.

'How much will I have to pay for a Giglio?'

'Are you prepared to spend around five thousand dollars?' said Marta. 'That's about par for a baby blue chip.'

'On your say-so.'

'What delightful fun!' said Marta, picking up her gloves. 'Pay the waiter, Raimondo, and let's go spending some of your money. It will be almost as thrilling as buying a painting for oneself.'

'Do you think he'll like it?'

'Raimondo, dear, I'm far from the expert you make me out to be. Very far from it. Only if you say so, I may know a little more here than you do. Let me put it investment wise. Giglio is not a Jersey Standard or an IBM. He's not paying any dividends yet, but some day he's going to move up and split. Given that premise, what is there not to like? It's a reasonable prediction that your man's acquisition will appreciate in value. Does that answer it?'

'For *me*, it does. What's the annual inflation-appreciation curve, Marta, about five to six percent per annum?'

'About that, I think.'

'Do you think Giglio's work will keep pace?'

'Conservatively, I think it may even do a little better.'

'Then it's good art,' said Ray. 'Let's go, Marta.'

'Raimondo, dear,' said Marta, 'I can see now that you're a genuine art lover. There are facets to you I've never appreciated.'

'That's because you've never had a chance to know me. I put my ignorance into your long, slender, pale, and capable hands.'

Marta took Ray's arm as they walked out. 'It's nice to have a man around, even if he's only a philistine. A bright philistine, though.'

'Manipulate me, kid. I may even surprise you and shape up.'

Marta squeezed his arm. 'I'd like nothing better.'

CHAPTER 27

Tony Saldana finished reading a copy of the letter which Ray had sent to Amerigo LoCroce. Ray had written in Italian:

DEAR DON AMERIGO:

It is only after one has been out of America for an extended period of time that one comes to truly understand what a benevolent as well as a powerful country the United States is. When upon my return I finally stepped on American soil, I was seized with an irresistible impulse to kneel down and kiss that soil. At all events, I have returned and hope to resume my duties in a manner which will meet with your approval. Although I have never had the honor of being associated with Amerigo LoCroce, his principles and philosophy are as familiar to me as those of my late godfather, Don Oliverotto, may his soul rest in peace.

Don Oliverotto often told me that he was privileged to be your friend. To commemorate my safe return, and to express high esteem toward yourself, I have taken the liberty of sending you Giglio's oil-on-canvas 'Morning in Rome.' Since Giglio is known to be one of your favorite painters, it is my hope that this addition to your already celebrated collection will afford you much pleasure and satisfaction.

With profound respect,
RAIMONDO RAFFAELE OCCHIACCO

'Pretty fancy,' said Tony. 'Real Mustache Pete stuff.'

'I wrote it by hand,' said Ray. 'I hope the grammar is okay. He's a fusspot about those things.'

'You couldn't prove it by me,' said Tony. 'When did you send it?'

'Three days ago.'

'So now?'

'We wait.'

While waiting, Ray thought back on his long-delayed entry into the Business under the aegis of Oliverotto. It had really started after his return from the Harvard School of Business. MBA and all, he had had to make his beginning the hard way. In fact, because of that college degree, otherwise neutral fellow members persisted in putting sardonic challenges in his way. Their unspoken attitude was: 'Try this problem on for size. Did they teach you in college how to take care of *this* one?' It took Ray six months to get his first two profitable crap games going. Within another six months, he had purchased a percentage of a restaurant with the profits from the crap games. Despite the fact that he and his partner were being robbed by the cooks, the waiters, and the bartenders, they still made money. The peculations of the thieves were kept within reasonable bounds by a real fear. The net profits from the games and the restaurant Ray put out on the street in loans. He was finally underway and found himself working harder than ever. He learned that he had to protect himself not only from outlaw competition but from higher-ups who constantly sought a higher cut. True, the boys had given him a license, but he had put much time, trouble, and money into building an organization that could give the public satisfactory service. By that time, he also had a few numbers controllers under him. A troublesome parasite were the police and minor politicians. They took, but they didn't always deliver protection. If outlaws muscled his crap games, he couldn't to squawking too much to the boys upstairs; it would make him lose respect. And, of course, he couldn't go to the law like a legitimate businessman. The precinct house was a sizable expense. Each patrolman on the beat received fifty dollars a week. The going figure for sergeants was one hundred a week, for lieutenants, three hundred a week. Beniamino made up an envelope each week for the sergeant bagman who came around for the captain. It contained four century-notes. That was additional insurance to keep people off Ray's neck. That didn't end the law-and-order problem. With considerable regularity, downtown switched the plainclothes squad in the area. The new squad never had trouble discovering where to seek the payoff.

Ray assessed the benefits of membership in the Organization realistically. It conferred no riches on one, immediately or deferred. Membership was simply the granting of a license—more accurately, a franchise to ask for something, or to enter an investment group. Even if you were approved for a percentage of a venture, you, yourself, had to produce the original funds for your percentage of the investment. That was *your* business, not the Family's. All *they* did was to give you the opportunity and the protective umbrella. Certainly, if a soldier or a *capo* could drag a hundred thousand dollars together—nobody cared how—and a junk deal surfaced, the investor was given an opportunity to take a percentage of it and make a quarter million on his hundred thousand. He could also lose his investment if something went sour. The Family guaranteed nothing. Aside from that, a soldier always had a protected job. Even an unambitious mediocrity could make a couple of hundred a week with little or no work. An ambitious hard worker could open a legitimate bar, restaurant, or some other enterprise, and the boys would throw him their custom. As in the legitimate securities market, there were always assorted joint ventures available, provided one had necessary capital. One could always put out money on the street, and the boys would help the lender keep the borrowers current. Above all, it was important before entering a business to obtain the imprimatur of a higher-up. Still more intelligent, it was advisable to give the lieutenant or the subboss his cut before you even started making money. That was sensible insurance, a premium for your franchise license. Or, if you wished to run a crap game, you first arranged for approval, the protection, and the cut off the top for the higher-ups. The principle was similar whether you were the sole proprietor or a partner in a joint venture. One thing was certain, you had to work as hard as in any legitimate business. Naturally, the more capital you piled up, the larger were the ventures into which you could go. If you encountered trouble, the boys would help you legally. The purchase of legal talent was a cooperative operation. There were benefits, but it was far from being a gravy train. There were other angles which Ray had personally avoided but which he had okayed for Nicky Polo and Beniamino. They would come to him and say, 'We want to buy a piece of a caper. An outlaw booster is setting up a private jewel heist.' Only they said 'Indian,' not 'outlaw.' Ray would say, 'Go ahead with your own money. This is between you and the Indians.' Then Nicky and Beniamino would proceed to lend the booster or boosters money, through a third party, with which to set up the heist. If and after the caper came off and the merchandise had been fenced, Nicky and Beniamino could make a profit of two hundred percent without personal involvement. Sometimes the caper went sour, but, then, so did the stock market. And, of course, there were no long-term capital gains taxes on such operations.

One could also purchase a percentage of a large wager on a fixed sporting event. The going rate in those days was one quarter of one's winnings to the higher-ups who compensated the fixer of the event with a given percentage of the total. Sometimes investors in such ventures tried to welch on the twenty-five percent service charge. That was rush and unintelligent. The least that happened was that the welchers lost their franchises.

Finally, one could invest in the Nevada gaming industry, if one was fortunate enough to command that sort of capital. But buttons usually lacked not only the financial affluence but the social standing to be invited in. As in the legitimate world, there was a direct relationship between rank and affluence and investment opportunities.

As Ray's organization prospered and he rose in the world, Beniamino, Nicky Polo, and, later, Tony Saldana were promoted to *caporegime*. At this point, Ray directed them to farm out to nonmember associates, activities which were no longer consonant with their dignity. Eventually, the Organization frowned formally on member involvement directly in junk distribution, safe, loft, jewel, furs, and liquor robberies and hijackings, the blue industry, movies, books, photographs and records, call-girl agencies, collection agencies, sucker-trade clip joints, and after-hours stores. Nonmembers were permitted to operate in these areas as long as they paid off. If such nonmembers violated verbal agreements, the Organization simply passed the word to the law instead of utilizing its own muscle. The police then moved in on the errant free-lance nonmember, not from zeal to enforce the law, but to shake down personal profit for themselves. The police liked this arrangement for still another reason: It provided them with a performance record.

The summons came during an evening eight days after the dispatch of the Giglio. Tony Saldana and Ray were in the study playing gin when Fats Mazzi knocked on the door and entered. 'Excuse me, Don Antonio,' he said. 'Man on the phone that says he's calling from the railroad station right here in Mineola. He says some picture was received.'

'What's the man's name?' said Tony.

'Jimmy Scott,' said Fats. 'Real name, Giacomo Scozzari. I know him. He's like a butler there.'

'What else did he say?' asked Tony.

'Nothing,' said Fats. 'He's got a message for Don Raimondo. Personal.'

'Where's Dumdum?' said Tony.

'Holding down the gate. He knows Jimmy, too.'

'You know this Jimmy Scott when you see him?'

'Yeah,' said Fats. 'I seen him at the races, it wasn't more than three months ago. We was picking a few horses together.'

'Will you recognize him?'

'Yeah. He couldn't of changed that much in three months.'

'So get in the car, go down, and pick him up,' said Tony. 'Before you bring him in here, you and Jack frisk him good.'

'He sounded right.'

'Then frisk him twice. Make him take his pants and shirt off.'

'He won't like that,' said Fats.

'Go ahead, Fats. You're wasting time.'

When Fats closed the door, Ray said, 'I had an idea he'd move this way. Oliverotto was like that also. He disliked the phone.'

'It's a good idea,' said Tony. 'These days you can never tell about phones. I don't like to use them myself no more than I have to.'

'That's only part of it,' said Ray. 'It isn't only a matter of security, although I'm not minimizing that. It's part of their personal way of doing things. I ran into it in Sicily, even a little in Rome. They still follow the *personalismo* pattern. The phone is too mechanical. Some *pezzo* wants to talk with you about something, he has a phone at his elbow, he still sends a messenger.'

'They don't have to worry about bugs over there,' said Tony.

'Nothing like here,' Ray agreed. 'But even if there were no bugs at all, they prefer to pass the word by man, not by wire. The idea is it's more human, more civilized. Also, more class.'

'That's Mustache Pete thinking,' said Tony.

'You'd be surprised. It's still strong in the old country. Form and face is very large. I think I have Amerigo figured all right. I should hit it off with him fine.'

'You think the picture did a job?'

'That, and the letter. These old boys love to do things obliquely, slantwise, without words. It's the old Sicilian game of *astutezza*. They modestly disclaim it, like Oliverotto used to, but privately they consider themselves the foxiest people in the world.'

'Who thinks about these things?'

'I do,' said Ray. 'I like to figure these angles. Remember, I'm just back from there with fresh reminders. Like, why are our people the way they are?'

'Who cares?' said Tony. 'I'm an American.'

'*You* are. I'm talking about the people over there. If the Americans had been muscled as many times as those islanders by different mobs, they'd also start thinking underground fashion, like the OSS in the big war. Hell, Tony, you're too young to remember it. Maybe I'm exaggerating a little, but it's a fact. They naturally do things in a roundabout way. I'm not kidding. They start learning how to shake tails before they're old enough to jerk off. After a while, it becomes natural.'

'Hell, I don't think that way,' said Tony.

'Why should you? Outside of a phone which might be bugged, what have *you* got to worry about? The U.S.A. is wide open. If you don't believe me, go take a trip to the old country, you'll see what I mean. Over there, kids start figuring angles even before their mother squeezes them out of the belly. Tony, boy, you're lucky you got yourself born on this side of the water, and don't forget where you heard it.' Ray sighed. 'It would have been nice if my old man had waited an extra year or so before he knocked me out of the oven.'

'Hey, man,' said Tony, 'you've became a real flag waver.'

'You'd better believe it,' said Ray. 'Visit Europe and love America. Even if you get busted here, it's still home.'

'Okay, Ray, I'll run up a flag next Fourth of July.'

'Goddamned right. It's a good example for the kids.'

He began dealing again and they played in silence for another half hour. Tony perked up his ears. 'That's tires on the gravel. I think that's them.'

Another fifteen minutes went by and Fats Mazzi and Jack Dumdum brought a man into the study between them. The man was short and stocky of build, with black hair, a clean-shaven face, and cold, impassive black eyes. He was a chunky peasant type, with strength in his arms and short legs and a head that was too small for the breadth of his body. A definite western Sicilian type, thought Ray, with Saracen genes reaching far back into his ancestry. A basso house retainer, as distinctive in his way as a Welsh corgi.

'This here's Jimmy Scott,' said Fats Mazzi. 'He's a friend of ours. He's okay.'

Which meant they had frisked him.

'Thanks, boys,' said Tony. 'Just leave Jimmy here.'

Fats and Jack Dumdum walked out.

'Sit down, Jimmy,' said Tony. 'Make yourself comfortable.'

'With your permission, Mr. Saldana,' said Jimmy. He seated himself carefully.

Tony got up and poured a glass of wine for Jimmy.

'Thank you, Mr. Saldana,' said Jimmy. He sipped slowly.

'You have a message for me?' said Ray.

Jimmy looked at Ray. 'Don Raimondo? Yes. The old man sends you his regards. He says thank you. You will come to our house for lunch with the old man and Mrs LoCroce next Tuesday at one. Mr. Saldana is also to come.'

'Me?' said Tony. 'I didn't think the old man knew me.'

'He knows you, Mr. Saldana,' said Jimmy.

'That's the whole message?' said Ray. 'For that you drove here all the way from Princeton?'

Jimmy half smiled. 'The old man don't like telephones.'

'How is he?' said Ray.

'In good health, Don Raimondo. He said to tell you he likes the picture.'

'Who painted it?' said Ray.

'Giglio,' said Jimmy.

'You want to stay here tonight, Jimmy?' said Tony.

'Thanks, Mr. Saldana,' said Jimmy, 'but I got to get back. The old man don't like me away from the house all night.'

'Okay, Jimmy,' said Ray. 'Tell Don Amerigo respectful regards from Mr. Saldana and myself. We shall be there.'

Jimmy got up and bobbed his head without speaking.

'Go ahead,' said Tony. 'Fats will take you back to the station.'

When Jimmy left, Tony Saldana said, 'You think maybe you should bring along something for his wife? Like a good piece of antique jewelry?'

Ray shook his head. 'He wouldn't go for that. It would be a sort of presumption. With these people, you act like their women aren't there.'

'You ever met the man? You know him at all?'

'Only from what Oliverotto used to tell me. He digs culture. He goes to concerts, art galleries, art auctions. He reads a lot of books.'

'I heard even when he was active, all he did was read books,' said Tony. 'Yet he got along fine with that troop of his. He never set no world on fire or made ten million bucks, but he always got along. He must be all of seventy-five now. It looks like he's going to die in bed. Which is more than I can say for a lot of guys.'

'True,' said Ray. 'Amerigo is what I would call one of our anachronisms. He didn't have to make a lot of money. He gets the equivalent of it in respect. That's what counts with him.

Because he's disinterested, everyone trusts him. He settles beefs when nobody else can. The commission always listens to him when he gets up.'

'Well, whatever the man's got,' said Tony, 'it's going to be spread pretty thin. I hear he's got about twenty-five grand-children.'

When Ray and Tony entered the house of Amerigo Lo-Croce, Jimmy Scott, in a white coat and white gloves, led them into the library of the house. Amerigo and his wife were waiting. Amerigo was tall, thin, healthily tanned, with a good head of white hair. Ray and Tony bowed slightly as they shook hands with the old don.

Amerigo presented the two visitors to his wife, a tall, slim, white-haired woman with a pleasant expression. When she put out her hand, Ray bent over and kissed it. In Italian he said, 'A great honor and a pleasure, *Signora* LoCroce.'

Tony looked startled and followed suit.

Don Amerigo smiled and said to Ray in Italian, 'By all means, let us speak our mother tongue. How very thoughtful of you to think of me, Raimondo! Dear Oliverotto taught you good manners. It isn't common nowadays.'

'Don Oliverotto,' said Ray, 'and my recent sojourn in Italy as a refresher course. The strongest impression which I brought away from there was that our people are the most courteous in the world.'

'But of course,' said Don Amerigo. 'Italian courtesy is the best because it springs from the heart. French manners are artificial and have always been.'

The luncheon proceeded very slowly, with Jimmy Scott and a maid serving.

'The painting pleased me immensely,' said Don Amerigo. 'I commend your taste, Raimondo.'

'It was not mine, Don Amerigo,' said Ray modestly. 'I had expert guidance. Since your own knowledge in this area is formidable, I didn't presume to depend on myself alone.'

Don Amerigo acknowledged the compliment and launched into a technical discussion of Giglio's work which Ray did not understand. He glanced at Tony. It was a cinch they had lost

Tony long ago. Maybe the old chick understood what was being said. Tony was beginning to fidget. Ray shook himself alert and reminded himself of the rule: When in doubt, listen raptly and look interested. And the next commandment: Nothing so commends us to others as our ability to listen appreciatively to the eloquence of others.

The interminable luncheon finally came to an end.

Mrs. LoCroce excused herself. Jimmy Scott, who was in the room, pulled back her chair. She rose and so did the three men. When she left, Don Amerigo said to Ray and Tony, 'Well, gentlemen, let's go into my study.'

That study was a second private library with shelves of books to the ceiling. Two big bay windows looked out on a stretch of lawn. Don Amerigo sat down in a leather swivel chair behind his desk and pointed to the wall behind him.

'Well, there's your painting, my boy. Very good. You have taste despite your disclaimers. It was a thoughtful gift and I am pleased.'

'I'm delighted to hear you say it, Don Amerigo,' said Ray.

The don reached into a cabinet behind the desk and took out a bottle of grappa and a tray of small glasses. He filled three glasses. Ray and Tony each took one.

'A little grappa is very good after a meal,' said Don Amerigo. 'Nothing better for the digestion.' He rolled a little over his tongue.

'To your good health, Don Amerigo,' said Ray and tasted his. He glanced at Tony from the corner of his eye and reflected that Tony was profiting by his exposure to this urbane fashion of doing things.

'Well, Raimondo, my dear boy,' said Don Amerigo at last, 'up to this point, your handling has been dextrous. You have observed the amenities and that is only proper. Some people nowadays unfortunately consider such steps a waste of time. On the contrary, they actually expedite the execution of business, as you shall see. So, then, Raimondo, since yours is obviously not a mere social call on a retired old man, what is on your mind? How can I be of service to you? You see, when the time arrives, I can come directly to the point.'

'It was Don Oliverotto's wish that I should get in touch

with you,' said Ray, 'if I was ever confronted by a difficult problem.'

'Yes, yes, of course,' said Don Amerigo with the faintest tone of impatience. 'That is all understood. Now, come to the heart of it.'

He heard Ray out without interruption and without change of expression.

'Both Colonel Colquhoun and your attorney were entirely correct,' he finally said. 'That Immigration and Naturalization file record of yours must be abstracted. It must be pulled out and lost if your well-disposed judicial friend is going to do you any good.'

'I don't have the connections, Don Amerigo,' said Ray. 'I have been away.'

'It can be done,' said the don. 'It has been done. It is not easy. And, of course, it is also very expensive.'

'Of course. I expect that. Whatever is necessary.'

'Perhaps I can help you. I have a number of good friends both in New York and Washington.'

'I shall be most grateful, Don Amerigo. My case will come to trial within three months. The prosecution's investigators even now may be planning to examine my file, so time is short.'

'I understand.'

'I'm prepared to pay immediately.'

Don Amerigo waved his hand. 'It's unnecessary. I'll give you the final figure when it is done.'

'I'm heartened to hear you say "when," not "if," said Ray.

'I think we'll be able to do something,' said Don Amerigo casually. 'But enough of this matter for the moment. You'll hear further from me through Giacomo.' Don Amerigo lit a wine-soaked crooked Parodi, leaned back in his chair, and puffed forth a cloud of smoke. 'You handled Poggio correctly. About Don Leonardo, I'm not so sure.'

'Ah,' said Ray without expression.

Don Amerigo nodded. 'It's no longer a secret in the right places. Don Leonardo complained before the commission about you and I took your part. Poggio was your internal affair and the commission so ruled. As to your methods of extracting payment from Leonardo, while they frowned, they also ruled in your favor.' He stared at Ray curiously. 'Some interesting stories are beginning to make the rounds concerning your activities while you were abroad. Are you aware of that, Raimondo?'

'No.'

'Well, they are. I've traced their source back to Don Leonardo. I suspect they will be his method of retaliation. While you were correct in sparing his life he may prove to be a source of embarrassment for you.'

'What sort of stories?' said Ray.

'Material which could certainly affect you unfavorably. Newsworthy, apocryphal, and obviously set in motion by Leonardo.'

'Have you spotted anything, Tony?' said Ray.

Tony shook his head.

'The substance of these unconfirmed rumors is simply this,' said Don Amerigo. 'While abroad, you allegedly conspired with an Arab guerrilla organization to assassinate Robert Kennedy. This group was behind Sirhan. You gave them financial aid.'

'Nonsense.'

'Of course. The motive would be believable. Kennedy did initiate deportation proceedings against you.'

'That is true.'

'And you did do business with such an organization while abroad.'

'They were not interested in Kennedy,' said Ray. 'My business with them had nothing to do with Kennedy.'

'True or false,' said Don Amerigo, 'Leonardo has a very solid bone to worry on. Watch it. Watch it very closely. I suspect it may eventually prove more troublesome than your impending trial on the unlawful reentry charge.'

CHAPTER 28

When Ray had returned from Cambridge with his sheepskin in his hand, Uncle Oliverotto said to him, 'I think you should now get out of the neighborhood. You have no more family here.'

'I have you,' said Ray.

'Me you'll always have,' said Oliverotto, 'as long as I live. Get an apartment in a nice neighborhood, quiet clothes. People judge a man by how he lives and dresses. That way, people will respect you. Anyhow, you're no cheap hood, you're the godson of Oliverotto, for whom I have plans.'

'Maybe they'll think I feel I'm too good for them.'

'Let them think what they want. Since they don't think, it's not important. The world is changing. Now we need business-men who understand balance sheets, not life-takers and pine-apple-makers. For you, the bridge is broken. Go.'

'Okay,' said Ray, 'but I'll stay in Brooklyn to be near you.'

'Then look around in Brooklyn Heights, by the river,' said Oliverotto. 'Get a building with elevators and a doorman. Lots of Wall Street people there. They're only fifteen minutes from their racket.'

So Ray leased a good apartment in Brooklyn Heights, opened a charge account with Brooks Brothers, whose modes were fashionable at that time, and became indistinguishable from the Wall Streeters. When he came visiting, the old man nodded with approval. 'That is what I meant. Your suit says you are *un uomo agiato*. What do they call the style?'

'Ivy League.'

'*Lega d'edera?*'

'All it means is "conservative," ' said Ray.

'A very nervous language, this English,' said Oliverotto. 'Always new traps.'

'I've got Benny living with me,' said Ray. 'He'll be getting married one of these days. Till then, I'll keep him close.'

'A good idea. That boy is an ox, a bull, a faithful watchdog. Since he's an innocent without brains, the sooner he's married, the better. Give him wine, food, and a few *puttane*, and he's like a child in a *confetatureria*. He should be nailed down by the church with an honest girl. Until then, look out for him, as he looks out for you.'

'I thought you didn't hold with the church,' said Ray.

Oliverotto raised his eyebrows and nodded thoughtfully. 'There are no simple whites and blacks about such questions, my son. The priests can be very useful in keeping order among the thoughtless ones. It makes things better for us.'

Ray smiled. 'Benny's always after me to live it up. "Hey," he says, "what's the use of making money if you're working all the time? Make a party with lots of broads." That's how he talks.'

'Young unmarried men must have women,' agreed Oliverotto. 'It's the most natural thing in the world. But the *puttane* and show girls you sleep with, don't bring them into your house. They'll make it dirty. Let Beniamino break his balls on them on the outside. It will keep him from mischief till he's married. Use Lorello's place, the Burlington. Anything goes there, and Lorello owes me favors. You're always safe there.' He shook his finger at Ray. 'But, remember, your business is not to spend yourself plowing whores. Too many women become one big hole in which you can drown yourself. You should be thinking of settling down with Marta.'

'I'm thinking about it,' Ray had assured him.

And with that the old man had had to be satisfied.

In the matter of the United States versus Raymond Hodgkin, accused of illegally reentering the United States, Judge Breckenridge had engineered a victory for the defendant.

'Well, Howard,' said Ray, 'you murdered that United States Attorney.'

L. Howard Willis lounged back behind his desk and stared

at Ray quizzically. 'You know, Ray, not that I'm looking a gift horse in the mouth, but it was too easy. I can't imagine how he could have come into court so grossly unprepared. And why.'

'He did ask for a postponement,' said Ray.

'We were lucky there,' said Willis. 'Any judge other than Breckenridge would have granted it, especially in a matter as vital as that. I must admit Breckenridge handled it very deftly. He tipped the balance our way without laying himself open to bias or judicial error. It was his prerogative to deny the U.S. Attorney's request for additional time.'

'The government may appeal on the grounds that the court granted all of the defense's requests for delays and denied the prosecution's very first one.'

'I concede that the government's request was certainly not frivolously based,' said Willis. 'And yet, I know from past experience, the government will not appeal. They're going to drop the matter. You're in the clear, Ray, if you except our good friend, Mr. Lathrop.'

'What about Lathrop?' said Ray.

'He telephoned me yesterday. He sounded like a king cobra with its hood spread.'

'What's he browned-off about? Because the U.S. Attorney blew the case?'

'You know quite well what he's angry about,' said Willis. 'The missing Hodgkin file. That reflects on *his* department and affects *his* case. If it isn't located, they won't have an easy time getting underway against you.'

'They must have one miserable filing system there,' said Ray.

'I'll grant you that. They should have computerized it a long time ago, just as the government should have mechanized the postal system years ago. From my own experience, I've always had difficulty in obtaining permission to examine a client's file. They stall you for months as a matter of policy. It's inherent in the nature of the bureaucratic animal that he simply dislikes imparting information. I recall one case I had where I experienced several months of delay in securing the file I required. I finally made a personal visit to I and N headquarters in Washington. We found it all right. It had

403

been misfiled by only a few hundred numbers. So your luck may be explained as another instance of clerical foul-up. The Hodgkin file is probably tucked away in some overlooked corner.'

'I suppose Lathrop is hunting it,' said Ray.

'Like a hound dog trying to dig out a fox. Not that it's going to do the U.S. Attorney any good at this point. It's Lathrop's own case that he's furious about. Do you recall my mentioning that man's personal clout with the Attorney-General?'

'Quite well.'

'Then don't write him off. I don't think we've heard the last of him.'

'For instance?'

'I'm not sure,' said Willis, 'but knowing Lathrop, it's safe to assume that he's really going to rip the guts out of a few offices to find out what really happened. His official jurisdiction is New York, but his unofficial arm reaches considerably farther. If there's been monkey business, someone's going to be crucified.'

Amerigo LoCroce was grave and regretful. 'Raimondo, my dear boy, the news I have is not good. The man who performed the service which you required of me, he has been in touch with me. Not once, but several times. He is a coward. He has lost his nerve.'

Ray sighed and braced himself.

'This man,' continued Amerigo, 'has received a subpoena and must appear before a federal grand jury.'

'So?'

'He tells me he is going to clear his conscience and confess everything to the grand jury.' Amerigo paused and his lip curled scornfully. 'These people! They have no sense of honor, of the fitness of things. Dogs, cowards, old women.' Amerigo turned placid once again. 'He was compensated most generously for his services. But what can you expect, Raimondo? They don't have our values. They were not raised in our disciplines.'

Ray shrugged philosophically. 'I may as well have the rest of it, Don Amerigo.'

'Yes,' said Amerigo reluctantly, 'you will need it. His name is Connors and he is a supervisor in the New York office of the Immigration and Naturalization Service. I'm sorry it has had such a wretched outcome.'

'Don Amerigo,' said Ray, 'if this man has caved in, it in no way reflects on you. I am most grateful to you for everything you have done. As you pointed out, one can't expect outsiders to maintain closed ranks.'

'True,' said Amerigo. 'Now, it's up to you. You will have to take appropriate steps to protect yourself.' He scribbled a few numbers on a slip of paper and passed it across the desk to Ray. Here is the man's New York address. He also owns a fine large house and grounds in Stamford, Connecticut. A beautiful estate. I doubt whether Mr. Connors was able to purchase and maintain this estate on his salary as a government employee.'

'Thank you, Don Amerigo,' said Ray, 'I deeply appreciate everything you have done.'

On the drive back to Mineola from Princeton, he examined the technical aspects of the problem. The abstraction and destruction of the dossier had set him back thirty-five thousand dollars, twenty-five thousand to the now-repentant seductee, Mr. Connors, ten thousand to the LoCroce seductors. Don Amerigo had done his best and was now saying, in effect, You have the ball, Raimondo. It is your play now. Take it down the field. I've knocked myself out investing forty thousand dollars in something which looks as though it's going down the drain, thought Ray. Forty-two thousand actually, if I throw in that watch for Marta. Then he began reproaching himself. Aren't you calculating a little too closely, Scrooge? You bought a present for a nice girl and it doesn't belong in the investment column. How cheap can you get? And, again, any monies paid to Amerigo and his people were well worth it for future goodwill. All Amerigo's boys had gotten was ten grand. That finking sonofabitch Connors had gotten the biggest mouthful. So forty grand was forty grand. Over and above that, how much was his own time and effort worth? That was an intangible, but the total investment would have to be safe-

405

guarded and insured. If only to force Mr. Lathrop, district director and Jesus Christ, Junior, to fold up his hood and coil back down into his swivel chair. Behind Ray's self-control, Lathrop's attitude during that visit to the district director's office with Willis had stung. Behind his spoken words, what Lathrop had actually said was, 'I'm going to nail you to a T-frame, you goddamned wop gangster. I'm going to kick you out of this country permanently. If I can put you in a federal penitentiary for a couple of years for openers, I'll do that also. If I can get the Italian government to bury you in Poggio Reale, or Regina Coeli, or the Ucciardone, I'll do it. You're scum, as far as I'm concerned, a lousy mobster, and this is what I am going to do to you.' A, B, C—just like that. Okay, Mr. Lathrop, thought Ray, if that's how you want to play, you leave me no choice.

'Don't get off the track, Tony,' said Ray. 'From here on in, we stick to operational questions. Where? When? How? By whom?'

Tony reflected. 'How about Giovannino, this man you brought over? He needs a little action. He could be like a race horse that ain't getting enough exercise.'

'Ordinarily, I'd say all right. He could chop down that son-ofabitch like a wild goat. He could squash him flat like a cockroach. But this is new turf. We don't have that much time and I can't take any chances on a foul-up. If there was one, it wouldn't be Juan's fault. No. We'll have to bench him for this inning.'

'If it was an ordinary Family hit,' said Tony, 'I'd say go ahead and use Fats and Dumdum. But with an outside mark, some funny things are liable to happen. You know how these outsiders are. You can never depend on them. They never cooperate.'

'You have to expect that,' said Ray. 'They don't know any better.'

'Sure,' said Tony. 'The thing is, I don't want Fats and Dumdum getting mixed up in this kind of action. They'd do it all right if I told them to, but I need them here. Do they get busted, it can throw out my whole numbers business. The controllers are afraid of them. I hope you don't mind, Ray.'

'Absolutely not,' said Ray. 'I agree with you.'

'How about Nick and Beniamino? They got a good man available?'

'They have the same problem you have,' said Ray. 'I think then we should bring in someone from out of town. But the thing is, we should move quickly.'

Tony closed his eyes hard and finally snapped his fingers. 'My old man.'

'Uh uh,' said Ray. 'Don't call him up.'

'I'm not going to,' said Tony. 'I'm going to call Frankie Falcari in Boston. He's been with the old man for eighteen years. A real crack enforcement man. He always has a few hungry young buttons on the string. I can phone Frankie right away.'

'Not from here,' said Ray.

'It's safe from his end,' said Tony. 'It's a joint in Scollay Square where he gets calls from ten to midnight every weekday evening.'

'Does Falcari know Fats?'

'Sure. Fats used to work for him. Then when I came down here, the old man told Frankie that I should bring Fats down here with me. You know, like a fat old dog. Hell, Falcari used to know Fats when he wasn't fat.'

Ray looked at his watch. 'There's time. Call in Fats and give him enough of the scoop. Tell Fats to drive into downtown Brooklyn and make the call from a public phone booth. He is to say to Falcari, "Send us down right away a good kid with some brains as well as balls." Whatever Falcari asks will be okay.'

'Franky won't ask nothing,' said Tony.

'If he does, Fats is to say okay. We want the boy's name and when to expect him. Tell Falcari none of our people. I want an outsider.'

'He usually has a few Indians available. They're not too bright, though.'

'We'll do the thinking for them,' said Ray. 'Start Fats off. Yeah, Tony, one more thing—if Falcari has some Indian up there he doesn't want to see again up in Boston, that's all right also.'

'Yeah,' said Tony. 'Hey, Ray, you know, that's a good idea. It will be cleaner that way.'

Fats Mazzi made his report the following morning. 'Boy by the name of Gus Churny, something like that. He'll be here tomorrow. I'm to pick him up at Kennedy.'

'Polack?' said Tony.

'Sounds like,' said Fats.

Tony gave Fats both the New York and Connecticut addresses of Connors. 'You and Jack go up to Stamford this weekend just to check. If this man Connors works here in town, the odds are he doesn't get to spend except Saturday and Sunday up there. Also stake out his New York pad every day, when the man leaves in the morning, when he gets home, does he come out again at night. Get the guy's whole pattern. You'll have to finger the mark for Gus so he can figure the best way to take him. You and Dumdum run this together. I want the man fingered right.'

'I catch,' said Fats and left.

'Okay,' said Ray, 'let's run it through again. Where? Most probably right here in town, though up in Stamford would be quieter. When? As soon as possible. By whom? We have a boy. How?'

'How?' said Tony. 'What's there to figure?'

'A few things,' said Ray. 'The object of a normal hit is usually intimidation and punishment with maximum publicity, so everybody will get the propaganda value of the message. Mr. Connors is something else, neither revenge, profit, intimidation, nor punishment. I want him out of the way as quietly as possible. I don't even want it to look like homicide.'

'You're kidding,' said Tony.

'I'm not,' said Ray. 'I don't want to extract anything from this hit. I just want Mr. Connors quiet, peaceful, and silent.'

'Let him disappear, like Poggio,' said Tony.

'That was also different,' said Ray. 'With Poggio his personal family was also being punished. Al won't be legally dead for seven years. That means his wife can't collect insurance for seven years, and I happen to know that Al had quite a bundle of it to keep them in the style to which he had ac-

408

customed them. Also, his wife can't remarry for seven years. That's what the church says and she's an obedient believer. So she and her children are in a bind and that is how I wanted it. Connors is different. I want it to look as though he died of a heart attack.'

'Yeah?' said Tony. 'How do you swing that?'

'Like this. Ever heard of a cyanide gun?'

'No.'

Ray took from his pocket three aluminium tubes, each one of which was eight inches long. 'What do these look like?'

'Dollar Havana cigars,' said Tony.

'Right,' said Ray. 'Each one of these tubes is called a cyanide gun. Each one contains a five-cc plastic ampul full of hydrocyanic acid. Inside the tube there is also a gadget for puncturing the plastic and releasing the pressure. They used to make the ampul out of glass with a gadget for breaking the glass. The only drawback there was that the operator might leave a bit of glass around and a smart investigator can draw a few conclusions. The cyanide gun isn't exactly a secret.'

'So how does it work?' said Tony.

'All right,' said Ray. 'Now the way the button uses one of these, he has to get up very close and fire it right into the mark's face from a distance of a couple of feet. The hydrocyanic acid vaporizes and the man dies. Enough cops don't know about this gimmick, and there's an even chance they'll call it heart failure.'

Tony was unimpressed. 'I'd say it's sort of unreliable, especially if you use it out in the open. Maybe the man will just get sick and not die. Some doctor gets to him in time with the right medicine, it can cause trouble.'

'There are such medicines,' said Ray. 'For instance, if a man knew in advance he was going to be hit with a cyanide gun, he'd take a sodium thiosulphate pill ahead of time. After he gets hit with the gas, if he keeps his head and inhales amyl nitrate fumes, he has a good chance of pulling through. That's why we haven't made too many cyanide hits. It's too uncertain, so when it's used they usually give the mark a couple of forty-five slugs in the face for insurance. But Connors is different. He isn't likely to be carrying around sodium thiosulphate and amyl nitrate in his pocket.' Ray tapped the three aluminium tubes. 'I want Gus to use all three of these so Connors can have a really good coronary, or whatever. Also, inside it works better, if Gus can set it up that way.'

'Supposing he blows it?' said Tony.

'Then we have to go in fast and take Connors any way,' said Ray. 'The key word is "quiet." I want him hit quietly.'

'Okay,' said Tony. 'I'm sold. All I want is there shouldn't be no trouble.'

'Sure,' said Ray.

Fats Mazzi at the wheel of the old Chevy stopped to pay the toll at the southern end of the Whitestone Bridge. He went through, tucked his fat head on his left shoulder, and settled down in the fast lane of the Hutchinson River Parkway. Gus Czerny, beside him, yawned and lit a cigarette.

'What's the matter, kid?' said Jack Dumdum from the backseat. 'Tired?'

'Yeah,' said Gus, 'kind of. I didn't get no sleep at all for the last couple of nights.'

'Yeah?' said Jack with a show of interest.

'Yeah,' said Gus. 'I'm in bed laying this broad in the hotel, minding my own business, when I get this call from Frankie.'

Gus's flat down-east pronunciation of the word as 'ca-a-all' obscurely irritated Fats. 'Yeah?' he said, 'You and Mr. Falcari are that close buddies you call him "Frankie"?'

'I don't know about being buddies,' said Gus. 'I don't have to "mister" nobody. I don't believe in it.'

'You're pretty good, eh kid?' said Jack.

Gus lounged easily over against the right-hand door, flourished his left hand in which he held the cigarette, and dropped some ashes on Jack's pants leg. 'Maybe you'd better ask Frankie that, Pop. All I know is, he gives me the tough ones nobody else can handle.'

'And you deliver every time, eh kid?' said Jack.

Gus wore his hair almost shoulder length. He turned around, brushed the long brown ringlets back from his forehead, and smiled at Jack. 'Whatsamatter, Pop, you constipated tonight or something?' He glanced at Fats. 'Hey, Blubber,

410

maybe you better stop at the next gas station so Baldy here can take a crap.'

'All I was askin' was about your experience, kid,' said Jack mildly. 'This is a very special job.'

Gus yawned and lit another cigarette. 'You heard about the McNaughton brothers, Pop?'

'A little,' said Jack.

'I took them both,' said Gus, 'with nothing but a tire iron and an ice pick.'

'What'd you have to punch so many holes in them?' said Jack. 'You like to puncture people?'

'Yeah,' said Gus. 'It gives me a big fat laugh.'

Fats Mazzi kept his eyes on the road. 'Nince sensayuma you got there, kid. You think you'll be able to handle these gas tubes like I showed you?'

'If you showed me right,' said Gus, 'and if the guy is where he's supposed to be, I'll handle it.'

'You don't get nerves or nothing before a job?' said Jack.

Gus yawned. 'Come up to Ba-a-ahstn, Pop, and ask around. Nerves and me ain't even been introduced yet.'

Fats stared ahead into the night and swung the jalopy skillfully around the curves of the excessively narrow, sinuous, and obsolete Hutchinson River Parkway. 'Stop bugging the kid,' he said. 'He'll do okay.'

'I was just asking,' said Jack placidly. He relapsed into silence, stared at the back of Gus's oversized brown hair-mop, and ran his fingers thoughtfully over the top of his own naked skull. He had hair also, a scant fringe down near the back of his neck which disappeared entirely as it approaches his ears. Maybe he should get himself a wig. Why did this noisy little punk-bastard have to have so much hair and he so little? Couldn't it have been arranged so they could split the hair fifty-fifty? There would have been plenty to go around for both of them. This young sonofabitch might look almost human with a haircut. And he, Jack Dumdum, would enjoy some soul comfort if he only had a little mat on top of his naked head. If there was anything which Jack detested, it was being called Baldy. By his close friends who were men of his own age, okay. By Fats Mazzi, who was no beauty himself and with

411

whom he had worked for fifteen years, all right. But where did this snot-nosed Hunky get off with that kind of lip? Frankie Falcari, eh? Frankie, no less. Frankie this, and Frankie that.

'As soon as I get finished,' said Gus to the two fingermen, 'you boys take me straight to Kennedy. I'm catchin' the first plane back.'

'Geezus, kid!' said Fats admiringly, 'where'd you get all the energy? What's the big rush? Stick around a couple more days. You do a good job, maybe my boss tips you something extra.'

'Shove it,' said Gus. 'I gotta lotta fuckin' to catch up on. When you're twenty-two like me, you got a lotta livin' to do.' He grinned at Fats. 'I guess you've forgotten. Hey, Fats, when'd you tear off your last piece?'

Fats sighed and did not reply. He halted at the Merritt Parkway tollboth, paid the toll, and sped on. 'Like I told you,' he said, 'there's twin beds in the master bedroom. I don't know which one he'll be in. We cased the joint during the week when nobody was there. There's two bedrooms and a den, like, downstairs. The man and his wife is upstairs and there's another little room up there. So you got nothing to worry about the kids. They're downstairs.'

'I got it in my head,' said Gus. 'I been studying the floor plan. What I'm thinking about, if this gas is so good, supposing the chick gets a lungful of it? Or don't you care?'

'We care plenty,' said Fats patiently. 'Only the guy. Do it like I told you.'

Fats swung off the Merritt Parkway at the first Stamford exit ramp, turned north, and drove along a two-lane concrete road for four miles. Then he took a right turn onto a graveled road. He finally slowed up in front of a low stone wall. A small fluorescent sign mounted in the angle of the wall said CONNORS. The house was set well back behind two hundred feet of lawn. 'The place looks different at night,' he said and automatically checked his rearview mirror. The road behind him was black and empty. He turned off his headlights, swung into the graveled driveway, and rolled very slowly toward the service side of the house and the kitchen side. In the spacious turning area he backed the Chevy around so that it was facing outward and ready to roll. 'Go ahead, kid,' he said to Gus. 'We'll wait for you. Here's a key to the kitchen door. I made it from a wax impression. It's nothing but one of those ordinary kitchen door locks. I greased the hinges good. Wear your gloves all the time. Remember, you go in the back door, straight forward down the center hall, and up the stairs. The big bedroom is on the right. You got it?'

'Got it,' said Gus.

'You got the tubes and the little gas mask I gave you?'

Gus patted his pocket, slid out of the right front seat, and walked rapidly toward the kitchen door. Fats and Jack Dumdum watched him turn the key, open the door, and disappear into the house.

'Nice boy,' said Fats tonelessly.

'Yeah,' said Jack Dumdum. 'The younger generation. You can't talk to them no more. Did I talk like that to older people when I was that age, my old man would of busted my head.'

'You're over thirty, you're an enemy,' said Fats Mazzi. 'You got no hair, you're two enemies.'

'You think we'll have to go in and check his work?' said Jack.

'Yeah. Don Raimondo said no slop job. I'll tell you, this boy ain't built up my confidence any about how good a worker he is, you know what I mean?'

'It's a pity we got to junk this heap,' said Jack Dumdum, 'especially just after I tuned it and souped it up good.'

Fats agreed. 'Yeah, it's kind of a waste. I'd say it's good for another ten thousand miles at least.'

'Easy,' said Jack.

Fifteen minutes after he had entered the house, Gus emerged and slipped into the front seat of the Chevy. 'Let's go.'

'No hurry, kid,' said Fats easily. 'Nobody can see us from the road. So what happened?'

'Nothing,' said Gus. 'I go up to the bedroom like you said. The guy's in the bed on the left side. I put on the gas mask and give him a shot of gas right in the puss. He kind of woke up and began to cough and strangle. The dame starts to wake up. I slap her in the puss with a towel full of ether.' He spread

413

the ether-impregnated towel across the seat. 'Don't smoke till this dries out.'

'Throw it outside for a while for Christ's sake,' said Jack. 'You want to give us a headache?'

'So?' said Fats.

'So she's conked out good,' said Gus, 'and I carry her into the other room, the little one. She didn't open her eyes or nothing. Then I went back and the guy's still choking and groaning kind of low. This time I pinched his nose. The guy opened his mouth and I shot the gas into it. Both tubes. Then I brought the dame back in and put her to bed.'

'You didn't leave no fingerprints nowhere?' said Fats.

'I always wear gloves on a job like this,' said Gus resentfully. 'Give me credit for a little brains. I do a job a month for Frankie and I ain't slipped yet.'

'Did you leave the windows open?' said Fats.

'Like you said,' replied Gus.

'Okay, kid,' said Fats at last, 'you keep Jack company. I'll just go in and check. No peep outa the kids downstairs?'

'None,' said Gus. 'Their door is closed.'

Fats took the kitchen door key from Gus, drew on thin rubber gloves, and let himself into the house. Despite his girth he had small feet. He trod as lightly as he could up the padded staircase strip. He was thankful for the lack of creaking. If Gus had done his work properly, both the man and his wife should be out. He tiptoed over to the woman and caught the odor of ether. Finally, he took a chance and shone a pencil-thin flashlight down on her. The sounds of her breathing were audible. That was all he was interested in. Ideally, he wanted her to stay doped-up as long as he had to be in the room; then she could wake up as soon as they were clear. Now the man. Fats turned to the left-hand bed. If Gus had done only a third of the job he said he had done, there was nothing to worry about. For this part of it, he needed no flashlight. He picked up Connors' right wrist and held it, pressing his thumb on the pulse and concentrating intensely. Nothing, as far as he could tell. No pulse. Connors was wearing pyjama bottoms only. Fats knelt down ponderously, laid his right ear against the man's heart, and concentrated hard. No heartbeat. Connors' flesh felt

414

cold and clammy. Fats rose slowly to his feet and shone down the pencil flashlight. Connors' eyes were open wide and staring. Fats tapped the pupils of both eyes roughly with the tip of the flashlight. If that didn't get a rise, nothing would. No reaction. The fink was dead all right. Satisfied, Fats closed down Connors' eyes, tiptoed down the stairs, and let himself out. He carefully wiped the kitchen door around the area of the keyhole and turned the key. Then he returned to the Chevy.

'Well?' said Gus angrily, 'you satisfied?'

'You did okay, kid,' said Fats placidly. 'No wonder Frankie likes you.'

'So cut the bullshit, man, and get me to the plane.'

There was silence in the car until they were speeding down Grand Central Parkway past La Guardia Airport.

'Yeah,' said Fats reflectively, 'you work real smooth, kid.'

'Hey,' said Gus craning his neck, 'where the hell you going? This ain't the way to Kennedy.'

'There's lots of ways of getting there, kid,' said Fats. 'You're from Boston, right? So leave the driving to Greyhound.'

He swung off the parkway, sped through several dark, empty streets, and turned right on Queens Boulevard heading back toward Manhattan.

Gus thrust his hand in under his jacket and snarled at Fats, 'What're you giving me, creep? You ain't heading for Kennedy.' At that instant, Jack Dumdum dropped a loop of nylon cord over Gus's neck. The ends of the cord were twisted around Jack's crossed fists. Slowly and carefully, he drew the cord taut, putting his two hundred pounds of beef and muscle behind the effort. He grunted, panted, and continued to tighten the loop.

Gus's sphincter finally let go. The reek and stench hit both fingermen like a palpable gas.

'All right already,' said Fats without turning his head from the road.

'A little more,' grunted Jack. 'This cord is on to stay. It ain't going nowhere.' He bowed his back and tautened his powerful arms. The nylon noose finally cut through and buried itself in the already-dead Bostonian's flesh.

'Where to, Mr. Dumdum?' said Fats.

'Drive me down to my junkyard, James,' said Jack. 'And while you're at it, open up the window. It stinks in here.'

'Yessir, Mr. Dumdum,' said Fats.

CHAPTER 29

Terry Antolli crossed his legs and solemnly regarded the toe of a scuffed, stained, steel-shod work boot. He dug into the side pocket of his worn, shabby leather jacket and dragged out a crumpled pack of Camels. With a worried scowl on his unshaven face, he pulled out a bent, wrinkled cigarette and carefully straightened it. With one large, black-nailed hand, he lifted the table cigarette lighter from the supervisor's desk, examined it, and scratched his head. His partner, Bob Baldassare, who wore a heavy black sweater over a sweat shirt, placed his greasy Army fatigue cap on the supervisor's desk. He brushed back his scant crew-cut black hair.

'Hold it, Terry.'

Terry Antolli lit his own battered Camel and held the flame close so that Baldassare could light up.

Both men, both in their middle thirties and work-muscled, were too uncouth to be New York City taxicab drivers. They passed well enough as longshoremen or construction laborers coming off the job after a tough day. They passed muster in any Tenth Avenue bar and grill. 'Two boilermakers. My friend here's buyin'.' One neutral glance from the bartender and customers in any joint along the piers, as far east as Eighth Avenue, along Amsterdam or Columbus in the sixties, seventies, or eighties, along Bleecker and a dozen other areas, and they were forgotten. Their unshaven, wind-burned faces, Manhattan-grayed and wizened by a thousand weather changes and the overhanging murderous city, were accepted as part of the scene. They were laboring New York. They were the guys who borrowed from the shylocks on the docks and who placed daily bets when the book came around. They were

417

also the boys who could be counted on to get into the crap game in the lower recesses of the half-finished building where they had been hammering concrete frames, connecting pipe, or securing sheet metal ducts. They were the city's hardhats, of the city, yet invisible. Too many segments, circles, echelons, levels, and strata of the city looked through their tough gray faces and did not see them. And yet, they were of the city. They owned a piece of it. They despised and resented those mindless hordes who blindly pushed through and over them. In all of their movements, gestures, words, and expressions, Terry Antolli and Bob Baldassare plainly replied to their fellow New Yorkers, 'Fuck you, all of you. If it wasn't for us, this whole goddamned burg would spring a leak, burn out its bearings, bust a gut, and drown in its own shit. If it wasn't for us, you creeps would starve to death, freeze to death, or melt in your own blubber. And, on top of all that, if it wasn't for us, you wouldn't be able to make a phone call or get to work. And if you did make it down to your office or loft, or whatever, you'd have to climb up twenty flights of stairs because the elevators were out, like the garbage collectors and the grave diggers. So fuck you all twice, you goddamned helpless creep-bastards, and fuck this goddamned town of yours which we're holding together for you with spit. Number One is looking out for Number One. Yeah, right.'

That was why Terry Antolli and Bob Baldassare were agents of the Federal Bureau of Narcotics.

Henry Bosch, supervisor of the Manhattan office of the Federal Bureau of Narcotics at 90 Church Street, eased open the collar of his clean white shirt and loosened his necktie. He drew out a fresh cigar from the breast pocket of the jacket hanging behind his chair. Then he heaved up his number elevens on the desk before him and leaned back with his hands clasped behind his neck.

'You gave us twenty thousand dollars,' said Terry Antolli to Henry Bosch, 'and we finally bought a kilo of junk from this Chris Kyriakos. What I'm bitching about is the bureau's policy on evidence buy-money. What do they expect us to do, stop the whole traffic into the Port of New York cold on twenty grand? If you want us to get past Kyriakos, we need more money.' He glanced at his partner. 'Right, Bob?'

Bob Baldassare snuffed out his cigarette and deftly slipped a wad of Copenhagen snuff into his left cheek. 'Terry's right, chief. The bureau's getting more chicken-shit each year about laying out buy-money. That's how they want us to work? Okay. So give a little dough. Meantime, we're the boys who freeze off our balls in the all-night stakeouts waiting for someone to show.'

'My wife beefs to me all the time,' said Antolli. ' "What! No overtime for all your extra night duty? Marry a narco and sleep alone. I should have had my head examined before I married one. Quit the bureau. Get another job, or I'm going to get a divorce." '

'No money,' finished Baldassare, 'we don't get farther up the pipeline. That's about the size of it.'

Henry Bosch regarded his two agents with paternal affection. 'I wish both of you would bathe more often. You both stink. I mean, your feet, not your work. And you, Bob, stop using my wastepaper basket for a cuspidor. In fact, stop using snuff in this office.'

'I'm serious, chief,' said Antolli.

'So am I,' said Bosch. 'We're dealing with Congress and the taxpayer. They haven't the vaguest notion of our problems. It's repugnant to Congressional thinking to lay out money to buy narcotics with the taxpayer's dollar at inflated Syndicate prices.'

'The bureau knows damn well that a federal court won't accept one junk buy as conclusive evidence,' said Baldassare. 'The U.S. Attorney has to have the solid evidence of two or, still better, three buys, so his own job will be easier.'

'We've been through all that already, boys,' said Bosch sympathetically. 'Just maintain surveillance on Chris Kyriakos. Sooner or later, he's going to lead you to Ysidro.'

'Chris is getting edgy,' said Antolli. 'I've been stalling him too long already. The last thing he said to me: "You want to handle direct with Ysidro Barbaganza, you gotta be ready to buy five keys. A hundred grand. You got that kinda dough? If not, don't waste Ysidro's time." If he gets us taped in his mind as one-key boys, we don't get anywhere near Ysidro.'

'The stuff will have to be destroyed,' said Bosch. 'You know bureau policy. It's good tax money down the drain.'

'They want and they don't want,' said Antolli. 'Then how do you expect us to get evidence that will hold up? We could pull Chris in right now. So we'd have one one-key distributor and that would be the end of it.'

Henry Bosch reluctantly agreed. Getting up to the next rung of the ladder and deeper into the pipeline was every narcotics agent's dream. 'And if you show Chris that kind of money, do you really think he'll set up a meet with Ysidro?'

'No question,' said Antolli. 'And it'll be the first break we've had in seven months of work.'

Henry Bosch sighed, opened his desk drawer, and threw an envelope across the desk toward Terry Antolli. 'Twenty thousand there in marked bills. That's a down payment to show you're not crapping around. You're out to buy weight. You get to meet Ysidro and check out the stuff, you'll give Izzy himself the balance. You tell Chris that.'

'They'll come up with it, don't worry,' said Antolli. 'And we'll have to cough up eighty grand.'

'By that time,' said Bosch, 'we'll be ready to move in and hit them all. We've finally got it coordinated. When you meet Ysidro, just stall him long enough so we can tail him to his source of supply. That's the boy we want. You notice how the scene is changing? Only a few years ago, a five-key wholesaler like Barbaganza would have been a Syndicate man. But strictly.'

'Not any more,' said Baldassare. 'The boys are crowded right at the top of the ladder. Even up to the ten-key level, they're leaving it to the Indians.'

'Well, that shows some progress,' said Henry Bosch. 'They're hurting. I hope they're hurting a lot. The man Ysidro Barbaganza deals with, he's a Syndicate man. Up to thirty keys, perhaps. That's the man in whom we're very much interested. If we can get to him, we can get to the high brass, the top importer.'

'It takes gelt, chief,' said Antolli. 'We'll do the work, but'— he shook the envelope at Henry Bosch—'this is the shovel we need to turn over the rocks.'

'You've got it,' said Bosch.

'Thanks.'

'I won't let you down,' said Bosch. 'If you need eighty thousand more, I'll scrounge it somewhere for you, if I have to go out and make a personal loan.'

'Much obliged,' said Baldassare dryly. 'Who would take a poor civil servant's signature for that kind of a loan?'

'A Syndicate shylock,' said Bosch wryly. 'I'll tell you this, we've got a lot riding on what you boys started seven months ago. Look at that map behind me. We've got the net hanging ready as far south as Trenton, north to Providence, east to Bayshore, plus all of metropolitan Jersey. The New York and the New Jersey state police, the New York Police Department, and the FBI are all carrying spears in this production. For all I know, the Canadian Mounties may be in on the show. They don't tell me everything. There's more junk around this town now than I've ever seen before. By the way, Jimmy Cardone's coming up from Washington to sit with us here when we kick off the big play.'

For the first time, Terry Antolli was mildly impressed. 'The Assistant Attorney General?'

'Himself, representing his boss,' said Bosch. 'So, at this point, we're not going to get chintzy about a few more bucks. There are about two hundred agents scattered around between Providence and Trenton, standing by and waiting. You go ahead and tell Chris Kyriakos everything is okay. You want to buy five keys. You want to buy weight. You want to meet Ysidro. When we find out who Izzy's boss is, we'll be on third. Good luck, fellas.'

Both agents rose from their chairs. 'Okay, chief.'

Henry Bosch swung his big feet down from the desk. 'Take a couple of days off. Have a good hot bath and get reacquainted with your wives.'

Bob Baldassare turned and grinned at the supervisor. 'Hey! Thanks, boss.'

Robert Reynaldo was high enough up to be out of nickname country. Nicknames were for bums and Reynaldo was no bum. He resided quietly, one cipher, immersed in an ocean of his

421

fellow cliff-dwellers on the Upper East Side of Manhattan. The furnishings of his two-bedroom apartment in that luxury building were neither better nor worse than those of the neighbors above and below him to whom he had not been introduced. Reynaldo was a typical Manhattanite who made it a point not to become acquainted with anyone or to speak to the tenants whom he met in one of the high-speed elevators. Reynaldo's apartment, 16–E, was not the dwelling place of a typical Manhattan family, if there was such a thing. He did not keep his wife and three children there. They dwelt permanently in a very pleasant air-conditioned, five-bedroom house on a waterfront lot in a gold coast development in Fort Lauderdale, Florida, in the boating part of town, east of U.S. Highway 1. This was boat country. Each householder had his own private dock. To each dock was moored at least a thirty-five footer, properly maintained in shining white paint and gleaming brass. Reynaldo didn't want his family up in Manhattan, anyhow, no matter how good the neighborhood. No place in Manhattan was any good for raising children properly, even the Silk Stocking District. Reynaldo flew down to Fort Lauderdale to spend weekends with his family. On weekdays, he labored in the vineyard, keeping the five-key men like Ysidro Barbaganza happy. He had on his list other five-key wholesalers who sold at a profit to one-key distributors like Chris Kyriakos. The one-key men were beyond Reynaldo's purview. His contact stopped at the five-key level. The marketing structure, as in any legitimate business, was pyramidal. There were only a few Reynaldos in the entire greater New York complex. And over the Reynaldos were the prime importers who had purchased big weight from the overseas exporters.

Robert Reynaldo did not envy Don Leonardo Codi, for whom he worked. He was sufficiently high up and satisfied with his arrangements. Surveying the two previous decades retrospectively, Reynaldo was well satisfied that he had had no contact with the police for so long that the law had forgotten of his existence. He had climbed up the hard way, first as a punk delivery man, a mere messenger, then a pusher, then an independent retailer with a crew of twenty pushers under him.

That was in the old days when connected people were still involved in such low echelons of the business. When Reynaldo was finally made, in addition to his junk action he won entree into equally remunerative opportunities in extortion, hijacking, and loan-sharking. During World War II, he had made his first substantial nut through merchandising counterfeit OPA stamps and coupons. When the war ended, he gave up all other activities and concentrated on junk, the riskiest and yet the most lucrative of all the enterprises he had tried. There was more profit in junk than in all the other action combined. Ten years before, Reynaldo had risen to become a *caporegime* in the Codi Family and a trusted lieutenant with whom the old man could deal directly. It was during the fifties that Don Leonardo had set up Reynaldo in this luxury apartment. Codi imported as much as fifty keys at a time from overseas. He entrusted Reynaldo with at least twenty-five keys at a time to be sold to the five-key wholesalers.

At his present level, Reynaldo did not actually see or handle the merchandise. Local deliveries were made directly to the wholesaler's car by a stash man who was unknown to the wholesaler, and only when the car was unoccupied. Reynaldo's delivery contact was the man who supervised the stash from which his particular consignments were drawn. He didn't want to know more than that. His particular forte was purity of the merchandise, strength, the constantly fluctuating wholesale market price, and the ratings of the wholesalers with whom he dealt. Len Codi, as top man, floated at the Reynaldo level and sometimes stayed overnight in the Reynaldo apartment to sand down the corners of some pending deal. Len Codi of Sands Point was the prime importer who bought in Rome, Marseilles, and Milan for delivery in New York City or Montreal. He had the last word on the cutting of the merchandise to a level that would be acceptable to the wholesalers and that would insure his profit margin. That was vital. Only Codi knew where all of the stashes were. He set the prices at which all those on the Reynaldo level should sell to the wholesalers. Codi took the major risks and Robert Reynaldo was satisfied to implement policy laid down for him. Reynaldo was, in effect, a vice-president in charges of sales, working for a commission.

That Codi should take the major share was only logical. Reynaldo's compensation was based on a commission for every kilo sold to wholesalers on the Barbaganza level. Depending on current market price, such commissions ranged between nine hundred and fifteen hundred dollars per kilo, with a median during the previous four years of eleven hundred dollars per kilo. But Reynaldo's was a relatively riskless operation. It was enough to maintain his family luxuriously in Fort Lauderdale and still leave a surplus for investment. Reynaldo definitely preferred the benefits of being a commissions-earning executive in the structure to the headaches of ownership. His operation was smooth and efficient. He had to know the wholesalers with whom he dealt, and did. He occasionally extended short-term credit on his own responsibility. He met his customers only by appointment and never at the apartment. A typical deal was closed for not less than five keys. Money changed hands before the okay was passed for the stash man to deliver the merchandise to the wholesaler. The rich and varied techniques of delivery did not concern Reynaldo. This department was not his responsibility and the top stash man was responsible directly to Len Codi for any foul-up. Finally, Reynaldo's problems as a sales executive were minimal because the attractive fact was that, in this business, the demand was always greater than the supply. It was a seller's market. It always had been and always would be. There always were other problems, of course, and, if one was a worrisome type, one could find them. But if one was a worrisome type, one didn't belong in junk in the first place.

Considering that Len Codi was at the tip of the pyramid, it was statistically unlikely that he would ever run afoul of authority. Well, hardly ever, but the odd chance was always present. It did not happen often, even to those on the second level like Robert Reynaldo, but it did happen. It had happened to a top figure like Don Vitone Genovese, usually through some stupidity or carelessness or greediness well down the merchandising line. It was for these lower-level banana skins that men like Henry Bosch worked and waited.

The Banana skin through which Len Codi finally took a pratfall was no fault of his. He was hit by a domino effect over which he had no control. Nor had Reynaldo been at fault. Nor had Ysidro Barbaganza, who had bought five keys from Reynaldo in good faith and who had sold one key to Chris Kyriakos in equally good faith. It was Chris Kyriakos who had committed the *faux pas* of selling his one key to a customer whom he did not know well enough. It was not enough just to know the customer. You had to know him thoroughly. But such thoroughness could sometimes crimp a good sale and Chris had violated his own precepts of business and his innate sense of caution. Because of greed, the desire to clinch a quick sale, Chris had failed to check out his customers completely. That was where the chain had cracked. The two customers, Terry Antolli and Bob Baldassare, like all good narcos, were consummate actors. Their own mothers would have sworn they were a couple of tough outlaw Indians running a retail stash and a chain of pushers, Indians who didn't easily get nervous. Because, at the retail level, while junk was at its most lucrative, it was also at its most nerve-racking. It came down to this: If you retailed one twenty-grand kilo weekly, you could clear weekly a sixty-grand profit after pusher commissions and minor miscellaneous expenses. Not bad, but only for those who had no nerves and no imaginaion, because you could get busted or crossed or hit in a thousand different ways. But as long as you weren't, it was sixty-grand profit a week.

Chris Kyriakos was frankly surprised when his two customers plunked down twenty thousand dollars as a twenty percent payment on a five-kilo order. The prospect of that kind of money left him excited enough so that at least two of fifteen shadowing agents picked up the trail to Ysidro Barbaganza. Henry Bosch finally had a truly gratifying fix. Ysidro was kept under round-the-clock surveillance by teams of agents, while Antolli and Baldassare took a well-deserved breather at 90 Church Street. A full month crept by before Ysidro led the shadowers to the next link. Henry Bosch personally happened to pick up the phone when a laconic agent phoned in the address of Robert Reynaldo's Upper East Side apartment to which Ysidro had been followed. He beamed as he put down the receiver. 'Terry, Bob, I think we've finally hit pay dirt. You know, it's like climbing up the sheer side of a rock cliff, step by step. You hammer in a spike, you test it for weight, you step into a sling hanging from the spike, and then you start hammering in a new one just above your head. That's how this business works.'

'What gives?' said Antolli.

'Ysidro has delivered,' said Henry Bosch. 'We finally know the man from whom he buys. Put your shoes on, boys, you're hitting the street again.'

The night on which the bureau cracked the Robert Reynaldo link in the climb to the top was a warm and muggy one. Ten FBN agents had had the high-rise staked out for the entire previous week. The heart of the job was always waiting—sitting in a car, shifting afoot in a doorway, sweating, freezing, but always waiting, and watching, too, which made it work. On the big night, the agents knew that Reynaldo was not at home. They had already tapped his telephone line with the approval of a federal judge. It was a corner building fronting on Second Avenue. Two agents sat in two taxicabs as drivers in front of the building. Another agent-cab driver held down the side street. Three agents held down the subterranean garage of the apartment house, one of them watching the elevators to the upper floors, the other two, ostensibly garage attendants, scanning the street and the driveway. That accounts for six men. Two more agents had taken up stations at the back or tradesman's entrance to the twenty-story apartment building. The two final men were posted in darkened store doorways directly across the street from the building watching the main entrance. Terry Antolli and Bob Baldassare had drawn that duty. They waited stolidly and chain-smoked as they watched the main entrance.

'This Reynaldo, he could be out of town,' said Baldassare.

Terry Antolli shook his head. 'Not with the kind of business Ysidro's doing these days. It's like Christmas at Macy's, busy, busy, you know? Reynaldo's in town all right. He's probably just out having a little fun. These guys are naturally night people. They eat breakfast at four in the afternoon.'

'My arches have collapsed,' said Baldassare. 'It's a good thing my wife understands. A lot of women wouldn't stand for a life where their husbands spend their nights watching an

426

apartment building from a doorway across the street.'

'You ain't just whistling "Sorrento," kid,' said Antolli.

Baldassare touched his arm. 'That's our boy, I think. Can you make him out?'

Antolli peered intensely at the man who was approaching the main entrance on the other side of Second Avenue. He took a small pair of night-vision binoculars from his pocket and focused on the prospective quarry. 'Some guys laugh at these, but I say why strain your eyes? He tallies with the description all right. Imagine! We've never even seen the man.' He glanced at his wristwatch. 'Three-fifteen A.M. Helluva time for a man to be coming home.'

Robert Reynaldo came down Second Avenue heading south. He had his front-door key out, ready to fit it into the lock. One of the agent-cabbies before the building left his cab and went over to Reynaldo. 'Excuse me, sir, I think you're the fare I'm supposed to be waiting for.'

Antolli nudged Baldassare. 'Let's go.' They trotted swiftly across Second Avenue and slipped in between the main entrance to the building and Reynaldo. To the Cabbie, Antolli said, 'Okay, Herb.'

Reynaldo was shaking his head and saying good-naturedly enough, 'You got me mixed up with someone else, cabbie. I'm just coming home.'

'Your name Reynaldo?' said Antolli.

Reynaldo's lined, saturnine face was expressionless as his restless, hard, dark eyes swept up, down, and over his questioner. Baldassare had a snub-nosed .38 muzzle in Reynaldo's back.

Reynaldo raised his hands above his head. 'Okay, so you're heist guys. My wallet is in my breast pocket. Go ahead, take it.'

Baldassare prodded the gun muzzle hard into Reynaldo's back. 'Drop your hands and open up the door.'

Reynaldo shrugged and obeyed. The three men walked inside the lobby.

Antolli drew out his identification wallet which carried his FBN badge. 'We're federal agents. You're under arrest.'

'Yeah?' said Reynaldo. 'So what do you want with me?'

'We want to look through your apartment,' said Antolli.

'You have a warrant?' said Reynaldo calmly.

Antolli handed one over while Baldassare kept the gun muzzle against Reynaldo's spine. Reynaldo took his time about reading the federal search warrant. He finally handed it back. 'Okay. But you won't find a thing in my place.'

'Let's go,' said Antolli.

Baldassare held the front door open and the two agent-cabbies in front of the building joined them in the lobby. The four agents rode up in the elevator with Reynaldo between them and escorted him down the corridor to 16–E.

'Anyone inside?' asked Antolli.

Reynaldo shrugged. 'This is my own place. Nobody lives here but me.'

'Let's go in and see,' said Antolli.

The five men walked into the apartment. One of the cabbie-agents switched on the lights. The other snapped a pair of handcuffs over Reynaldo's wrists and shoved him toward the couch. Reynaldo settled himself glumly and an agent, gun drawn, stood behind him.

Antolli and Baldassare immediately started a search of the apartment with the help of the remaining agent. They walked into the master bedroom, which contained twin beds and was luxuriously furnished. The occupant of one of the beds sat up. After the first shock of surprise, he calmly returned the stare of the agents.

'Bob,' said Antolli tightly, 'wouldn't you say we've bumped into the big fish himself?'

'Yeah,' breathed Baldassare, 'in person.'

'You're Leonard Codi, aren't you?' said Antolli.

The occupant of the bed continued to stare at the agents with cold, hard eyes and did not reply.

Antolli walked over to the night table beside Codi's bed and began examining the contents of a wallet. He disregarded a wristwatch, a handkerchief, and a handful of change. He extracted the vehicle operator's license from the wallet and showed it to Codi. 'This doesn't quite look like our stuff down in the office, but it's close enough. Credit cards, Social Security card, the works. Are you collecting Social Security, Len?

You're old enough. May as well.'

Codi did not reply.

'What do you say, Len?' asked Antolli.

Codi shrugged and maintained silence.

'Okay,' said Antolli. 'Leonard Codi, I'm an agent of the Federal Bureau of Narcotics. I'm placing you under arrest. And this is off the record, Len. I'm quite happy about it.'

Codi finally spoke. 'Why? What's the charge? I'm just an overnight visitor here.'

'Our records have you down as one of the owners of this apartment,' said Antolli. 'Let's complete the routine first. I'm hereby warning you of your rights. You don't have to answer any questions here. The usual—anything you say here will be held against you.'

Codi looked balefully bored. 'I deny that I'm an owner of this apartment. But what if I was? Is that against the law?'

'In this case, it is,' said Antolli. 'Large amounts of heroin have been sold from this apartment for the last few years and undoubtedly before that.'

'So what am I charged with?' said Codi.

'That's the charge so far,' said Antolli, 'coownership of a domicile from which illegal narcotics have been sold.' There was a bathrobe on a nearby chair and Antolli threw it over to the man in the bed. 'You might as well get out of bed and put this on.' When Codi did so, the agent snapped a pair of handcuffs on Codi's wrists. 'Go into the other room and sit down beside your friend.'

They all returned to the living room. The two handcuffed men sat on the couch in impassive silence.

'All right, boys,' said Antolli, 'call three more of them up here and let's start searching. I want you to really tear it apart.'

After three hours and the sweat of seven agents, the apartment was a shambles.

'I told you you'd find nothing up here,' said Reynaldo sardonically.

'No sweat,' said Antolli pleasantly. 'Bob, advise your namesake here once again of his rights. Spell it out for him. Let's do this by the book. Uncuff Len and let him get dressed. Then we'll go.'

Harlan Lathrop, district director of the Immigration and Naturalization Service, and James Cardone, Assistant Attorney General, were sipping coffee from paper cartons in supervisor Henry Bosch's office when Antolli's call came through. Bosch picked up the receiver.

'Chief,' said Antolli. 'This is Terry. Right. We've hit the jackpot. Len Codi himself and in person. Right. We're bringing him and Reynaldo down.'

'Pull off the entire crew and get them all down here,' said Bosch crisply. 'Are you one hundred percent sure it's Codi you've got there?'

'It's him all right,' said Antolli.

'Beautiful,' said Bosch exultantly, 'beautiful. We're going to activate the big sweep immediately. We're going to hit all the stashes and bring them all in. I think we've cracked this one. Thanks, boys. Get down here. See you soon.'

After Leonard Codi had been arraigned before a United States commissioner and released in one hundred and fifty thousand dollars' bail, Bosch, Lathrop, and Cardone met to cast up accounts and plan the next step.

'At this moment,' said Cardone, 'all we have against Codi is the minor charge, penalty ten years. The logical charge, importing heroin hydrochloride into the United States, receiving, concealing, selling, and facilitating the transportation, concealment, and sale of heroin—that would get him forty years.'

'A pity that narcotics offences are bailable at all,' said Bosch. 'In my opinion, they should be treated as capital offenses.'

'Your attitude's understandable, Henry,' said Cardone. 'Actually, it's an academic point as far as Codi is concerned. Ten years is an ample span for the government to drive a stake through his heart. Meanwhile, he's quite safe out on bail. He's not going to skip the country.'

'One hundred and fifty thousand dollars is nothing to that man,' said Bosch uneasily. 'I won't feel right till he's on ice, even for ten years.'

'Ten years is fine,' said Cardone cheerfully. 'Codi's no pullet. He'll never leave prison alive. So what's the difference even if we have to settle for the minor charge?'

'The satisfaction of crucifying the bastard, I suppose,' said Bosch thoughtfully. 'That's the difference. My people worked themselves numb for almost a year breaking this one open. I'd like to see Codi boiled in oil, slowly, in public, till he sings loud and clear the way Joe Valachi did.'

James Cardone chuckled ironically. 'That's the chaste beauty of our legal system, isn't it? Even the Codis get fair and impartial treatment. No discrimination. No boiling in oil, public or private.'

Harlan Lathrop had been listening, grim and expressionless. He now stirred restively but maintained silence.

'What's the matter, Harlan?' said Cardone. 'You're certainly not as chipper about this break as Henry here.'

Harlan Lathrop packed his pipe slowly and lit it before replying. 'I'm happy for all of us on this thing,' he said at last. 'Henry's boys deserve all our gratitude and I hope the FBN can turn Codi into fertilizer. I've got quite another problem, though, and, I think, a much tougher one.'

Cardone nodded sympathetically. 'You're referring to Hodgkin, of course. Too bad, though frankly, I don't see that it's tougher and more important. Breckenridge threw out our case, but you can't win them all, can you?'

'I wouldn't trust Breckenridge any farther than I could throw a dump truck,' said Lathrop angrily. 'Not from what all of us know about him.'

'That's quite another matter,' said Cardone tactfully, 'and, for the moment, it's neither here nor there. Breckenridge had clear sailing this time. We came into court with our pants already down and there's not a chance that Old Southern Comfort will be reversed. No reflection at all on your people, Harlan. You've always run a tight ship up here.'

'We didn't in this case,' said Lathrop bitterly. 'For my own reasons, I've gone along with an official verdict of heart failure for Connors. We all know he was murdered with cyanide and I'm not through yet.'

'All we have to do is to prove it,' said Cardone, his sardonicism disguising his sympathy.

'We will,' said Lathrop. 'We will. Hodgkin isn't going to get away with a thing. There's far more involved here than unlawful reentry and our renewed efforts to redeport him.' He glanced at Henry Bosch. 'I'm not here to poop your party, Henry. You're feeling good about Codi and I'm feeling lousy about Hodgkin. But my boy should interest you very much, Henry. He's your real case. He's far bigger game than Len Codi. Have either of you seen today's New York *Times* article on him, by the way?'

'Not yet,' said Bosch. 'Not with all the things that've been breaking here.'

'This should interest you also, Jimmy,' said Lathrop to Cardone. 'Please be patient and listen while I read at least part of it. It's quite long.' He read:

. . . No one knows at this point just when Raymond Hodgkin reentered the United States illegally. No one can pinpoint the lapse between the time of his reentry and the day on which, accompanied by his attorney, Mr. L. Howard Willis, he surrendered voluntarily to Harlan Lathrop, district director of the New York District of the Immigration and Naturalization Service. There are reasonable grounds for speculating that such an unaccounted time lapse did occur during which Hodgkin dispatched private business. After surrendering to the Immigration and Naturalization Service, Hodgkin made an appearance bond. He was duly indicted by a federal grand jury and was tried in a federal court on a charge of having unlawfully reentered the United States as a deported alien. The circumstances under which the government's case against Hodgkin were eventually dismissed by federal district Judge Warner Hanley Breckenridge are interesting, to say the least. A coincidentally intriguing circumstance is the death of Francis Connors, a minor Immigration and Naturalization official. Connors' department was responsible for the relevant material on which the government had hoped to base its case and on which a new deportation proceeding against Hodgkin was to be founded. In view of the United States Attorney's defective preparation, the dismissal of the case on grounds of insufficient evidence was inevitable. Rumor and speculation concerning the probable cause of death of Connors' will not be stilled ...

Lathrop raised his eyes from the newspaper. 'I'm not going to read it all verbatim. I'm just going to hit the highlights.' He continued:

... Connors was scheduled to appear before a grand jury to answer questions regarding the disappearance of the aforementioned documents. A theory of suicide has not been entirely discounted. With all of these questions still unanswered, there is additionally speculation that Raymond Hodgkin may have been involved in the background of the major new narcotics smuggling case which has just been broken by Henry Bosch, district supervisor of the Federal Bureau of Narcotics in Manhattan, and his staff of agents. There are unconfirmed rumors that Raymond Hodgkin exported a large consignment of heroin from Italy to Leonard Codi in New York City. Codi, a reputed Mafia boss, is presently under indictment on a charge of being one of the owners on record of an Upper East Side apartment from which large quantities of heroin were sold. James Cardone, Assistant Attorney General, who is in overall charge of the tangled ramifications of this case, is said to be in touch with Italian authorities regarding Hodgkin's alleged role as a narcotics exporter. There have been shadowy, anonymous, and apocryphal rumors that Raymond Hodgkin, while supposedly living in Italy under police surveillance, flew to Beirut, Lebanon, on several occasions to purchase either heroin or morphine base. During one of these trips, Hodgkin is supposed to have purchased a considerable quantity of narcotics from the Palestine Liberation Front, which is headquartered in Beirut. The PLF has had a long and notorious record of violence and extremism in the Middle East. The proclaimed political platform of this organization is virulently anti-American and pro-Soviet Union. It undoubtedly stands at the extreme terminus of the spectrum of

433

violence and advocates vociferously the total extirpation of the Israeli state. The essence of this report as it concerns Raymond Hodgkin is that the PLF had every reason (over and above the motive of financial gain) for seeking to utilize heroin as a weapon of psychological warfare against the United States....

Harlan Lathrop raised his eyes from the newspaper. 'Thanks for listening so far, gentlemen. Now, here's the clincher. Get this.' He read:

... it has been alleged, and with some plausibility, that the PLF bitterly hated the late Robert F. Kennedy, that it had long planned to have him assassinated, that it did, in fact, have him assassinated by employing as its tool a so-called programmed assassin, Sirhan Bishara Sirhan. The 'one man' theory of this political murder has been officially blessed and approved by the Los Angeles Police Department, which conducted a major investigation of the assassination. Nevertheless, many students of the case have continued to theorize on relatively sound grounds that Sirhan was indeed a programmed or a hypnotized assassin. The question arises: What, if any, was Raymond Hodgkin's role in this affair? Reasonable motives to cover both Hodgkin and the PLF are not lacking. There is, in fact, an embarrassment of riches. The fact that Robert Kennedy came out openly as pro-Israel in the California primaries of 1968 and that he advocated immediate shipments of arms to Israel would cover the PLF's motivation adequately. How does Hodgkin dovetail into this picture puzzle? It is a matter of record that Raymond Hodgkin was bitterly hostile to the late Robert F. Kennedy, who inaugurated the proceedings through which Hodgkin was eventually deported. Witnesses are still available who can testify to the fact that Hodgkin regarded his feud with Kennedy as a personal vendetta. It has been alleged that during a farewell dinner which some of Hodgkin's associates tendered prior to the mobster's deportation he, Hodgkin, is said to have risen to his feet and stated: 'I'd like to kill that —— Kennedy. Somebody should kill him. Sooner or later that Bobby-boy is going to get his buckwheats.' 'Buckwheats' is supposed to be underworld argot for 'just deserts in a particularly severe and vindictive fashion.' If there is any substance to the foregoing basic premises, it could be demonstrated that both the deportee and the PLF had common motives for seeking the destruction of Robert F. Kennedy.

Harlan Lathrop dropped the New York *Times* on Bosch's desk and removed his spectacles. He blinked his eyes to ease the strain and stared thoughtfully into the distance.

Bosch stared expectantly at the Assistant Attorney General.

James Cardone looked about and grimaced. 'It's a potful of rattlers, isn't it? And we'll have to stick our hand into it. Okay, we will. If there's anything to this, it's worse than rattlers. It's like trying to unsnarl a tangle of fishing lines on a heaving deck during a fifty-mile-an-hour wind.'

'Any ideas?' said Lathrop dryly.

'One,' said Cardone. 'Len Codi. He's the logical man to clear up the great Raymond Hodgkin mystery for us.'

'You can't torture Codi,' said Henry Bosch regretfully.

'No,' said Cardone, 'but we can question him in relays. And keep on questioning him. And questioning him. We do it very well. There's an outfit called the FBI, gentlemanly young fellows who wear gray hats and blue suits. They smile and they ask questions till the top of a man's head caves in.'

'Bosses don't crack,' said Bosch.

'Now you're being romantic, Henry,' said Cardone. 'Bosses do and have cracked. But just in case this one doesn't—and, honestly, he doesn't look too tough to me—I'm going to make him 'ncarugnutu with the boys, if I have to manufacture the story out of whole cloth. In other words, Len Codi is going to be billed as a canary whether he wants the role or not. It's one of the stalest tricks in the book and it works.'

'Not with everybody,' said Bosch. 'I've tried it.'

'Not with everybody,' agreed Cardone, 'but with Len Codi, yes. As I have that man analyzed, Len Codi comes first with Len Codi—first, last and always—and to hell with the Organization. If there's the slightest suggestion of danger to Codi's tender epidermis, he'll sing loud and clear. In the old days a Len Codi would never have made it as a Mafia boss. No guts, no character, no honor. So I'm sanguine. In fact, I have a feeling we won't have to go that far.'

Harlan Lathrop smiled for the first time. 'If you can swing it, Jimmy, I'll buy you——'

'What'll you buy me?' grinned Cardone. 'You want Hodgkin badly, don't you, Harlan?'

'Very badly.'

'Well, maybe we'll be able to deliver him. In one way or another, and God willing, we'll deliver him to you or to the devil.'

'Amen,' said Lathrop solemnly.

CHAPTER 30

Warren Carruthers, Assistant United States Attorney in charge of the Codi prosecution, was an American variation on a comfortable and now moribund British myth. This myth had, in the golden years, proudly proclaimed that only the well heeled and the well born were qualified to offer devoted and disinterested public service. Warren Carruthers, Princeton, BA, 1957, Yale Law School, 1961, well groomed, personable, and tennis-fit, exuded *noblesse oblige* and benevolence arising from a Gibraltar of eternal verities (Carruthers toweling, sheeting, ticking, and bedspreads, since 1842). His natural courtesy was equaled by a bland and equally natural lack of imagination. He now listened to Counselor Morton Perlman with an attention which was happily unpolluted by quizzical gingery overtones. Carruthers, from the depths of his cotton-batting security, was essentially a good-natured man and tolerant enough to accept the Perlman's as members of a noble profession.

'My client, Mr. Codi,' said Morton Perlman, 'is willing to plead guilty to a charge of coownership in an apartment from which narcotics have allegedly been sold.'

'And the rest of it?' said young Mr. Carruthers.

'In return for immunity from prosecution on a charge of conspiring to import heroin,' said Perlman, 'my client will reveal the identity of an important narcotics exporter.'

Carruthers nodded with the easy amiability of a high-bracket resident practicing in a charity clinic. 'Mr. Codi is willing to name the exporter from whom he obtained the narcotics he has wholesaled?'

'I'd rather reword it,' said Perlman. 'We're only saying that

437

Mr Codi will name an important exporter, specific quantities, dates, amounts of money and their disposition, methods of shipment, consignees, and the present location of such narcotics.'

'Your client will give us a conspiracy case against Reynaldo?' said Carruthers.

Perlman nodded. 'Strictly speaking, all you have against Reynaldo at this point is the minor charge. In return for immunity, my client is willing to deliver Reynaldo and several other people, including the prime exporter.'

'Assuming that the government considered your client's proposition,' said Carruthers, 'I suppose he's aware that his life would be in constant danger.'

'Quite,' said Perlman. 'As part of the immunity package, my client would expect effective sanctuary in confinement.'

'Sanctuary in a federal penal institution?' smiled Carruthers.

'I find your complacent negativity somewhat disturbing, Mr. Carruthers,' said Perlman dryly. 'Why *not* sanctuary? Isn't the United States government powerful enough to ensure the safety of those to whom it has made a commitment? Has Uncle Sam abdicated entirely?'

Typical of this breed, thought Carruthers. Let's be charitable and unbigoted, Warren. Aloud, he said, 'Spell it out for us, Mr. Perlman. Give us good faith and solid facts instead of vague promises and hints. Give us a case and we'll think about it.'

Young Lochinvar will have to run to his boss with the package, anyhow, thought Morton Perlman. Aloud, he replied, 'We're prepared to give you a strong case and to save the government a lot of money.'

Carruthers shrugged. 'I doubt whether you could give us anything which we don't already possess. You and I and Mr. Codi know that he is one of the principal importers of heroin in the United States. We have enough evidence against your client to imprison him for forty years.'

Morton Perlman was soberly conceding to himself that this Ivy League nebbish might, in his innocuous way, be something of a horse-trader. With four kings pat, everybody could be a

438

regular tiger. Perlman felt about the Codis as a hard-working syphilogist felt about syphilitics. He wanted to get shut of the case.

'Mr. Carruthers,' he said evenly, 'I'm trying to work out a bona fide deal which will be acceptable to all parties. My client will plead guilty and accept ten years' confinement if the government can safeguard his life. In return, he will deliver this particular case, gift-wrapped.'

'The United States government, Mr. Perlman, doesn't enter into deals.'

'Plus one additional thing,' said Perlman.

'What is that?'

'The solution to the murder of Robert F. Kennedy,' said Perlman. 'Facts which will substantiate a conspiracy theory.'

The vague prospects of fame stirred excitement through the bland, mannered sludge of Carruthers' soul. 'Can you give me something on account now, Mr. Perlman?'

'For the boys upstairs? Of course. I understand.'

Vulgarian, thought Carruthers tolerantly.

'Mr. Carruthers,' said Perlman, 'we'll give you all the facts you will require to prove that Raymond Hodgkin, alias Raimondo Raffaele Occhiaccio, was directly involved in the programmed assassination of Robert F. Kennedy.'

'Hodgkin, eh?'

'You're familiar with that matter, no doubt.'

'I wasn't personally involved in it.'

'Congratulations,' said Perlman in a tone which strained Carruthers' tolerance severely. 'Do you really believe that Mr. Kennedy was murdered by one man, by that lunatic Sirhan Bishara Sirhan?'

'No comment,' said Carruthers pleasantly. He could afford to coast and listen. The Perlmans, fortunately, offered the Carruthers no serious competition.

'Sirhan acted under hypnosis,' said Perlman. 'He was a programmed assassin.'

'And what, pray, is a so-called programmed assassin?' said Carruthers.

'I'm listening to you with the third ear, sir. But I assure you that our information will not prove fanciful. We can give you facts which will incontrovertibly prove that Raymond Hodgkin was involved with a political group behind Sirhan.'

'Sirhan was a mercenary working for cold, hard cash,' said Carruthers disdainfully. The day before one of the newspapers had carried an editorial asking why the federal authorities were dragging their heels about arresting Raymond Hodgkin and questioning him regarding conspiracy aspects of the Robert F. Kennedy assassination. Perhaps, speculated the editorial, there were some answers which Raymond Hodgkin could supply regarding a link between the Palestine Liberation Front and Sirhan Bishara Sirhan. Did PLF in fact, conspire to murder Kennedy? And was Hodgkin in any way involved? Even if he, personally, were not, perhaps he could supply the answers to some of these questions. The editorial had concluded with a tart suggestion to the authorities that Hodgkin be immediately subpoenaed to appear before a federal grand jury to answer some questions or before a specially convened commission to reopen the matter of Kennedy's death.

'Was Hodgkin actually involved with those PLF people?' Carruthers asked casually.

'Yes.'

'All right. One thing at a time. I take it that your client is prepared to sell out his accomplices?'

Perlman shrugged. 'He wants a clear understanding with the Department of Justice that he will be in no way connected with the importing charge when the government presents its case. Your chief defendant will become Reynaldo. My client will give you sufficient evidence to convict Reynaldo on an importation charge. Mr. Codi seeks the government's promise that he will be incarcerated in some remote military post rather than routinely in a federal institution.'

'I can't promise you a thing.'

'Naturally,' said Perlman, aware that it was the wrong thing to say. But he couldn't resist the opportunity to needle junior a little.

'However,' said Carruthers, 'in view of the—ah—magnitude of your promises, we'll take the matter under advisement. You'll be hearing from us.'

'Thank you so much, Mr. Carruthers,' said Perlman.

He closed the door behind him thinking, Thank you so much Mr. Uncle Sam Carruthers.

Harlan Lathrop was willing to give Morton Perlman blanket assurances even before receiving specific details. Henry Bosch was not. James Cardone the Assistant Attorney General and final arbiter, was neutral. 'I appreciate how both of you feel,' he said. 'Harlan wants Raimondo's scalp. Henry wants Codi's. Personally, I'd hate to see Don Leonardo sitting it out safely in some military base in Guam or Alaska while the smaller fry are subjected to the full rigors of the law.'

'You do make those special arrangements now, of course,' said Lathrop.

'We have been quietly for the last few years,' said Cardone. 'It has become evident that in dealing with these Organization figures we simply have to be flexible if we can derive some advantage from such a policy. This administration has finally begun to realize what a really formidable adversary the Organization is. We've come a long distance from the years when officialdom wouldn't even admit that there was such a thing as the Organization. It isn't often that you get one of them to talk. Look at how much trouble the government had coaxing Joe Valachi to sing. And he was only a soldier right down at the bottom of the Organization structure. If there's anything at all to the story Perlman's trying to hand us, we'd certainly be willing to work out something with the military to keep Codi away from the knackers. Consider, Joe Valachi was only a soldier and there are still open contracts out on him all over the place, perhaps a half-million dollars' worth. Think how the bounty would rocket up for a Family boss like Codi! It would be unprecedented and, in an Organizational context, revolutionary.'

'You're the boss,' said Henry Bosch.

'Someone has to be,' said Cardone. 'It's Justice's function to decide if a deal will be made and on what terms. I'm personally inclined to give Perlman his advance guarantees and I'll so recommend to the big boss. I know how Perlman feels. He just wants to shove clear of this and it's about as good a deal as he can make. If Codi pleads guilty to the lesser charge, we'll have him for ten years. That's long enough and we'd lose nothing. If his story is bona fide, I wouldn't even risk an Army post or a Marine base. I'd have him held in a ship at sea.'

'He won't like that,' said Bosch. 'He'd find a tossing ship's brig pretty confining.'

'It would be confining, all right,' agreed Cardone. 'But, after all, he made no specifications about comfort. All he requests is safety. Security he'll have, because he'll never come ashore. If inbound, he'd be transferred at sea to an outbound vessel. And his existence would certainly be more hygienic than in a Mexican or Turkish jail.'

'What about the possibility of escape in a foreign port with the connivance of members of a ship's crew?' said Lathrop.

'He'd never get to a foreign port,' said Cardone. 'The Navy will give us full cooperation. No fear on that score. I envision an arrangement whereby a custodial skipper would transfer the prisoner in irons before entering port. In other words, Codi would be constantly transferred from ship to ship, so that only the commander of the last vessel responsible for his custody would have knowledge of his whereabouts. Confidential knowledge. But we're getting ahead of ourselves, gentlemen. We haven't even come to a decision as to whether or not to accept Perlman's proposition. I think that we should.'

'Do you really think so?' said Bosch dubiously.

'Rest assured, Henry,' said Cardone. 'Len Codi would be no Lieutenant Philip Nolan. He'd never rate deck liberty. He'd never be allowed out of his cell to mingle with a ship's crew and conceivably to corrupt them. He'd be secure and safe enough from the Organization and from temptation. As safe as four steel walls could make him.'

'He'd never survive ten years under such a regime,' said Bosch more cheerfully.

'Precisely,' said Cardone, 'and it would be quite in order. Codi himself would have consented to the conditions of his incarceration. That would be the security we'd offer for the relative brevity of his imprisonment. We lose nothing because Codi will never survive ten years of solitary in a ship's brig. I'll make book on that without having to gamble. The man's at least sixty-five today.' He looked at Henry Bosch. 'Henry, you

442

and your people have turned in a superb performance of devotion to duty. Rest assured, by the arrangements which I propose, you can write Codi off permanently.' He turned to Lathrop. 'As for your end of it, Harlan, I'd venture you have everything to gain by our making a deal with Perlman. If there's anything at all to this conspiracy angle on the Kennedy assassination, we'll be able to bury Raymond Hodgkin for good. We'll be able to proceed against him in a way which will make civil deportation proceedings seem like a Sunday school picnic. Gentlemen, I move we accept.'

'Seconded,' said Henry Bosch.

Don Leonardo Codi, hitherto free on bail, had suddenly disappeared from his usual places of resort. His *caporegimes* could not find him at home. His wife, speaking truthfully, could not say where he might be. His friends——? Len Codi had no friends. His business associates had been busted and were incommunicado. The word went out swiftly and quietly across a national network and it was not from motives of fraternal concern for Brother Leonardo. The grapevine passed the question through the Tombs, the Queens County Jail, and the Raymond Street Jail, to Sing Sing, Great Meadows, Auburn, and Dannemora. Thence to Lewisburg, Danbury, Atlanta, Milan, Leavenworth, and McNeil's Island. And even Terminal Island, an unlikely little federal backwater. Thence to Cook County Jail and the Washington, D.C., jail. Thence to the big houses in Walla Walls, Folsom, San Quentin, Canon City, Colorado, Lincoln, Nebraska, and McAlester, Oklahoma, and numerous less illustrious bastilles en route. There was no point in checking Vegas or Miami Beach or the big tracks. Len Codi simply wasn't that kind of man. Or the right nightclubs, or the call-girl agencies. Oh, my God! No. None of this was the shrunken little bastard's bag. Just what *did* he do with himself when he wasn't busy piling it up like a shadowy, avaricious spider? Come to think of it, no one could really say. His wife said that he sat at home in a bathrobe and lambskin slippers on his feet. Yeah, six slippers, one for each foot. Or did spiders have eight feet? *Ma!* No Len Codi.

The commission didn't relish the situation at all. Its members had no taste for mysteries. Could Uncle Angelo in some way be involved? If so, the commission disapproved of such secrecy as somehow unethical. 'I dislike it exceedingly,' said Amerigo LoCroce. 'I strongly recommend, gentlemen, that you push the button.'

'Shut down everything, Don Amerigo?' said a fellow solon. 'Isn't that a bit premature?'

'Nothing is premature where Don Leonardo is concerned,' said Amerigo. 'He is a walking cancer, a one-man bubonic plague. He is a broken mirror, a curse, one of the living dead. He is probably making a deal at this moment with Uncle Angelo.'

'The man isn't here to defend himself,' said the other statesman severely. 'A little charity, Don Amerigo.'

'My bones are old and sensitive to changing barometric pressures,' said Amerigo. 'I have a feeling for *stregoneria* and treachery.'

'With all due respect for your intuition and sagacity,' said the commission, 'we will wait.'

'Gentlemen,' said Amerigo, 'I bow to your collective wisdom.'

Two weeks after Len Codi's disappearance, Ray came down into the study of Tony Saldana's house in Mineola to join the owner of the house for breakfast. Tony was already seated at the table and Fats Mazzi was waiting on his master.

Ray seated himself at the table facing Tony.

With a sober expression on his face, Tony passed a copy of the New York *Times* across the table to Ray. 'You seen this story about yourself?'

'Not yet,' said Ray.

'Maybe you better read it,' said Tony.

Ray read:

... as in the case of the death of President John F. Kennedy and in that of the Reverend Martin Luther King, Jr., the conspiracy theory refuses to die. Thus far, the version of the Robert F. Kennedy assassination that has been accepted as official is that of the Los Angeles Police Department—

namely, that Robert Kennedy was assassinated by one man, Sirhan Bishara Sirhan.

Considering the questions which have now been raised about the trips which Raymond Hodgkin made to Beirut and about his alleged dealings with the Palestine Liberation Front, an organization which does, in fact, exist, and whose political views are sufficiently known, perhaps the version of the Los Angeles Police Department may now be questioned by reasonable men. It resolves itself to one question: Did Sirhan act as a lone assassin, or were there others behind him? Many knowledgeable, cautious, and conservative individuals are now inclined to reject the theory—a fascinating one, admittedly—that Sirhan was in some way hypnosis-prone, that he was somehow programmed or conditioned as a murderous automaton to commit the deed. Up to the present moment, this publication has taken the editorial position that, even if Sirhan had others behind him, he was motivated by pecuniary profit; *i.e.*, he was neither hypnotized nor programmed.

Sirhan's possible motivations have been reviewed *ad nauseam*. The explanation that an obscure, poverty-stricken Sirhan killed wealthy and famous Robert Kennedy is surely simplistic. Unless we are going to reject all of Sirhan's statements wholesale in a spirit of hostile subjectivity, we must weigh some of them. Following his apprehension, Sirhan stated with apparent sincerity that he greatly admired the man he had murdered, that he, Sirhan, would have voted for Robert Kennedy for President. On the other hand, Sirhan explained his deed in terms of his patriotism as an Arab. He killed Robert Kennedy, he insisted, because the Senator had promised to send fighter planes to the state of Israel. But, as has been pointed out by investigators, Kennedy made this promise in a speech delivered on May 26, 1968. However, when Sirhan's notebook was examined, it was found that the assassin had made a written record as early as May 18, 1968, to the effect that Robert Kennedy would have to die. Such written reminders, apparently made by Sirhan to himself, appear repeatedly throughout the notebook. Proponents of the conspiracy theory base themselves on the fact that Sirhan has insisted steadfastly that he had no remembrance of ever having made these entries in his notebook. From this fact, such proponents conclude that Sirhan was proceeding under hypnosis and that, therefore, there was some sinister group masterminding Sirhan as their weapon. If there was in fact such a group and if Raymond Hodgkin was associated with that group, certainly the questioning of Raymond Hodgkin in this regard would be in some way justified and might lead to certain clarifications.

Proponents of the conspiracy theory found it significant that Sirhan, after his arrest, acted in an eccentric and bizarre manner. That is simply their opinion, not some official conclusion. A police officer, for instance, studying Sirhan after arrest, stated that the suspect's eyes were permanently dilated. That is to say, Sirhan's eyes did not react to an intense flashlight beam played by the officer and remained dilated. The officer then concluded that Sirhan was either under the influence of alcohol or some kind of a narcotic when he committed the murder.

Much is made of the fact that Dr. Bernard L. Diamond, the psychiatrist who examined Sirhan in his cell, was of the opinion that Sirhan was susceptible to hypnosis. Dr. Diamond stated that he had successfully hyptonized Sirhan on more than one occasion. The psychiatrist noted that on each occasion when Sirhan was emerging from a hypnotic trance, an episode of trembling or shivering was observed. Dr. Diamond further stated that, under hypnosis, Sirhan repeated the written injunctions to himself to kill Kennedy. Additionally, according to the psychiatrist, Sirhan obeyed instructions posthypnotically. The well-known cell bar climbing incident is an example. Sirhan, emerging from hypnosis, carried out the psychiatrist's order. Obviously surprised, Sirhan explained his action as due to restlessness, boredom in confinement, and a need for some kind of exercise. The psychiatrist was unsuccessful in jogging Sirhan's memory of the murder by hypnotic suggestion. To the hypnotized Sirhan, Kennedy was apparently not dead. Dr. Diamond's suggestion is that certain blocks were implanted in Sirhan's memory to prevent him from revealing the identity of those who had conditioned him. The psychiatrist demonstrated the possible existence of such blocks in a series of experimental questions put to the hypnotized Sirhan.

All of this makes for interesting conjecture. Proponents of the conspiracy theory would have us believe that susceptible individuals may be placed in a state of high suggestibility during which they may be made to execute certain acts. A word which has assumed a degree of popularity in the average man's mind, perhaps because of pseudoscientific connotations, and a dramatic and even sinister aura, is that the individual was 'programmed.' The concept of programming or brainwashing was popularized in a best-selling novel several years ago. It has been suggested that an individidual somehow can be programmed or conveniently processed so that he will not only perform a certain act, such as the perpetration of a murder, but that he will also forget that act and also the identity of those who had programmed him.

At this point, the conspiracy theory and its supplementary theory of programming tends to escape the disciplining corset of scientific objectivity into a somewhat fanciful and dubious realm of parapsychology. Although it makes for a good story, it still has to be demonstrated scientifically that certain individuals may be processed to commit an act and then to conveniently forget both act and processor.

It is not the intention of this writer to speculate pointlessly about such esoteric matters. We are interested in the role which Raymond Hodgkin did or did not play behind the scenes. We know that he spent three years in Europe during his deportation period. There are authorities in Europe, one of them a high Italian police official, who can clarify some of Hodgkin's movements. This unidentified police official alleges that Hodgkin made one or more trips to Beirut during this time span. Also that Hodgkin negotiated narcotics transactions with an Arab guerrilla organization. Whence arises a deduction, still unproven, that Hodgkin dealt with the same political organization which had programmed Sirhan.

Ray folded the newspaper carefully and put it down. He stared across the table without expression. 'A real can of worms, hey Tony?'

'Yeah,' said Tony. 'Worms with rattles on their tails, maybe.'

'I think I'd better make a move right now.'

'Finish your coffee. What you got in mind?'

'Amerigo,' said Ray.

'Yeah. That's a good idea. This shit'—Tony indicated the folded newspaper—'it's like dry brush soaked in gasoline.'

'Tell Fats to bring the car around,' said Ray. 'We're heading out to Amerigo's now.'

'You ain't got no appointment.'

'How true! No appointment.' Ray rose from the table. 'Where the hell's Fats? I want him to move his tail.'

'He was here just a minute ago.' Tony got up from the table, went to the door of the study, and yelled, 'Mazzi!'

Fats came puffing in. 'Yeah, boss. Jimmy Scott's here. I just went to let him in.'

Ray and Tony exchanged glances. 'Send Jimmy in,' said Tony.

Jimmy Scott walked in, cool and impassive as always.

'Good morning, Mr. Saldana. Good morning, Don Raimondo.'

'What's the word, Jimmy?' said Ray.

'Don Amerigo wishes to speak with you immediately. I'm to drive you out there in my car now, you and Mr. Saldana.'

'In your car?' said Tony. 'We don't take ours?'

'That's what Don Amerigo said.'

'Do you want some breakfast and coffee, Jimmy?' said Ray.

'Thank you, no. I think, maybe, we better get going.'

Ray and Tony followed Jimmy Scott out of the house and got into the backseat of the Oldsmobile station wagon in which Jimmy had come. The house basso drove carefully but very fast. He maneuvered, swung, and kept pushing drivers out of the fast lane. He came up behind a Greyhound bus and tried the same tactic on the bus, unsuccessfully. He finally swung into the middle lane and passed the bus on the right. 'Sonofabitch is nothing,' muttered Jimmy. 'Big, that's all.'

'Relax,' said Ray.

When they reached Amerigo's house, Jimmy escorted his two passengers into the house and took them directly to Don Amerigo's study. The old man was seated behind his desk reading the New York *Times*. He looked up with a smiling expression on his face. His eyes were not smiling.

'Ah, Raimondo, my boy,' he said, extending his hand. 'How good to see you. And you, Antonio.' He also shook hands with Tony Saldana.

'We came as soon as Jimmy brought your message, Don Amerigo,' said Ray.

Amerigo LoCroce wiped the smile from his face entirely. 'Have you been reading the newspapers, Raimondo?'

'Yes.'

'All the news that's fit to print. I think you have a problem, Raimondo.'

'I'm listening, Don Amerigo.'

'I won't waste time. My sources of information are reliable. They've been carefully built up over the years. That's why the commission listens to me. Most of the time, anyhow.'

'They respect you,' said Ray.

Amerigo LoCroce waved his hand. 'We have no time for further amenities. Follow me, now. Don Leonardo Codi, your friend and mine, has been talking to the Department of Justice, to the Assistant Attorney General, James Cardone. They didn't have to break him down. He went to them to sell information in exchange for favors to Leonardo Codi.' Amerigo spat.

'Where is he now?' said Tony.

Amerigo shrugged. 'We're inquiring. There's an open contract out on Codi for a half million dollars, if and when.'

'As of when?' said Ray.

'Only last night,' said Amerigo. 'You wouldn't have had a chance to hear about it. You know about Reynaldo? Yes? He will certainly get the ax now. The Indians also, naturally, but they are not our problem. All that, I think, is only a part of Codi's deal with Uncle Angelo.' He turned to Tony. 'You Antonio, you, Beniamino, and Niccolò Polo are also very hot. I think that all three of you should drop whatever you are

449

doing and concentrate very hard on finding Leonardo Codi.'

'If we don't find him sooner,' said Tony, 'he'll have to come out in open court to testify.'

'True,' said Amerigo, 'that's the only chance you will have at him. If you don't take him then, forget it. Cut and run.'

'So we got a breathing spell,' said Tony

'A short one,' said Amerigo. 'For a while. But Raimondo has none.'

Ray started to speak, but Amerigo LoCroce waved his hand.

'Whatever you have to say, Raimondo, is not now important. Whatever it is, it isn't the point at issue and I'm not really interested. Let me sum it up quickly. I have learned that Codi told the Justice people that a certain saracino, the *questore* of Rome, no less, gave him the story on you. And what is this story? One, Roberto Greco sent you, while you were living in Rome, to Beirut to purchase drugs for him. While you were in Beirut, you did business with an Arab political organization which was interested in killing Robert Kennedy. They dealt with you because they had heard that you wanted to revenge yourself on Kennedy because he had deported you.'

'So?' said Ray.

'So, according to Saracino, you did business with them and also contributed additional funds to their cause so they could set up the killing of Kennedy.'

'A good story,' said Ray. 'I couldn't care less about their politics. I know nothing of Arab–Israeli differences.'

'It's not important what you don't know or don't care about. The substance of the story from Codi, who says he had it from Saracino, is that you were a mover in an Arab political conspiracy to kill Kennedy. Also that you had plenty of believable motives for wanting to see the man dead.'

'How did you get this information?'

'What does it matter? What do I care about this story? Keep your eye on the target, Raimondo. Cardone, this Assistant Attorney General is an ambitious politician. He very much likes this story about you being involved in the killing of Kennedy. He loves it. He is going to make big capital out of it. He is going to reopen the case and make a big production out of it to advance himself. And you are going to be the star actor in his play. The Department of Justice, spearheaded by Cardone, is moving to take you and do this to you.' Amerigo picked up a pencil from the desk and snapped it in half, and then into quarters.

'I'm listening.'

'Listen good, Raimondo. You must leave immediately.'

'Leave the United States?'

'Right away. Now. You don't have even twenty-four hours' margin.'

'I have nothing with me. No clothes. All my money is in the safe deposit box.'

'Unimportant,' said Amerigo. 'I advance it and Antonio repays me. I have clothes for you already packed.'

Ray looked surprised.

'Sometimes I think perhaps you are a child, Raimondo. Giacomo Scozzari is a man almost your size. His clothes are good enough. A couple of suits, a coat, a hat, that's all you need. How much is in your safe deposit box?'

'About a million,' said Ray.

Amerigo opened a drawer of his, took and removed two large envelopes. 'Here is the money in big bills, Raimondo. Antonio will settle with me. You will also find in the envelope an American passport, should you need it. Open it up. Look at your picture and your new name: Enrico Pellegrino. You are a pilgrim, all right, Raimondo. And here is an El Sereno visa and a letter to my friend Jorge Enriquez. He is strong in the present junta. Minister of Justice, I think. He'll take care of you.'

'When do I leave?' said Ray.

'Tonight, from here. Giacomo will drive you to Bayonne and put you aboard a freight ship. Here is also a seaman's passport made out in the name of Pasco Vergaza, an El Sereno national and a member of the ship's crew. The ship's captain expects you and has been alerted.'

'Weapons?'

Amerigo waved his hand impatiently. 'You need nothing for the moment. When you do, the captain will supply you. He is our man and all arrangements have been made with him.'

'I want Torres with me,' said Ray.

'Who is Torres?' said Amerigo.

'A Spaniard I brought over from Rome.'

'Why do you make this point? Is it important?'

'I will need him with me,' said Ray. 'He is a top man.'

'A bodyguard,' put in Tony Saldana. 'A very good one.'

'So,' said Amerigo. 'You cannot go to get him now. We will send him on to you when you are settled.'

'This is important to me,' said Ray. 'I will need Torres where I am going.'

'I will have him sent to you,' repeated Amerigo. 'That's all. There's nothing more to be done for the moment. Antonio, you will stay and have dinner here. Then you can drive one of our cars back to Long Island.'

'It's good to have you in our corner, Don Amerigo,' said Tony

The old man nodded and calmly lit a cheroot. 'In a way I envy you young men. Such excitement! I think I would like it for myself. When I was a young man——' He looked at Ray. 'Are you listening?'

'Yes, Don Amerigo.'

But the old man began to laugh. 'I know how you feel, my boy. But it will all turn out all right. Believe me. I've been through these things.'

'With all due respect, and do not think me importunate, Don Amerigo,' said Ray. 'Only send me my Spanish man at arms and I'll take it from there.'

'Yes, yes,' said Amerigo testily. 'This Torres, this paragon. He will leave on the next banana boat to El Sereno. And, now, let's go into dinner, my friends. The mark of a good man is his ability to dine calmly and enjoy his food while the wolves are howling on the other side of the gate. That is the proof of a man of good stomach. Am I not right, Raimondo?'

'As usual, Don Amerigo,' said Ray, 'you have summed it up.'

CHAPTER 31

El Sereno was only one of the smaller squares on a ragged Latin American chessboard which was beginning to quiver from the Rio Grande to Cape Horn. The America of this ill-omened Hispanic heritage had been rumbling, groaning, and functioning after a fashion for more than three centuries and the seams had always held. The little people, the Indios, the mestizos, and the lesser breeds who enjoyed no pull and no access to the Bite had continued to grope and had tried to solve the puzzle under the triggered rat trap. They had always had their fingers smashed. As each convulsion ended, the generals, the prelates, the *hacendados*, the fat-cat *caciques*—in short, the *gente gorda*, the people of standing—exchanged glances and patted their brows with an unobtrusive handkerchief. The social quakes in recent decades were coming more closely spaced, each new disturbance treading on the still-uncollected litter of the preceding disturbance. It was no wonder that decent citizens who already enjoyed a piece of the action sighed for the simpler old days, when absolute space had been more spacious and when absolute time had been longer than in this psychotic mid-twentieth century. A currently fashionable scientist–philosopher reduced the phenomenon to some lucidity. 'This is what has happened,' he said. 'Our world is now smaller in an absolute sense. It is now running on far closer tolerances, on fewer bearings, when, in fact, it requires more bearings and more frequent lubrications. Our social engine requires a tune-up but no one seems willing to pay for one. Each man shrugs and says let the Yanquis do it.'

In the capital city of El Sereno, Ray Hodgkin said to Juan

Torres, 'What a pity, Juanito! You have arrived here about four centuries too late. The gold is all in the cathedral altars or in Merrill Lynch's vaults via Swiss investment advisers. The Indios are all dead.'

'I still see enough of them about,' said Torres.

'I mean the free and innocent Indios,' said Ray. 'Those who died in the mines for the love of God and the gain of their masters.'

'My stomach is not great,' said Torres mildly. 'Those in power today who steal, I look at them and I think to myself *Muy bueno*, they steal a little for Juan Torres also. How much does a man need for his old age?'

Ray laughed and clapped Torres on the shoulder. 'Ah, Juanito, what a modest man you have become! No. I say you should have arrived here with the first wave of spoilers, with those who brought the true faith, the sword, and the rack. You could have carved yourself out a kingdom and had a hundred thousand Indios digging in your mines.'

'To every man his time and portion,' said Torres. 'As that old Jew, Solomon, once said: 'Where there is much, there are many to consume it. And what has the owner but the sight of it with his eyes?'' He was a foxy one, that Jew.'

'Bullcrap,' said Ray. 'You Spaniards are always clear off the table at either end, right out of sight, either monks embracing poverty like a beautiful whore or as avaricious as ten thousand devils. Why can't you be middle-of-the-roaders like we Italians?'

'Who knows?' shrugged Torres. 'We attained maturity too late. And perhaps we worried too much about some Moorish–Jewish taint in our veins. And, lacking the proximity advantage of you Italians, no doubt we developed the bad habit of taking Holy Mother Church too seriously. As for my personal situation, a soldier is indeed like a monk. There are long spans of abstinence relieved by brief, glorious episodes of blood and carnage. I don't mourn for the women with whom I shall never sleep. I don't regret the wealth I shall never have. I am Juan Torres and I wouldn't trade places with God.'

'Spoken like a true Spaniard,' said Ray, lifting his glass. 'To your health, Juan.'

They drank and Torres said, 'Will we make it, Don Raimondo?'

'That Cardone and the Department of Justice are beginning to apply the heat heavily,' said Ray. 'They want me badly. Lacking me, they are leaning on the boys hard. From the news Amerigo sends me, it isn't good. But I'm beginning to think like you. As the days go by, I fear less and less.'

'That is the only way,' said Torres.

'That last lot of junk on which Al Poggio tried to cheat me,' said Ray, 'the seventy-five keys. I see now that I should have held onto it and brought it down here. I could have bought the entire government with it. Do you know what Jorge Enriquez told me the other day? He said that if the junk traffic were really stopped here, it would throw the whole country into a depression. It would deliver El Sereno to the Communists.'

'An unnerving prospect,' said Torres gravely.

'With a straight face, Enriquez told me, "Our citizens are so poor because you Yanquis have never really helped us. That is why our poor Indios continue to chew the coca leaf to dull the pangs of their misery." I said to him, "What do you people do with the three hundred million dollars the American taxpayer sends you annually?" He replied, "We use it to buy arms to protect ourselves from the *Communistas*. What would your State Department say if the Reds took us over?" I said, "They'd be worried shitless, Jorge." And they would. After all, Juanito, political liberty is more important than bread, especially if you're crammed with caviar.'

Torres smiled, 'Which side are you on, Don Raimondo?'

'Oh, I suppose I'm with the thieves all right,' said Ray. 'I just wish they wouldn't be so sanctimonious about it. Crooks are crooks, but when they're hypocrites into the bargain, they begin to smell pretty high.'

In a crude, crummy, primitive way, El Sereno was another Lebanon, at least a potential Lebanon which could be cleaned up and organized properly. The military junta on the one hand and Jorge Enriquez and his cabal on the other supported the administration of the *presidente*, Dr. Sarabia-Ruiz. *El presidente* was eminently satisfactory to all parties. He was not only a thief, but a weak and submissive thief, which made him vulnerable and amenable to pressure. Everyone who had something to say about controlling *el presidente* and his administration backed him in return for a piece of the action. United States anti-Communist subsidies, coffee, bananas, a little oil, tourism, and narcotics kept the treasury of El Sereno going. The United Nations Commission on Dangerous Narcotics had been bleating for a good many years about the fact that El Sereno was one of the principal narcotics depots for the South American continent. The UN delegates listened to the commission's reports perfunctorily and promptly scattered to dip into Manhattan's fleshpots. It was pleasant to be a UN delegate, particularly for those representing the so-called undeveloped countries. The opportunities in New York City to conduct private business were rich and varied. The El Sereno delegation to the United Nations had a long and stable working relationship with the six Organization Families of the Greater New York complex. This delegation acted as bagmen for outbound Organization funds. This function was shared with the El Sereno embassy to the United States. Once under diplomatic seal and underway, it was clear sailing. After reaching the capital of El Sereno, the funds were properly apportioned and allocated for Montevideo, Panama City, Vaduz, Ticino, Zurich, Basel, Beirut, and Nassau. Ray made use of his enforced exile in El Sereno by reorganizing and tightening this distributional link for the Organization. In any case, dishonesty on the part of diplomatic couriers was minimal. The Organization had a good intelligence system and a long arm in each country. The administration in El Sereno was a typical example. They played it straight with the American Organization because it was better business to do so. The politicians in power were generously supported and the diplomatic couriers were liberally compensated. As for the minor internal rackets—gold and diamond smuggling, the pornography traffic, the flesh trade, assorted contraband—all these matters were left in the hands of the local *caciques*. This was what the American Organization asked of the El Sereno politicians: Get our funds safely transferred and deposited. We shall expect proof of deposit. In return, your country is your protected territory and we'll throw you business in the rackets we're too busy to handle. You help us and we'll more than help you.

Surveying the El Sereno scene, Ray conceded with a kind of rueful admiration that even Sicily at its worst was honest and wholesome as compared with this Latin American structure. Even Lebanon was a model of virtuous government. As for the United States of America, it was a paradise of severe and incredible rectitude compared to the joyous and wholesale corruption below the border.

'Observe,' said Ray to Juan Torres, 'the intrigue and treachery of these El Sereno politicians is too intricate for Americans to grasp. The double double cross is a commonplace down here.'

'You should be able to cope,' said Torres.

'True,' said Ray, 'but I'm fed up with this tropical paradise already. I'm just waiting for the green light so I can clear out and return to New York.'

But, even as he spoke the words, Ray knew that there would be no green light, not according to the reports which he was getting from the United States.

The heat was on, a qualitatively different kind of heat this time—nuclear, rather than soft coal. Conventional heat in the past had always involved the motions of a cleanup limited to a large city—New York, Chicago, Los Angeles, Philadelphia, Cleveland, or Detroit. It had always been a diverting morality play to bemuse the voters and to make new headlines for the politician producers. In Amerigo LoCroce's memory, these morality plays had never gotten out of hand. A special prosecutor, or two, or three, were usually appointed who selected blue ribbon grand juries. During the second act, the grand juries began handing out indictments like traffic tickets. When that kind of carnival got under way in New York City, the press usually had a wonderful time speculating on the political implications behind the new production. The standard explanation with which the press had been wont to play was that it was the upstate Republicans who were trying to stink up the evil Democratic machine in New York City. Such cleanup drives offered fun and prizes for everyone, a variation on the old Roman gladiatorial games. With considerable fanfare, a

457

few minor hoods were thrown into jail, the newspapers sold many copies, thus delighting their advertisers, Republican legislators in Albany thumped their chests, hack magistrates commenced reporting for work on time, assorted Democratic officeholders with their hands in the cookie jar were fired, and, after a time, the fervor petered out and everyone went home with a righteous glow and a hangover.

This new heat wave began in the usual way. As it gathered momentum, the wind as well as the temperature began to rise. This was going to be a hurricane, said the Organization's anxious hurricane watchers, and no ordinary hurricane. The word flashed out from the shores of the Atlantic to the shores of the Pacific. This was going to be a coordinated nationwide pogrom against the Organization and only a powerful agency could be behind it. The first overt symptoms of the new distemper were disquieting. Police departments in every major city were employing ruthless extralegal rousting techniques which had the Organization's lawyers taking triple doses of aspirin and tranquilizers. 'What gives?' demanded their shocked and indignant clients up and down the land. 'Haven't we been playing fair with the police? What has happened to our expensive connections in the city halls and in the state houses? If we're not paying off enough, if they want more, why don't they just say so?'

'It evidently isn't that kind of a roust,' explained the lawyers lamely.

'And the judges and the district attorneys aren't cooperating either,' complained the clients bitterly. 'Haven't they heard of the Bill of Rights and of habeas corpus? Don't they know that we have a Constitution and a Supreme Court in this country? We pay taxes also. They can't do this to us.'

'They can't,' agreed the lawyers, 'but they're doing it. It's a new ball game.'

'What's the name of this ball game?' demanded the clients.

'That's what we're trying to find out,' said the lawyers. 'In the meantime, pull the master switch. Stop everything.'

And everything stopped.

Up and down the big cities, the police departments began smiting both the connected and the unconnected, both the free-lance Indians and those who were mobbed-up, with cold, co-ordinated ferocity. When the accused finally appeared in court, more dead than alive, the courts took no official notice and set outrageously high bail. When defense attorneys protested, even mildly, that excessive bail was unconstitutional, they were themselves jailed for contempt, worked over by the police, and disbarred in record time by their local bar associations.

The Communists have taken over, said many citizens to themselves, and a great disquiet lay over the land.

When juries brought in guilty verdicts, judges imposed maximum fines and prison terms to run consecutively. When juries brought in not guilty verdicts, judges rejected such verdicts and pushed for the immediate selection of new juries. A biting Napoleonic wind blew through the land—the defendant is presumed to be guilty until he has proven himself to be innocent beyond the shadow of a doubt—and the prosecutors and the judges waxed terrible. Judges with a reputation for leniency and defense attorneys who appealed adverse verdicts too vigorously began to suffer harassment from their bar associations, from the Department of Justice, and from the Internal Revenue Service. The outlaw Indians and the amateurs who lacked the wherewithal for competent legal counsel were swiftly steamrollered in the hurricane's early stages. High administration figures began to appear on national TV hookups with pronouncements that the American taxpayer was fed up with criminal trials hampered and protracted by frivolous technicalities. The American system of criminal justice was about to receive a face lift and shift into third gear. There would be no more expensive and interminable circuses such as the Manson trial in Los Angeles. There would be no more vaudeville shows such as the one which the Chicago Seven had put on for the benefit of poor Julie Hoffman. Under ruthless administration pressure, the Congress passed not only a broad-based law to legalize wiretapping evidence in criminal cases with generous discretionary powers to courts and police departments but also a national no-knock search-and-enter law, *sans* search warrants. The new conservatively weighted, hard-nosed Supreme Court had already hinted that it would regard these two pieces of legislation benevolently and that it would

459

uphold the Department of Justice. The new State of the Union message edified the voters with old copy-book maxims: spare the rod and spoil the child: as ye sow, so shall ye reap; if thy finger offend thee, whack it off; and many other wise saws to a like effect. And with sophisticated concepts in the fashionable new mode, to wit: 'There is much talk of ecology these days and of the evils of pollution. It is possible that rampant criminality, slovenly permissiveness, craven abdication of responsibility on the part of those who have irresponsibly reproduced themselves, and contempt for the rights of others are also a form of pollution, a pollution as undesirable as smog, sludge-choked lakes and harbors and mercury-poisoned streams. We are confronted by a social cancer and this administration will employ whatever surgical procedures are necessary.'

The new Congress doubled all existing penalties in the United States criminal code. Select committees rolled up their sleeves to formulate a constitutional amendment spelling out the crime of conspiracy to commit organized crime. State legislatures began to write legislation that attempted to define organized crime as precisely as burglary, automobile theft, murder, and statutory rape. Congress finally passed a law which made it a crime to belong to any secret organization where allegiance to such an organization assumed disloyalty to the Constitution and the laws of the land. The act of joining such an organization presumed an intent on the joiner's part to conspire to violate the laws of the United States. This law, despite its less than satisfactory wording, was upheld by the United States Supreme Court.

And the panic was on.

Word went out confidentially that police efforts to elicit information from suspects would be interpreted benevolently by courts. Habeas corpus was shelved by tacit consent and suspects brought into courtrooms on stretchers received no particular consideration. The concept of trial by jury began to be questioned by several potent Senators. The gist of the attack was: 'What is so sacrosanct about twelve good men and true? Why twelve? Why not six? Or three, or two? Or none? What is so remarkable about this so-called common law concept which we have inherited from England, as the history texts tell us? Surely, that petrified, mummified little island kingdom is not the custodian of eternal verities and wisdom shall not perish with it. America's problem is considerably more complex than homogeneous and compact England's. Our mechanical obeisance to the jury system is choking us and creating intolerable logjams. Indeed, in civil matters, juries are totally unnecessary.'

Thus, in many states criminal trial by jury was dispensed with entirely on the grounds that the taxpayer could no longer afford the interminable and costly process of selecting jurors. Where an appeal did reach the Supreme Court, that august body upheld such dispensation of jury trial as necessary and desirable on an emergency basis. 'Our follies of the past have beggared us,' concluded the Supreme Court blandly, 'and beggars cannot be choosers. Let us, by all means, have dispatch.'

But the new climate was not entirely weighted on the side of vengeance and punishment. The Second Circuit Court of Appeals Council issued the first unprecedented rule ordering criminal cases in federal courts to be brought to trial within six months or the charges to be dismissed. The other circuit courts of appeal throughout the entire country soon followed suit.

In the meantime, many states which had retained the death penalty added new offenses such as armed robbery and burglary (if committed by night and if some individual was lawfully within the said burglarized premises at the time) to their lists. The city of Los Angeles had long and justly been celebrated for its passionate romance with the automobile. In a burst of zany enthusiasm inspired by its perennial and ineffable mayor, Mr. Samuel Yorty, the city of Los Angeles elaborated exuberantly on its muncipal vehicular code. The city of Los Angeles now let it be known that automobiles parked overtime would be subject to a mandatory fine of one hundred dollars for the first offense. All moving vehicular violations were subject to a mandatory penalty for the first offense of five hundred dollars. Driving an automobile while intoxicated, or driving without a proper operator's license was made a felony with penalties of five years in a state penitentiary or a ten-thousand-dollar fine, or both. Certain worthy citizens of Los Angeles demurred and protested that, since the city still lacked an adequate public transportation system and since most citizens were still utterly dependent on their automobiles for the pursuit of their daily bread, these new penalties were unrealistic. To which the mayor, a celebrated expert on foreign policy and particularly on the Vietnam War (which was still continuing), replied with nasal wisdom, 'All fines thus collected by the city of Los Angeles under the new traffic code will be turned over to the federal government to facilitate the prosecution of our just cause in Southeast Asia. Since the federal government finds itself so financially strapped at the moment, I think it would be a fine patriotic gesture for the people of Los Angeles to make this unique contribution in achieving our final victory in that part of the world.' The citizens of Los Angeles, overwhelmed by their mayor's sublime and selfless patriotism, acceded in a state of patriotic shock. Bicycles became popular overnight in the city, the smog blanket drifted into adjoining counties, and Mayor Yorty was considered by *Gulp* (*Look*, *Time*, and *Life* had already gone broke) as a serious contender in the next Presidential election.

The city of Los Angeles, like a dependable veteran clown, was always good for laughs, of course, but the Congress was in no laughing mood. It further enacted legislation which abrogated a condemned individual's right to appeal his or her death sentence to the United States Supreme Court. The condemned individual could appeal as far as the supreme court of the state which had condemned him (or her) and no farther. Senator Strom Thurmond, the grand old bourbon of South Carolina, had fathered this particular piece of legislation and expressed himself as deeply gratified with its reception, as a vindication of his states' rights philosophy.

The police everywhere were using their guns and clubs freely and a frantic opposition in Congress, in state legislatures, and in editorial columns were screaming: 'Police state! The unthinkable has come to pass in America! It has happened here!' The politicians of the administration in power said: 'Why police state? The great silent majority is behind us. It opposes the pampering of criminals. It opposes judicial circuses at their expense. It opposes wrist-slapping jurists and crippled police departments. It demands swift severe justice for the guilty. The great silent majority wants a cleanup.'

The professional polltakers decided to test the waters and the national mood on these questions and surfaced with some disquieting findings. The great silent majority was apparently supporting the hard-nosed administration position anent law enforcement. Not by spectacular margins, but supporting it. Since professional polltaker results were more sacred in the American pantheon than mother, municipal tax-exempts, and reverence for revealed religion, the dissenters were quelled, cowed, and quite discomfited.

The winds of change were beginning to bite.

Politicians who had been accepting payoffs got the message and even stopped answering their phones. Newly appointed federal judges turned in their signed letters of resignation on the same day that they were sworn into office. Many states amended their laws making judicial offices appointive rather than elective. In such cases, the presigned letter of resignation was made an integral part of the procedure. The executive branch was now to the judicial branch as Grant had been to Richmond. The police murmured, 'Oh, brother!' limbered up their club arms, and settled accounts privately with those who had been irking them through the preceding decade. The IRS and the FBI made a shambles out of the dignity of the state of Nevada by invading the sacred precincts of casino counting rooms during the hallowed counting hour. When the state of Nevada attempted resistance, Justice and Treasury enforced the new policy, not only with U.S. marshals, but with federal troops in full battle regalia. Sundry state, county, and municipal officials throughout the state of Nevada were indicted for malfeasance and misfeasance in office. The casino patrons began drifting away and business fell alarmingly.

Even though all the wheels had stopped turning in Chicago and in its environs, all of Cook County was put under martial law and a big federal dragnet went out. When the mayor of Chicago inquired of Mr. James Cardone, Assistant Attorney General, the admitted fiend behind this villainy, why Cook County was being treated so harshly, Mr. Cardone replied, 'No particular reason yet, Mr. Mayor. But, in case you get any quaint ideas, we just want to show you who is boss.' Chicago understood such logic and Mr. Cardone became an illegitimate hero in the Windy City for the next two weeks. 'It ain't bad,' said many Chicagoans.

The crap layouts were locked away in Bel Air, Beverly Hills, San Francisco, Grosse Pointe, Saratoga, and all of the joints in Metropolitan Jersey across the river from Manhattan. Newport, across the river from Cincinnati, escaped martial law because it was mysteriously destroyed by a conflagration which the authorities decided was the work of some mad arsonist. Since such arsonists tended to be suggestible and imitative, Gretna, the 'Cicero of the South' in Jefferson Parish, directly across the Mississippi River from New Orleans, also went up in flames. So did the Mexican cities of Tijuana and Mexicali, directly across the border. The *caciques* in Mexico City shrugged their shoulders, raised quizzical eyebrows at one another, and murmured, 'This Señor Cardone is *muy macho*. He has very big balls. But no matter. When this gringo fever has run its course, they will rebuild Tijuana and Mexicali for us and our cities will be more beautiful than before. This time we must have inside toilets in all the whorehouses.'

Dade County in Florida was put under martial law and the city of Miami Beach sustained a federal roust which left it trembling and debilitated. For the first time in anyone's memory, peaceable Northern bookies down at the beach for a warm profitable winter found themselves grading Florida's back roads in chain-gang shackles.

The small fry—the unconnected Indians, the heisters, the jewel boosters, the paperhangers, the pimps, and the fences— took down their shingles, went to ground, and zipped their entrances closed behind them. The cops, it appeared, weren't even bothering to book such suspects after apprehending them. If such people were at all known to the cops they were given a running start and gunned down while resisting arrest. 'Aaa-yah!' murmured the admiring pezgordos in El Sereno and Mexico, D.F. 'These *Yanquis* have added a piquant touch to our time-honored *ley de fuga*. This is the *Yanqui* way of saving the gringo's tax dollars. *Los Estados Unidos* is truly a benevolent country.'

The unconnected little folk who serviced Organization enterprises in the United States—stickmen, pit bosses, housemen, blackjack and stud dealers, call girls, musicians, bartenders and food handlers—walked softly and worked harder. Business was poor. Low echelon associates employed by Organization soldiers—runners, bookies, straight collectors, muscle collectors, controllers, pineapple men, pistols, moneylenders, stinkbomb specialists, blue photographers, and blackmailers—were told to take a vacation without pay. Those with a little bundle followed the racing meets or drifted down to Miami where they were told, 'Behave yourselves down here, boys and girls, or you're liable to find yourself talking to your heads, courtesy of Uncle Sam. Yes, you can go to the tracks here but there are no bookies.' Those who lacked the wherewithal holed up in their mildewed furnished hotel-apartments throughout the nation's tenderloins, played gin for buttons, finished their booze, watched the boob tube, and yawned at one another.

'Boss,' said Fat Mazzi to Tony Saldana, 'some of these people that have been working for us are coming around saying they're already broke. They want an advance on their pay.'

'They do?' said Tony. 'They'll get an advance all right, a lead advance right through their goddamned eyes. Tell them to stay the hell away from us. I don't want to see the cheap crumbs till I'm ready to call them back. Don't they know there's a pogrom on?'

'Yeah?' said Fats. 'What's that?'

'Like the early Christians in the lion's den, stupid,' said Tony.

'Some of these people liable to starve if they don't get on relief or something,' said Fats.

'Good,' said Tony. 'It couldn't happen to nicer people. Get me the address of the Welfare Department. I'll send the commissioner a letter saying not to put any of those bastards on relief.'

Beniamino closed down all his operations. So did Nicky Polo. The Leonardo Codi Family lay in ruins, hammered flat by the fist of James Cardone of the Department of Justice.

Bob Hope, having already crossed Vietnam off his itinerary, decided to give his next Christmas benefit show in the sober and nervous cities of grass-roots America. His quips about Attila Cardone were well received and roundly applauded.

Every Family along the Eastern Seaboard between Boston and the Tampa–New Orleans axis closed down their shutters and began living on their fat.

The fix disintegrated everywhere at every level like a tired condom in a saucer of sulphuric acid. The police captains, the county sheriffs and supervisors, the ward heelers, the party committeemen, the lobbyists, and the state legislators applied for unlisted telephone numbers, zipped up their tepees, and began rediscovering the joys of family life. Billy Graham opened the biggest revival meeting of his distinguished career in Madison Square Garden and unprecedented numbers of people came forward to testify and receive God in their hearts. Historians began to think of the period as the Era of the Big Heat and many clergymen patterned their sermons on the theme. 'Surely,' they proclaimed, 'a new judge has arisen in America and he will purify the land and make it once more acceptable to God.' Since Americans were characteristically inclined to be courteous to preachers, they grunted noncommittally and waited in patience.

The Federal Bureau of Investigation, the Federal Bureau of Narcotics, the Internal Revenue Service, the United States Customs, and the border patrols of the Immigration and Naturalization Service coordinated their efforts and networks and brought up all manner of exotic fish from the depths, fish with tumors and exquisite excrescences on their unhealthily phosphorescent hides.

Harlan Lathrop and Henry Bosch came to view a few roundups and lineups in Ellis Island, where an emergency stockade had been established under Marine Corps and Coast Guard custody. Terry Antolli and Bob Baldassare came along with their boss, Henry Bosch.

'Where did they find them?' asked Bosch. 'Are they really human?'

'Once, I guess,' said Antolli. 'There are all kinds of strange growths and life forms in the sewers of big cities when you drag deep and long enough.'

'Cardone has really started something,' grumbled Bosch. 'When you begin stirring up the mud on a river bottom, you never know what you're going to bring up. Just what are we going to do with all these specimens that we've dragged to the surface?'

'I know what I'd do,' said Antolli.

'What would you do?' said Lathrop ironically.

'I'd run them forty miles out to sea in barges and scuttle them,' said Antolli.

'Easier said than done,' said Lathrop. 'These life forms, as you call them, are human for all that. We still have laws in the United States. Jimmy Cardone has gone too far.'

'Frankly, I think it's great,' said Antolli.

'Back in Italy around 1922,' said Lathrop, 'Mussolini gave a hard-nosed cop named Caesare Mori carte blanche. He ran the same kind of a dragnet through Calabria and Sicily trying to smash the Mafia. Do you know what happened? Mori got exactly nowhere. All he did was to drive the *mafiosi* out of Sicily and into the United States.'

'Beginning to have second thoughts, Harlan?' said Henry Bosch.

'I am indeed,' said Lathrop. 'I think these cavalier extra-legal methods are going to fly back and hit us in the eye like a big cow flop.'

'That's Jimmy Cardone's responsibility,' said Henry Bosch, 'and that of the Attorney General, and the President of the United States. They wanted Operation Cockroach and, by God, they've gotten it.'

'It's fortunate that we've got the Vietnam War wound down to the point where we have enough troops for domestic police work,' observed Lathrop.

'Let's hope the shit doesn't hit that electric fan in the Middle East until we close down Operation Cockroach,' said Bosch. 'Jimmy Cardone still hasn't gotten the big cockroach who sparked all this. You also want him, don't you, Harlan?'

'Hodgkin?' said Lathrop. 'I certainly do. But I rather think we're using a hundred-ton steam hammer to smash one roach. I'd say we're overreacting a bit. After all, it hasn't been proven

467

that Hodgkin was involved in Robert Kennedy's murder. Even if he was, Kennedy wasn't first cousin to God or anything near it. Hodgkin should be treated like any other fugitive.'

'For instance?' said Bosch. 'El Sereno hasn't honored American demands for the extradition of Ray Hodgkin. Should this country send in the Marines to drag him out of there?'

Lathrop smiled sourly. 'That would be quite as bad as this domestic police terror which Cardone has let loose, wouldn't it?'

'Cardone's idea is to put so much pressure on the Organization,' said Bosch, 'that they themselves will figure out a way to bring Hodgkin out into the open. They can get him back to the U.S.A. and throw him into our lap, and they won't have to use the Marines either.'

'Is Cardone going to make that kind of deal?' said Lathrop.

'Maybe,' said Bosch. 'The first Organization rule is that the good of the whole supersedes the good of any individual member. The boys understand very well what Cardone is doing and why. They'll throw Hodgkin to the wolves somehow, in an effort to deflect the heat from themselves. Hodgkins come and go, but the Organization goes on forever. At least, that's what they think and hope.' He turned to Antolli. 'Terry, much as I sympathize with your suggestion of Operation Scuttle for all these subhuman squids, cuttlefish, crabs, eels, worms, sea snakes, roaches, and other vermin we've dragged up from the depths of what's laughingly known as the underworld, I'm afraid we'll just have to house and feed them until Cardone makes up his mind what he wants to do.' He stared dubiously at the crowds of prisoners jammed into the cages. 'I suppose they could be rehabilitated in some way. But I ask myself, Why? We already have too many deserving people who rate federal assistance, attention, and money. My, my! How did the United States ever permit such a monstrous mountain of human excrescence to develop?'

'Part of the pollution picture,' said Antolli laconically. 'Ecologically speaking, it would be useful if they could somehow be turned into fertilizer. The underdeveloped countries need fertilizer badly. Maybe the CIA has some department that could handle the problem.'

Harlan Lathrop stared bleakly at Antolli. 'No fertilizer, Antolli. This is America, not the Third Reich. These prisoners are still human beings, not garbage. The government will hold them and process them and eventually turn them loose. Frankly, I'm sorry I was even indirectly responsible for having gotten Cardone started on this sweep. Ray Hodgkin wasn't worth it. I'd like to see the damage that's already been done reversed. I want a return to the status quo.'

'Reactionary,' said Henry Bosch.

At the boss, the subboss, and the *caporegime* levels, all further meets were called off. In the duplexes on Fifth Avenue and Park Avenue, in the patrolled estates of Forest Park, in the electronically secured properties dotting Bel Air, in the helicopter-patrolled ranches in Wyoming, Montana, Arizona, and New Mexico, in big twin-diesel sportfishermen around the Bahama out islands, the top dons of the Organization relaxed. Well, it was nice to take a break and to have a drink. It was good once in a while to catch one's breath and get the long perspective. Like everything else, this big heat would simmer down and the wind would blow itself to sea. In the meantime, who in the hell and what had started it? That fink, Len Codi, *naturalmente*. And the fellow that Amerigo LoCroce had been defending so hard, that Ray Hodgkin. This mess is Amerigo's baby and he will have to get us out of it.

CHAPTER 32

Amerigo LoCroce was trying not to think of the problem of Raimondo Occhiaccio that he had brought into being. In his mind the unwelcome shadow of the inevitable conclusion was already forming. The responsibility was his. He would soon have to initiate a meeting of several key bosses to propose a stroke which would cut the Gordian Knot. It should have been named the Cardonian Knot. All that the cutting of this knot promised was the springing of a trapdoor. It would all end with everyone who counted, including himself, dancing on air. Perhaps we should have paid more attention to chess, thought Amerigo ruefully. Mr. Cardone is a very fine chess player. If the venerable, hallowed rules of the game did not meet Cardone's requirements, he made up new ones as he went along. To those who asked, 'By what right?' Cardone, in effect, spun a loaded revolver and replied, 'Here is my right.' He had already contacted LoCroce secretly and said, 'Well, what do you think of the things we've already accomplished?'

'When the wind rises,' Amerigo replied, 'ordinary men must bow their heads.'

'It will rise even higher,' said Cardone. 'There's a warfare on earth between us and who do you suppose will win?'

'That's not for me to predict,' said Amerigo. 'I won't be around to see the outcome.'

'You hope,' said Cardone. 'It has been said that old men dislike violent change. If you wish to end your life pleasantly in Princeton, I suggest that you cooperate with us.'

Amerigo spread his hands. 'Why do you come to me? I'm only a small, retired manufacturer of women's garments. What can I accomplish?'

'Much, despite your modesty,' said Cardone. 'You know what we want.'

'Why don't you extradite him?'

'They're sufficiently anti-American down there,' said Cardone cheerfully. 'They laugh at us. Like children, they're aware that their weakness protects them and so they spit on extradition treaties. The Department of State has decided against applying conventional pressure. The United States can't allow itself to lose face before a trivial banana republic misgoverned by bandits. In the simpler past, we would have landed Marines and brought him out.'

'True,' agreed Amerigo, 'force is no longer fashionable.'

'And a good thing, I suppose,' said Cardone. 'Still, we do want Mr. Hodgkin and intend to retrieve him. By unconventional means, since the orthodox channels are barred to us. We do have the resources, you know.'

Amerigo LoCroce bowed his head respectfully. 'I'm only a private citizen. The Assistant Attorney General of the United States flatters me with his confidence.'

James Cardone grinned amiably. 'Come, come, Mr. LoCroce. I, too, am of Italian ancestry. Why don't we shelve this elaborate old country play-acting and deal plainly with one another?'

'By all means, Mr. Cardone.'

'Consider, then,' said Cardone, 'we're seeking to retrieve Hodgkin alive. Never doubt, we'll eventually succeed. It's simply a matter of expediting the process. When we do take him, we'll open his mouth and he'll tell us many things to your grave detriment. Do you question our ability to do so?'

'Considering the storms you've raised thus far,' said Amerigo mildly, 'I'd be the last man to question it.'

'How lucidly you reason!' said Cardone. 'What a credit you might have been to your adopted country!'

Amerigo LoCroce sighed.

'Sighs are for what might have been,' said Cardone. 'You and I must deal with problems as they are now, not as we might have liked them to be. Do you recall Caesare Mori?'

'I know of him, Mr. Cardone. However, I had been an American citizen for many years before Mori commenced his operations in Sicily.'

'Mr. LoCroce, what Mori attempted there is nothing to what the American government will do to your Organization if you don't cooperate. If you wish to close your years peacefully, I suggest you deliver Hodgkin, as the lesser of two evils. Alive, I might add, in good health and in a condition to speak clearly. He wouldn't be of much use tongueless, for instance.'

Amerigo shrugged. 'Others may not be as ready as I to cut their throats.'

'I've heard you're a very eloquent man, Mr. LoCroce. You should be able to persuade your friends. Perhaps you can convince them that Hodgkin will not violate *omerta*.'

'You're saying he will?'

'*Omerta*, Mr. LoCroce is effective only in countries with a sentimental regard for the suspect's rights.'

'And isn't the United States such a country?'

'It certainly has been up until now. Your Mr. Hodgkin will have the distinction of breaking new ground. I expect him to sing like a cage full of happy canaries.'

'How brutally you put it! You're handing us, to state it vulgarly, a snatch contract to be turned against us.'

'Hardly,' said Cardone. 'A contract implies a return consideration of value. All I'm offering is a personal reprieve to you.'

'You ask me to play Judas?'

'I ask you nothing. I tell you. Hodgkin alive or the Organization dead. What choice do you have?'

'I must consider it at length.'

'Save that fine logical mind. You have no choice, I assure you. All you do have is three months in which to deliver Hodgkin to us, alive and coherent. In the meantime, the pressure stays on—all the way.'

'And if we perform the task which you have laid on us?'

'No bargains and no promises, Mr. LoCroce. As long as this administration remains in power, hostilities will continue.'

'There may be a reaction. You will not retain power indefinitely.'

Cardone laughed. 'You're grasping at straws, Mr. LoCroce. Whichever way the American voter decides, you and your friends will not survive. Whatever else we fail to accomplish we'll make crowmeat out of you.'

Amerigo LoCroce shrugged and rose. 'May I be permitted to leave, Mr. Cardone?'

Cardone nodded. 'Three months.'

Amerigo bowed slightly. 'Good night, Mr. Cardone.'

'Good night, Mr. LoCroce,' said the Assistant Attorney General.

So had it gone and what was one to say? He, Amerigo LoCroce, and his brethren were being hoisted on their own petard. Which proved conclusively that all of these fine philosophical speculations were vanity and a waste of time. All that counted, in the final analysis, was institutional power and leverage.

Each of the five bosses who had been summoned to attend this rump session of the national commission had received a verbal invitation to attend the thirty-fifth wedding anniversary of Mr. and Mrs. Thomas Zitu. The affair would be held in a private banquet room at Pucci's. Since Pucci's was more than ordinarily quiet on Tuesdays, the celebration honoring the Zitus was posted for 9 P.M. on a Tuesday evening. This couple had not been wedded for thirty-five years and were, in fact, nonexistent. Correctly decoded, the message stated that a matter of grave emergency had arisen.

Ordinarily, considering that it was the Zitus who were being honored, nine top executives would have attended this meeting. One of them, Don Leonardo Codi, had disappeared from the haunts of men into the federal maw and had still not been located. His attorney's, presenting writs of habeas corpus in the wonted places, were treated like blacks, Jews, Chicanos, Orientals, and other undesirables applying for membership in the Burning Tree Golf and Country Club—that is to say, politely. The attorneys were further given delicately to understand by the appropriate bar association that, in their own interest, they would be wise to select future clients with greater care. 'It would seem,' L. Howard Willis had observed to junior partner Marta Peruzzi, 'that the Bill of Rights has been temporarily suspended. This new arbitrary climate will

473

soon overtake the ordinary law-abiding taxpayer. When it does, he'll scream and the walls will echo their sympathy. He's going to relearn a simple truth: Better for ten felons to escape than for one innocent to suffer. Let's economize, by all means, but not in the administration of justice. There are ten thousand other rat holes of extravagance to be stopped up. I couldn't disagree more with Cardone's philosophy. From now on, Marta, until further notice, this firm will limit itself to civil matters.'

'Have you heard anything from Ray?' said Marta, already knowing the answer.

'Nothing,' said Willis. 'I imagine there's quite a fox hunt going on at this very moment.'

As to the Zitu affair, another executive, James Verdiano, a man in his late sixties, was in a terminal coma at Columbia Presbyterian Medical Center. Two others, Nicholas Tasca and Louis Sonnino, were with their wives, sunning themselves in Laurance Rockefeller's Caneel Bay Plantation. They had been duly notified and had returned word to Don Amerigo Lo-Croce, the manager of this meeting, 'Affectionate congratulations to the Zitus. Exercise your full freedom in selecting our anniversary gifts to them.' That gives me three votes out of a possible seven, reflected Amerigo. He had made exceptional security arrangements. Four electronics technicians had painstakingly searched the banquet rooms for bugs and had finally pronounced the banquet room antiseptic. At Amerigo's order, they also installed a high-frequency scrambler that would neutralize any bugs which they might have overlooked. Four armed buttons in the garb of waiters assumed guard posts at 5 P.M., two men in the banquet room proper, and two in the locked corridor leading to it. They would remain an additional two hours after the meeting had ended. This corridor, which opened on Pucci's main delivery entrance in an alleyway, was separated from that entrance by a steel door locked on the inside. Two additional exits, similarly locked and branching off this corridor, led into adjoining buildings. A button covered each of these exits. Two buttons had taken up unobtrusive posts before Pucci's front doors. Three others covered the alleyway.

Amerigo himself had selected the evening's menu and it was

somewhat on the ascetic side. A lean man, he possessed a life-long cultivated disinterest in food for its own sake. Two of the four guests, also lean, John Risalaimi and John Piccillo, could take food or leave it. The other two, Aldo Muro-Lucano and Andrew Albanesi, were plump, jovial men and knowledgeable gourmets. No matter, thought Don Amerigo, the nature of this evening's discussion will not be conducive to hearty appetites and good eating. My penitential selections will suffice. Muro-Lucano and Albanesi will benefit by an unaccustomed abstemiousness, survive, and remain more alert through the evening.

These four men had many additional aliases and variations for use in their various enterprises. These, however, were their true and official names by which their parents had known them.

Despite the fact that Amerigo, as manager and convoker of the meeting, would chair it, John Risalaimi was accorded the place of honor. Risalaimi's confreres were impressed with and trusted him because of his disinterest in personal gain. Like a well-managed mutual fund, John Risalaimi disbursed all dividends and capital gains to the Family's *caporegimes* and soldiers, leaving nothing for himself beyond a modest management fee. What greater proof of integrity and personal purity? The Organization was Risalaimi's only mistress. His personal worth had been variously estimated as somewhere between twenty-five thousand and sixty thousand dollars. A stark demonstration of virtuous poverty! His fellow dons, excluding Amerigo LoCroce, respected such a proof of pecuniary chastity. Amerigo tended skeptically to probe for motives behind the motives. He looked about the table. He and his four associates represented considerable wealth in a hundred different enterprises, yet it was a feather in the balance. Nothing, but nothing, could approach the power to levy and collect taxes with the consent of the governed. And the Organization was a long way from that. Nothing could approach the benevolent and now irritated apparatus behind Mr. James Cardone. I might have done as well, reflected Amerigo soberly, to have remained one of the consenting governed and to have restricted myself to the manufacture of women's garments. *Ma!* It was time to begin.

Amerigo LoCroce rose from his chair and formally greeted his four guests. He succinctly reviewed the facts of the Occhiaccio affair and reported the gist of his interview with James Cardone. Since John Risalaimi was the likeliest prospect for that critical fourth vote, Amerigo bowed amiably to the philosopher *mafioso*. 'Don Giovanni, as the senior and most respected brother here, I believe we would all welcome your comments.' Amerigo sat down thinking, Don Giovanni (Robespierre the Incorruptible) Risalaimi will soon clinch this business. Risalaimi rose, stared about him, and said:

'Thank you, Don Amerigo, for a well-organized and enlightening report. I guide myself by one rule: The good of the Organization must always take precedence over the good of any individual member. In my opinion, we should not be intimidated by Mr. Cardone's threat. We should disregard his demands for Occhiaccio's person, not on a point of honor, but because our compliance would adversely affect our Organization. I move that Occhiaccio be destroyed immediately. Whether or not he had anything to do with the Kennedy matter is irrelevant. Realistically assessing the enemy's resources, I don't doubt they'll open his mouth in record time.'

Risalaimi sat down and Amerigo LoCroce gave the floor to Andrea Albanesi.

'Don Amerigo took it upon himself to spirit Occhiaccio out of the country,' said Albanesi. 'Therefore, Don Amerigo is morally responsible for Occhiaccio's life. Aside from that, I think it unfitting that Occhiaccio should be so unceremoniously condemned, particularly since he is not here to explain and defend himself. Occhiaccio has always been a staunch, proven, and respected man. We aren't, after all, dealing with a mere button. In abandoning him with such rude speed, we do ourselves an injury. Whenever one ruler falls, all rulers bleed. I am dissatisfied and call on Don Amerigo for a more equitable solution.'

Amerigo LoCroce rose and said, 'Thank you, Don Andrea. I accept full responsibility for Occhiaccio's present situation and have no excuse to offer. If, in your collective opinion, my conduct merits punishment, however severe, I'm ready to accept it willingly. We have, meanwhile, deviated from the problem before us. I regard Raimondo Occhiaccio with the same

476

affection as did his godfather, the late and well-beloved Don Oliverotto. Be that as it may, we're presently confronted by a *de facto* suspension of the Bill of Rights. I agree with Don Giovanni Risalaimi that if we comply with Cardone's demand the government will loosen Occhiaccio's tongue. Don Raimondo will make Joseph Valachi, that accursed Joe Cago, sound like a dead canary with cancer of the larynx. Therefore, Occhiaccio must die.'

Don Aldo Muro-Lucano rose to protest. 'I think we should comply, at least ostensibly, with Cardone's demand. We should retrieve Occhiaccio through our connections in El Sereno. Very well. But we should have Occhiaccio's memory hypnotically blocked before turning him over to the federal authorities.'

Don Giovanni Risalaimi rose to reply. 'A plausible suggestion, Don Aldo. I know just enough about this esoteric field to doubt whether it is possible. I would even suggest that memory blockage by hypnotic methods is a mere myth. Even if it were possible, I doubt whether it could be accomplished within Cardone's ninety-day ultimatum. Aside from that, our decision will stink dishonorably in the nostrils of those who serve us, trust us, and give us their loyalty. If we cravenly sell a brother, blocked or unblocked, to the enemy, we sign our own death warrant. In such case, I would expect no man to mourn for me and I would not mourn for myself. Munichs have never paid off. I say dispatch Occhiaccio like a man, in a clean and orderly fashion, and take your chances with Cardone. You will have less to lose thereby.'

Amerigo LoCroce took the floor and produced the telegram from Caneel Bay Plantation. 'Gentlemen, since I have already received the proxies of Don Niccolò Tasca and Don Luigi Sonnino, those in favor of condemning Occhiaccio hold a majority.' He nodded toward John Piccillo, who had not yet spoken. 'We haven't yet heard your views, Don Giovanni. While intending no rudeness, I must stress, in the interests of speed, that those views are academic. Let me only add that there are precedents for the position taken by Don Giovanni Risalaimi and myself. In a far less serious case, we abandoned a respected associate to the law because the pressure was too great. I refer to Lepke Buchalter who, though non*mafioso*, was

at least as important as Raimondo Occhiaccio. Lepke Buchalter was thrown to the law to deflect heat from our Organization. True, he went to the electric chair in silence. In view of the
magnitude of the present stakes, however, the government will
not content itself with merely executing a silent Raimondo
Occhiaccio. I refer, of course, to the golden publicity value of a
reopened case on the death of Robert Kennedy. Occhiaccio
will speak and speak abundantly, even if the government has
to draw out every centimeter of his intestines and examine
them under a microscope. Even if it were possible to successfully block his memory, as Don Aldo has suggested, Cardone
will find means to unblock him, even if that ordeal eventually
turns Occhiaccio into a vegetable. Cardone is a formidable and
merciless man. I make these additional comments only out of
courtesy to Don Giovanni Piccillo. As matters now stand, we
have four votes in favor of execution.' He turned to Piccillo.
'Don Giovanni?'

'I'll vote with the majority,' said Piccillo rising. 'I'm a long
way from home and know far less about this case than Don
Amerigo and Don Giovanni Risalaimi. Moreover, I have the
utmost confidence in Brother Risalaimi's judgment and integrity. I should like to add one more observation which no
one else here has seen fit to mention. According to Don
Amerigo's account, Raimondo Occhiaccio, in violation of a fun-
damental Organization law, had a federal official put to death.
A minor official, true, but it was a serious lapse on Occhiaccio's part, and it undoubtedly precipitated this federal land-
slide. It seems to me that Occhiaccio is in good measure responsible for his present predicament. You have my vote for
execution and that is all I shall say.'

'Thank you, Brother Piccillo,' said Amerigo LoCroce.
When the task of taking the formal final vote had been completed, he continued: 'I move that Don Raimondo Raffaele
Occhiaccio he formally condemned to death and that a nationwide open contract to that effect be issued. I also move that
any member, anywhere, at any time, and by whatever means,
who can successfully destroy him and produce satisfactory
proof of his death, be paid two hundred thousand dollars from
commission funds earmarked for such purposes.'

Don Giovanni Risalaimi rose to his feet. 'I second the motion and would further suggest that we at least act out the gesture of inviting Occhiaccio back to the United States for a confidential conference. We should inform him, through Jorge Enriquez and other intermediaries, that we have closed new connections in the Department of Justice. We should give him full assurances that, if he returns, the matter can be adjusted and that the dogs of justice will be called off.'

'Occhiaccio is too old a hand, too wily and suspicious a fox, to be talked into that kind of trap,' said Amerigo. 'He won't take the bait.'

'I don't expect he will,' said Risalaimi, 'but we should make the attempt. The odds are improbable, but it may save us labor. Simultaneously, I move that we activate a crack hit team to enter El Sereno and take him. Don't underestimate the difficulties of such an undertaking. Nor should we sell Occhiaccio's security arrangements short. We'll require carefully selected men and they will need much luck.'

'So moved,' said Amerigo.

Andrea Albanesi took the floor. 'The blood of this matter is on Don Amerigo's hands. He'll have to sleep for the rest of his life with Raimondo Occhiaccio's ghost. I move that Don Amerigo be invested with the responsibility of selecting, briefing, and supervising the execution team. I also move that he be held personally responsible, specifically, that his life be forfeited if the mission fails. But whether we succeed or fail in this operation, I say that we have all emerged with dirty hands, diminished prestige, and no credit to ourselves.'

'Thank you, Don Andrea,' said Amerigo. 'I accept your rebuke and your criticisms. There's no need, gentlemen, to put Don Andrea's motion to a vote. If you all agree with him, I accept responsibility for the mission and the penalty for failure.' He looked around at his four fellow dons. 'Does anyone else wish to speak?'

Risalaimi rose to his feet. 'I do,' he said mildly. 'I've just had a complete change of heart and thinking. We've been wasting time being polite. We've also been making foolish statements and unsound decisions.' He removed his jacket and rolled up his shirt sleeves. 'Let's now stop don-ing each other and come to the guts of it. Andrea is dead wrong in criticizing Amerigo and in sounding off. If you trace Occhiaccio's course from the moment he carelessly signed that tax return to the moment he killed the federal man, you'll agree he has no one but himself to blame for his present fix. A poet once wrote, if I recall the Latin tag, *Faber quisque fortunae suae*—"every man is the architect of his own fortune." Secondly, I now feel that the contract bid is not only grossly overliberal but actually unnecessary. The money can be better employed elsewhere. So much for that. Thirdly, I retract all I said before and now move that we do not, for the present, publicize an open contract against Occhiaccio. To do so would alert him, advertise our intentions, alienate his *caporegimes*, and complicate our task. Fourthly, I don't think Amerigo alone should be saddled with the responsibility. Andrea's remarks are so much sheer nonsense. I now move that we five tackle a plan of action immediately, if we have to remain here all night. We should have it underway by morning at the latest. Remember, there's only one problem before us: to kill Occhiaccio as expeditiously as possible. No hypnotic brainwashing.' He glanced at Muro-Lucano ironically. 'No buttons blundering around El Sereno trying to gun Occhiaccio down. Let's keep it simple and homey.'

'What do you have in mind?' said Amerigo.

'Love and greed,' said John Risalaimi. 'I've never seen it to fail yet. Specifically, that gang in El Sereno has given Occhiaccio sanctuary thus far because he has paid off. We can easily outbid him. We should do so immediately through the El Sereno embassy here in Washington. We, the Organization, carry more weight than Occhiaccio, the individual. What happens? The El Sereno gang regretfully expells Occhiaccio. Why? Ostensibly, because the CIA and the Department of Justice are harassing them unmercifully and threatening to foment everything from a revolution to a volcanic eruption in poor El Sereno if they persist in protecting him. The performance of that fire-breathing Mr. Cardone will certainly reinforce their excuse.'

'You mentioned love,' said Albanesi.

'Ah, love!' said Risalaimi. 'The divine indefinable. In conjunction with greed, it's a hammer against an anvil. Greed and treachery force Occhiaccio into the open. Love and trust will smash him flat.' He turned to John Piccillo. 'You're the big cowboy in this crowd, Giovanni. Do you still own the Trinidad Ranch in Baja?'

'Still,' said Piccillo. 'The Gomez brothers have been running it for me for the last eighteen years.'

'The governor of Northern Baja is still your good friend?'

'Es mi *compadre*,' said Piccillo.

'Then it will serve nicely,' said Risalaimi. 'We, Occhiaccio's good friends, invite our Wandering Jew to take refuge in that desolate region.'

'And why should he accept?' said Amerigo.

'Love and trust,' said Risalaimi. 'This woman, Marta Peruzzi—does Occhiaccio love her?'

'He loves no one,' said Amerigo.

'But she loves him?'

'Faithfully.'

'Then he must trust her.'

'I would say so,' agreed Amerigo. 'One of the few he does.'

'Splendid!' said Risalaimi. 'We should be grateful for at least one weakness in the man. Attend me now! We fly Marta Peruzzi down to the Trinidad. A little vacation in a remote, unspoiled area, let's say.'

'Why should she consent?' said Albanesi.

'What won't a woman do to see the man she loves, to touch him, to speak with him?' said Risalaimi. 'We, Occhiaccio's devoted brothers, plan to fly him secretly from the Trinidad to São Paulo, Brazil. We propose to reestablish him there for a few years, in a bustling city with a large Italian population in which we have many friends. La Peruzzi will buy this, for no woman's brains are proof against the heart. She'll fly on wings of love to this brief, tender interlude.'

'And then?' said Albanesi.

'And then?' Risalaimi spread his hands. 'God will point a way.'

Piccillo laughed. 'Very pretty.'

'I'm glad you think so,' said Risalaimi. 'To work, my friends.'

CHAPTER 33

The big twin-prop aircraft circled once over the Trinidad ranch and came straight in eastward toward the Gulf of California. It sped down the rough airstrip leaving behind clouds of red dust. With another two hundred yards of strip to go, it lurched to a halt.

Off the runway, Ray and Higinio Gomez stood beside the pickup truck loaded with drums of aviation gasoline.

'It is your wife, *señor*?' said Gomez.

'Yes, my wife,' replied Ray.

The pilot remained in the cockpit. The man beside him got out with Marta's two bags. He carried them over to the jeep some fifty feet away in which Torres was sitting at the wheel. Then the pilot came out and helped Marta to the ground. She was wearing a light tweed traveling coat over a sweater and tweed slacks. She had a bandana bound over her hair. Although the sunlight was weak on this day, oversize dark glasses masked her face. She saw Ray and ran toward him, stumbling a little over the stones and loose gravel. She threw her arms around him and kissed him on the mouth. He took her in his arms and kissed her back. 'Marta, this is *Señor* Higinio Gomez, my host.'

Marta decided not to trust her Spanish. She held out her hand and smiled.

Gomez took her hand lightly for a second and nodded. '*Mucho gusto, señora.*' To Ray, he said, 'I have to get the plane refueled.' He got into the truck and drove it onto the runway and alongside the plane.

Again, Marta kissed Ray and he pressed her in his arms. 'Let me look at you,' she said a little breathlessly. 'A beard!'

'It's easier than shaving. No water heaters down here.'

She stepped back to examine him. He was leaner and heavily tanned. The hair at his temples was gray-white and the trimmed beard streaked with gray. He looked dour, older, and perhaps because of the weight loss, taller. He was wearing a short sheepskin-lined jacket over a khaki shirt and trousers. The trousers were jammed into short, dusty cowhide boots. He had a holstered revolver strapped to his waist.

'Why the gun?' said Marta.

'I wasn't even aware of it,' said Ray. 'Around here, a gun is like your pants.' He put a straw sombrero on his head and drew her closer. 'Let's go. Juan's waiting. As you heard, Gomez thinks you're my wife. Officially, you're *Señora* Occhiaccio. Juan knows you're not, but he plays along. Anyhow, welcome to the Gomez spread.'

'I thought it was Mr. Piccillo's.'

'Gomez, Piccillo, what's the difference?'

When they reached the jeep, Torres got down and removed his sombrero.

'This is my brother, Juan Torres,' said Ray. '*Mi hermano adoptivo.*'

Torres bowed stiffly over Marta's hand and smiled through his beard. 'An honor, *signora*,' he said in Italian.

Marta smiled back. This tall, grim-faced, saturnine Spaniard didn't look prepossessing. Neither did Ray, for that matter. Torres was garbed like Ray, except that he carried a much larger revolver in his holster, a .45. He blended with the arid, desolate coastline and the somber blue mountains scowling off on the western horizon.

'So this is Baja,' said Marta.

'A tiny corner of it,' said Ray. 'The poor man's Ultima Thule. Get into the jeep. I have to talk to the pilot.'

He walked back to the plane on the airstrip.

Higinio Gomez had connected a hose from one of the drums on the truck to the aircraft's port fuel tank. He was slowly hand-cranking in the fuel.

The pilot, a tall, lanky, heavily tanned young man in levis and a windbreaker, grinned in friendly fashion. 'Mr. Hodgkin?' he drawled. 'I'm Johnson. Glad to meet you.' He jerked his thumb toward the fueling operation. 'Slow work by hand, but Mr. Piccillo keeps top aviation gas down here for us.'

'Did you come straight from Phoenix?' said Ray.

Johnson nodded. 'We picked up your wife at the ranch and came right on down. Nice, smooth flight.'

'How's Mr. Piccillo?'

'Fine. Said to give you his regards.'

'Anything else?'

'He said to tell you he'll be down this weekend. Either me or one of the other boys will fly him in.'

'Why don't you just give the whole scoop?' said Ray with an edge of impatience.

'Well, the way I got it, we're to fly you, your wife, and your friend to Mexico City.'

'In this plane?'

'Oh, sure. It's got the range. We'll top off our tanks in Guaymas just across the Gulf. Then we'll head down by way of Mazatlán and Guadalajara. We may come down in Guadalajara to take on some more fuel, and then go right on in. I'm supposed to fly you as far as Mexico City.'

'What about Mr. Piccillo?'

'He'll wait here till I get back. He's got flight connections fixed up for you and your friends from Mexico City out, but he didn't give me details. Your wife, all she's got to do is take a commercial nonstop flight to New York.'

Vaguely dissatisfied, Ray nodded. 'Glad it's this weekend. I've had enough hunting and fishing this last month to last me a long time.'

Johnson squinted at the darkening mountains to the west. 'Must be some real good deer hunting up in there.' He zipped up his windbreaker and shivered a little in the chill wind blowing in from the Gulf of California. 'Hot as a bastard along this coast in summertime, but it ain't that way now.' He studied the sullen, darkening sky. 'Probably have some headwinds going back.'

Higinio Gomez had already topped off the aircraft's tanks and had driven his pickup well off the airstrip.

'Got enough fuel?' said Ray.

'Plenty,' said Johnson. 'No sweat.'

His partner was already in the right cockpit seat waiting.

Johnson shook hands with Ray. 'Well, take care now, Mr. Hodgkin.'

'You, too,' said Ray. 'See you this weekend.'

'Me or Bill Roberts. And you'll be on your way.'

Johnson waved his hand, climbed into the aircraft, and slammed the door. He made his way to the left cockpit seat. The port prop began to turn lazily, and, after a tentative false start, the starboard prop. They began to spin steadily and Johnson revved them up a little. The plane turned slowly and taxied back to the end of the runway. There it pivoted once again and the engines revved up to full throttle. Then the plane roared down the airstrip, lifted, and sped out into the gloomy Gulf of California.

Squinting into the dust, Ray watched it disappear into the murk over the water. He turned and slowly walked back toward the jeep.

'Sorry to keep you waiting,' he said to Marta. 'I was just getting the latest.'

'When is it set for?' said Marta without expression.

'This weekend.'

Marta shivered. 'I'm cold and hungry. I hope you have adequate accommodations here for a soft, spoiled New Yorker.'

'The best,' said Ray swinging into the jeep on Marta's right.

Torres put the jeep in gear and headed toward the dirt track and the dim yellow illumination of the Gomez ranch house.

'Juan lives in the main house,' said Ray. 'I have a smaller separate place for us a piece up the road from it. A bungalow, I guess you'd call it. It's not the Carlyle, but it's livable.'

'I hear you have a lot of scorpions here,' said Marta.

'They stay sort of sleepy in the winter,' said Ray. 'Like the snakes. But, just to make sure, I'll give you a flashlight. We'll get cleaned up a little. By that time Higinio's wife should have it all on the table.'

Ray and Torres sat on a massive cedar bench at the table. They faced the tall, deadpan Higinio Gomez and Augustín, a lean, silent, catlike younger edition of his father. Marta, as the guest of honor, occupied the only chair in the room, a heavy affair upholstered in worn leather and red velvet, as grand as an extinct Spanish title. The walls of the big drafty room in

485

which they sat were roughly whitewashed. The floor was laid in patches of broken multicolored tiling, cobbles, and slabs of dark-gray slate interspersed with slabs of dark-reddish porphyry, onyx, and chalcedony. The stark wall was relieved by a big calendar picture advertising the Santo Tomás Wineries. It was an idealized lithograph from the past, of the grape harvest celebration. The benevolent beaming padres in black-and-white habits sat at table with the *gente principale* pledging one another in purple brimming bumpers, while the docile *Indios*, slight in build, watched from the sidelines and the *niños* laughed and cheered.

Three Coleman gasoline lanterns cast a harsh, uneven glow over the table. On the other side of the room, a ponderous iron-bound chest secured with a huge padlock stood on the floor. Hanging over the table on the wall were two .22 rifles and three 30/30 Winchesters, all well oiled, clean, and cared for.

Torres, wholly at ease, conversed in low tones with Gomez. The Indian answered without change of expression in monosyllables. Augustín remained silent and listened intently to their dialogue. *Señora* Gomez stood in the doorway leading in from her kitchen and listened to the conversation. The table was set with big clay platters of broiled yellowtail, clay bowls of rice, beans, tomatoes, olives, and peppers. As the tortillas were consumed by the five diners, *Señora* Gomez brought out a fresh stack from the kitchen and placed them on the bare wooden table.

'I caught that yellowtail myself right out here in the cove,' said Ray to Marta. 'It weighed at least forty pounds. In fact, I caught four of them this morning. Higinio has already salted down the other three.' *Sotto voce*, he added, 'The women don't sit down with their menfolk. She'll eat after.'

'What about me?' said Marta.

'You don't count. You're from another planet.'

Higinio Gomez uttered a soft word and his wife brought over and set out on the table tall flagons of wine in woven basket sockets. 'These wines are from the Santo Tomás vineyards up the peninsula,' said Gomez. 'They grow some very good grapes up there.'

As one of the platters was emptied, Gomez, without turning his head, raised a finger. *Señora* Gomez immediately retreated

486

into the kitchen and returned with another bowlful of beans, rice, or fish.

'No refrigeration here,' said Ray to Marta. 'It isn't money. By Baja standards, this is a prosperous rancho. There's power at the tip and up at the border, but not in the waist. Sort of a frontier area.'

He joined the dialogue between Torres and Gomez with an adequacy which made Marta apprehensive for her stumbling Spanish as she struggled to follow the local colloquialisms.

'*Signora*,' said Torres helpfully in Italian, 'their tongue here differs somewhat from what I've spoken in Spain and North Africa.'

'Big difference,' said Ray in English. 'It's a kind of specialized frontier language. They have a lot of words which aren't used down in mainland Mexico. You have to look at a map to see how cut off you are. Most of the population is crowded some fifteen hundred miles from here as a lazy crow would fly, on the Guadalajara–Morelia–Mexico City–Vera Cruz line. That isn't much by U.S. standards. But they've got some roads and mountain ranges down here, *mamma mia*! To most Mexes, Baja might just as well be the moon.'

Marta made an attempt to be cheerful. The four men about her were forbidding and, in a bleak, special way, antique. Antique? Or was it alien? Whatever it was, she felt separated and barred out by more than the flight-miles between New York City and the Trinidad Rancho. Gomez and his son couldn't be pure Indian, because the older man was unusually tall for an Indian. Their harsh, withdrawn impassivity was barely softened by a veneer of formal Spanish courtesy, the kind they couldn't have learned from books. Ray had mentioned that they were illiterate.

'Mr. Piccillo gave me a package for *Señor* Gomez,' said Marta to Ray. 'The man from the plane left it here instead of taking it over to the bungalow.'

'I noticed it,' said Ray. He reached over and put the package on the table. 'For you, Higinio, from *Señor* Piccillo.'

Señora Gomez began clearing away the bowls and platters. Gomez refilled the wine glasses. Ray took out a package of cigarettes and offered it to Gomez, who extracted one carefully and murmured his thanks. He lit it from an American matchbook and offered his lit cigarette so that Ray could light his own. 'It's polite to light your own first so you don't waste matches,' said Ray to Marta. 'Higinio, let's open your package.'

'By all means,' said Gomez. He unwrapped the heavy, brown-paper-wrapped parcel. It contained four boxes of ammunition for the Winchester and four boxes for the .22's. Augustín's eyes lit up with happiness and Gomez nodded. 'It was very thoughtful of *Señor* Piccillo,' he said to Marta. 'Please thank him for me when you see him.

'He'll be here this weekend,' said Marta.

'Ah, true,' said Gomez. 'And what is in this metal box? Not shells, surely.' He opened it. It contained a set of sparkplug socket wrenches, six graduated screwdrivers, and twelve graduated, open-end wrenches. Gomez beamed as much as his Indian impassivity would permit. 'Ah, you have no idea how much such things mean to us. It's not money. Getting to market, that's the problem. In my truck, it takes me five days to Ensenada. The tools I can buy there, they break in my hand.' He handled the new wrenches lovingly. 'These are of good quality.' He touched Augustín's shoulder with restrained paternal affection. 'If this young one used more than one bullet to bring down a deer or a wild pig, I'd be surprised.'

Augustín looked embarrassed and half smiled.

Carefully, Marta placed one Spanish word after another. 'Do you have other children, *Señor* Gomez?'

'Four daughters of school age, between eight and fifteen,' said Gomez. 'There is no school here. They live with my brother, Vincenzo, and go to school in San Ignacio. He has a rancho near there. We are going there tomorrow for a week. My wife, she misses the girls. We don't see them enough.'

'Tomorrow?' said Ray.

Gomez nodded. 'That is our life and our pleasure. We go there for a week. They come here for a week or a month. It does not matter. I have five other brothers with ranchos in this country so we have enough visiting to do.'

Ray finished his cigarette. 'My wife is tired. She's had a long day. I think we'll go to bed.' To *Señora* Gomez he said, 'The fish was unusually good, *señora*. As always, our thanks to you for your hospitality.'

The heavy woman smiled from the doorway. 'It is nothing, *señor*.'

'Sleep well,' said Gomez and his son echoed him silently.

'Good night, all,' said Ray. 'See you in the morning, Juan.'

'Good night, Don Raimondo,' said Torres.

Ray and Marta left the ranch house and headed up the dirt track by flashlight. When they entered Ray's separate dwelling, she held the flashlight while he lit two Coleman gasoline lanterns. 'I've gotten so used to these things, I don't even miss electricity anymore.'

'They're so formal,' said Marta, 'so polite.'

'That's the only good thing those goddamned Spaniards taught these countries. Also, in a place like Baja it pays to be polite. Or, put it another way, it doesn't pay to be impolite.'

The room had whitewashed walls covered with serapes. An oversized double bed of dark carved wood filled up most of the room. It also contained a dark, theatening wardrobe, an old carved desk, and three armchairs in various states of disrepair. Three Winchester rifles and a shotgun hung on the wall over the bed.

'You keep a lot of guns around here,' said Marta.

'This is gun country.'

'This Spanish furniture——'

Ray grinned. 'I know what you mean. It's a Spanish thing. They believed in building for the ages. Like English shoes and Egyptian pyramids.'

Marta put her arms around Ray's neck. 'This country makes me nervous.'

'You're not the only one.'

'How does it stack up with El Sereno?'

'Not in the same league. Baja isn't picture postcard stuff. It's mean. It couldn't care less about people and lets you know it.'

Marta sighed. 'Well, we're leaving this weekend.'

'That another thing. We have to talk about it. In the meantime, let's get to bed before we freeze.'

They undressed and got under the covers. Marta snuggled up to Ray.

'Does anyone know you're down here?' said Ray.

'Only Mr. Piccillo. Why?'

'Just asking. How did you work it at your office?'

'Nothing to it. I told them I was taking off a couple of weeks to visit relatives in Houston. I did fly to Houston. From there I took a local flight to Phoenix, where Johnson picked me up and took me to the Piccillo ranch. The next day he flew me down here.'

'Does Piccillo have a big spread there?'

'Sounds like it. I didn't see anything.'

'Instead of falling on you and making love,' said Ray, 'here I am asking you a lot of fool questions. I'm a lousy lover.'

'You always were. It's all right. I'm used to it.'

When Ray made love to her finally, she gave herself feeling shy and critical at the same time. He was physically competent but his heart was obviously not in it.

'You perform well, my forty-eight-year-old lover,' she said finally. 'You've had a lot of experience, haven't you?'

'Some.'

'But you weren't with it. Aren't you glad to see me?'

Ray kissed her on the cheek. 'More than you can imagine.'

'I know you don't love me. Have you ever really loved any woman?'

'You're as close as I've come. It's a failing like baldness or myopia. Okay. But your being here has given my morale a boost.'

'Which it needs, I take it?'

'Considering how things have broken so far, yes. Are you happy to be down here?'

Marta laughed. 'Only because you're down here. Why else would anyone struggle down to this God-forsaken backwater? It's calculated to give a New Yorker nightmares. This is Gomez country.'

Ray chuckled mirthlessly. 'He belongs. You and I are just tolerated. Juan, now, he could belong if he wanted to.'

'Let's talk about us. We don't have that much time.'

'Did Piccillo give you the score on the itinerary?'

'Yes. What do you think of it?'

'It stinks.'

'Why?'

'Because I don't control any part of the situation. It has

degenerated to a matter of faith, than which there's no better noose. Did Piccillo tell you what happened in El Sereno?'

'Yes.'

'Maybe the American government was leaning on those sonsofbitches. Maybe it wasn't. You can't believe a word Enriquez says.'

'What do you mean?'

'I haven't put my finger on it. All I know is when you don't control a situation, you're gambling, you're a sitting duck. I'm being asked to believe certain things and I don't believe that easily. I have to know for sure.'

'Don't you trust Piccillo and LoCroce?'

'Maybe. Maybe not. Put that aside for a second. I don't like the fact that you're down here without leaving word behind.'

'You're off base,' said Marta. 'Do you think I'd give anyone an inkling of your whereabouts? They've got all the dogs loose.' She looked at Ray. 'Did you have anything to do with this Kennedy thing they've been headlining?'

'Absolutely nothing.'

'That's good enough for me. Well, what are we going to do? Don't be afraid. I'm not going to break up.'

'Of course you're not. But this, as the English would say, is a sticky situation.'

'How are you fixed for money?'

'Plenty,' said Ray. 'No problem there.'

'You can make a new life for yourself in São Paulo for a few years. Considering everything, it's a logical solution. You can't return to the U.S.A. while this administration's in power. Certainly not while Cardone is out panting for your blood.'

'What's the use of kidding around? They have plenty of other things on me. You know what I've been.'

'I don't particularly care,' said Marta. 'For me, you're it, and I'm tired of beating about the bush. I say, go to São Paulo. I'll return to New York, wind up my affairs, and meet you down there. We'll get married and make a new life for ourselves. São Paulo isn't Baja, after all.'

'Brazil now has an extradition treaty with the U.S.A. There'll always be a shadow over us. The Organization would have a perpetual half nelson on me. Weighing everything, it would be to their advantage to eliminate me, sooner or later. All they'd have to do is tip off the American government and it's all over.'

'Do you trust *me*?' said Marta.

'You and Juan Torres. That's as far as it goes. I wouldn't want to see you stranded in a foreign country away from friends, profession, New York City, everything.'

'We'll figure out something,' said Marta with forced cheerfulness. 'We'll solve this one together.'

'I haven't told you the half of it,' said Ray somberly.

Marta sighed. 'You may as well. Let's hear the worst and get it over with.'

Ray kissed her. 'Not now. Let's make love instead. Whichever way it breaks, my eyes will be open. I just don't scare.'

She felt his hardening maleness against her body and stared at him in the darkness. 'That's a proof of it, I suppose.'

'It's a proof of something. Don't ask me what.' Once again he pressed his lips against her mouth.

She sighed, closed her eyes, and relaxed in his arms.

Afterward, they lay back side by side, tired and content.

'Let's get a night's sleep,' said Ray. 'Things may look clearer in the morning.'

They finally fell asleep with their arms around one another.

'On this peninsula,' Gomez had said to Ray and Torres, 'all of us have to improvise and strive for self-sufficiency. Here, we are all like the *fayuqueros* who are constantly on the road. What the gringos throw out as hopelessly dead, we utilize. If there is no life in it, we resurrect it and extend its existence. Take a smooth tire. We jam, sew, and bond old rubber into it and make of it a solid tire. If not that, a kind of *alpargatas* or a dozen other things. But how does one improvise brake lining? There are those who stop to pray at a hilltop shrine before starting down the grade. But sometimes the Holy Virgin is not listening, eh, *señores*? It's the road, the accursed road.'

'Have you ever been in Mexico City?' said Torres.

Gomez regarded Torres as though he had asked about Atlantis. He shrugged. 'Never. What would I do in Mexico City, or even in Tijuana, that *poso del mundo*? This is my country.'

'Why doesn't your government build a road through here?'

Gomez laughed. 'You do not know our government, *Señor* Torres. They know this country exists but they put it from their minds. Sometimes I hear talk in Ensenada. But I only get there two or three times a year. Perhaps someday the government will build a road through this country. So I hear. But only when people settle here. But there are, as you see, no people. So the Government does not build the road. So the people do not come. What fool would settle his family here, unless he is like myself who was born on this land?'

They walked out to the shed where Gomez showed them the deer and goat meat which he had salted down and which was drying in the sun. 'The last time I went to Ensenada, I brought back many things—paper and pencils, fishing lines and hooks, tools for the truck, and the outboard motor on the boat. We depend on that boat for our food. There are many fish in the gulf. But we must have a boat to go out there and get them. And the motor must be treated like a newborn child, always, lest it be spoiled. I bring back motor oil and ammunition. There is much game in the hills, but one must go out and shoot it, yes? I bring back salt, flour, slab bacon, and kerosene.'

Ray pointed out the corral, which contained the stacked fifty-gallon drums of gasoline. 'How does this stuff get down here?'

'Ah, the gasoline. That's the staff of life down here. *Señor* Piccillo buys a bargeload at a time up in Bahia de los Angeles about once a year and a big turtle boat tows the barge down here. It is much work to unload the barge.'

'You could make it easier for yourself,' said Torres. 'I see how you and Augustín pull up the boat on rollers when you return from the fishing. That is heavy work even when *Señor* Occhiaccio and I help. I will help you to construct a track with a cable on a drum and the boat can be hauled up more easily.'

'We have no wire cable here.'

'Get some the next time you're in Ensenada,' said Torres. 'I'll show you how to build such a track.'

'I shall not be going to Ensenada for another four months.

493

No matter. It's not the hard work. We, Augustín and I, are used to it. That is how we have always done it, bring up the boat on the beach with roller-logs by brute force.'

'What's the difference?' said Ray. 'But you're happy here, that's the main thing, no?'

'What is happy?' said Gomez. 'I could not imagine living anywhere else. In truth, if you travel through this country, you will see I am a rich man even if *Señor* Piccillo were not my partner of the name. Come, I'll show you.' He led Ray and Torres out to the planted fields. 'The gulf is filled with fish which we salt down. The hills are full of deer, wild goats, and wild pigs, and in the mountains the big horn sheep. We cure the skins and sun-dry and salt down the meat. Here I grow dates, figs, olives, peppers, little tomatoes, citrus fruits, and much corn. The land is good. It's true we don't get much rainfall, but I have here three good wells.' He pointed to the windmill and the ponderous creaking waterwheel, which brought up water from the deep underground wells and spilled it into the cistern. 'The water, ah, that is precious. We keep a drumful or two near the house and learn to conserve it. We cannot waste our water.'

After Marta had arrived, Ray said to her, 'I'm glad I didn't come here in the summer. This land has more rattlesnakes in it than people.' He pointed to the hills. 'There are literally cities of big boulders out there, whole condominiums, apartment complexes. There must be hundreds of thousands, millions, of rattlesnakes in there—whole colonies of them, all sunning themselves on the boulders and living in the caves. They hibernate in the winter, but in the summer, Gomez says, you can hear the zingales going all night. Even in the winter, when you walk around here, you watch out and keep your distance if you want the rattlers to do the same. And don't tangle with the cholla bush. I swear to God, they've got a brain, they're alive. All you have to do is brush against them and they come off on your clothes and the spines start working into your skin. If you try to take them off, the spines come off in your fingers and start stabbing your fingers. The right way if you hit a cholla is to get a pair of pliers and carefully pull off the ball. I read a book about some Belgian Jesuit who banged around this country in the eighteenth century. Twenty-five years of it. Imagine! I know how he felt. He hated it. The people were hopeless and the land was savage. He said he used to lie on his pallet on the ground on the summer nights in his travels and he used to hear the zingales whirring all around him. Bringing salvation to the *Indios*. *Mamma mia!*'

'True,' said Torres, joining into the conversation. 'This is the land of serpents, a hundred, a thousand, a million. What is there here to disturb them? They are in command. This land, despite the vegetation, reminds me of the Atlas and the southern Sahara in that it's wholly hostile or, at best, indifferent to man.'

'Surely, you're not afraid of this place, *Señor* Torres?' said Marta.

'Not Juan,' interrupted Ray. 'It scares the hell out of me, though. Juan is sort of used to the wide open spaces, but I've always been a city boy.'

'Let the weekend come fast,' said Marta.

'Amen,' said Ray. but he waited for the weekend ambivalently and discussed the prospects confidentially with Juan Torres.

'Do you recall,' he said, 'that night in Beirut when we brought the morphine base into Cadri's warehouse?'

'Quite well,' said Torres. 'It could have been a trap. But, fortunately, it turned out otherwise.'

'This is another such trap.'

'Is this your natural suspicion or something concrete?'

'Perhaps this country has sharpened something in me. The droughts, the floods Gomez has told us about, the snakes, the cholla, and the loneliness.'

'A bad country,' agreed Torres, 'an accursed country. São Paulo will be a definite improvement.'

'Perhaps someone is playing games with us as with children.'

'Why?'

'The Gomez family is leaving for a week.'

'It's normal,' said Torres. 'These ranch families are always visiting among relatives. What else is their life? Are you reading something into it?'

495

Ray shrugged. 'Gomez has an Indian's sixth sense for trouble. Or he may even have had instructions from Piccillo.'

'Gomez, I think, is as honorable and straightforward as any other manifestation of nature around here—the floods, the droughts, the cactus, and the snakes, which you dislike so much. If you wish, though, I can ask Gomez.'

Ray shook his head. ' "Ask" means "kill." That would be unwise. If he goes in good faith, it's foolish to ask. If not, we'd have to kill the wife and the son also. If Piccillo has instructed him, what would we gain by killing? The Gomez clan would hem us in and I think we'd die very slowly. No, we have no differences with Gomez. It will even be better that the family should be away from here.'

Torres touched the .45 at his waist. 'The father and son will take a twenty-two apiece. That's all they usually carry on a visit. We'll have six Winchesters and plenty of ammunition.'

'Can you fly a plane?'

'No.'

'Neither can I. The pilot and the plane will be important to us.'

'All this is supposition,' said Torres.

'I didn't become a boss and survive to forty-eight by stumbling into traps like a stupid pig.'

'Now you're growing angry.'

'True,' said Ray. 'My paranoia.'

'What about *Signorina* Peruzzi?'

'We'll have to stash her out of the way. I think perhaps they used her as an innocent bait to get us into this cul-de-sac.'

'Well, I'm glad someone is innocent,' said Torres dryly.

'Assuming I've got it figured right, they're organized and I'm alone. Eventually they win. If you want out now, take off with Higinio and Augustín. They're not interested in you.'

'Thank you, Don Raimondo. You've been speculating and I've been listening. If there are grounds for your thoughts, I wouldn't want to miss the outcome. Two men, forewarned, can give a good account of themselves. But I think perhaps you err on the side of excessive mistrust.'

'Perhaps,' said Ray. 'Perhaps.'

Higinio Gomez had the pickup already loaded with provisions. *Señora* Gomez and Augustín sat in the cab. Higinio came over and Marta came out of the ranch house. Gomez shook hands with Ray, Torres, and Marta.

'Regards to Vincenzo and his family,' said Ray. 'Have a good time.'

Gomez got behind the wheel of the pickup, started the engine, and crept up the grade to the dirt track in low gear. He waved his hand.

'*Vaya con Dios!*' called Torres waving back.

The truck trundled down the road in a cloud of dust. Ray, Torres, and Marta turned back to the ranch house.

'Marta,' said Ray, 'we're making a change of plan.'

'Now what?' said Marta.

'I think we've been set up. You, too.'

'What do you mean, set up?'

'I don't think Piccillo intends to carry out that itinerary.'

'What then?'

'A hit. And, if I'm right, it will naturally include you. Nothing personal on their part, of course.'

Marta turned to Torres. 'Is he always like this, *Señor* Torres?'

'Ever since I've known him, *signorina*,' said Torres.

'Ray,' said Marta, 'you're crazy.'

'Maybe,' said Ray. 'Maybe not. How would you like to spend tonight on the beach, alone, about three or four miles from here?'

'I wouldn't. I'd be scared to death.'

'It won't be bad. Just a little chilly. We'll fix you up with a few tarps, a sleeping bag, and some blankets, and you can spend the night under the jeep. Nothing's going to come down from the hills to bother you or up from the sea.'

Marta stared at him. 'Are you serious?'

'I've got a feeling I've got to play this hand tight. Even if you think I'm cracked, go along, just for tonight.'

'Piccillo and Johnson are due down here tonight?'

'Right. So just humor me along.'

'Very well, I'll humor you along. What do you want me to do?'

'Nothing,' said Ray. 'Juan, gas up the jeep. There are six

empty jerry cans in the tool shed. Fill them up and load them into the jeep. Also some tarps, blankets, and a sleeping bag. You drive Marta down the beach around the point where it can't be seen from the house. Leave her there with the jeep and walk back. Do it now.'

'Why can't we have dinner together at least?' said Marta.

'I don't know when they'll come in,' said Ray. 'You eat dinner alone.'

'All by myself on that lonely beach? A thousand miles from nowhere?'

Torres was apologetic. 'We'll take along food and I'll leave you a pistol. Do you know how to use one?'

'No,' said Marta.

Ray began laughing. 'Baby, I know this is a helluva way to treat a girl, but please cooperate. When we get back to New York, I'll not only take you to Pucci's, I'll buy you the damn place.'

'You mean "if," ' said Marta.

'This country is basically harmless if you approach it rationally,' said Torres. 'Coming as you do from a large city, I can appreciate how you feel. I'll position the jeep high up on the beach well away from the high-tide mark. You'll be dry under the jeep. No harm will come to you.'

'Better get going, Juan,' said Ray.

Torres went off and Ray kissed Marta. She clung to him and said, 'You've plaited a daisy chain of paranoid speculation.'

'That's what Juan keeps telling me. Go ahead, kid. It'll be a cool, lonely night, but safe. If Piccillo is playing it straight, no harm done. If not, I'm calling. We'll know soon enough. Keep your chin up.'

'I hope you know what you're doing,' said Marta. She turned and went off to join Torres at the jeep.

CHAPTER 34

Ray and Juan Torres faced one another across the table in the ranch house.

'If we're not on the airstrip to meet them,' said Torres, 'they'll become suspicious.'

'If we are, we'll be wide open.'

'How will you judge?'

'If Piccillo comes alone with the pilot, they live. If there are others, we open fire.'

'Johnson had another man with him,' said Torres.

'He was nothing. I'm talking about real buttons.'

'Can you recognize them?'

'You can smell them. And if they're here on business, they won't be carrying just handguns. Not down here.'

Torres nodded. 'I can't argue with that.'

They heard the faint drone of aircraft engines overhead.

'That's them,' said Ray. 'Douse the lanterns. If Piccillo is alone, don't bother with him. He probably hasn't handled a gun in thirty years. If the pilot gets out of the plane, I'll be surprised. He'll want to sit on his ass safely in the cockpit. It's who else will be with Piccillo and the pilot, that's what counts. Let's go.'

They walked out of the ranch house into the darkness and crossed the hard-packed dirt yard to the drying shed. In this shed, Gomez salted and stored his fish and meat. Ray and Torres had prepared their position behind the salting bin. It was constructed of rough-hewn planks, the interior lined with galvanized tin and half filled with coarse rock salt. In the darkness behind the salting bin, they had a clear field of fire on the entrance door to the ranch house. Six loaded Winchester rifles and the shotgun lay on the ground beside the bin.

The engines of the airplane were now loud and low overhead.

'They'll be landing in a few minutes,' said Ray. He lit a cigarette. 'Time for a couple more.'

'How do you feel?' said Torres.

'Excited. A little bit.'

'I think you hope you're right.'

'Maybe.'

They sat down on the ground against the wall of the shed with the rifles handy before them. The salting bin shielded them from sight. By bending and peering around the side of the bin they could still see the entrance to the house.

The engine noises died.

'They've landed,' said Torres.

'Settle back. It'll take them another fifteen minutes to stumble over here.'

Torres rose to one knee, picked up a Winchester, checked the loading, and sighted along the barrel toward the doorway. 'These are fine little weapons, Don Raimondo. I like them.'

'This is the gun that conquered the Wild West—according to Hollywood, so it must be true.'

They heard footsteps approaching, coming down the slope from the dirt track and toward the backyard. Someone shouted, 'Hodgkin? Gomez? Anyone home?'

'That doesn't sound like Piccillo,' whispered Ray. 'That's a younger American voice. And it isn't Johnson either.' He stood up straight behind the salt bin and placed his Winchester against his right shoulder in the classical firing squad shooting stance, left foot forward, his weight balanced on his right foot. Torres moved out a little to the side of the bin. He placed his rifle against his shoulder and settled down comfortably on one knee.

Two tall men came into view. Each one of them carried a Thompson submachine gun. One of them drawled, 'The bastards must be drunk or asleep.'

The other man peered into the dark doorway. 'Maybe they took off with Higinio for San Ignacio.' He played a flashlight into the interior. 'Hello, in there! Anyone——'

Ray trained his gun sights carefully on the face of the man behind the inquirer. His target was in right profile and the cheek shone white in the moonlight. Ray squeezed off the trigger gently. Simultaneously, Torres fired into the broad back of the inquirer, squarely between the man's shoulder blades. The crack of both rifles exploding in the confined space of the drying shed was magnified several fold.

Ray's target sank to his knees and dropped his submachine gun. The second man, whom Torres had struck between the shoulder blades, staggered and whirled around, his weapon blazing wildly as he held down the trigger.

Still on one knee, Torres barked, 'Now! Rapid fire!' He fired a second, third, and fourth cartridge into the face of his target. The man dropped his automatic weapon and crashed to the dirt, face downwards, hands outspread.

Ray came out from behind the salting bin and walked in shadow to the opening of the shed. The man whom he had hit was stirring on the ground and still clutching his Thompson. Ray took deliberate aim although the distance was only fifteen feet. He fired two bullets into the prone man's head.

John Piccillo came running down into the yard. 'Claflin!' he shouted. 'Mike. What the hell——' He looked all about him.

From the doorway of the shed Ray said, 'Hold it, Johnny.' He drew a bead on Piccillo's heart.

Piccillo peered at him, unbelieving, still only half seeing the speaker. 'Ray? Ray Occhiaccio? Is that you?'

'It's me, you sonofabitch,' said Ray. He fired point-blank. The stocky, white-haired don clutched at his chest and fell to his knees. 'Saluto, Don Giovanni,' said Ray. He fired once more and struck Piccillo between the eyes.

Torres was now out in the open. The pilot came running into the yard, a revolver in his hand. Torres took leisurely aim and brought him down with a shot in the chest. Ray walked over to the pilot, fired into the pilot's head, and kicked the body over on its back. 'It's Johnson, all right.' He picked up one of the Thompsons from the dirt and began blasting slugs into the four prone bodies till the magazine was empty. He tore off the magazine and threw it on the ground. Reversing the Thompson and gripping it by the end of the barrel, he

501

brought down the stock on Piccillo's white head, crushing the skull. Then he threw down the empty Thompson.

'They're all very dead,' said Torres.

Ray walked over to one of the tall men who had carried a Thompson, the man whom Torres had killed and who lay in the dirt on his face. He turned the body over with his toe and shone a flashlight into the man's face. 'These aren't regular buttons. Just local cowpoke talent, from the way they came charging in here. Maybe they thought they were herding cows. So I was right.'

'You were right,' said Torres.

'You killed the pilot,' said Ray reproachfully.

'A pity. I forgot myself.'

'You forgot yourself?' Ray laughed. '*Ma!* The airplane is of no use to us now.' He picked up the unused Thompson. 'There may be others in the plane. What do you think?'

'I doubt it.'

'If there are, curiosity may bring them out. I'll wait for them here. Go get Marta and the jeep.'

Torres walked off across the field taking a shortcut down the slope to the beach. Ray went back into the drying shed and sat down behind the salting bin with the Thompson cradled in his arms. He lit a cigarette and relaxed. He was dozing when he heard the noise of the jeep being driven into the yard. He started up guiltily and came out of the shed holding the automatic weapon at the ready.

Marta was pale and disheveled. She looked around her at the scene of slaughter in the moonlight and seemed to slump for a second. Ray handed the Thompson to Torres and put his arm around Marta's waist. 'It's all finished, kid. It's all over.'

'I seemed to hear it from where I was,' said Marta in a dead voice. 'What happened?'

'What I thought would happen,' said Ray. 'Let's go in.' He half dragged her into the house and pushed her toward one of the beds. 'You lie down here like a good soldier and try to get some sleep. If you can't, here's something to help you.' He handed her a bottle of tequila, half full. 'Take a few shots and relax. And don't come out. We have some more work to do.' He walked out of the house and slammed the door behind him.

Torres was still standing over the four bodies with the Thompson in his hands.

'Let's get them loaded into the jeep,' said Ray. He lifted out all except one of the loaded jerry cans from the back of the jeep and set them near the doorway. Working together, he and Torres tossed the four corpses into the back of the jeep. He carried out the unused Winchesters and placed them on top of the corpses. Torres handed Ray the Thompson and got behind the steering wheel of the jeep. They drove up the incline and headed for the airstrip. The plane stood sharply silhouetted in the moonlight.

Without headlights, Torres drove cautiously in low gear and slowed down further as he approached the silent aircraft. 'There could be others,' he said. 'Perhaps on the ground in the darkness, perhaps in the shadows on the other side of the plane.'

'Fuck 'em,' said Ray. 'Let's go.'

They drove up alongside the open airplane door and Ray fired a burst into the interior. 'Come on out, boys,' he shouted. 'It's all over.'

There was no response.

'That's all there was,' said Ray. 'Let's get to work.'

They got down from the jeep and dragged the four corpses, one at a time. They carried them around to the aircraft's open doorway. They hurled the corpses into the plane. Ray carried over the full jerry can of gasoline and threw it in on top of the tumbled corpses.

Torres backed off the jeep to a safe distance. Ray fired a weaving burst from the Thompson at the jerry can, ran, and dropped to the ground as the fuselage exploded into a mass of orange-yellow flames and clouds of dense black smoke. He picked himself up from the ground and ran on toward the jeep. 'The fuel tanks will catch in a little while. Let's go.'

They drove back to the ranch house.

'A nice action,' said Torres. 'But perhaps unnecessary.'

'How do you mean "unnecessary"?'

'As in the Greco business. We'll never know now whether it was necessary to kill the Grecos and those other two in Beirut.'

503

'Better safe than sorry.'

'Ah, Don Raimondo, you're a very conservative man. Too conservative, I think. You're never sufficiently willing to take a chance on the intentions of others.'

'These automatic weapons tell their own story,' said Ray.

'Perhaps.'

'They weren't carrying them to sing Christmas carols.'

'Perhaps.'

'As for Greco, he was deadly. No, no, Juan, I've been calling them right so far.'

Marta was sitting at the table. The tequila bottle was untouched. Ray went over to her and put his hand on her shoulder. 'How do you feel?'

She shuddered. 'Don't touch me.'

'They were going to kill you also,' said Ray.

Marta stared at him with tense, hard eyes. 'What makes you so certain?'

'Do you think they'd have let a valuable eyewitness like yourself get away? These were very antisocial people, the kind they don't teach you about in law school.'

'I saw three dead men out there,' said Marta in a strained voice.

'Four.'

'You seem almost cheerful. I'm getting the impression that you enjoyed killing those men.'

'While I didn't exactly enjoy it, I didn't mind it either.'

'Really? How do you feel when you're killing someone, Ray?'

'That I'm helping the pollution problem along.'

'You mean that, don't you?'

Ray stared at her. 'You're not that shocked, Marta. Now you've learned a little about the reverse side of the coin. Now you can return to New York and be a better lawyer.'

Torres came into the room and sat down on the bench.

'What are your plans, Don Raimondo?'

'We leave Higinio a stack of money to clean up the trash. It'll speak for itself. Then we load up the jeep and head for Tijuana. Do you have all those papers Amerigo LoCroce gave you when you came down to El Sereno to join me?'

504

Torres patted his pocket. 'Enough passports to go anywhere. An American one, a British passport, even a Mexican passport.'

'Then you're all set. Here's my idea. We hit the border—it shouldn't take us more than three or four days, three days if we push hard. Marta can catch a plane for New York. You're free to go anywhere you wish, Mexico City, the U.S.A., or back to Europe. I still have plenty of cash in the house. Help yourself.'

'And you?' said Torres.

'I'm turning myself in at the border,' said Ray.

Marta looked up from the table. 'What did you say?'

'I'm surrendering to the U.S. Border Patrol,' said Ray. 'I'll tell them I'm wanted by the Department of Justice. They'll make all the arrangements from there, probably from San Ysidro.'

'Why are you doing this?' said Torres slowly.

Ray brought out the special little wallet. He removed the two Silver Stars and placed them on the table. 'Do you remember in Italy when we spoke of these?'

'I remember,' said Torres.

'I've been thinking about it for quite a while. I want to square my account with the United States of America. I like these.'

'Ah,' said Torres softly. 'Now I remember. You're a patriot. You said you loved that unforgiving woman and perhaps she would kill you.'

Marta looked from Torres to Ray. 'What woman?'

'It's a manner of speaking, *signorina*,' said Torres. 'Don Raimondo has a certain affair of the heart with America.'

'Oh, God!' said Marta.

'Relax, kid,' said Ray. 'I'm just turning myself in.'

'They'll crucify you, you idiot. They'll boil you in oil.'

'Not quite. They'll give me forty years for exporting heroin into the United States. Then they'll execute me twice, once for Al Poggio and once for Francis Connors.'

'They'll drag you through a concrete mixer first,' said Marta. 'Very slowly.'

'They won't have to,' said Ray. 'I'm going to tell the federal government everything they want to know—names, dates, money amounts, anything they ask. Then there's also the unlawful reentry rap.'

'Your three lieutenants,' said Torres. 'They were, how would you say, accomplices in the Poggio killing. They also will be executed. Not by way of reproach, Don Raimondo, but I also was involved in that affair. Will you send your friends to the executioner?'

'I see no choice,' said Ray. 'From me, what America wants, America gets.'

'Antonio Saldana was very faithful and loyal to you,' said Torres. 'He will die. So will his two servants, the fat one and the one without hair. And Beniamino, and Niccolò Polo.'

'That's right,' said Ray.

'Amerigo LoCroce will go to prison, if not to the electric chair,' said Marta. 'He helped you.'

'I think he was among those who condemned me,' said Ray. 'Which was as it should be, I suppose. But, even if he helped me, it no longer matters.'

'I am now also an accessory in some of your affairs,' said Marta. 'The very least that will happen to me is that I'll be disbarred—the very least.'

'Are you worried about that?' said Ray.

'I have more serious matters to worry about now,' said Marta. 'The shock of recognition.'

'How can you talk like that?' said Ray mockingly. 'You're an officer of the court, Marta. As a professional upholder of the law, you should be approving my intentions. About these four we just took care of down here, they were scum, nothing.'

'You'll rot in a solitary cell for forty years,' said Marta with controlled dryness. 'Your teeth and hair will fall out. You'll go blind and insane.'

'I'll even pay them for my room and board,' said Ray, 'so I won't be a drag on the taxpayer's back.'

'Don't be so quick to brag,' said Marta. 'Your name will stink. People will spit when they mention it.'

Ray laughed. 'Do you remember what Jesus Christ said? "Blessed is he who gets the business for My sake," or something like that. How did it go?'

506

Juan Torres stared at Ray with cool, objective interest. 'So now we have Jesus Christ in the picture. But you were never a religious man.'

'I'm not,' said Ray.

'Do you believe in a life after death?'

'No,' said Ray.

'Or in God?'

'Well, yes. Female gender. America.'

'Of course,' said Torres, 'that woman of yours.'

Impatiently Ray rapped the two Silver Stars on the table. 'Look, I've tried to explain it to you. I've got this thing with the U.S.A. It's time I stopped weaseling around and squared accounts with her. Do you understand? I owe her. I have to be clean with her.'

'All the other people Juan and I mentioned,' said Marta. 'They'll be sucked down into the whirlpool with you.'

'That's how the ball bounces,' said Ray. 'Whatever the government wants, I'll give them. No holding back. Like confession. They'll ask questions and I'll give them answers, the truth, the whole truth, and nothing but the truth.'

Torres shrugged. 'Is this your irrevocable decision, Don Raimondo?'

'It is,' said Ray getting to his feet. 'Let's get started.'

He turned and headed for the door. Torres drew the .45 revolver from his holster and fired twice into Ray's back. Marta screamed. Torres rose from his bench and walked over to the door where Ray lay on his face. He fired twice into Ray's head and holstered the revolver. Then he bent over and patted the dead man on the shoulder. 'Good-bye, Don Raimondo.'

Marta began crying softly.

Torres went over and touched her shoulder lightly. She raised her face. 'I did it in love and friendship, *signorina*. He was an exceptional man but always unpredictable.'

Marta composed herself with an effort and asked the question without words.

'Courage!' said Torres. 'We must give him decent interment. With his medals. A lonely country in which to be buried. But I agree with you, it's better than rotting in prison for the rest of his life.'

'And then?'

'We must leave Higinio Gomez money. That was a sound suggestion. Then you and I, *signorina*, must drive across the border. I think, perhaps, I should like to become an American citizen and find out more about this America of Don Raimondo's. You are a lawyer. Perhaps you will be able to help me?'

Marta did not reply.

GLOSSARY

Borgata: Lit.: Village, hamlet. Slang: The basic unit of the Organization, the Family.

Buttons: Button men, soldiers, workmen, rank-and-filers in the Organization. The lowest-level position in the Organizational authority structure.

Caid (Arabic): Judge, magistrate. Slang of the Corsican Organization in Marseilles: Lieutenant, *caporegime.*

Capodecina (Synonym: *caporegime*): Lieutenant; literally, head of ten men (a *decina* can run higher, up to twenty-five or thirty men).

Caporegime (Synonyms: *caporegima,* lieutenant, captain, *capodecina*): Position on the third level in the hierarchical authority structure of Organization Families. The active supervisory level between the boss and the soldiers or button men. Function equivalent to that of a platoon leader.

Confettureria: Sweetmeat shop, confectionary store, candy store.

Consigliere (Synonym: counselor): Staff advisor to the boss and/or subboss (*sotto-capo*) of a family on inter- and intra-Family problems. His advice lacks the mandate of an official order in the chain of command.

Cosca: Lit.: leaf of the artichoke (*cacocciola*). Slang: Group, section, Family. A local alliance of Sicilian Mafia units. P.: *Cosche.*

Dei gusti non si discute: There is no accounting for tastes.

Gabellotti: Lit.: Excisemen, customs officers. Here: *Mafioso* tax collectors to whom the titled Sicilian landowners had farmed out their estates. The *gabellotti* collected from the peasant tenants and remitted a net amount to the absentee

509

landowners after deducting their own commissions.

Lega d'edera: Lit.: League of ivy. (Translated literally, the American colloquialism has no meaning for Oliverotto.)

Omerta: Slang: *The Mafioso* code and conspiracy of silence. A persistent cultural concept which frowns on cooperation with government authorities and with the police; *i.e.,* the police should never be permitted to enter an affair of honor, discussing Family affairs with strangers involves loss of face, self-respecting men should face a hostile world with a blank wall of silence. Implicit manliness, self-respect, honor, and courage.

Pineapple man: Specialist button man in the fabrication and/ or employment of explosive devices for purposes of exortion or of killing.

Puttane: Prostitutes, harlots, whores. Sing.: *Puttana.*

Regima (Synonyms: regime, *decina, brigata,* crew, circle): The organization of button men reporting to a lieutenant or *caporegime (caporegima).*

Sicarii: Bravi, cutthroats, hired assassins, ruffians. Sing.: *Sicario.*

Soggiorno obbligato: Lit.: Compulsory sojourn. Regional detention. Compulsory residence under police surveillance in a prescribed administrative area.

SURVIVAL ... ZERO *by* MICKEY SPILLANE

All that was left of Lippy Sullivan was a chalked outline on the floor of a cheap bedsitter and a small pile of sawdust that had been used to soak up his blood. Another pointless murder to go in the 'Unsolved' files of the police department.

But before he died Lippy had managed to make one last telephone call—to his old friend Mike Hammer, private investigator. The call was going to land Mike in a lot of trouble with the police and the CIA when he learned more than was good for him about a new intelligence game involving germ warfare ...

552 09482 X—**35p**   T132

THE BIG KILL *by* MICKEY SPILLANE

Mike Hammer thought he knew everything about babes. But this one was different. This one was sleeping peacefully in a bar on the East side of town while outside bullets were blasting the silence of the night and the screech of tyres carried a murderer away.

So now the babe was all Mike Hammer's responsibility— and what could a tough private investigator know about looking after a one-year-old kid? But he did know that he was going to tear the town apart to find the jerk who'd made the kid an orphan—even if it meant the end of a beautiful relationship with a well-stacked brunette ...

552 09483 8—**35p**   T133

A SELECTED LIST OF CRIME STORIES
FOR YOUR READING PLEASURE